Vengeful Gods MC

The Complete Series

Crystal Ash

Vengeful Gods MC playlist

Rise Against - The Violence
Me First and the Gimme Gimmes - Straight Up
Halestorm - Heathens
Mushroomhead - Holes in the Void
Stone Sour - Song #3
The Civil Wars - Devil's Backbone
Egypt Central - White Rabbit
STARSET - Monster
Thrice - Black Honey
Cilver - I'm America
Linkin Park - Burn it Down
Dorothy - Gun in my Hand
Atmosphere - Graffiti
Badflower - Animal
Nirvana - Rape Me

Listen on Spotify: crystalashbooks.com/VGMC

Glossary & Pronounciations

- **Tezcatlipoca** (Tess-CAHT-lee-POKE-ah): An Aztec deity of the night sky, hurricanes, sorcery and divination, jaguars, war, and more.
- **Astarte** (As-STAR-tay): A Canaanite and Phoenician goddess of war, love, healing and hunting
- **Jandro** (HAN-dro): Short for Alejandro, one of Rori's fathers
- **Mija/Mijita** (MEE-ha/MEE-hee-tah): My daughter, derived from *mi hija*
- **Viejito** (Vee-HEE-toe): Old man, diminutive form
- **Callate** (CAH-yah-teh): Shut up
- **Paloma** (pah-LO-mah): Dove

Faithless

Crystal Ash

Content warning

This series takes place in a dystopian world and contains graphic violence, foul language, and sexually explicit scenes.

This book also contains people who are enslaved (gladiators/sex workers).

The epilogue contains blatant misogyny, as well as references of violence against women, and implied sexual assault of a male character.

Prologue

Santos

I had never seen anything like it before. Blood and carnage covered the sands. Audience members in the colosseum were standing, yelling and pumping their fists at the grisly scene below. My fellow gladiators stood at my sides, shoulders stiff with tense grips on their weapons.

None of this was unusual. But the violence happening right then on the sands was unprecedented, at least in my four years as a gladiator.

The pitmasters had unleashed a black jaguar, its spots in the glossy coat visible only at certain angles in the harsh sunlight. That in itself wasn't usual either. They loved to throw large animals into the fights. I'd fought jaguars before, and they weren't even the biggest of cats. They'd set loose lions, bears, bulls...even full-grown elephants.

It took fifteen gladiators to take down the last elephant, a male in his prime. Five men had been either crushed to death or gored on those massive tusks. But eventually, the big beast fell. The animals always did, often taking a few gladiators with them.

But this one. This black jaguar that may have even been small for its species, killed everything in its path. Nobody could even scratch it.

It darted like a shadow across the sands, leaving blood and detached limbs and entrails behind. When it slowed or paused, all I saw were its bloody teeth before it became a blur again.

At first, the pitmasters threw a few gladiators at it, one by one. Then they sent two at a time. Then three. Then five.

The last one in the group of five was running away, dragging a bloody, maimed leg behind him. The cat followed at a leisurely pace, then crouched down and wiggled its rear end before pouncing on the man.

This creature was playing with us.

"They're gonna run out of gladiators," the Ghost muttered to my left.

I tightened my grip on my twin machetes in response, hoping that wouldn't be the case. We were easily replaceable, sure. All they had to do was enslave more able-bodied men, put a weapon in their hands, and throw them out into the pit.

But being short on gladiators meant fewer fights, which was bad for business. They already had to replenish our numbers at a steady rate, considering a handful of us died every single day.

I was banking on them calling this fight soon. Sending fighters out to this demon of a jaguar might as well have been putting live men through a wood chipper. We were dropping like flies, and no one stood a chance.

But the crowd was going nuts over it. So this could potentially get dragged out for the sheer entertainment value.

The jaguar dragged the last man by the throat to the center of the pit, leaving a trail of blood behind. It released the body, letting it fall limply into the sand, then turned to face the rest of us behind the gate.

Something happened the moment the animal's eyes met mine.

A sensation overtook me that nearly brought me to my knees. This jaguar was no animal or person but...*more*. It was time and history, bloodshed and the purest devotion. It had seen the rise and fall of empires, centuries of colonization and genocide. This thing was timeless, ageless. And all of this perspective happened to be contained in a snarling, four-legged package that walked straight toward me.

Tezcatlipoca.

The word ran across my brain, making me shiver in the hundred-degree heat, and I knew it was this entity's name.

"Butcher." The pitmaster called for me and angled his head. Before I could even process what was happening, the gate in front of me opened, and I was shoved forward. I heard Ghost hiss out a protest, but there was nothing he could do. If I was picked to fight, I couldn't refuse. None of us could. Nor could I turn around, to try getting away from the fight. Cowardly gladiators were captured and corralled separately for the bare-knuckles fights, in which a mob of five other men were tasked with beating him to death.

Now, nothing stood between me and whatever this thing parading as a jaguar was. I stepped out from under the awning of the building into the harsh sunlight. The crowd reinvigorated itself, the noise elevating to a roar when they saw me.

I was a crowd favorite. It was them who had named me the Butcher, after all.

Normally, I liked to play it up for the audience and give them a good show. Not because I enjoyed it, but it kept me alive and made me valuable as a fighter. The resort even sold charms of my twin machete blades in the gift shops.

But right then, showmanship was the last thing on my mind. I could actually die today.

I held those blades out to the sides, forcing my feet toward the cat-shaped shadow in the pale white sand when all I wanted to do was fall to my knees before this creature.

I was human and unworthy. A sack of flesh, only 28 years old. A slave, and barely even a person. I hadn't made a single decision for myself in four long years. What was I to this thing that could take my life with one bite to my windpipe?

When I was nearly ten feet away from the jaguar, it sat down.

It just calmly planted its hindquarters on the ground and tilted its head at me like a curious housecat. My breath felt stuck in my chest, and I circled my wrists to make my blades dance. The weight of them was comforting, a natural extension of my arms, but the last half hour of watching this animal slaughter grown men could not be erased from my mind.

Don't be afraid, Santos. I will not harm you. The voice was vast and deep, penetrating my ears while also rolling over my skin; as comforting as a hug, and powerful as a building collapsing on top of me.

"What?" I whispered, then I really did fall to my knees. I hadn't heard my given name spoken to me in years, even before my time as a gladiator. The Ghost was the only one who knew it, but he couldn't call me that name here. Anything that gave us identities and humanity was forbidden.

You are under my protection, my dear son.

The voice was just as ancient and timeless as the energy I felt from this being. I was humbled in the presence of someone, or something, great but no idea what.

"Who are you?" I said, lowering my eyes to the sand. If the crowd was still going, I couldn't hear it past the pounding of blood in my ears.

In the simplest terms for you to understand, I am a god. You know one of my names.

"Tezcatlipoca." The strange word that had stamped onto my brain now rolled off my tongue, despite it being in a language I'd never spoken before. "The Smoking Mirror. Ruler of the North." I dared to lift my gaze to the golden eyes of the feline in front of me. "Have you come to free us?"

It is not that simple, Santos. There is much to be done. Many pieces must come together at the right place. The right time. The jaguar's tail flicked as he regarded me. *I have two primary roles in this manifestation. One is as your protection. I will be your guard and invisible shadow, Santos. Follow my guidance, and you will reach the freedom you seek.*

I released a shaking breath, unable to believe this was happening, that this nightmare I lived every day could actually come to an end.

"And your other role?" I asked.

A wave of scorching heat passed over me, oppressive and painful. It constricted my throat and forced my palms down to the burning sand. The weight of something impossibly heavy, like the entire colosseum filled with people, seemed to press down on my back.

I realized this was the weight of Tezcatlipoca's anger.

Vengeance, the god answered.

Chapter 1

Rori

"Whew!" I slammed the shot glass facedown, tilting my head back to savor the burn of liquor down my throat until it turned to warmth in my belly. Releasing the glass, I pointed to Lily across the table. "One more shot for the birthday girl!"

Flushed and giggling, my friend shook her head. 'No, I'm done!' she mouthed while her hands moved in fluid sign language.

"Aw come on, Lil!" I was proficient in signing but at the moment, was too drunk to move my hands in any eloquent way, let alone remember the gestures. She got my meaning, though. Plus, I was loud enough that she could probably hear me with her hearing aids. "Is your birthday," I slurred. "You gotta go all out."

Lily's boyfriend, my twin brother Daren, pushed a tall glass of water toward her. "Stay hydrated," he reminded her in a warm, gentle tone that reminded me of the way our fathers spoke. "I'll share the last shot with you," he added with a smile. His sign language was just as fluid and effortless as Lily's, which made sense considering they'd known each other since they were five years old.

Lily accepted the water and gulped it down, a coy look on her face while Daren and I waited for her verdict. "Okay, fine. One more, only if you'll share it with me," she relented.

I slapped my palm down on our table as I slid out of the barstool. "I'll make it a double, then."

But the happy couple were too wrapped up in each other to catch what I'd said. Lily leaned against Daren's shoulder and his arms went around her with a kiss on her forehead. I headed for the bar, shoving down the pang of longing in my gut.

I loved them both dearly, but sometimes I envied that they had found each other so easily. Lily had been new in Daren's kindergarten class at school, which wasn't equipped to accommodate her needs right away. She didn't know anyone yet, and my shy twin was determined to be friends with her. They'd been inseparable ever since.

Lily spent so much time at our house that our parents learned as much sign language as they could to communicate with her. To no one's surprise, she and my brother started dating in high school.

Fast-forward to now; we were all twenty-three. Daren and Lily had an apartment together and were planning a wedding. He was the head mechanic at our dad Jandro's auto shop and was set to take over the business when dad retired. Lily was now an ASL teacher and interpreter.

In both love and life, the two of them just seemed to have it so...easy.

I shook the thought from my head as I pushed my way through the crush of bodies in the bar. I was drunk and in my feelings. No one deserved forever love and success more than those two. They were my best friends, my family. I wanted only the best things for them, honestly.

As for me? I was a hot mess by comparison. Daren and I might've been born minutes apart, but we couldn't be more different. He had always been quiet, calm, and studious. I was loud, boisterous, and impulsive. A tornado of sunshine, as my mother called me.

And unlike my twin, no prospects for love or career had fallen into my lap. It wasn't for lack of trying. Just nothing, so far, had seemed to work out. I wasn't all that bitter about it, but some guidance from the universe would be nice. I wouldn't say no to a clearly laid out path with a neon sign that said, *Here, Rori. Do this, and you'll live happily ever after.*

I knew life didn't work that way, but again, I was currently in my feelings.

I eventually made it to the bar, coming face-to-face with Bryce, the owner. He was a man in his fifties, hair and beard streaked with gray, and a longtime family friend, practically a fifth father to me. Some of my earliest memories were of him and my dad, Reaper, teaching me to ride a bike and later, a motorcycle.

Bryce peered at me shrewdly, lifting a bushy caterpillar eyebrow at my approach. He could probably smell how drunk I was.

"One more round," I said, circling my index finger in the air. "On my tab."

"You're cut off after this, Rori," Bryce grunted as he set up the shot glasses on the bartop.

"Yeah, yeah. I get it."

"How you gettin' home, young lady?"

"Walkin'," I answered, throwing a thumb over my shoulder. "I'm crashing on the lovebirds' couch." Daren and Lily's apartment was just a couple blocks from the bar. I'd parked my motorcycle at their place earlier, and we'd all walked over here together.

Bryce seemed satisfied with that and poured our drinks without comment. He hesitated over the fourth shot though, and lifted his head to look around. "Where's the fourth member of your merry band?"

"Dunno." I wanted to resist looking around myself, but I had no self-control while drunk. I craned my head to scan over the crowd, head swiveling. I was tall for a woman, just under five foot ten, but it was a busy night, and I couldn't see Torrance anywhere. He was probably fucking some girl in the bathroom.

Oops. My drunk ass said that out loud, and Bryce gave me a

disapproving look. "He better not be getting up to that in *my* establishment," he grumbled.

"Hey, Daren's the only one with a leash on him. Don't look at me." I had actually been able to *not* think about Torr for an hour or so. But now the mental image of him thrusting into some girl propped up on the bathroom sink turned my stomach.

"You kids kill me." Bryce shoved the shots toward me, but I caught the smile under his beard. He and his wife didn't have kids of their own, so he was like an honorary uncle to me, my siblings, and all the other kids in town we grew up with.

"But you *love* us." I gave him my cheekiest smile as I gathered up the shot glasses in my hands. "Thanks, Bryce."

He waved a hand, shooing me away from the bar as he turned to serve another patron. It took all of my drunken concentration to not only hold the drinks but sidle my way through the crowd back to our table. I went slowly, careful not to spill the precious liquid that numbed both my heartache and general lack of clarity about my life.

I spotted Torrance finally, about halfway back on my journey. A beautiful brunette clung to the sleeve of his leather jacket, brows drawn together and lips frowning like she was upset. Torr seemed to be pulling away, his free hand gesticulating as he talked to her. I couldn't make out their conversation, but it looked like an argument.

Typical Torr. Breaking hearts and vaginas, sometimes in the same night. A lot of people didn't understand how he, a capital-P player, and my brother Daren, utterly devoted to one girl since he was *five*, came to be best friends.

The thing was, Torr didn't hide that finding love was the absolute last thing on his mind. He was at least honest with every girl he hooked up with. His utter lack of commitment wasn't his best personality trait, sure. But playboy tendencies aside, he actually was a solid friend and a really good guy.

Which made it really, really hard for any woman not to develop feelings for him. My pathetic ass included.

But I would never let myself become one of Torrance Knight's many flings or one-night stands. So I kept my trap shut and hid it all behind a numbing waterfall of booze. Although, I probably gave myself too much credit. We'd known each other for thirteen years, and in all that time, he'd never looked at me that way. To him, I was nothing but his best buddy's sister.

Astarte.

The strange word entered my brain out of nowhere, like someone had planted it directly in there. I stopped in my tracks, drawing my gaze to the window where a white dove sat perched on a tree branch outside. It just stared at me with its beady bird eyes, looking ghostly with its white feathers against the night sky.

The fuck?

I closed my eyes and shook my head. Okay, maybe I should have stopped drinking at that last round. But I knew my limits. My parents had allowed me tiny sips of booze since I was a toddler. Right then I felt good-drunk, but not sloppy-drunk. And I'd definitely never drank to the point where I was hallucinating.

"Hey, Ror!" someone yelled through the noise.

I opened my eyes to see Torr coming toward me, the pretty brunette gone. He cut through the crowd like a shark through water, everyone subtly ebbing away to give him room. His towering height certainly gave him that power, but there was also just something about *him* that made people want to stay out of his way.

He wasn't scary, but intimating? To those who didn't know him, absolutely. Torr had a hell of a glow-up in high school, muscles filling out his skinny frame and a cool, detached confidence taking over the haunted skittishness he'd portrayed as a child. Shit, I thought he was mute when I first met him. He didn't speak for a week, and even when he was safe, he had the demeanor of a wild animal that had been caged and abused.

People used to think Torr and Daren were twins. They both had that quiet, dark-eyed broody thing going on. My brother was a total sweetheart underneath, but Torr was hard to sum up in one word. And that word was definitely not *sweet.*

I'd known him for years and still found it hard to describe him. In school, he was known for protecting kids from bullies. But he'd beat the bullies so badly, they spent weeks in the hospital. Some of those fights resulted in battery charges and short stints in jail. He had a lot of anger, a lot of violence churning within him. He'd always been a good friend to Daren, Lily, and I, not to mention warm and respectful to our parents. But I still didn't feel like I really *knew* him.

And yet, he was the subject of all my dirtiest fantasies.

Fuck my stupid heart. And my vagina.

"Good, you didn't drown in pussy," I said when he got closer.

"Unfortunately," he sighed dramatically.

"Take a couple of these, will you?" I thrust the shot glasses at him. "I'm worried about spilling."

"I wondered why you stopped suddenly like a ghost possessed you." His hands were warm, but thankfully dry, as they brushed mine. I didn't want to think about who or what they touched tonight.

"So who did you send away crying this time?" I asked, both because I was a masochist and because I didn't want to dwell on that weird moment with the bird in the window.

"She didn't cry, thank fuck," he grumbled. "But that was Kay. She works in the governor's office."

"Trying to get those arrests scrubbed off your record?" I teased as we made our way back to the table together. "Probably shot yourself in the foot there."

"Nah, I don't give a shit about that. But she's a single mom, told me she was down for the casual thing because her kids come first and all. Tonight, she can't stop talking about how they need a strong father figure and that I would be so good for them. So, I ended it."

"Would it really kill you to settle down with a nice ready-made family?" The words hurt as they left my chest, but as soon as I downed this shot, I knew it wouldn't hurt as much.

"First of all, I knew her for all of three weeks. Second of all..." We reached the table and set the drinks down. Torr turned to me, smirking, with his shot still in his hand. "You're one to talk, Aurora Wilder."

"Touche." I rolled my eyes and raised my drink, turning toward Daren and Lily.

I knew he was only teasing, but I still hated how much Torr's words stung. He wasn't wrong. I had a bit of a reputation for being the female version of him. But for me, it was different. I genuinely *wanted* love—the constant, passionate kind that my parents had.

The only kicker was, I wanted it with multiple men. My mother, with her four devoted, loving husbands was exactly what I dreamed of for myself. They had essentially raised me to not settle for one partner, so why would I?

But their arrangement was still an unusual one in our fairly small town. And my attempts at dating multiple people had been met with derogatory remarks and heartache. It sucked, and I hated the double standard that made people respect Torr for playing around, while treating me as a warning sign.

Today was not about me, however. I put on a big smile as the four of us toasted our drinks and said happy birthday to Lily once again. Last call was made soon after, and I decided not to push my luck with Bryce and try for another round.

We chatted about work and mundane things while nursing waters until the crowd started to thin. Daren, ever the helpful one, started bussing tables until Bryce shooed us all out. Once we left the bar and hit the sidewalk, I realized that I needed a little extra concentration to walk, but I was otherwise fine. Daren and Lily walked ahead, arms around each other while Torr and I trailed behind.

"Smoke?" Torr held his pack out in my direction, a cigarette already dangling from his full lips.

"Yesss." I took the cigarette greedily. Smoking was not my usual thing, and I was certain I'd regret it in the morning. But the nicotine buzz hit so much harder after a few drinks, and I really wanted to float away on a high right then.

I expected Torr to just hand me his lighter like normal, but instead he turned and stepped in front of me, forcing me to stop walking or else I'd crash into him. His dark eyes were shadowed in the dim streetlights. When he held up the lighter, flicking the spark wheel, the flame's light danced over his cheekbones and nose, high-lighting all the sharp features of his handsome face.

Our gazes remained locked as I leaned forward a few inches to light my cigarette. I sucked in a long drag, our staring contest contin-uing as he lit his own. The flame's light disappeared and his face was cast in shadow again. We released our smoke in unison, the toxic clouds mingling in the air between us, molding into one before dissi-pating into the night sky.

Then I broke the spell with a snort. "What the fuck was that? Your latest seduction technique?"

"You wish." He smirked before turning to walk alongside me again.

"Yeah, right," I scoffed, maybe a little too loudly.

He let out a dry chuckle, more smoke exhaling from his nostrils. "It's just fun to mess with you, Ror."

I know, I thought but only grunted in reply. That was just Torr. He flirted with everything that had a pulse. I was the fool for reading into it.

Something bright caught my eye. I glanced up, thinking it was the moon or an especially bright star, but no.

It was that fucking bird.

The same creepy white dove that had stared at me though the window of the bar was now perched on a tree branch hanging over the sidewalk. I stopped walking but not because I wanted to. Some-thing seemed to hold me in place, something outside of my control.

"What the fuck are you?" I muttered under my breath.

It answered me, with the same ancient, omnipresent voice I'd heard earlier. *I am called Astarte, and I am your destiny, Aurora Wilder.*

Chapter 2

Rori

The neck pain woke me up first.

I rolled over with a groan, then promptly rolled back at the sensation of teetering on the edge of a cliff.

Ah, that's right. It was coming back to me now. Torr ended up crashing at Daren and Lily's place too, so he got the big couch while I squashed myself onto this tiny-ass loveseat. I vaguely remembered complaining drunkenly that Daren and Lily needed more bedrooms for us to crash comfortably. Daren said something about us paying rent, then I said something along the lines of, "Fuck you, but I love you," and that was the last I remembered.

I stretched my arms and legs, which meant throwing them over the arms of the loveseat. My throat was dry as a bone and a little scratchy. I knew I shouldn't have had that cigarette.

The memory of Torr lighting it for me came to the forefront of my mind and replayed like a movie. I knew I'd be recalling that moment again and again—the way his dark eyes bore into me, how the light and shadow played across his face, the smoke swirling around his silhouette like he was some mysterious figure in the night.

I would think back to it while daydreaming, because I was that pathetic. I was no better than the girls orbiting around him, desperate for a scrap of his attention.

I rubbed my forehead, keeping my eyes closed. He was across the room right now, his long frame stretched out over the couch. It was kind of unusual that he didn't find some other girl to take home. His place was only a few blocks up from here. But I suppose even players had their off days.

Slowly, I lowered one leg to the floor, then the other, pushing myself up to sitting. Whispers and gentle sounds of movement came from the kitchen, which meant Lily and Daren were already up. Damn early birds.

Ugh, no. Don't think about birds.

That whole shit with the dove was so weird and had never happened to me before. As I padded to the kitchen, I wondered if maybe I should cut down on drinking. I liked to party; I mean hell, my whole family did. But anything to do with hallucinations freaked me out, which was why I wasn't a hard-drug type of girl.

Lily signed a cheerful, "Good morning!" to me as I shuffled over to their breakfast bar.

I gave a small wave and said as I signed back, "Good morning, birthday girl. Thank you," and accepted the mug of coffee she held out to me.

Daren had his back turned, tending to something sizzling on the stove. Some kind of breakfast sausage from how it smelled. "Hey Ror, next time you come over," he said over his shoulder, lazily signing one-handed so Lily wouldn't be left out of the loop, "can you bring another carton of eggs? We're getting low."

"Sure, but text me later to remind me." My ASL wasn't at the level where I could say everything one-handed, so I set my coffee down to answer. "You know I can't remember shit first thing in the morning."

Lily chuckled as she brought plates down from a cabinet. "How are you feeling?" she asked.

"Thirsty and a little sore from your loveseat, but I'm otherwise fine," I told her, knowing she would want the honest answer.

She shook her head as if in disbelief, then playfully bumped Daren with her hip. "I'm always amazed at the alcohol tolerance of you two. I had half the amount of drinks and still needed headache medicine when I got up this morning."

"That's our biker tolerance," Daren said with a laugh, then kissed her temple. "Steel Demon genes, whatever you want to call it. It's a blessing and a curse."

"Why a curse?" Lily asked before handing him a plate.

"Because we don't always know when to stop," I answered for my brother while his hands were busy plating up food.

Our dads didn't make it a secret that they had used drinking as a crutch, though that was mostly in the past. Shadow had been especially careful about his intake for as long as I could remember.

Probably the most important thing about growing up in a family of bikers was that they didn't hide bad shit about the world from us. Me, Daren, and our younger siblings all knew that our parents had been outlaws when the world was in turmoil. The Collapse of the United States over thirty years ago meant territories were unstable, with laws and order going completely out the window.

Wars over territory and resources were constant back then. My parents' accounts were backed up by our history classes in school.

There had been a big war just outside of our territory before I was born, with all of my parents playing key roles, that ended in victory. They had become heroes, local celebrities. To this day, everyone in our town, Four Corners, knew who they were. My parents left their outlaw ways behind and started legitimate businesses when the territory was still young and had been here ever since.

Even though Daren and I had grown up happily, with a loving, supportive family, our parents didn't hide that the past war and turmoil left lasting damage. Reaper didn't have full use of his left hand. Jandro, Gunner, and even our mom had scars from gunshots and stab wounds. Shadow was covered in scars, including a large one on his face that cut through his eye. He was the "scariest" of my dads, but what most people didn't know was that he was one of the kindest, most loving people on earth.

Daren and I were fully aware of the sacrifices they'd made so that our lives could be better. Right then it made me feel a little guilty for my pity-party feelings last night. So what if I didn't have four hot boyfriends, or even one? Who cared if I didn't have my life fully figured out at twenty-three? At least I'd never seen a day of war in my life.

I tried to hold on to that sentiment as Torrance noisily rose from the dead, groaning as he stretched and then the loud thump as he rolled from the couch to the floor. He still looked half-asleep as he stood, following the smell of food to join us in the kitchen.

Wearing nothing but his boxer shorts, of course.

"Fuck, smells amazing," he mumbled, dropping into the chair next to me.

"Make yourself at home, why don'tcha?" Daren dropped a plate of eggs and breakfast sausage in front of his best friend, then playfully smacked his shoulder. "I told you, Lil. We should be charging both of these losers rent."

"Hey man, you're lucky I left my chonies on. I'd be buck-ass naked if I was at home. Can't sleep with clothes on." Torr grabbed my coffee and slurped it loudly.

"Excuse you!" I swiped it back from him mid-slurp.

"I was actually thinking we should swap out the loveseat for a futon," Lily signed to Daren, a smile pulling at her lips. "So it could be folded down and overnight guests would be more comfortable."

"Nooo, don't encourage them," he pretended to whine as he pulled her into a hug, laughing as he cradled her head in the center of his chest.

"Love you too, bro," I muttered into my coffee mug.

"Look at these two. It's too early in the morning for so much damn cuteness." Torr made a gagging sound as Lily hugged around

Daren's waist. She looked up at my brother, and their smiles of love and adoration matched perfectly before they kissed.

"Absolutely disgusting," I said, playing along with Torr.

"Hey, you want to keep sleeping on the loveseat or not?" Daren shot back.

"I'm perfectly good with the couch. Mr. Sleeps Naked over here just needs to find his naked ass in some damsel's bed more often. Or I dunno, his own."

Torr turned to me, stretching up so the full length of his abs and torso were on display. "And deprive you of this stunning view? I could never be so cruel, Rori."

"I dunno, you're looking a little squishy here." I reached out and pinched some skin on his stomach. Of course, there wasn't much to grab because he was wrought with muscle, and I was full of shit. "Been slacking in the gym?"

He shrugged, completely unaffected by my teasing. "Just doing some *new* workouts," he said with a salacious grin. "Lots of hip thrusts, if you get my drift."

"Ew. You're grosser than them." I angled my gaze back toward Daren and Lily, though something bright caught my eye in the kitchen window. The sight nearly had me dropping my coffee cup. "Mother-*fuck!*"

The white dove was right there, perched on the windowsill and staring at me.

You cannot ignore me out of existence, Aurora. The voice raked over my brain and skin, taunting me.

Oh shit. Shit. Shit. This was bad. I wasn't drunk anymore. Why was I still hallucinating?

"Hey, Ror? You okay?" The voice sounded far away, like it was coming from the opposite end of a tunnel.

My chest felt tight, and it was hard to get a breath. The rapid pace of my own heartbeat seemed like it was trying to choke me. What the fuck was happening to me?

"Rori, hey!"

The weight of a hand fell to my shoulder, fingers gently squeezing to bring my attention back. It worked, a little. Torr was leaning in close to me, the scent of him calming. It was his hand on my shoulder; his warm, dark eyes searching mine with concern.

"You're shaking like a leaf," he said, his brows pinching together. "What's wrong?"

"You need to lie down, sis?" Daren asked me, his expression also concerned. "You went really pale all of a sudden."

"No, no. I, uh..." I brought my hands to my face, rubbing my eyes like that would make the hallucination go away. When I looked again, the dove was still there, preening its feathers. Mocking me.

"I need to go home." I stood abruptly, nearly making my chair fall backwards but Torr caught it. "I just...yeah, not feeling great. Want to lie down in my own bed, you know?"

"Are you sure you're okay to ride your motorcycle?" Lily's hands moved swiftly as she asked the question, chewing her lip in concern.

"Yeah, yeah. I'm good." I was so frazzled that I forgot to sign, so I repeated the words with my hands. "I'm sober, just maybe a little more hungover than I thought." I forced a smile, trying to lighten the mood. "Steel Demon blood isn't invincible."

Torr's hand went around my forearm in a gentle but commanding hold. "Let me take you home."

"No." I pulled my arm loose. "I'm fine, Torr. Really." He was the last person I wanted in close proximity while...whatever this was was happening. Was this a psychotic break? Would I need to be committed to a mental hospital? As if it would hide my frantic thoughts, I walked away from everyone's stares to find my shoes.

Nobody said a word while I laced up my boots, not even the stupid bird, thankfully. I purposely kept my gaze away from any of the windows as I grabbed my keys from the bowl on the side table.

"Text me when you're home, Rori," Daren said as I headed for the door.

"Me too," Torr piped up.

"What, do I have six fathers now?" I grumbled.

"Pull over and call me if you're not able to ride safely," Torr added. "I'll pick you up and take you the rest of the way."

"Fucking hell, it's a ten-minute ride! And I'm sober, like I said. No need for all the hand-wringing."

"Just check in with us anyway," Torr said. He was using that bossy tone that all the girls hanging off of him melted over. Well, it wouldn't work on me.

I mean, I knew it came from a place of caring, so I'd do it. But it was still annoying. I'd been riding since my toes could reach the foot-pegs. I didn't *need* to check in with them like a child.

"Fine, whatever." I swung the door open, calling out over my shoulder, "See you guys later," before I closed it behind me.

Once away from their worried faces, I hurried to my bike and instantly felt a sense of comfort when I sat in the familiar seat. My parents got me this bike for my eighteenth birthday, and it was my greatest treasure. Jandro custom-built it, along with Daren's bike, since we shared the same birthday, while Gunner had everyone else helping him source the parts for our gifts. I can only imagine it took months, maybe even close to a year, to piece together both bikes.

I turned the key and welcomed the roar of my machine coming to life. Riding was the only thing I knew I wanted to do for the rest of my life. It was freedom and exhilaration unlike anything else in the world. My bike and the road were always there for me whenever life kicked me down, like when guys decided I was too slutty to be a serious girlfriend.

Riding was healing, and I needed it right now more than ever.

I pulled out of Daren and Lily's driveway, not looking at my mirrors until I was out on the main road.

Sure enough, I saw a white dove flying behind me.

Chapter 3

Torrance

The white dove flew away from the windowsill just as Rori left the apartment. Daren and Lily watched it too, all three of us puzzled as to why it spooked her so much.

"Do you think Rori's okay?" Lily signed to Daren, worrying her lip between her teeth.

"I dunno," he admitted, pulling his girlfriend into an embrace when she started leaning into him. "I've never seen her act like that before."

I could only nod, chin in my hand as I pondered her behavior. As her twin, Daren knew Rori best. If he'd never seen her in that state before, that was really alarming.

Something we could all agree on though, was that Rori was fearless.

In all the years I'd known her, I'd seen her enraged, heartbroken, or hurt over some douchebag who didn't deserve her. She was at times moody and sarcastic, with an especially sharp tongue that came out when she drank. But I'd never seen her *afraid*.

This was the first time I'd seen Aurora Wilder, the daughter of the bikers who'd once ruled the lawless southwest, express genuine, unabashed fear.

My mind was made up in an instant. "I'm gonna follow her."

I went to the couch for my clothes and turned when I heard a soft snort behind me. Lily grinned as she signed at me, "Good luck. She'll have your balls in a vice if she finds out."

"She won't find out. I'll stay far enough behind."

"Like usual," Daren muttered under his breath, the words not meant for my ears, but I heard them anyway.

"What was that, D?" I finished getting my pants on and shook out my shirt before putting it on. "If you're gonna say something, say it with your whole chest."

"I said, like usual," he repeated in a normal voice. Next to him, Lily sucked her cheeks in and widened her eyes in a, *oh shit, here it comes,* kind of look.

"And what's that supposed to mean?"

"Means you'll keep watching her like a hawk but be too chicken-shit to actually date her."

A tense silence fell, and Lily took the opportunity to leave the kitchen, which I was grateful for. Daren always signed when she was around so she wouldn't be excluded from conversations, which was fine under normal circumstances. But I didn't want an audience for *this* talk.

"Rori doesn't want to date *me,*" I reminded him. "And besides, she's your sister, bro."

Daren held up an index finger. "One, of course she doesn't, not with the way you're acting now. And two, you know I don't give a shit about that. The four of us hang out all the time anyway. You two are always squabbling like a married couple as it is."

I did *not* want to get into this with him. The sound of Rori's motorcycle was already fading, and I needed to have eyes on her to make sure she was okay.

"Daren," I sighed, shrugging my leather jacket on. " No offense, bro, but you're a terrible fucking matchmaker if you think me and your sister would be good together."

"If both of you pulled your heads out of your asses, maybe it could work." He whipped a dish towel in my direction. "But what do I know? I've never run away from the person I fell in love with."

"Yeah, good for you." I got my shoes on and headed for the door. "I'll see you later. Tell Lily I said 'happy birthday'."

"Yup. Later."

I headed for my motorcycle, parked alone now that Rori's was gone. She'd said our rides matched one time a few years ago, so we always made the effort to park next to each other. Two peas in a fuckin' pod.

"When I'm president of a club, you can be my VP," Rori had teased. "Only the best bikes get to ride next to mine."

"And what if I want to become president?" I'd asked her.

"You'd have to kill me for it." She'd laughed. "Rules of the road."

Once my steed roared to life, I eased onto the road, deciding to loop around and take a different route to her family home. Even if she didn't see me behind her, there was a chance she would hear my bike. It wouldn't be as obvious that I was following if I spotted her from a different direction.

Rori. Gorgeous, infuriating Rori.

I hated that Daren was right. It pissed me off how perceptive he was sometimes. Like he had a sixth sense for the things I tried to bury in a vault.

Everyone asked me why I could never keep the same girl around, why I couldn't just settle down and commit to someone nice. The excuse I gave was always accompanied by a smirk and a shrug. "I'm twenty-five, not forty-five."

I'd never spoken a word of the truth to anyone, but Daren had apparently caught on somehow. Every girl I hooked up with was a poor attempt at a distraction. A means to get Rori fucking Wilder out of my head.

Newsflash: it never fucking worked.

When I closed my eyes at night, it was always the wild, fiery biker princess with the short bob of blonde hair that I saw. Instead of being excited to see whoever I was fucking at the time, I always looked forward to hanging out with Daren or the parties at the Steel Demons' house because she was always there.

Shit, I got half of my tattoos from her dad Shadow's shop because she worked the front desk part-time. I'd schedule my appointments for when she was there, and we'd talk while her dad or one of the apprentices worked on me. It was just convenient that Shadow was the best artist around for hundreds of miles.

I'd known for years that Rori was the only one I could see myself with long term. But Daren was wrong about one thing. She truly did *not* feel the same way about me. If she did, I would know.

Rori was bold. Ever since we were teens, she was never shy about making her interest in a guy known. At parties, I'd seen her walk right up to a guy, kiss him, turn around and kiss his friend, then lead both guys to a bedroom and close the door.

Yeah, she wasn't shy about wanting multiple men either. And honestly? She deserved it. I'd have no qualms about sharing her with a guy or a few, as long as they were good to her and she was mine too. I knew deep in my marrow that I'd never so much as look at another woman again if I had her.

But I was never one of the guys she kissed and dragged to a bedroom. I was the guy she treated like, well, a brother.

We were friends, sure. Close enough and trusting enough that we could rely on each other in times of need. But our relationship rarely went beyond a surface level—partying or riding together, cracking jokes and giving each other shit. And every day I tried to be satisfied with that while I buried my cock in someone else.

I came to a four-way intersection and slowed to a stop. Looking to my left, I saw a glint of short blonde hair in the sunlight before Rori turned another corner. She appeared to be driving fine, which was a relief to see. When it was my turn to go, I continued on straight, hoping to catch sight of her again at the next block.

My strategy worked, and Rori had no idea I was following her. Lily was right in saying she'd be pissed if she knew, but, well, Rori didn't have to know.

If the chumps she dated couldn't appreciate her enough to stick around and actually watch out for her, it might as well be me.

As she crossed the bridge over the long, skinny lake that cut through our town, I maneuvered onto a side street to make sure she wouldn't spot me. This side of Four Corners was older and not as condensed as the downtown area where Daren's apartment was. The lots here were bigger with more land per household, especially on the other side of the bridge where Rori and her family lived.

She'd be safely in her own driveway moments after crossing, so once she made it, I turned my bike around, satisfied that she was okay. My phone buzzed with a text a few minutes later, and I checked it at a stoplight.

Rori: Made it home, Dad #5. Satisfied?

Torrance: Good girl ;)

Rori: Ew, don't be weird.

I STARTED TYPING out a joke about spanking her, then quickly erased it. Rori and I liked to push each other's buttons. We flirted, sometimes said raunchy shit, but always as a joke, always in front of other people. But a text was private. For some reason, that felt a step too far. Too intimate. The last thing I wanted to do was accidentally make my real feelings known. That would only make shit awkward. So I replied with a quick, "hope you feel better" and shoved my phone back in my pocket.

Chapter 4

Rori

I parked in the driveway next to my parents' motorcycles and paused for a moment after turning the engine off. My mom's bike was here, thank fuck. She was the one I really needed to talk to.

I didn't know if the hallucination had continued during my ride. I was too freaked out to look in my mirrors after the first time.

Smoothing out my hair, I took a deep breath and retrieved my phone to text Daren and Torr that I'd made it. Daren replied instantly with a simple thumbs-up emoji. Torr's reply came when I reached the front door, calling me a good girl.

I snorted and told him not to be weird. That whole praise kink shit was never my thing. At least, the guys I'd been with had never done a convincing job of it. Getting them to talk dirty, whether it was praise, degradation, or just telling me what the fuck they liked, was like pulling teeth more often than not. I was lucky if I got a quiet moan most of the time.

I bet Torr's good at it, though.

Ugh, I needed to focus.

I went inside, the familiarity of the home where I grew up

instantly comforting me. With five parents, me, Daren, and my two younger siblings, it was always a full house. Torr had even lived with us for a few months back when Daren and I first met him at ten years old. Plus, Lily has been hanging out with us since we were five. I could only imagine how exhausted my mom was, looking after *six* children in the house while also balancing her demanding career as a doctor.

I never remembered her being especially tired or stressed out though, and that was probably due to the fact that my dads were always present and involved. They took many burdens off her shoulders and were happy to do so. When Mom came home from a long day and us kids were still at peak energy, she'd say hi to us quickly, then one of my dads would put a glass of wine in her hand, send her to the bathroom with an already-filled tub, and shut the door behind her.

Our household was chaotic at times but always loving and happy. A family with multiple husbands just made sense to me. I didn't understand why other people thought it was so strange.

It was quiet when I walked in. My dad Gunner sat next to my youngest brother, Nolan, at the kitchen table, the two of them poring over what looked like math homework. Nolan was fifteen and a lot like Daren in that he was perceptive and enjoyed figuring out all kinds of puzzles. Whereas Daren preferred hands-on puzzles like cars, motorcycles, and sign language, Nolan excelled with numbers.

"Hey, Ror." Gunner looked up at me with an easygoing smile. He was the least outwardly threatening of my biker fathers with his friendly smile and cool, relaxed demeanor. Few people knew he was also one of the deadliest. He taught me everything I knew about weapons and self-defense. Before he retired, he worked as a military strategist, often with my grandfather, who had also been the general of the Four Corners Army.

Not that it mattered but Gunner was also my bio-dad. Pretty obvious when only the two of us had blonde hair in the family. His was pulled back in a ponytail, still lush and full with only a few wisps of gray in it. I could never stand the texture of our hair—not quite straight but not curly either, some weird wavy thing in the middle. My waves had a mind of their own, so I kept my hair chopped in a short bob no longer than my chin.

"Hey." I approached the table and rested my hands on the back of a chair. "Where is everyone?"

"Lucia was at a sleepover last night. She'll be home later," Gunner said, referring to my seventeen-year-old sister. Lucia was *gorgeous*, the spitting image of our mother, and incredibly popular. She had a large circle of friends and was always out somewhere with them. I had no doubt she'd find multiple men to adore her one day.

"Shadow had a tattoo client today," Gunner went on. "Your mom, Jandro, and Reaper are out back. How was Lily's birthday?"

"Good!" My voice went high with false cheer. "It was good, we had fun."

Gunner's face darkened. My parents always knew when something was off. "Everything okay, Ror?"

"Yeah. Just, you know, tired. A little hungover even though Bryce cut me off." I tried to make my voice normal, but I knew I couldn't hide everything from him. "I do want to talk to Mom about something, though."

That was code for I needed her for women-only-business, and my dad nodded with understanding. The whole while, Nolan kept his head down, punching things into his calculator or scribbling on his homework page. I wasn't offended though. My baby brother sometimes got hyper focused when he was deep in a complex puzzle.

Gunner stood as I rounded the table, heading for the sliding door that led to the backyard. He pressed a kiss to my temple as I passed him. "Here if you need anything, okay?"

I gave him a grateful smile. "Thanks, Dad."

Outside, Reaper and Jandro looked to be repairing part of the chicken coop while my mom watched them, holding a sleeping chicken in her arms. Mom was the first to spot me, shielding her eyes from the sun as I approached. "There she is! How were the birthday celebrations?"

"Good." I repeated what I told Gunner inside, putting on a smile, but it dropped the instant I saw the white dove settle on the fence behind everyone.

"Just good?" Jandro hadn't seen my face yet, since he was stretching a roll of chicken wire across some posts which Reaper held steady. "Did you get Lily to dance on the bartop? Get Bryce to flash his titties?"

Reaper grimaced. "Ugh, God. Why, Jandro? Nobody wants to see that."

Mom was the only one who noticed my expression, and she pinned me with her knowing doctor's stare. "Rori, is something wrong?"

My dads instantly stopped what they were doing and whipped around to face me.

"I'm fine!" That annoying, fake squeak entered my voice again as I fought to keep my eyes away from the fence. "I just wanted to talk to Mom real quick."

"Ah, girl stuff?" Jandro's worried face relaxed with the question, though Reaper was still scowling.

"Yes, girl stuff," I confirmed. Mom was a gynecologist, so I'd talked to her privately about "girl stuff" plenty of times in my life. Of course, that had nothing to do with hallucinations of birds following me everywhere, but as a medical professional, she would know what steps to take, at least.

"Here." Mom handed the chicken she'd been holding to Reaper. "Take Mimi while us girls chat."

He grunted in protest but cradled the chicken to his chest, who had woken up from the commotion with a few annoyed clucks. I knew he didn't care for raising them, that was mostly Jandro's domain, with some help from Mom. But like everyone else in our household, Reaper loved fresh eggs for breakfast, so he didn't complain. Much.

"Oh, before I forget." I snapped my fingers, turning to Jandro. "Daren wants another carton of eggs."

My father made a dismissive noise while rolling up the excess chicken wire and putting his tools away. "Tell that boy to come get them himself. He never comes over anymore."

"Let him be." Reaper slapped Jandro's back with his free hand. "Daren's a man, about to get married. Let him enjoy his independence." He kissed my forehead and squeezed my shoulder as he walked by me. "Love you, sugar cube. Hope everything's alright."

"He can enjoy his independence and still come over to see his dads once in a while! Sheesh," Jandro kept grumbling as they went into the house.

Once it was just me and my mother, my defenses immediately began to crumble. "Mom..." I choked out. It was getting harder to breathe. My chest and throat seemed to tighten and close up with panic.

She was right there, as she'd always been. Her arms went around me in a protective embrace. Because I was a few inches taller, she pulled my head to shoulder and petted my hair, kissing my forehead. "Let's sit down, sweetheart. Everything's going to be fine."

I allowed her to lead me to a bench, feeling like a child again as she soothed me. Everything seemed to be hitting me right then. I was so confused, so scared.

"Take a deep breath. Slowly," she said, gently rocking me. "You're breathing. You're healthy. You're not dying. I'm right here. No matter what's going on, you will be fine, Rori." When I calmed down enough to finally speak, she said, "Whenever you're ready, I'm listening."

"I'm...I think I might be schizophrenic or something," I blurted out. Not the most eloquent thing to say, but my mind was all kinds of jumbled. "Mom, I'm really scared."

The powerful, calming tone of her voice didn't change. "What makes you think that, sweetheart?" Her palm passed up and down my back in soothing, repetitive patterns.

"I've been having hallucinations. It started last night, and I thought I drank too much. But it kept happening this morning." I lifted my head from her shoulder, staring into my mother's bright hazel eyes. "Mom, am I gonna have to be committed?"

"One thing at a time, love." She cupped my cheeks, holding my gaze on her. "Have these been visual hallucinations? Auditory?"

"Both," I said.

"Are you hallucinating right now?"

I shifted my gaze to look past her, where the white dove now stared at me from atop the chicken coop. "Yes. I keep seeing the same white dove since last night. It followed me from the bar to Daren's house, then from there to here." I closed my eyes, wishing my brain would stop fucking with me. "I know it's not real. I just want it to stop."

My mom was silent for a long time. I just knew she was trying to tell me in the gentlest way she could that I *would* have to be committed and likely on a cocktail of medications for the rest of my life. Of course, she couldn't diagnose me herself since it wasn't her field, but one of her colleagues would.

The worst part was knowing that it probably wouldn't be safe for me to ride, and that was absolutely heartbreaking. I was only twenty-three, for fuck's sake! I didn't know *what* exactly, but there was so much I wanted to do with my life.

Eventually, my mom said, "Are you talking about the white dove on top of the chicken coop?"

My eyes snapped open in shock. "You see it too?"

"Yes." Her voice hardened to one I didn't recognize. "I can see it, Rori."

I felt a huge rush of relief and then more confusion. If she could see it too, then I wasn't hallucinating! But then...what the fuck?

Mom's head snapped around to face me. "The dove has talked to you? Has it told you its name?"

"I...what?"

"Answer me, Rori. What has it said to you?"

I'd never heard my mom speak so harshly before. Now it was her breath coming out in short, panicked puffs. My fearless mother, Mariposa Wilder, motorcycle club queen and battle medic of wars past, didn't just look afraid. She looked terrified.

I swallowed, but there was no moisture left in my mouth. "Its name is Astarte," I said. "And it said it was my destiny."

"Oh no..." Mom whispered with the smallest shake of her head. Then she turned to face the dove, anger coursing through her words. "Listen, you will *not* take my daughter! Not after everything *we* did! Do you hear me?"

An odd sensation rumbled over my skin, and I somehow knew it was an amused reaction. Something like laughter.

Mariposa, child of Freyja, the voice chuckled. I felt it in my head, on my skin, everywhere. *You know how this works. Your daughter is already mine.*

Chapter 5

Rori

I was so fucking confused.

Over the next twenty minutes, my mother refused to explain another word. She only said that all my fathers needed to be here for a family meeting. She called Shadow at the tattoo shop, telling him something in a hushed whisper before hanging up the phone after a few seconds.

The next thing she did was send Nolan to our grandparents' house down the street, which confused me even more. Rather than a family meeting, it seemed more like some kind of parental intervention.

Shadow must have left his shop immediately after getting off the phone with Mom, because his loud motorcycle rumbled up the driveway just as my other parents and I settled into the living room. I sat cross-legged in the big armchair, hugging a pillow to my chest as he came through the door. A looming, scarred figure with black hair to his broad shoulders, Shadow made grown men swallow and step back when he entered a room.

He also worshiped the ground my mother walked on and was the first to hold me whenever I had a meltdown as a kid, whether from a nightmare or a scraped knee.

I didn't know exactly what he did for the Steel Demons back in the day. Everyone said he was an enforcer, which could have been anything from slitting throats to making sure people were loyal to the president, Reaper.

I knew in my gut that he had killed people. All my dads and probably even my mom had. Their softer sides were private, reserved for at home with our family and friends. The public only knew their deadly sides, and Shadow was said to be the deadliest of all of them.

"Rori," he grunted out softly, crossing the room to my armchair in two long strides.

"Hey, Dad—uh, hi." To my surprise, he dropped to his knees in front of the chair and hauled me to his chest in a protective bear hug. He even bowed over me, as if the house were caving in and he was trying to shield me from a collapsing roof. My family and I were close, but it had probably been a decade since he hugged me like this, if not longer.

He held me like I was a little girl, using his size and strength to protect me like I was tiny and vulnerable again. And that was what clued me in to how serious this really was. I was a grown woman, one that had learned to hold my own and take care of myself, and my most protective father wanted to shield me from it all.

I gripped the edge of his cut at his shoulder, allowing myself to burrow into his embrace for a moment. "Dad, what's going on?"

Shadow lifted his head. "Have you filled her in?"

"Not yet," Mom answered. "We wanted everyone to be here."

"Yes, please, fill her in whenever you're ready," I snapped, annoyed with all the secrecy.

Shadow released me and went to sit on the couch next to Jandro while my mom opened the sliding door all the way. "You might as well come in. We all know what you are," she yelled outside.

The dove flew in moments later, perching on the stair banister while I felt myself curl up into a ball again.

"Astarte," my mother said in a clipped tone. "Tell us what you want with our daughter."

That is between Aurora and I. It does not involve you, daughter of Freyja.

Everyone else in the room flinched as if something unseen had touched them all at the same time. "Shit, been a while since I heard a god inside my head," Gunner said, rubbing his temple.

Something clicked into place, a missing piece of my parents' past that made the big picture much more clearer.

"What did you say?" I demanded. "A *god?*"

An oversimplification but one that will do, Astarte commented.

"You're a god?" Shadow looked like he wanted to wring the dove's neck and serve it up on a barbecue. "And you've chosen *our* daughter?"

That is correct.

It was so strange to hear a voice inside my head, especially knowing now that it wasn't a product of my own brain.

"Why? We did our part," Jandro growled, also staring murderously at the bird. "Why are the gods coming for our children now?"

Times change. Situations change. There is unrest that must be quelled, and I need a human. This *human.*

Reaper stood up, and everyone's eyes swayed to him. He'd been quiet since the whole thing started, observant and calculating. As the Steel Demons president, his word was once law. If anyone could make this situation go away, it would be him.

"Our children are not sacrificial lambs for your causes," he told Astarte with a deceptive amount of calm. "Our sacrifices to the gods have already been made, ten times over. You have no right to come in and use our daughter for whatever game you're playing. *We* accepted our bonds and did our duties so that our children would be safe. The war is over, and like Jandro said, we did our part."

Your war is over, yes. But this is no game. Another war is brewing under all of your mortal noses. It grows out of control, day by day. If I wait as long as your gods did, it will be too late for humanity.

Your gods? What the hell did she mean by that?

Before I could ask for clarification, Shadow jumped to his feet. "Then let us go instead. Rori, she..." he trailed off, gaze falling to me. "She doesn't know about all of this."

Obviously, I thought, still feeling completely in the dark while everyone else argued with this bird-god.

Your time has passed, Astarte said. *You've had your days to prove yourself, Son of the Sisterhood. A new generation must step up to the mantle.*

Shadow froze, his whole body going rigid like a block of wood. "What the fuck did you call me?" he demanded, a viciousness in his voice I'd never heard before.

Next to him, my mother wrapped an arm around his bicep and her lips went to his shoulder, as if to comfort him. That or to prevent him from actually killing this bird, which he seemed intent on doing.

Aurora doesn't know about that either, does she? The dove made a soft cooing sound. *Leaving children in the dark does them no favors. Humans always seem to forget this.*

Reaper stepped closer to the dove, his nose mere inches away from its beak. "Rori was never supposed to meet gods. You were never supposed to interfere with our lives again. Hades, Horus, and Freyja said they wouldn't!"

None of this seemed real. I felt like I was watching some strange alternate reality, my life playing out in a bizarre, fictitious version of the real thing. Hades and Freyja were a dog and cat we had when Daren and I were kids. Horus was a trained falcon that belonged to Gunner around the same time. I knew they were named after gods in ancient myths, but they weren't actual...

A memory hit me so hard it took my breath away. No, it was a dream. A memory of a dream I hadn't thought about in years. But it crashed to the forefront of my mind as vividly as ever.

I was around twelve years old and dreamed I was in a desert. There was nothing but dry, sandy earth and scattered bushes around me. There were mountains far away in the distance, and I remembered feeling hot. A scorching, dry, oppressive heat like I was inside an oven. Each breath felt like I was inhaling sand.

"Miserable, isn't it?"

I turned around to find a man standing a few feet away, when I had been alone moments before. He looked like a younger version of my dad Reaper, with brown hair, green eyes, and a warm smile.

"Who are you?" I had asked him.

"I'm Daren," he'd said. "It's nice to meet you, Rori."

"That's my brother's name."

"Yeah, you kinda got my brother's name too." He'd smirked, charming and teasing.

It clicked for me right away. I had seen flashes of him in dreams before, but never photographs or anything. My parents had told plenty of stories about him, though.

"You're my *uncle* Daren."

"That's right, kiddo."

He was Reaper's younger brother and had died years before I was born. Reaper's real name was Rory, which he hated and never went by. My nickname was a means to tease him at first, but it stuck, and he'd always said it was much better as a girl's name.

"What is this place?" I had asked my uncle's ghost.

"When you come here in a few years, it'll be called the Great Wasteland. Back when your dad and I used to ride through it? It was the Nevada desert."

"When *I* come here?"

"The gods will lead you here," he'd said, nodding at the mountains like they were the ones telling him this. "It will be dangerous and the most difficult thing you'll ever do in your life. But you're the only one who can, Rori."

"I don't *want* to be here. I want to go home."

Uncle Daren had turned to me then with a kind smile and knelt to talk at my eye-level. "I know, kiddo. It won't be for a while. Sometimes grown-ups have to do really difficult things. But it's okay. You won't be alone." He gave an affectionate squeeze to my shoulder and there, the dream ended.

I'd had dreams of my uncle for as long as I could remember, and I always believed *he* was real. Something like an angel, guiding and protecting me. Reaper told me that he dreamed of his little brother too, at times. But I had completely forgotten his cryptic message about gods until now.

In the present, my parents were still arguing with Astarte, one of the gods who I could only assume would lead me through the Great Wasteland as my uncle had told me.

Hades, Horus, and Freyja finished their business with you, Astarte was saying. *They are not part of this.*

"They wouldn't allow this," Gunner said. "They won't interfere, but they said they would remain present to watch over and protect our family."

I'm sure your trinity gods will continue to do so, but that does not mean they will interfere now.

"They never were just animals, were they?" I piped up.

Everyone seemed to have forgotten about me, despite the conversation being *about* me. A hush fell over the room as my parents exchanged glances, as if deciding telepathically what they should tell me.

"By the time you came along, they were just our pets," Reaper said. "But before that, during the war, no." His gaze slid to my mom, who gave him a subtle nod. "Hades, Horus, and Freyja *were* gods in animal vessels. Just like Astarte here."

"They bonded to us," Gunner added. "They gave us...gifts which enabled us to win the war."

"Humanity would have been headed for extinction if we had lost," Jandro said. "So we were prepared to make sacrifices and fight with everything we had. But..." He turned a narrow-eyed glare to Astarte. "The human population has been increasing. Territories are stabilizing. It's been twenty-six years of peace and progress. So can you understand us losing our shit over a god coming back after all this time and demanding our oldest daughter?"

The threat that looms is in its infancy, but its power is continuously growing. If another decade passes with it going unchecked, all your sacrifice will have been for nothing. All the progress of the past twenty-six years will be undone.

"What exactly would I be going up against?" I asked. "Another god?"

Other humans, for now.

"So why are gods getting involved if it's a human issue?" Mom asked.

It always starts with humans, Astarte answered cryptically. *But it may not end up that way. It seems you forget, Mariposa. Gods are human concepts given personification. When you give those concepts power, you deify them. War, love, fertility, prosperity. Each of these ideas have gods attached because humans gave power and personhood to them.*

"None of us have forgotten," Reaper snarled. "But why does it have to be Rori? Why *our* daughter?"

The dove fluffed up its feathers and promptly smoothed them down, looking directly at me. *This is simply the path she is meant to take.*

Chapter 6

Rori

Astarte flew away soon after dropping that bombshell, but I knew the dove would return. Reaper came to kneel in front of me, taking one of my hands in the silence that followed. "Sugar cube, you don't have to do this. No matter what that god tells you, you have free will, and you can say no."

"Love." Mom came up behind him and placed her hands on his shoulders. "You know that's not true. I know you want to protect Rori, but please don't lie to her."

Reaper let out an angry huff of breath, staring at her hand like it offended him. "We didn't do everything we did just so the gods could come back and take our kids from us, Mari."

"Rori, what are you thinking?" Jandro leaned forward from his place on the couch, the side of his face coming to rest against my mom's hip. "You've been quiet, mija. Do you have any questions?"

"I don't...I don't know." I ran my fingers over my scalp, still unnerved by the sensation on my brain that came from a god speaking to me. "I'm glad I'm not hallucinating, I guess."

No one laughed. At this point, I was starting to wonder if mental illness would've been an easier outcome.

"What...do I even have to do?" I scanned the room, looking at each of my five parents. "What did you guys do?"

They all exchanged looks again, that silent communication between partners that had known each other for over twenty years. With a pat on his shoulder from my mom, Reaper got up from the floor and returned to the couch. My mom squeezed in between him and Shadow.

"The gods we had bonded to us in different ways," Reaper began. "Hades, a god of death, chose me. He came to me in the form of a Doberman." My father paused and laced his hands together before continuing. "And I...reaped for him. I carried out kills on his command. In exchange, he protected me from death. Even though there were times where I got *very* close."

"He protected all of us," Jandro added. "Our bonds to him were different, but I'm certain he had a hand in all of our survival."

"Freyja bonded to your mother." Reaper angled his head toward her.

"I heard a kitten crying," Mom said, just above a whisper. "And I found myself tied to this beautiful black cat in ways I couldn't explain."

"What did you get out of it?" I asked.

"Freyja is a goddess of love, healing, and fertility. All of us, and every patient I worked on, healed rapidly from their injuries. I had some skills back then, but Freyja's guidance was...intuitive. I just *knew* what to do." She gave a small smile to Shadow next to her, who returned the look. "I think she was a bit of a matchmaker for us too."

"She was," he confirmed. "But Freyja was also a goddess of death. I don't know how exactly, but she worked with Hades in some sense."

"She did," Jandro confirmed with a nod, his eyes unfocused, his mind somewhere else.

"Horus is a sky god. He never talked to me much." Gunner had his elbow propped up on the arm of the loveseat, his gaze out the window. "Not until later, but I could see through his eyes. Falcons have binocular vision, and it was great for battlefield tactics." His smile in my direction was almost sad. "If I miss one thing about those days, it's the sensation of flying."

"Horus also gave me my sight back." Shadow absently scratched the long scar cutting through his brow, eyelid, and cheek. His eye underneath the scar was white, while the uninjured eye was dark brown. "Even improved my vision so I could see better in the dark."

"Is that how you always caught me sneaking to get cookies out of the kitchen at night?" I asked.

He grinned. "Yes."

"You got the dad-vision turned up," Jandro added.

Soft chuckles rose from everyone, but the humor was short-lived. We all fell back into a pensive silence. The situation felt too grave for cracking jokes.

"So Astarte is going to give me...some special ability?" I asked. "It doesn't even sound like this god likes me very much."

"Seems like it, but we don't know what that'll be," Mom said. "Everything we had was slightly different."

"What kind of animal vessel is that anyway?" Jandro muttered. "A pigeon? What a shit bird. If our girl's gotta go out there, she deserves an eagle or some shit."

"It's a dove," Shadow informed him dryly. "There's lots of symbolism attached to them."

"Whatever. Same thing as a pigeon. Fucking rats with wings."

"Says the guy who calls his chickens *'magnificent swans',*" Reaper muttered.

"My girls *are* magnificent!"

"Guys, can we focus?" Mom cut in before looking at me. "What else can we answer for you, sweetheart?"

Silence fell again as they all waited. It almost felt like they were expecting something from me.

"I don't know, like..." I spread my hands, shaking my head as I looked toward the ceiling. "What do I do? How do I deal with being chosen by a god? I don't even know what to ask!"

"It's a lot to take in," Mom said. "But it will become clear to you."

The answer felt placating. Patronizing. It was a non-answer, and that only made me more frustrated.

"So I *have* to do this?" I asked in the silence that followed. "Like Astarte said. It's the path I'm supposed to be on?"

Reaper was the one that answered. "Every time I resisted Hades, he made a point of reminding me just how...*human* I was. And that he was something more. Humans may have brought gods into existence, but they are *more* than us. They exist outside of the bounds of time and physical space. They know things we don't, and everything they have us do is for a reason." The look on his face was pained, like it killed him to say it. "So yes, sugar cube. Your mom is right. There is no getting out of this once you're chosen."

My chin went up and down in a nod, even though I didn't feel like I was *really* understanding. I had all this information coming in but none of it was processing. I knew the words, but the meaning, the gravity of the situation wasn't sinking in.

I was still the same directionless woman from last night, drinking and partying my feelings away for the town's heartbreaker. Like tons of others born after the Collapse, I was trying to find purpose in a world that was still recovering from irreparable damage. There was no reason why a god should choose me.

Only one thing was clear to me, a persistent need itched under my skin.

"I'm going for a ride," I said, standing abruptly.

I loved my family more than anything, but I was sick of them staring at me like this. Like they were waiting for me to accept this mission proudly, the prodigal daughter finding her purpose at long last.

I needed the road to clear my head.

"Helmet," Shadow barked as I walked past the couch.

"Yeah, yeah," I grumbled back.

———

I TORE through town on my motorcycle, then turned onto the winding road that would lead to a secluded pond just outside our borders. The location must have been a park for families and children before the Collapse. Rusted metal play structures were in a fenced-off area next to the pond, which was shallow and little more than a mud hole.

Daren, Lily, Torr, and I used to come here as teens to drink and just be dumbasses. My brother once stole one of Reaper's clove cigarettes that he liked to hide, and all four of us nearly choked on the intensity of it. When Reaper found out, he was so pissed that he told Daren and I to finish smoking it. We tried, both threw up before we could, and never stole from our parents again.

I eased back on my bike, reducing my speed once I left town and let the curving road guide and sway me through the landscape. The wind in my hair was cool at this time of year, but it would start warming up soon. It never got too cold in this region, not that I'd really spent much time anywhere else.

My family and I went on rides, sure. We camped and went on road trips every summer. I'd seen much of the land that was once a single country, before the central government fell apart and it became a bunch of warring territories. I'd never lived anywhere but in Four Corners though, and I'd never gone on a multi-day ride alone.

Would this mission from a god really be so terrible if it took me somewhere new? My parents were all worried, even angry. I knew they'd suffered in the war and didn't want the same for me, but it didn't sound like that was what I'd be walking into. But then again, Astarte hadn't revealed much.

The only thing that seemed certain was my lack of choice in the matter. And that in itself made me want to dig my heels in and tell that bird to fuck off. I was perfectly content in my small town life—riding motorcycles, working part-time at the tattoo shop, drinking the night away while pining over a man I couldn't have.

Perfectly fucking content.

The ride ended too quickly, and I pulled up to the gravel area next to the pond while my thoughts still churned. I sat atop my bike for a minute, just looking at the place where my friends and I had once been blissfully ignorant troublemakers. It felt different than I remembered. None of us had come here in years, to my knowledge.

I turned off the bike and swung my leg over to dismount. My boots crunched over the gravel as I headed for the playground, hopping the short, barely-standing fence with ease. I sat in one of the rusted, creaking swings, my legs stretched out in front of me and dragging along the ground. Bending my knees to pull my body forward, I allowed myself to gently swing.

The rumbling of a bike pulling up next to mine moments later wasn't surprising in the least. Neither was the tall rider with tousled dark hair walking toward me after he'd parked. My gaze remained impassive as he approached, watching songbirds and dragonflies fly over the surface of the pond.

Torr sat in the swing next to me without a word. He offered me a cigarette, which I accepted, again, without a word. He lit mine for me and then his own. We swung lazily back and forth, taking drags with no conversation for a few minutes.

"Stalking me now?" I asked him when my smoke was halfway done.

He made a small huff of laughter, the corner of his mouth pulling up. "I was running errands in town when you tore through like a bat out of hell. I'm sure the next ten blocks could hear your bike. Didn't know what to think, especially since you'd just texted that you got home."

Yeah, speeding through town probably wasn't the best idea. In a place like Four Corners, people would likely ask my parents what the hell that was about. We weren't the only biker family, but we were the most well-known.

"Everything okay, Ror?" Torr asked when I didn't respond.

"Not really," I admitted, my chest clenching painfully. How much could I even tell him?

"Well, what's up?" Torr tossed his cigarette butt and scraped his boot over it as he swung forward. "Who do I gotta put in the hospital?"

I snorted out a laugh. Typical Torr, solving problems with his fists or his dick. "It's nothing like that. My parents just kinda...dumped some news on me."

"Like what, they kicking you out or something? You need a place to stay?"

"No." I stared at him, a little unnerved by his prying. He'd never been this...protective over me before. "It's...I dunno. Family stuff."

I regretted the words once I said them. While *I* never thought of Torr as a brother, he and Daren were as close as brothers, their bond forged during that time he lived with us. My parents essentially considered Torr to be another son. Even after he was placed in a foster home, my parents made it known that he could stay with us at any time. Which he often did. In every way that mattered, he *was* family.

If my words bothered him, he didn't show it. He just nodded and kept swinging lazily next to me.

"Thanks for the smoke, but you don't have to stay with me," I told him.

"Would you rather be alone?" he asked.

It took a while for me to answer. "No," I admitted. That was the last thing I wanted. I didn't feel prepared to handle this on my own. My thoughts would just end up spinning in circles. I wanted someone to tell me what I should do. Or at the very least, provide an outside perspective.

"Then I'll stay," Torr answered, like it was the most simple matter in the world.

My knee-jerk reaction was to crack a joke about him having somewhere better to be, like hitting up one of his many booty calls. But in reality, I was grateful for him being there. I'd never have him in the way my chest ached for him, but he'd always been a solid friend.

And friends trusted each other. They gave each other support and guidance. Torr was fairly closed off when it came to his own feelings, but he'd never made me feel bad for wearing my heart on my sleeve. Hell, my heart was on every single stitch of clothing I wore when I was drunk. Whenever I cried into a bottle about a guy cheating on me or dumping me because I was "easy", Torr and Lily would take turns holding me in equal measure. I'd lost count of how many times I'd woken up, hungover and puffy-faced, with my head in his lap, his calloused fingers stroking gently through my hair.

The only thing I kept to myself was how I really felt about him, because we all knew that would end disastrously.

So I couldn't keep quiet about *this*. He'd go around and start asking questions if I suddenly up and disappeared, anyway. My dads were hardasses, but Torr was just as stubborn. He'd get to the bottom of it eventually.

Torr offered me another smoke and chuckled in surprise when I accepted. "Something must be really fucked for you to be smoking this much," he observed.

I took a deep drag, letting the nicotine hit all the right neural pathways before I answered him.

"Do you believe in gods, Torr?"

Chapter 7

Torrance

"Gods?" I repeated. "Like, more than one?"

Rori shrugged, flicking the end of her cigarette with a delicate finger. "Anything bigger than us, really. Higher powers, that sort of thing."

I paused to light up and inhale. "Yeah, I guess so."

She looked surprised at that, eyebrows lifting. "Really?"

"Yeah. Not in a religious sense, but I've always believed in something bigger than us. Why would humans have evolved to search for greater meaning if it's not there? Looking for those answers has always been a part of us, since we've lived in caves and shit. Maybe it's the searching itself that matters, and not the answer, but we all have that drive to find things that aren't right in front of our face. It's imprinted in our DNA."

Rori's lips curled with a soft smile. "I didn't know you had such a philosophical outlook on things."

"You never asked." I tried to soften the words with a smirk, taking another pull of my cigarette. I wished she'd ask me what I'd imagined that mouth doing, especially as her lips pursed to drag on her own cigarette.

"I've never believed in anything." She looked almost embarrassed by the admission, her amber eyes flicking away. "Like, sure, I don't know all the answers. But I've never really cared either, you know? I'm just one person. Who am I to figure out how the universe works? There are people way smarter than me who can't agree on what it all means, so why should I worry about shit beyond my own day-to-day life?"

"Nothing wrong with that either," I said.

Rori glanced back at me. "You don't think that sounds bitchy and self-centered?"

"Nah. But I feel like it's more personal than that, though. If something makes sense to *you* and makes *your* life feel meaningful, then who gives a fuck what so-called experts say? And by the same token, if you *don't* feel like you're missing anything by not having gods or something bigger in your life, that's cool too."

Rori sighed and tilted her head back, stretching the long, pretty column of her throat. "What if I didn't think I was missing anything until a god literally flew into my life?"

"Um." I braced my feet on the ground to stop my swinging and look at her more shrewdly. "What do you mean, Ror?"

"I left Daren's this morning all out of whack because I thought I was going crazy." She tossed her cigarette down almost violently and scraped over it with her shoe. "If I tell you, you'll probably think the same thing."

"I already know you're not crazy," I said. "But I can tell something's weighing on you, and you're thinking about it really hard. If it's family shit, like you said, I'll stay out of it. I'm here for you though, Ror. Just say the word, and I'll shut the fuck up while you get whatever it is off your chest."

She pushed back a wave of thick, blonde hair. "I mean, you are basically family."

I tried not to outwardly cringe at that. Sure, Daren and I were as thick as thieves, practically brothers ourselves, but I never saw *her* as my little sister. She had a point though. Her family was really the only family I ever knew.

I barely remembered my life before I ended up in Four Corners. The clearest memories were how badly my feet hurt. The soles of my shoes had worn out, and my blisters were bleeding. I remembered how hungry I was after walking for what had felt like days. The skin on my nose, ears, and neck had been made raw and red from the sun.

Night was falling as I happened upon Four Corners for the first time at twelve years old. After trekking alone through the desert for who knows how long, thinking I would surely die, I'd never been so happy to see civilization again. Even so, I had remembered a vague warning as I entered the town. Something about not trusting people, not letting anyone find me.

I wasn't ready to die yet, so I took that to heart. I snuck into a building with large roll-up doors and hid in a dark corner behind a large, metal contraption. There was just enough room for me to curl up between the big metal thing and the wall, where my exhausted body finally fell asleep.

I slept so hard that I didn't hear the roll-up door open the next morning, but I felt the stabbing rays of sunlight and roused just in time to hear a man say, "Que mierda? Who— what the fuck?"

Now jolted awake, I went to scramble away, but the man had me cornered. He crouched low, eying me with confusion but not anger or malice. "Easy, son. You're alright," he said in a gentler tone. Not removing his eyes from me, he yelled over his shoulder, "Hey, Lark. Call Mari. Tell her it's an emergency."

"Yeah! Everything okay, Jandro?" a voice called back.

"Found a kid sleeping next to the Mustang's V-8." To me, he said, "You got a name?"

I just shook my head, curling up to make myself smaller.

"That's okay. Looks like you had a rough night." He tilted his head, inspecting me from the painful, blistering sunburn on my face to the holes at the bottoms of my shoes. "Rough several nights, by the looks of it."

"Papi?" A boy about my age came up to him then, wrapping his arms around the man's neck as he looked at me curiously. "Who's that?"

"Do me a favor, mijo." The man hugged around the boy's waist and kissed his mop of dark hair. "Get a cup of water from the sink in the break room, okay? He needs our help."

The boy took off running, his father watching him for a moment before returning his gaze back to me. "I'm Jandro, and you're in my shop, kid." He smiled at me, warm and at ease. "My boy is Daren. He's ten, looks about your age."

The sound of running water in a nearby room made me realize how thirsty I was, how much everything hurt, and that I didn't want to be alone anymore. The warnings kept going off in my head, memories of some faceless person yelling and shaking my shoulders. My mother, maybe?

Don't trust anyone, you hear me? You can't let any of them find you. Promise me, Torrance. Say it back to me. Again, promise me.

I was made to repeat my promise over and over, but I couldn't remember by who. Even now, it was a blank hole in my memory. I repeated my promise over and over, miles after I'd been told to start walking. The muscle memory of the words on my lips was probably the only reason I remembered it at all.

It was important to whoever had sent me off. But fuck, I was so tired and so fucking thirsty. And this guy seemed nice. Like, he took care of his kid rather than send him on a death march in the middle of nowhere.

"I'm Torrance," I whispered through my parched, aching throat. "I'm twelve."

"Well, Torrance." Jandro rubbed his jaw, still looking over me with that curious but kind gaze. "I don't know what you've been through, but you're going to be okay from now on."

Jandro did more for me in that moment than any parental figure ever had until that point, I knew that much.

Next to me in the present, Rori was silent for a while after calling me family. She chewed her lip, staring at the ground as she swung back and forth.

"So?" I prompted. "If I'm family, you gonna bring out the skeletons in the closet or what?"

She stopped swinging and met my eyes again. "They're some serious fucking skeletons. I'm still processing it all. And like I said, it sounds crazy."

I took a stab in the dark. "Because it has to do with...gods?"

"Yes." She sighed and held out her palm. "I'm gonna need another cigarette."

———

Rori and I had killed off my pack by the time she finished explaining it all to me. Once she fell quiet and I sat back to just process all of the information, my fingers itched for another smoke to help me sift through it. Because she was right. It was a fucking lot.

"That's not at all what I expected to hear," I admitted, raking a hand through my hair. "I thought one of your dads had a spiritual awakening or some shit and wanted to go off and live on a mountaintop by himself."

"None of them would do that," she snorted. "Okay, maybe Shadow."

"Nah, he's too devoted to you all."

Shadow was the scariest motherfucker I'd ever seen in my life. He made Jandro look like a puppy. He hadn't said much to me when I first came to live with the Steel Demons. It wasn't until maybe two weeks later, after I started school and came home with a black eye from some bigger kids, that Shadow approached me.

"Do you want it to stop?" he'd asked me. When I'd barely nodded, trying my best to keep my tears at bay, he said, "Follow me."

I followed him out to the backyard gym area where he pointed at a large dumbbell on the ground. "Pick that up."

I did as he said, imagining crashing the weight into my bullies' faces.

"Lift it over your head," he instructed. "Arm straight."

It took some grunting and effort, but I got it up, holding the dumbbell aloft like a trophy.

"Good. Now put it back down on the ground."

I did so with a confused frown.

"Pick it up."

I did as I was told, the weight feeling heavier this time.

"Lift it over your head."

My arm trembled as I raised it this time.

"Good job. Now put it down. With control, don't drop it." He pinned me with that scarred, pale eye as I released the weight, panting for breath. "I know you feel weak right now, Torr, but keep doing that over and over, and you *will* get stronger. Not just here." He tapped one finger to my shoulder. "But up here." He touched that same finger to the side of my head. "Daren works out with me three days a week if you'd like to join us."

I'd hit the weights every single fucking day since then.

It was an outlet I didn't know I'd needed. Every time I questioned why my birth parents didn't want me, why they left me out in the desert to die, I added more plates to a barbell and let the pain be my answer.

To this day, even though I was in my prime and Shadow was in his fifties, I never could beat that guy's deadlift or his bench press.

"You're right," Rori said, drawing me out of the memory. "Maybe Shadow would've done that before he met my mom though. Everyone teases him about how he was too shy to talk to her and that she pretty much had to pursue him herself." Rori's smile faded, her hands twisting on the chains of the swing on either side of her. "But no, it's gods. They helped my parents win the war years ago, and now one of them has come for me."

"Yeah, that's...a lot."

Silence fell over us again until Rori asked, "What are you think-ing?" Like she couldn't stand the quiet any longer.

"Honestly?"

She swallowed. "Yeah."

"I'm thinking there's no way in hell I'm letting you do this alone."

Rori blinked, then shifted in her swing to face me directly. "Wait, hold on. You believe me, though?"

"Of course I believe you." I couldn't help the laugh that escaped. "Why would you lie about something like this?"

"I wouldn't, but I mean, this sounds nuts, doesn't it?"

I shrugged and reached for another cigarette before remembering they were all gone. "The whole world has been pretty fuckin' nuts for while, Ror. Since before we were born. It actually doesn't surprise me to hear that something else is brewing."

"Me neither, but come on, *gods*?"

"Why not?" I countered. "We fucked up pretty badly to have had a Collapse in the first place. Maybe some things are still out of the cosmic balance or whatever."

"I swear, Torr." She rubbed her forehead with a groan. "I could tell you unicorns flew over my house and we need to race them on a rainbow track, and you'd be like, 'Cool, when do we start?'"

"Hell yeah, I would. That sounds dope." I let her roll her eyes before continuing. "But really, it makes sense for me to come with you. Your parents have fought their fight. Daren and Lily got each other to think about, so they shouldn't go. I know you can handle yourself, but it only makes sense for you to have backup."

Rori shook her head, the worry clear on her face. "I *don't* feel like I can handle this, I'm way the fuck out of my element here. But that doesn't mean you need to get involved, Torr."

"Actually, that's even more reason for me to get involved," I pointed out. "If you're not prepared, who else is gonna save your damsel ass?"

Rori laughed so hard, she nearly fell off her swing. She hated being referred to as a damsel, so I teased her with it as often as I could. For all of her confidence and boldness, I could see the insecurities she tried to brush off. Always comparing herself to her twin brother. Stepping out of her parents' tall shadows. She truly was the brash, take-no-shit biker chick everyone knew, but sometimes she played it up to hide some of those fears.

You could be a damsel, I thought. *Just for me. I'll keep your secret safe.*

"Fuck you," she threw at me once she recovered. "How are you gonna live without pussy on tap, huh? It's gonna be slim pickings out in the desert. Unless you're into fucking cacti and tumbleweeds."

I was used to her throwing that in my face, but it still cut me every time. A repeated reminder that she would never want me.

"I'll live," I answered dryly.

"Sure," she scoffed, turning to rock back and forth in her swing again. "I won't see you for months when we get back because you're gonna be buried in an avalanche of ass." She paused, tilting her head. "*If* we get back, that is."

"We will," I said. "Besides, I'm Daren's best man. I'm gonna have to come up for air sometimes."

"Ew."

"You're the one who said 'avalanche of ass', not me."

"And I already have regrets," she sighed. We sat in silence again for a few moments until she nudged the toe of her boot against mine. "So you're really coming with me?" Her voice went quiet, almost a whisper.

"Hell yeah." It wasn't even a question in my mind. As if I'd last a single minute sitting on my ass here in Four Corners while she rode off into the great unknown by herself. Even if she'd never told me, I'd still find out and chase her down. "What's a damsel in distress without her Knight in shining chrome?"

"Torr!" Rori palmed her forehead. "You did *not* just make a pun with your last name."

"I sure as fuck did."

"I'm gonna kill you before this is over," she groaned, covering her face with both hands.

"Well, until then, I'll be your backup. Your right hand, whatever you need."

She peeked over her fingers and her eyes crinkled with a tiny, but genuine smile. "Thanks, Torr."

I nodded as I stood from the swing, immediately stamping down the fluttering in my chest. "We should probably tell your folks, huh?"

"Yeah." She rose from her swing as well. "Let's get this show on the road, I guess."

A white dove settled on the fence surrounding the playground as we headed toward our bikes. I glanced at Rori, but she had no reaction. There was no fear or confusion in her eyes now, only resigned acceptance.

Well, now.

The voice in my head made all my hairs stand on end. It felt ancient and everywhere, in my head and on the surface of my skin like a breeze. Possibly feminine, but it was hard to tell. I stared at the dove, who just cooed at me impassively.

This will certainly be interesting, the god said.

Chapter 8

Rori

"**T**orr's going too?" Gunner raked his hands back through his hair, gripping it like he wanted to rip the strands out.

"I am," Torr confirmed, standing next to me.

"And he knows...?" Mom trailed off, looking between the two of us.

"All of it," I said. "The present god, the past gods. I told him everything you all told me."

We were in the kitchen, the two of us having come back just as my parents were having lunch.

"So you're just accepting this?" Shadow leaned back in his seat, his arm draped over the back of my mother's chair. "Both of you?"

"It doesn't seem like I have a choice," I said.

"It's true. You don't." Jandro was stone-faced, all the humor gone as he regarded us from across the table. "And I fucking hate that." He brought a fist down on the table, startling everyone. "I hate that *we* gave up so much, and it wasn't enough. We *still* couldn't keep you safe from this. I'm sorry, mijita."

"Papi," I breathed, using the name I called him as a little girl. "It's okay. It's not your fault."

"She's right." Reaper leaned over and squeezed his shoulder. "We can't blame ourselves. We had no way of knowing this would happen."

"But the gods probably did," Gunner pointed out. "And they couldn't have warned us? I hate this too. It's fucking bullshit."

"We *all* hate it," my mom said, raising a hand. "None of us wanted this for our kids. But that doesn't change the fact that it's happening. And," she hesitated, lowering her palm, "Astarte is probably right in the sense that Rori is better equipped to handle such a threat than anyone else of her generation."

"Because she was raised by us," Reaper said, his chin lifting with pride.

"Yes, exactly."

I swallowed heavily, hoping no one noticed. I didn't feel like I was equipped with a goddamn thing. For all I knew, I was going against a tank with a slingshot.

"We've taught Torr well too," Gunner said, eyes falling to the man at my side. "You still shooting at the range?"

Torr nodded. "Couple times a week."

"Still lifting?" Shadow asked with a small smile. Anyone could tell Torr was ripped just by looking at him. He and Daren hit the gym together every morning.

"Shit, I gotta beat your deadlift one of these days," Torr answered.

"Hm. Not likely, kid," Shadow said coolly.

"If there's one thing I can feel comfort in, it's that he'll be with you," my mom said to me before turning a grateful glance to Torr. "Thank you for doing this. We love you like one of our kids, so my mothering side is in pieces over this, but at the end of the day, I'm glad it's you with her, Torr."

I noticed Torr standing a little straighter, his chest puffing out slightly. "You're all the closest thing to a family I've ever had, so when Rori told me about this, it was a no-brainer. I know you'd never ask this of me, but she also shouldn't be out there alone. I promise she'll be safe and back home in one piece."

"If it was any other kid giving me that speech, I'd send him out the front door with my foot up his ass." Reaper glowered. "But you're not just any other kid, Torr. You *are* our family too." My father stood, extending his hand. When Torr went to take it, Reaper grabbed his forearm and pulled him into his chest, clasping his other arm around Torr's back in a rough hug. "I know you'll take care of Rori. But get yourself home safe too. You hear me, kid?"

"Yes, sir."

They released each other and Torr glanced back at me, his expression a little dazed. That often happened when someone got close to Reaper. Bryce once joked that he never knew if Reaper was going to hug him or stab him.

I met Torr's gaze and nodded with another hard swallow. The inevitable couldn't be delayed any longer. "Guess we should start packing."

———

I MANAGED to go a whole half hour of picking out the lightest, but most usable items from my wardrobe for the trip before my fathers started hovering. One of them barely knocked at my bedroom door before all four of them crowded their way in.

"Jesus, you guys can still knock!" I shoved the underwear I'd laid out into a side pocket of my saddle bag.

Jandro paid no mind to my panty selection and immediately assaulted me with a bear hug. Unsurprising, since he was easily the clingiest of my dads. He'd be happy to have me live under his roof until I was well into my forties.

"We're not gonna see you for shit knows how long," he murmured into my hair. "So don't get mad that we want to spend every last second we can with you."

A painful twinge pulled at my chest, and I melted, returning his hug. "I don't know what I'm doing, Papi," I whispered into his chest.

He let out a shuddering breath as he rubbed my back. "You don't know yet, but you will. I promise you will. Trust in your god. Astarte won't lead you astray."

"But I don't *know* that," I protested. "I've never trusted in anything like this."

"I know, mijita. Believe me, I know how terrifying this is."

"You'll have Torr," Reaper reminded me from where he stood a few feet away. "He'll have your back, no matter what. I believe you can trust Astarte, but other gods...they may try to manipulate you. So don't trust *all* gods, only the one bonded to you."

"Great. I can't wait to hear about where that piece of advice came from."

Reaper smiled but it didn't reach his eyes. "I'll tell you the story another time."

"If all else fails, trust in yourself," Gunner said. He stood tall, eyes sharp and alert like a general on a battlefield. "Your instincts, your reflexes. I didn't train you to shoot left-handed for no reason. We've taught you everything you need to know, Rori. You just need to believe in it."

I nodded, wishing I could steal his cool, controlled demeanor for myself. "Thanks, Dad."

Gunner softened immediately, his lips quirking into a lopsided smile as he held his arms out. "Come here."

I released Jandro and went to him, slipping into his solid hug. He was my father by blood, and while all four men played equal roles in raising me, my bond with Gunner was just a little unique, a little different. Not closer necessarily, but different. I'd never hoped so strongly that I inherited his instincts for weapons and strategy. They just might save my life on this trip.

I looked at Shadow, who'd remained silent since walking into my room. He wasn't even looking at me but glowered at the clothes and supplies strewn on my bed. I had a feeling he wasn't looking *at* my stuff though, but that his mind was somewhere else far away.

"Any sage advice for me, Dadow?" Like with Jandro, I used the name I called him as a child.

His gaze snapped to me, and the look in his eyes actually made me jolt in fear. I'd never seen it before in my life. This giant of a man had always made me, my mother, and my siblings feel safe and loved, but I barely recognized him at that moment.

"Don't ever trust anyone who says they're with the Sisterhood of Bathory. You got that?" The words came out harsh and biting, like he was scolding me.

"Yeah, Dad." I could feel myself shrinking in Gunner's arms.

"I fucking mean it, Ror. You see someone who claims that, you get the hell away. Keep Torr away from them too. They'll use you to get to him."

My eyes narrowed with confusion. He was making zero sense. "Use me how?"

"Doesn't matter. Just stay far fucking away. I'm talking if they're in the same town as you, go to another town. Don't even let them *talk* to you, Ror. I—"

"Hey, hey." Reaper approached him, settling a hand on the other man's chest. "Take it easy. You're getting worked up."

Shadow turned his gaze on him, his jaw clenching and pupils like pin pricks. "Reap, you know I'm not exaggerating."

"I know, man. But it's upsetting you, and that's not helping Rori. She's smart, she'll know what to do."

"Aurora, *promise* me." Shadow returned his gaze to me, serious enough to ignore Reaper and use my proper name. "Promise me right now you won't have anything to do with them."

"I promise, Dad. I swear." Eager to reassure him, the words tumbled out of me quickly. "Sisterhood of Bathory, got it. I'll avoid them completely."

Only then did Shadow relax, his fists unclenching at his sides as a heavy breath escaped his chest. "I love you, Ror. I just don't want a fraction of what happened to me, to us," he glanced at Reaper, "to touch you. There's rotten, evil shit out there that shouldn't exist, but it does. And if I could prevent you from being exposed to any of it, I'd do it in a heartbeat."

"I know, Dad. I love you too." Sliding out of Gunner's embrace, I went to him. "But I gotta be a big girl too and fight my own battles."

"Nooo," Jandro whined, rubbing his face.

"Yeah," Shadow huffed in agreement with him. "That part, you fighting battles, scares the shit out of me."

"All of us," Reaper chimed in. "We were all just saying earlier, your mom too, that *this* is the hardest thing we've ever done. Letting you go."

"What the fuck, guys?" I blinked rapidly and wiped at my eyelashes before moisture could collect on them. "You're getting all sappy on me."

"Don't tell anyone," Reaper chuckled, kissing my brow. "Or we'll lock you in the garage."

"Not a bad plan." Jandro rubbed his chin. "She'll be safe in there, so will our reputation."

Gunner laughed. "You say that like she won't take a hammer to the walls to escape. Remember that?"

Like I could forget. He brought up my epic tantrum from eight years old at every opportunity. "That was an *accident!*" I reminded him. "I just really didn't want to be in time-out; I didn't know it would go *through* the wall."

"A lesson in repairing drywall that I never want to repeat," Shadow sighed, but he smiled at me. "We know you'll kick ass out there, Ror. Your dads are just always gonna worry about you."

"I know." I leaned against him and let him wrap me in a tight hug. My chest ached already, knowing how much I would miss them all.

———

TORRANCE ARRIVED EARLY the next morning, just as the sun rose. Everyone in my house was up and about except for Nolan and Lucia. My parents talked in hushed whispers so as to not wake them. I guzzled down coffee and forced eggs down my throat despite not feeling hungry. I would need the energy for the ride.

Torr immediately got roped into breakfast too—no one escaped being fed when the Steel Demons served up a meal.

"Did you say anything to Daren?" he asked, sitting across the table from me.

I nodded. "On the phone last night. He was...weirdly calm about it. When we hung up, he was just like, 'See you when you get back, sis. Love you.'"

My forkful of eggs paused on its way to my mouth. I wondered then if he had similar prophetic gifts to his namesake, our uncle Daren who passed and visited me in dreams. It never occurred to me until then, but it made sense. My twin had always been the wise, quiet one, while I'd always been a doofus.

"He expects us to be back in time for the wedding, I bet." Torr looked up and smiled as my mom placed a cup of coffee next to his plate. "Thank you, Mari."

"I mean, the wedding's six months away. How long do you think this will take?" I asked.

We both looked toward the kitchen window, where Astarte peered at us from atop the chicken coop again. *As long as it needs to take*, she answered cryptically.

"And where exactly are we going?" Torr asked.

Somewhere far and not on any map.

"Fantastic," I grumbled. "Somewhere in the Great Wasteland, I take it?"

On the northern side of it, yes.

"Even better."

Torr and I ate until we couldn't anymore and my parents couldn't pretend to be occupied with other things.

"Rori?" Mom cleared her throat while two of my dads squeezed her shoulders. "Did you want to say goodbye to the littles?"

I nodded, swallowing the dry lump in my throat as I got up from the table. Even though they were teens now, Lucia and Nolan were respectively six and eight years behind Daren and I. We knew they looked up to us, and we felt our own share of responsibility in raising them.

I went to Lucia's room first, finding her fast asleep on her stomach. Like a typical seventeen-year-old, clothes were tossed in piles all over her room and pictures of hot male celebrities were haphazardly taped to her walls. She was sprawled out on her bed, all arms, legs, and long, dark hair.

Pushing back a lock of her hair, I bent to kiss Lucia's cheek and whispered, "I love you, baby sister. I won't be gone for long."

Her brows pinched together, and she stirred with a soft groan but didn't wake up. I stood from her bedside and left the room quickly, knowing that if I stayed, I'd be tempted to slide under the covers and sleep next to her like we used to. Sister sleepovers, we had called them.

Nolan's room, on the other hand, was meticulously clean and organized. He was very particular about how and where things were placed. My baby brother was barely older than a toddler when he started making his own bed in the morning because he didn't like how our mom did it.

Unlike Lucia, he was also a light sleeper and roused the moment I stepped into his room.

"What time is it?" he groaned, rubbing his eyes.

"Early," I said. "You don't have to get up, I just came to see you."

He blinked, confusion etched into his features. Like my other siblings, it was unclear which dad he came from. I saw a lot of Reaper in him but also some Jandro. "See me for what?"

I pointed to his bedside. "Can I sit?"

He nodded, sitting up higher.

I crossed the room and sat down on his comforter, completely at a loss of what to tell him. I'd half-hoped to just kiss him and say goodbye like with Lucia. I figured our parents would tell him the most difficult parts, if they felt he was ready.

"I have to go away for a little while," was what eventually came out. "But I'll be back."

"Go where?" Nolan's eyes narrowed. "For how long?"

"I'm not sure about either of those things," I admitted. "There's a lot I don't know other than that this is an important job that I have to do."

"Is it, like, dangerous?"

"Maybe." I couldn't find it in me to lie to him. "But Torr's coming with me. So I'll be okay." I brushed my knuckles against his jaw in an effort to wipe away his frown. "Don't worry. Your big sis can handle it."

"What aren't you telling me?" he demanded. The poor kid couldn't stand *not* knowing things, and I felt for him. I hated keeping him in the dark, but I also wasn't his parent. I didn't even fully know what I was getting into, so I had no idea how much was safe to tell him.

"A lot. And I'm sorry for that." I ruffled his hair, and he slapped my hand away in annoyance. "Mom and Dads will be able to tell you more."

"Yeah, right." Nolan grunted, flopping back down in bed. "They never tell me anything."

"They will," I said. "When you're older." Our parents hadn't really opened up to Daren and I about their war stories until we were eighteen, going into our early twenties. Looking back now, I understood why. Those weren't stories for kids, not even smart teenagers.

"But you're leaving now, right?" Nolan asked. "Why do I have to be older to know why my big sister is leaving right now?"

Tears sprung to my eyes, and I quickly blinked them away. Fuck, this was hard. I knew where he was coming from. Shit, I could still remember being fifteen myself and feeling like everything was so unfair. He was frustrated, and that wasn't his fault. As badly as I wanted to alleviate that for him, I knew protecting him was more important.

Maybe the battles my parents fought couldn't fully protect me. But if *my* battles could protect Nolan and Lucia, then I would do whatever it took.

"Listen, big guy." I fought to keep my voice steady. "I love you, okay? And this will all make sense one day, I promise. But right now, all you need to know is that this is something that *I* need to do. For you and Luce."

Nolan just made an annoyed noise, turning to face the wall away from me. I tried not to take offense to it. He didn't know how serious this was, what Torr and I would be risking. All he was thinking about was that he was being left out of the loop. And he wasn't wrong.

Steeling myself, I stood up from the bed and repeated the words Daren had said to me over the phone. "See you when I get back."

When I left his room, Torr and my parents were already gathered outside. Torr sat on his motorcycle next to mine, his engine already humming gently. One by one, each of my fathers walked up to hug me and offer final words of wisdom.

"Eat good, mijita. Don't take shit from nobody," Jandro said. "And remember to change your fucking oil. Don't let your bike suffer, okay?"

I snorted. "I will, viejito."

"Call us for help if you need it," Reaper told me next. "For anything, sugar cube. Even if we're not hovering over you, we're right here. You're *never* alone, understand?"

"Thanks, Dad." I nodded, my throat drying out again.

Shadow came up to me next and said nothing for a long moment, just held me against his broad chest until he pulled away, his hands still on my shoulders. "You're stronger than you think you are," he said. "There will be times when you want to give up, but you won't. You're going to hold on, because you have it in you. Trust me on that."

There was so much experience and personal meaning layered

into those words, like he'd said them to himself hundreds of times before. I only nodded, meeting his gaze to show that I understood. Then I turned to my last father.

"Trust your instincts, Rori. Your aim is true, you know why?" Gunner whispered into my ear as he hugged me. "Because you're *my* fucking daughter."

I was already getting swept over by emotion, but that last sentence did me in. My eyes squeezed shut as I took a shuddering breath, clinging to his shoulders.

"We love you," Gunner said, gently rocking me from side to side. "And we're so fucking proud of you."

"I haven't even done anything," I whispered back. "I don't know *what* to do."

"You're taking the first steps. You've accepted the responsibility. That's huge." He pulled away, hands cupping my shoulders as he looked at me. "No matter what happens, we're so fucking proud." His hands dropped away as he stepped back with a lopsided smile. "Just come back to your old dads, alright?"

"Will do," I said shakily, forcing a smile. With another deep breath to center myself, I turned to my mother.

She stood off to the side while my fathers had fussed at me and now smiled as I approached. "You remind me of myself," she said, pulling me into a hug.

"Clueless, scared shitless, and in way over my head?" I asked, holding onto her tightly.

"Yes, exactly. All of that." She pushed her fingers through my hair. "Those feelings are normal, Rori. They don't mean you're not ready for this. You know what else I see?" Mom pulled back and held my face in her hands. "Someone a lot braver and more prepared than I was. I know you don't feel like it, but you *are*, my love. You were a warrior the day you came out of my womb, screaming bloody murder and kicking your brother in the head."

I let out a very undignified snort, but my mom's words did the trick and eased a little bit of my tightly wound fear. "Thank you,

Mom. You don't know how much it means to know you believe in me."

Now she blinked back tears right before bringing my face down to kiss my forehead. "Always, my daughter."

When we separated, I still felt clueless, scared shitless, and in over my head. But also a little steadier. A little more determined to see this through, if only to return to my amazing family again that much sooner.

I went to my bike and climbed on, my tentative steadiness turning rock solid the moment I sat on that machine. The world was mine when I rode, gods or no. This was freedom, and this was power. As I turned the key and felt the engine roar to life, I couldn't imagine arriving at my destiny any other way.

With a quick nod to Torr, I shot out of the driveway. Together, we followed the dove flying just ahead.

Astarte led us northwest, toward the Great Wasteland.

Chapter 9

Torrance

We followed Astarte through miles and miles and *miles* of desert. With the exception of a couple of pit stops, Rori and I rode nearly the entire day. I'd never admit it to her, but my ass and balls were aching like crazy by the time night started to fall. She'd been riding years longer than I had and probably never got sore from riding anymore.

Around dusk, Astarte perched on a rusted sign, which teetered dangerously to one side and was riddled with bullet holes. I had to tilt my head and squint to read, *Welcome to Carvers, Nevada*. Damn, so this was a pre-Collapse place. No one my age ever called it Nevada, only the older folks did.

You will rest here for the night. I shuddered at the sensation of Astarte's voice. It felt like fingertips dragging over my brain. Rori didn't seem to have the same reaction. I wondered if she'd gotten used to it.

"Where?" Rori looked around, and she had a point. There wasn't much to see.

In the tavern, child. In the morning, you will meet your first contact in that same location.

"*That* place?" Rori sounded incredulous as she nodded toward a building that had seen better days. Dust caked the windows and exterior walls. The siding was warped with age and some parts were tagged with faded graffiti. Neon signs in the windows advertised liquor and food, although their illumination of all the dust made the offers feel a little suspicious.

Windows covered the second and third stories of the building, and I could only assume those were rooms for the overnight travelers like us.

"Come on, it's not so bad." I nudged Rori with an elbow. "Imagine if Bryce's place was also a motel. That's what this is."

She rolled her eyes toward me, her expression dripping with disapproval. "Don't insult Bryce's like that."

"I mean, sure, it'd probably be less dusty, but Bryce isn't exactly a clean freak."

"We can't stay anywhere else?" Rori looked at the dove.

The answer came with a straightforward, *No*.

"Alright," Rori huffed, not sounding convinced as she popped up her kickstand.

We drove up the short distance to park in front of the building, and I waited until we turned the bikes off to keep ribbing her. "I thought you loved roughing it on camping trips," I said, following her to the front door. "This is just like that."

"I know my sleeping bags are clean and where my food comes from on those trips," she shot back. "This...I don't know anything about this."

"It's an adventure." I reached in front and pulled the door open for her. "And remember, I've got your back."

She glared at me on her way inside, but her mouth tipped up with playfulness. "Your eternal optimism is already exhausting."

"Sounds like a stamina problem for you, not me." I stepped in behind her, head swiveling around the dark room as I allowed the door to close behind me.

We'd walked right into the small bar-slash-restaurant area. Only a few wooden tables with benches lined the walls, most of them empty. The long bar at the far end, backed with rows of dusty liquor bottles, was similarly empty.

The bartender, a woman in her sixties with salt and pepper hair, looked up and squinted at us as we entered. "Can I help y'all?" she called across the room.

The few people, maybe eight in total, occupying benches and barstools turned to look at us as we crossed over to the bar. Rori paid them no mind, but I glared at the men who blatantly ogled her.

"Hi," Rori said cheerily to the bartender. "We'd like a couple of rooms for the night, please."

There was a pause as the bartender eyed us. "Separate rooms?"

"Yes, please."

I ignored the uncomfortable little prickling in my chest as I planted my feet wide, crossing my arms and meeting the eyes of everyone who stared at us until they looked away. While the bartender flipped through some pages in a logbook, Rori glanced over her shoulder at me, her brows drawn in confusion. I was standing close to her, probably hovering. But none of these perverts were about to get an unobstructed view of her ass in leathers. Absolutely the fuck not.

"Sorry, miss." The bartender looked up. "Only got the one room available. Will that work?"

"One room?" Rori repeated, looking around the bar. "Are you sure? It doesn't seem very busy tonight."

"We're doing some renovations," the bartender clipped out. "You want it or not?"

Rori pushed a hand back through her hair, her fingers landing on her bare nape. "Well, does it have two beds?"

Damn. Just twist the knife and announce to the whole world that you don't want me, I thought.

The bartender's eyes slid to me once before answering. "I think so. I'm not sure, though."

"You're not sure?"

The woman held up her logbook, the pages of which had been copied and recopied so many times, the room information was barely visible. "We don't have computers up here yet. We're all working with what we've got, miss."

Rori sighed. "Well, I guess we'll take it then."

While she filled out our information in the book, I went out to get our saddlebags from the bikes. When I returned, Rori had our key and angled her head toward a rickety-looking staircase. I followed her up, floorboards creaking with each step I took. The landing brought us to a short hallway with doors on either side.

"This is us." Rori went to a door with the number six and inserted the key. I wondered if we were both holding our breath as she turned the knob and swung it open.

"Fuck," she hissed.

I barked out a laugh.

There was only one fucking bed.

"Where the fuck is that bird?" Rori crossed the room and opened the window, sticking her head out to night air, supposedly looking for Astarte.

"Relax, it's no big deal." I slid the bags from my shoulders and placed them on the bench at the foot of the bed. "They have cots in these places, right? I'll sleep on that." I went to the closet and found it empty aside from a few wire hangers. "Or the floor, I guess."

"You're not sleeping on the floor." Rori pulled her head back in and shut the window. She turned toward the bed hesitantly, like she didn't want to look at it. "Looks like a queen, so there should be plenty of room."

"Aside from my feet hanging off the edge, sure." I sat in the single, small armchair and started to take my boots off. A queen bed was actually pretty small for a guy my size, and Rori was a tall woman too. My bed back home was a king, not only because it was long enough to support my whole frame, but it was spacious enough to feel like I was still sleeping alone when anyone spent the night.

A queen bed would put enough space between Rori and I, but just barely.

"Do you snore?" Rori asked, perching on one side of the frayed quilt covering the mattress.

I snorted. "How many times have we both crashed at Daren and Lily's place and you still don't know the answer to that?"

She wrinkled her nose. "Well, I sleep pretty hard when I'm fucked up." With a sigh, she tilted her head back to look around at the walls and ceiling. "But I don't think I'm sleeping a wink in here, regardless."

"You can kick me if I snore." I slipped my fingers into the collar of my shirt. "Also, uh."

"Oh God damnit, I forgot." Rori stood from the bed with a groan. "You sleep naked. Maybe you should take the floor, I don't want any cooties."

"Sure, if you want." I shrugged, pushing down the jab like I always did. "But I'll keep my boxers on, I just get really hot. And I use protection and get tested regularly, by the way." I hated everything about that last sentence that came out of my mouth and wished I could take it back. Maybe it was the ride and the long day, but she had me feeling so damn defensive.

Rori's mouth wobbled. "Sorry. I was just poking fun, but that was mean. I'm sorry, Torr. I'm an asshole when I'm tired and stressed."

"It's nothing. Here, just give me a sheet and a pillow."

"You're not sleeping on the floor," she insisted. "Just don't strangle me like an anaconda, and we'll be good."

"My anaconda is far gentler than that, I assure you."

"*Okay!*" She made a sound halfway between a groan and a laugh as she came to rummage through her bags. "I'm taking a shower, unless you wanted to get in first?"

"Nah, go ahead."

When she disappeared into the small bathroom and closed the door, I flopped back onto the bed with a sigh and pulled out my phone.

No reception, which was pretty much what I expected. Cellular service was spotty in most places, except for well-established territories and only if there were peace treaties between those territories. At least Sevier, a neighboring territory to Four Corners, was finally in the process of manufacturing new phones now. Everything we used now were relics from before the Collapse.

Rori's parents, Bryce, and all the other old timers talked about how technology used to advance so quickly. Before the Collapse, they had powerful computers that were so sleek, fast, and could perform all kinds of functions. Electric vehicles and the automated machines that built them. Speakers that you could talk to and order things that were delivered straight to your house.

That kind of growth happened at a snail's pace for Rori and my generation. There were just fewer opportunities to learn the things of the past, and those who knew enough to teach it were dying off.

I played some puzzle game on my phone until I heard the shower shut off. Then I tried and failed to focus on my game instead of imagining Rori step out of the shower, her bare skin glossy with water as she swiped a towel over herself. The mental image of her naked was too much to bear, and I dropped my phone, palming my erection with an annoyed grunt.

Maybe I'd wait until she was asleep, then slip out of bed to sleep on the floor after all. The fact that she insisted on two rooms, and then her utter disappointment at the lack of two beds, got under my skin more than her usual jabs.

We partied together, crashed together, told dirty jokes, and flirted all the time. We'd known each other for years, and yet had never been in the position to share a bed. I'd be a gentleman and not touch her, of course. But for some reason, her repulsion of me bothered me to the point where I'd rather take the floor than force her to share a mattress with me. She'd never outright tell me that it made her uncomfortable, but I knew she'd be relieved to wake up in bed alone.

The bathroom door opened, and Rori stepped out in a cloud of steam. She was dressed in sleeping shorts and an oversized T-shirt, thankfully saving me from seeing the impression of her nipples against anything tighter, like a tank top. Her hair was brushed back, the wet strands sticking to each other and ending at chin-length. Normally her hair was so voluminous, hovering around her face like golden clouds, but I liked the slicked back look on her too.

Who was I kidding? I liked everything on her.

"No lead poisoning?" I asked, watching her rub a towel over her hair in the mirror.

"Not enough to croak yet, at least," she chuckled. "The water's hot, which was a pleasant surprise."

"That's good."

She turned, hanging the towel on a hook as she came toward me with a thoughtful expression. "Do you remember what else Astarte said? Something about a contact tomorrow?"

"We'll meet our first contact in the morning here," I said. "You think this place serves breakfast?" I laughed when she wrinkled her nose. "I'll taste-test everything for you, princess."

"It's not that, dick." She gave a playful shove to my shoulder before flopping down on the bed next to me. "The word *first* has me worried. Like this is some kind of top secret covert mission in those old spy movies. How many contacts are there going to be? And are they humans or...?"

Gods was the unspoken word she left hanging on the end of that sentence.

"I dunno, Ror. We'll find out when we meet them, I guess."

She grabbed a pillow and hugged it to her chest as she turned to face me on the bed, drawing her long legs up to sit cross-legged. Funny how she called me an anaconda when I'd love nothing more than those legs to wrap around my hips and squeeze the life out of me.

"What do you think this whole mission is going to entail?" Rori's chin rested on top of the pillow, brows knitted together as she thought out loud. "Are we just receiving instructions from various mysterious contacts? What if they tell us to, I dunno, hurt people without any clarifying details?" She jerked her head up abruptly, pinning me with a wide-eyed stare. "What if we're on the wrong side of this, Torr?"

I snatched the pillow from her and softly whacked her over the head with it. "Don't *what-if* yourself to death. That's not gonna help us. We'll find out more tomorrow. And if shit looks fishy, we'll plan accordingly."

"You ass!" Rori dove for the pillow, but I swung it out of her reach. With nothing to hold on to, she barreled forward into my lap. I half expected her to scramble away, but to my surprise, she pressed her palms into the tops of my thighs, pushing herself up until we were eye-to-eye.

"How are you so calm and collected about this?" Our faces were inches apart, and I could feel the warm puffs of air from her lips as she spoke. "How does your mind *not* race with all the worst possible outcomes, Torr? Whatever you've got, I want some, because I wish my brain worked like that."

I shrugged, practically sitting on my free hand so I wouldn't be tempted to run my fingers up one of those arms braced on my thighs. "Being left for dead taught me pretty quickly that it's not worth worrying about things I can't control."

Rori blinked those forest green eyes and eased back slowly, her fingers dragging a few inches down my legs before her hands returned to her lap.

"You deserved better than what your parents did to you, Torr. I don't know if I, Daren, or my parents ever told you that, but it's true."

I shrugged again. "The point I'm trying to make is that you can't run through scenarios in your head, trying to predict an outcome, because it'll never turn out the way you think it might. You'll just get yourself worked up for no reason."

"My dad Gunner would disagree," she argued.

"He made predictions as a tactician with the knowledge he had available to him. His battle strategies were based on his expertise in the field, not wild guesses. Your predictions are based on your anxiety."

"Well, shit. Ouch."

"All I'm saying is, it's better to hear what the facts are and then plan accordingly."

Rori sighed before she snatched the pillow back from me. I saw it coming, but I let her take it anyway. "You're right," she sighed, hugging the pillow to her chest again. "I know you're right. I just... can't turn my brain off."

"I know." I leaned forward and tickled the bottom of her foot, something I always did to distract her from an anxious meltdown when we were kids. "I'm here for that too."

"Stop!" She laughed, flinging her foot out and narrowly missing kicking me in the chin. With all the times she had kicked me when I tickled her, I was surprised I still had all my teeth.

"Try to sleep," I told her. "And when your mind starts racing, imagine kicking me in the face. I'm sure those thoughts will be a lot more satisfying."

She scoffed, tossing the pillow back up to the headboard. "Thanks, Torr."

Rori scooted across the bed to her side and reached for the lamp on the nightstand. I stripped down to my boxers and climbed in, careful to stay close to my edge so I wouldn't accidentally touch her. Once I pulled the sheets up to my chest, Rori clicked off the light, and the room plunged into darkness.

"Goodnight," I heard her whisper softly from across the bed.

"Night, Ror."

I adjusted my pillow, settled in, and waited, listening for when her gentle breathing deepened so I could move to the floor.

Chapter 10

Rori

I woke up exhausted, feeling like I needed another eight hours just to feel normal. I had fallen asleep faster than expected, probably because we'd ridden all day and it was my first long ride in several months. My body's weariness made up for the fact that my mind ran like a hamster wheel.

Groaning, I rubbed the sand from my eyes. Why did my body feel so heavy? Oh wait, there was an arm thrown over my waist.

Torr's arm.

I noticed the dark lines of his tattoos first, the half-sleeve of swirling gray smoke that solidified into a snow-capped mountain on the top of his shoulder. His forearm was a golden tan from the sun, visible veins and corded muscles stretching down to a strong hand with long fingers.

My breath paused in my chest, and I laid there for a few seconds, frozen. I became aware of his deep, even breathing directly behind my head. Not snoring, thankfully. His chest wasn't quite pressed against my back, but I could sense the solidness and heat of him all the same.

Unfortunately, I needed air to live, so I started breathing again, forcing the inhales to be as slow as possible so as to not disturb him. So I could make this last a little longer, before he realized what he'd done.

Or had *I* instigated this? A quick look told me no, I was still on my side. Torr had been the one to cross the invisible boundary in our bed, and it secretly thrilled me.

He slept on, breathing deep and steady, so I began turning over as slowly and quietly as humanly possible. The sight of his sleeping face nearly made me gasp. He was *so* beautiful. Did he always have those freckles? I'd never noticed them before. But of course, I'd never woken up in bed next to him either.

Tons of women must have gotten this view and woken up the same way I did. But I couldn't bring myself to be jealous right then. He was here with me, not with any of them.

The thought brought a cold dose of reality, like icy water to the face. He wasn't *with* me, not really. He hadn't even wanted to sleep in the same bed. If I hadn't insisted on it, he would probably be on the floor now.

I wanted to touch him and curled my hand into a fist just so I wouldn't be tempted. He wouldn't welcome that, not from me. The only reason he came on this ride with me was because there was no one else. Lily needed Daren more than I did. My parents weren't fighters in their prime anymore. Torr put aside his own wants and was being an incredible friend by doing this. I had to be grateful for that and not hope for anything more. To do so was selfish.

Torr pulled in a deep breath and stirred, rolling to his back with a soft groan. That arm lifted away from me as he rubbed his eyes.

"Mornin', sunshine," I greeted.

"Hm?" He lifted his head and squinted one eye at me. "Aw, damn it."

"What?"

"It's nothin'," he croaked, his voice rough and groggy with sleep.

I pushed back my blanket and began to slide from the bed. "Sorry

I'm not the chick you were dreaming about." The words came out harsher than I intended.

Torr groaned, scrubbing his palms down his face. "S'not that, Ror."

"I'm kidding." I walked around the bed, grabbing my leathers and a fresh shirt.

"I was gonna move to the floor after you fell asleep," he said, lacing his hands behind his head so that his biceps and the wide expanse of his chest were on display. "But I guess I conked out before that happened."

"Why? I told you the bed was fine." I went to the vanity just outside the bathroom and pulled a brush through my hair, trying to distract myself from the little stab of rejection in my chest.

"Just to give you some space. Make you more comfortable."

I could almost believe the sweet sentiment in his words. Torr was masterful at letting a girl down easy.

"Well, all turned out fine." He must not have realized he was practically spooning me moments ago, so I wasn't about to mention it. "You sleep well?"

In the mirror, I watched Torr bring one hand down to rest on his chest. "Yeah, better than I thought I would. Guess it was a pretty grueling day. You?"

"Yeah, same. You ready to meet this mysterious first contact?"

"Yeah, let me get a quick shower in."

He pushed back the cover and I busied myself with my toiletries as he gathered up some clothes, wearing nothing but his snug boxer briefs. I kept avoiding eye contact as he approached me, all the way until he squeezed into the tiny bathroom and shut the door. Then I tilted my head back and let out a long sigh before looking at myself in the mirror again.

"Get a grip, bitch," I told my reflection. "You're just making this harder on yourself."

I got dressed while Torr showered, then after he was decent, we headed down the rickety stairs together.

"Did the all-knowing Astarte tell you anything this morning?" he asked as we entered the main room with the bar and tables.

"Nope. Not a peep." The room was even emptier than last night, with only the bartender, one grizzled older man sitting at the bar, and one table occupied by a group of three men.

"Want to take our chances with breakfast?" I asked Torr.

"Hell yeah, I'm starving."

He grabbed us a table while I went up to the bartender. The breakfast selection was simple but plentiful. Eggs, sausage, toast, and country potatoes for five Territory Credits, or TCs as they were most often called.

TCs were a relatively new currency, only put out into circulation about ten years ago. Six of the most stable allied territories came together and forged an agreement to make TCs their de-facto currency. This was to encourage more trade between the territories and make it easier for their traveling citizens to buy and sell goods across each other's borders. Many of the smaller territories and neutral zones had also adopted TCs for everyday use.

The days of bartering goods and services were something my parents' generation had been accustomed to for years, so a standardized currency had received some pushback from them. Especially Gunner, who prided himself in negotiating good deals.

"You can keep the eggs, my homie's chickens lay much better ones," I could imagine him saying with that charming grin. "And I'll give you two TCs for the rest of the spread, what do you say?"

I went to sit across from Torr at a table once I put our food order in. For a moment, we just stared at each other, saying nothing.

"So now what?" My anxious ass couldn't help but break the silence first.

Torr shrugged, propping his elbow on the table and then resting his cheek on his fist. "Guess we wait. We didn't get a description or a code word or anything, right?"

I leaned back while the bartender came over and dropped a pot of coffee and two mugs on the table, waiting until she left to speak. "Nope. We are well-equipped spies for this mission, clearly."

Torr only chuckled as he poured coffee for both of us. Our food came out a short while later and we dug in, mostly quiet as we ate. None of it was terrible, but my dads definitely wouldn't approve of the eggs. They were small, and the yolks were pale. I could imagine Jandro walking back to the kitchen himself with a lecture on how to raise chickens properly so they gave you large, nutritionally-dense eggs.

The activity in the room didn't change much as we ate. The guy sitting at the bar left halfway through our meal. The three men at the table talked quietly among themselves as they nursed cups of coffee.

We finished our food and the whole pot of coffee without incident. Torr and I locked eyes when the bartender cleared our plates.

"Don't say it," Torr warned.

"Now what?" I said at the same time.

"Damn it." He laughed and playfully kicked me under the table.

"It's nearly noon, right? Morning's almost over. What do we—"

The front door opened, spilling light into the room. The brightness of the outside was quickly blocked off though, by the dark figure stepping into the room.

And by the massive black wolf at their side.

Holy shit. I was too stunned to let the words leave my mouth, especially as the figure and their wolf turned toward us and headed straight for our table.

Neither Torr or I moved when the two of them paused in front of us. The figure lowered their hood, revealing herself to be a dark-haired woman. She looked to be a few years older than me, possibly in her early thirties.

"May I sit?" the woman asked in a soft voice.

"Um, sure." She could only be the one we were waiting on, so what else could I say?

Before I could scoot on the bench to make room for her, Torr got up and gestured to his bench, offering her his seat. "You can talk to both of us easier this way." He slid in next to me, and I was grateful for his presence at my side.

"Thank you," the woman said politely, sliding into the free seat with all the grace and poise of a princess. Her wolf jumped onto the bench beside her and rested its head in her lap.

Looking straight at her now, it dawned on me that she was really pretty. Naturally so, yes, but she also made herself that way. Her eyebrows were perfectly shaped and filled in, and her long, curling lashes were clearly extensions. Aside from her lashes and brows, there was no hair on her face, like she even removed the soft peach fuzz that every human being had. She wore no makeup, but her face was a smooth, pristine canvas.

"My name is Gwen," she said in that soft, polite voice. "And this is Lupa."

The wolf lifted her head at the sound of her name, looking at her human expectantly for a moment before laying her head back down.

"I'm Aurora. I go by Rori," I said. "This is Torrance."

"Torr," he said with a small wave.

"So you're our, um, contact?" I broached.

"I suppose I am," Gwen said with a small shrug. "Lupa brought me here. She said I would find the woman who is the light and the man who is her guard."

Torr glanced at me, his brow furrowed in confusion and I laughed softly. "Aurora is a type of light," I told him. "You know, like the aurora borealis?"

"The what now?"

"You know, the northern lights. Those greenish-blue lights in the sky that happen near the north pole? Those are auroras."

"Huh," he mused. "I never knew that."

Aurora is also a goddess of dawn. The ancient, feminine voice trailing gently over my brain was not Astarte's. It took me a second to realize it was Lupa, the wolf. She propped her head on the table and gave us a sweet, doggy smile. *You're touched by gods not only through your parents, child, but in your name.*

Torr and I looked at each other first before glancing at Gwen across the table. "Well, I'm glad we're not the only ones who can hear that."

Gwen smiled, her shoulders relaxing. She'd been so poised since the moment she walked in, I hadn't realized she'd also been stiff as well. "It's a trip, isn't it, when you first hear them in your head."

"I actually believed I was hallucinating," I admitted. "Until my mom let me know that the same thing happened to her and my dads."

"My parents were called on by gods too," Gwen said.

I rocked forward, bracing my palms on the table. "Are you serious?"

She nodded. "Lupa first came to me a few years ago. My mission has been ongoing." Her dark brown eyes traveled over us curiously. "And now it seems to have intersected with yours."

"We don't even know what it is," Torr said. "We just followed Astarte here and were told to wait for you."

"Ah, yes." Gwen tilted her head, her smile growing. "It's fun when you're only given information in bits and pieces, isn't it?"

"A fucking blast," I deadpanned.

"I wish I could tell you more about your own path." My heart sank when she said that. "But all I know is what I've been tasked to give you." Her eyes darted between us again. "Pardon me for asking, but are you two a couple?"

"No," Torr and I answered in unison. "No, we're just friends," I added to clarify.

Gwen narrowed her eyes, her lips pursing into a frown. "Are you two...close?"

"I mean..." Torr and I shared another look, and my hands folded nervously on the table. "We've known each other for thirteen years. He's basically a member of my family so, yes, you could say we're close. Platonically."

"I see." Gwen's eyes slid to Lupa, who licked her muzzle and opened her jaws in another doggy smile. "Well, I'm meant to help you get somewhere, and the place you're going has very strict rules for entry. Depending how uh, truly *platonic* your friendship is, you may have some difficulty gaining access. Or you may not, I don't know you well enough to speculate."

Now it was my turn to narrow my eyes at her. "What exactly are you saying?"

Gwen's shoulders stiffened again, her ramrod posture returning. "You will have to convince the staff at this establishment that you are a married couple."

Chapter 11

Rori

"Excuse me?" Torr sputtered. "Married?"

"Not *just* married, but happily so," Gwen went on. "This place is a resort that appears to cater to honeymooning newlyweds."

"What the hell are we looking for in a place like that?" I demanded.

"I don't know," Gwen said. "I'm sorry, I wish I could tell you. What I can tell you is that this place is very mysterious and exclusive. They don't publicly say what any of their amenities or attractions are. You have to apply to be a guest, and they've never outright said what the requirements are. But the pattern we've noticed is that only married couples and single women have had their applications accepted."

Torr and I fell quiet. "That *is* strange," he mused.

"Let me rephrase." Gwen placed the edges of her hands on the table so that her palms faced each other. "Married couples and single women who can afford it. The other catch is that the cost is very high. Even the application fee is exorbitant and nonrefundable."

"I have a good nest egg of TCs saved up," I said.

"Whatever you have won't be enough," Gwen said while I tried not to feel insulted. "That's where I come in. I'm going to sponsor your application and attendance fees. But you two also need to look the part, and I don't just mean acting like you're married." She leaned back, pulling her hands into her lap. "You two need to act and look like you come from wealth. And I mean *serious* wealth."

Torr leaned forward, placing one elbow on the table as he rubbed his jaw. "And who are *you*, again? How exactly do you know all this, let alone have the funds to get us in?"

Gwen's dark eyes hardened. Her perfect posture didn't crumble under his stare, and my respect for her only increased. It took serious balls to stand up to Torr when he was trying to be intimidating.

"I'm the publicist for a Blakeworth family," she said. "One of the Elite Eight."

Ah, so now the perfectly groomed brows and eyelash extensions made sense. The Blakeworth territory was known for having an obscenely wealthy elite class whose favorite past times included flaunting that wealth and crushing anyone beneath them into the dirt. Many of the citizens in Four Corners had been Blakeworth refugees, fleeing the outrageous laws and human rights violations that applied to everyone *but* the elite class.

I knew they were briefly involved in the war my parents had been in. One of my favorite stories was about how Shadow, his brother—my uncle Grudge and his club—and my mom, were wanted fugitives in Blakeworth. The Blakeworth governor had kidnapped my aunt Kyrie, the woman who would become the wife of Grudge, T-Bone, and Dyno, who ran the Sons of Odin MC. They all rescued her on that mission but knew they would be shot on sight if they ever returned.

"So you're a Blakeworth bootlicker, huh?" Torr's mouth twisted disdainfully.

"No. That's just my day job." To her credit, Gwen kept calm and not at all defensive. "What I'm actually doing, with Lupa," her gaze slid to the now-sleeping wolf next to her, "is providing resources and escape routes to those carrying all of the elite's bloat. The *real* citizens." Her eyes blazed with a passion I hadn't seen up until that point. "And from the inside, I'm dismantling the elite class, brick by brick."

Silence fell over our table while the pieces slowly began to click together in my head. "So this resort," I said. "Who runs it? The elite Blakeworth families?"

Gwen shook her head and spread her hands. "There's lots of speculation being thrown around, but no one knows for sure. My employers don't have any involvement, but they have been guests. Their friends claim no involvement either, though a son of *that* family claims to know an investor but apparently has been sworn to secrecy. It's one of those things where everyone seems to know something, but no one can locate the source."

"And probably half of them are lying," I said. I sure as hell didn't trust people with an obscene amount of wealth and power.

"Yes," Gwen agreed. "That's also a likely factor."

"How long has the resort been around?" Torr asked.

"About five years ago was when invitations to apply began circulating. I never heard anything before that, so construction must have been top-secret."

"And no one knows *anything* about what goes on in there?" I asked.

"That's correct. And those that have been guests in the past aren't saying a word. Apparently, they lose the privilege of returning if they divulge anything."

"Well, if that doesn't sound fucking shady, I don't know what does." I drummed my fingertips on the table and looked at Torr, but his focus was across the table.

"Sorry I called you a bootlicker," he mumbled.

"That's alright." Gwen smiled gently. "I've been called worse."

"It's admirable that you're doing this," I said. "I can't imagine the anxiety of working for a rich asshole family who would do terrible things to me and my family if they knew—" My mouth slammed shut, but I realized my misstep too late. "Sorry, I wasn't thinking."

"It's okay. My family is fine." Gwen raised a palm. "They're safe and far away in another territory. One of my dads is actually an accomplished hacker, so the false emergency contact information I gave to my employer cleared with no issues. They have no idea where my family is."

"Good. Still, that can't be easy." I smiled, feeling an odd sort of kinship with her. "How many dads do you have?"

"I have three."

"That's nice. My cousin has three. I have four."

Gwen's polite smile went into a full-on grin. "Our lucky mothers."

"Uh, so." Torr cleared his throat. "What's next? We tell everyone we're...married? Get ourselves some colored contacts and rich people shit?"

"Right." Gwen's expression went serious again. "You need suitable transportation too. How did you two arrive here?"

"Motorcycles," I said.

Gwen shook her head. I expected as much but still felt myself deflating inside. There was no other ride I preferred over my bike.

"I can store your vehicles in one of my employer's garages. They'll never notice. And I'll lend you one of their cars to take to the resort. Actually." She paused, tapping a finger on her chin. "I'll come with you in a separate vehicle. Your stay will likely be a month long, so I'll bring along changes of clothes and things you'll need. I just need to take your measurements, because everything has to fit like a glove."

"A *month?*" Torr balked. "People really go on honeymoons for a month?"

"In my employer's circle, three week vacations of any kind are the minimum," Gwen explained. "Any shorter than that and you will be looked down upon as frugal. Four weeks to three months are more typical."

"Jesus." Torr rubbed his forehead.

"What do we need for this application?" I asked.

"I'll handle all of that." Gwen waved her hand. "It's sent electronically, so when I finalize today, we should have an answer by tomorrow." She looked at Torr. "You asked about colored contacts. Yes, I'll get you both several pairs. When you're at the resort, you'll want to change them out regularly. It'll be expected of you to coordinate your eye colors with your outfits or jewelry."

"Jesus," Torr said again. "Fucking rich people."

"Aww, honey!" I wrapped my arms around his bicep, leaning my head on his shoulder and batting my eyelashes with a cheesy smile. "We can have matching irises like a couple of psychos!"

"Do *not* ever call me honey again."

The corner of Gwen's mouth tilted up as she watched us. "Any other questions for me?"

"Is there any other reason why you're helping us?" I asked. "Aside from your god leading you here, plus sticking it to rich assholes. Is there anything personal in this for you?"

She took a moment to answer, one hand stroking through the wolf's thick fur. "People have been disappearing. People I...knew. Worked with, in secret. Just missing, with no rhyme or reason."

Torr and I looked at each other. "You think that's related to this resort?"

"I don't have any proof, just a strong gut feeling." Gwen frowned at Lupa, like she was frustrated at the wolf goddess. "If anyone knows about the disappearances, they're not saying anything. These are not elite folks, either. Just normal people."

"So the elites don't care and aren't doing shit to find them," Torr said. When Gwen nodded, he added, "I'm sorry."

"The weirdest thing is," Gwen looked up at me, "you know how vulnerable people are usually the ones kidnapped? Women by themselves, teens, children, you know."

"Yeah?"

"That's not the case here. It's strong, able-bodied *men* going missing. Guys you'd never pick a fight with for no reason."

"Sorry to ask." Torr held up a hand. "But what makes you think they're being kidnapped? What if they're just getting the hell out of Blakeworth?"

"Because they're leaving spouses, children, and all their belongings behind." Gwen's voice hardened. "Because when the first kidnappings happened, a group of friends organized to protect their own streets since no one else would. They were gone before morning. Four men between twenty-five and thirty-five, none under six feet tall, all vanished into thin air."

Gwen's jaw clenched and her lip wobbled, her dark eyes blinking away tears. I could sense what she left unspoken—that one, maybe more, of the missing men had been especially important to her. If my deductions were correct, she was keeping together extremely well. I'd be a raging, feral animal if someone I loved was taken from me.

"I'm sorry," I said, feeling the urge to reach across the table and hold her hands. "I want to tell you that you can count on us, but I guess that's an empty promise if we don't know what we're dealing with."

"Yes. I really wish I could tell you more about what you're getting into." Gwen sniffed and quickly composed herself, folding her hands on the table. "But it's safe to say, you should probably assume the worst."

The worst being...what, exactly? I wondered. Slave labor? Human experimentation? My mind, already prone to running wild with ideas, started flipping through worst-case scenarios. In doing that, a question bubbled up, and I voiced it before getting lost in the spiral of my head.

"What's this place called?"

"Mystic Canyon Resort," Gwen answered.

———

WE RETURNED to our room later, where Gwen took our measurements for our rich asshole disguises, as Torr called them. If Gwen had any thoughts about two platonic friends sharing a room with one bed, she didn't say anything.

"What do you think?" Torr asked me when she'd left. "Do you trust her?"

I didn't have to think for very long. "Yeah," I said, confident in my answer. "I do. You?"

He nodded sharply, his expression determined. "I do too."

We stayed one more night at the tavern, and this time, Torr didn't bring up sleeping on the floor again.

I didn't wake up to his arm around me the second morning and got annoyed by the heavy disappointment in my chest.

At breakfast, Gwen informed us that our application had been accepted. In two days, we would arrive at Mystic Canyon Resort.

"That quick?" Torr held out a strip of bacon to Lupa, who gulped it down with a crazily wagging tail. "I thought all our clothes and shit had to be custom-fitted."

"It's a rushed order on my employer's account," Gwen said. "The tailors know not to keep them waiting."

"Is that how you're funding this whole thing?" I asked her. "On their dime?"

A sly smile curved her lips. "Of course. I can't afford any of this on my personal earnings."

I frowned. "Is it safe for you to do that?"

"I know how to cover my tracks," she answered with a coy smile. "And this stuff is a drop in the bucket to them, so covering anything is honestly overkill. They're at the level where they still have exponentially more money coming in than going out. If I really wanted to drain them, that would take a lot more effort that would definitely raise eyebrows."

"Fucking rich people." Torr broke another bacon strip in half and gave a second piece to Lupa. "I like the Robin Hood shit, though. At least you're stealing something from them."

"Well, it's not exactly going to the poor in this case," I mused.

"It's still a worthwhile cause." He scratched Lupa's ears as she licked her lips. "Just to find out what the fuck is going on in that place."

"I agree," Gwen said. "I'm all but certain this is the only way to get in." She took in a shaky breath. "After the kidnappings started, some people went out to find Mystic Canyon. They also disappeared and never came back."

Torr leaned forward. "Is the place guarded?"

"I don't know, but I can only assume so. It's out in the middle of nowhere. The invitations have directions but no actual address. So it's possible they might have perished from heatstroke or something else along the way. I'm not sure, though."

"Whereabouts is it?" I asked.

"About three hours north of here."

I huffed out a soft laugh. "Everyone was right. The pieces are all coming together." Astarte hadn't said a word since that first night here, but she hadn't needed to. She led us right where we needed to be and no further. I was still utterly clueless, but at least I knew more now than I did before.

"If you don't mind, I'll have some of my people come and pick up your bikes today," Gwen said. "They're trustworthy and will handle your vehicles well. You have my word they'll be stored in a safe location."

"Can it wait until tomorrow?" I asked. "I'd like to go on one last ride before I'm not able to for a whole month."

"Oh, sure." Gwen tilted her head with a curious expression. "Riding is pretty important to you, isn't it?"

"It's everything to me," I admitted. "Kind of runs in the family."

She smiled lightly. "Oh, I know some people just like that."

"Yeah?"

Gwen then seemed to get a bit flustered, clearing her throat as the color in her cheeks deepened. "Enjoy your ride," she said, standing from the table abruptly. "I'll see you tomorrow."

Rori

Torr glared at the huge makeup kit Gwen had set down on the small desk in our room the next morning. "This is why we had to get started so early? Makeup?"

"Blakeworth's elite are always heavily made-up. You have to look the part to not arouse suspicion," Gwen explained, opening the kit to reveal a small horde of brushes, pallets, eyelashes, lipsticks, and even small gemstones. "I'm not a professional, but I can do you both up enough to get by. When you arrive, they should have makeup staff for you, since they don't allow guests to come with their own servants."

"Wait, wait." Torr held up a hand. "What do you mean you can do both of us?"

"Blakeworth men wear makeup too," I told him. "You didn't know that?"

"No! Why would I?"

"I'll do Rori first, since she'll take longer," Gwen said. "In the meantime, Torr, would you mind shaving your face? Your foundation will look patchy if you put it on over stubble."

"Ror?" The high note of desperation in his voice was hilarious.

"You heard the lady." I sat in the chair Gwen pulled out for me. "We're top-secret agents going undercover, remember?"

I held back my snicker until Torr finished stomping around in search of his shaving kit, then went grumbling into the bathroom.

"He's a good sport, he'll get over it." I closed my eyes as Gwen pinned my hair back and soon felt the gentle mist of a cleanser on my face.

"When was the last time you had a makeover?" she asked.

"Probably when my little sister wanted to use my face as a finger painting canvas. She's seventeen now."

Gwen chuckled as she wiped my skin clean and began applying a primer. "Well, lucky you are about to get one every single day for a month."

"That sounds kind of exhausting, actually."

"I hear you. As soon as I'm off the clock, the first thing I do is wash my face."

I let her work on me in silence for a few minutes before asking, "Do the makeup staff get paid over there? At the resort?"

There was a long pause before she answered. "I don't know."

My jaw went rigid. Blakeworth faced all kinds of backlash from other territories because of the supposed terrible working conditions for laughably little pay. Many even believed they used slave labor. But the territory was so secretive about their economy, always diverting attention with their flashy elite class to show how prosperous and well-off they were.

"I guess that's something we'll find out," I mused.

My ass was numb and my limbs stiff by the time I was finally done. My eyelids felt heavy, and when Gwen let me turn to the mirror, I saw she'd glued in long, wispy feathers alongside my false lashes. She'd also put in bright, crystal blue contacts in, so my normally dark green eyes were straight up freaky-looking. Everything from my eyeshadow to my blush and highlighter shimmered with an almost blinding effect.

"Holy shit," I muttered. "Feels like I'm about to go to a costume party."

Gwen laughed. "Nope, this is an everyday look. You'll get used to it, though."

"I kind of hope not."

We dragged Torr into the chair together. He thankfully didn't put up a fight and was finished much quicker than I had been. He chose an emerald green for his eye color, and I popped the lenses in while Gwen worked on his face. When she was done, the difference was subtle but jarring.

She'd contoured his face, shaped and filled in his eyebrows, applied some neutral eyeshadow shades, and that was pretty much it. He still looked like himself but too...polished. Torr's freckles were gone, as was the rough stubble on his jaw and the small scar through his eyebrow. He'd gotten it from a fight with a playground bully, and Daren and I had taken turns applying pressure to it while we waited for the school nurse to come.

He wasn't that charmingly disheveled, rough-and-tumble guy I'd had a crush on since I was ten. Now he looked like he could put on a suit and recite the slimy words of a politician.

"That bad, huh?" He smirked, and I realized I must have been staring at him for a while.

"Uh, no, actually." I tried to recover smoothly. "You make a very convincing rich asshole."

"Great. You're not a bad rich bitch yourself."

"A match made in heaven," Gwen laughed as she put away her supplies.

Oh shit, that was right. We were supposed to act like we were married.

"Hey, don't I need a big, flashy rock or something?" I extended my fingers, trying to imagine some obnoxiously large ring on my finger.

"Oh, right! I almost forgot." Gwen reached into her pocket and pulled out a small box. "Torr, do you want to do the honors?"

For some reason, my heart beat crazily against my ribs when he took the box and opened it. Torr let out a long whistle as he held it out to show me. "Damn. Now that's a ring."

My breath stuttered. I was not usually moved by jewelry, but this one was just *pretty*. It was a large, single black stone, cut and polished so that all its faces threw off glassy reflections like deep pools of water. It was held to the silver band with four large prongs.

"It's a black diamond," Gwen said. "They're more rare, so the elites love them. The simple setting is also fashionable right now. Of course my employer bought like ten of them in one trip, so I just snatched one that looked like it would fit you."

"Hang on. Let me do this right." Torr dropped to one knee, his eyes locked to mine as he reached for my hand.

"What? Torr, no." I pulled my hand back, my throat choking with emotion. Why? Why did he want to do this? It was just Gwen in the room. We didn't have to play pretend right *now*.

"Come on, just let me." His voice went low with that sultry, masculine growl that worked to charm all the women. Myself included, even though I knew all of this was fake.

"You don't need to commit to your character this much," I muttered, letting him take the hand I'd pulled away.

His eyes dropped to my outstretched hand, the ring finger extended like it couldn't wait to receive that rare piece of jewelry from him. Fucking traitor, that little finger.

"No matter what happens in there," Torr said, eyes returning to my face as he slid the band over my knuckle, "I'm your guard at every turn. You'll always have me."

My chest started to ache with how long I'd been holding my breath. Even my teeth started to hurt from clenching my jaw. I hoped he couldn't see how my whole body trembled with every emotion I fought to prevent from rising to the surface.

I was a swirling maelstrom inside, pissed and hurt. It felt like he was mocking me, putting on this fake display when he knew the real thing would never happen between us. It felt so painful, I wanted to scream or slap him.

But Torr would never intentionally be that cruel. He remained blissfully unaware of my feelings, so he must have thought a fake proposal would be funny. He looked so solemn though, on his knee as he carefully slid that band over my last knuckle. The ring was a perfect fit, which was just the extra, cruel cherry on top.

"We come out of this together or not at all," he said before releasing my hand and rising to his feet.

A few feet away, Gwen busied herself with putting her makeup away, acting like she totally didn't see fake marriage vows between two platonic friends. Fuck me. We hadn't even made it into the resort yet, and I was already fucking up this act.

"What next?" I asked distractedly to no one in particular. "Clothes?"

"Um, yes!" Gwen sounded relieved at the subject change. "I have your gown over here, Rori. Torr, your suit is in the garment bag hanging on the closet door."

Torr's brows pinched together, like he was confused or even insulted that I didn't acknowledge his fake vows. But his features quickly smoothed over as he crossed the room to get his clothes.

I turned to the bed where a long, flowy gown made of some satiny material was laid out before me. It was a deep, rich pink, almost burgundy in color. I wasn't big on pink in general, but the dress was pretty, and I knew Gwen would pick a flattering color for me. I brought my left hand out in front of me, staring at the ring Torr had placed just moments before. The stone's glassy surface reflected the pink hues of the dress, and I wondered how long it would take before the charade was too much for me. How long until I couldn't hold back anymore and cracked?

Closing my fist, I let my hand drop back to my side and refocused on the dress. *One day at a time*, I told myself. *One minute at a time if I have to.*

———

AN HOUR LATER, our bikes were being loaded into a trailer being pulled by a truck, and Gwen showed us to two luxury vehicles waiting in front of the tavern. Torr practically drooled as he approached "our" car, some kind of vintage Rolls Royce.

"I've always wanted to drive a car like this." He walked a slow, appreciative circle around the thing.

I, on the other hand, just hated that it had four walls and a roof. It might as well have been a cage. I'd always hated riding in cars ever since I was a baby. My parents complained I'd send them to an early grave because I'd always open a car door before it stopped moving. Nothing beat the freedom of a motorcycle, and a heavy stone of sadness settled in my chest knowing it would be a whole month before I rode again.

Torr seemed to sense the melancholy rolling off me, and he came around to give my shoulder a squeeze. "It won't be forever," he said, as if he knew exactly what was getting me down.

I gave him a small nod and allowed him to guide me to the passenger side with his hand on my back. He opened the door just as Gwen pulled up in front of us in her large luxury SUV, the backseats crammed with "our" things for our "honeymoon".

"Just follow me," she said before rolling up the tinted window.

Torr and I settled into the car, and he push-started the ignition. "Think she'll let me go fast in this thing a time or two?"

"Don't risk it," I said. "She has to give this back to her employer at some point."

"I know, I was just kidding."

The silence was heavy between us as we drove. I spent most of the time staring out the window at the desert rushing past us. Part of me wanted to bring up the whole business with putting the ring on my finger, mainly to ask what the fuck that was about? At the same time, I was scared of the answer I would get.

Torr didn't push for conversation, and I wondered if he was

mulling over that same moment as I was. Probably not. Torr was like a mountain—everything just rolled off of him. Was it just two nights ago that he lectured me about not holding onto things I couldn't control?

Well, my control over my feelings for him was slipping. And I wasn't sure how to reel that in, especially now that we had to play the part of a married couple.

Looking upward, I was completely unsurprised at the flying speck in the sky. Astarte kept an easy pace with us in the car and apparently still had nothing to say. Would she even step in to course-correct if we fucked up? Who knew? My parents talked about bonds and abilities with their gods like there was a relationship. Gwen and Lupa certainly seemed close. But me and this dove felt like reluctant coworkers at best.

The drive was no less than three hours, but it felt like no time at all before Gwen's tail lights lit up, and we slowed behind her. I straightened in my seat, craning my neck to see what was ahead.

There was...nothing.

Only more desert stretched beyond her front bumper, and I was utterly confused as to why she stopped.

"Is something wrong?" I wondered aloud, hands going for my seatbelt.

Torr's hand stopped mine, his palm touching the ring on my finger. "Stay put. I'll check on her."

No sooner had he said that than a woman in a crisp black suit seemed to pop out of nowhere and approached the driver's side of Gwen's car. The sight made me wonder if I was hallucinating again. "Where the fuck did she come from?"

"Hang on." Torr hit a button that opened the car's panoramic sunroof and lifted up, poking his head through the top of the car. He flopped back in his seat seconds later. "Ah, I get it."

"What?" I demanded.

"There's a canyon up ahead, I could just see the edge of it just now. We're on a slight incline, so it's harder to see when you're sitting."

"Oh, so that's where the resort is?"

"Must be."

I stretched up to look myself, and he was right. A sheer drop-off was maybe thirty feet in front of Gwen's car. Across the divide, I could see just the top of the far canyon wall. The rock looked smooth, even polished, like it was carved by human machinery instead of nature.

Dropping back to my seat, I saw the suited woman talking to Gwen through her lowered window. She had to be verifying us as guests, and I hoped we were flying under the radar as well as Gwen assured us we would be.

Several long moments passed until the woman nodded definitively and looked toward us with a beaming smile. She waved and began to approach our car while Torr rolled his window down, but it was my side of the car she came to. Torr fiddled with the buttons for a moment until he got my window to lower.

"Welcome to Mystic Canyon Resort!" the woman said. "You have passed all the qualifications for entry, and we hope you enjoy your stay. I'm Nella, the guest services manager, and will be showing you around today."

"Thank you."

Nella continued before I could ask any questions. "I have staff on their way up to retrieve your things, including valet service for your vehicle. If you would like to pull up just in front of your assistant, our valet driver can take your car to the lot, and we can enter the lift to begin our tour."

"Thank you, that sounds...*lovely*." I tried my best to sound like a snooty rich person while finding it curious that she spoke exclusively to me, never glancing once at Torr.

Nella stepped away as he rolled our windows back up, and we slowly maneuvered in front of Gwen's SUV.

"I'm already creeped the fuck out," Torr muttered.

"You and me both."

"She stared at you like she wanted to eat you."

"Why wouldn't she just come to the driver's side?" I wondered.

"Shit, *I'm* glad she didn't."

"Dick." I shoved at his shoulder, but a smile never cracked his face. All of this was becoming very real.

There was a concrete pad, essentially a lone parking space, directly in front of Gwen's car, and Torr drove onto it. We were only a few feet away from the edge of the canyon now, and I stared at some kind of metal frame drilled into the side of the canyon wall nearby. It looked like a cage with only four bars making a rectangle shape, the top maybe eight feet above the lip of the canyon.

The questions in my head were answered when a glass and metal box slid up from the inside of the canyon wall and nestled into the top of the metal frame. Four people stepped out of the box, all women in the same crisp black suits as Nella.

An elevator! I realized, the word screaming out in my head. I'd never seen one in real life, much less stepped inside one. I was pretty sure Torr never had either.

Two of the women approached our car and opened the doors for us. "Welcome to Mystic Canyon Resort," they said in unison with warm, welcoming smiles. "We'll take your vehicle to the valet lot now," said the one at my door.

Torr and I stepped out, and the woman who opened his door slid into the driver's seat. The rest of the staff went to the back of Gwen's car and quickly unloaded our things. I clasped my hands in front of me, shoving down the uncomfortable feelings of someone else carrying my stuff. When you rode motorcycles, everyone was responsible for their own goods.

A whirring, grinding sound made me whip back around. "Torr!" I hissed, grabbing his arm.

"I know," he said, placing a warm palm on my back.

The concrete pad, and our car on it, was descending straight into the fucking ground.

"I apologize for the noise of our car lift," Nella said, eying her fellow staff member in the driver's seat like she was the one responsible. "We will replace the machinery immediately."

"Ah, no, that's okay," I protested, forcing a smile with a hand on my chest. "It just startled me, that's all."

"Which is unacceptable. You are our guests." Nella lowered her head in a show of humility. "Every part of your stay with us should be comfortable and pleasant."

Little dramatic, but okay. I just gave her a tight-lipped smile and a nod, unsure of how else to react. Thankfully, Gwen exited her car and came around to the front.

"This is where I leave you." She was also wearing a crisp suit, though it was an emerald green with gold trim. I assumed it was her regular work uniform. She also wore a full face of makeup, though it was more understated than mine.

"Thank you for everything," I said to her with genuine gratitude. Really, she had gotten us here. All we did was show up and do what we were told.

"See you in a month?" Torr's arm slid around my waist in a firm, possessive hold as he asked her the question.

"Yes, of course." Gwen inclined her head respectfully, as I was sure she would do for her employers. Though she glanced up quickly, catching both of our eyes. "Enjoy your honeymoon, you two."

Oh, right. That was why Torr put his arm around me.

"We will." I smiled and leaned my head against his shoulder.

One of Nella's staff slammed Gwen's trunk closed as they got the last of our things, so with a final, curt nod at us, she got back in her car.

And then we were alone at this mysterious resort with its creepy staff.

"If you would please follow me." Nella extended her arm toward the elevator before heading that way. The others had already taken a trip down with our stuff and a new, empty glass cage stood waiting for us.

I held my breath as I stepped from the natural ground into that cage, hoping I gave off the air of someone who rode in elevators all the time.

"Holy shit," I muttered under my breath, my eyes going wide at the view of the canyon.

I was quiet, but Nella heard me anyway. "Magnificent, isn't it?" The door slid closed, she pushed a button, and we began a gentle descent. "The founders wanted it to look exactly like ancient Rome, and I'd say we came pretty close."

Taking up most of the canyon, carved deep in the earth, was a giant outdoor colosseum.

Chapter 13

Devin

Santos stood at the tiny window of our shared dorm when I came in after breakfast. His two machetes lay on the side table, freshly sharpened and gleaming in the morning sun. He stood like a statue, feet wide and hands clasped behind his back, wearing only a pair of boxer shorts.

I shamelessly admired his ass as I reclined in my bunk. He didn't do guys but wasn't bothered that I did.

"Keep standing there for another twenty minutes, if you don't mind." I groaned as I stretched, my calves and feet hanging off the ridiculously small bed.

"Why?" he asked with a soft chuckle.

"One, I have a great view of your back and your ass. Two, you're blocking out the sun, and I want to get a nap in before training."

He cast a smirk at me over his shoulder. "You might be fighting for bed space for that nap."

As if waiting for his cue, our third roommate, Santos' black jaguar, Tezcatlipoca, jumped onto the bed with me.

"Ow, Tezca!" Paws the size of my hands braced on my chest as the big cat made himself comfortable right on top of me.

The jaguar only huffed in amusement and leaned down to lick his sandpaper tongue against my jaw. He loved to groom my beard for some reason.

"Fuck, you're heavy, and your breath stinks." I shoved back against Tezca but only succeeded in sliding myself out from under him. He settled himself down on the bed, while I only got the very edge. Sighing, I brought my feet to the floor and leaned back against the big cat's flank. "What are you looking at, anyway?" I said to Santos, who'd returned to staring out the window.

"More resort guests just showed up," he answered.

"So?" I gathered my hair up and began winding it into a topknot at the crown of my head. If I wasn't going to nap, I might as well get stretched out for training.

"Something's weird about them. Come look."

I finished tying up my hair and stood to look over his shoulder. I had a few inches on Santos in height, but he had me beat in muscle mass and savage brutality that crowds loved to see in a gladiator. My talents lie in being fast and swift. My opponents always lost sight of me before I delivered the killing strike.

Hence why he was dubbed the Butcher and I, the Ghost.

Through the window and across the canyon which had been our involuntary home for the past four years, I saw the guest elevator descending with three people in it. One was Nella, the vile bitch who was the guest manager of this so-called resort. The guests were a couple in their twenties, a woman with short blonde hair and a dark-haired man. Their arms were around each other, so honeymooners probably. Their eyes were on Nella as she gestured around the canyon, no doubt giving her welcome speech filled with her cleverly woven bullshit.

"They look pretty typical to me," I said to Santos. "What's weird about them?"

"I dunno, something's off." His dark eyes narrowed, rapt on the couple like they were a puzzle he was trying to solve. "The woman's body language is stiff. Like she doesn't want to touch him."

"They're hundreds of yards away. How can you tell?"

"Appearances are off too. Their clothing looks like Blakeworth, but they just...don't look like Blakeworth stock to me."

"So what are you thinking?" I returned to sitting on the bed, where Tezca was already asleep with a bit of his tongue poking out. "That they're the ones big kitty here says we're waiting for?" I patted the jaguar's flank. He stirred but didn't wake up.

"Maybe. I don't know, could be nothing." Santos finally turned away from the window, rubbing his eyes. "Ever since he told us that, it feels like I'm reading into every little thing."

Young gladiators often prayed for miracles. They asked their various gods to rescue them, to be kept safe in the pit, or for a quick, painless death on the sands. If they lasted a year or more, like us, they often became too jaded to have any hope left. We certainly had been. The two of us were skilled fighters, but it was also our celebrity status, our entertainment value, that kept us alive.

But for Santos and I, our answered prayers came years after we'd lost hope and in the form of a black jaguar. Or rather, a god taking on the form of a black jaguar. He was brought out for the gladiators to slaughter during an event, but the clawed, fanged shadow killed everyone who neared him instead. Everyone except us.

Tezcatlipoca had said rescue was coming. Not right away but one day. He gave us hope, but hope was a heavy burden when you had to fight for your life, day in and day out.

It was relatively easy to make Tezca our pet. He wouldn't leave our side, and we were valuable gladiators who brought income to the resort. So they just let him stay with us. It kept the pitmasters from breathing down our necks and the other gladiators from attempting to kill us in our sleep.

Yeah, the pit wasn't a place to make friends. Santos and I were somewhat of an exception in that we were already acquainted. We'd been taken from the same place—another prison, just not one where we'd been forced to fight. He and I had been housed there together, along with a third guy, Hudson, who had been left behind. Who even knew if that poor bastard was still alive?

"Has he said anything to you?" I nodded at the snoring jaguar behind me.

"Nah, nothing." Santos pulled on his pants and then secured his belt around his hips.

"So it's probably not them, right?"

"I dunno. He doesn't always tell me shit." Santos slid the machetes into their sheaths on his belt. "Sometimes it's fucking riddles, and I don't know what he means."

While both of us had heard Tezca speak, his primary bond was to Santos. An Aztec deity paired up with a Mexican guy made sense, I guess. It would be nice if a Chinese dragon would appear to save my half-Asian ass, but no luck so far.

"Well, that couple was with Nella, so you know she's gonna bring them down here to inspect the livestock," I said bitterly. "We can do some inspecting right back."

Santos sat down to lace up his boots, glancing up at me. "Which one were you inspecting more, the girl or the guy?"

"They were too far away to see clearly. But probably the girl. Guy didn't look like my type."

"Yeah, girl was cute." There was something in his voice that sounded a bit like yearning.

I held back from saying a sarcastic remark. Despite his reputation for brutality in the pit, Santos was, for lack of a better word, soft. Not in a bad way. I actually admired him a lot for holding on to that part of himself. Even after our years in captivity, he held on to that desire for a long-term partner and a family. The guy wanted love, and while I couldn't fault him for that, I wondered how he could still believe in such a thing at all.

Especially with how Nella exploited him to the guests. She was no better than a fucking street pimp, serving him up like fresh meat.

"Come on, Butcher. Let's keep you sharp." Before getting up, I gave two more pats to Tezca's flank, and that woke him up with a snort.

Santos and I both laughed at the big cat. Tezca was our sleek, prowling ray of black sunshine in this hellhole. Sometimes it was hard to believe the goofy animal was also inhabited by an ancient god.

The jaguar rolled over and slid down from the bed, now alert with ears pricked forward as he followed Santos out the door, an ever-watchful guard. I followed after the cat, already armed to the teeth like usual. Not that anyone but Santos could tell.

The pitmaster eyeballed us as we came out into the hallway, muttering under his breath as he took a headcount of all the gladiators coming out for training. The sun wouldn't be directly over the canyon for another couple of hours, so the sands were nice and cool when we entered the pit in the center of the colosseum.

Santos and I immediately separated, as was our routine. We didn't act like friends in front of the others, especially the pitmasters. Once they saw friendships, or worse, romantic or sexual relationships developing, they liked to set those fighters up against each other. Everyone knew Santos and I were roommates and had come here from the same place, but all that meant was we got along well enough to not try to kill each other outside of the pit. After four years of being here, it seemed to work. We had never once been scheduled against each other and were both still alive to show for it.

Tezca circled around Santos protectively while the guy got to hacking at a training dummy with a couple of batons. Santos had whittled down the wooden batons until they were the same weight and balance as his machetes.

My training, however, couldn't be practiced on an inanimate object.

I stuck to the shadows, slowly circling the perimeter of the sand pit while the other gladiators stretched and warmed up. The veteran fighters gave me dirty looks as I passed. They knew what to expect from me. It was a shame they didn't seem to realize my training was beneficial for them as well as myself. Only the most honed senses, the sharpest ears and reflexes, stood a chance against my attacks. And during training time, they were lucky I wasn't actively trying to kill anyone.

The newest fighters, on the other hand, would be in for a hell of a surprise.

I spotted the fresh meat from a mile away. The newest gladiators all hung out together, which was their first mistake. Alliances and friend groups only got people killed here, especially if they weren't smart enough to keep it discreet like Santos and me. The two nearest pitmasters were already leaning their heads together, talking quietly between themselves while nodding at the group with sinister smiles.

The group of four were also easy to spot because of their pasty-as-fuck skin. In time, if they survived, they'd be darkened by the brutal sun like the rest of us. After spending the first few weeks as red as lobsters, of course. This lot must have done years in solitary confinement somewhere. A couple of them squinted and shielded their eyes like they'd never been outside before.

In fewer words, they were a perfect warm-up for the day.

I continued my walk, studying them in my peripheral vision while looking straight ahead. One of the veteran gladiators, the Animal, glared at me as I approached him.

"Don't fuck with me today, Ghost," he snarled at me through blackened teeth. "I'm not in the fuckin' mood."

"You're safe from me today, spider monkey." Just for fun, I liked to call him a different animal every time we interacted. He flew off the handle every time like clockwork, *except* for when I called him an axolotl. He only flipped me off and yelled slurs at me for a whole minute, so I think he liked that one.

Spider monkey however, did not have the same effect.

He picked up one of his clubs with a heavy grunt, bringing it back over his massive shoulder to wind up for a swing. "I fucking told you, I'm not in the fucking—"

I was behind him before he finished drawing back his arm. In the next moment, I held his wrist with one hand and had the tip of my dagger pressed into his spine with the other. The Animal froze, his body in a precarious balance. If he resisted my hold and tried to swing his arm forward, his spinal column would run straight into my blade.

I had the knife positioned between two vertebrae, and he'd seen how cleanly I severed spines during my fights. I had left people paralyzed from the waist down dozens of times. And they never figured out why, because they never saw me coming.

And if the Animal didn't resist and continued following gravity, he'd fall backwards onto my knife anyway.

"Lucky for you, titmouse," I said, "I'm not in the mood to deal with you today either."

I heard his teeth grind in anger and his furious huff of breath. But we both knew he couldn't risk moving until I released him.

Which I did, because two pitmasters were storming our way.

"What the fuck is going on?" one of them demanded, while the other rested his hand on his taser gun at his belt.

"Nothing, sirs." I stepped away from the Animal and lowered my gaze to the ground. "Just tussling a bit to warm up for training."

"Yeah," the Animal agreed, his gaze lowering like mine. "No trouble here, sirs."

The pitmasters turned around and were gone in the next moment. Scuffles were normal between gladiators during training. They just wanted to make sure no one killed each other prematurely and messed up the fight schedules. Spectators usually had a lot of money riding on those fights.

As soon as the pitmasters were out of earshot, the Animal whirled to face me. "Fuck with me again and I'll skull-fuck you right back 'til I puncture one of your lungs and you're drowning in my cum. Then I'll take your scrawny ass while you suffocate and keep going until your corpse is cold. Am I clear, Ghost?"

I kept my face expressionless as I turned to leave. "Don't threaten me with a good time. Later, alligator."

"I know where you sleep," he called after me.

It wasn't until I was a good thirty feet away that I allowed myself some deep breaths. Well that was...unsettling. Rape threats were a dime a dozen here, but that was especially graphic. He must have been really pissed. It was a good thing I slept in the same room as a jaguar whose kill record nearly matched mine.

I lifted my head and continued on my walk, bypassing the group of new gladiators. I was no longer in the mood to teach any young ones some hard lessons. Santos was by a water station, taking a quick, rationed drink under the watchful eye of more pitmasters as I continued past him.

"You alright?" he muttered under his breath, not looking at me.

"Yeah," I answered, not breaking my stride.

I would be fine, once I walked off the mental image the Animal had put in my head. That was another thing about dealing with gladiators. You could never, ever let their threats rattle you.

Once that happened, you were already dead.

Rori

"Here is the spa, where we have the most *amazing* skin treatments and massage options. There's also a nail salon and a lash, brow, and wax studio if you ever need any regular maintenance."

"Mm-hm." I held onto Torr's arm, already bored by this tour, but plastered on an *Ooh, yes! Very interesting* smile every time Nella turned to look at me.

"And right next door is the gym with all of the state-of-the-art equipment." The suited woman opened the door to let us look through.

Torr let out a low, appreciative whistle, his eyes flicking around to all of the weights, squat racks, and barbells. "Definitely gonna spend some time in here."

"Meathead," I teased with an elbow to his ribs.

He wrapped an arm around my shoulders, pulling me into his side as he dropped a kiss to my temple. "Just keeping the goods in shape for you, honey."

I gave him my best glare when Nella turned her back. He was making me pay for calling him honey before, and being especially smug about it, since I couldn't tell him to eat a dick while Nella was around.

He turned me toward his chest with the arm around my shoulders, bringing me closer to talk privately. "What are your thoughts so far?"

His breath tickled my ear and the weight of his arm was comforting, grounding. Whatever fancy cologne Gwen had sprayed him with smelled amazing, and I hated that I wanted to press my face to his chest and inhale him.

"This place is fucking creepy," was what I told him instead.

The path under our feet was mosaic tile in a dazzling colorful pattern. The different areas of the resort were carved into the sides of canyons, accessible by elevators and ornate bridges. Everywhere we went had stunning views of the canyon walls and the colosseum, which was probably the whole point. Rich people paid big bucks for nice views, it seemed.

"Here's the cafe, right next to the aviary." Nella gestured to an open patio with spotless white furniture and dozens of green plants to amp up the tropical look. Beyond the patio was a large, dome-shaped cage.

"We have the largest collection of exotic birds in the world," Nella explained. "Many of these species are already extinct in the wild, but you can enjoy their songs during your morning coffee, afternoon tea, whatever suits you."

I couldn't get over how sad that was as we walked on to the sounds of many different bird calls. How hopeless would that feel to be the last of your species and caged in a desert canyon far away from home? To be nothing more than exotic background noise? My gaze lifted skyward, but I saw no sign of Astarte. It sure would be sweet, karmic justice if she dropped a little present in one of the patio guest's drink.

"You two are quiet." Nella turned to look back at us as we followed the mosaic path around the cafe and aviary. "Is everything to your liking?" She looked directly at me, still all but ignoring Torr as she had since she approached our car.

"Yes, it's beautiful!" I chirped, spreading my lips wide into another performative smile. "It's all just...I don't know where to begin."

"I've saved the best for last." Nella beamed. "The colosseum entrance is just up ahead. We can go directly to the sand pit in the center and see the gladiators perform their morning training."

My brain scratched over that last bit of information like the vinyl record player in Bryce's bar. "Did you say gladiators?"

"Of course! They're our biggest attraction. To fill up the colosseum, we sell tickets to the fights without granting access to the rest of the resort. But our resort guests, like yourselves, have private VIP boxes that offer the absolute best views of the action."

"These are *actual* gladiators?" Torr piped up. "Like, slaves that fight to the death, gladiators?"

Nella frowned at him over her shoulder. "If you have ethical concerns, sir, I assure you that these fighters are among the worst criminals in the world. We are doing humanity a favor by allowing them to release their pent-up aggression on each other rather than innocent victims."

Torr and I exchanged a look. Yeah, she sounded *way* too sure of herself. Also, what a convenient explanation for a bunch of men to have gone missing.

The ornate mosaic tile turned to concrete as we went through the colosseum's underbelly. The open, airy space of the canyon gave way to dark corridors that soon opened up into brightness again.

The sun was high, directly over the colosseum, and I had to squint against the glare on the bright sand. Across the sand pit, roughly thirty men were either sparring with practice weapons or exercising alone. Nella said something to another staff member, the first male one that I'd seen. Actually, it looked like all of the colosseum staff were men, with holsters on their belts that carried tasers, handguns, and police batons.

The uniformed man nodded sharply, then brought his fingers to his mouth to let out a shrill whistle. Immediately, all the gladiators dropped their practice weapons and came jogging across the pit toward us. When the male staff member held out his palm, they stopped.

"Line up," he barked.

The confusion must have been clear on my face as the men arranged themselves in two parallel lines, standing shoulder to shoulder. What the fuck was this about?

Torr and I, along with Nella and the male staff member, stood on a wooden platform that was elevated slightly above the sand pit like a stage. We could see all the fighters clearly from this vantage point. They stared straight ahead but didn't meet our eyes. Well, most of them didn't. A couple of younger guys in the back snuck upward glances at me. Their shoulders and nose bridges were red with sunburn, their complexions much paler than the other gladiators. Seemed they were the new guys.

"The Mystic Canyon gladiators are the best fighters you've never heard of," Nella said proudly, looking out over the men. "People come from all over to see them, and we often sell every seat in the arena. There is nothing more thrilling to watch, I can guarantee you that. If you two are the gambling types, you can place bets on the fights in the office over there."

When she looked away from them, a tall, slender Asian man glanced up at her with a death glare. There was pure murder in his dark eyes and no question that he absolutely loathed her. Just as quickly as it happened, his features smoothed over and he blankly lowered his gaze again. He was so sneaky about it, I almost missed it and wanted to smile.

"Do any of the fighters catch your interest, ma'am?" Nella's voice grew quieter, husky. A secret smile pulled at her lips.

"Interest? Uh, well..." I scanned their faces, slightly overwhelmed by it all. These weren't professional fighters. Their beaten down gazes and tattered training gear told me that. A professional boxer came into Bryce's bar once, and everyone treated him like a celebrity. He wasn't as flashy as Blakeworth elite, but he dressed well and bought rounds of drinks for everyone who was there. It was clear he had money to go along with his fame.

These men had nothing to their name.

Nella had talked about them like they were racehorses. We even stood above them like they were animals in a pen. Everything about this was wrong. Sickening, even.

Astarte, what the fuck am I supposed to be doing here?

"I mean, they all look like very capable fighters." I forced the words out through a tight throat and a boulder in my stomach. "I'm, uh, looking forward to seeing them in action."

The guy next to the Asian man glanced up, and our eyes locked for one heart-stopping moment that felt like minutes. He looked Latino, with dark hair shaved close to his scalp. The most beautiful, thick eyelashes framed his large brown eyes. He almost would have looked doe-eyed, boyish and innocent, if it weren't for his eyebrows drawn together in a scowl and his mouth pressed into a hard line. Dark stubble coated his lower jaw, and another dusting of dark hair covered the flat, sculpted planes of his chest.

Equally sculpted shoulders and biceps flared out wide, his wrapped hands resting on his hips where he had two machetes strapped. I had been mistaken, there was nothing innocent about this man. He was positively lethal.

"I don't mean as fighters," Nella continued with that secret smile. "Some of them are also very nice to look at, yes?"

My face burned. Shit, she'd caught me checking out the machete guy. I jerked my gaze away, eyes landing on the Asian man next to him. He was beautiful in an ethereal way, like those seductive fae men in fantasy stories. His glossy, black hair was long and tied up high on his head, showing off high cheekbones and a knife-sharp jawline. His muscles stretched out long on his tall frame, willowy and graceful. To be a gladiator, he must have been just as dangerous as the machete guy, but he looked almost too beautiful to be a fighter.

"Is that why women watch the fights?" Torr asked with a playful smile. "For the eye candy?"

Nella ignored him, as she usually did, and I had a passing thought to call her out on it. She knew he was my 'husband', and it was just getting rude at this point.

"Some of our gladiators also serve another purpose," she said carefully. "One that is mutually enjoyable for both the guests and the fighter."

Torr stiffened next to me and went still, as if he'd stopped breathing.

"What's that?" I had to ask before my mind went wild with ideas, because she couldn't possibly mean...

"Should you wish to sample them for sexual pleasure, we are happy to arrange it. I can point out the ones most skilled in the bedroom, if you would like."

My mind went blank, which never happened. It was like I couldn't even process what she had said. My body, however, reacted with a chill over my skin and a horrific twisting sensation in my gut. These men weren't just forced to fight... but to fuck. What kind of fucking nightmare bizzaro world had we landed in?

"Isn't that dangerous?" I asked when my brain started up again. "I thought these were the worst criminals in the world, and you let them...*sleep* with guests?"

"Not all of them are qualified, of course. And we have strict safety protocols in place for the ones who are," Nella assured. "To be honest, it was requested over and over by our guests, and who are we to say no?"

Well, you'd be exploiting them a little less, so that's something.

"But we're married." Torr's arm was a heavy weight around my waist, pulling me closer to him. "I thought this resort was for couples. Why would you offer men for a, uh, sexual service?"

Nella looked directly at him, probably for the first time since we stepped foot in this place. "Mystic Canyon accepts couples, yes, but also single women who qualify. We are a female-centered facility.

Our focus is to create a relaxing, pleasurable retreat for female guests, and we're proud to be the only one of our kind. Their male partners are welcome, of course, but they are not our primary audience. Should the woman wish to sample other options, we merely provide the opportunity to do so. Her husband is welcome to participate if he so chooses."

"So there isn't a sample of lady gladiators for the men to choose from?" Torr's question was sarcastic, but it made my gut churn even harder.

"No, there isn't." Nella looked almost offended by the question. "Women have been used, degraded, and dehumanized by men for thousands of years. There is none of that here. At Mystic Canyon, women are empowered and treated like queens, as they should be."

If they can afford it, I thought bitterly.

"How altruistic of you," Torr muttered.

"So." Nella went back to ignoring him and turned to me with a pleasant smile. "Are there any you would like to try? I'm happy to give you my personal recommendations, if you like."

Fucking hell, she acted like she was talking about dresses in a clothing store. If pretending to be Torr's wife wasn't hard enough, I also had to act like I was down with sexual slavery? It was a miracle I hadn't thrown up right into the sand below. This was abhorrent on all levels. Probably one of, if not the most, evil things human beings could do to each other.

And it started to dawn on me why Astarte called on me for this. Kidnapping people. Forcing them to fight and have sex. This evil had to be rooted out. It could not be allowed to spread. This place was already obscenely wealthy from the clients it picked, so they had to be planning for even more growth. More enslavement.

But what the fuck could *I* do? A place with this much money also had power. And what kind of people were involved? Who was at the top, pulling the strings? Who hired Nella and the armed guards? They were finding these people somewhere.

I felt like a mouse going up against a wolf. I was one person, a nobody. Sure, I had Torr with me, but two people weren't an army. Not against something *this* big. Fuck, I had never wanted to ask my parents for advice so badly.

The answer is right in front of your face. You know what to do, child. Astarte's voice came through, powerful and gently chiding as a parent's would be. The white dove flew down moments later, perching on one of the empty colosseum seats a few rows away. She cooed softly and preened her feathers.

Steeling myself with a breath, I met Nella's smile with one of my own. "We can spend time with the gladiators alone? My husband doesn't have to be there?"

Torr's head whipped in my direction, staring daggers into the side of my face.

"Yes, of course," Nella said. "For safety reasons, we can only permit you one gladiator per session. If you're interested in group sex, your husband will have to be the additional person."

"No, that's alright. One is fine." I ignored Torr's stare burning into my temple while I scanned the fighters below again. No matter what, I kept coming back to the man with the shaved head and pretty eyelashes. "What's he like?" I asked with a lift of my chin. "The one with the machetes."

Nella hummed with approval. "Ah, yes. The Butcher is a popular choice among our guests. One of our best lovers, as well as one of the most brutal fighters you will ever watch. His events are not to be missed." She pulled a slim notebook from inside the pocket of her blazer and flipped through pages. "He's booked up with several appointments this week, on top of an upcoming fight, plus his training schedule. I can set you up with him next Tuesday, but no sooner than that, I'm afraid." She looked up. "Is there anyone else you would like to try? The Tormentor has availability tonight."

"That's okay. I can wait until Tuesday," I said. "In the meantime, I think we'll settle in and enjoy what else the resort has to offer." I grabbed Torr's hand, leaning into him, but nearly yelped when he squeezed my hand in a death grip. The guy was *not* happy.

"Excellent. Your session with the Butcher will be Tuesday afternoon." Nella scribbled it down in her notebook and slipped it back into her jacket. "I'll send a reminder card to your suite."

"Thank you."

We turned away from the enslaved men in the sand below us and left the colosseum for our opulent suite in the resort.

Chapter 15

Torrance

"You're not actually going to fuck him, are you?" The words flew out the moment Rori and I were alone in our suite, which was bigger and grander than her family home back in Four Corners. There were multiple huge bedrooms, a gourmet kitchen, a deck with a pool and hot tub with unobstructed views of the canyon, and tons of plush couches and armchairs centered around an ornate glass fire pit.

"I don't know." The dismissive answer hit me like a slap.

Dumbfounded, I watched Rori as she breezed from room to room, checking out the massive suite. She looked everywhere but at me. But I was fucking used to that, wasn't I? She never looked at me.

"Rori, he's a *slave*." The word burned my mouth like poison. "He can't consent to having sex with you. Jesus, I can't even believe I'm saying this. This whole place is way more fucked up than I imagined." I headed straight for the extensive liquor cabinet in the kitchen, then stopped myself right before opening the glass door. Fuck, I needed a drink, but all this top-shelf booze was likely bought with slave labor. I wanted to burn this whole place down and wash myself clean of its stink.

"I know." Rori leaned against an armchair, rubbing her forehead. "I'm using the time to talk to him, find out more about this place."

"So what's with the, 'I don't know' then?"

She spread her hands, palms up, as she shrugged. "I mean, what if he gets in trouble if I *don't* fuck him? What if they see it as, like, he didn't please me or whatever and he gets punished?"

"Listen to yourself. That's your anxiety playing the what-if game again."

"But it might not be, Torr. You saw how beaten and broken down those men were. Who knows what they do to them?"

"Well, we know they fight to the death and get whored out like rentable dildos." I rubbed my mouth, spinning around in search of a bathroom. Ah, there it was, between the kitchen and bedrooms, the size of a conference room with a walk-in shower taking up one entire wall and a bathtub the size of a small swimming pool. "God, this place makes me sick," I groaned.

"Me too."

I turned back around to face Rori. "Not so sick that sampling the goods is out of the question, huh?" I knew I was being an asshole, but in that moment, I just couldn't bring myself to care.

She narrowed her eyes at me. "Torr, I'm just trying to be realistic. Of course I don't want to take advantage of a guy in that situation, but if the alternative is him getting beaten to death? Sure, I'll have sex with him to save his life."

"Fuck." I turned away again, physically unable to look at her.

"We don't know what we're actually dealing with here," she continued. "So talking to him and getting more information is our number one priority."

"Yeah, and what if they've thought of that, huh? What if he's so beaten down and brainwashed that he reports you to fucking Nella once you start probing?"

Rory scrubbed her hand down her face, smudging her makeup. "I'm not an idiot. I won't be obvious."

"Maybe not, but who knows if we're on her radar already?"

"We've passed through all of their security measures, thanks to Gwen. If they had a whiff of suspicion, we wouldn't be here." She smiled wryly. "Listen to me. Telling *you* not to be paranoid for a change."

"This place just makes my skin crawl. Nella looks like she wants to throw *me* in the gladiator pit."

Rori gave me an appraising look from head to toe, and it was really fucking annoying how my stomach flipped in response. Even now, with a slightly better idea of the deep shit we were in, I wished she wanted me.

"I could see it," she said with an approving tone.

"See what?"

"You, fighting half naked in the sand pit. The crowd'll pay good money for that."

"Enslaved and fighting for my life every day, you mean?" I snapped. "Maybe having my dick rented out to the highest bidder too, while I'm at it?"

Her face fell. "Sorry, Torr. I'm just trying to make light of the situation a little."

"Well, I don't find it funny. But then again, this place doesn't cater to *me*, does it?"

"You're right. I'm sorry, it's awful. If it was women in that situation, I wouldn't be making jokes."

A small amount of tension bled out of me. I knew she'd be able to see the double standard. But it was the mental image of her and a gladiator alone in a room that kept my teeth grinding.

"I don't want you to see that guy," I bit out. "Cancel that appointment. Please."

Rori pinned me with a hard stare. Fuck, she was really going to fight me on this. The smudged makeup on her face now looked like a mask of war paint. And it was way hotter than the glammed-up look she'd been wearing all day.

"Do you have any better ideas for finding intel?" she asked.

"Not right now, but let's take some time to get our bearings here.

You talk to the ladies at the spa. I'll talk to other guys in the gym. You know, get a lay of the land first."

Her gaze hardened. "So how many gladiators are you willing to let die because you want to be slow and careful?"

"If we're *not* slow and careful, it could be *us* getting fucked over."

Rori threw her hands up in exasperation. "I'm not seeing the guy until three days from now. We can certainly do both methods."

She was right, and it was a good plan. What better way to find out what was really going on than private one-on-one time? But fucking hell, the thought of her in close proximity, alone, with one of them, made me want to send my fist through a wall.

Not because it was potentially unsafe or that our cover could be blown. No, it was all over the simple fact that she'd be alone with another man. And she wasn't completely writing off having sex with him.

After watching her head off with other guys so many times, I couldn't begin to understand why this time made me especially ragey. Maybe because it was just the two of us without a buffer of friends to keep me distracted. Maybe because finding my own piece of tail in this place wasn't an option. Or maybe, just maybe, I had secretly hoped this trip would bring us closer in a new way.

When she'd woken up in my arms that morning and didn't immediately pull away while I pretended to sleep, I stupidly thought we might be able to head in that direction. But that was just me when it came to Aurora Wilder. Stupid.

Now, being in completely unknown territory with only each other to look out for, evidently made me even stupider.

"I just don't want you to do it," I hissed through clenched teeth. "Seriously, Ror. I got a bad feeling about it, and I don't want you to meet up with the guy."

Rori stood from the chair, staring me down. She hadn't taken her heeled shoes off yet and was almost as tall as me. Her shoulders squared like she was ready to fight.

"You don't dictate what I do here, Torr. You came to back me up, remember? That doesn't mean you boss me around. If I have a chance to talk to someone with no interruptions, no eavesdropping, I'm going to take it."

I couldn't stop the next words that came out. "And a ride on a cock, too. To protect the guy and your cover. Awesome. Great plan, Rori."

She reeled back with a surprised huff of breath. "Are you jealous, Torrance Knight?"

The large, airy suite suddenly felt cramped and cluttered. I needed space. I needed to lift heavy shit until I collapsed. And I really needed Rori to stop fucking looking at me like that.

"Pick which bedroom you want," I told her, turning away and heading for the massive bathroom. "I'm hitting the gym."

Chapter 16

Rori

Torr and I didn't talk much the rest of that day or the next. The tension between us was beyond awkward. He seemed pissed off at me, and every moment of being in the same room together felt like navigating a minefield.

I picked the smallest bedroom to sleep in, and he chose the one farthest away from mine. Every time I tried to make casual conversation while in the suite together, he'd ignore me or answer with a grunt.

After spending our first night in the suite, I let him know there would be a gladiator fight that evening and that it would be smart for us to attend. He mumbled out something like, "Okay," chugged the rest of his coffee, and left for the gym.

I decided to give him space and not push him. Whether he was angry at me specifically, or the fact that this glamorous resort openly profited off of enslaved people, he needed to get it out of his system so he could focus. It was jarring, seeing Torr so frazzled. I knew he had a lot of pent-up aggression, but he usually seemed in control of it. Working out was his outlet, but now he acted dependent on it, like a drug.

While he did that, I spent too much time sitting and thinking. Because I had to keep up the guise of being from Blakeworth, I spent a good chunk of my day in the makeup chair, both for my daytime and nighttime looks.

The maid assigned to help me with makeup and clothes was a young woman named Paige. She had bright red hair pulled back in a long French braid and lots of freckles dotting over her pale skin. Her vivid green eyes were shrewd as she skillfully contoured my face and applied a new set of fake lashes and colored contacts.

For my evening look to attend the fight, I chose a dark pink eye color, bordering on purple, and Paige picked out a dress and makeup colors to coordinate. Like most of the resort staff, with the exception of Nella, she was quiet and agreeable. I wondered how much of that was the persona she put on for her job and how much was actually her.

"How long have you been doing makeup?" I asked, eyes closed under the soft brush sweeping over my skin.

Paige hesitated before she answered. "Since I was five, maybe six." The brush fell away, and I felt a fingertip gently dab at my eyelids. "The daughter of the family my parents worked for always threw away old makeup pallets in favor of buying new ones. Some of the colors were never touched, and they were so pigmented. My sisters and I would pick them out of the trash and practice on each other." Her finger pulled away and I opened my eyes to find her looking at me with a worried expression. "I'm sorry, ma'am. I didn't mean any offense, I just ramble too much. I swear the makeup was thrown away, I never stole it."

"Hey, it's okay." I held up a hand and smiled. "I believe you, and I like hearing you talk. It's why I asked the question. And besides," I lowered my hand and returned to looking vacantly straight ahead, "listening to you keeps me out of my own head."

Paige wiped her hands on a small towelette and picked up another makeup brush. "That's kind of you, ma'am. Most of the guests prefer us not to speak unless absolutely necessary."

"Sounds boring as fuck."

She laughed softly and returned to painting my face. "You don't speak like other guests either. Both in your accent and the words you use. It's refreshing, if I may say."

"You may say anything you want," I told her. "I mean that. Don't worry about offending me or talking too much. I'm used to people speaking their minds with crass words."

A pang of homesickness hit me. I missed my loud, rough-necked family. Everyone said foul words and didn't pull any punches when expressing their opinions, but they were always genuine. The love and loyalty back home was real.

Here? Everything was too fucking fake.

Once I settled into the suite yesterday, I dug out my phone and walked laps around the place, trying to get a signal. I got nothing, and that was probably by design. The resort probably couldn't be kept a secret if guests could freely send texts and photos. I didn't know when I'd be able to make a quick call simply to let everyone know I was alive, and that just made my homesickness worse. Now with Torr giving me the cold shoulder, I felt even more alone in this place. A single word of encouragement from my mom or any of my dads would have put a little pep in my step.

At least I had Paige to talk to.

"Do you come from a big family?" I asked.

"Not really," she said. "Just me, my sister, and my two parents."

"Did your mom and dad both work for a rich family?"

Paige hesitated and I popped an eye open, watching her hand hover nervously over a selection of lipsticks. "I don't...exactly have a father," she mumbled, avoiding my gaze.

"Two mothers?" I guessed.

Her nod was hesitant, and my heart broke as she searched for judgment in my eyes. "I have two aunts who've been married over twenty years," I said. "Well, neither one is blood-related to me, but they're still my family, and I love them. Oh, and I have three uncles who are with each other plus a woman, my other aunt." I grinned at

Paige's open-mouthed shock. "So yeah, my family's pretty big. And there's all kinds of fun relationship combinations. It's pretty great. Just more people to love and support you."

"I...wow. Pardon me, ma'am. I've never heard of such dynamics."

"Like I said, you don't have to censor yourself around me. I've heard it all, due to the sheer amount of people in my life. I find silence to be pretty eerie, if I'm being honest." The only kind of silence I liked was the steady roar of my motorcycle and the wind in my face. Fuck, it had barely been a day and I already missed riding something fierce.

"Can I ask where you're from, ma'am?" Paige asked.

Shit. I bit the inside of my cheek, remembering what Torr said last night. The staff could report anything suspicious to Nella. I had to be more careful and probably already spilled too much.

"Blakeworth." I silently prayed she had worked somewhere else and wasn't familiar with the elite families. "A cousin helped us with our resort application as a wedding gift, and we were thrilled to be accepted."

"Congratulations!" Paige's tone betrayed nothing as she applied a final swipe of lipstick before she capped the tube and stepped away. "You're all finished, ma'am. Is everything to your liking?"

I leaned toward the mirror, inspecting the look. She put wispy green feathers in my lashes and stuck small green gemstones at the corners of my eyes to contrast with my pinkish-purple irises. My eyeshadow was a dark, smoky purple and my lips the color of a ripe plum.

"Thank you, Paige. I love it." I turned to smile at her. "You do great work. I look like a sorceress."

She dipped her head in respectful nod. "If I may say, ma'am, thank you for the opportunity to work with you and...to talk with you. I felt inspired while creating your look, and, well, I enjoyed doing it."

A warm glow filled my chest, and I smiled so hard I was sure I'd crack the lipstick. "Thank you for the conversation. I enjoyed talking to you too. Maybe I..." I stood from the chair, smoothing my hands down my dress. "Maybe I could keep you to myself while I stay here. Would that be alright with you?"

Paige's mouth gaped open and closed a few times before she bowed her head. "I would be honored, ma'am! I...I'd love nothing more than to assist only you. I, holy shit!"

Her muttered curse made me laugh. I liked this woman, and while I would remain cautious about what I told her, I felt like I could trust her. "How should I go about that?" I asked her. "Just tell Nella that I want you assigned to only me?"

"Yes, ma'am. Her extension is by the phone on the side table in the foyer. You can just leave a message for her, and she'll see to it."

"Perfect. Say, does that phone make outside calls?"

Paige shook her head. "No, ma'am. Only within the resort for whatever services you may need."

I thought so, but it was worth a shot. "Thanks, Paige. And you can call me Rori, by the way."

She blinked. "Ma'am?"

I shook my head. "Don't know who that is."

A smile pulled at her lips, and she looked from side to side like she was about to say something utterly scandalous. "Alright, um...Rori."

"It's fun to be rebellious, isn't it?" I grinned at her and did one last check in the mirror. "Thank you again."

"It's my pleasure." She did a little curtsy. "Will you be coming back here after the event? I can prepare your room for bed."

"That would be amazing, thank you." I didn't know exactly what all that entailed, but she seemed excited to do it.

A knock on my bedroom door had us both turning around. "Come in, Torr," I called, recognizing the signature pattern of his rapping.

A few seconds passed before he appeared. Despite picking the smallest bedroom, it still had its own mini foyer, sitting area, walk-in closet, and luxurious bathroom before the actual room with the bed in it, which was also stupidly big. Torr's heavy footsteps bypassed all of that to stand before us, and damn, what a sight.

He was in his workout pants and sneakers, topless except for the towel around his neck, which he used to wipe the sweat from his forehead and neck. His skin was flushed, breaths ragged like he literally just stepped off the treadmill. After barely talking to me for a full day, I couldn't imagine why my room was his first stop after the gym and not the shower closest to his own room.

"Hey," I said, keeping my gaze firmly above his collarbones.

"Hey, Ror."

Torr dropped the end of the towel he'd been using to wipe his face. He studied me from head to toe, mouth flattening with displeasure. I tried not to take it personally. I looked fucking hot, thanks to Paige. It was the whole rich-lady facade he hated, not how *I* looked in particular. Still, it stung that he looked at me with such disapproval.

"So, there's a dress code for this gladiator fight?" he grunted out.

"For us, yes. We're guests of the resort, so we're in the VIP boxes, remember?"

"Right."

Paige stepped forward. "I can call a male staff member to assist with your clothes and makeup for the event, sir. We have several who—"

"No, that's alright." Torr turned to leave, presenting his wide, muscular back to us. "I can manage on my own."

He left the room, and Paige and I both let out sighs at his departure, albeit for different reasons.

"Sorry about him," I said. "He's a fucking grump lately."

"It's no problem, ma—um, Rori." She gave me another salacious smile. "You're very lucky, if you don't mind me saying so. He is, well, very nice to look at."

"Don't I know it," I mumbled, my own mood now souring. I'd enjoyed looking at Torr so many times over the years I'd known him, even before he packed on all the muscle. Always looking, always yearning. Never having.

It felt especially cruel now that we were posing as married, and he couldn't even pretend to like me. We had this gigantic suite to avoid each other now. For a moment, I missed the little bed we were forced to share in the tavern. I missed how easy it was to distract myself with riding, drinking, and other guys back home.

I sure as shit didn't feel lucky.

Chapter 17

Rori

Torr and I walked with our arms linked to a section of VIP boxes on the colosseum's floor level.

Just outside of our box was a lounge area with a bar, a few tables, and plush seating. We put on fake smiles as we mingled and made introductions with some of the other guests, lying through our teeth about who we were. It was easy, really. Everything was a subtle power move, a sly one-up to show you were better than the person you were talking to.

Torr held me against his side with his arm around my waist, spinning all kinds of bullshit about who we were, where we came from, and how he proposed to me with the exact, rare black diamond I'd wanted. He was a natural at charming people, and I just followed his lead. I leaned into him and extended my hand to show the ring off, letting everyone *ooh* and *ahh* over the rock. I hadn't taken it off once since he'd put it on my finger back at the tavern.

I'd been sitting and staring at the thing a lot more than I'd like to admit, especially since things had gotten awkward between us. I felt like an idiot for even entertaining the idea that his vows had an ounce of truth to them. We'd only been here a matter of hours before he stormed off. So much for guarding me at every turn.

We settled into our box after roughly a half hour of mingling. The drinks and appetizers we'd ordered waited for us on a low table in front of a pair of chairs that looked more like thrones. Beyond the massive window and a short barricade, we had a perfect view of the entire fighting arena.

Torr sighed with a groan as he sank into his seat, letting his body slide toward the polished tile floor.

"It's fucking exhausting dealing with these people," he said.

"You were a natural out there," I told him. "You're really good at that."

"Acting like a rich asshole?"

"No, just schmoozing, networking. Whatever you want to call it. You just know how to work a group of people."

There was a beat of silence. "Thanks, Ror."

I reached for my champagne glass, mainly to keep my hands occupied. "Are you gonna be okay watching this?"

"I'll get through it."

He grabbed his own glass and downed it in one gulp, then pulled the bottle from the ice bucket to top himself off. Then he threw back his second glass just as quickly as the first. If by *get through it* he meant becoming completely obliterated by the time the fights started, he was well on his way.

Part of me wanted to comfort him, to reach for his hand or shoulder. But he was still treating me coldly in private. It was like a light switch, how he flipped on the charm and affection when in front of others, then shut me out the moment we were alone. He'd even scooted his chair away from me, keeping a good few feet of distance between us.

As tempting as it was to try breaking down this barrier between us, I wasn't going to capitulate to his mood. I was his only ally here. If he wanted to shut me out and stew in his own head about this fucked up place, so be it.

I sipped daintily at my drink and watched the colosseum seats fill through the large window of our box. The sky darkened and huge floodlights cranked on with a hum of electricity. Torr and I had to shield our eyes and blink while the lights were adjusted, pointing directly at the sandpit to illuminate it like a spotlight.

There would be two main fights tonight, according to the schedule. The second one, featuring the Butcher, was the most highly anticipated. The program didn't give any details about who his opponent was or what the fights would entail. Surprises were the best part of the fights, as some of the other guests had just explained to us.

A group of four young men walked out onto the sand from one side of the colosseum. I recognized one as the sunburned fighter from the lineup yesterday. His shoulders had already darkened and began peeling.

The crowd's low murmur shifted into loud booing. All four men huddled with their backs together, weapons and shields pointing outward. One yelled back at the crowd. Another waved his middle finger in the air. Some audience members even started throwing things down into the pit. I saw food, drink cups, crumpled paper programs, and all kinds of random items landing on or near the four men. The fighters raised their arms and shields against the thrown objects, protecting themselves as well as each other.

"They're fighting as a team?" I wondered aloud.

"Doesn't seem very gladiator-like," Torr muttered, leaning forward.

Two figures emerged from the opposite side of the sand pit, and the crowd immediately shifted to cheering. The figures raised their arms, turning in circles as they looked back at the audience. These two were clearly seasoned fighters, covered in scars, muscle, and dark tans from long hours in the sun.

"Who are they?" Torr asked, leaning toward me to see the paper program.

"The Animal and the Hatchet," I answered.

"And the four musketeers?"

I blinked at the written name. "The Maggots."

"Huh, that's harsh."

There was no announcement, no referee to signal the start of the fight. The veteran gladiators simply rushed at the group of four, weapons raised while screaming war cries.

Two of the Maggots broke off from their tight formation to dodge assault, leaving their comrades exposed. One guy immediately got a sword through his gut, the sound of metal through flesh unmistakable.

I jumped in my seat, covering my mouth. The champagne I just swallowed threatened to come right back up. The sight before me almost didn't seem real.

"Better get used to it," Torr said grimly. "That was just the first strike."

The man who got stabbed didn't appear to believe it either. He just looked down at the bleeding wound on his stomach until his opponent withdrew the sword and stabbed him again, this time through the neck.

When he fell, bleeding from two mortal wounds, the gladiator who made the first kill of the night spread his hands to the side, waving them up and down as he spun in a circle, getting the crowd riled up. They started chanting *"Ani-mal! Ani-mal! Ani-mal!"*

The Animal's partner, the Hatchet, went after one of the Maggots who had broken away from the group and was now running the perimeter of the sand pit. The running man grabbed doors and gates, trying everything that looked remotely like an exit. He jumped over a short fence and started climbing up the front of the stage where Torr and I stood yesterday.

I blinked and then there was a small ax in the center of his back.

"Oh my God!" I cried.

He was still trying to climb out, and the Hatchet only laughed, juggling two of his namesake weapons for a moment before the blades sailed through the air at the other man. The Hatchet's victim fell, and he turned to one of the armed guards with tasers and batons at their belts.

"Aren't you going to get those back for me? That last one was my favorite!" He let out a deep belly laugh, and the crowd's chanting shifted to, *"Hat-chet! Hat-chet! Hat-chet!"*

Seconds later, the three hatchets sailed over the short fence and landed harmlessly at their owner's feet. He picked them up and raised them in the air, the crowd's noise reaching a new level of frenzy at the sight of those blades covered in blood.

In the middle of the pit, the Animal and one of the two remaining Maggots were trading blows. The Animal was big and slow but seemed to be biding his time, while the other man moved in quickly and took aggressive shots. The other guy's emotion was clear on his face, his jaw clenched and the rage potent in his eyes. Whether his anger was directed at his opponent for killing his friend or at the two who broke away and ran off like cowards, it was hard to say. Probably both.

The newcomer was a skilled fighter but struggling on the shifting, sandy ground. I held my breath when he missed a forward jab with his sword, exposing his side to the Animal. The other gladiator didn't hesitate and brought a meaty fist encased in brass knuckles to the man's side. The crowd started chanting for the Animal again as the Maggot rolled and scrambled to get away.

"Come on, throw some fucking sand in his eyes!" I hissed.

Torr let out a mirthless laugh. "Rooting for the underdog, huh?"

"I guess so." I chewed one of my nails and fully expected all ten fingers to be bitten down to stubs by the end of the night. "Those guys don't belong in here. That one that ran was scared shitless."

Finally, the man scrambling on the ground tossed a handful of sand up at the Animal, buying himself a few precious moments to roll to his feet. The two of them had neared our box, and I got my first clear look at their faces.

He's kind of cute. The thought was more sorrowful than admiring. If he survived tonight, I wouldn't be surprised if he were added to the sexual services menu.

The Animal swung a spiked club, narrowly missing the other man's head. The Maggot dodged low and drove his sword into the Animal's gut. Smartly, he pulled away, withdrawing his weapon in the blink of an eye. The Animal was enraged, roaring wordlessly as he pursued the other man. His stomach was badly bleeding, but the injury didn't seem to slow him down.

Their fight had gone down mere feet in front of our VIP box, blocking our view of the rest of the pit. When the Animal and the underdog moved their fight along, it seemed we'd missed some other action.

The Hatchet was now kneeling in the center of the pit, with one of his own axes held against his throat by the other Maggot. As the other two fighters came closer, the man holding the Hatchet hostage said something to the Animal. It looked like a threat, a *do-something-or-he-dies* kind of command.

The Animal just threw his head back and laughed. "We're all destined to die, you fucking worm! Kill him! Cut his throat with his own weapon! He won't hesitate to do the same to you."

That moment of distraction was enough for the Animal's opponent to finish the job. He thrust his sword through the back of the veteran gladiator's neck before he could say anything else. The Animal made a gurgling sound as blood poured from his neck, running down his chest to mix with the blood from the wound in his gut.

You could hear a pin drop in the colosseum as the Animal fell to his knees and then face-planted dead on the ground. Only after he fell did an uproar carry throughout the audience. They were an angry, yelling mass shouting and gesturing at the fighters below.

"Bet some folks just lost a lot of money," Torr said.

The Hatchet tried taking advantage of the upset by the Animal's death. He grabbed his captor's forearm, trying to wrestle the ax back into his own possession, but the other man caught on. The Maggot wrenched his arm free and this time did not hesitate.

He buried the ax blade under the Hatchet's chin, and pulled it across, releasing a river of blood. He must have gone deep, because the Hatchet died much quicker than the Animal.

The two men who had appeared to be on the same team now stared at each other across the sand.

"What happens now?" I asked. "Did they win?"

A new energy took over the crowd, starting as a low murmur but quickly taking over the whole colosseum. I even saw other resort guests in their VIP boxes standing up and pumping their fists. Within moments, a new chant emerged.

My blood ran cold as the horrific realization seeped in.

"There's no 'they'," Torr confirmed with a bitter shake of his head. "At the end of a fight, there can only be one man standing."

"Kill him! Kill him! Kill him!"

Chapter 18

Santos

I could only give a sad shake of my head from the sidelines. The baby gladiators, Maggots, as they'd been called, looked horrified at the realization of what they had to do. They'd stuck together since being shipped to this hellhole. Now one would have to kill the other.

If they refused, more fighters would be released onto the sands. One man standing was the only rule.

"I tried to warn 'em," the Ghost, Devin, said with a regretful tone. "After training yesterday morning, I pulled Animal's killer aside and told him not to look too cozy with his boys."

"They never listen," I muttered. "They have to learn the hard way, like we all do."

It still wasn't easy to see. Part of, if not all, of your humanity was lost the moment you killed someone you once considered a friend. Even an acquaintance. Some of the kills that got to me the worst were the guys I had sparred with or just talked football with for a sense of normalcy. That was the main reason Devin and I acted like strangers in front of everyone's eyes. We likely wouldn't be able to bear standing across the sand from each other like these two were.

Both of the Maggots just looked at each other, not moving, until the crowd got bored and started throwing shit again.

"Glad I'm not going out there today." Devin started flipping one of the many hidden knives he kept on him. "At least the Animal's dead. Sick fucker."

I grunted out an agreement, though the bastard's death wasn't all good news. He'd been a favored fighter for the gamblers and had been something of a cult leader among the gladiators. Not that he had any leadership skills to speak of, he was just big, mean, and a fucking ruthless killer. People didn't want their skulls bashed in when he was in a foul mood, so they kissed his ass. His death created a power vacuum among his minions, and they'd be squabbling to take his place.

The seasoned gamblers would also be taking a huge loss. Even against four Maggots and the Hatchet, the odds had been highly skewed in the Animal's favor. Now that precarious balance had been upset by a scrawny dude with a sunburn.

The dude could fight though, and he had my respect for that. But it was his first time on the sands, and he'd have to prove himself time and time again.

"Ooh, they're arguing." Devin sounded like he was watching a TV drama.

I crossed my arms, scratching the stubble on my jaw as I watched. The two guys were circling closer to each other, both of them red-faced with anger as they shouted. The Animal's killer was repeating something like, "You ran! We were supposed to hold tight, but you ran and got them killed!" The sword was in a loose hold at his side, but his opponent clung tighter to the axes in each of his hands as he shouted arguments back.

The whole colosseum seemed to wait with bated breath, not daring to look away and miss who would strike first. In the end, it was the Hatchet's killer who raised his weapons against his friend.

The Animal's killer brought his sword up to block the attack. Metal sang as axes and sword clashed. Then there was a crunch and an "Oof!" as the Animal's killer drove his elbow into his friend's nose.

"Quit trying to be a good guy," I muttered. "There's no way for both of you to leave the pit alive. You want to be merciful, end it quickly for him."

With blood pouring down his face and a look of malice that wasn't there before, the ax wielder recovered and swung again. He was wild and uncoordinated now, sloppy. The swordsman dodged his friend's attacks easily, the hurt and anger in his eyes morphing into a grim determination. He waited until the axes finished another wide, lateral swing, then drove his sword through the other man's ribs.

The swordsman had clearly aimed for the heart in a valiant attempt to make his friend's death quick and painless. But he was off by several inches, and the man at the business end of his weapon would remain very much alive for a few minutes.

All the gladiators watched with grim silence as the two men crumpled to the sand together. One dying and being cradled in his killer's arms, the other with his head bent low and probably whispering all manners of regrets and apologies. We'd all seen it before. This was the consequence of getting attached to anyone.

The swordsman pulled his weapon free and, with a shaking hand, stabbed his friend again to end his suffering. My respect for him went up even higher as I watched the ax wielder finally go limp. Most wanted to hold on, to prolong their final moments with loved ones for as long as possible. He gave his friend one final kindness and sent him to a quick death.

A rough pat on my shoulder came from the Ghost. "You're up next, Butcher boy. Carve us up some steaks."

"Yeah." I shrugged his hand off and rolled my shoulders, then my neck.

While waiting for pitmasters to carry off the body and escort the last fighter from the sands, I pulled my machetes from their sheaths and rotated my wrists around to warm them up. Tezca rubbed the length of his body against my legs, circling me tightly.

He usually came out to fight with me, mostly because no one wanted to deal with trying to corral the jaguar who'd killed a dozen of us. Every pitmaster that attempted to got a nasty bite or a scratch. One even got a bad infection in his hand and had to stop working.

The jaguar got free rein of the colosseum, a privilege even most of the employees didn't have.

Outside under the floodlights, the crowd had quieted down to a murmur. They were probably still reeling over the shock of the Animal's death. By the next fight though, they'll have moved on and picked a new favorite. We were expendable like that, going up and down in value like my grandfather's baseball cards.

Once the fighters were gone and the bloody sand had been quickly raked over, the gates in front of me swung open, and the audience exploded with new life.

The noise was deafening, even down where I was. I raised one machete in the air, turning around so everyone got a chance to see my face. Maybe I smiled, I didn't know. Putting on the act of a crowd-pleasing entertainer had worn thin for me. I was on autopilot for this shit. My singular focus was getting through this fight to live another day.

For what, I didn't know exactly. Tezca said change was coming, and I had to believe him. The talking jaguar god had been at my side for months. Despite more of the same since his arrival, I had to believe him. If I didn't, what else did I have to live for?

As I hit the center of the sand pit, I lowered my eyes from the stadium seats to the VIP boxes on the ground level. These were the resort guests who dropped a year's salary at my old job to get the best views.

The VIP boxes were protected by a half-wall barrier, armed pitmasters, and tempered glass windows. Gladiators weren't allowed guns, but it wouldn't surprise me if that glass was also bulletproof.

My eyes stopped on a woman behind the glass. Short, blonde hair in soft waves hit the edge of her jaw, showing off a graceful neck and slender shoulders. It was the same woman from the elevator, the one who had a personal appointment with me in a couple of days.

She sat a few feet away from her male companion, who I still wasn't convinced was her husband. They weren't talking or looking at each other, just staring blankly out at the sand. That honestly wasn't unusual with many of the resort guests. Many of the couples seemed to only tolerate each other, at best.

The woman's eyes caught mine, and our stares locked for a single, electrifying moment. She moved first, raising her glass a few inches as she mouthed, *Good luck.*

I jerked my chin down in a quick nod before turning to face the gates my opponents would come out of. By now, she must have heard other guests talking about me, or more specifically, my skills that had nothing to do with fighting. If she were anything like the others, she probably hoped I'd live through this fight just so our session wouldn't be canceled. These elite types all thought they were gods, after all. Everything on earth existed to serve them.

But damn. I'd be lying if I said I didn't want to miss that appointment either. Just like when I first saw her come down the elevator, I got a different feel than the other guests. Some buried part of me dared to wonder if our time together would be different too, if even fun.

God knew I was fucking tired of the same old shit. Both on the sands and in bed with the guests.

The far gate lifted slowly, and I gave another quick swing of my wrists to make my machetes dance. I never knew ahead of time what would come out of that dungeon. No one did, except the pitmasters scheduling the fight.

My heart sank at the sound of low growls and then a series of barks. I fucking hated killing animals in here. At least gladiators understood what they were getting into. These were likely stray dogs that had been rounded up, starving and aggressive out of pure necessity.

The pack shot out in a streamlined formation, running until they formed a circle around me and Tezca. These pups were hungry alright—their ribs on display and bodies scarred from previous fights.

Tezca and I faced opposite ends of the circle. I knew his back was arched and heard his feline warning growl over the dogs. He'd take care of a few while I carved up the rest.

What a fucking waste.

The first dog lunged for my leg, and I swung low. As the two halves of its body separated and the top half went rolling across the sand, another dog jumped, its teeth aiming for my neck. I swung the machete in my opposite hand, sending the dog's head flying like a soccer ball across a field.

It was a brutal dance of carnage, one that I hated with every fiber of my being. But the crowd loved it, and it was partly because of their passion that I continued to live. They stood from their seats, chanting, *"But-cher! But-cher! But-cher!"*

When I was finished, dogs lay slaughtered in pieces all around me and *on* me. I would have done anything for a private moment to throw up and take a shower, but I had more fighting to do.

I had barely caught my breath when the gate opened again, and a huge beast of a man came running straight for me. He wore a helmet that looked like something those medieval knights wore and spiked armor from his wrists to his shoulder. To complete the medieval getup, his weapons were two spiked maces. The man was pale, filthy, and I didn't have to speak to him to know he was half-crazed.

If I could see his face, I might have recognized him. Or maybe not, since he clearly hadn't been part of the regular gladiator population for a long time.

Sometimes, if we needed disciplinary action, we weren't thrown out in the middle of the pit right away. No, depending on the pitmasters' mood, gladiators would be tossed into a windowless dungeon with no light or human interaction for months. On top of the isolation, they would be creatively tortured. I'd heard stories of electrocution, sleep deprivation, forced injections of drugs, and all manners of things that weren't necessarily painful but fucked up a person's mind beyond saving.

It made me think of Hudson, Devin and my friend who'd been left behind when we were shipped off to this place. He'd been separated from us weeks before to fulfill an esteemed, special purpose, as they had said. We never saw him again but had heard his anguished screams every day until they loaded Ghost and I onto the truck that brought us here.

The crazed knight stumbled out toward me, swinging his maces blindly. I couldn't imagine he had a good field of vision in that helmet. He missed me by a mile, and the momentum sent him careening into the sand.

Uproarious laughter came from the crowd, making my skin prickle with discomfort. This man had undergone torture that they couldn't even fathom, and they were laughing at him.

This type of fight was familiar to me, sadly enough. I was supposed to let the man bumble around like a court jester. He was little more than a rodeo clown, just some grim comic relief before I sliced him down.

He fell down more often than he was able to stand, run, and take swings at me. I couldn't bring myself to laugh with the audience, not even to pretend. While dodging his wild swings, I tried meeting his eyes through the slit in his helmet. Did he recognize me? Would I ever recognize who he was?

He never said a word though, only mumbling and grunting as he came at me again and again.

At some point, he went sprawling onto the sand by tripping over his own feet. The crowd's laughter was more subdued this time, which meant they were getting bored. Time to end this soon.

The man wasn't getting up though, and the crowd started shouting and jeering at him to get up and fight.

"Come on, man," I muttered under my breath. "Let me give you the respect of killing you standing up, alright?"

My gaze lifted, and I found myself looking at the blonde woman in the VIP box. Neither she nor her companion were laughing. She leaned forward, her shoulders tense. Her fingers were clasped so hard in front of her, the knuckles were white. Her eyes were glued to the armored man on the ground, eyebrows knitted together and her mouth a thin line.

Some motion caught my eye, and I lifted my gaze higher to see a white dove fly down to perch on the slanted roof of her private box.

In the sand at my feet, Tezca cautiously stalked over to the man on the ground and sniffed around his head. The jaguar then pressed his forehead against the man's helmet, leaning in to run his cheek and neck against the man, nuzzling him as he so often did with me.

"Kill him! Bite his throat!" someone yelled from the crowd.

The taunts and shouts faded as I felt a sense of calm coming over me. A reassurance and settling I so rarely felt in this place. The only other time I had was the day I met my jaguar. The man's body, which had been tense and twitchy since the moment he ran out, had calmed into stillness.

After a few moments, Tezca walked away, and the man pushed himself up to standing. He turned slowly to face me, his mannerisms completely different from the wild, uncoordinated lashing out from before. The eyes behind the slit in the helmet met mine, focused and lucid for the first time.

"Are you ready?" I asked, my voice tight.

He nodded once and I brought up my machetes, crossing them in front of my chest as I stepped forward.

"I'm sorry." I wasn't sure what I was apologizing for, but it felt like something that needed to be said.

"Me too, kid," he answered.

I slashed my blades down in two perfect arcs. A red X formed across the man's torso. I made sure to hit the arteries in his neck too. Blood pumped out in steady bursts from the cuts, and after a few seconds, he fell once again.

This time, with dignity.

Chapter 19

Rori

I couldn't take my eyes off of him.

The Butcher was swift and brutal as he fought, but there was a beauty to his movements, almost like a dancer. He moved with precision and confidence but nothing overly flashy. Aside from the entrance he'd made, he acted as though the audience wasn't even there.

And when the pale man came out, dressed like a laughingstock of a knight and falling down everywhere, the Butcher made no attempt to humiliate him further. He ignored the crowd's taunts to kick the other man while he was down, to shove a machete up his ass, and every other cruel, vile thing they yelled out. No, the Butcher waited until the man could stand up, and they even appeared to exchange a few words before he cut the man down.

I'd been so entranced with watching him, I didn't even notice Torr's eyes burning a hole in the side of my head until the staff dragged the knight's body off the sand.

"What?" I demanded.

"Enjoying the preview of what's to come later?" Torr asked, his voice heavy with derision.

"Being cut up with machetes is actually *not* one of my kinks," I shot back. "And like I said before, my plan is to talk to him, not fuck him."

"But you haven't ruled it out." Torr pulled the champagne bottle from the ice bucket and drank directly from it. I held my hand out, but he didn't offer me any. "And you've been eye-fucking him since he walked out there."

I dropped my arm, letting it flop against the side of my chair. "What is your fucking problem?"

"I could ask you the same thing."

"Torr, we're supposed to be working together." I put my hands in my lap and turned to face him. "When you're not ignoring me, you're picking fights with me. I know this shit is difficult to see. I know it's hard to pretend to be like the other guests. But we have the same goal, right?"

"I don't know." He took another swig from the bottle. "You tell me. What is that goal, Rori?"

I put my elbow on my knee, bringing my hand up to cover my mouth. The VIP box seemed private, but I still wanted to be careful. "We have to shut this place down. I don't think it's just the gladiators they exploit. I was talking to my maid earlier and...she didn't outright say she was enslaved, but I could read between the lines."

"Fuck." Torr rubbed his eyes and took another pull of champagne. "And how are the two of us supposed to do that?"

"You see the Butcher's jaguar?" I nodded toward the sand pit, where the fighter and his animal companion paced in the center. Shit, was there even more fighting to come?

"Yeah, so?"

"What if it's a god like Astarte? Did you see how it protected his back? When it rubbed against the other man and then he stood up?" Torr remained silent, his brow furrowed as his mind put the pieces together. "That's why I need to talk to him. I'll bet you he's the one we needed to meet. Maybe he can...I dunno, get the gladiators to revolt. Tell us what we need to know."

Torr's eyes shifted toward me. "You didn't see the jaguar around when they lined up during training."

I stared at him, confused. "Okay, so? Astarte isn't exactly glued to me at all times, either."

"I'm pointing out the fact that you were up for fucking—I'm sorry—*talking* to him before ever knowing he had a jaguar."

"Torr!" I barked so loudly, my voice echoed off the glass window. "Why the fuck is that such a stick up your ass? It's a perfect opportunity to find more intel, and you're acting like it's some big fucking betrayal."

"You know why."

He continued hogging the champagne bottle, so I snatched it out of his grip because I sure as hell wasn't going to have this argument sober.

"Is it *really* because he's a gladiator and can't consent? Or is it something else? What do you want me to do, pinky-swear that I won't fuck him? Why is it such a big fucking deal to you?"

Torr stood abruptly from his chair, towering over me for one intense second that felt like minutes. His shoulders and jaw were so rigid from held-back energy, I thought for a moment he might hit me.

Or throw me against a wall and fuck me, if he was that bent out of shape about me *potentially* fucking someone else.

The familiar fantasy hit my frontal lobe, playing out like it had so many times before. Torr lifting me by the waist so I could wrap my legs around his hips. Kissing me like he needed my air to breathe. Walking forward until my back hit a wall and pinning there while we fumbled with passion and desperation to get clothing out of the way of our goal.

I'm right here, I thought, meeting his heated gaze. *I'm right fucking here. You don't want me alone with another man? Prove it. Show me the real reason why.*

Torr broke his gaze away, his shoulders cutting stiffly through the air as he crossed the space to the door in a few strides. "I'm gonna finish drinking out there." He angled his head toward the guest lounge on the other side of the door. "Probably won't head back to the suite until later. Gonna need some space."

He didn't slam the door behind him, but he might as well have from the way I flinched at the sound.

Alone in the VIP box, I turned slowly to face the sand pit again. The Butcher was in the middle of another battle, another free-for-all with other gladiators like the first fight had been.

"Fuck Torr," I said to the small, empty room I now had to myself. "Fuck me."

I settled back into my chair and grabbed the half-empty champagne bottle. Bringing it to my lips, I leaned back, kicked off my shoes, and placed my feet on the table in front of me. My skirt slid up my legs, exposing me from my feet to just about my knees.

I drank my fill, both of the expensive booze and the beautiful display of strength and grace from the Butcher. Torr thought I was eye-fucking him before? That was nothing compared to this.

I watched the sweat roll down his neck to disappear under his thin shirt. The shape and tension of the muscles in his arms and shoulders as he swung the machetes at his opponents. I watched his tongue dart out to lick his lips and the intense focus in his dark eyes. His eyelashes were so thick and full, beads of sweat clung to them like tears. When his shoulders and chest rose and fell with great gulps of breath, I wished I could see that motion on a repeating loop.

When all motion stopped, I realized it was over.

Roughly a dozen gladiators had been released to the pit for this final fight, and now only the Butcher stood, with his jaguar at his side.

He stood in the center of a massacre, all manner of blood and gore surrounding him. He was exhausted but appeared uninjured. Everyone in the audience was on their feet, chanting his name, pumping fists, and clapping.

The Butcher didn't acknowledge them, though. He looked straight at me.

I watched his gaze start at my ankle, then travel up the length of my bare calf. When our eyes met, I raised my champagne bottle in his direction and shot him a smile.

"Well done," I said, even though he couldn't hear me.

He gave a small nod in return, the corner of his mouth ticking up for one mere second. It was barely a smile, but it sent my chest pounding all the same.

———

I RETURNED to the suite alone, not bothering to check in with Torr when I left the VIP box. He'd been sitting at the lounge bar, engrossed in conversation with the beautiful bartender. She'd laughed uproariously at something he'd said, tossed her dark, braided hair over her shoulder, then leaned across the bar to stick her cleavage in his face and whisper something in his ear.

Whatever. If he hooked up with her, he'd be an even bigger asshole for trying to dictate what *I* did. And a hypocrite at that.

I glanced over my shoulder after passing him and wished I hadn't. It still hurt that he didn't pull away from her but smiled all lazily and flirtatiously instead. It still hurt that his gaze flicked down to all the business happening in her bra.

I hated that we'd been thrown into this crazy mission full of secrecy and corruption and things were still exactly as they'd been back home. Torr flirting with, and almost definitely fucking, the prettiest woman in the room. Me shoving down my feelings and trying in vain to distract myself with other men. Same old fucking bullshit.

His weird possessiveness was new, though. For a minute, I thought it might be due to him wanting me after all. What else was I supposed to think when he got all squirrelly and ran off to the gym when I'd semi-jokingly asked if he was jealous?

But it was crystal clear to me now. He'd rather flirt with a boobili-cious bartender than be near me. For fuck's sake, why did he even want to come with me if he couldn't stand to be around me? We barely looked like a honeymooning couple and had spent most of our time apart since we'd arrived.

My thoughts stewed, roiling around my head like a stormy sea as I walked back to the suite. Once there, I headed straight for the bar next to the kitchen. It would probably cost Gwen's employer extra to keep this place fully stocked, but I couldn't bring myself to care. That champagne bottle had barely touched my tolerance, and I was intent on getting obliterated. I grabbed a whiskey bottle and headed for my bedroom.

Paige, the sweetheart, had made my bed, folded down my sheets, and laid out a soft, neatly folded robe on the bed. She placed a note on the garment, handwritten in a pretty, feminine script: *Rori, dial *6 for maid service and ask for me if you need a bath, food, or anything else for your evening. I'm happy to be of service! -Paige*

"Too damn sweet," I muttered, setting aside the note and robe so I could flop onto the bed without ruining them. It would be nice if I could smuggle Paige out and take her with me whenever we left this place. She and her family would be happy and free in Four Corners.

I swallowed a big pull of whiskey, sinking down into the mattress as the liquor made a warm path down my throat to my belly. I could almost pretend it was someone's hand, or a mouth, moving down my body like that.

A frustrated sigh left my chest. We had a whole month to spend here and were off to shit-tastic start. I knew in my gut I was right about the Butcher's jaguar. That gladiator was the one I needed to talk to, and on some instinctivel level, I knew it before I ever saw the black cat prowling at his side. But even if the Butcher and I got a plan together, how much could I really do if I didn't have Torr to back me up?

How far would he really go in *not* supporting me?

Round and round went my mind with questions. The only reason I wasn't speaking them aloud was because I didn't have anyone to listen. If Torr were here, he would tell me it was just my anxiety.

I took another pull of whiskey with an annoyed groan. Closing my eyes as I swallowed, I imagined the Butcher's fingers trailing from my jaw, down my throat, between my breasts, and settling on my belly.

Only...I imagined his touch continuing further down, a hunger in his dark eyes as he watched me with rapt attention. With my own hand, I followed the path I imagined him taking, sliding a palm down my thigh to bring the dress up higher, until it bunched around my hips.

I was just on the edge of tipsy, pleasantly warm and languid with just the slightest buzz in my brain. But it was enough to quiet my racing thoughts and replace my fantasies about Torr with those of someone completely new.

I couldn't believe how easily I pushed Torr from my mind and slotted the Butcher seamlessly into the same place. Whenever I had tried to fantasize about other men before, it never worked. Thinking of them just didn't stimulate my body and brain the way Torr always had. But for some reason, my brain chemicals decided that the Butcher was just what I needed.

In my mind, his hand gripped my thigh, kneading it before traveling to the space between my legs. Maybe he'd cut my underwear off with a machete, that'd be hot.

Imagining it was his hand doing the work, I rubbed myself. My head went back, eyes firmly shut to stay in the fantasy. Instead of my own two fingers sliding across the thin material of my panties, they were his. Hands much bigger than mine, with callused fingertips for added friction, stroked my lips with a firm pressure that continued up to my clit.

My skin, my breathing, and heartbeat, everything reacted to his touch. I arched on the bed, splaying my legs wider as I sighed under my—no, *his*—ministrations. If I peeked, I'd definitely see dark, hungry eyes framed by thick lashes drinking me in. Those eyes would drop, traveling the length of my body before zeroing in to watch where his hand played with me.

What did the Butcher's voice sound like? Was he a dirty talker? Would he tell me how I looked to him stretched out on the bed like this? Would he describe all the ways he wanted to fuck me in filthy, clear details? Or would he just watch silently during the foreplay, observing me closely for what I liked and responded to the most?

His mouth would definitely be occupied if I had anything to do with it. He had nice lips, and I wondered if he allowed kissing when he met with guests.

He's enslaved. He can't set boundaries or say no to anything.

That was Torr's voice in my head, and it was as sobering as a bucket of ice water to the face. My eyes snapped open, and I pulled my hand away from between my legs, panting hard. A flash of anger hit me, and I reached for the whiskey bottle on the nightstand, pulling another long, burning swig.

Chances were high that I wouldn't actually fuck the Butcher, despite Torr's utter lack of faith in me. But he sure as hell was not going to come barging into my brain and ruining a harmless fantasy, especially after being such an ass tonight.

Determined, I brought my legs together and slid my panties off, then slingshotted them to a dark corner of the room. After settling back and spreading my legs again, I closed my eyes and allowed the Butcher to explore me bare this time.

I was wet, my flesh swollen and sensitive. The Butcher traced my lips with his fingers before pushing them inside my mouth. I sucked and licked at the digits, imagining his groan as he thought of me sucking him in other places. Those wet fingers skimmed down my body, leaving trails of heat before they teasingly circled my clit hood.

A whimper escaped my mouth as I arched higher for more, then those fingers trailed down and stroked inside me. My teeth sank into my lower lip, hips lifting off the bed to match the thrust of the Butcher's hand. I imagined his breath ghosting over my skin, maybe even kissing my hip and lower belly as that mouth moved closer to where his fingers played.

It wasn't the same as a tongue but flattening my palm over my clit was close enough to let my imagination take over. The Butcher licked over the sensitive nub while his fingers curled and spread inside me, demanding a response from my nerve endings with every stroke.

I had no restraint, no self-control, and no desire to draw this out with teasing. Once the orgasm started building, I headed straight there, accelerating like I just hit the gas on a straight stretch of road.

The release locked up my muscles, sent my hips spiking up to grind against the Butcher's face. I could feel him riding out my pleasure, keeping steady on all the right spots to carry me through the peak and descent.

When I finally fell back to the mattress, limp, panting, and sweating, I didn't dare open my eyes. Reality could wait because I wasn't ready to face it yet.

I'd much rather stay in the fantasy of someone, the Butcher, crawling up the bed to lie next to me and hold me in my sleep.

Chapter 20

Santos

My appointments with guests were the only times I was allowed a long shower, complete with hot, running water. So I made it count.

I shaved my face and manscaped, lathering myself up everywhere. Then, when I dried off, I made sure I kept smelling decent with a few spritzes of cologne. Less was more, as I'd learned from experience.

I dressed in loose, linen pants and a matching shirt. My feet were bare, and my trusted machetes were back in my room in the bowels of the colosseum. I always felt the most naked without my weapons, but they wouldn't serve me here. No matter how much I occasionally wanted to murder the guests.

I gave myself a final once-over in the bathroom mirror, then nodded at the pitmaster to let him know I was ready. It was always the male staff keeping watch over those of us who met privately with guests, just as a precaution.

My guard's face was blank as he patted me down for hidden weapons, his expression never changing as he unlocked the door and held it open for me. I went through the short corridor and stopped before the door at the other end. He unlocked that one for me while I waited, then held it open as I crossed the threshold.

The guard didn't enter the lavish room with me. He would stay on the other side to give us privacy, keeping the door unlocked just in case I, or the guest, hit a panic button during our time together. Then he'd be able to rush in at a moment's notice.

In my four years of being at Mystic Canyon, I'd only heard of a panic button being used once. A gladiator had taken a guest hostage in hopes of negotiating for his freedom. The staff had been able to diffuse the situation and the guest was unharmed, but that guy was immediately thrown into the next fight—a brutal five-on-one. Devin was the one who put him out of his misery with a knife thrown to his frontal lobe.

After that, they almost stopped whoring us out, but Nella wouldn't have it. She claimed the demand for fucking gladiators was still high among the guests, despite the risks. So the service remained, just with extra security measures. Apparently, the guests also had to sign a liability waiver too, saying they knew and assumed the risks for spending time alone with dangerous criminals.

As I'd come to find out, it was because of those risks that we were in such high demand, not in spite of them. Some people rode motorcycles, lit things on fire, or took drugs for a thrill. And some liked to fuck unhinged killers.

My current guest, who had been sitting on a loveseat, stood abruptly as I walked in. My heart did a little extra kicking motion in my chest. I'd been antsy for days about this session, the pretty blonde who'd requested me personally and watched my last fight from her VIP box. There was no tangible reason for this private spark of excitement behind my sternum rather than the resigned dread I usually felt. And yet it was there all the same.

With a few exceptions, I was not attracted to most of the guests and loathed the type of the sex the majority of them wanted from me. It was usually a grin-and-bear-it type of thing, but maybe this time, I could actually enjoy it a little.

"Good afternoon," I said with my politest tone and smile. "No need to stand for me. Make yourself comfortable."

"Hello," she returned in a soft, husky voice. "Thank you for, um, seeing me."

Her smile was nervous, and she clasped her hands in front of her like she didn't know what to do with them. Ah, a newcomer then. Every once in a while I got one of those. The first order of business was making her comfortable.

"It's my pleasure. Would you like something to drink?" I made my way to the minibar while she settled back on the loveseat and smoothed out invisible wrinkles in her dress.

She seemed to perk up at the prospect of a drink. "Do you have whiskey?"

I paused, hands frozen in midair for a second. We had every spirit and fermented alcohol the guests could desire, but whiskey was an unusual choice for a woman. It threw me a little, but I recovered quickly and grabbed two short tumblers.

"Will a pre-Collapse single-malt do?" I asked, showing her the bottle.

Her eyes, an unnaturally bright turquoise from the colored contacts she wore, widened. "I don't think I've ever drank anything pre-Collapse before."

I kept the surprise off my face. The Blakeworth elite loved their relics from before the Collapse. They hoarded aged wine and spirits from that time like it was gold. "It's extremely difficult to find these days, but we have more whiskeys if this one isn't to your liking."

I poured a small taste into one of the glasses, but the woman waved her hand at me to continue. "I'll take a full pour, I'm sure it's excellent."

I obeyed silently, pouring myself slightly less alcohol than her. If she was nervous, she'd want the edge taken off. And I couldn't allow myself to drink much and risk running into performance issues. Curiosity or not, I was here to get a job done.

Instead of swiping the drink out of my hand like I was a waiter, the guest held my gaze and kept her drink level with mine. "Cheers," she said softly, toasting me as she had during the fight.

It was getting harder and harder to keep the surprise out of my expression. Already, this woman was treating me closer to an equal than a body hired to do a service.

"Cheers," I returned, touching my glass to hers.

She held my gaze as we took our first sip, but I broke eye contact to sit on the loveseat next to her. We were close, but still far enough for me to not crowd her if she was nervous.

"Are you enjoying your stay here?" I set my drink on the side table and turned to give her my full attention. The guests loved talking about themselves like they were on a date with someone who actually gave a shit, actually wanted to fuck them. I knew how to fake it well enough, but with this woman, I was genuinely curious to hear what would come out of her mouth.

"Yes. I am, thank you."

Bad liar, I thought, my curiosity piqued to a new level. The words were stilted, forced out after a moment of hesitation and a tight smile. She took another drink, and I wondered how many whiskeys she'd need before those pretty lips started spilling truths.

"What has been your favorite part of the resort so far?" I leaned back against the arm of the loveseat, putting on an air of being open and relaxed.

Her eyes sharpened, and I wondered what their natural color was. "Watching you fight."

I smiled wider. It wasn't an especially unique answer, but she was telling the truth. And when she said it, I wanted to gloat and beat my chest. "Thank you, that's very kind."

"You're very precise with those machetes, and your technique is incredible. I know they call you the Butcher, but the way you fight is so much more than a messy hack-and-slash job." She took another sip of her drink. "Did you fight before becoming a gladiator?"

"Um..." I rubbed my chin, stalling with an awkward laugh to cover up my surprise. Blakeworth elites didn't know shit about fighting, aside from its entertainment value. They loved the blood I spilled and how brutally I cut up my opponents, not my technique. Who the fuck was this woman? "I was a mercenary in a past life," I admitted, figuring the truth was the easiest.

"Really?" Her head tilted, a golden, wavy strand falling across her forehead. "Who hires mercenaries these days?"

"Crime syndicates, usually the ones wanting to take over territories. But I haven't been in that game for about six years, so who knows if any of them are in business anymore."

"You ever work for any motorcycle clubs?"

"Nah. Bikers tend to run pretty tight ships. They're big on loyalty among members and don't usually hire outside help." I picked up my drink again, if only to keep my hands occupied. "You ask a lot of interesting questions."

It probably wasn't the smartest thing to say. We were supposed to be agreeable with the guests, to stroke their fragile egos and make them feel even more important than they already believed they were. It was frowned upon to give direct statements that may put them on the spot or make them uncomfortable. If someone got offended and complained to staff, I'd have one hell of a beating to look forward to.

But this woman was unlike anyone who had requested my services before. And to my relief, she didn't seem offended.

"I'm just curious, I guess." She smiled again, taking another sip of whiskey like she drank it all the time. She never even coughed or made a face at the taste. "I haven't left home much, so it all sounds very adventurous."

"Where are you from?" I scooted closer to her, sensing that she was becoming more comfortable, and felt pleased that she didn't pull away.

Her lips pursed, and she made a soft exhalation like she was about to say an F sound, but then she quickly changed her mind. "F—Blakeworth."

I didn't hide my smile or my skeptical look as I allowed myself another small sip from my drink. "You have secrets. I understand and respect that." I stood firmly in forbidden conversation territory now but was enjoying myself too much to care about the consequences. This wasn't the usual tired, rehearsed small talk before getting down to business. This was a real conversation, something I experienced so rarely.

"Just know that anything you tell me is confidential," I said. "The privacy of our guests is of utmost importance." Okay, that was a rehearsed line, but with her, I actually wanted to know. Of all the drunken and drugged-out confessions I'd heard before, the basic details of this woman's life were the ones that I wanted to collect and hoard. What was her name and the real color of her eyes? Where was she really from? Was that man actually her husband?

"Really?" Her eyebrows went up in surprise. "You're not mandated to report anything to the staff?"

Another interesting question that I filed away. "Intimate details about our guests, no."

"But other things?" I paused to consider my answer. "If it would endanger other guests or interfere with how the resort is run, yes, I am supposed to report things of that nature."

Her wry smile returned. "But do you?"

"Why?" I grinned back at her. "Do you have nefarious plans for this place?"

"If I did, would I risk telling you?"

I swallowed the remainder of my drink, put it down, and moved in much closer, until my thigh pressed against hers, and I could take her delicate chin in my hand.

"That might depend on how well I do today, won't it?" Flirting and banter were great, but she'd come to me for a purpose, and we only had an hour. Now that her nerves were gone, it was time for me to do my job.

The woman's pupils dilated, and her lips parted on a soft gasp. Damn, I might even enjoy kissing her. That usually wasn't on the table for these kinds of sessions, but if she was on board, I sure as hell was.

I leaned into her, allowing my eyelids to fall closed, only to find fingers pressed to my lips at the last moment. My eyes popped open, and I saw her eyebrows knitted together in some conflicted emotion as she leaned away.

Panic fired through me like a gun going off. Oh shit, I read this completely wrong. Where did I fuck up? If she was stopping me, she was definitely going to complain to the staff. Fuck! I was usually good at this shit.

I slid back until a good two feet of space separated us on the love seat and cast my eyes downward. "I'm sorry." My mind raced, grasping at things to say to hopefully avoid the beating from the pitmasters that would surely come out of this. "I'm very sorry. I... completely misinterpreted and did not intend to make you uncomfortable. I can have them send in another gladiator, if you wish."

"No, don't apologize." The woman reached across the distance to place her hand on my forearm. "You did nothing wrong. *I'm* sorry."

I could only stare at her, even more thoroughly confused. Guests were never wrong. They never had anything to apologize for, no matter what they wanted. If something wasn't to their satisfaction, it was *our* fault. Always.

"I'm sorry," she said again. "I'm...new to this and probably still not ready to...you know, sleep with you."

I swallowed. "Would you like someone else instead?"

"No! I meant in general. I don't think I can sleep with anyone being, you know, offered here. It just doesn't feel right."

"Oh. Okay." My throat remained a tight knot, but my heart rate started to calm. It had been so long since I'd been around anyone who had ethical issues with prostitution. I had forgotten there were people like that at all. "So you're not going to tell anyone I didn't...satisfy you?"

Her expression turned horrified. "No, of course not! In fact, I'll tell them the opposite."

"You really will?"

"Yes! You did nothing wrong. I would never throw you under the bus."

A sigh of relief left my chest. "Thank you."

She shook her head, looking around the ornate room furnished and decorated for the sole purpose of satisfying guests. "It's terrible that you even have to thank me for that."

"That's just how it is." I couldn't stop looking at her, couldn't stop wondering how this woman ended up among the elite clientèle of this place. She seemed almost...normal. And yet lovely and fascinating. If I wasn't so relieved about not getting reported, I'd be bummed about not sleeping with her. She seemed like a girl I would pursue if I was, well, not enslaved.

"Well, I like talking to you." She tilted her head again in that way that made her hair shimmer. "Would it be so bad if we spent the rest of our time doing that?"

"Not at all." A weight felt lifted off my chest now that I didn't have the pressure of satisfying her sexual needs or her ego. I propped my arm on the back of the loveseat. "And the feeling is mutual."

Her smile was warm and sultry. "Do you say that to all the girls?"

"Yes, but with you, it's the truth." Damn, she made it so easy to flirt and just pretend to be two people getting to know each other.

She played with some loose fabric on the couch, reserved but no longer nervous. "My name's Aurora. I go by Rori."

"Aurora." I rolled the R's in her name, enjoying the vibration of it in my mouth. "That's beautiful."

"You're a show-off with that tongue, huh?"

I laughed. "If I really wanted to show it off, we wouldn't be having a conversation right now."

"Hm, maybe next time," she mused.

My eyebrows lifted. "Are you saying you'd want to see me again after this?"

"I mean, we got off to such a great start." She chuckled.

"We sure did. I'll never forget it, Aurora."

Her next smile seemed a bit sad, and I felt it too. She'd be here for a few weeks, at most, and then leave. Maybe we'd have sex, maybe we wouldn't. But sitting and talking as two people, just because we could, was such a rarity for me. I wasn't bullshitting to flatter her. I'd remember this for however much longer I lived.

"What's your name?" she asked.

"I'm the Butcher." My response was automatic. Real names were forbidden, especially to the guests. Our names humanized us, gave us an identity outside of our roles. But fuck, I *wanted* to tell her.

"You know what I mean." Aurora's look was playful but stern. "I gave you mine."

I sighed, disappointed that I could no longer live in the fantasy of being on a date with her. Reality had to whisper in my ear and remind me of the consequences. "I'm really not supposed to tell you that."

Her face fell, the realization dawning on her. "Oh, I'm sorry."

"It's not your fault."

"It's pretty unfair, huh?" She leaned closer to me. "What you go through here."

I thought of the last beating I got. It was a few months ago, shortly after Tezca had arrived. The guest wasn't satisfied because I didn't choke her hard enough.

I thought of the Tank, a ruthless fighter and a decent enough guy, for a gladiator. He was made bait at last month's animal-mauling fight because he developed feelings for a guest, to the point of being convinced she would free him and they would run away together. The guy ran his mouth too much and died in an excruciatingly painful way—ripped to shreds by a pack of starving dogs. And the guest he fell in love with? She added me and a few others to her rotation to replace him.

Unfair? That was the fucking understatement of the year.

"You could say that," I answered through the tightness in my chest.

Reality kept me alive, so I had to stay firmly anchored to it. No matter how much good conversation, laughter, or flirtations I shared with Aurora, she didn't feel a thing for me. She wasn't here to save me.

Aurora looked like she was about to say something, then jumped in her seat, pulling her feet up to the cushions. "Oh my God, is that...?"

My head snapped around to where she was looking, where Tezcatlipoca sat like a cat-shaped shadow with yellow eyes. Fuck! My blood pressure spiked for the second time that day. He was absolutely *not* allowed anywhere near the guests.

"Tezca!" I hissed. "What the fuck are you doing here? Go!"

He ignored me, naturally, and walked forward. The black jaguar went around the coffee table and approached Aurora. I thought I was going to have a stroke when he placed his fucking chin on her knee and looked up at her with wide *please-pet-me* eyes.

"Well, hello." Her voice was calm, even amused as she reached a tentative hand out toward his head. She glanced at me, fingers pausing in midair as she asked, "May I?"

Not that she needed my permission to touch a god, but I nodded. "If you promise not to tell anyone about this either."

"I promise. My lips are sealed." Her palm came down on the big cat's head, and his eyes closed, lifting his head to press against her hand. "Oh, you are just beautiful," she cooed, scratching his ears. "Aren't you? Such a handsome boy, yes. Oh!"

Aurora yelped with surprise when Tezca jumped on the loveseat, effectively shoving me out of the way while he lie across her lap. She laughed as he flipped over to his back, silently demanded more scratches under his chin and on his belly. "You remind me of a cat I had growing up."

Her nails raked gently over his neck and ribcage, fingers smoothing out to rub in circles over his belly. Tezca opened one eye to stare at me, taunting me as if to say, *she could be running her hands all over you, but too bad.*

"Is he usually like this?" Aurora massaged Tezca's front paw pads, gently pressing on the muscle that exposed his claws, the sharp curve as long as my pinky fingers.

"He's never like this," I admitted. "Not even with me."

"I guess he likes me." Tezca flipped over so his chest and chin rested on her legs, and she stroked down his long back to his tail. "Well, I feel the same way, Tezca. You are just absolutely gorgeous."

The tip of Tezca's tail tapped against my thigh. *Yeah, I'm jealous, you jerk. Is that what you wanted to hear?* I thought.

He answered, not with words but with a feeling pushed into my mind. It took me a moment to recognize it as trust. It was the same way I felt around him and Devin, and it made me pull in a surprised breath. He was telling me we could trust Aurora, if even challenging me to try.

Well, if this wasn't a day full of surprises.

Aurora glanced up at my sharp inhale, her hand pausing on Tezca's back. "You okay?"

I nodded, swallowed, then took another breath. "My name is Santos."

Chapter 21

Torrance

"I'll take another, Andie."

The bartender paused, narrowing her eyes at my empty drink. "You're getting started awfully early today. You sure you don't want to slow down?"

I shot her a stony look right back, not having any of her fake concern. "You can give me a water to chug too, if that'll make you feel better."

She shrugged and took my empty glass, then placed a cup of water in front of me. I nursed it while she poured me a fresh whiskey and was grateful when she disappeared to the other end of the bar.

Andie and I had gotten to know each other pretty well over the last few days. When I wasn't working out to the point of collapse in the gym, I spent nearly every waking moment at this bar.

Rori and I had barely seen each other, let alone spoken to each other, since the gladiator fight. She had been right to confront me in that VIP box. I was being a total ass and knew it would only get worse the closer she got to her private appointment with that fighter.

I avoided her because she deserved better than seeing me go apeshit. I didn't trust myself around her, and even if she had sworn up and down she wouldn't fuck the guy, it probably wouldn't have reassured me at all.

Instead of manning up and being honest, I, of course, went to drink and chase tail. Because that was how I dealt with not having the woman I wanted. That was how I dealt with getting passed over for someone else. Again.

I had every intention of hooking up with Andie after the gladiator fight. She had even invited me to a vacant guest suite, which she had access to because her friend was a maid. But no matter how sloshed I was, no matter how badly it hurt to watch Rori eye-fuck that gladiator, I couldn't bring myself to say yes.

So I made a lame excuse about having drank too much, and said I'd be back the next night. I got back to Rori and my suite late. Her bedroom door was closed, and the whole place was dark. When I got up the next morning, she was already gone.

I worked out, showered, ate. Checked out the gentleman's club and golf course in the resort, got bored, then came to the bar. Andie invited me back again. And again, I couldn't say yes.

She gave up trying after that, and I couldn't blame her. I almost suggested it myself the day Rori went to see the gladiator, but I had *really* obliterated myself, to the point of passing out at the bar. I woke up to a maid gently shaking me and informing me meekly that she needed to clean.

I went to my suite and crashed for a few hours. At some point, I was awake enough to hear Rori's bedroom door open and close, then the soft voices of her and her maid.

So it was done then. Great.

Part of me wanted to storm over there, rip the door off its hinges, and demand to know what happened. Part of me wanted to know everything she'd done in explicit detail. Was he actually good in bed? How many times did he make her come and in what ways?

The other part of me wanted to throw the covers over my head and pretend none of this was real, and that was the side that won out.

That day had come and gone, and it still wasn't sitting with me any easier. Not knowing what happened was the worst part, but the thought of swallowing my pride and asking Rori made me want to drink myself into oblivion again.

I had to just...figure out how to be okay with the possibility that she'd done him.

Might as well tell a fish to learn how to breathe air.

On top of all that, we were supposedly meant to be doing something important here, important enough to get gods involved. Rori may have found things out from the Butcher, or, considering she hadn't yet told me anything, maybe not.

Sure, I wasn't exactly making myself available to her, but there were only so many places I could go here. If she needed me, she was smart enough to find me.

"You're a fucking bastard, Torr," I mumbled into my drink before swallowing it down.

It was easy to ignore the shouts and the scuffling sounds. This bar was just outside the underbelly of the colosseum, and gladiators were training in the sand pit. But when someone shouted, "You lost me five thousand TCs, you piece of shit!", that got my attention.

The bar staff, on the other hand, put their heads down and became particularly engrossed in their work. Andie turned her back to the corridor heading to the pit and began slicing lemons to add to her already-full stash in the refrigerator.

I heard more yelling, thuds that sounded like kicks and punches, and began sliding from my barstool. "The hell is going on?"

Andie's head snapped around. "Don't get involved."

I heard an electric crackling sound, like a taser or cattle prod, then a yelp of pain.

My feet carried me toward the dark corridor, not wanting to believe what I was hearing but too horrified to stop. "Are they beating up a gladiator in there?"

"Sir, please!" A maid jumped in front of me, then lowered her eyes meekly. "You are an esteemed guest here, please do not bother yourself with the staff's disciplinary actions—"

"Excuse me." I went around her in a wide circle, fearing I'd be too rough if I'd touched her, because I was already seeing red.

It wasn't her or Andie's voice I heard anymore, yelling at me to stop and not get involved. It was teachers at school and other sixteen-year-olds like me, trying to pull me back from a defenseless kid getting ganged up on by bullies.

This situation wasn't any different. I'd gotten too many black eyes, broken noses, and bruised ribs of my own to let that kind of humiliation happen to someone else, no matter who they were. From the moment Shadow put a dumbbell in my hand and told me to pick it up and put it down over and over again, I knew I'd use the strength I'd gained for those who couldn't defend themselves.

The lighting was dim in the colosseum's underbelly, so I followed the sounds to a dark corner. Sure enough, four of the male colosseum staff stood in a circle, surrounding someone crumpled on the floor. One had his taser out in his hand.

"Can't believe this little bitch killed the Animal," one of them sneered, then spit on the man on the ground. "You call yourself a fucking gladiator?"

Another one kicked the guy who, to his credit, didn't scream or beg. Come to think of it, he hadn't said a peep except for when he got tased.

All four shitbags were so preoccupied with the guy on the ground, they didn't even notice me walk up to them. Most bullies were like that, as I'd found out over the years. Pea-brained and single-minded.

I snatched the one asshole's taser first. He barely had a moment to look up in surprise before my fist crashed into his jaw. He whirled away like a spinning top, and only then did his friends get the memo.

The next guy that came for me got his buddy's taser right to his fucking gut. I kicked his knee so it bent in the wrong direction with a satisfying crunch. His scream gave me wicked tinnitus, but I still had two of the gang to deal with.

They tried to arrange themselves in front and behind me, typical dumbass bully behavior that I'd seen a thousand times. I backed up to a wall and lifted my hands, feigning surrender. As I expected, the dumbfucks thought they had me cornered and lowered their fists.

"You're a guest?" one of them said, gawking at my clothes. "Why are you getting involved? This doesn't concern—"

My left hand snapped out with the taser while my right fist connected with the other guy's nose. Both guys went down, one convulsing from electricity, the other groaning as blood spurted from his face.

None of the four dickbags were mortally injured, though they were in a world of pain. I stood in front of the gladiator they'd been beating up, blocking their path to him while they watched me with wary, confused eyes.

"What the fuck is wrong with you?" asked the first guy I'd hit, rubbing his swollen jaw.

"Could ask you fuckers the same thing." I dropped the taser and shook out my fists, resuming a fighting stance. "You want more? I got all fucking night."

"You're gonna get kicked out of the resort," hissed the one whose knee I fucked up, listing heavily to one side. Okay that might be semi-permanent damage, but I wasn't sorry. "And you'll be blacklisted from ever coming here again," he went on.

"Aw, damn. Can't wait to go up to my room and cry about it."

"You really have no idea what you've done." The four of them started edging toward the doorway, keeping their eyes on me like I'd pummel them again if they turned their backs.

"You're gonna regret this," another one of them echoed.

"Oh no, I'm fucking shaking."

They weren't amused by my deadpanning and slunk out the door like the slimy pieces of shit they were. Only after I no longer heard their footsteps scurrying away did I turn to see how their victim was faring.

"Hey. You alright?" I held my hand out to the guy, but he ignored it.

Rather than accept my help, he scooted back to use the wall as a support. One hand pressed to his ribs while he slowly stood to full height, his face grimacing, although he still didn't make any sounds of pain.

"They were right, you know," he growled at me in a low voice. "You made a big fucking mistake jumping on them."

"Well, you're fucking welcome, I guess. Didn't know you liked having your ribcage used as a soccer ball, but I'll remember that next time." I turned to leave, not offended or entirely surprised by his reaction. The sad thing was, some victims of bullies didn't always believe they deserved help.

"Hey," he called when I'd almost made it to the exit.

I stopped and looked back at him. "Yeah?"

"Why'd you get involved, anyway?"

"Because what they did is fucked up. And to be honest, I was in the mood for spilling some blood."

He let out a derisive snort. "Welcome to my world."

He was tough, this guy. And not just physically strong. I could only imagine the headfuck of not only being thrown into a fighting pit and beaten up by guards, but being forced to kill a friend. And here he was, standing tall and rolling his shoulders like it was all water down his back.

"Yeah, I guess." I paused, then turned all the way around to face him. Come to think of it, it had been a while since I'd talked to another guy, just man to man. Shit, if Daren was here, he'd be right at my side, taking those assholes down. My best buddy would probably be piggybacking this guy to the hospital, he was such a saint. Unlike me. "I don't know how you can stand it," I blurted out.

"Stand what?"

"All of it. Everything you have to do out there." I jerked my head toward the sand pit. "Being whored out to female guests. Dealing with those pricks ganging up on you when you can't even fight back."

The gladiator shrugged one shoulder with a scoff. "When the

alternative is bleeding to death for the mass' entertainment, what else can you do?"

"Yeah, you're right. Sorry. I can't even imagine what that's like."

He cautiously dropped one hand from his ribs and tried to take a deeper breath, wincing a little. "Sometimes that's just the hand you're dealt."

I still wasn't ready to head back to the bar, to face Andie and whoever else saw those assholes run with their tails between their legs. The consequences would come, and I'd shoulder them like a man. But not quite yet. I especially wasn't ready to tell Rori that I'd fucked everything up.

"You got a name?" I asked the gladiator.

He shook his head. "We don't do real names. That shit's burned and buried." He straightened a little taller anyway. "Since I defeated the Animal, they've been calling me the Hunter."

"Right on. It's fitting, with the way you fight. Really strategic. Congratulations, by the way. On surviving that, I guess."

"Thanks." He gave a lopsided smile, one that showed he was enjoying this bro-talk as much as I was. "That was my first fight here. I was shitting bricks, you know? I *knew* I was gonna die, I was so fucking scared."

"I don't blame you. Where'd you come from?"

The smile instantly disappeared from his face. "Somewhere really fuckin' bad. Honestly, I don't know if this place is any worse. At least I can make a name for myself here."

My eyes narrowed. "Seriously? What's worse than here?"

The Hunter met my stare, squaring his shoulders. "What's it to you? If you're trying to take me on as your new charity project, I'm not interested."

"What? No, it's not that." I looked down, realizing that he was still seeing me as a resort guest and from the perspective of miles stretching between our social classes.

Well, fuck that.

"Look, can I trust you to keep your mouth shut?" I asked. "At least for a little bit?"

He cocked his head but humored me. "Sure. We gladiators aren't exactly all buddy-buddy with each other. And I'm obviously not getting along with the staff."

"Right, makes sense. Well, my name's Torrance. You can call me Torr. And this shit?" I pinched at the fabric of my shirt, looking around as I lowered my voice. "It's all bullshit. I'm not one of these people."

The Hunter's expression didn't change, though I saw his gaze sharpen. He was observing me for any twitchy, lying behavior. "How are you here then?"

"I'm still not sure exactly. Connections, I guess. But we're undercover, sort of. Trying to sniff out this place, and yeah, it's fucking rotten."

"We?" he repeated. "You mean, you and your wife?"

I wish.

"She's not actually my wife, but yeah, the two of us are just regular folks from Four Corners."

"Shit," he breathed, eyes widening. "So, what, you're here to like...free us?" He whispered the word so cautiously, like he didn't dare believe it.

"That's just the beginning. We want to find out who's on top, funding all of this. This whole fucking business model is just sick, and we want to root it out for good."

The Hunter's jaw hardened. "Get us out. Burn this place until it's nothing but a scar in the ground. Do what you came here for, and I'll tell you about where I came from. I have a feeling I know who's at least supplying fighters to this place."

"That'll help us a ton," I said. "We want to stop it. This whole place has made my skin crawl since I set foot in here. It's just... fucking inhumane."

He continued to observe me coolly. "I haven't been a gladiator long, but I'm pretty sure this is a big, complex machine that I've been a cog in for years. You won't be the first to try putting an end to it. But I sure as fuck hope you're the last."

Chapter 22

Rori

"No jaguar hanging out with us today?"

The Butcher chuckled, sending me a warm smile over his shoulder as he poured drinks for us at the mini-bar. "No, I think he'll leave us alone today."

"Aw, too bad." I propped my elbow on the back of the couch. "He's the whole reason I was excited to see you again so soon," I joked.

By some fluke in the schedule, I'd been able to see the Butcher, er, Santos, again only two days after our first appointment. I was a lot less nervous this time, less conflicted about my feelings for Torr, who seemed hellbent on avoiding me for the past several days.

That was fine. I could at least spend time with someone who pretended to be interested in me.

Although Santos didn't give me a lot of fake vibes. He, too, seemed warm and relaxed today. A nice change after he'd been so worried about being reported the first time we met. After his jaguar had showed up, we'd small-talked about mundane things until our time was up. There had been a little tension and awkwardness hanging between us then, but I didn't feel any of it now. The nerves in my belly were solidly about spending time with a guy I was attracted to, and if things went in a physical direction, I just might let it happen.

"I can do my best jaguar impression if you want," Santos said, coming around the couch with our drinks. "Crawl around on all fours, lick myself in unseemly places, stretch across your lap in hopes of head scratches."

"Hmm, tempting. Your head does look very scratchable." I accepted the whiskey from him. "Thank you."

"If you ever need a scratching post, it's there for you." He settled on the couch next to me.

A laugh burst out of me. "Wait, am *I* pretending to be a jaguar now?"

"Hey, fair's fair." His smile and warm, dark gaze made me bashful to the point that I had to take a drink just to have a break from the intensity of his eye contact. "So, what have you been up to since we last hung out?"

Oh, nothing. Just being completely shut-out by the guy I'm in love with and thinking of you while I masturbate so I'm not focused on him.

"Not much," I said, keeping my tone casual. "Going to the spa, breakfast at the cafe, dinner and drinks. The usual. You?"

The pause before he spoke stretched on long, giving me the sense he didn't believe me, but he humored me enough not to address it. "The life of a gladiator is much more boring than that," he said with a smirk. "It's just eating, training, sleeping. Watching your back and preparing for your next fight."

He didn't mention his private time with other guests, which I was morbidly curious about. Nella hinted that he was popular, so how often was he in this room with other people, having sex with them? Did he have regulars that kept coming back?

I wanted to know everything, but couldn't bring myself to ask. I asked Torr about his sex life all the time, at first thinking it would help me get over him. But my feelings never went away and hearing about what he did with others only hurt me more. Santos felt like the beginning of a crush, and I knew the end result would only be the same. Hurt and rejection that I'd only brought upon myself.

"How often do you fight?" I asked instead.

"It's different for everyone, but since I'm a headliner that draws crowds, I'm out there once a month. Guys that are lesser-known, they're tossed out there once a week sometimes."

"Wow, doesn't seem like a lot of recovery time."

"It's not, which is actually by design to weed out the weaker fighters. If you keep proving yourself, keep winning, you earn longer recovery times and little perks here and there."

"A jaguar bodyguard seems like a hell of a perk," I mused.

Santos laughed softly. "Yeah, they don't exactly hand out kittens for us to bond with."

"How *did* you end up with Tezca, if you don't mind me asking?"

He paused again for a while, this time seeming as if he was wrestling with how much to tell me. "Tezca was released into the pit during a fight, a pretty routine thing. But he just...kept killing everyone."

My eyebrows shot up. "Holy shit."

"He couldn't be captured, couldn't be beaten. Gladiators were dropping like flies. And then they sent me out."

I cocked my head, waiting for him to continue. "Well, I'm glad to see you're still here."

"Yeah, me too." Santos laughed dryly. "I went out there, and he... spoke to me."

Dark eyes flicked up to mine, gauging my reaction. "Did he tell you his name?" I asked.

Santos blinked. "Yes. How did you know?"

"If you've noticed a white dove hanging around me, it's the same situation. Her name is Astarte. She chose me."

"Yes!" Santos shifted on the couch, sitting straight up as he faced me. "Tezca chose me. He said that...something was in motion and that he would be my protection."

"Astarte led me out here," I said, relieved to get it off my chest. "So it's probably no coincidence we've met."

Now Santos cocked his head, a grin pulling at his delicious mouth. "So you're not really from Blakeworth, are you?"

"No, Four Corners," I said. "And the guy I'm here with, he knows everything."

"Is he really your husband?"

"No."

Santos nodded as if that confirmed what he'd already guessed. "Boyfriend?"

"Definitely not."

He grimaced. "He's not your brother, is he?"

"No!" I laughed.

"So, it's...platonic?"

I hesitated before answering and knew he took note of the silence. Those eyes missed nothing. "We've been friends a long time. But, on my end at least, my feelings are... complicated."

It felt good to be honest. I'd never breathed a word of my feelings for Torr to anyone. But I felt like I could trust Santos and that he wouldn't be judgmental about the situation.

Santos nodded again, nothing changing in his expression. "And on his end?"

I shrugged and took a long sip of my drink. "You'd have to ask him."

The handsome gladiator made a dismissive noise, leaning back as he spread his powerful body across the loveseat. "He's a fool if he's not crazy about you."

My stomach flipped. "That's sweet of you to say."

"I'm not blowing smoke up your ass. I mean it."

I couldn't help the smile as I looked away from him bashfully. "You don't even know me."

"I know enough."

I shook my head, but my smile only grew wider from the attention he poured on me. "Callate," I told him with a soft laugh.

His eyebrows lifted, and a pleased grin spread over his face. "A white girl that speaks Spanish? I'm half in love with you already."

Heat burned my face like I'd just stuck my head in an oven. No man that I wasn't related to had ever told me they loved me, even as a joke.

"My mom's Latina," I told him, awkwardly ignoring that last thing he said. "So's one of my dads. I grew up speaking both languages."

Santos' eyebrows went higher. "*One* of your dads?"

"Yeah. I have four." I covered my eyes with a soft laugh, only somewhat pretending to be embarrassed. People had all kinds of reactions to my family's dynamic, and while I usually didn't care, I found myself anxiously wondering what Santos thought.

"Like, all at the same time? I don't mean any disrespect, I'm just curious."

"Yeah. They've all been together almost thirty years. Well, none of my dads are together-together. They're just with my mom."

"They don't get jealous?"

"Not that I've seen. They're all best friends with each other." I straightened my spine, feeling a little defensive of my family. "It's worked out great for us. Me and my siblings are all so close, and we're supported and loved by all our parents. I wouldn't change my family for anything."

"That sounds amazing." I was relieved that Santos' tone sounded genuine. "I'm a little envious, honestly. I had it pretty rough growing up."

"I'm sorry to hear that. We don't have to talk about family if it's a sore spot."

He shrugged, his expression and body completely at ease. With his arms draped over the couch like that, he really did look like a jaguar—all powerful, dark muscle forming sweeping, graceful lines that I couldn't stop looking at. A predator at rest.

"There's just not much to tell. I was an orphan. Been a little street punk for as long as I could remember. I was a small kid, so getting by was tough when I had to fight for food and shelter. I was a crafty little shit though. I learned how to get by and just took it day by day." Santos rubbed his chin, his eyes lighting up with amusement. "Kinda like how it is now."

"You're a survivor," I said. "That's how you got through it all. The fights, everything."

"Yeah. It surprises me sometimes that I'm still here when I've known a lot of people, either smarter or stronger than me, that didn't make it."

"You need some of both, I think. Sounds like you have a good balance of smarts and muscle." His story reminded me of Torr's, and the thought of the two of them trading war stories, maybe even becoming friends, was oddly pleasing to my brain.

"I dunno, maybe." Santos drank me in with those warm, beautiful eyes again. The look he passed over me made me want to burrow into his chest to find out if that big, powerful body of his was as huggable as he looked. "I think luck plays into it too."

"Luck or gods, you think?"

"That's the question, isn't it?" His smile was slow and just as warm as the gaze he fixed on me. "Maybe that's what luck is, an extra little nudge from the gods."

"You think they're up there, content to just watch us most of the time?" I went to take a sip from my glass but found it empty. "But when they feel like it, they'll give us a little poke in one direction or another?"

"I mean, if they can inhabit animals and speak directly to our minds, what's off the table?" Santos ran a palm over his buzzed hair, and I remembered his offer to lie in my lap for head scratches. "But what I want to know is," his hand fell to his lap, "why did the gods bring together a beautiful girl from a good family and a street punk turned gladiator?"

There he went, making my face hot again and probably as red as a tomato. I didn't know how to respond to compliments and flattery. The guys I had dated back home were punks too, wannabe bikers usually, but none of them had talked to me like this. So my only natural reaction was to ignore and deflect.

"Do you want more to drink?" I got up from the couch abruptly, circling around the back of it on my way to the minibar.

Santos was up in a flash, prowling around the other side of the couch to cut me off. My breath stuttered as he towered over me, not as tall as Torr but enough for my head to tilt back. Still a good kissing height though. *Now where did that thought come from?*

Not to mention he was also a broad, muscular wall, his hands and feet widened out slightly as if anticipating my going around him.

"What are you doing?" The question almost sounded playful, his eyes alert and a wry smile pulling at his lips. A jaguar ready to pounce.

"Getting another drink?" I hated that my answer came out like question. Why the fuck did my spine turn all noodley when it came to him? "I'll get you one too." I held my palm out, thankfully sounding much more sure of myself.

"No." The single word rumbled from a low place in his throat, a growl. "You don't do that. I'll get us drinks." He held his palm out, mimicking my gesture. "Give me your glass."

Part of me wanted to cave, to melt under the firm weight of his words, but another side was dying to see how far I could push this.

"I'm perfectly capable of pouring drinks for us," I said, standing my ground.

"It's not that you're incapable." His voice went lower, and I found myself leaning closer to hear him. "It's just not your role here. I serve you. Not the other way around."

"You do more than enough for others already," I shot back. "Let me do this one small thing for you, please."

Santos took a sharp inhale, looking away for a moment. He licked his lips and...fuck, I swore I even saw him biting his lower one. Could he possibly be enjoying this as much as me? Why was this back-and-forth arguing such a turn-on? My core was pulsing, and every inch of my skin was alight and eager for his touch.

"What if I told you..." He paused, drawing out the moment. Teasing me like this really was foreplay. "That I genuinely enjoy serving you? Not because that is my duty at this resort, but because it pleases me, as a man, to do something for *you*, Aurora."

It took all my focus to not let my eyelids flutter half-closed when he said my name like that, all seductive with his rolling Rs.

"Then you are welcome to serve me when you're no longer a gladiator," I said. "But when you're in a position where you can't say no...I can't let you do that. It feels wrong."

That slow feline smile returned, and God damn it all, it almost made me whimper with need. It became achingly clear in that moment how long ago I'd been touched by a man. Months, coming up on a year almost. I desperately wanted Santos to touch me, but only if this fucking enslavement situation wasn't a factor. Fuck, it was hard to remember that annoying little detail right then.

"That's a tall promise, to even speculate about a future in which I'm not a gladiator." His gaze flicked once to my lips. "That kind of hope sends men to early graves. I've seen it happen many times."

"I'm not trying to make promises I can't keep." My skin became prickly, uncomfortable. "I just...don't want to exploit you."

A long pause stretched on after that, and I couldn't shake the fear that it widened the distance between us, like the mouth of a canyon.

"You're not exploiting me, Rori." He went for the glass in my hand, but I swung it out of his reach.

Our eyes met again, and the playfulness there drained all the tension from the room. The two of us stood frozen like statues for a second, then I jumped into action. "You'll have to catch me if you want this!" I yelled, running away.

Santos' laugh was gorgeous, deep and musical. I felt it in my ear moments later, because he caught me easily with an arm around my waist, lifting me off the floor. His hold on me was loose though, probably in an effort to not hurt me. I was able to wriggle free to his frustrated cursing and started another lap around the furniture.

I made it to the back of the couch, and he faced me off from the front. We must have looked ridiculous, feet wide, giggling as we stared at each other, feinting to the left and right to throw each other off.

After a stand-off for nearly a minute, the victory went to the gladiator. Santos made a convincing dive to the right, then bounced back the other way before I could change my direction.

"Damnit!" I laughed when he caught me by the waist again, lifting me up like I was a dainty little thing that was closer to five feet tall than six.

"And now my prize." Santos held me pinned against him with one arm, holding his palm out expectantly with the other.

I hesitated a long time before placing the glass in his waiting hand. Both because I was a sore loser who hated admitting defeat, and because of the fact that I enjoyed the firm heat of his chest against my back. Maybe too much.

Likewise, Santos seemed hesitant to let me go. His arm unwrapped slowly from around my waist, fingers trailing along much like how I imagined they would when I touched myself.

"All that just to pour a girl a drink, huh?" I said, panting slightly.

"Not just a girl," he corrected, unscrewing the whiskey bottle. He poured two fingers in the glass and then held it out to me. "For you. The dove to my jaguar."

"There you go, being sweet again." I accepted the drink. "Thank you."

"It's my pleasure." He turned to me, all smoldering and sexy. "And I truly mean that."

"Santos..."

There was so much I wanted to say, much of which didn't seem appropriate, considering this was only our second time meeting. I wanted to promise him that he wouldn't die a gladiator, that I would do everything in my power to give him and the others normal lives again. Not just the fighters, but those like my maid, Paige. Talk about giving a dangerous amount of hope. What could I do? I only had Torr to help, and barely, at that.

If only I were my father, Reaper. With a single command, he had not only an entire motorcycle club, but an army behind him. Back in his day, I figure he had the firepower to torch this whole resort until there was nothing left but rubble and ash.

"Yes, Rori?" Santos answered his own name with my own, an eagerness to his voice that was delicious and tempting. But our time was limited, and he needed to be a free man yesterday.

"Can you tell me what Tezcatlipoca has told you?" I asked. "About what's coming? What steps you should take?"

His chin lifted with surprise. "Back to serious business, huh?"

"Yeah." I returned to the couch and sat down. "We need to figure out what the gods want us to do. How we're supposed to..." I paused for a breath, feeling the weight of my words before I spoke them. "Free everyone and shut this whole fucking place down."

Santos sat down so heavily next to me, he practically fell. "Damn, so you're serious-serious."

"I really am." I grabbed one of his hands, wrapping my fingers around the warm, callused skin of his palm. "I have no idea what I'm doing, but yeah, I *want* you to have a future where you're not a gladiator. I want that for you really fucking badly."

Santos blinked several times but said nothing. Then I felt his rough hand squeeze around mine just as his gaze fell to my lips.

A harsh banging sound tore through the moment, making me startle.

"Time's up, your session is over," the guard called through the door. "We'll give you three minutes to get dressed."

Chapter 23

Torrance

"Hey, we need to talk."

I finally found Rori at the cafe the next morning, seated next to the aviary with a cup of coffee, an everything bagel with all the seeds and seasoning scraped off, and her nose in a paperback novel.

She lifted her eyes, an icy blue color today, slowly over the top of her book, then licked her fingertip before she turned the page and dropped her eyes back down. "Do we?"

"Yeah, Ror. We do." I looked around. She was relatively secluded over here by the giant cage filled with exotic birds, but there were still guests and staff milling about the cafe. I'd much rather talk to her in the privacy of our suite. "Like, right now. It's important."

"Huh. That's interesting, considering we haven't talked at all in the last four, oh no, five days." She picked up her coffee, eyes never lifting once from her book. "Surely it can wait until I finish this chapter."

Shit. I should have known that would have come back to bite me in the ass. "Look, I'm sorry. I've been a dick and a hardass about the whole gladiator thing."

I'd been more than that. I'd been a fucking mess. In the moments where I'd seen her briefly, from a distance or passing by each other in the suite, she'd looked...radiant. And not just from the clothes and makeup. She was glowing like she was on top of the world, with confidence in her steps and a secret smile.

I knew it was because of that gladiator, and that fucking killed me. I couldn't even pretend I was upset about the whole sexual slavery thing anymore. She was enjoying every moment of her time with that guy, and it clearly wasn't all sexual. Rori didn't just look well-fucked. She looked smitten, like she was in a new and highly satisfying relationship.

Fuck. Me.

"Hm," was all she responded.

"Rori," I hissed, eyes darting around again. "This is fucking dire. Like, we might have very limited time here. Hours, if that."

"I'll be done with this chapter in a few minutes. This is a great scene." Her teeth peeked out with a small smile, biting her lower lip. "They're about to have an orgy."

Oh, great. We were on the verge of getting kicked out or killed, and she was reading smut.

"Rori!" I ground my teeth to keep myself from yelling. "I fucked up bad, okay? I got in a fight with some staff. So they're most likely fucking onto us."

That got her attention. She lifted her head, the book falling away from her chest as she stared at me. "What did you say?"

"If you would really like to hear me out, I suggest we go somewhere more private."

She set the book down on the metal bistro table, moving slowly as if she were unsure. Then to my utter relief, she said, "Okay. Let's go to the suite."

"Thank you," I sighed.

As she stood, she carefully picked up her napkin covered in the scraped off seeds that were on her bagel. She went to the giant bird cage, stuck her arm through one of the bars, and shook the napkin so its contents fell on the floor. A flurry of wings and bird calls descended on the discarded seeds like it was the first time they'd seen food in a week.

"I can't save all of them," Rori said, returning to my side. "But I can make life a little better for them."

We walked to the suite in silence. I tried to keep my pace relaxed and not look like I was rushing anywhere. After an eternity, I opened our door for Rori and stepped in after her, locking it behind me.

"So, what happened?" she asked, leaning against the kitchen counter with her arms crossed. She was still closed off and angry at me. But I could handle that as long as she heard me.

"You know those armed guards that work the colosseum? I saw a group of them beating the shit out of a gladiator."

"Which one?" she demanded, eyes widening.

Not your boyfriend, don't worry. "The guy that won the first fight we watched. He killed the Animal and his buddy that he came in with. They're calling him the Hunter."

Rori's shoulders visibly lowered with a sigh of relief. "So what'd you do?"

"Jumped in and stopped it. Pretty sure I broke a guy's leg. Got a good few hits in on all four."

"*Four?!*"

"Yeah, they were totally ganging up on the poor bastard. He's okay, though."

Rori nodded. "That's good, I'm glad."

In all the years we'd known each other, she'd never condemned me for getting into fights. She knew I was defending those who were weaker, after all. She even used to try joining in, but Daren and I forced her to stay out of the way of flying fists.

As we got older, Rori and Lily would distract teachers and staff so I could make sure to end the fights before they were broken up too soon. I was usually done when Daren pulled me back, slapped the shit out of me, and told me it was enough. If it weren't for him, I very well could've been locked away for murder at sixteen.

"But now we've got a target on our backs," I said. "By now, I'm certain Nella is aware, and she's just figuring out what to do with us."

"If they think we're still regular guests, they'll probably kick us out." Rori chewed her thumbnail. "If they suspect something else... who knows?"

"Exactly my thoughts," I said. "Which is why I think we should beat them to the punch and get the hell out of here ASAP."

She blinked. "You mean, just up and leave? Now?"

"Yeah. Get some good walking shoes on. Let's take the elevator up and just go until we find a signal so we can make phone calls. Then we'll regroup and come back with some firepower."

"Torr." She shook her head. "We can't."

"Sure we can. Look, I told that gladiator about us, why we're really here. He might be able to help us out. It's a long shot, but it's something. But we have to get out of here first, together."

"I can't, Torr."

"Why the hell not?"

"I'm seeing Santos tonight."

"Who the fuck is Santos?" It dawned on me right after I said it, cutting through me like a machete's blade. "Oh, wow." I rubbed my jaw. "Gladiators are forbidden from giving their real names, and y'all are on a first name basis, huh?" It was worse than I thought.

Naturally, Rori ignored me. "I can let him know what's happening too. The more gladiators who know, the better. Maybe they can organize a revolt while we're away. And by the time we're back, they'll be ready."

"How many times have you seen him?" Nothing else was on my mind. Not our exit plan, nothing. I could only think of Rori being intimate with this man, getting closer to him in a matter of days than we had in thirteen years.

"Twice." She bristled, her expression going as frosty as those fake contacts she wore. "What does it matter to you, anyway?"

"Have you fucked him?" For days that felt like centuries, I'd wrestled with the unknown, and it was fucking torture. The answer might hurt like a bitch, but I *had* to know.

"Oh God, fuck off, Torr. I'm not having this fight with you again."

"We're not fighting. It's just a question."

"It's never just a question with you, and I'm fucking sick of it! I'm done. I don't want to do this with you." She turned, heading for the liquor bottles on the minibar. It was late morning, early for drinking, but who the fuck was I to judge?

"What are you saying?" I followed after her, my panic riding high now. "What do you mean, you're done?"

"I'm done with you being an asshole and getting all up in my business about who I'm seeing." She aggressively opened a whiskey bottle and started pouring. "You've never cared about who I fucked before, and I don't believe for a second that it has to do with him being a gladiator. I don't even want to know why anymore. I just want it to stop, Torr."

My heart started to sink like a lead balloon, and it may have even been in pieces. "So you *have* slept with him?"

"Oh my God, did you hear *anything* I just said?"

"It's a yes or no question, Rori."

"I don't have to tell you jack-*fucking*-shit."

"I know you don't, but fucking tell me anyway!" The last word was accompanied by my fist slamming a side table so hard, I left a dent in the polished wood surface. "Please," I added, my tone betraying how fucking weak I was for this woman.

Rori only stared at me with an expression of complete bewilderment, her drink hovering on its way to her mouth. A timid knock came from the other side of our door, echoing through our uncomfortable silence.

"Rori, ma'am? Is everything alright?" came the hesitant voice of her maid.

"Now's not a good time," I answered. "Come back later."

Rori's drink came down hard on the counter, spilling whiskey with the force of its impact. "You don't talk to her like that," she snapped. Paige is a friend, not a servant."

God, I was royally fucking everything up.

"Sorry," I said under my breath. Then louder, "I'm really so fucking sorry, Rori." The list of things to apologize for seemed too big to rattle off, so an all-encompassing apology seemed the most appropriate.

"You'd know I was getting close to her too if you'd actually, you know, talk to me." She looked past me to yell at the door. "I'm okay, Paige. I'll be out in a few minutes."

"Okay!" came the timid reply through the door.

"You're right." My hands clenched at my sides with the need to wrap around her, to pull her into my chest for real this time, not as an act. "You're right about everything, Ror. I shouldn't have shut you out."

Rori held up her left hand, examining the black diamond I'd placed on her finger back at the tavern, which felt like an eternity ago. "So much for guarding me at every turn, huh? Good thing I didn't need you anyway."

And yet I don't see you taking that ring off. I swallowed back that retort, despite it burning hot in my throat. If I wanted a fighting chance of us getting out of here alive, I had to keep my defensiveness in check. I had to leave behind all my jealousy, all the bitterness of the chances I'd lost. Chances I never took because I was too afraid of losing her.

Sure, she'd only met with this gladiator twice, and it might not go anywhere. But he wasn't some small-town guy like all the ones she'd had before. I'd known all of them, known they weren't good enough for her. But the Butcher wasn't just a man, he was a force. He might actually see her worth. Might actually take her from me.

And acting like a jealous, sad sack wasn't going to keep her. Shit, it might be too late at this point. I could already feel her slipping away.

"I meant those vows when I said them," I told her. "And I'm

sorry that I let my pride rule me and didn't guard you like I should have. I really fucking regret that, Rori." She narrowed her eyes, but I went on before she could respond. "I also said we would come out of this together or not at all. And I still have every intention of doing that. But Rori, I cannot stress how much we need to leave *now*."

She shook her head, and I wanted to punch the end table again with how fucking infuriating and stubborn and gorgeous she was.

"Santos deserves to know what's going on," she insisted. "But we can leave immediately after. Just lie low until I get back."

"Right," I snapped, my threadbare control snapping like a single strand of hair. "I'll just wait here with all the lights off while you take one last ride on your gladiator rodeo. Brilliant fucking idea."

"I haven't fucked him, Torr! Jesus fucking Christ!" She threw the whiskey glass across the room as she shouted. It bounced and slid across the floor but didn't break. "Not that you'd fucking believe me, but there it is. Satisfied?"

Oh I was, more than I would ever admit. Something possessive and toxic inside me felt immensely pleased that she hadn't gone through with it. Rori's heart followed where her sex life led. I'd seen it happen many times. If she hadn't pounced on this guy, she wasn't falling for him.

Yet.

"I do believe you." I shoved my hands in my pockets, jerking my chin down in a quick nod. "Fine then. Go let him know what's up."

Rori was still fuming, her chest rising and falling with harsh, furious breaths as she glared at me. "This is the last time I'm going to ask you," she said, her voice just on the edge of calm. "Why do you suddenly care about who I'm fucking, when it has never mattered to you before?"

My throat closed up as though my heart had jumped in there to choke off my words and protect itself. "You really don't know?" I forced out.

She swung her hands out to the sides, then let them flop against her legs with a *duh* expression. "Now would be a great time to use your words and actually *talk* to me, Torr."

Oh hell no. This was the last place I wanted to be, putting my heart on the line to Rori fucking Wilder. I didn't do that for anybody, especially not her.

I wanted to scurry off to the gym and lift until I was a puddle of sweat on the floor. Or better yet, bend her over that counter and *show* her how I felt. I wouldn't stop until she was an orgasmic mess, wouldn't that be enough? My love language was nonstop orgasms, but saying it in words was too damn much.

Rori scoffed in response to my silence. "That's what I thought." She then moved coldly past me to the door and left.

Chapter 24

Santos

Two private sessions with guests in one day was always exhausting, mentally and physically. Especially when the day began with one of the guests I hated most, an heiress named Blair who believed the whole world should kneel at her feet. The only thing that made it bearable was knowing my day would end with Aurora.

On both occasions, my time with Rori had passed too fucking quickly. An hour with her felt like five damn minutes. Whereas an hour with Blair felt like a year.

Holding Rori's hand toward the end of our last session felt more intimate than any of the sex I'd had in the last four years. When the time came, I never wanted to let her go.

"How soon can I see you again?" she'd asked immediately.

That question and the eagerness in her voice made my chest swell so much, it felt like I'd swallowed a balloon. "I should be free tomorrow evening," I'd told her. "Book me as soon as you're out of here."

"I will." When our hands separated, it felt like she took a piece of me with her.

My routine was the same this morning—shower, shave, a spritz of fragrance. But every motion felt like swimming through mud. I didn't want to be here. Hell, I never wanted to be here until *her*. But right then, I would have traded anything to not do this appointment. My lack of choice in this matter had never felt so painfully apparent until now.

I walked out into the room with boulders in my stomach and cement blocks on my feet. My smile at the morning guest felt like the corners of my mouth were being pulled apart by fish hooks. "Good morning, Blair."

"Butcher," she crooned, assuming what must have been a seductive pose, one foot on the floor with the other propped up on the back of the couch. "I've been waiting for you to come split me apart."

The gown Blair wore was some sheer lacy material, leaving nothing to the imagination. Her chest was so augmented, her breasts looked like flotation devices. I knew every cosmetic surgery scar she tried to hide with body paint and fake tanner, because she had come to see me many times before. Blair had two obsessions: looking as physically perfect as possible, and rough, if even dangerous, sex.

There was a time when I almost felt sorry for her. What happened in this woman's life to make her reach for an unobtainable, idealized version of herself, while craving such degradation in the bedroom? She never even wanted aftercare. She only ever wanted me to be as brutal to her on this couch as I was out on the sands. If I'd been allowed to bring my machetes in here, she'd probably be thrilled.

That desire for the rough stuff was shared by nearly all of the guests I serviced, to varying degrees. They wanted the fantasy of the Butcher, to flirt with danger and experience my persona like an amusement park ride. Wild, thrilling, heart-pounding, but ultimately, completely safe.

Only Rori wanted the real me. Santos Antonio Jimenez.

I tried to swallow at Blair's spread open display, but no moisture remained in my throat. "Something to drink before we begin?" I turned to the minibar, blatantly stalling. Fuck, I really didn't want to do this. Not when I had to face Rori right afterward.

Why I felt some strange sense of loyalty to her, I had no idea. We'd spent a total of two hours together, nowhere near enough to form any kind of bond. But damn if those two hours weren't the best time I had in years. Maybe my perspective was all fucked. I'd been in this shithole so long that I latched onto the first pretty woman who talked to me like I was a fellow human being.

But Tezca told me to trust her, and she had a companion god too. No matter how logically I tried to look at it, we had simply been destined to meet. To what end, I didn't know. But right then, every cell in my body revolted at the woman currently lying on the couch, and wished it was Rori instead.

"The only thing I want to drink is your cum," Blair crooned from the couch. "I want you to make me choke on it like last time."

I made some kind of dismissive noise while pretending to be busy at the minibar. She liked it when I was mean to her, so I could keep stalling and denying her a bit longer. My dick was not excited in the least, though. Fuck, I should've popped one of those erection pills this morning. I could not imagine getting through this any other way.

"Hurry, Daddy," she whined. "I need you to fuck me until I bleed."

I had just swallowed a shot of the same whiskey Rori and I had shared yesterday and nearly threw it back up when I heard that. "I'll fuck you when I'm good and ready," I said, adding a hard tone to my voice.

The truth was, the hardcore domination stuff had never appealed to me. It didn't matter who it was with. I was a brutal, relentless fighter by necessity, not because being violent turned me on. But that was all these people wanted, and I was so beyond fucking sick of playing that act.

Before falling asleep last night, I got turned on by the thought of resting my head in Rori's lap. I imagined her scratching my head like we'd joked about, running those nails over my neck and back.

And I hadn't been joking about being happy to serve her. I wanted to earn her head scratches, her smiles, her approval. Hell, maybe even her love. Because I already knew I could trust her. I *knew* she wouldn't exploit or abuse me like I had been for nearly half my life. And that only made me want to worship her even more.

God, if a woman like that could actually love me? That kind of happiness didn't seem possible.

"Butcher," Blair barked from the couch. "You are wasting my time and my money. I pay for you to use your cock, not stand around with it in your hand."

I whipped around and launched myself at her, making the couch rock from the weight of my impact. Blair wore dark blue contacts today with little swirly golden designs in the irises. Those eyes flashed with fear as I straddled her, bringing one hand to her throat. She moaned, and I squeezed harder, which only made her writhe underneath me. If I felt between her legs, I knew she'd be wet.

"I'll use my cock on you," I growled, rubbing the soft organ with my free hand. "I'll use it in all your filthy holes until you're screaming for me stop, and then I'll fuck you even harder. Is that what you want?"

"Yes, please," she begged. "Destroy me, Butcher. Tear me apart like a filthy whore on the street."

I hate this. I hate this. Holy fucking shit, I hate this.

No amount of touching myself was working, so I racked my brain for ideas. The last thing I wanted to do was touch her with my fingers or mouth. She loved when I shoved her head down on my cock, but I didn't want to do that either, plus then she'd know I wasn't getting hard. We weren't allowed to use toys because the risk of injury to the guests was too high.

God damn it, what the fuck was I going to do?

I released Blair's throat and lifted off of her. Before she could complain, I roughly manhandled her into another position, pressing down on her upper back so that her face and chest were shoved into the couch cushions.

"Oh yes!" she cried out, lifting her hips in the air to rub her ass against me. "Take my ass, Daddy. Shove it in, and fuck me rough."

God, if she would just shut up, I might be able to fantasize about something else to get through this. But that grating voice and those demands that made my skin crawl kept me firmly in the limp zone.

"You're *my* little whore to use." I lifted the sheer, shimmery fabric of her gown over her hips, staring at her bare, wet cunt in an attempt to feel any-fucking-thing below the waist. "Be quiet so the other gladiators don't take you from me."

"Oh, I would love for the others to use me! I want all of them to defile me and stuff me full of cum."

Yeah, right. She'd end up dead if that were to really happen. I wouldn't wish such a fate on anyone.

When Blair arched deeper and pressed back, I stopped her with a hand on her hip to keep her from rubbing on me again. The grab was rough. She mistook it for things getting started and practically trembled with anticipation.

"Ohh yes! Give it to me hard, and make it hurt. I can't wait any longer."

Well, that was definitely not happening. And so much for keeping quiet. The seconds ticked by, and it was becoming increasingly clear that this wouldn't end well for me. I couldn't stall anymore, and no part of me had the stomach to even fake it through this.

Sorry, Rori. I'm going to be in rough shape when you see me.

I stood from the couch and lowered my gaze to the floor. "I'm very sorry, Blair. But I can't perform the duties as requested."

"What?" I heard a rustle of fabric as she most likely moved from her position, and my downcast gaze saw her feet touch the floor. "What do you mean, Butcher?"

"Regrettably, I am unable to perform, ma'am. My sincerest apologies." I was supposed to offer another gladiator to her, but no way would I subject any of the guys to this headfuck.

"What are you talking about? You're a male in your prime, what's wrong with you?"

"I'm afraid I don't know. Maybe my training this morning exerted me too much." I didn't even know why I was making excuses. It was all bullshit that didn't matter.

"Fucking idiot," she huffed. "If you can't do it yourself, I will *make* you perform."

Blair got up from the couch and approached me, making a grab for the front of my pants. My arm shot out on pure instinct, catching her wrist in my grip.

"Don't touch me," I hissed.

She looked at me with surprise at first, then pure loathing as she pulled her arm free. "You don't have the right to refuse me! You are here to do exactly what I want and nothing less. So do as you're told, gladiator, or I'll have you locked in the black box."

I ground my molars. The rotten bitch would threaten me with the sensory deprivation dungeon, the same prison that drove the crazed knight mad for months before they sent him out to be killed by me.

Blair apparently took my silence for compliance, her hands going to the waistband of my pants again. That action, that fucking entitlement, pushed all the threats and consequences from my mind.

Fuck the consequences. I wasn't a sex toy anymore.

I shoved Blair back by her shoulders. "I said don't fucking touch me!"

Her arms windmilled as she fell back on her ass. I'd pushed her harder than I meant to, but she wasn't hurt, just stunned that I kept exercising a right I supposedly didn't have.

"The panic button is under the coffee table. Call them in, fuck it. I don't care. As long as I don't have to fuck you anymore." I started pacing, just waiting for her to give the order to send me to whichever hell she chose.

"What did you say?" Blair asked in a low, malicious voice as she moved slowly, easing herself back up to the couch.

"I don't want to fuck you anymore." I was already dead, most likely, so why stop at half truths? The dam was broken, so I might as well let it all out. "I've never wanted you. I've hated every moment of being with you. So send me to the black box, I don't give a fuck. At least I won't have to touch you ever again."

"I see." She sounded calm, eerily so. Her ego was so overinflated, none of what I said probably hit where it hurt. Though I'd hopefully scratched the surface.

Blair stood from the couch and calmly crossed the room. She went to the doorway I usually came out of and knocked softly. The door opened, and a few minutes of quiet conversation passed. Then she turned and walked across the room to the guest doorway, not glancing at me once as she passed through.

"Butcher." A pitmaster appeared in my doorway and beckoned me forward. "Your session is over."

I went to him, ready to be escorted to the bowels of the colosseum. A sudden, panicked thought flashed through my mind that I must have fucked up seeing Rori tonight. Shit, what would they tell her? As a paying guest, she could demand to see me. But would she?

A sharp pain cut across my jaw, jerking my head to the side. I tasted blood, and realized I'd been too in my head to see the hit coming. Another one crashed into my gut, and it felt like a battering ram swung into my stomach.

I doubled over, and my legs seemed to stop working, so I fell to my knees. My vision swam while I tried to catch a breath. When I looked at the hand that had clutched my stomach, red blood streaked across my palm. I patted my stomach again, wincing at the pain and wetness that was definitely my blood.

I looked up to find three pitmasters standing over me, all of them brandishing fancy brass knuckles with spikes on the ends. Shit.

"Not every day we get to whale on the fuckin' Butcher," said the middle one gleefully, lifting his brass knuckles to admire them more closely.

"Hey!" The left one snapped his fingers in my face, prompting a snarl from me. "Your sandy ass has another guest to serve tonight. Don't fuck it up this time."

"Yeah, stand up. Show us whatcha got," the third one piped up.

I was beyond sick of everyone ordering me around, but I also had too much pride to remain on my knees for these assholes. With no small amount of effort, I rose to my feet. My stomach muscles screamed in protest, spasming from my injury. The spikes didn't go deep from what I could tell, but they hurt like a bitch.

No sooner had I stood to full height than a hit came swinging for my jaw. I dodged it, but then got a crash of metal to my temple that made my skull ring like a bell. I went down again, my vision darkening. More drops of blood fell on the floor, and all I could think about was cleaning it up before Rori stepped in it.

Another jarring blow came to the back of my head, and then darkness swallowed me up.

Chapter 25

Rori

I paced the opulent room for nearly ten minutes after my appointment was supposed to start, and Santos was still nowhere to be seen. Thoughts raced through my head while I chewed down the nail on my index finger. Did he not want to see me after all? Well, it wasn't like he had a choice, which just heightened my anxiety even more. Maybe he didn't have any open spots today or was with another client. No, Nella managed his schedule and would have said something.

"What the hell?" I grumbled, my feet intent on wearing a hole in the rug. I was so frazzled after seeing Torr, and it made me extra anxious to see Santos. I needed the distraction of those warm eyes and that gorgeous smile, even if it was for the last time.

The door across the room finally creaked open, and my heart leaped at the sound. "You know, it's rude to keep a lady waiting." I spun to face him, grinning, but all humor fell away as my jaw dropped open. "Santos!" I cried, rushing to him. "What happened?"

His face was bruised, swollen, and scratched deeply in several places, like his jaguar had swiped at him, although that was impossible. He also held a hand to his stomach and took small, pained steps into the room. "Sorry to keep you waiting." His voice was quiet, scratchy, defeated. And it broke my heart.

"Come sit down." I took one of his arms. "You can lean on me. I'll get you water."

"I can walk," he said but grimaced as I led him toward the couch.

I let him keep his pride, despite wanting to throw his arm over my shoulder and force him to use me as support. He sat down with a groan, and I rushed to the minibar for water and some cloth napkins. The scratches on his face looked fresh, and some were still bleeding.

Once settled next to him with my supplies, I wet a napkin and reached for his face. "Turn your head, let me see."

He leaned away from me instead, shaking his head. "No. It's not your job to take care of me."

"Right now, it fucking is," I snapped. "Come here, Santos. Please." The last word came out softer, a genuine plea. "I don't like seeing you hurting. Let me help." I leaned forward with the cloth again, and he remained still, so I took my chance.

He allowed me to dab at his jaw and temple for a few silent minutes. "Who did this to you?" I asked, getting up to check the other side of his face.

"Doesn't matter."

"Yes, it does."

"Really, it doesn't." He lifted those dark eyes, which now looked empty and sad, to mine. "It's just what they do to us."

"Why?" I could only imagine the injuries were from staff. If it had been another fighter, they never would have been able to land any hits on him. Santos had only been hurt this badly because he couldn't fight back.

"Because...I refused to do as I was told." He looked at me with so much pain and unsaid emotion, I couldn't bring myself to look away. "I'm sorry, Rori."

"Sorry?" I lowered the bloodstained napkin and touched the one unmarred spot on his cheek. "You have absolutely nothing to be sorry for. This is not your fault."

"I was so looking forward to seeing you." He looked away, a mirthless smile pulling at his lips. "I'm sorry I had to ruin our time together by being all busted up like this."

"Stop it. You're not ruining anything." I let my head fall to his shoulder. "I'm just worried about you."

"Don't be. I'll be alright." His arm moved behind me like he was going to wrap it around my shoulders, but then he froze with a grimace and a hiss.

I lifted my head, poured more water on the napkin, and straightened up. "Where else?"

"Rori," Santos sighed. "Enough. You don't have to nurse me."

"Yes, I do!" My hands shook, just as my eyes blurred with tears. "I care about you, okay? I can't just act like nothing's wrong when you've been beaten up for no reason. I hate that they do this to you, that you don't have choices, and you're treated like this. So *please*, just let me care about you like you deserve."

"Hey, don't cry." I closed my eyes and felt rough thumb pads sweep tenderly over my cheeks. Santos' voice was soft and so close that I felt his breath over my lips. "Don't cry for me, Aurora. I'm not worth it."

"Yes, you are," I choked out. "You're worth so much more than what they've made you here."

"You barely know me."

"I know enough."

He chuckled lightly at my repetition of his words from yesterday and leaned back, his hands falling away from my face.

I sniffed and opened my eyes, composing myself. "Will you please let me look at your other injuries?"

He sighed, and the deep breath made him wince and touch a hand to his stomach again. "If you insist."

"Shirt off, then. Do you need help?"

"No, I got it." Santos leaned forward, pulling the black linen shirt from his back. He sat back and hesitated once it was over his head, keeping his arms in the sleeves and his stomach covered. "It's really not as bad as it looks."

"Off with it." I went to pull the shirt off one of his arms, and he begrudgingly allowed me. The moment he was uncovered from the waist up, my blood ran cold. "Santos…"

It was definitely as bad as it looked, if not worse. His torso was covered in dark blue and purple bruises overlaid with those same deep scratches and what looked like puncture marks. Small, round lacerations all evenly spaced apart in sets of four. And there were hundreds of them all over his chest, stomach, ribs, arms, and back.

"What are all these from?" It took every ounce of self-control to ask the question calmly when all I wanted to do was scream. "Brass knuckles?"

"Spiked ones, yeah."

"Fuck."

I went to clean a few that still leaked blood, clenching my teeth to keep my jaw from shaking. But the tremors in my hands gave me away, as did the hot, burning tears springing to my eyes again.

"Rori, it's okay." Santos took my hands, the roughness of his palms a soothing texture against my icy rage. "I'll honestly be fine. It's all surface stuff, they can't damage me permanently. I make this place too much money, remember?" I heard, rather than saw, the forced smile in his voice. "I'll be sore for a while, but I promise I'll live. It's what I do best."

"I'll kill them," I heard myself say. Tears fell, and my vision cleared, the sight of his bruised, welted skin solidifying the promise in my mind. He had to be in so much pain. "I'll kill whoever did this to you."

Santos let out a soft huff of breath, barely a laugh. I felt his hand on my cheek, then he was looking at me. The warmth in his eyes had returned, and the smile he wore was genuine, the one that made my heart flip-flop.

"No woman has ever said she'd kill for me before." His thumb touched the corner of my mouth.

"I'm fucking serious." I placed my palm over his hand and laced my fingers through his. "You haven't seen me fight yet, but I can. And for you, I will."

"I believe you, Aurora." He stroked my lower lip with his thumb, eyes rapt where he touched me.

"I don't have a lot of time left here," the words came out in a frantic rush, urgency hitting me like a train. "Torr assaulted some guards, and we're likely to get kicked out soon. But we're not done here, Santos. I won't let you die as a gladiator."

His brow furrowed, mouth flattening. "Kicked out? They'll never let you back in."

"Well, we're not exactly coming to the front door and knocking politely."

That smile returned, although sadder and more subdued than before. "I'm so glad I met you. You're an incredible woman, Aurora."

"You don't even know me," I teased.

"I know enough," he returned, eyes lighting up.

We had gotten so close at some point. I was one outstretched leg away from straddling his lap, and our noses were nearly touching. My lips ached from wanting to kiss him so badly. With the way he kept stroking my mouth, it seemed we had similar ideas.

Neither of us spoke for a while. It felt like a tiny, fraying string held us apart, the final barrier between us threatening to snap at any moment. When it finally did, the two of us crashed together like storm clouds.

We met in the middle, and there was nothing tentative about that kiss. I opened my mouth to him, and his tongue swept in, tasting like desperation, like this first kiss might also be our last. The thought had my tongue caressing his, and I tasted bits of blood. Worried I'd hurt him, I pulled back to sip at his soft, plush lips, but he was having none of that. Santos wrapped an arm around my back and drew me closer, deepening our kisses until there was no space left between us.

I barely needed to move, but kissing him wasn't enough. My leg flew over his lap, and he drew me down with a tender hold around my waist. Our lips never separated as I settled into him, resting my hands on the sides of his neck. I kept my forearms lifted off his chest until he ran a light touch from my wrist to my shoulder.

"You don't have to be careful with me," he murmured, kissing the edge of my jaw.

"I don't want to hurt you more than you already are." My head tilted back, shamelessly offering my neck to his mouth, and he obliged me, running a sensual trail of kisses from my earlobe to my shoulder.

"Imagine how hurt I'll be if I never see you again." Santos kissed the hollow of my throat, moving higher up the front of my neck.

"You will." Our mouths connected in another kiss, and I gave a little tug on his lip with my teeth. "I swear on both the gods protecting us, I'll come back for you."

Santos looked unsure, his eyes flicking away for a moment. "Even if you do, what happens when that guy realizes how perfect you are and wants you for himself?"

I barked out a bitter, pained laugh. "Torr has never shown any interest in me in all the years I've known him. He's not about to start now."

"I'm not so sure about that."

"He knows how I am. How, you know, I was raised with multiple dads. And he's never been a sharer, so it's a moot point."

"Ah, right." Santos leaned back, his expression studious. "You're never going to end up with just one guy, huh?"

I shrugged. "I'm not wired that way, but it hasn't worked out for me so far, so who knows?"

His hold tightened on my waist as he let out a little scoff. "You're fierce, brave, beautiful, and ruthless. You deserve rooms of men."

I laughed a little, leaning forward to kiss him. "I only want one man right now."

This time, I allowed myself to melt against his chest. Santos only wrapped tighter around me, pulling me closer until our chests were flush. He brought one hand to my knee, running a hard grip up my thigh as he pushed my dress up to my waist. His touch continued up and behind me, grabbing my ass in a rough squeeze that made my hips roll forward—and make contact with the stiff erection in front of me.

"I want you, Aurora," he groaned, nipping at my throat again.

"I want you too, Santos." I was needy and hot, fighting the urge to rub against him and soothe the pulsing ache between my legs. "But…"

He was still a gladiator. I would be using him. I didn't want this unless he had the complete free will and inalienable right to say no.

Santos seemed to follow my train of thought and held my chin between his thumb and forefinger. "That's not what this is. You don't see this as a transaction, right?"

"No, but…"

"*I* want this. For me." He cupped my cheek, kissing me tenderly. "You wanted to do something for me yesterday. Will you give me this?"

I let out a soft laugh of disbelief, rocking my forehead against his. "This is what you want? To be with me?"

"It's all I want."

Another '*you don't even know me*' hovered on the tip of my tongue, but I stopped myself, realizing how serious he was.

And how much I wanted the exact same thing. Right now, while I still had him.

Chapter 26

Rori

Ikissed Santos in reply, sealing the deal for both of us. He returned it with equal fervor, pulling me in with that possessive hand on my ass, and I let myself slowly crash into him.

Santos shoved away all of my dress fabric that was pooling around us, his hands running up my thighs to my hips like he couldn't get enough of me. His cock was long and thick behind his pants, and I wanted to shove away his clothes like he was doing with me. But I forced myself to wait, to run my aching core over him from base to head. My hips lifted and lowered, simulating riding him at a slow, tantalizing pace.

"Mm, should've known you'd be a tease." He grinned, holding my waist to guide my movement.

"Foreplay isn't just for women, you know." I leaned in to kiss his neck and maybe also to kiss some of his bruises. I wasn't fucking joking about killing whoever did this to him.

"I know. It's just..."

I nipped at his earlobe when he trailed off, and a sexy moan rolled out of his throat when I ground harder against his erection. "Just what?"

"I was gonna say it's been a while since I've done this, but that's not exactly true, is it?"

"That wasn't sex. You were being used." I eased back in his lap and pulled at the ties on his linen pants. "I bet you weren't even being pleasured, were you?"

"Mm, no." His dark eyes fell between us to where I'd freed his cock and stroked him. He was so hot and rigid, the thick length of him pulsing against my palm. "Not like this. No one's ever touched me like you."

I had a feeling he was flattering me again just to be sweet, but the words made me smile and flush with heat all the same. I wanted to believe him. And damn it, he deserved to feel good after everything he'd been through.

Sliding backwards off his lap, I held his gaze as my feet hit the floor first, then my knees as I separated his thighs to make room for myself.

"What are you doing, paloma?" His voice was low, eyes hooded behind those dark lashes. His fingers trailed over my arms, my shoulders, and neck. He touched me like he was endlessly in awe of me and stared at me like my beauty was something to marvel at. I knew I wasn't a cave troll or anything, but no one had ever looked at me like *that*.

"Giving you what you want." I kissed one of the bruises on his ribs, just barely brushing it with my lips so as to not pain him. Then I kissed one on his lower stomach. "What you deserve," I added.

"I want to please you too." Santos traced my cheekbone with his thumb. "I want to make you come and hear you say my name as I get you there, over and over."

"You will." I placed a kiss on the deep line in his hip crease, squeezing harder around his cock as I stroked upward. "When I come back for you."

"Aurora," he rasped in frustration.

"Santos," I answered, looking up at him. "I can't be selfish with you. Not right now. Please, can you understand that?"

Before he could answer, I lowered my mouth to him, sliding my lips and tongue over his blunt head until his chin tipped up with a moan.

"I...guess I can live through this," he sighed in answer.

I laughed a little, then dragged a long lick from the sensitive tip to the base of his cock. "Besides, you're injured," I pointed out, licking my way back up. "I want you fully recovered and far away from this place when you fuck me."

"Can't happen soon enough." Santos caressed my neck, pushing my hair out of the way as I savored him with my mouth. "Fuck, you're so beautiful. You feel, uh, so fucking good..."

His praise encouraged me, and I started to suck him in earnest, working the entire length of him with my hand and mouth. In truth, it was all his nonverbal reactions that made me feel like a fucking goddess. His soft moans and hisses of breath. The subtle rolls of his hips to drive deeper into my mouth. The way his grip tightened on my hair or shoulder when he felt especially good.

Too many times I had given blowjobs where it felt like I was slobbering on an inanimate object, not a person experiencing pleasure. It got my anxious spiral rolling, wondering if I was doing it well enough or if the guy actually liked me. With Santos, I had none of those thoughts. His responsiveness was not only reassuring, it turned me the fuck on. I didn't have to touch myself to know my panties were soaked.

My hand went there anyway, partially to soothe my clit that was aching to be touched but also to see his reaction.

Santos' cock jerked against my tongue, his breaths getting even more ragged. "Oh yes, touch yourself for me. I want you to come. Be a little selfish for me, paloma."

It wouldn't take long. I was slick, and my flesh was so sensitive to every rub I made with my fingertips. Santos was getting close too, his grip on me tightening while he stiffened and swelled inside my mouth. I felt his hand reach lower, diving inside the bodice of my dress to find my breasts.

I was moaning too now, wordless and muffled with my mouth stuffed full of him. My orgasm was building hard and fast while I rubbed myself and Santos rolled my nipples with those callused fingers.

"You really want to know why I got beat?" he rasped, his voice tight.

"Mmm!" I took him further down my throat, sealing my lips down his solid length.

"Come for me first." He laughed when my moan turned into a throaty growl of frustration. "Your pleasure is the price for knowledge. Show me how much you like sucking my dick."

Oh Jesus. Not only was he a responsive lover, he could tease and talk dirty too. I couldn't afford to fail at torching this place and freeing all the gladiators. Not when I'd just found the perfect man.

And the part I couldn't get over? He wanted me too.

"Don't stop, just like that," Santos groaned, kneading a breast in one hand while he stroked my neck and face with the other. "You're so perfect, so good to me."

My breath was shortening, the building orgasm coiling tighter in my clit like a compressed spring. Sucking down Santos became a race to see which would come first—me, him, or my need to breathe.

He spilled on my tongue with a ragged groan, hips pistoning to drive his releasing cock through the seal of my lips. His sounds of pleasure, and the salty taste of him, spurred my own orgasm to let loose. The spring uncoiled, stretching free. My legs clamped shut as they shook, trapping my hand against my clit as I swallowed every thick pulse of Santos' release.

I let him fall from my mouth when he grew soft, resting my cheek on his thigh as we looked up at each other. He was so fucking sexy, sitting back on the couch with his knees wide, chest rising and falling as he caught his breath. With his powerful physique, the injuries dotting his skin, and the light sheen of sweat coating him, he looked like a sated god of war.

"Come here, paloma," he rasped, cupping my cheek.

I rose from the floor, accepting his embrace. He turned me sideways, draping my legs across his lap while those powerful arms encircled my waist. Santos kissed me deeply, possessively, holding me tightly in a way that showed that he never wanted to let go.

The tenderness of it nearly made me want to cry. I wasn't used to this either, any kind of cuddling or afterglow following anything sexual. I didn't even realize until right then that he was probably the first guy to initiate this with me.

Maybe this was what I was missing, genuine affection freely given. It was like how my fathers always were with my mother. At least one of them was always touching her just because they loved to be connected to her. Kissing, cuddling, even holding hands, were things I always had to fight for with a guy, and I always initiated.

Santos was acting like I'd already saved him, and this was just a blowjob.

"Don't you have something to tell me?" I whispered, my lips brushing his.

"You're the sexiest fucking thing I've ever seen," he said, kissing me again. "And your mouth, fuck." He touched his thumb to my lip, his smile lazy and sated. "These lips are magical."

"You know, you're very good at using charm to be distracting." I almost said, *you remind me of Torr,* but I thought better of it. "But I'm not easily distracted. What were you going to say before?"

"Hm, you'll have to remind me." He kissed my mouth again, then the bridge of my nose. "Because I am very easily distracted, and this gorgeous face hasn't been kissed enough."

"Santos!" I laughed as he moved on to my cheek and my neck. God, why couldn't this last forever? Finally, an adorable, sweet, funny man who was also hot as fuck and wanted me just as badly as I wanted him. Right when I had to leave too, and I could only hope he would still be here when I came back to storm the castle. "You know what I'm talking about. I paid the price for knowledge, so tell me why they did this."

He kissed my shoulder and then rested his forehead there for a moment, barely even a second, when the knock came to the door.

"Time's up. Three minutes to put your clothes back on."

"Fuck," we said in unison.

"I hate this," I whispered, wrapping my arms around his shoulders. "I hate this so much."

"Me too. Rori, listen." Santos pulled back and held me by the shoulders, his face gravely serious. "They're most likely going to put me in isolation after this. As further punishment."

My heart felt like it stopped and then clenched with fear. "Isolation? What does that mean for you?"

"It means..." He inhaled sharply before continuing. "I might not be the same person when you come back. It's like sensory deprivation, real fucked-up psychological shit."

Torture. He meant psychological torture.

My hands found his, linking through his fingers as if to create a type of netting that would never separate us. "Then we've got to get you out *now*."

"That's not possible, paloma. I'm sorry."

I started to rise from the couch, keeping our hands linked. "Come with me through the guest door. We can run. You can hide in our suite until—"

"There will be at least a dozen pitmasters between there and here," he said. "It'll never work."

"We have to try!" I brought our joined hands to my chest. "I can't lose you when I just found you."

It was a dramatic, probably embarrassing thing to say. But it was how I honestly felt in that moment, and I had always been one to wear my heart on my sleeve.

Santos, thankfully, said nothing of it. He only slowly untangled our hands to hold me against his chest. "Go, and bring the cavalry when you come back," he said, lips against my forehead. "I'll...hold on and do what I can here. I have a friend who might be able to unite the gladiators while I'm isolated."

"That'll help," I admitted. "If we have a united front on the inside while we come from the outside, we can't lose."

"It won't be easy. Gladiators only look out for themselves."

My hands went to his face, and our mouths met in a kiss that had me simultaneously burning and melting from passion. Fuck, it was all I could do to not drag him from that room and start running *now*, but I knew logistically it would be insanely difficult. It would be easier for me and Torr to go, gather support, and come back.

But fuck, it killed me to leave him.

"I'll come back as soon as I can," I promised in a hurried whisper, knowing our time was running out. "You stay strong in there for me, okay? Not just for me but for you. For the life you're going to have after this."

Santos' smile was easy and almost infuriatingly calm. "Don't be scared for me, paloma. Surviving's what I'm best at, remember?"

"Entering in twenty seconds!" called the guards from the door.

Shit, shit, shit. That was no time at all. What could I do besides kiss him some more? So I did just that, and he kissed me back with a bone-crushing embrace.

"Entering now!"

"I refused to fuck a guest," Santos whispered before he was abruptly pulled away from me.

"What?" I was dazed from kissing him, heartbroken at the sight of three guards leading him toward the door. One of them had spiked brass knuckles hanging from a loop on his belt, and it hit me right then. These were the ones that 'punished' him, and he was telling me why.

"Because I only wanted to be with you." Santos' eyes were dark and intense as he was walked across the room.

"Excuse me, gentlemen!" I called out. "Can I ask you three something?"

The three guards paused and all whipped their heads toward me. "Yes, ma'am?"

I smiled sweetly. "I just wanted to see your faces. Thank you for your service."

Chapter 27

Rori

My bravado ended the moment I stepped out of that room, but my mind latched onto the faces of those guards, burning them into my memory. I headed back to the suite, fighting every impulse to turn around and wrestle Santos free of those men. He needed me. Torr didn't.

I didn't know what to expect when I returned. The chances of Torr being there or not were fifty-fifty in my mind. With a shaky breath, I opened the door to find him stretched out on the longest couch with only a single lamplight illuminating the whole space. Night was creeping in quickly, filling spaces with darkness and shadows.

Torr swung upright as soon as he heard me, pinning me with a hard expression. "You okay?"

No, I wasn't. My heart wanted to crack open at the question, but I kept it together, pulling in another breath, which unfortunately made my nose sniffle. "You ready to go?"

Torr stood, approaching me with long strides. "Have you been crying?" Again, he completely ignored what I said and reached for my face.

I jerked away from his hand, well past my limit with him. "No. Let's just go."

"Rori, what happened?" He would not get out of my way and succeeded in cupping his palm against my cheek. Such a different feel to Santos' hands, and it seemed so incredibly cruel that he'd be affectionate and caring with me now. Too little, too fucking late.

"Stop, Torr." I batted his arm away, taking several steps back to move around him. "You were in such a big fucking hurry to go, so let's *go*."

"Not until you tell me what the fuck happened in there." He grabbed my upper arm, spinning me to face him. His jaw and cheekbones cut harsh lines from the shadows, and my mind flashed back to when he lit my cigarette under the lamplight. "Why are you upset? Did he hurt you?"

"No! Jesus fucking Christ!" I pulled my arm free, swung it back, and stopped myself from using the momentum to punch him. That was not me. Torr was pissing me off beyond all belief, but he was not my enemy. "I blew him, okay?"

Torr froze. I wouldn't have needed a punch to knock him over. My pinky finger would have done the job. "What?"

"I gave him a BJ. Went down on him. Sucked him off." I waved my hands in front of me in a mocking *ta-da* motion. "You're gonna keep harassing me until I tell you, so there it is, Torr. It finally happened, are you happy? And I'm upset because he got his ass kicked for me. I actually fucking like him, and he's gonna get tortured while we're off taking who-knows-how-long to get enough muscle to torch this place."

"Shit. Rori, I—" Torr raked a hand through his hair, looking more flustered and uncomfortable than I'd ever seen him in my life. He usually kept it all locked away in a safe, but right then, he seemed moments away from bursting.

"I'm sorry he went through that. Is *going* through that. I wasn't going to ask you what you did with him. You're right, it's none of my business. I just...don't like seeing you upset."

"Huh." I turned in the direction of my room so I could change clothes and pack. "That's a first."

"No, it's not."

The forcefulness in Torr's tone made me stop in my tracks and look back at him, confused. "What?"

"I've always...cared about you, Rori. As more than a friend. More than my best friend's sister." His throat bobbed with the force of his swallow. And in the silence that followed, the noise of that swallow seemed to echo in the room.

"Wait...what?" My brain felt like it short-circuited. How long had I been fantasizing about hearing those exact words? That the gorgeous man who everyone wanted felt the same way about me as I did him? It had been so long and, since meeting Santos, I began to let go of that yearning for Torr. Now that he was telling me what I wanted, it was almost nonsensical.

He shifted uncomfortably and cleared his throat. "Look, I'm not good at this emotional stuff, but I'm trying." He licked his lips and inhaled sharply as he looked down at his shoes. "It's true. Like, the real reason I've never been able to commit to anyone is because...I always compare them to you." He looked up, the vulnerability plain on his face. "I always wanted to spend my time with you because... you've always been there for me, and you're just...perfect."

"Are you fucking kidding me?" I understood that he was putting his heart out on the line, probably for the first time in his life, but I was still pissed. "You're telling me you spent years chasing tail all over Four Corners because you didn't have the balls to say, 'Hey Rori, let's go out on a fucking date'? Is that seriously what you're saying right now?"

Torr's mouth hardened. "I wasn't the only one sleeping around, remember? What was I supposed to think when you'd drag two dudes off to a bedroom at a party, huh? You never did your little come-hither thing at me, so why would I try?"

"Don't turn this around on me! I'm not responsible for what comes out of your mouth." I stabbed my index finger at my own chest.

"You *knew* I wanted something real, something more than hooking up. You were *there* when I cried about getting dumped. I told you about every single failed relationship and how much it hurt me that they never worked out. And here you are, going from woman to woman, making it very fucking clear that you want nothing lasting. So what was *I* supposed to think, Torr?"

He started shaking his head, looking away from me. "Forget I said anything."

Oh, fuck that. "What? No, *you* opened this can of worms. Let's talk about it." I went around and planted myself in front of him.

"Rori, move," Torr growled.

Oh, how the tables had turned.

"I'm not going anywhere." I spread my feet wide, placing my hands on my hips.

"I don't want to talk about this anymore."

"Too bad." I cocked my head at him. "We've known each other for thirteen years. You never had *one* opportunity to ask me out? Or just, like, kiss me? Just to see if maybe I felt the same way you did?"

"Nah." He shook his head. "It wasn't for lack of opportunity. I just knew it'd never work out."

"Why not? You never even tried!"

He shrugged, the movement jerky and stiff. "Just wasn't a risk I was willing to take."

"I can't fucking believe you, Torr." I pinched the bridge of my nose. "Why are you like this?"

"Like what?"

"Just...so emotionally constipated!" My hands flew up in frustration. "Did it ever occur to you I might want you back? That if you had just been real with me, I would have said yes? I would have given us a chance, at least."

"No." He swallowed hard, shaking his head again. "No, I couldn't have even asked you out. I was ready to go to the grave having never taken that chance with you."

I was on the verge of tearing out chunks of my hair. "Fucking *why?*" I cried out.

"Because the last people who were supposed to love me left me in the desert to die!"

The silence following his shout created a void in that room, nothing but pure emptiness. And then it slowly filled to the brim with all kinds of realizations.

Torr kept everyone at arm's length, even Daren. He poured all of his energy into lifting weights so that he'd never need anyone but himself to protect him. When others needed protecting, he did so with an onslaught of fists and years of pent-up childhood fury. Despite my family opening their home and arms to him, he always held back, just a little. He was always on the fringe, never fully allowing himself to be part of us. Because family, to him, meant abandonment.

And he never let himself fall in love so that his heart would never be broken again.

"Torr..." His name was a whispered plea on my lips, and then it was me reaching for his face. He stiffened at my touch but thankfully didn't pull away. "Remember this?" I brushed the back of my fingers against his cheek, letting the black diamond gently run across his stubble. "You can still keep this promise. You and I are in this together, okay? You're never going to lose me."

He was quiet for a long time, so long that I wondered if he'd locked everything away again until he said, "How do I know that?" in a choked whisper.

"Trust." My hand slid around to the back of his neck. "You're going to have to unclench your emotional butthole and trust me a little."

I was expecting more of his stoicism but he actually laughed, his forehead lowering to brush mine. "See, this is why you're perfect."

"I'm not." I placed both hands around his neck, letting my nails drag along the tight muscles there. "But I'm here. And..." My throat tightened. It was my turn to lay it all out there. "And I'm yours. If you'll have me."

Torr's hands fell to my waist in a heavy, solid grip. "What about your gladiator?"

"That depends," I mused. "Would you let me keep him?"

His fingers closed into fists, bunching up the fabric of my dress. "Probably. As long as you keep me too."

We drifted closer together in a proximity that was familiar, yet these touches were completely unknown territory. "Never shut me out again," I said, meeting his eyes. "Talk to me, and don't bury what you're feeling. And I promise I'll never let you go. But if you shut me out again, that's it. We're done."

Torr nodded, his arms sliding around my back. "I'll do my best to not fuck it up." One hand returned to my face, his thumb measuring the distance between our lips as he whispered, "I'm sorry about how I acted. Then, now. All of it. Forgive me?"

"Yeah." Our noses touched now, the warmth of his mouth heating mine. "I still need you, Torr." I traced his mouth once before adding, "I still love you."

His kiss tasted like a drug I'd been craving since I was at least sixteen, maybe younger. It was a heady rush that made my knees buckle, but he was thankfully there to catch me. All the years of yearning, wishing, wanting, hit me like a motorcycle at full speed. And the reality was still better than I'd imagined.

Torr held me flush to his chest, an urgent tightness in his grip that suggested he still had fears about me leaving him. That would take time to alleviate, and I was patient. I'd waited this long for him after all.

We parted for a breath of air, and I dragged my lips across his jaw to his ear. "Not going anywhere," I whispered, untucking his shirt to dive my hands underneath. "You might share me, but you'll always be mine."

"Yours," he groaned, palming my ass with both hands. "I've only ever wanted to be yours."

"You want your name tattooed back there?" I pressed lightly on his chest, making him walk backwards until he hit the couch, then shoved him down to lie on it. "Just say the word, and I'll do it."

I straddled him and together, we got his shirt off. All of the times I'd seen him topless, made excuses to touch him but not too gratuitously, it was laughable now. My hands ran shamelessly over his abs, his sculpted arms and shoulders, smoothing over the flat planes of his chest. He grabbed my wrist, stopping my hand directly over his heart.

"That's where I'm tattooing your name." He grinned. "And I'm gonna have your dad do it."

"Ew, no! Do not bring my dad up right now."

He laughed, then speared his fingers through my hair and closed his fist, bringing me down for a possessive kiss. "Let me try to be sweet," he growled against my lips.

I ground my core against his bulge, pressing into the friction separating us. "Try again without mentioning any of my family members."

"We should fuck on Daren's kitchen table when we get back. I always thought it was the perfect height for that."

"Torr!"

He cackled gleefully, and I had to admit the moment of pure joy lighting up his usually-brooding face was beautiful to see. Even as I squeezed a hand around his throat, glaring at him as hard as I could, I was laughing too.

"I'd kill you if I didn't love you so much." I was smiling too hard to sound threatening, and his grin pressed to mine, hands running up my thighs.

"You already kill me." His teeth scraped my lips as his fingers headed for the space between my legs. "You knock me dead all the fucking time."

"See, now you're being sweet—ah!"

He shoved my panties aside and touched my bare skin, palm and fingers stroking in a thorough, confident exploration of my pussy.

"You're so wet already," he groaned, eyes meeting mine. "Did your other man get you warmed up for me? How nice of him."

Torr stroked two fingers inside me, and I moaned, rocking forward onto his hand. He didn't sound jealous or spiteful, to my surprise. Maybe it was wishful thinking, but he actually sounded... pleased? It was one hell of a turn-on to think of him and Santos working together, that was for damn sure.

Who knows if I'd be able to keep them both, or if they'd even get along well enough to *want* to share me. But those were thoughts and discussions for another time, when everyone was safely out of this infernal place. And when I wasn't on the verge of coming from Torr's fingers hitting the most perfect spot inside me.

"Fuck." He gave no other warning as he grabbed my hip with his free hand, shoving me backwards off his legs as he rolled up. His fingers continued to work inside me, thumb rolling my clit as he brought his legs behind him and continued pressing me back.

"Torr, what—"

He pressed me down flat on the couch, brought one of my legs over his shoulder, and dove down to seal his mouth over my clit.

"Oh, *fuck!*"

My hips spiked up so hard, I would've worried about him chipping a tooth if he wasn't already attached to me. He grabbed my ass with his free hand, supporting me while I writhed and bucked against his sensual mouth. Holy shit, his lips and tongue...he was doing some kind of light, constant suction over my clit which I'd never felt before, but it was fucking divine. Gone were the days of men just jamming their tongue against it with no finesse. Torr treated oral sex like an art form.

His fingers worked in perfect tandem with his mouth, spread and curled inside me for maximum friction as he hit that same, perfect spot over and over. I was still sensitive from the orgasm I'd given myself earlier and building up to another one fast. My last coherent thought as my head pressed back with a choked cry, was that maybe there was some benefit to Torr being a manwhore after all. He sure as fuck knew how to please.

The orgasm hit me like the most delicious stroke of lightning, amplified by Torr continuing to work me through the peak and descent until I pushed his head away. Grabbing a fistful of his dark hair, I pulled him up for a breathless kiss. My wetness coated his lips and tongue, and I absolutely loved it.

Through messy, desperate kisses, we both pulled apart his belt and undid his pants. I barely had a moment to touch him, to give his heavy length a stroke, before he notched it at my entrance and pressed all the way forward in one fluid thrust.

"Oh...God!" I clasped onto his arms, my breath stolen at the sudden intrusion filling me up.

"Too much?" He pulled back with a knowing smirk, grin spreading wider at my reaction to the slide of him through me. Cocky fucking asshole.

But he was *my* cocky asshole, and I'd make sure he'd never forget it.

"Don't you dare stop." I squeezed around his hips with my legs, drawing him in again as I locked my ankles behind his back.

"Not on your fucking life." He made sure my panties were still adequately pulled aside before thrusting in earnest, abs flexing like a damn porn star.

"You don't have to look so smug." My hands slid around to his back, pulling him down until we were chest-to-chest, and he settled perfectly between my legs.

"I just can't believe this is real." Torr's head went down to the pillow next to me, his nose touching mine. "I'm exactly where I want to be."

I kissed him, wondering how many '*I love you*'s would make him uncomfortable. He wouldn't say it back to me for a while, if ever. But I knew he was showing me, telling me in his own emotionally-constipated way. He was trying, and I had to meet him where he was, plus make him feel safe whenever he took a chance to be vulnerable.

"You're getting good at this being sweet thing." I hugged around him with my whole body, sinking into his delicious thrusts while running my nails up and down his back. "So fucking good," I added, though the compliment had nothing to do with his sweetness. He took long, deep strokes, stretching me wide and ensuring I felt every glorious inch of him. I moaned against his shoulder, taking the occasional biting kiss of that dense muscle whenever he pressed in especially deep.

"Fucking best I ever had," he groaned into my neck, hips crashing into me more forcefully.

I laughed with a small nip to his earlobe. "You don't have to protect my ego."

"I'm not, Rori." His head lifted, eyes blazing into mine as he cradled my neck and shoulders. "You know why you're the best?"

My heart crashing against my ribcage had nothing to do with the sex becoming more vigorous. "No. Why?"

"Because you're fucking *mine.*"

He swelled thicker inside me, and I saw stars with every drag of his cock through me. My head pressed back, and he smothered my moans with deep, passionate kisses that told me more than the words *'I love you'* ever could. He angled my hips higher, striking down with powerful thrusts that hit my clit on every impact. I was screaming into his kiss, the pleasure coursing through me like a fiery river.

"Come for me," Torr said in a rough demand. His muscles were locked, tense and bulging as he pounded into me relentlessly. "Give me all your fucking pleasure, Rori. I need it."

The fire burned and consumed me in an explosive release, pulsing through my blood and licking across my skin. Torr spilled more heat inside me with a ragged growl, his body surging as he rode his own pleasure until he carefully lowered himself on top of me.

I was hot, sweaty, and short of breath, but no way was I going to shove him off me. I raked my fingers through his hair, running my nails over his neck and back until he shivered.

In return, Torr traced his index finger over my arm, spelling out three short words.

234

Chapter 28

Torrance

I woke up on that same couch with a Rori-sized blanket draped on top of me. Her dress was gone, discarded sometime between the second and third round we went last night. My eyelids were still heavy with sleep, the best fucking sleep I'd had in nearly a week. I smoothed my hands up and down a long, naked back, the warmth of her skin lulling me back to dreamland.

"Question for you."

I startled, nearly dropping to the floor. "Jesus, it's creepy when you wake up and immediately start talking." Rori did that sometimes when we both crashed at Daren's house. One minute she was out like a light, the next, she was busting her brother's nuts for running out of eggs or coffee.

"Shush. I'm perfect, remember?" I felt a kiss on my collarbone and the scrape of a short fingernail circling my nipple. "You couldn't stop telling me that last night."

"Mm, perfectly creepy." I locked my arms around her and brushed a kiss against her forehead while I worked on the whole waking-up thing. "What's your question?"

"You were never going to tell me how you felt, back home." I opened my eyes to find her chin propped on my chest, looking straight at me. Her icy contacts were gone and her natural forest green eyes met mine. "I guess I'm just wondering what changed when we got to this place."

Everything.

I had to pause for a deep breath, fighting the urge to clam up and deflect. Rori and I had broken new ground. To be the man she deserved, I had to be honest with her. Especially when she asked difficult questions.

"Back home...I think I took for granted that you'd always be around. Here, I realized I could actually lose you."

Rori frowned. "To what?"

"Your gladiator, for one. I dunno, I just kind of had a gut instinct that something would happen. Shake up the life we were used to back home. I thought pushing you away would make it easier to get over you. But," my hand trailed up her spine to wrap around her shoulders, "it just made me more desperate to keep you."

"You're stuck with my creepy ass, Torr." She returned her cheek to my chest. "I don't know exactly where things are gonna go with Santos, but he's worth saving from this place."

"So's the Hunter. He seems like an alright guy." My thumb stroked back and forth on her shoulder as I thought. "I'm willing to bet most of those gladiators are decent, normal dudes forced into bad situations and not all mass rapists or whatever."

"I'm thinking the same thing." Rori's hand made a fist on top of my chest. "And they're getting them from somewhere, in steady supply. To get killed and abused every day."

I drummed my fingers on her arm. "As much as I love lying here with you, it's almost morning. We should've left hours ago."

"Yeah, let's head out." Rori sat up, and I reluctantly let my arm fall from her shoulders. "One more question," she piped up.

"Yes?" I held her waist, obsessed with the heat of her skin and the gorgeous lines and shapes her body made. After only imagining touching her for so long, now I could never get enough.

"Why did you really come with me?"

At least that was easy to answer. "Because I don't ever want to be without you."

Rori froze, like that shocked her. Then she leaned down and held my chin as she kissed me. "I know you can't say it to me right now, and I'll never pressure you to do so," she whispered. "But I love you, Torr. I hope you believe me when I say that."

You're the only person I've allowed myself to fall for. I love you so much it fucking scares me.

The words rang out like a bell in my head, but they never reached my throat. I swallowed, cleared my throat, still nope. There was a complete disconnect from my mind to my mouth, and it pissed me off. Rori deserved to have those words said back to her, but I might not be the man to say them. Despite knowing and feeling the depth of those words for her, it felt like my ability to speak them was on the other side of a vast canyon.

The last time I had said them, I was discarded and left completely alone.

"I do believe you," I choked out. "I'm sorry I can't—"

"No, Torr. You have nothing to be sorry for." Rori held my face, smiling gently as she kissed me again. "Know that I love you. Know you're enough, and it'll all be okay."

I held her tightly for a final long kiss, wishing she could absorb everything I felt through my embrace. Not just my love but my gratitude that she accepted me like this, that she was patient and demanded nothing of me but my honesty.

That she was still my best friend.

I swatted her hip as our kiss ended. "Let's go, creep."

She groaned in annoyance as she slid off my lap, rising from the couch. "I don't know which is worse, creep or damsel."

"There's always honey." I watched her hips sway as she walked naked toward her bedroom, then ran up behind her to smack her ass.

"Ah!" Rori darted into the room and playfully glared as she

peeked out from the behind door. "Definitely not that. I actually kind of like creep."

"Damsel it is then." I started toward my room, eager to dig out my jeans, boots, and leather jacket. No more of these fancy threads for me.

"Fuck you," Rori called.

Love you too, I wanted to call out in return. But damn, that heart-mouth disconnect tripped me up again. I really needed to work on that. More than anything, I wanted to see her face when I told her I loved her.

No more than five minutes could have passed when an insistent knock came pounding at the door.

"Shit."

Rori and I came out of our rooms at the same time, both dressed in jeans and leather, and looked at each other.

"Can we go out a window?" I asked her.

She ran to check when more hard pounding came to the door. "Mr. and Mrs. Renault! This is Nella, the guest services manager. It is imperative that I speak to you right away."

"No dice." Rori shook her head as she came back from the window. "It's a sheer drop into the canyon, not even any window sills or roofing to stand on. You want to hide? Fight?"

I clenched my fists, working through the scenarios in my head. Hiding was no good, they'd tear the suite apart and likely knew it better than we did. Fighting was also dicey, especially since we had no weapons. Nella had likely arrived with backup, and roughing up more staff than I already had was likely to cause more problems than fewer.

"We will enter the room in thirty seconds if you do not comply!" Nella's voice called. Damn, she was not fucking around.

I held my hand out to Rori. "I think we need to face the music and see what we're dealing with."

She took my hand with a nod, lacing our fingers together and squeezing. "Together or not at all."

I love you. I brought the back of her palm to my lips and kissed it before we headed to the door together.

Rori unlocked the door with her free hand, standing slightly ahead of me as she swung it open. "Hello, Nella."

The woman was fuming mad. The scowl she always reserved for me was now aimed pointedly at Rori. The six armed guards behind her, though, were expressionless.

"Are you aware of what your husband has done?" Nella asked.

Rori stood a little straighter. "I am."

"That he inserted himself into routine disciplinary action, assaulted and gravely injured *four* of my staff?"

That was a bit of an exaggeration. I only *gravely* injured one guy.

"I'm aware," Rori answered.

"We do everything in our power to see to our guests' entertainment and comfort," Nella said stiffly. "But we have a zero tolerance policy for getting involved in staff duties and harming those who work here. You two are to leave the premises immediately."

"We figured as much." Rori nodded and smiled politely. "We don't want to cause any further trouble and will be on our way."

Nella blinked, and her expression cracked a little, like she wasn't expecting us to be so compliant. "Very well," she said stiffly. "We'll escort you out."

I released a breath, not realizing I'd been holding it as we stepped over the threshold. Nella led the way, while the guard flanked us on either side and marched at our backs. Rori and I kept our hands connected as we walked, the two of us on high alert. People gawked and whispered as we walked past, but they weren't my concern. I was trying to figure what the catch was, which trapdoor someone would open that would shoot us to the middle of the sand pit to be the bait for the next fight.

Once the elevator was in view, I started to relax a little. Maybe a walk of shame was a big deal to these people, or maybe being banished from the most exclusive resort in the world was considered punishment enough. Big whoop. We'd be back. Just not as fucking guests.

Nella stepped onto the large, concrete platform, and Rori and I followed behind her. The elevator was at the top of the canyon, making a slow descent toward us. Rori leaned her temple on my shoulder, and I kissed the side of her head as we waited.

The glass cage was halfway down the canyon wall when Nella turned to face us with an expression of smug, evil glee.

"Take him," she ordered.

My arms were grabbed faster than I could process, and I was yanked backward off the platform, my hand torn from Rori's.

"No, Torr!"

I heard Rori's cry of protest but was forced to the ground and could no longer see her. Metal cuffs slapped over my wrists, locking them behind my back. Well, at least I still had fucking legs and elbows.

I rolled over to my back, kicking out, and got one guy in the nards. He hissed in pain and backed away, cupping himself, but that still wasn't much of a reaction for how hard I got him. He had to be wearing protection, fuck.

Another guy leaned over me, and I headbutted him. The opportunity gave me a split second to roll up to my knees and check on my woman. Rori was fighting like a hellcat against two of the guards, but they both restrained her to the point where she couldn't do much. Nella just stood off to the side, all smug bitch power pose.

That split second was one too long, sadly. A fist cracked into my jaw and sent me back face down into the dirt with no way to block it. I scrambled to get my feet under me again, and hot, crackling pain zipped up through my whole body. Fucking tasers.

"You fucking rotten bitch, call them off!" Rori screamed. "Let him go!"

"Mm, I think not," Nella said. "I think he'd make a fine gladiator, actually."

It took all four of those guards to start dragging me toward the colosseum, and I made sure they fought for every inch they took me away from her. I kept getting punched, tazed, and restrained until my vision went dark and I could no longer hear Rori swearing to kill them all.

———

I couldn't figure out if the oppressive darkness was due to my surroundings or being unconscious. My body felt solid, so at least that was a plus, even though everything ached like hell.

Trying to get myself oriented, I rolled with a groan to discover I was on a lying on a hard, dusty floor. It smelled musty here, like there was little fresh air to go around. I blinked my eyes, then brought a hand up in front of my face and wiggled my fingers. Nothing but darkness. Shit, had I been blinded?

I brought my hand to my face and felt around. Yeah, it was sore and swollen in places, but my eyeballs were still there. Either something had been done to my eyes or I was truly in the darkest fucking pit on earth.

"Who's there?"

I scrambled upright, searching my inky black surroundings for the disembodied voice. It sounded like a man, but I had a small flash of hope that it was Astarte. "I could ask you the same thing," I answered.

"Who are you? I don't recognize your voice." Definitely a man.

"Once again, I could ask you the same fuckin' thing."

There was a huff of breath, almost like a laugh. "Hang on. I'm going to walk towards you."

"No thanks." I swept my arms around me as I started moving backwards, away from the voice. "How do I know you don't have a weapon?"

"Dude. You think even if I had one, I can see any better than you do?"

"I dunno, man. I don't know where the fuck I am."

There was a long pause. "Are you a gladiator?"

"No. Not yet, anyway."

Another pause. "A guest, then?"

I was really starting to hate that word. "You could say that. Although given where I am, you could say I'm not very welcome anymore."

"Fuck," the guy whispered. "You're him. Did she escape?"

Footsteps rushed at me, and I felt the presence of a big, muscular guy right in my face. "Whoa! Hold on, I'm right here." My hands stretched out to put space between us, and they landed on a wide set of shoulders only inches in front of me.

"Rori. Aurora," the guy said, leaning into my palms. "Did she get out? She said she was getting out. If you're in here, did she make it?"

Oh shit. I knew exactly who this was.

"You're Santos."

I heard a hiss of surprise and then felt two arms swiftly break the contact of my hands on his shoulders. "How do you know my real name?"

"Rori told me. And...I dunno." I shook my head even though he couldn't see. "We were right at the elevator, and they separated us. I got knocked out before I saw what they did to her."

"Fuck!"

I felt Santos' presence back away and heard the shuffling of pacing steps a moment later. I wanted to do the same, but I knew Rori better than he did and felt the overwhelming sense to reassure him.

"She'll figure something out, man. We won't be in here too long."

"That's what I'm worried about," he grumbled. "If she finds out we're both in here, she'll want to spring us so bad, she won't stop to consider all the pitmasters in the resort coming after her." The pacing stopped. "What did she tell you about me?"

"Well, she likes you. A lot. And...she told me what happened last time she saw you."

The pause that followed was the longest one yet. "Why would she tell you what we did?" He sounded a touch possessive, which I couldn't blame him for, but not angry. It seemed more like he was curious, which made me wonder how much Rori had told him about us.

I took a deep breath. This felt like a horrible idea, considering I would be stuck with him in this pitch black cell for who knew how long. But he was someone Rori cared about, and he deserved to know the truth. If he couldn't handle her being with both of us, well, then he wasn't right for her anyway.

"When she came back from seeing you, we talked and...well, aired out a lot of things that had been unsaid for too long and kind of...turned over a new leaf."

This next pause was brief, and then soft laughter filled the air. It slowly grew louder, unconstrained, and nearly hysterical. "I *knew* it."

"Knew what?"

"That the fool she came here with would finally wise up before she slipped through his fingers."

Okay, I deserved that. "Yeah, you're right," I sighed. "I was that fool, but not anymore."

"And now she's your girl. Congratulations."

"Well, she's yours too."

I didn't have to wait long for a reaction. The gladiator shuffled over to me until his shoes gently bumped into mine. He touched my shoulder and followed down the length of my arm until he found my hand. Then he clasped his hand against mine.

"Guess we might as well get to know each other."

Chapter 29

Rori

"Torr! Torr! Fucking wake up! Torr!" I struggled hard, fueled by fury, but the armed guards barely budged as they restrained me between them. I could only scream my throat raw as the four other guards dragged Torr's limp body away.

Straight to the colosseum.

When I realized we were in the elevator heading up, I called on every technique my fathers had taught me to get out of a hold. But because there were two of them and we were in an enclosed space, I couldn't get any leverage. I couldn't even kick my feet out because my legs had nowhere to go. My guards each had a leg braced in front of mine with both hands clasped tightly to my arms.

There was no fucking escape.

It still didn't keep me from fighting. Once we reached the top and the glass door opened, they took me a few steps forward, then released me. I spun around, ready to throw punches and kicks so hard they'd need kidney transplants, only to find two gun barrels pointed at my chest.

"Walk away," one of the guards said. "If you start now, you might find someone to pick you up before you die of heat stroke."

"Fuck you," I spat. "I'm not leaving without him."

"You take one step toward this canyon, you're vulture food." The other guard cocked his weapon. "We're giving you this chance to live because you're a woman. But you will never come near here again or breathe a word of this resort. If you do, there will be consequences."

"Like what?"

"Trust us, you don't want to know. The resort owners have the means to enslave you and your whole family."

If there was just one of them with a gun, I could have had a chance to take it from him. But two was too risky. Still, I wanted to laugh in their faces. They had no fucking idea who I knew or what I had at my disposal.

But I wasn't about to show all my cards. I wanted them to underestimate me. And most importantly, I needed a healthy amount of backup to get Torr and Santos out alive.

"Alright." I started to turn away, toward the empty, barren desert. "You won't see me again."

"If we do, we won't give you a second chance."

As much as it prickled my skin to turn my back, I started walking away. Seconds later, I heard the sound of the elevator heading down to the canyon floor.

I looked eastward. The sun would be rising soon, and then I might be in trouble. This was the Great Wasteland, and I had no food, water, or wheels to get me anywhere. Shit, where would I even go? That tavern we stayed at was a good three-hour drive away, and there was no cell reception there. Home was even farther away.

My hands flew over my jacket and jeans pockets in a panicked rush. A huge sigh of relief deflated my lungs when I found my phone. I pulled it out and turned it on. No reception and only 12% battery. Fuck.

I turned it off to conserve the battery and returned it to my pocket to look around again. Where could I go? *Come on, Rori...*

My gaze settled on the brightest part of the sky again—east. That way was Sevier, my Aunt Kyrie's territory. I had some other family there too, probably closer to me if I was estimating correctly. It would still be hours away, but it was closer than home, and I should be able to make phone calls as I got closer.

Resolved, I started walking toward the rising sun.

I had only gone a few hundred yards when a certain dove chose to settle on top of a cactus and coo at me.

Now I really wished I had a gun.

"Oh, fuck you!" I yelled up at the bird. "Huge fucking help you've been, thank you very much! Do me a favor, and just fuck off, alright? I don't need you, Astarte."

Yes, you do, Aurora. The bird shook out its feathers. *Now more than ever, you do.*

"You know what? I'll take my chances, thanks."

I am not a pet you can dismiss, child. Astarte's voice pressed like a tangible weight against my skin. *You cannot perceive all the threads woven into your destiny, but I see them all. And without me, those threads will tangle and choke you like a fly in a spider's web.*

"Yeah, great job keeping me untangled from the shitshow that just happened. Torr and Santos could be dead or tortured, and for what?" I spread my arms out, looking up helplessly to the god. "What the fuck is the point, Astarte?"

Typical human, she scoffed. *Always so short-sighted.*

"Then fuck off and leave me alone!"

The dove flew off, and while I was grateful for the peace, I couldn't shake the sense that Astarte could see everything. My future, my thought process. My decisions and motivations, like she was both inside my head and also zoomed all the way out with a bird's eye view of the map of my life.

Whatever. As long as that deity stayed out of my line of sight and didn't talk to me anymore.

I was pissed, and since I had nothing to shoot or hit, I put all of my anger into walking east. The sun peeked over the mountains in the distance, gradually revealing itself fully. And on I walked.

The sun rose higher, and I kept walking long after feeling the uncomfortable prickle of a sunburn on my nose and cheeks. After some time, I noticed my shadow in front of me, gradually getting longer. My feet had started aching hours ago, the pain fading to numbness now. I didn't even want to think about my hunger and thirst. That would send my mind into a panic, and I didn't want to venture off-course in a futile search for water.

One foot in front of the other. Again. And again. And again.

At some point, the sun started to set directly behind me, and I felt its fiery blaze on my neck. I knew I had to have walked miles, but I couldn't begin to guess how many. I felt myself starting to sway, exhaustion settling in when my pissed-off determination ran out. As the eastern sky began to darken, I didn't know how I was still upright, let alone moving.

And in a few hours, I'd be in trouble with no shelter and no sun to guide my way. I wasn't much of a star navigator.

Shadow's oddly poignant advice came to me at that moment. *You're stronger than you think you are. There will be times when you want to give up, but you won't. You're going to hold on, because you have it in you.*

"I dunno, Dadow." I could only mouth the words through my cracked lips. "I don't know if I have any more in me."

When the ground beneath my feet felt different, I looked down and had to stare for a few moments before my exhausted brain could process the information.

I was standing on a road. A decently well-paved stretch of highway.

Looking up, the reflective highway sign was riddled with bullet holes but still readable. The red stripe across the top said INTER-STATE. The big white numbers underneath that on the blue background read 80.

Somehow, I put the brain cells together to pull out my phone and turn it on. I stared at it so long, my battery dropped down to 10%. It was with a mixture of disbelief and pure exhaustion that I could only stare at the single tiny bar of cell reception.

Eventually, my aching fingers managed to open up my contacts and call one of the few numbers that actually had a chance of finding me before I perished out here. I brought the phone to my ear and prayed the call wouldn't drop.

The phone rang once. Twice. Thrice.

Once there was a click on the line, I didn't wait for a hello. "LJ, it's Rori." My voice was as rough as sandpaper. "I'm in trouble, and I need a big fucking favor."

Of course, my excitable-as-a-golden-retriever cousin talked right over me and didn't hear a thing I said. "Hey, Ror! What's up? Haven't heard from you in a while. What's new?" There was a shuffling and then I heard his voice farther away. "Carter, guess who it is? Our favorite cousin! What? Of course it's Rori! Nah, I don't know where she's at."

"Lark!" I yelled into the phone, but my throat was so dry it came out like a whisper. "Stop talking for a second! I need your help."

He finally went serious and quiet over the phone. "What's going on, Ror? Where are you?"

"Somewhere in old Nevada, about three hours north of Carvers. I'm on the old interstate 80. I'll explain later, but can you head west and pick me up?"

There was a pause, and I had a moment of terror that the call had dropped, but finally LJ spoke up. "Yeah, cuz. Me and Carter can be there in a few hours. You okay? You need food? Water?"

"Please...and thank you."

"Is Daren or anyone with you?"

"No, and don't fucking call him," I rasped. "Or my parents either. I need to handle some shit and don't want them to worry."

There was another long pause on the phone. LJ was three years older than me and somewhat of an older brother figure. It could go either way that he'd insist on tattling to my folks or be down for what I was about to tell him.

"Should we bring guns?" he asked finally.

"Arm yourselves, just in case. But we don't need the whole armory. Yet."

"Yet, huh? Sounds like you're gonna need it later."

"Yeah, I'll also need bikes." I clenched the phone in my hand. "And a whole lot of fucking firepower."

Epilogue

Hudson

I hated women.

There was nothing in this world that I despised more. I hated their manipulation and lies, their abuse and humiliation. Nothing from their mouths could be trusted. I'd never met a man as joyfully sadistic as every single woman I'd met here.

Almost every man I ran across in here had been confused, bewildered. And then soon enough, terrified. But at least they eventually got the sweet release of death.

As for me? I was still here. And every day was hell.

Santos and Devin weren't afraid, though. They made this place almost bearable. We had each other's backs. Even though Santos was weak, always looking for an extra second at the prettier ones, he understood the situation we were in. This hell that had thrown us together and become our lives.

Now Santos and Devin were gone, and I had nothing left. I was pure hate, barely held together by a man's body.

I hated their smug smiles, their laughter and taunts. But what I hated most of all was that my cock still got hard for them.

Sexual pleasure was a long distant memory, growing fainter by the day. I felt nothing. My body was a machine, responding to stimuli as it slowly broke down from overuse. One day, it would be beyond repair. That was the only thing I looked forward to, when I would be useless and they would finally be rid of me.

I fantasized about killing them, abusing and torturing them in the same way they did to me. What I would give to see fear twist their features, hear their pathetic cries for help, feel the life get squeezed out of them under my hand. How would it feel to turn the tables and release this burning, bitter hatred that churned inside me like a constant, angry sea?

I hated that even malnourished and weak, I could still kill them if I wasn't shackled all the time. I wouldn't even have to find a weapon, my bare hands would be enough. But I couldn't even remember the last time I had free use of my limbs.

These weak, evil creatures didn't care about fairness, didn't care that I'd never dreamed of hurting a woman before they captured me.

They made me into this.

I was an ordinary man once, just trying to get by like everyone else. I made the mistake of accepting a drink a pretty woman bought for me, then woke up here.

I hated them for everything they took from me.

The current one rolled off of me, and I barely noticed. Dissociation was a skill I'd honed well in this place. I didn't have to look at her to know she was on her back, knees to her chest and her hips tilted up as her labored breathing slowed.

"You're going to give me another daughter," she said cheerfully. Like this was some consensual thing, a decision we made together. She was lying in the bed next to me like we were both involved in what just happened. Now *that* was a fucking joke.

I would have vomited if I could still feel anything. Instead I said, "I hope this one makes you bleed to death."

The woman scoffed. "You are so ungrateful. You have the privilege of creating the next generation of Sisters, and you do nothing but stare at the ceiling and complain. You're lucky your body is nice and your seed is strong. Otherwise, you'd be a moon sacrifice or blood bag."

I'd rather be anything than this. Dead would be most preferable.

The woman turned to face me when I didn't answer her. In some distant part of my brain, I recognized that she scooted closer to me. Her hand came to my chest, her head on my shoulder.

"You don't *have* to be chained up, you know," she murmured, brushing her lips over me. "If you would just...accept your role in this. You would be given so much freedom, veneration even. You would be one of the few men respected in our society, the father who gave us life and made us multiply."

Even if I believed her, I was too dead on the inside to find any enticement in her offer. My heart, my will, my resolve—it had all rotted and withered to nothing but ash. I was only waiting for my outside to match the inside.

She sighed, as if disappointed that I didn't respond again, and lifted away from me. The absence of her touch was only a mild relief.

"The next Sister will clean you before she takes you inside her."

She rolled off the bed, and the mattress creaked as she stood up. Clothes rustled. A toilet flushed. A door opened and closed. All background noise, compartmentalized to a distant part of my mind.

Like always, I sent up a prayer that the next woman would be kind enough to smother me with a pillow.

And for the first time, there was an answer.

Your suffering is temporary, Hudson. You have not been forsaken. Hold on.

My head snapped up from the pillow, looking around the barren room. "Who's there?"

I am with you. With Santos and Devin. You are not alone. Vengeance will be had, my dear son. Hold on for me, just a little longer.

The voice was in my head, but it also ran over my skin like a tangible touch. The first and only one I'd welcomed in years. I was either losing my shit for real or my countless prayers were finally being answered.

"Who are you?" I whispered.

A gust of wind howled violently, and my head snapped to the single small window in the room. The night sky was dotted with stars. I could see them even through the tree branches that scraped against the glass like a monster trying to break in.

I am everything their goddess wishes she could be, the voice said. *I am war. I am sorcery and desire. I am vengeance.*

———

TO BE CONTINUED IN HARMLESS - VENGEFUL GODS MC BOOK 2

PRE-ORDER AVAILABLE NOW:
https://books2read.com/VGMC2

———

Want to read about Mari's adventure with the Steel Demons MC? Their series is complete and begins with Lawless.

Start reading now: https://books2read.com/SDMC1

Harmless

Crystal Ash

Content Warnings

This book contains mentions of:

- suicidal thoughts
- sexual assault against men and women (not graphic or on
  the page)
- Gun violence and gunshot wounds
- misogynistic and abusive thoughts toward women

Chapter 1

Devin

I flipped one knife in my left hand, catching the handle on every second turn in the air. With my right hand, I moved a smaller blade across my knuckles like my old man had taught me to do with a quarter when I was a kid.

The wooden target, with its faded circles of paint and hundred of tiny nicks on the surface, sat fifty yards away from me, but I wasn't looking at it. I wasn't looking at anything in particular, but I sure as hell was listening.

All of the gladiators noticed Santos' absence. The Butcher was famous in and out of the pit, not that he'd ever wanted the fame. Everyone also noticed that Tezcatlipoca, his jaguar, seemed to hover around me like a shadowy four-legged bodyguard.

I didn't particularly know or care what conclusions the others drew from this, not even if it made me a target. Even if I didn't have a two hundred and fifty pound black jaguar prowling around me protectively like I was his cub, I was the Ghost. No one could touch me.

On top of that, I was annoyed. On edge. If I let one thing get under my skin, I was liable to let one of my knives fly until—oopsie—it landed in someone's eye socket.

Everyone sparring in the pit was talking, except for the one person I wanted to hear from. Aside from my missing roommate, that was none other than the very jaguar currently sitting on his haunches, panting in the sun as he stared out across the sands.

"You know where Santos is. You're just not telling me." I caught the knife I'd been flipping and let it fly. The blade hit the wooden target with a thunk just to the left of center-mass. Not bad for throwing with my non-dominant hand, but had I been cool and not so twitchy, it would have hit dead-center. My emotions were getting to me, and that made me sloppy.

I never let anything get to me. My survival depended on my aim, and if my aim was fucked, I was just another corpse in the pit. For four years, the carnage of this place had always passed through me, never sticking with me. Guys disappeared all the time, whether their last act was fucking a guest or bleeding out on the sands.

But never Santos.

We were each others' anchors here, a friendship made through being forced to endure the unthinkable. First, in that hellhole before the gladiator pit, and then afterward.

It had been three days since he went for a personal appointment with that woman and never came back. Come to think of it, I hadn't seen her or her supposed husband either.

"Not a peep, huh?" I muttered out of the side of my mouth, the question aimed at the jaguar who was, in fact, not a jaguar.

Tezcatlipoca was some kind of deity, divine consciousness, what-have-you, that was currently occupying the body of a jaguar. He had a connection with Santos, but I had also heard the jaguar speak directly into my mind. What I'd heard sounded like riddled nonsense, but I would have taken anything, even a clue in pig-Latin, to know where Santos was.

Or if he was even alive.

But after three days and counting, Tezca didn't seem interested in revealing any of that to me.

"Not that it's important or anything," I said, approaching the target to retrieve my knife. "But I care about Santos. I'm pretty sure you do too. So, anything you can offer would be great."

The jaguar moved to the shade next to the row of targets and plopped his belly down in the sand with grunt.

"You're making it awfully tempting to stab you."

Tezca rolled over, twisting his spine as he brought his paws up and his belly to the sky.

"Really? You think *now* you deserve belly rubs? Or are you just taunting me?"

He stretched his neck out, offering his chin up for scratches.

"Only if this is an even exchange, cat. I give you scratches, you tell me where the Butcher is. That's the deal."

I got nothing. No words, in any case. The closest thing to a response I got was a feeling of frustration, separate from my own. The sensation stroked along my brain, similar to when I heard the jaguar god speak to me. Tezca was annoyed with me, like we were playing charades and the answer was completely obvious to him, but I kept making the wrong guesses.

"I dunno, Tez." I turned around, stalking several paces away to set myself up for target practice again. "I don't get it."

"You're not the only one."

I whipped around, knives ready, letting my instincts and keen hearing guide me to my new target—the source of the voice that had somehow managed to sneak this close to me.

The Hunter lifted his chin to give space to my blade that found itself nuzzled snugly against his skin. A red bead of blood welled at my knife's edge, growing round and dark before it ran a crimson trail down his throat.

"What don't you get?" I asked him. "That you missed a spot shaving down here?"

"Take it easy." He held his palms open and out to the sides, while his swallow made his throat bob and press my blade in deeper against his skin.

"You must not know what happens to people who try to sneak up on me," I mused.

"I didn't try. I did." A cocky smile spread across his lips, despite the fact that his life was literally hanging on the edge of my knife. One wrong move and he'd have another smile right under his jaw. "Guess I'm not that bad of a hunter after all, huh? I caught me a ghost."

"Might need your eyes checked, Hunter. It seems I'm not the one who's caught."

I kept the pressure against his neck rock steady, and the kid finally seemed to get the picture that I wasn't a nice guy and therefore not letting him go.

"Look, I just wanted to talk." He held in his breath, trying not to press against the blade any more than necessary and add to the blood running down his neck.

"I'm not much of a talker." In my spare hand, I brought up my second knife and let it dance across my knuckles again. "I let my knives do the talking."

"I wanted to ask you about the Butcher."

"Why would I know anything?"

Santos and I were careful to not appear outwardly friendly to the other gladiators. Any whiff of friendship would be used against us. We'd seen it dozens of times with the fighters who became close as brothers, or lovers. They had always been set up to fight against each other, one forced to kill the other.

Our mutual survival depended on acting indifferent toward each other. We'd been brought here together and luckily ended up as roommates simply because it was logistically easiest for our overlords. Only in those private moments in our room, lying awake in our beds at night, did we allow ourselves tiny shreds of vulnerability with each other.

It never got sexual, because Santos didn't swing that way and I wasn't going to push that boundary, especially not when he'd been exploited enough by the guests. Sometimes it was a vent session, a mutual exchange of I-can't-fucking-take-it-any-longers. Other times, one of us had to drag the other out of unfathomably dark mindsets. The kind where Santos teased the edge of his machete along his wrists or I stared at my knives a little too long, knowing how easy one stab through the neck would be.

In an environment that was truly every man for himself, we were extremely lucky to have each other. And we made every effort possible to protect this rare friendship we had from outside threats.

Apparently, the fucking Hunter saw right through all that.

"I know you two are tight. You make a good show of not acting like it, but I could see it. Plus, his jaguar's protecting you."

I didn't allow my face to flicker. "Even if that were true, what's to stop me from slitting you open right now?"

"My value has shot up since I killed the Animal. I'm set to take the Butcher's place in the next fight."

"Your head must be all kinds of fucked if you think I care how much money is riding on you." It was true that I'd get in trouble for killing a valuable gladiator outside of a scheduled fight. Maybe take some beatings, get thrown in the isolation dungeon, yawn. Like I wasn't already numb to all the punishments of this place.

"And I want to help!"

The Hunter's last statement was made on a desperate rasp. I didn't realize I'd pressed my knife in a fraction deeper until I saw he was on his toes, trembling as he fought to keep the kiss of sharpness away.

I pulled my blade back by a hair's width, using my peripheral vision to make sure no pitmasters would interrupt us. "Help with what?"

"Revolt. Escape. Getting free and telling these assholes where to shove it."

Only then did I fully pull my knife away, partially out of shock, but mostly out of pity for the delusional bastard. This kid didn't need me to kill him. If he was being serious, he'd do that all on his own.

The Hunter doubled over, taking his first deep breaths in probably a full minute while he pressed a hand to his throat to stem the bleeding.

"What the fuck are you talking about? Actually, no, don't tell me." I held a palm out to him as I turned to face my targets again. "I don't want to be part of this stupid idea or know why you'd want to get the Butcher involved."

"I think he's already involved," the Hunter wheezed. "Something's going to happen, or is happening already. We need to be ready."

"You're a new gladiator, so I'll make it clear for you." I started flipping a knife again, warming up my wrist. "There is no *we* in this place. The moment you start teaming up with people, making friends, they'll be sure to ruin that by throwing you all in the pit until only one of you survives. That was why you and your three buddies got sent out to fight together. You want to watch another friend you've murdered die in your arms?"

There was silence behind me for a while, enough for me to sink three knives into the bullseyes of three separate targets.

"No," came the quiet answer behind me. "I don't want to murder anyone. I want out of here."

"Then *you* will be murdered. Those are your only choices." I spared a glance at him over my shoulder and actually felt a drop of sympathy for the guy. He was just in shock. Santos and I called it BGS— Baby Gladiator Syndrome. Sometimes the new fighters were in denial, unable to accept their new reality at first. They were desperate for a way out that wasn't as a corpse.

"No, it's not anymore." The Hunter came around to stand in front of me, blocking me from retrieving my knives from the targets. The bleeding on his neck had barely slowed and it continued in a rivulet down his neck and chest. "Listen, I talked to a guy, a guest. Well, he was posing undercover as a guest, but he was here to gather information." The Hunter leaned in close to me. "He and the woman he came with. They're getting this place shut down and all of us out."

I closed my eyes so he wouldn't see me rolling them, willing myself to have patience with this child of a man. "I'm sorry, but he was lying to you."

The Hunter jerked back as if I'd struck him. "What makes you say that?"

"Because everyone lies. You think I haven't heard it before? Every once in a while, a guest gets a savior complex and wants to feel good about themselves. So they pony up the cash to bring a hot young thing home." I poked him in the chest as I said that. Yeah, the Hunter was hot, but naivety was such a turn-off for me. "If they happen to choose you, congratulations. You're now enslaved in a fancy house instead of a gladiator pit. And eventually, the novelty will wear off, and they'll get bored of you. Next thing you know, you're starving to death in a dungeon because they don't care to feed you."

He paled but blew out a determined huff. Damn, this kid was stubborn.

"That's not what this is. They're from Four Corners, not this upper class crowd."

I frowned. All I'd ever heard of Four Corners was that it was a pipe dream. A mythical, promised land where everyone had rights. Not dripping in riches, but no slavery either. A place where you could live a normal life, have a normal job, and generally go do whatever you wanted. After what my life had been for the last six years, anything resembling *normal* sounded like a fantasy.

And from what I knew about the guests that came through here, they were allergic to anything simple and normal. Everything had to be extravagant, from their possessions to the stories they told other people. It was that old expression of keeping up with the Joneses, but on steroids. There was nothing in these people's worlds that wasn't a one-up contest.

So, if someone had been wanting to take the Hunter home as a pet, they wouldn't dream of claiming to be from somewhere as mundane as Four Corners.

"Which guest was it?" I found myself asking.

"Uh, dark hair. Good-looking fucker and, like, naturally so. You know how a lot of them look plastic and fake? He didn't look like that. And I saw him with a woman, also naturally really pretty. She was tall for a girl, short blonde hair. You remember Marilyn Monroe from way back when? Hair and face kinda like that."

"Fuck." I tipped my head back to the sky, even though I knew in my gut who they would be.

"What, 'fuck'?"

"That woman. The Butcher had seen her for...personal appointments."

"Oh, so they hooked up? Lucky dude. That guy, Torrance, he said she wasn't actually his wife."

"He's not *lucky* to be rented out like a blow-up doll," I hissed, even though I had an inkling that wasn't entirely the case with this particular woman.

I remembered when Santos first pointed them out to me, coming down the elevator into the canyon when they first arrived. He kept insisting there was something odd about the couple, although I wrote it off at the time. Tezca had told us to prepare for something, and he seemed convinced it was them.

Santos had been all googly-eyed about that woman, to the point where I'd bet my knives he'd sleep with her for free. He'd been twitchy, nervous, before he left to see her for the first time, and grinning like a cat that ate the canary when he got back. I didn't ask for details, and he didn't give them, but it was a hell of a change from the somber, hollow-eyed look he'd have coming back from other sessions.

He'd gone to see her at least two more times, all eager and excited like a kid going on dates. And now he had fucking disappeared.

"I don't care what this guy claimed." I shoved past the Hunter, walking up to pull my knives out of the targets with rough yanks on the handles. "The Butcher went to see that woman, and now he's vanished. I don't trust her or that guy she came with."

You can trust the Light and the Guard.

The words hit me gently, like someone running their hand over my head, but it was so unexpected that I tripped over air, stumbling over my feet as I whipped around, blades out. When my gaze landed on Tezca, the black jaguar lounging calmly in the shade, that was when my pulse kicked into overdrive.

The Hunter can be trusted as well, Tezca added. *But do not trust the false messenger.*

"The what?" I whispered in disbelief. "Who is that?"

"Hey, Ghost? You alright?"

My head jerked to the side, realizing only then that the Hunter had been speaking to me the entire time I'd been listening to Tezca. "What'd you say?"

"That couple has disappeared too. I've been asking around, and no one's seen them. There was some commotion a couple days ago and someone said they saw those two getting kicked out."

I refocused on the jaguar, who blinked slowly at me with those sharp, lantern-yellow eyes. *I'm supposed to trust him? And them?* The questions were both wondering thoughts as well as seeking confirmation from the deity within the animal.

The answer I received was not in words but as a feeling so strong, it was almost a physical sensation on my skin. A pair of hands on my shoulders, urging me forward. An overwhelming sense of affirmation that I was on the right path.

I turned to The Hunter, clarity honing my instincts. "We need to talk to the gladiators."

Chapter 2

Rori

I hobbled out of the bedroom, my feet still tender and aching from my day-long trek through the desert. I went to rub an itch on my nose and winced. My sunburn was peeling, which made my skin itchy as hell, but the new layer underneath felt tenderized and near painful to touch.

My two cousins, LJ and Carter, oh-so-helpfully watched me wobble from their guest bedroom to the kitchen table like a newborn gazelle.

"How do you feel?" The question came from Carter, the older of the two brothers.

"'Bout as good as I look. Did you leave me any coffee?"

"I'll get it." LJ jumped up from the table, rounding the kitchen counter to grab a mug.

He was always a sweetheart, the sunshine to his brother's brooding dark cloud. I didn't know what Carter's deal was. Maybe my aunt Noelle and uncle Lark were stricter with him, since he was the first-born and all. They all seemed happy when our families got together, though.

LJ placed a mug of coffee and two slices of slightly-burnt

buttered toast in front of me, and I beamed up at him. "Thanks, LJ. Did you know that you're my favorite cousin?"

"Aww, you're mine too, Ror."

Carter just rolled his eyes as his little brother plopped back down in his seat. "So what the fuck's going on?"

The single bite of toast I'd taken turned to sawdust in my throat, and I swallowed it down with lukewarm coffee. "I'm gonna need your guys' help. Probably the Valkyrie Network's help too."

"I gathered that. But I need to know what exactly I'm helping you with."

I swallowed again, steeling myself as I recalled everything that had unraveled so quickly in the last few weeks. My eyes lifted to the window at the sound of fluttering wings. It couldn't have been very loud, but I was attuned to that infernal bird and couldn't do shit about it. Sure enough, Astarte, the goddess inhabiting a white dove, peered at me from the windowsill.

"Torr and I came upon something terrible that's being kept secret. We went undercover and it's..."

"Where *is* Torr?" Carter pinned me with a hard stare. "Why were you alone when we picked you up?"

"He got..." I tried to force another breath through my closing throat, "...captured."

LJ reached out, putting his hand on my arm. "Captured where? By who?"

I went for the glass of water on the table, gulping it down with the realization that I was probably still dehydrated. My cousins waited patiently as I took my fill and recomposed myself. Torr needed me to have my shit together. So did Santos. I would never be able to get them out if I was a blubbering mess, so I zipped it all up and breathed until I was calm enough to speak.

"There's a resort hidden in a canyon in the desert. The super-rich pay a lot of money to go there, I'm talking Blakeworth elite types."

"Rich people doing shady shit, what a surprise," Carter drawled.

"What are they doing there?" LJ piped up.

I took another calming breath, making sure not to close my eyes, or else I would see nothing but the carnage of the gladiator pit, the abuse that had been done to Santos, and Torr being dragged away from me.

"They enslave people," I choked out. "Mostly men to fight as gladiators. The, uh, attractive men are also pimped out to the female guests as sex slaves. There are female staff there too who could use help." I rubbed my forehead, as if I could wipe away my maid Paige's look of terror when she first talked to me, all because *she* believed she talked too much. "Basically, these ultra-wealthy folks get to do whatever they want to those beneath them."

"Fuck," LJ breathed, eyes sliding toward his brother.

Carter only cracked his knuckles. "So we're fucking up some rich assholes' playground and getting Torr out? I'm in. What do we need?"

A smile pulled at my lips for the first time since my cousins had picked me up. No, longer than that, probably. The last time I smiled was probably when Torr and I were naked in that suite.

But I loved that Carter was a man of action, always ready to go. He and LJ were the right people to call for this job. Carter wasn't even 30 years old, and yet he was one of the most accomplished riders of the Valkyrie Network, an organization that smuggled people out of oppressive territories, like Blakeworth, and brought them to safe havens like Sevier and Four Corners.

I shook my head as I smiled, waving my hand in a *no* gesture at him. "Not just Torr. Everyone."

Carter lifted one dark eyebrow. "And how many people is *everyone?*"

I did the quick math in my head. "All the gladiators, plus service staff, might be about...thirty?"

"Thirty people!" LJ exclaimed.

"I don't actually know how many gladiators there are. They... you know, lose so many and then bring in more."

"Where do they get more?" LJ asked, peering at me with all the curiosity of a child.

"Prisons, it seems. When they're not kidnapping men off the streets."

"A better question is, even if we *can* rescue thirty fucking people, where are we going to put them?" Ever the logistical one, Carter cocked his head as he continued staring at me. "The most we've ever moved at one time with the Valkyrie Network is ten people."

"I was hoping we could use the safe houses," I admitted. "If they're not currently occupied."

Carter scrubbed his face and blew out a long breath. "One of them might be free. But it still only has four rooms to sleep in. Even if we pack 'em in, we can fit maybe ten or twelve people in there before shit gets too crowded."

"I'll figure something out," I insisted. "I'll call Aunt Kyrie. She might be able to house people somewhere too."

"She's definitely gonna be pissed about something like this happening so close to Sevier," LJ mused.

My aunt Kyrie, a former governor of Sevier, was the one who started up the Valkyrie Network. Her three husbands, my uncles who formed the Sons of Odin MC, were in charge of finding riders daring and brave enough to sneak into war-torn territories, many of which ran like dictatorships and even forbade their citizens from leaving said territories. Hence the need for bikers who were proficient with weapons and could ride fast. Although there had been a few close calls, no riders or refugees had ever lost their lives since the Network's inception.

Each of my dads had volunteered to ride for the network a number of times, rotating so three of them always stayed home with my mom and us. My mom hated the danger but knew how important the work was. On her days off, she and some colleagues would give free checkups to new refugees in Four Corners. In one form or another, everyone did their part to help out.

A few years ago, all four of my fathers decided they were finished riding for the Network and passed the torch to the younger genera-tions like Carter. Daren, LJ, and I would be eligible to volunteer when we turned twenty-five, and Torr had just become eligible this year.

Now that my uncles were older as well, they had recently hung up their cuts and promoted their most trusted Sons of Odin members to run the Network. Rumor had it that Carter was rising up the ranks and would likely receive a President patch within the next ten years.

Multiple branches of my family, from my blood relatives to my biker family, had all dedicated their lives to rebuilding our post-Collapse world. My aunt Kyrie had dedicated most of her life and her political career toward helping others, so she definitely wouldn't sit on her ass and do nothing about fucking Mystic Canyon Resort.

"So what can you guys help me with?" I looked back and forth between my two cousins. "I need riders, firepower, vehicles to trans-port people. We're going to need food and water too. Probably clothing."

"Firepower for sure." LJ nodded enthusiastically. "Vehicles too. Uncle Jandro actually just fixed up and donated some vans to us—"

"Hold your damn horses." Carter cut him off with a slapping palm to the shoulder, then looked at me. "I'll have to check our inven-tory, see what the Network's plans are for the next few weeks. We have resources already allocated for certain missions, and you're kinda asking for stuff with zero notice or intel, Ror."

"I know, and I'm sorry. I'm not trying to take away from other people in need." My fingers curled on the table, nails biting into my palms. "This just feels so urgent because Torr is there. And..."

"And someone else?" Carter's eyes narrowed with the question. For being so damn stony, he sure could decipher my emotions.

"Maybe," I admitted. "But I swear it's not just guys I have a thing for—"

"So you *do* have a thing for Torr!" LJ sat back in his seat like a great realization had floored him. "I knew it. For, like, ten years, I've known it."

"Seriously, though, that place is awful," I said, ignoring my younger cousin. "Some of those gladiators might actually be violent psychos, but I don't think most of them are. They're normal people who got taken advantage of, and they need help."

"That's most of what we deal with in the Network," Carter said. "We're used to it. And we try to prioritize our efforts to the most dire situations. So trust me, I've seen some awful shit."

"Well, this is pretty fucking dire. People are literally being killed for entertainment." I stood from the table. "Alright, see what kind of weapons and cars you can set aside for me. I'm gonna call Aunt Kyrie and see what she can do."

"Aye-aye, captain." It almost sounded mocking, but I knew LJ was too sweet to be anything but sincere. He stood as well, gave me a quick hug, and headed for the basement, where their armory was most likely kept.

"Anything else you need?" Now Carter's tone, on the other hand, dripped with sarcasm.

I wheeled around to face him. "Just don't be a dick, alright? I know I'm interrupting the Valkyrie Network's very carefully crafted schedule and you're going to have to shuffle some inventory around, which I *do* appreciate, it's just..." I waved my hands around help-lessly. "People are dying in there, daily. And with every passing second, I'm worried Torr could be next."

Carter's face softened just a fraction, his expression showing an echo of sympathy. "I get it, Rori. I felt the same way when I first joined the Network. There's a sense of desperation, that you have to move as quickly as possible to save as many lives as possible."

"Yes, exactly," I breathed.

"Here's some advice I hope you take to heart." He crossed his arms, resembling a stern, younger version of his dad, my uncle Larkan. "Drop that mindset. Let go of it, right now."

I returned his stare and the arm-crossed position, not ready to back down. "Excuse me?"

"If you go in rushed and half-cocked, you'll be sloppy. And when shit goes sideways, you won't know what to do, and you'll panic. You'll make mistakes that will probably cost people their lives. A successful mission counts on being prepared, having backup plans for your backup plans. And that takes time to get that all lined up." Carter rapped his knuckles on the table and stood, continuing to look me square in the eye. "Go ahead and call Kyrie, see what kind of supplies you can get. But I also want you to write down a description of this place. Draw a diagram if you can, and do not skimp on a single detail. We need to know what we're getting into."

"And what if Torr doesn't have that kind of time?" I demanded. *Or Santos, or Paige, or, fuck, anyone.* "What if planning everything down to the letter is what costs people their lives?"

Carter gave me a sorrowful look over his shoulder as he headed for the same door his brother went through. "No matter what you do, you can't save everyone."

Chapter 3

Santos

Adjusting to life in complete darkness wasn't the hard part, especially when there was someone to talk to. The shitty part was when one of the ceiling panels opened, and light flooded our dark little dungeon home. Torrance and I were too busy shielding our blinded, pain-filled eyes and retreating to the shadowy corners of the cell like cockroaches.

The pitmasters opened the ceiling quickly enough to drop food or water, blind the shit out of us with the spotlight they always used, then close things back up again while our optical nerves dealt with the whiplash.

Every day, Torr and I tried to be ready. But they never opened up at regular intervals. We could faintly hear the hustle and bustle of the colosseum outside of our prison, so even though we didn't have any light to go by, we could make educated guesses on what time of day it was.

It had been quiet during this last drop, and Torrance and I had been catching some sleep, so we could only surmise that it was the middle of the night. The spotlight had jolted both of us out of a dead sleep, on top of killing our eyes. It was disorienting as fuck, to the point where I didn't know where I was for maybe thirty seconds.

That was good ol' psychological torture for you.

"Hey, you good?" I heard Torr's voice from somewhere across the room when everything had darkened again.

"Relatively speaking," I groaned, rubbing my eyes in an effort to get the flashing storm clouds out of my vision.

"We got a brick painted to look like bread again." I heard a *tap-tap-tap*, like he was pounding the rock-hard loaf against the ground. "And like two inches of water that smells like fucking backwash."

"My favorite," I deadpanned.

I heard the shuffle of footsteps coming closer and waved my hand out in front of me until my fingers brushed against Torr's pant leg. He clasped my hand and stuck a handful of hard bread into it. "Bon appetit."

"Thanks."

We ate without conversation, our chewing the only sounds as we choked down the stale bread with nasty water.

It wasn't long before Torr got up and started walking the perimeter of our pitch-black cell, his hand running along the brick wall keeping us in. When his feet nudged my hip, I scooted forward from where I leaned against the wall, and he kept walking.

Another day of pacing in the hamster wheel. What else could we do?

"How long do you think it's been?" he asked on his second lap around.

"Going off the sounds of activity outside? Three days, give or take a day."

"How can you even keep track? Can't see shit to make markings on the wall or anything."

"Well, counting to three is pretty easy for most people. The longer we stay here, though, the funkier time's gonna get."

"That's what I'm saying. There's no sense of time in here. No context, no stimuli. I can't even tell how big this room is. Feels like I'm losing sense of up and down too."

I noted the hint of panic in his voice and had to remember he wasn't like me. Even if he wasn't as rich and privileged as the actual guests who came through here, he'd probably never been imprisoned. Never been thrown into an isolation room like this one. Never been sleep deprived or starved as a punishment.

Psychological torture was a bitch though, often even worse than physical. And we were in Mystic Canyon's favorite torture chamber.

"You need to calm down," I told him. "You're falling for what this room is made to do—screw you up mentally. They know it fucks with your senses, that's the whole point. Remember that, and keep your wits about you."

"Fuck, man. Every time I want to take a deep breath to chill out, it feels like there's a weight on my chest."

"Yeah, it's humid as fuck in here," I said. "Just do your best."

Torr's steps continued to shuffle along the perimeter, so to avoid getting kicked by him again, I scooted forward to sit closer to the center of the room.

"You been in here before?" he asked after a while.

"Not this one specifically or for this long."

A memory surfaced of before I came to Mystic Canyon, when Devin and Hudson were forcefully dragged away and I was left alone to imagine what kind of horrors were being inflicted on them. They came back about twelve hours later, hollow-eyed and tight-lipped, their wrists, ankles, and necks covered in raw, angry red marks.

"You gladiators," I could imagine Torr shaking his head in disbelief as he spoke, "must have nerves and balls of steel from this shit. I thought I could handle a dark room, but I'm wilting over here, and you sound rock steady. Like a Buddhist monk or something."

I let out a soft laugh. "We're all forged by our environments. I'm sure it would be the reverse in a different situation."

Torrance was quiet for a moment, then I heard a scraping noise, like he was sliding his back down the wall to take a seat on the ground. "You know what? You're a nice guy for a gladiator."

"You met many gladiators?" I snorted.

"Fine, I take it back."

We both scoffed at that.

"I can see why Rori likes you, is what I'm trying to say," he added.

I stiffened. Aside from acknowledging that we had both been with Rori in the beginning, we had avoided talking about her. She told me a little about the whole sharing thing with her one mom and four dads. The idea would take some getting used to, but I wasn't opposed to it.

Having that kind of thing work seemed to hinge on the people involved most of all. How well everyone got along, if personalities meshed, and if things were all balanced. And I just didn't know Torr well enough to say if I was willing to share Rori with him.

But it was ultimately up to her, I suppose. She and him already had a history. I was the outsider trying to find a way in.

"When did you and Rori meet?" I asked.

"When we were kids. I was twelve and she was ten."

Oh, damn. That was a *long* history with them. The possibility of seeing myself alongside them wilted like a plant starved for water.

"My birth parents just kinda fucked off and left me to die," he said casually. "So I lived with her family for a few weeks until a suitable foster home was found. But they became my family. Her twin brother's my best friend, so I was over there hanging out with them all the time."

My head lifted. "So you saw how her family was like, huh?"

"Oh, you mean her four dads? Yeah, it was weird at first, but you got used to it. And they ended up being like dads to me too. Good thing, 'cause they're great role models, you know? Those guys love the hell out of their woman and make it known, never complain about her in private or sneak around on her like my foster dad does. Nah, Rori's dads also taught us all kinds of cool shit like how to ride motorcycles and shoot guns. Great family. Good people."

"That sounds nice," I said remotely. It must have sucked to get abandoned, but it seemed like the guy ended up alright. Well, up until the point that he landed in a dungeon with me.

There was a rustling sound like Torr was shifting his weight. "What about you? You got family somewhere missing you?"

I shrugged even though he couldn't see. "I'm sure I got blood relatives all over the place, but no one who would claim or miss me. The closest thing to family I've got is Dev—"

My mouth shut abruptly with the realization that I almost just gave his real name. Shit, even if I hadn't, I shouldn't be revealing my friendship with another gladiator.

"Who?" Torr pressed.

"Nothing. I don't have any family."

"Dude." He sighed. "I'm in this dark, dank hole with you, trying not to lose my shit. I'm not gonna rat you out to the resort people. Rori's coming back, and we're gonna get out. We need to trust each other, at least with basic information."

I sighed and scooted back toward the wall, letting my head rest on the solid brick. I wished I had my machetes on me, not to use them, but to sharpen them or work out my wrists—do something with my hands.

Even if Torr was lying, which I didn't think he was, or if Rori didn't come back for whatever reason, it wasn't likely the resort staff would use any information against me. There was nothing more they could do to me. This cell was the last one punished gladiators sat in before they got sent out to be disposed of in a fight.

I was either getting out or I would be dead soon. There were no other options.

"There's a gladiator called the Ghost," I said. "His real name is Devin. We were imprisoned together before coming here, then got shipped to Mystic Canyon together. We've gotten to be pretty good friends, so he's the only one I would call family."

"That must be huge, having someone at your back in a place like this. I imagine most people gotta deal on their own."

I smirked in the darkness. "Imagine if you didn't have me to talk to in this cell."

"Shit, my mind would be gone already."

If I had to be honest, Torr being here was helping me to stay sane too. Talking to another person was grounding. I could guesstimate the distance between us with how his voice traveled and the sounds he made when he walked around. And instead of letting my thoughts roll around endlessly in my head, I could express them and get feedback that wasn't just an echo.

"There was another guy with Devin and me," I said, suddenly in a talkative mood. "His name was Hudson, and if we do get out—"

"We will," Torr interjected.

"Devin and I are going to want to find him," I said. "Once we're in the clear, that's going to be objective number one for us."

"Rori will make it happen, I'm sure. Do you know where he's at? Another gladiator pit?"

"No. I don't know what or where it was exactly. It was just...hell. Imagine a prison in hell, that's what it was."

"It's not like that description makes my imagination go wild or anything. Did they dangle you naked over bonfires or something?"

The mental image made me laugh despite how vastly uncomfortable I felt talking about that place. I could see why Rori liked Torr too. He had a goofy side that made you feel more at ease despite uneasy situations.

"No, but...you know how I was brought out of the pit to, uh, service guests?"

"Yeah."

"There was some of that there too, only it was a lot more forceful. Like, we'd be tied down and shit."

"Jesus Christ." Torr's words were muffled like he was rubbing his face. "What a fucking nightmare."

"That wasn't even all of it. We weren't forced to fight, but some guys left and never came back. We'd hear screaming, and sometimes there was blood dripping through the cracks in the ceiling. We'd walk past a guy in a cell who'd be covered in bleeding cuts all the time."

"What...*the fuck?*" Torr's tone was bewildered. "Are you fucking with me, Santos?"

"I'm not."

"That sounds like straight-up horror movie shit."

"All three of us said the same thing. We kept hoping to wake up and find out that none of it was real."

"How the fuck did you end up there?"

It had been a while since I'd told that story. "I was grabbed while I was just out walking after a job. I'd actually fucked up the job, because the client wanted his cheating wife killed, and I didn't take out women. That was just my personal boundary."

"What were you, a hitman?"

"Kind of, yeah. More of a mercenary. Anyway, I broke into the house like I was supposed to, had my machete against her throat and told her what the deal was. Then I told her she needed to get the hell out of Dodge and that I'd take care of the rest. I was going to fake a bloody murder scene, tell the client I'd dumped the body, and it was all done."

It was interesting recalling that memory right then. I examined each event of the night, walked through every step I took, wondering which one, if any, would have altered the course of my destiny.

"Did it work?" Torr pressed.

"Beautifully," I said. "She made her escape, I painted the scene and got out, then I was on my way to meet the client and collect my pay. He was a rich Blakeworth fuck, so he was waiting in my part of the city, the underbelly, all dirtied up under a disguise." Torr snorted, and I rolled my eyes. "Right? So I was gonna meet him in a bar. I was on the same street and could see the door up ahead." I went quiet, knowing this next part was where I'd fucked up.

"I take it you didn't make it." An astute observation from Torr.

"No," I whispered. "A little girl ran up to me out of nowhere. She was wailing, sobbing, in so much distress. She was dirty and barefoot, such a sad little thing. This kid grabbed my hand, trying to pull me somewhere. I pulled back and just tried to get her to calm down. I couldn't understand what she was saying, she was hysterical. So I crouched down to her eye level." I closed my eyes. "That was when they got me."

"Jesus, how?" Torr asked. "I've seen you out there. You're a beast."

"Chloroform, my man." I chuckled mirthlessly. "They waited until I was distracted and close to the ground, put the shit over my nose and mouth, and then a bag over that so I couldn't escape the fumes. Next thing I remember, I woke up sitting in a cell across from Devin."

"Fuck, that's some shit."

"Yeah." I rubbed the back of my neck. *Then, six years later, I got a talking jaguar and I'm falling for a girl who has another man.* Not that I got any bad vibes from Torr, but I didn't need to reveal my whole hand just yet. He probably already knew I had it bad for Rori anyway.

Torr cleared his throat. "Got a personal question, if you don't mind."

"Shoot."

"After all that, do you still feel the same way about killing women? Is it still a boundary for you?"

A laugh burst out of me from seemingly nowhere, echoing off the brick walls. But I knew where that sound came from—the deep part of my soul that had gone as black and empty as a bottomless pit.

"Absolutely the fuck not."

Chapter 4

Rori

I dropped onto the couch, dying to get off my still-aching feet. "I can't thank you enough, Aunt Kyrie. This is more than I could have asked for."

I knew the woman had resources, but she'd really come through for me. She had two safe houses reserved for us, plus a warehouse full of blankets, clothes, toiletries, basic first aid supplies, and non-perishable food. She was also arranging for fresh water and food and a doctor to come check on our soon-to-be escapees for more serious medical issues.

"It's my pleasure, sweetheart. Nobody deserves what those people are going through." I heard a distant tapping on the phone, like my aunt was drumming her fingers on her desk. "Something about this resort sounds...I don't know, familiar, but that's not quite the right word."

I sat up. "You've seen something like this before?"

"No, but the exploitation of men, specifically at the hands of women, reminds me of something one of your uncles went through as a child."

I gripped the phone harder, pausing before asking, "Uncle Grudge?"

"Yes," she confirmed softly.

Her husband, Grudge, my dad Shadow's half-brother, had been rendered mute as a result of his tongue being removed. He could make some sounds with his throat and lips but primarily communicated in sign language. It was because of both him and my brother's girlfriend Lily that our whole family took on learning how to sign.

With Shadow's scarred appearance and Grudge's mutilation, it was clear that they had both been through horrific ordeals when they were younger. I hadn't yet made a connection between them and the gladiators, but what if there was one?

"Has he told you what happened?" I asked Kyrie.

"Yes, but," shesaid, pausing. "It's not my story to tell, Rori. I can ask him—"

"No, it's okay." I stopped her. "I don't want to dredge up bad memories for him. Besides, it was so long ago, way before I was born, right? It probably isn't related. No one at this place had their tongues removed that I saw."

"Even so, I'm going to tell him what you told me," she said. "If he thinks there's a connection, he'll say so. And you know all three of them will want to help."

"What happened to enjoying retirement?" I laughed.

"I found T-Bone and Dyno hitting each other with golf clubs the other day. I don't know *how* they still have so much energy and testosterone, but they need some kind of outlet."

"My dads will probably be the same. They'll have to go on old-man rides together and leave you and my mom in peace."

Kyrie laughed, and I heard the smile in her voice. "We could use a girls' day. Val and I miss the hell out of Mari and you kids."

"I miss you and Val too and even those old farts."

"Oh, you'll be seeing Val soon." Kyrie's voice brightened, and I knew her smile was growing wider. "She'll be running those supplies over to you."

"Really?" I straightened again, but this time out of excitement at seeing her daughter, another one of my cousins. "That'll be badass. It's been too long."

"She's just like you, can't keep her off a motorcycle. I swear you two should have been sisters."

"Yeah." I sighed through an uncomfortable pang in my chest.

I loved my little sister Lucia to the ends of the earth and missed her like crazy. We had an easy sibling friendship, bonding over books, gossip, and boys, but we otherwise didn't have much in common. She didn't get my love of riding and hated that motorcycles were so loud and always kicking up dust.

Aside from my parents, only Daren loved riding like I did. And Torr, but he and I had dropped all pretense of acting like siblings, hadn't we?

Aunt Kyrie's voice cut in before my mind could drift to those last moments with Torr. "Well, I'll let you go, sweetheart. I've got to dispatch all these supplies and get these safe houses cleaned up for you."

"Thank you so much, again," I said. "You're the best, Aunt Kyrie."

"Absolutely. It feels great to be doing *real* work again, instead of going to charity functions where only a fraction goes to those who really need it." She finished off that thought with a grumble before her voice became chipper again. "It was great to hear from you, dear. Let's do that girls' day once all these people are rescued and those responsible are tossed in a grave."

I couldn't help but laugh. The woman had come from a well-off family, the daughter of a governor. She was well-educated, a natural player in the political arena, and on the surface, prim and proper. Kyrie could blend seamlessly into the Blakeworth elite crowd and no one would bat an eye.

But she married three bikers, and at her core, was a biker bitch through and through. My aunt looked as pretty and fragile as a glass shoe, but if need be, she wouldn't hesitate to smash the heel off and fight dirty with the jagged edge.

"Can't wait. I love you, Aunt Kyrie. Give your three old men my love."

"Love you too, kiddo. And I will."

We ended the call, and I pulled the phone away from my ear to look through my recent calls. Kyrie and I had talked for nearly an hour, but she wasn't my first call of the day. My call to Gwen had gone straight to voicemail, which worried me.

She was the one who'd arranged for Torr and I to get into Mystic Canyon, from faking our application paperwork to dressing us up. As a publicist for one of the Blakeworth elite families, she'd been able to carefully siphon money, clothes, and even cars from her employers.

Since capturing Torr and tossing me out, the resort staff must have dug deeper to discover our ruse. And I had a sneaking suspicion that any repercussions wouldn't fall on the wealthy family who'd supposedly vouched for us, but on Gwen.

I tapped her number again and brought the phone to my ear. "Fuck," I muttered, ending the call a second later when her voicemail greeting instantly connected. If anything happened to Gwen, it would be our fault. My fault.

I stared at my phone screen for a long while, willing it to light up with a call from her. When nothing happened, I sighed and scrolled down to my mom's number, tapped it, and brought the phone to my ear.

It rang several times before going to voicemail, which wasn't unusual. She was probably working.

"Hey, mom, it's me," I said after the recording beep. After that, my mind went blank for a moment. What should I tell her? Leaving my mom a message was such an autopilot process for me that my brain actually stuttered to a halt when it came to revealing actual details on what had happened.

"Um, I'm okay. Safe. I'm with LJ and Carter right now. I just wanted to let you know so that you wouldn't worry. I'm going to be out here for a little while longer, but I'm hoping I can make it back home soon. I miss you. I'll call again when I can. Love you, bye."

I ended the call quickly, my throat burning. If I stayed on any longer, I'd spill everything about Torr and the resort, then she'd send my dads out to retrieve me like a lost little lamb. But this was my fight, and I had to see it through, no matter how badly I wanted to rush back home to where I knew I'd be safe at all times.

The reason I actually called her was because I knew she wasn't likely to answer. If it had been one of my dads, they'd pick up and immediately grill me for details, and I'd cave. Chances were high they'd see me calling and immediately head for the nearest parked motorcycles.

It was sweet, and I was lucky to have a family unit that was so caring and protective. But my mom had a different perspective than them, a more nuanced one, perhaps. My fathers' instincts were to run out and save me at a single hint of trouble. My mother knew I had to spend this time in the trenches, figuring out how to fend for myself. She'd get my message and let everyone know I was okay.

God, I missed them though. I'd never been away from my family this long. And it had only been, what, a week? A week and half?

I missed all the male voices talking over each other, the smell of coffee and fresh eggs in the morning, the shit-talking and rough-housing out of love. I missed the parties we threw at every excuse—birthdays, holidays, anniversaries, celebrations. Sometimes our house got so busy and rowdy with friends and family that I'd head out for a ride just to have some alone time, some peace.

But all that noise *was* peace. It was warmth and love and life being lived.

I was so caught up in missing my family and home that I jumped when my phone vibrated in my lap with a call. Looking at the screen, I frowned. Unknown number. Definitely not my mother calling me back.

I let it ring for another few seconds, steeling myself for whatever was on the other line before I answered. "Hello?"

"Rori? It's Gwen."

"Oh, thank fuck!" I sagged into the couch, relief shooting through my sore limbs. "I've been trying to call you."

"Yeah, I ditched my old phone. Rumors started flying around my employers' circles that something happened at the resort. So I took some vacation time and decided to make myself scarce for a few weeks."

"So you're okay, then? You're safe?"

"Oh yeah, I'm good. Lupa and I are staying with family. Nobody from Blakeworth knows where I am."

"Good. That's good." I raked a hand back through my hair. "Shit, I was worried."

"I told you one of my dads is a hacker, right? I know how to make myself untraceable."

I smiled even though she couldn't see me. "I'm glad."

"So, I take it you and Torr are not at the resort anymore?"

I swallowed, my throat going dry again. "I'm not. Torr still is and...he's in trouble. I'm working on a plan to get him out."

"Oh no! The place was that bad, huh? Or worse?"

"Worse," I sighed, and gave her a brief run-down of events from when we first touched ground in that canyon to being separated and me forced out at gunpoint.

"Holy shit," she breathed. "I don't even want to think about how many missing people have gone through that place."

"Yeah, getting kidnapped just to be thrown in a colosseum to die? It's sickening."

"What can I do to help?" Gwen asked, or rather, demanded.

"Nothing." I practically barked into the phone. "They're probably already looking into you since you dropped us off. So you stay hidden and safe until this blows over."

"Rori, I can't just sit on my hands while you're—"

"Thank you, Gwen, but you've done enough. You got us in, and now we know someone's dirty little secret. We just have to find out who's it is." *And blow it the fuck up.*

"I'm already involved. I might as well help," she insisted.

"Gwen, please." I rubbed my forehead. "I fucked up, and Torr's still in there because of me. If something happens to you, I don't want that on my conscience. I won't be able to handle it. Please."

Silence stretched out over the phone. "You're serious," she said finally.

"Yeah." I rubbed my forehead. "We kinda fucked the whole thing up. Bad. And other people got caught in the crossfire." *Like Santos and Paige. I know Santos is strong, but God, I hope Paige is alright.*

Some crackling and shuffling came over the speaker like something was fuzzy with our connection.

"Gwen? You still there?" I glanced at my phone screen to check my reception bars. All good on my end.

"Yeah, sorry!" she said after a few seconds. "Lupa just told me something, and it startled me, so I dropped the phone."

My pulse started to pick up for no apparent reason. Lupa was like Astarte and Tezcatlipoca, a deity in an animal vessel. In Lupa's case, a wolf.

"What did she say?" I almost dreaded the answer.

"She said to tell you that all is unfolding as it's meant to. Trust yourself and try not to worry. You are on the right path, Rori."

I closed my eyes and tried to conjure up the patience to keep this frustration away. "Tell her thank you for me."

I heard a bark and soft howl in the distance, to which Gwen and I both laughed softly. "We're thinking of you and Torr," Gwen added. "If there's anything we can do, please let me know."

"Thanks. I'm glad you're okay."

"Trust in Astarte too, Rori." Gwen's voice was firm, like she knew my faith in the winged goddess was shaky at best. "She's there to guide you."

"I'll try," I answered with a sigh. "I know you probably can't give me your number so call back in a few days, alright? I'll update you."

"Will do. Be safe, Rori."

"You too, Gwen."

I ended the call and glanced at the window behind the couch just in time to see the white dove perch on a tree branch. It was hard not to glare at the animal, and not only because her feathers were so damn bright. Supposedly, Astarte was here to guide me, but she'd remained silent the vast majority of the time.

The few times she did deign to speak with me, it was some vague, riddled mumbo-jumbo, like I was supposed to figure it all out like a puzzle.

I didn't have time to solve puzzles. Not when Torr, Santos, Paige, and everyone else in that hellhole needed me.

"Would be nice if I could get a little more *specific* guidance on what the fuck I'm supposed to be doing," I muttered more to myself than anyone, but of course, that was when Bird Almighty chose to respond.

You're still not understanding, Aurora, came the goddess' voice raking over my brain like a chastising mother. *I cannot interfere with your free will. I cannot change the course of actions already taken.*

"Then why are you even here?" I wanted to throw my phone at the window. "What good is your so-called guidance?"

When you are conflicted, I can show you a path. When darkness is all you see, I can be a beacon to show you the way out. But you must choose to take those actions, which will lead to events, which leads to more actions to be taken.

"But you are hoping for a certain outcome, right? You're trying to prevent something bad from happening. That's your ultimate goal, and I'm your tool to do so. So why not just tell me the best way to make that happen? Why sacrifice Torr and Santos for this?"

For you, the journey is just as important as the outcome, Aurora. Every decision you make lays the foundation of the woman you will become. I am here for when you are truly lost, but for the most part, you know the answers. The dove shook out her feathers, resembling a puffy ball before smoothing them all down again. *And I never said your men will be sacrificed, but they are important keys of your journey.*

"Will this plan work?" I pleaded quietly. "Will we really be able to pull this rescue off? So many lives are riding on my decisions, and I *need* to know. It's killing me."

You'll know soon enough, Aurora Wilder.

Chapter 5

Devin

The Saint was a fairly new gladiator who had quickly made a name for himself. He earned his fighting name in a twist of irony, from the upside-down crosses tattooed next to his eyes.

Other fighters began rallying around the Saint after the Animal had been killed, kissing his ass in an effort to make him their new cult leader. It was interesting to watch from the sidelines. Some people were completely aimless without anyone to follow. And others turned out to be natural-born leaders.

The Saint wasn't a loud, brash guy like the Animal had been. Like Santos and I, he had mostly kept to himself, and at first seemed like an unusual choice for the other fighters to rally around. He'd been tested, of course. Not everyone liked or respected him, so a pecking order had to be established. I'd heard of three fighters, all on separate occasions, sneaking into the Saint's room at night to kill him in his sleep. He'd slaughtered every single one and brought trophies as proof to the breakfast table the next morning.

Just like that, he'd not only proven he wasn't one to fuck with, but that he could also bring a group of bloodthirsty men to heel. Which was exactly what we needed if we were going through with this whole organized escape plan.

I volunteered to speak with him during training hours, to which the Hunter seemed relieved.

The Saint was sharpening a spear as I approached him head-on. Coming up from behind would likely end in death, or at least a bloody neck, as the Hunter had figured out when he approached me. It was an important lesson to be learned in the gladiator pit—if you're not a threat, it's smarter to let the other party see you coming.

"To what do I owe the pleasure?" I was ten feet away and the Saint didn't even lift his head when he asked the question.

I scanned the colosseum. We were near the center of the fighting pit in plain view, but no one was close enough to eavesdrop.

"How would you like to get the fuck out of here?"

He paused in his sharpening, the tattoos at the corners of his eyes compressing slightly as he squinted up at me. "That can mean any manner of things. Are you propositioning me? I'm flattered, Ghost, but men aren't my delicacy of choice."

I didn't know what threw me first, his overly-formal speech or that he immediately thought I was offering to fuck.

"That's...not what I was asking," I said, lowering my voice and walking closer. "I mean out of *here*. Escape."

He smiled as if amused, then lowered his head, returning his attention to his spear. "Just when I've been chosen as the shot-caller? Interesting approach to knock me off my throne, I'll give you that."

"I'm not after your position, I don't want it." My eyes continued scanning the arena, and I pulled out a couple knives to mess with in order to look less suspicious. "We've got a real shot at fucking this place over. But we need to organize. You're the one with the most influence over the fighters."

"Yes, I am," he said matter-of-factly. "What are you proposing? An uprising?"

"Help is coming from the outside." I flipped a knife in the air, caught it, and held it up, pretending to examine the blade. "We need the fighters aware and ready, and most importantly, to keep their mouths shut until it's time."

"When is this outside help coming?"

"I don't know."

"Okay, so who are our kind rescuers?"

Tezca's words returned to me. *You can trust the light and the guard. But do not trust the false messenger.* All fucking riddles. Some names would have been great, but all I knew was that the guy's name was Torrance. Who knew if that was even a real name?

"I'm not sure. But they posed undercover as guests here," I answered.

The Saint snorted. "So you don't know who's coming or when. What do you expect me to tell the fighters?"

"You're their leader." I shrugged. "You speak well. Be persuasive."

"And why should I put any amount of trust into what you say?" He peered up at me again, those tattoos making his glare look sinister. "The pitmasters put you up to this, didn't they? Are they trying to see if I'll actually go through with an uprising so they'll have a reason to shoot us all down?"

"Why would they kill us en masse? They need us."

"Only temporarily, until they find more bodies," he pointed out.

"Listen." I sighed heavily, caught my knife, and brought it to my side. "The Butcher is missing."

"I've noticed."

"He's my friend, okay? We've had each other's backs for years, and I know his real name."

"Which is?"

I hesitated. The Saint could take Santos' given name and run directly to the pitmasters. Or worse, Nella. Both of which would immediately throw me into a fight I wouldn't be allowed to win. He knew the risks of asking for and receiving such information. But he needed something if he was going to help us, and I had nothing else to give him.

"I won't tell you his," I said. "But my name is Devin. Devin Ito."

The Saint straightened, his face going slack with surprise. "You're either incredibly foolish or you believe in this cause that strongly."

"I do," I said. "I'm done here. I'm finding my friend and getting the fuck out or getting killed trying."

The other man narrowed his eyes again. "Is anyone else in this with you? Or are you coming to me on your own?"

"The Hunter is with me," I said. "He's the one who actually spoke to the undercover guest."

The Saint crossed his arms over his chest. "I'll need his name as well. That is my price."

"I don't know it."

"Then get him over here."

I looked around, then whistled and motioned when I spotted the Hunter trying to look busy while swinging a sword around. He jogged over, and I gave him the rundown of what we had just discussed..

"You told him your *name*?" The young fighter stared at me in disbelief.

"Talk louder, please," I hissed at him.

"Are you fucking nuts?" he whispered aggressively.

"Maybe, but we don't have any other collateral to give him. I'm Devin, by the way. You might as well know too."

"Fuck." He grabbed at his hair and turned around, looking at all the gladiators in the distance.

"I'm waiting," the Saint mused, testing the sharp edge of his spearhead.

The Hunter turned back to face him. "We need your name too. It's only fair."

"You're getting my fighters to organize and prepare for an uprising with no other details, and that is it." The Saint glowered at the Hunter. "No other extras. Your given name, Hunter. Or you get nothing from me."

The Hunter's eyes shifted to me, and I gave a slight nod. I hated to put him in this position, but we had literally nothing else to give.

"It's Levi," he said quietly. "My name is Levi Cooke."

———

I SHOULD HAVE EXPECTED it when, hours later after a quick shower and returning to my room, Nella requested me in her office. Tezca did not seem interested in coming along, and promptly jumped onto the bunk bed the moment I vacated it. At least the pitmaster escorting me went pale as a sheet the moment he saw the big cat. Tezca enjoyed taking bites and swipes of those who fucked with Santos and me.

My mood soured the instant I stepped into the guest services manager's office. It was a luxurious room, with Nella's long, polished wood desk at the far end and a bank of windows overlooking the canyon behind her. There were bookshelves and a sitting area with two chairs to the left, a loveseat with a coffee table to the right. The floor was covered in a plush, patterned rug, and the ceiling vaulted high above my head, making the room feel like a cathedral. A perfect place for my sins to be judged.

"Thank you for coming, Ghost," Nella said with her fake pleasantness. Like I had the choice not to come. "Please have a seat."

She gestured toward one of the chairs in front of her desk, and I obediently walked forward while the pitmaster stayed by the door. I dropped unceremoniously into the chair and waited.

There were papers on her desk. My file, perhaps. Although why anyone bothered to keep paperwork on the gladiators was beyond me. We came in and got out all in the same ways.

"How are you, Ghost?" she asked, flipping through the papers like she was my accountant or something, catching up with me before getting down to business.

If I hadn't been patted down and stripped of my weapons, I'd have driven my blade through her neck already.

"Why am I here?" I responded instead.

She actually had the balls to look offended that I didn't want to waste time bullshitting with her. "We've noticed you spending more time socializing with one of the newest fighters lately, the Hunter. Is there anything you'd like to tell me about that?"

I shrugged with a shake of my head. "He needs guidance and fighting tips. When I kill him in the pit, I don't want it to be too easy."

"So you're training him?"

"Just passing the time, but sure, I guess."

"Would you say you've gotten attached to him in any way?"

"No." Any other answer or deflection would have looked suspicious.

"We also noticed you talking to the Saint earlier today. Anything you'd like to share about that conversation?"

"He's the new shot-caller, so I was just paying my respects."

"Really? You never did that with the Animal."

"I didn't respect the Animal. I do respect the Saint." At least that was the truth. And from this line of questioning, it didn't seem that Nella knew the Hunter and I had shared our real names, which was a relief. She wouldn't have bothered with all the fake pleasantries if that were the case. She was just being a nosy bitch.

"Are you feeling more social now that your roommate is gone?" Nella sent an evil smile my way.

In an instant, I could have jumped from the chair, leaned across the desk, squeezed the air from her throat, and demanded to know where Santos was. But if he was still alive, her knowing of our friendship could not only put me in danger but him as well.

So I shrugged again. "It's whatever. At least I've got his jaguar to keep me company."

Nella frowned, and I mentally snickered. *Yeah, and don't you forget it, bitch.*

She and the pitmasters hated having the jaguar around, but there wasn't much they could do about it. Any attempt to capture or shoot Tezca was met by the aggressor being mauled, if not killed, by said jaguar. Everyone was safest when they left the big cat alone, much to Nella's dismay. A force with teeth and claws—not to mention unnatural speed and strength—protecting gladiators meant her grip of control on us was slipping.

"I'm going to ask you something, and if you value your life, I strongly suggest you answer me honestly." She paused for dramatic effect, and I resisted the urge to fill the silence with a long fart noise. This woman thought she was so powerful, so intimidating. But it would only take a crack to the foundation to collapse her fortress. The only problem was, her fortress was heavily guarded.

"Are you and the other fighters planning something?"

"No." Again, short and to the point. To lie effectively, I had to give her nothing to work with. Most people were bad liars because they subconsciously felt guilty for lying, were afraid of the consequences if found out, or a mixture of both. Good thing both guilt and fear had been beaten out of me years ago.

"Are you lying to me, Ghost?"

"No, I'm not." My hands and feet remained still, my gaze rock steady while her eyes bounced all over me in search of tells.

Nella's brow pinched. A small, frustrated huff left her nostrils at her inability to find a chink in my armor. So she switched tactics, her face relaxing.

"I'm glad to hear it. Just a reminder, you would be rewarded well for coming forward with any information if the fighters *are* planning something. You could have a suite of rooms to yourself, not just a dorm. Running water that's heated. Meals brought to you. All kinds of comforts that would be very well deserved."

Right. And then I would be promptly killed by the Saint and his crew the moment I stepped foot among the fighters. What a great deal that was.

As if reading my mind, Nella added, "You would be guarded for your own protection, of course. I know the other fighters wouldn't react well to you receiving special treatment."

Shadowed by pitmasters at every turn, even better.

"I'll keep that in mind," I said, feigning a tiny bit of interest in her offer, only because it would have looked suspicious if I didn't act like I wanted cushier accommodations. "But for the time being, I have nothing to tell you. May I go now?"

Nella pursed her lips. Actually fucking pouted. "You're so eager to leave? I was looking forward to catching up with you, Devin."

I didn't expect her to use my real name, and damn it, it got to me. My fist tightened on the end of the armrest, teeth clenching in my jaw. Keeping my expression as calm as I could, I said, "Yes, I am eager to leave. I loathe every minute in your company."

"Devin." My name came out as a grating whine on her lips. "That really hurts my feelings. I thought we had so much fun together."

She was seriously pouting across the desk, sticking out her bottom lip and using her arms to push her cleavage together. Fuck, I hated this game. I hated how she used us, not just for sex and fighting, but her stupid little roleplaying fantasies too.

Using my name and pretending like we were star-crossed lovers or some shit? She used our humanity like we were toys to play with. She did the same thing with Santos, even trying to pit us against each other like jealous guys in a love triangle.

"Do I have your permission to leave?" I asked through gritted teeth. I refused to play, but I couldn't actually go anywhere unless she let me.

"I don't want you to leave," she whined. "I want you to stay and show how much you've missed me. Work has kept me *so* busy, you know."

"The day I'll never see you again will be the best fucking day of my life," I answered. "Second only to the last day I see you, which will hopefully be when I finally kill you."

Nella jerked back, her face shocked. Maybe some part of her actually believed the delusion that we were in some kind of relationship, but I wasn't about to start feeling sympathy for her now.

"Just so we're abundantly clear," I said, leaning forward. "I will celebrate your death. And I will never, ever miss you."

"Get out, Ghost," she hissed, getting back to business. "One more word and I'll have you beaten for threatening a superior."

Ha. I win this round, bitch, I thought with a smile, although I'd never give her the satisfaction of saying it out loud.

I left the chair and had just made it to the guards posted at the doors when she called out, "Oh, I almost forgot," in an all-too pleasant tone. "You're fighting the Butcher the day after tomorrow."

Chapter 6

Rori

"This is it?" I frowned as I scanned over the list of names and supplies, trying to visualize everything in my head.

"Uh, yeah. You're welcome." Carter huffed like he was insulted. "That's who and what we have to spare."

After spending the last two days telling my cousins everything I knew about Mystic Canyon, the list didn't feel like enough. Not for a surprise attack on a heavily guarded canyon resort. Although, without my cousins' connections and resourcefulness, I wouldn't have anything at all. I was grateful but nervous. We might be able to pull it off, but it wouldn't be easy.

"You don't look happy," LJ mused from his spot sitting on the kitchen counter.

Sighing, I put the list down and rubbed my eyes. "Thank you, guys. This is actually great, and I appreciate you both getting this together. I just worry about actually executing it."

"If the diagram you gave me is accurate, it should be doable. Given we stick to the plan," Carter said. "Everyone's been briefed, and they're ready to go on your order."

I scanned the names of the riders again, a few of whom I recognized as family friends and acquaintances, but many I didn't. These were Carter's people from the Valkyrie Network who were currently off rotation, some of whom were members of Sons of Odin MC.

If Carter vouched for them, then they were solid. Good riders, quick thinkers, and trustworthy. But it still bothered me that I personally didn't know most of the people I'd be riding and fighting besides.

And even more concerning, eighteen total people, including me and my cousins, didn't seem like enough to take down the whole resort.

Who knew if the gladiators would even see us as help? Santos said he'd do what he could, but could he realistically do anything after being dragged away by those guards? Maybe Tezca was communicating intel to him. Or, for all I knew, the big cat was as useful as my damn bird.

"So what do you think?" Carter pressed. "Are we a go?"

"Hang on." I stood, leaving the list behind as I headed for the small balcony off the dining room. "I need to think for a minute."

Ignoring Carter's grumbling, I went outside to the crisp, dry air. For once, the trees were empty as I scanned them.

"Figures," I muttered. "When I go looking for you, you're nowhere to be seen. When I don't want you around, you're hovering over me."

Only silence answered me and the distant cawing of a crow or raven. My uncle T-Bone had a raven named Munin who could mimic voices and allowed me to pet him. He was a much cooler bird than this fucking dove.

"You're here to guide me, so where the fuck are you?" I muttered.

You know, Aurora, a little respect goes a long way. The familiar, disembodied voice raked over my brain. *Please and thank you cost nothing.*

"Yeah, well, the feeling is mutual," I grumbled. "Straightforward answers would be most appreciated."

Just like your father, Asarte mused. *You mask feelings of fear and inadequacy with stone walls and sharp barbs. True strength is being open and vulnerable, Aurora.*

"This is not about me. I'm trying to ask you about this attack we're planning." I lowered my voice, knowing my cousins could over-hear if I got too riled up. "Is this a suicide mission? Am I going to cost seventeen other people their lives if we do this? And that's not even counting the people in the canyon."

The outcome of your attack will depend on the decisions you will make in critical moments.

I nearly slammed my forehead down on the balcony railing. "Just once. One fucking time. A yes or no answer would be amazing."

A force came out of nowhere, like an invisible vice pressing in on me on all sides. I felt excruciating pressure on my head, chest, arms, and legs. I could barely take a breath, and every attempt to move felt like trying to lift a car with my pinkie.

I am not your personal fortune teller, Aurora Wilder. I am not a toy you can pull off a shelf and demand answers from. You are a human woman who has known twenty-three years of life. In the millenia of humanity I've seen, do you realize how utterly insignificant you are?

"Please," I gasped, finding it harder to draw breath with each passing second.

I am not in your service. Do you understand? If you don't want humanity to fall, you will listen to me. Because I have seen your kind rise and fall.

"Okay!" I wheezed, desperately clutching my throat. "I'm sorry. I'm listening."

The pressure immediately lifted, and I slumped against the rail-ing, taking in lungfuls of beautiful, precious oxygen.

As I've said, Astarte's voice took on an eerie calm, *I cannot influence outcomes of events or your decisions. I am telling you to trust yourself, your own inner compass, Aurora.*

"But I—"

Stop. Stop running your mouth and letting your brain chatter take up all the room in your head. I'm telling you to cut through all of that and listen to the deepest, most instinctual part of yourself, Aurora. Listen to the part of you that has always been connected to me.

"What the fuck?" I groaned, still gasping for breath.

Astarte went silent and I knew she was gone, or at least not hovering over me anymore. As I caught my breath and found my legs underneath me again, it became clear that it wasn't just the goddess that went silent but all of my surroundings.

LJ and Carter lived in a small apartment complex, mostly consisting of fellow bikers and Valkyrie network cohorts. Usually, I could hear a neighbor or two talking, laughing, barbecuing, the roars of bikes and cars coming or going, but now there was nothing.

It was too damn quiet, and my own breaths and heartbeat thundered in my ears. My instinct was to fill the silence, work out this rescue plan aloud to myself or head back inside to chat with my cousins. Noise and chatter was comforting, familiar. This abject quietness left me feeling vulnerable and exposed.

I suppose that was the point.

Placing my hands on the balcony railing, I took a long, shaky breath. The kind you took before jumping off a cliff. And then I closed my eyes.

And I listened.

Chapter 7

Torrance

"You better quit that." Santos' voice came from my left, about ten feet away was my best guess.

"Why?" I didn't lose momentum, didn't lose a breath in my push-up routine. Without weights to throw around and test myself, bodyweight workouts were my only option, aside from crawling up the wall from going stir-crazy.

"You're going to exhaust yourself. We're not eating or staying hydrated enough to sustain working out like that."

"Relax, I'm not going that hard." I paused at the top of my push-up, walked my hands and feet back to the wall, then took my feet up the wall to go again, this time from a modified handstand position. "I'll be bored out of my skull if I don't move around."

"So move, but don't exert yourself."

"What are you, my mother?"

"I'm just trying to keep us both from getting killed."

"I know my limits. Just trying to burn off some energy, alright?"

"Alright." His voice carried a don't-say-I-didn't-warn-you tone.

I rolled my eyes, not that he could see, and kept going. "How do you stay sharp, Butcher?" I brought a fist to the small of my back to keep lowering and lifting myself one-handed.

"Mobility," he said. "Keeping my joints flexible. And spatial awareness. Devin taught me a lot about how to move and react."

"Yeah? What's his story?"

"If we ever get out of here, maybe he can tell you."

Only then did I stop, my pulse slightly elevated and only a bit of shallowness to my breaths. I brought my feet down to the ground, coming to sit with my back against the wall. "We will get out, Santos. Rori won't leave us behind."

There was silence for a while, then a sigh and some shuffling as Santos rearranged his sitting position. "I hope you're right. I really do."

"She will. I have zero fucking doubt."

"That's great, Torr."

I wished he could see my face. Not just because the pitch-black darkness routine was getting old but so he didn't miss the glare I was shooting him. "What the hell, man? I thought you believed in her too. What happened?"

Santos' laugh was dry and absent of any humor. "I've been enslaved for most of my adult life. Every shred of hope I ever had turned out to be for nothing. That's what happened. So, sorry for being skeptical of anything turning out differently this time."

I crawled forward until I found him, my hand coming down on the shin of one leg stretched out in front of him. "You thought the psychological effects of this place were getting to me? Well, I think they're getting to you now, buddy."

He snorted. "Probably, who knows."

I squeezed the leg my hand rested on. "No way, man. You're not giving into apathy now. You're fighting this."

"If you don't stop touching me, I'm gonna be fighting you."

"Sorry." I lifted my hand away. "Do me a favor though, Santos."

"What?"

"Think of Rori. Think of the last time you saw her. Picture her face. Imagine *her* touching you. Remember what she told you. Remember how you felt back then."

Santos had gone unnaturally still, and I knew his mind was back there, with her. I used the silence to examine how I felt while telling this other man to fantasize about his last moments with the woman *I* loved.

After a few long seconds of sitting with that, I realized I was...fine.

I was fine when Rori herself told me she wanted to explore things with him after all this was over. They were still practically strangers, but their connection was clear and undeniable. I didn't feel threatened by or jealous of this guy. Shit, I was starting to like him too.

I'd always known Rori would find multiple men to be with. And I was secure in knowing my connection with her was something irreplaceable, something neither of us had with anyone else. We had a bond that ran deeper than two partners. She was my home, my safe place. The only woman I'd allowed myself to fall in love with, even if I was too chickenshit to voice it.

Santos and I *had* to get out of here just so I could man up and tell her all that shit.

"You there, man?" I asked him after probably a full minute of silence. "You with her?"

"Yeah." Still, he sounded hesitant. "This isn't weird to you?"

"What, telling you to think about my woman to get you in the right headspace to survive? Nah."

He laughed dryly, with a bit more humor this time. "You're right, though. It's working. I'm remembering how...serious she was about coming back. How painful it was to be separated from her."

"You can believe her when she says she'll do something. I've known her for thirteen years, and she's never half-assed anything or gone back on a promise."

"I want to believe you, Torr. I do. It's just hard to go against the last six years of life experience." He made a soft sound, and while I barely remembered what he looked like, I could picture him smiling.

"Rori...she feels like a fantasy. Like she's not even real. The last time I saw her feels like it could have been a dream."

"She is real, my man. And this nightmare you've lived is about to end."

"I would love for you to be right." He sighed. "I really would."

More silence stretched between us for a while until I cleared my throat. "Uh, is it cool if I pat your shoulder?"

Santos laughed. A real laugh this time that echoed off the walls of our dungeon. "Sure. Just don't feel up my leg again."

"Deal."

I felt around blindly until I found his forearm, to which I followed up to a broad, round shoulder. As I slapped my palm there twice, I nearly got the wind knocked out of me from Santos smacking me right in the center of my chest.

"You're alright, Torr," he said, still chuckling. "You're not bad."

EVERYTHING CHANGED ROUGHLY A DAY LATER.

Light flooded our dungeon with no warning, sending Santos and I ducking and covering our faces to protect our sensitive eyesight. What had been white noise in the background became a deafening roar. I realized it was a chorus of voices, hundreds of them.

An audience.

"What the fuck is happening?" I groaned, squeezing my eyelids shut against the painful light.

"It's the side wall opening up," Santos answered. "Right to the sand pit. Looks like we're fighting."

Peeking over my arm only brought more searing pain to my eye sockets. "We're...*what*?"

"Come on, dude. Like you didn't know this would happen."

"How am I supposed to fight when I can't fucking see?"

"I dunno, figure it out quick. The seats are packed."

It was another full minute before I could even squint. I saw an arena with a sand-covered ground alright. And hundreds of people in the colosseum seats, shouting and waving.

A fight was already going on, from what the dark blurs zipping all over the pit told me. My eyes were having a bitch of a time tracking motion, let alone giving me details about what was right in front of me.

I turned back to the darkness, my senses too overwhelmed by everything going on outside, and that was how I got my first close-up look at Santos. I'd only seen him from a distance before, one of many figures out on the sands. Now seeing him up-close as a fellow man was something else.

His hair and beard were growing out, as I was certain mine had as well. He was a broadly built dude, which made it even more impressive that he could move so quickly. Intense, dark eyes met mine. That was the most familiar thing about him, the weight of his stare. I remembered the look in those eyes as he stared down his opponents in the fight I watched.

"Hey, sexy," I greeted.

That clenched jaw relaxed into a smile for a moment. "Back at you."

A cheer rising up made us both turn around. My eyes were slowly adjusting, and I could make out a figure lying still in the center of the arena while another raised his arms in victory. Blood darkened the sand around the victor's feet in big splotches. A pool of it surrounded the body on the ground, slowly growing in size.

The lone man standing spun to face the crowd in all directions, turning his body slowly until he faced us. When our eyes met, his face broke into a smile and he pointed his arm, which I now saw was holding a sword, straight at us.

"Son of a bitch," Santo hissed. "He's got my machetes. That fucking thief."

"Who is that?" I squinted, now seeing more clearly that the fighter's blade was shorter than a sword's and curved up at the end. Only one was in his hand, the other sticking out of the chest of the man on the ground.

"The Bulldozer."

"Well, even bigger problem." The Bulldozer gestured at us with his free hand, a mocking-friendly motion to come out and play. "He's armed and we're not."

"There's a rack of weapons we can grab. A lot of crappy, rusted-out shit, but better than nothing. It's to the right of us, but we have to make a mad dash."

"Do we stand a chance against this guy?" I watched the Bulldozer wave Santos' weapon around, grab his crotch, and stick his tongue out. True to his name, the guy was huge. And he knew fighting well enough to survive this long and stab a guy in the chest.

"If the two of us are armed?" Santos tilted his head from side to side like he was weighing the options. "Maybe."

"Okay, get weapons. Good plan. Anything else I should know?"

"Yeah." He leveled that dark stare at me. "Rori better be on her way right fucking now. Because they won't stop the fights until one or both of us is dead."

Shit, how could I forget that part? One man standing was the only rule in the gladiator ring.

"So we gotta stall for time," I said. "Potentially a *lot* of time."

"We can't let the audience get bored. As long as we're entertaining, they'll keep it going."

"Well, shit. How do we do that while not dying?"

"Improvise. Switch up your weapons. Get naked and run laps around the pit, I dunno."

"Fuck." I scrubbed my face because my eyes were still fucking killing me.

"One more thing." Santos took a long pause. "If you can make a kill, don't hesitate. Just do it. Make it quick and painless, if that's your thing. But if you hesitate, the other fighter *will* kill you first. Understand?"

"Yeah, I got it." I clenched my hands to hide the shaking in my fingers. Fighting and shooting were well-honed skills of mine, but I never imagined I'd be in a position to take someone else's life. Logically, I knew now was not the time to puss out. It was survive or die, as simple and brutal as that. But I'd never been in a position where I'd had to finish the job before, nor had I asked myself if it was something I was capable of.

Guess I was about to find out.

Not that I was about to bring that up to Santos. He had enough on his plate and didn't need to be shouldered with giving me a pep talk on top of everything.

For a moment though, I envied him. He seemed like a nice dude, and he obviously cared about Rori. But as his gaze focused on the arena, jaw clenched and brows down in concentration, I saw the cold, detached killer that this place had made out of him.

It wasn't that I envied what he'd been through, just that he could turn off all emotion and do what he needed to survive. He wouldn't hesitate. The fact that he was still here was living proof that he never had.

Me, on the other hand? I didn't know if I could turn off the human part of myself and become a killing machine.

No pressure or anything.

There was a metallic clanking sound behind us and I whipped around. Santos, smartly, didn't turn his back to the fighter on the sands but cocked his head in the direction of the new noise.

Another wall panel of our cell slid away, revealing a room on the other side. Or, rather, it was more of a corridor, because the space was packed with armed guards as far back as I could see. There had to be at least a dozen of them coming through the new opening, filing in and crowding our once-dark and closed off cell.

"Into the pit, prisoners," ordered the leader, a sadistic smile pulling at his face as he slapped a baton into his opposite palm. "Your sentence is death."

Santos and I moved to the far edge of the cell, where the first wall had opened up. His toes hovered over the shadow casting a line in the sand, darkness on our side, light on the other.

"Count of three, we run for weapons," he muttered. "One, two—"

"Get moving!" Something flashed in the corner of my vision—an arm swinging back, ready to bring a baton down on my head.

"Three!"

We took off, bursting into painful sunlight and burning sand. I didn't expect the ground to be hot, while also soft and shifting beneath my feet. Santos' blurry form was several paces ahead of me as I struggled to find my footing.

You better fucking get here, Rori, was my last thought before falling flat on my face and looking up to see a dark shadow looming over me.

Chapter 8

Santos

Torrance was no longer at my side when I made it to the weapons rack. When I looked back to find him? "Aw, fuck."

I'd forgotten that he wasn't used to the sandy ground because this surface was like second nature to me. He'd fallen, and the Bulldozer was right on his ass. I grabbed the first weapon within reach, not even taking note of what it was, and hurried back. A sinking feeling in my stomach told me he was already a goner though. The bastard couldn't even see yet.

The Bulldozer swung his—my—machete down, catching only a bit of Torr's shirt as he rolled out of the way. Torr then kicked the inside of the fighter's knee, making him scream and stumble, but the Bulldozer did not go down.

And I knew the big bastard wouldn't go down easily. He'd been here as long as me and Devin.

Torr went for an easy kick next—the gladiator's nads, but the Bulldozer was ready. He grabbed Torr's foot just as I sprang into action again. He started to twist just as I took a running jump and broke my weapon against his face.

What I'd ended up grabbing was a wooden stick, little more than a broom handle. I cracked my weapon so hard against the Bulldozer's nose bridge that it splintered apart. His nose erupted in a fountain of blood, and he released Torr's leg to grab at his face.

"Get a weapon!" I yelled at him, facing off at the Bulldozer with my now-splintered and broken stick. The bleeding gladiator had also dropped my machete, and I eyed the curving blade on the sand near his feet.

I couldn't grab it yet though. The enraged gladiator seemed to forget about the blood pouring from his face as he stared me down. "Butcher." He smiled cruelly, revealing jagged, blood-stained teeth. "You're alive after all." Without breaking eye contact, he lowered to pick up the machete. "Killing you myself will be so much sweeter now that I can do it with your own weapons."

"How'd you even find those?" I didn't really care to know. I was just stalling for time, backing away slowly, the splintered end of my stick pointing at the Bulldozer as he advanced on me.

"Went in your room when Nella had some fun with your roomie in her office. That big cat of yours didn't stand a chance."

He said both of those sentences to throw me off my game and get under my skin. And goddamn him, it worked. While I was trying to process Nella taking Devin again, and this big oaf actually laying a hand on Tezca, he moved in for a strike.

On instinct, I brought up my weapon to block, forgetting that it was made of wood. My mistake became clear when my own machete sliced through it cleanly, nicking me in the shoulder before I dodged the rest of it with a hiss of pain.

I went behind the Bulldozer and he spun, coming for me again, forgetting all about Torr who ran up behind him with a mace of some kind. Rori's man swung the weapon like a baseball bat, landing a hard blow on the Bulldozer's kidney.

"Took you long enough to find something," I muttered, holding my bleeding shoulder while the Bulldozer swayed unsteadily.

He swung at Torr, who successfully blocked the machete blow and kicked the gladiator in the stomach. Unfortunately for him, the Bulldozer barely budged.

While those two danced, the Bulldozer swinging my blade as Torr dodged and whacked him where he could, I went to look for another weapon. There was a short sword on the rack, not quite what I was used to, but it would work well enough. I grabbed it and grimaced at the weight. There was no way I could hold this thing with my bum shoulder. It felt like the muscles had torn, so I was already down to using one arm.

Not that I don't have faith in you, but any minute now would be great, Rori.

I switched the weapon to my other arm and ran over to help Torr. The Bulldozer was giving chase now, running after my buddy and swinging wildly while Torr did his damnedest to keep out of range of that blade. Every move missed him by inches, and he was bound to get sliced if they kept at it.

What the Bulldozer had in brute strength, he lacked in speed. I came up behind him and brought the sword down across his back, hoping to slice between his vertebrae. If I had my own damn weapons, I'd know exactly where to aim. The fighter's thin shirt sliced apart, revealing some kind of vest underneath.

"Goddamn it!" I ground my teeth against frustration and the pain in my arm. No gladiators had access to stab-proof vests. Sometimes we managed crude armor out of metal plating, but that thing could have only come directly from the pitmasters. Torr and I had sat in darkness with barely any food or water for days, and they still rigged this fight against us.

The Bulldozer only laughed when I realized what he was wearing. "What's wrong, Butcher? Don't want your pretty little weapon back?" He waved my machete in front of my face, mocking me.

"Take it off," I hissed at him. "Take that fucking vest off and fight like a real man."

"No thanks, but I'll remember your honorable words when I'm carving your insides out." He was holding the machete all wrong, waving it around with no finesse or respect for the weapon. "I think I'll keep your blades too. They're very sharp."

"They'll let you die too, you know," I said. "Their gifts don't mean anything. *You* don't mean anything. You think working with them will get you a leg up so you'll live longer, and maybe you will, in the short term." Torr was creeping silently up behind the Bulldozer, so I went on talking to keep him distracted. "But they're still using you, just like they use all of us. You're not a favorite. You won't be saved."

"You sound jealous, Butcher. Want one of these for yourself?" The Bulldozer pounded a fist on his vest. "Fucking the guests and being the crowd favorite not good enough for you?"

Torr took that moment to jump, his arm around the huge gladiator's neck and legs braced on either like he was taking a piggyback ride. He'd lost the mace at some point and held the Bulldozer's neck in a choke hold, his wrapped arm clasping his opposite bicep to cut off the fighter's oxygen.

Almost immediately, the Bulldozer's face turned a bright red, his eyes widening in panic from the lack of air as he fought to get Torr off his back.

"Now, get him!" Torr yelled, clinging to the massive fighter with his full body. The Bulldozer couldn't break the hold on his throat, so he was trying to elbow Torr in the gut.

I darted forward, aiming the sword low at the fighter's legs. He wore leather greaves to protect his ankles and shins, so I drove the sword through his thigh. Only a grunt escaped his mouth, and I couldn't tell if that was due to his pain tolerance or Torr's hold. I stabbed through his other thigh, dark red blood now pouring onto the sand as if from a fountain.

My jabs were quick, and I darted back to stay out of the gladiator's reach. "Torr, let go! He's going down!" I hollered.

The Bulldozer began leaning backwards, like a tree falling. His face was slack, as if he was unconscious already, and quickly losing color. And Torr still did not release his choke hold.

"Torr, let *go!*"

He finally did, but it wasn't fast enough. The Bulldozer fell backward with a crash, pinning Torr beneath him.

A moment passed where everything felt still. Even the people in the audience, whom I was barely aware of, seemed to be holding their breath. Then it hit me.

Oh fucking hell, neither of them were moving.

"Torr!" I dropped the sword, ran to the Bulldozer's hefty side and started pushing, trying to roll his dead weight off the other man. "Fuck, you better be just knocked out under there..."

I had only been shoving for a few seconds when a meaty fist snapped up, fingers clasping around my throat in a surprisingly painful hold. In an instant, my breath was gone. Stars and dark spots danced in my vision, but through them, I could see the Bulldozer's eyes. Open and alert.

And the grimace of effort on his face as he squeezed harder was equally clear. "We all die, Butcher," the gladiator wheezed through his broken nose and choked throat. "I'm just glad you'll die before me."

I clawed at his hand with the last of my flagging strength, desperate to break the hold over my airway, but there was no use. Fuck, why did I drop the sword?

My vision became mostly black, and my lungs burned. It was wholly unfair, but everything about a gladiator's life was. I was sloppy, weak, and uncoordinated from being imprisoned. Even with two of us against one, Torr and I never stood a chance.

This was an end I expected for myself. I just hoped Rori wouldn't be affected by my death too badly. She and Torr loved each other, but her and me? Maybe it was a good thing we never really got a chance to begin. She'd have enough to deal with, mourning the guy she'd known since childhood.

Devin would learn to move on. Nothing could mentally break that guy. Maybe he and Rori could save Hudson.

So many maybes... was my last thought before I gave in and stopped fighting to breathe.

Chapter 9

Devin

"Let me out," I demanded the pitmaster. "It's supposed to be my fight against the Butcher. He's taking *my* kill."

"Step back." The uniformed guard sneered as he slapped his electric prod against my chest, finger hovering over the trigger. "We had a last minute change in the fight. You'll go out when it's your damn time."

I paced back forth behind the gate, for once eager to run out into the sands instead of dreading it. I was forced to watch the Bulldozer collapse on top of the guy the Hunter had called Torrance and then choke Santos until my friend fell limply to the sand. The Bulldozer was now rolling slowly to his feet, despite still bleeding severely from his legs and nose.

That was the thing about this particular fighter. He was slow, and not very well coordinated, but fighting him was like a scrawny child going up against an armored tank. He had yet to lose a fight due to sheer endurance alone. He would not live past this day, but he still wanted to die on his feet.

I could have respected that if he hadn't just killed my friend.

And for Santos, I needed to be the one who ended the Bulldozer's life. It was the least I could do to avenge him.

"Let me out," I repeated to the pitmaster. "I'm up next. What are you waiting for?"

The asshole pulled the trigger on his prod, releasing a crackle of electricity. Before he could stick me with the business end, Tezca got between us and let out a low warning growl. The pitmaster hesitated, because the last guy who tried to electrocute the jaguar lost his hand.

That was when the gate decided to rise, granting me entry into the arena.

I didn't spare the pitmaster a second glance as I ducked underneath and sprinted out onto the sand. Tezca was right at my side and then ran ahead of me straight to Santos' side.

The Bulldozer was on his feet but unsteady and leaking blood like a faucet. My throwing knives were between my fingers the moment he faced me head on, and two were embedded in his eye sockets before he took his next ragged breath.

He didn't seem to know what happened, turning his head left and right as if wondering why he suddenly couldn't see. The realization hit him a moment later when shaking, bloodsoaked hands reached for his own face.

I sent a third knife into his thick neck, since his chest was protected by a convenient stab-proof vest.

The Bulldozer was dead before he hit the ground, which worked well enough for me. I was never one for prolonging anyone's death, no matter how vile they were.

We never knew who, what, or when they would send our next opponents out, so I retrieved my knives first before heading over to check on Santos. "Tezca," I hissed, eyes darting to all the gates and doorways that would bring new bodies into the pit. "Tell me something good, please."

The jaguar had his paws on Santos' motionless chest and was sniffing the man's nose and mouth.

"Is he alive?" I demanded.

Not quite.

I fucking hated how calm that voice sounded. "So he's...dead?"

Also not quite.

"Fuck." I looked up and around at the gathered crowd, feeling powerless. Nearly every seat was filled, with the audience yelling and gesturing, but I couldn't make out what they said. Nor did I care. None of this shit should have been happening out here, like we were animals in a zoo. If Santos was dead, I wanted to mourn him privately.

But that was a luxury none of us had.

I went over to the other guy, Torrance, just to give myself something to do. Putting my ear to his nose and mouth, I did hear breathing. So he must have just gotten knocked out when the Bulldozer flattened him.

He and Santos both looked unkempt, like they hadn't bathed in a week, and pale. Santos looked thinner than I remembered. Had the two of them been holed up together?

The fluttering of wings and a cooing sound brought my attention up to one of the gates. A white dove had settled on top of the archway and peered over at us, as if curious about the unconscious man.

In the next moment, several things happened at once.

The gate just beneath the dove started to open. And I heard a long, rasping, desperate breath of air behind me.

"Fuck," Santos wheezed and coughed. "Ghost?"

"Hey, dude." I didn't take my eyes from the silhouettes of fighters approaching. "Glad you're back, but it's not over yet."

Santos coughed again. "Protect him. I'm getting my machetes."

I didn't know if he was talking to me or Tezca, but I straightened as the Saint approached me calmly in the pit, a pair of short swords made with long cross guards to look like crucifixes in his hands.

The fighter clicked his tongue once, smiling almost pleasantly. "Where's our daring rescue party, Ghost?"

Shit. This was all bad if no one came within the next two minutes.

"I don't know," I admitted.

"That's unfortunate," he mused. "Because if no one is coming to our rescue, there is only one way this ends."

More fighters entered the pit from where he came, fanning out to the sides in an orderly formation. They looked like organized units now, but I knew if a signal didn't come from the Saint, all bets were off and everything would descend into chaos.

I spotted the Hunter, Levi, in one line of fighters, his eyes locked on us. *Wait*, he mouthed insistently at me.

"We have to stall for time," I said to the Saint.

"How much time?"

I shook my head. I didn't know if the woman would come within minutes, today, or even next week. "Just as long as possible."

"You know that won't work," the Saint warned. "They'll come in and start killing us themselves if we don't do our jobs."

The crowd started chanting, *Fight! Fight! Fight!* right then, as if on cue. Pitmasters started closing in, their electric prods crackling. Time was not a luxury we had, and we had nothing to bargain with to gain more.

"What do you say, Ghost?" the Saint pressed. "Business as usual?"

No, no. Not with all of us out here at the same time. I couldn't bring myself to make an attempt on Santos' life, or even the Hunter's.

A metallic hum and series of clanking sounds caught my attention, but it was just the banks of floodlights lighting up the arena. The sky had darkened and now we, the men caught between a hard place and death, were spotlit for the world to see.

The Saint sighed as if he were only mildly disappointed, then rotated his wrists, making those blades flash. "Well, it was a convincing attempt. I'll give you that."

"Wait," I hissed. "Just...spar with me. But don't let anyone make any kills."

"It's too late for that." He almost sounded apologetic. "Everyone's got their own life to save now."

"Wait...wait..." Torrance was rolling over now, coming painstakingly to his knees and then standing all the way up. "Rori's coming. She wouldn't leave us."

"When?" I demanded. "Because we are out of time."

"I don't know, I..." He rubbed the side of his head, wincing like he had a concussion. "You just gotta trust her."

The Saint made that wistful little sigh again, looked over his shoulder, then made a slicing motion across his throat to the other gladiators. Like a flipped switch, they turned on each other with every weapon they had—slicing, punching, stabbing, and bludgeoning the nearest man to death. The Hunter was backed into a corner, fighting for his life.

"No, wait!" I stepped up to the Saint, only to feel the edge of his sword on my throat.

"No hard feelings, Ghost," he said. "It's just survival."

He pulled back to swing, and I went for my knives, leaning into my instincts—my distribution of weight on the sandy ground and the finely tuned muscle memory of my arms—when the floodlights shut off.

I let a knife loose just as the entire colosseum plunged into darkness. It wasn't just the floodlights that were off, the entire canyon had lost power, from the looks of it.

The sounds of fighting ceased as everyone froze in shock. This was unprecedented. In my entire four years in this place, the resort had never fully lost power.

One small, dim light switched on near the top of the colosseum, and everyone turned to look at the source like moths to a flame. A figure stood in the announcer's box, which was rarely used. The figure leaned down, revealing herself to be a woman with short, blonde hair wearing a leather jacket.

"All spectators are to leave now if you don't want to get hurt," she said into the microphone, her voice reverberating across the arena. "The gladiator fights are over. Mystic Canyon Resort is fucking closed."

Chapter 10

Rori

There was no reaction to my announcement at first, only stunned silence. The spectators sitting closest to the announcer box looked at each other with confused expressions. I made a quick hand signal to LJ, who was hidden behind a pillar a few rows down from me. He returned the signal, stepped out of his hiding place, and fired a few rounds of his automatic rifle in the air.

That got people moving. And screaming. But it was the moving part that was important.

While the resort staff dealt with the chaos of a few hundred panicked, stampeding people, now we had to deal with the gladiators.

To keep any curious spectators from looking too closely at us, LJ lobbed a smoke grenade into the stadium seats. Riders from the Valkyrie Network guarded the sections of lower seats to prevent anyone from running out into the sandpit, which was where I needed to go next.

I left the small office and jogged down the stairs in LJ's section, patting his armored back as I passed him. "Good job, keep it up."

"Thanks, boss." He fired a couple more shots in the air to spook an especially slow group of people. "Let's move it, people! The resort is permanently closed for business. No, you may not ask questions, just move your asses."

Hopping over the final barrier, I was out in the fighting pit. And shit, Santos hadn't called it the sands for no reason. The ground was shifty, almost fluid beneath my feet. Every step felt like I was sinking in a little.

A group of men stood across the pit, watching me run toward them. There had to be at least a dozen fighters out there. With all the spectators that had been in the crowd, this looked like it was going to be a massive, battle-royale type of fight.

It seemed we arrived just in time.

I tried to scan faces in the darkness, looking for the two faces that had haunted my every waking moment since I was forced away from this place. One man started toward me, running at full speed, but with all the chaotic noise and lack of light, I couldn't make out his features clearly.

"Stop! I have a gun!" I shouted, drawing my weapon from my holster.

The figure didn't slow until he crashed into me, wrapping me in a hug that felt just as good and familiar as my motorcycle seat.

"Fuck, I'm so glad to see you." Torr's voice was muffled, his face pressed into my neck.

"Torr! Oh my God, are you okay?" I nearly buckled under the weight of him but held on just as tightly as he held me, my hands running up to his face and neck.

"You don't want to kiss me, creep," he warned. "I smell and probably taste like a sweaty asshole."

My laughter was cut short by the feeling of wetness on my hand. I pulled my fingers away from his hair to see dark, sticky blood coating my skin. "Shit, are you hurt? Did you hit your head?"

He pulled away and felt the back of his head with a grimace. "Had a little tussle, but I'll be okay."

"Torr, a head injury is serious."

"Damn, it's so good to argue with you again." He gave me that sexy, lopsided smile, but it was far too early to enjoy our reunion yet.

"Are *you* the one rescuing us?" The question came from a tall, leanly muscled fighter with crosses tattooed next to his eyes. He carried a pair of short swords at his sides, turning to me like he was ready to use them.

"Yes," I answered. "Surprised?"

"You could say that."

"My name's Aurora Wilder." I lifted my chin, projecting my voice so everyone in the fighting ring could hear me. "And I'm here with some capable fighters of my own. We're here to shut down the resort for good, but we need your help." I scanned the faces watching me, my heart leaping when I saw Santos among them. "Help us fight back against the people who have used you, enslaved you, and took away your humanity."

"What do you want from us?" someone called out.

"Nothing!" I spread my arms out. "You are free to go your own ways afterward, or come with us as long as you don't harm my people."

"Yeah, fuck this place!" yelled another guy.

I raised my hand before the hooting and hollering became too loud. "While we're here, I'm requesting you bring me four people alive." I tucked in my thumb to make the number 4. "Bring me Nella and the three guards whose preferred weapons are the spiked brass knuckles."

"I'm gonna kill Nella!"

"I'm asking that you don't."

Bright light filled the arena just as I said that, the floodlights humming as they re-powered. We figured there would be a backup generator somewhere. The darkness was just so I could have enough time to talk to the fighters.

Shouts and movement echoed all around the near-empty colosseum. The armed guards were getting into position at the exits, and I could only hope the gladiators would pick our side and hadn't succumbed to any kind of Stockholm Syndrome in this place.

"Need a gun, Torr?" I pulled my spare from the holster at the small of my back.

"Oh fuck yes, please. Loaded?"

"Yup."

I fired a shot at one of the nearest guards, catching him square in the chest. His hand came away bloody as he collapsed. "They don't have vests!" I called out. They must have never expected revolting gladiators to have guns.

Chaos erupted then, fighters running in all directions as they beat their chests and shouted war cries. I headed for a certain fighter wielding a pair of machetes, sidestepping and looking in all directions to make sure I wasn't a target.

"You really came back." Santos' warmth shone clearly through his features, despite looking thin and more than a little haunted with dark shadows under his eyes.

"Told you I would." I slid one arm around his back, only to get crushed into a full-body embrace against his chest. For a moment, the canyon, the battle, the whole outside world didn't exist beyond me and him. "You okay?" My gaze scanned over him, immediately zeroing on the dark, wet stain running from his shoulder to his elbow. "That arm doesn't look good."

"I got nicked, but it's not serious." Santos lifted and swung both machetes, and I noticed his injured arm didn't raise as high. "At least I got my babies back."

Like I was just gonna let that stand. I grabbed his good arm and tore off a chunk of his sleeve. With no words, only his amused smile, I wrapped the strip of fabric around the wound at his shoulder and tied it off.

"We have medics with us," I told him. "We'll get that taken care of properly as soon as we're out of here."

"Look at you, always taking care of me," he murmured.

I went to touch his face before remembering my fingers were now slick with his blood. "Somebody has to." As much as I wanted to sink into the warmth and intimacy of this moment, the sight of his injury kept me grounded in reality. Peaceful, tender moments had to wait. "You and Torr both look like you've been through it."

"We were. They kept us in the same cell." Santos flipped his blade in his hand to caress my cheek with his knuckle. "You could say we're best buds now."

I laughed. "Oh, really?"

"Yeah, your man's alright."

A four-legged shadow encircled us, Tezca's golden eyes gleaming as he stalked low to the ground, ready to hunt.

"Well hello, handsome." I stroked a hand down the jaguar's velvety back, and Tezca headbutted my hand in reply. "Was he with you?" I asked Santos.

"No. I think he was keeping watch over the Ghost." Santos nodded ahead to where the tall Asian man fought against the canyon's guards alongside the Hunter and the man with tattoos near his eyes. "Suppose we should help out." Santos rolled out his wrists, circling his twin blades in figure-eight patterns.

"The sooner we do, the sooner we can get everyone out of here."

Santos embraced me again, brushing a quick kiss on my forehead as he released me. "I owe you my life, paloma."

He was jogging away, Tezca loping at his side, before I recovered from my mental swooning.

Behind you. Northwest side of the arena.

I turned without hesitating at the sound of Astarte's voice, spotting one of the armed guards with his arm around a woman, holding her in front of him with his electric prod at her temple. The moment I recognized her terrified expression and that long, red braided hair, I sprinted up to that section of seats.

"Let her go!" I demanded, leveling my weapon at the guard's head.

Paige's eyes went even wider as she saw me. "Ma'am? Rori?"

"Stop the uprising or she gets 10,000 volts," the guard hissed, his finger shaking over the trigger of his weapon. "These have been engineered to kill, and I won't hesitate to use it on her."

I narrowed my eyes at him. "I remember you."

"You will! I'll kill this maid if you don't stop everything right now."

"No, you were the one who pointed a gun at me and forced me away from the canyon."

"Yeah, and I told you not to come back. Now people are going to die, and everyone you love will be enslaved."

I laughed, the sound wild and maniacal. "You said you let me go because I was a woman. What did you think was gonna happen?"

My first shot was fast and low, an aim from my hip. The electric prod clattered to the ground as he screamed. The guard clutched his maimed hand, blood pouring from the wound in the back of his palm.

"You like that? Neat little trick my dad taught me." I held out my free arm. "Come here, Paige. I got you."

The poor girl thankfully had enough sense to listen, hurrying to my side and allowing my arm to fall around her shoulders protectively. Holding her trembling form close to me, I took proper aim with my shooting arm, lining up my wrist, elbow, and shoulder.

Now it was the guard staring at me in fear, his mangled hand held tightly against his chest.

"You shouldn't have let me go," I told him. "Your biggest mistake was believing me to be harmless." I fired, and he fell dead in a crumpled heap.

Immediately, I turned to Paige, wrapping her up in both arms. "Are you okay? Did any of them hurt you?"

"W-what's going on?" She shook like a leaf, practically vibrating in my embrace. "I'm scared, I don't know what's happening."

"We're closing down the resort and freeing everyone." I pulled away, taking her face in my hands. "You're getting out, and then we can get you in touch with your family. You'll be able to go anywhere you want, but you have to listen, okay?"

Paige nodded shakily, and I tried not to take it personally that she probably had some amount of fear of me as well.

"Stay hidden and out of harm's way until this is over. We've got to fight our way out, but none of my people will hurt you, okay?" I wasn't so sure about the gladiators, but I knew at least my cousins and the Valkyrie Network riders wouldn't harm a hair on her head.

"Ah, ma'am? Aurora?"

"Yes?" I turned to face the fighter who had walked up behind me and stepped between him and Paige.

It was the Hunter, panting slightly, his bare torso slicked with sweat and blood. He held a hatchet in one hand and a short sword in the other.

"We've found the pitmasters with the brass knuckles. They're bringing them to the center of the pit now."

"Excellent, thank you." I immediately decided that I liked this guy. He seemed noble and honest, not to mention a stellar fighter.

He is trustworthy. A featherlight breeze over my skin and Astarte's words confirmed it.

"Hunter? Would you please watch over her?" I stepped aside to reveal Paige, who seemed calmer since he arrived. "Paige is my friend and was almost taken hostage. I need to make sure nothing happens to her."

The young gladiator straightened, his chest puffing out slightly. "I will guard her with my life."

"Again, thank you." I turned to Paige, giving her shoulder a little squeeze. "Stick with him, okay? You'll be safe."

Even though I had nothing to worry about, I stepped in close to whisper in the Hunter's ear, holding my weapon loosely at my side. "I will know if you hurt her or touch her in any way that she doesn't want. And I won't be merciful on you."

His jaw tightened. "I would never."

"Good." I gave his shoulder a little pat as I slid past him, heading back to the fighting pit.

Shouting and gunfire, with the occasional explosion of a smoke bomb, came from all around me as I walked. Someone had released the rest of the gladiators who hadn't been in the pit, and those were the ones the uniforms seemed to be going after at the moment.

LJ, Carter, and their riders were mostly guarding the exits—allowing guests to escape but not staff. A few others were combing through all rooms and offices of the resort, flushing people out of hiding places or hidden passageways. We knew there had to be procedures in place in case of a breach and figured there would be some amount of escapees.

That was fine with me. I wanted word to reach whoever was at the top of this operation. I wanted to remind them that they weren't all powerful, and they wouldn't get away with enslaving people for much longer.

I wanted them to know I would soon come knocking.

With head bent low and hands tied behind their backs, the three guards sat in a circle on the sandy ground. Two gladiators stood over them, one of them being the man with cross tattoos next to his eyes.

"A gift for you, Aurora," said the tattooed man with a smile, gesturing to the three guards.

"Thank you." I spent a quick moment taking him in. "What are you called?"

"As a gladiator, I was called the Saint." His smile stretched wider. "Now that I'm no longer enslaved, it would honor me to present you with my given name, Solomon."

My gut remained silent about this guy. I couldn't get a read on him, nor did I receive an endorsement of trustworthiness from Astarte. I would have to keep my guard up.

"It's good to meet you, Solomon." I held my hand out. "Welcome back to humanity."

He clasped my palm in a fast, respectful shake. "I'll leave you to it. Or do you wish for us to stay?"

"I'm good, thanks. Think I've got these dicks handled."

He motioned to the other fighter, and together, the two men jogged across the sand pit to join the fray elsewhere.

I turned my attention to the three men tied up on the ground and gave them my best psychotic bitch smile. "Hey, fellas. Remember me?" One of them flinched as I reached down and took the brass knuckles off his belt. That fearful reaction just pissed me off even more.

"So, these are your weapons of choice?" I slid the brass knuckles onto my fingers, testing the weight as I curled my hand into a fist. The finger holes were too big for me, but with a clenched fist, I could still hold the weapon in place. "You like to use them on gladiators who can't fight back, right?"

"Please..."

"It must be *so scary* for you, being surrounded by all these men who kill each other every single day." I tilted my hand from side-to-side as if I were admiring some diamonds on my knuckles. "I bet it feels good to tie them up and get some hits on them. Show 'em who's boss."

"Listen, we just do our jobs! If we don't do as we're told—"

"Hang on, let me try this." I curled my fist tighter, pulling my arm back until the spiked knuckles were next to my face. "I gotta see what all the hype is about."

The man in front of me shut his eyes and turned his head away from me. The other two also found something very interesting to look at away from me.

I waited, my anger calm and cold like a steel blade. I was patient enough to wait all day if it meant serving up this asshole a taste of his own punishment.

A whole minute passed before he was curious enough to take a peek, bringing his head forward just a few inches.

The sound of my fist connecting with his jaw was the most satisfying, sickening noise that ever hit my ears. There was a definite *pop* as I disconnected his lower jaw from his skull. The spikes gave me claws that rivaled a jaguar's, piercing his skin and dragging through the flesh to cut his mouth wide open. And the weight of those knuckles gave my punch the power and follow-through of a man twice my size.

"Damn, you were right." I returned to admiring the brass knuckles like they were a flashy engagement ring. "These are *so* much fun. I think I'll keep them."

The man's screams and protests got lost in the fountain of blood gurgling from his face. I might have cut a bit of his tongue too. Good thing I had my mother's stomach for gore and wasn't squeamish in the slightest.

"Rori!"

I turned to see Carter running toward me, his boots kicking up sand and his assault rifle barely swaying as he held it in front of him.

"What's up, cuz?" I held up the knuckles, about to ask if he wanted a hit on these assholes, but his expression made me reconsider. "Something wrong?"

"Uh, yeah." He stopped in front of me, barely panting. "I started to think this was too easy. But they've got backup coming."

"How many?"

"A shit ton. Coming in from the north. They're less than a mile away. We gotta evac now."

"Has anyone found Nella?" I demanded. "She's the one who runs this place, and I need her."

"No word yet. But you can bet your ass we'll all be trapped in this canyon if we don't leave *now*."

"Fuck..."

If Nella got away, nothing would be fixed in the long run. She and whoever her superiors were would just build another resort—with even better security measures—and enslave more people.

But saving a few lives was still better than letting everyone perish here.

"Alright, fine. Call it."

Carter gave a quick nod and put his fingers to his lips, letting out two loud, shrill whistles. I pocketed my new brass knuckles and followed him, not giving another glance or thought to the men tied up in the center. They were just grunts, hired muscle. Nella was the head of this operation, so it was her brain I needed to pick.

"Head for the elevators!" I yelled to fighters and service staff as we ran through the underbelly of the colosseum. "It's time to go!"

One of the maids darted out from a side room, her arms full of liquor bottles. A gladiator came out from behind her, took some of the loot to lighten her load, and they ran out toward the canyon floor together, holding hands.

"You seen Torr?" I asked Carter, looking around.

"He was searching for that bitch in charge last I saw."

A flash of red hair in my peripheral vision had me spinning on the balls of my feet. "Paige! We've got to go!"

"Coming!" She ran toward us, hefting a drawstring laundry bag over her shoulder. The Hunter was glued to her side, and as he checked their surroundings, he took her bag to carry it in his free hand.

They'd make a cute couple, I thought just as a sense of warning filled my body. All my muscles locked up, like I was being physically held back from going any further.

Take cover.

Astarte's instruction barely finished processing when I grabbed the back of Carter's shirt, dragging him off to the side until we were pressed against one of the curving canyon walls. "Stay covered!" I hollered at the top of my lungs to no one in particular. "Don't go out into the canyon! Paige, get back here!"

Bullets fired down from above us, and Paige and the Hunter went down.

Chapter 11

Torrance

The rain of ammunition came from nowhere.

All had been fairly quiet for a while. Santos and I had been tearing up the offices, looking for any documents about the resort or anybody important that was hiding.

"Oh shit! She just punched the fuck out of that dude with his own brass knuckles." The fighter stared out a window with a scenic view of the colosseum and the east-facing canyon walls. He let out a wistful sigh. "Damn, that's hot."

"I know, man, but we gotta focus." I felt around the heavy wooden desk, tapping my knuckles in search of hidden compartments. "You sure this is Nella's office?"

"Yeah, I mean this is where she brought me and Devin all the time." He didn't give me the specifics of why, and I didn't ask him. I figured it wasn't a monthly review on his accomplishments as a gladiator.

Just as my fingers ran over a tiny deviation in the smooth, polished wood, I heard a rapid series of pops.

"Shit!" Santos and I both dove below the window ledge for cover.

"Is that you guys?" He took a careful peek through the window. "Dressed all in black, shooting down over the canyon ledge?"

I shook my head. "Doesn't sound like the Valkyrie Network."

"Oh fuck, they're shooting down at escapees! Everyone's scattering."

My heart stopped in my chest. No one likely expected the resort to have backup. "You see Rori?"

"No."

"Shit."

"There's a fucking lot of them Torr, they're lining up all along the ridge."

I went to look myself and cursed again. Those who weren't shooting at people went up to Carter's truck and began looting what looked like food, blankets, and medical supplies. One of them promptly shot all four of the vehicle's tires.

That was especially bad for Santos, who needed his shoulder treated as soon as possible.

"Fuck." I checked the magazine of the gun Rori had loaned me. Four rounds left. I had used most of my ammo on the pitmasters who'd been guarding this office.

Santos tightened his grip on his machetes. "What should we do?"

"Find Rori," I decided. "If only one person makes it out of here, it has to be her."

The fighter gave a solemn nod, and we headed for the door together, only to be met by Tezca, his jaguar, on the other side.

Follow.

If the disembodied voice running over my brain wasn't enough, my feet trailed after the big cat like they were puppeteered by him.

"Here, you go." I pushed Santos in front of me so I could guard his back. From what he'd told me of the jaguar's kill streak, I figured the teeth and claws provided adequate cover in the front.

Tezca let us through all kinds of doorways and corridors, some of which were as pitch black as the cell Santos and I had been in together.

"Did you know all this was here?" I asked him as we made our way through a particularly twisty tunnel.

"None. I was only allowed in the pit, my sleeping room, and the chow hall." He paused. "And the sex room, I guess."

The tunnel stopped short, and the black jaguar sat on his haunches in front of a door. On the other side, we could hear shouts and commotion. And...was that Rori's voice?

"Let me open it." I slid past Santos and felt for a knob. When the door pushed open, it reminded me of when they'd shine bright lights into the prison cell to blind us. Spotlights were now positioned at the top of the canyon, shining down on the open area below.

"Torr?"

I looked to my left to see Rori, Carter, and a cluster of gladiators and service staff pressed against the wall.

"Oh, thank fuck."

"Oh, thank fuck."

We didn't laugh about speaking in unison, just wrapped each other in a tight embrace. "Santos and Tezca are here too."

"Have you seen Devin? The Ghost?" Santos scanned the faces of those pressed against the wall, shielded from the guns looming above. His jaw clenched tight when he didn't see his friend.

"I'm sorry, I haven't." Rori looked at him with a mix of determination and sympathy. "We'll find him, though."

"Maybe in an afterlife," Carter muttered. A barrage of shots came down from below, kicking up dirt and gravel while everyone pressed against the wall tried to make themselves flatter. "Because I don't see how we're getting out of here like this."

"They have to come down here at some point," Rori said.

"Do they?" Carter challenged. "And even if they do, can we wait them out? Because they can run for supplies whenever they want."

Santos pointed across the canyon. "Hey, is that—"

"Don't expose your arm!" Rori slapped his hand down against his thigh. "I did the same thing and almost lost my hand. Those assholes are actually decent shots."

The guy jerked his chin instead. "Is that the Hunter?"

"Yeah, and Paige." Rori's mouth tightened. "We had them go ahead of us just before the gunfire started coming down. They're trapped out there."

The couple were huddled together under a picnic table in a clearing smack in the middle of the canyon. Craters littered the table's surface, hundreds of small indents made from gunfire. For once, I was thankful to the resort for having top-of-line, cream-of-the-crop quality everything. Who knew a damn picnic table would be bulletproof?

"She keeps trying to run out there." Carter shot Rori an annoyed look.

"I can't just leave them!" she cried.

"He's right," I said. "We can't have you filled with bullet holes either."

"Fuck." Santos rubbed his mouth, his eyes narrowed on that table. "It's only a matter of time before a round makes it through."

"Ugh, don't say that!" Rori's hands dove into her hair. "We can't just sit here!"

"Unfortunately, that's the only thing we can do," Carter said.

We weren't the only ones taking cover against the canyon walls. People were lined up single file, avoiding the areas most exposed to those preying on us from above. Not everyone was lucky, though. Several bodies laid out in the clearing, unmoving as their blood pooled around them.

Our shooters weren't just sitting and waiting up there either. They walked the rim of the canyon, trying to catch people at different angles. The spotlight kept moving around, sometimes exposing people's feet as targets.

It was abundantly clear, though, that the shooters were in no hurry. They would wait us out if they had to. We were sitting fucking ducks.

"Should've planned for this," Carter grumbled with a shake of his head.

"Excuse me? No." Rori folded her arms and glared at her cousin. "If we'd been any later, these guys would have fought to the death. Can't believe I had to drag your ass out as late as we did."

"Well, maybe if we'd planned to mitigate being trapped in the canyon, we wouldn't be trapped in a fucking canyon right now."

"Fuck you, Carter. Now is not the time to pick a fight with me."

I cleared my throat, "Hey guys, maybe we should focu—"

A spray of bullets rained down, piercing the dirt just inches away from our feet. From out in the clearing, a scream rang out.

"Paige!" Rori cried. She leaned away from the wall as if she were about to run out, but Carter pulled her back.

I could barely see the woman under the table. She was curled up on the ground with the gladiator on his hands and knees over her, shielding her with his body. When he touched her hands or arms as if to reassure her, his hand came away bloodied, and he looked up at us with a grim expression.

"Is she hit?" Rori called out to him.

"Just a graze, I think," the Hunter answered. "But she's bleeding a lot."

"Fuck." Rori's hands went to her hair again. "We have to do something."

"I'm all ears, president," Carter snorted.

"Shut the fuck up! You can talk shit later, but my friend is hurt!"

"She'll survive a graze."

"Not if we're out here for hours and it gets infected! She's not a fighter, Carter. She can't just tough it out."

The woman under the table was sobbing loudly now while the gladiator tried to soothe her, his large hand applying pressure to her wound.

"I'll get her."

I didn't realize the words had left my mouth until everyone stared at me like I'd grown a few extra eyeballs.

"The fuck you will, Torr," Rori said.

Follow.

Everyone looked down this time at the jaguar who returned our gazes with bright golden eyes. That single word had led Santos and I straight to Rori moments ago. Was I really willing to follow the command a second time?

Follow and trust, Torrance. And stay low.

The big cat left the cover of the curving, canyon wall, and I did as he instructed. Despite the background noise of the others yelling at me, I followed.

Sure, it wasn't lost on me that I was walking into open gunfire and therefore scared enough to shit my pants, but there was something else besides that all-consuming fear. A strange sense of calm, like I just knew that everything would be alright.

The pinging of bullets all around me was a poignant reminder not to tempt fate too much, so I kept alongside Tezca, low to the point where I was practically crawling. Don't get me wrong, the jaguar was bigger than most cats, but he wasn't exactly lion or tiger-sized. The broad side of his body barely covered me, but he trotted along calmly, as if we were just going for a stroll in the park.

We reached the picnic table and I dove underneath, blocking the view of the Hunter and Paige from one side. I figured Tezca would go around to block the other end while I assessed the damage.

"Where'd she get hit?" The big gladiator was curled so tightly around the woman, I could barely see her.

"Her leg. Outside of her thigh. Shhh..." He petted her hair and soothed her with the arm that kept her protectively to his chest. His other hand was already stained dark red from putting pressure on her wound.

I took my shirt off, hating to use such a filthy thing, but slowing her bleeding was the number one priority. We'd have to worry about infection later.

"Let me tie this around her injury. You're gonna lift your hand when I say, just enough to put this over the wound, then you're gonna apply pressure again. Got it?"

"Yeah."

The barrage of gunfire continued all around us as we worked, the smell of gunpowder burning my nose. With an errant glance over the Hunter's shoulder, I realized Tezca wasn't blocking the other side. Where the hell was that jaguar?

Once Paige's tourniquet was secure, I ventured a peek around the canyon and was struck dumb by what I saw.

Tezcatlipoca was running laps through the canyon, drawing gunfire *away* from us. The cat wasn't so much a blur as it was a shadow, at times appearing flat and two-dimensional. But then I'd blink and he looked normal again, just fast as hell. It looked like the shots were hitting, but the jaguar never lost a step as he zig-zagged around the open, exposed floor.

"Damn, the Butcher has that cat well-trained," the Hunter remarked.

"Yeah." I fought to keep my head in the game, shaking off the jaguar's complete disregard for the laws of physics. "Listen, can you carry her and run? We'll be better covered at the wall."

"Yeah, of course." The gladiator tenderly shifted his arms around Paige. "I'm gonna put your legs over my arm, okay, hun? Tell me if it hurts."

Paige only made a few soft whimpering noises as the Hunter maneuvered her. Shock and adrenaline had probably set in now. Once they were ready, I turned my focus to the situation outside of our little picnic table bubble.

"Wait for my signal."

Tezca completed another loop around our end of the canyon, the jaguar practically levitating as he moved through space. Like a hornet colony swarming an attacker, all the guns on the rim swung to follow the shadow on four legs. For the moment, at least, we were forgotten.

"Now, let's go!" I scrambled out from under the table, staying nearby to guard the other two coming out.

Driven by some instinct or compulsion, I didn't know which, I pulled out Rori's borrowed gun from my waistband and pointed it at one of the distracted attackers on the ledge. My finger curled around the trigger and a shot rang out an instant later, the man crumpling to the ground.

"What the fuck?" I whispered.

It wasn't my shot that hit him.

"Torr, get *the fuck* over here!" Rori's hoarse screaming finally got through to me, and I sprung into action, heading for the canyon wall. The Hunter and Paige were already there, protected by a little alcove.

"You are going to give me a fucking heart attack—"

"There's someone else up there." I cut off Rori tearing into me and rendered her speechless. "One of them got shot, and it wasn't from me."

"Was it someone down here returning fire?"

"I don't think so. It looked like they got hit from behind."

"Carter?" Rori turned to her cousin. "Are any of your people still up here?"

"No. The ones posted at the elevator jumped down here to start hurrying people up. We're all down here."

Santos voiced the conclusion that all of our brains were struggling to comprehend. "Someone else is up there? Helping us?"

"We don't know that," Carter muttered. "It could have been an accidental friendly fire. Or worse, a competitor."

"Oh my God, look!" Rori pointed, forgetting all about her own rule of keeping arms out of sight.

More of our attackers were being taken out with extremely precise shots, to the point where their comrades were looking around as if confused. Most were even turning their attention away from us down in the canyon.

"I don't know who's giving it to us, but this is our chance." Rori popped a fresh magazine into her gun and yelled at the top of her lungs. "If you have a weapon, return fire now!"

She didn't have to tell anyone twice. Riders, gladiators, service workers, anyone who'd gotten their hands on guns, emerged from their cover just to gain enough clearance for shooting.

Now we weren't the ones who were trapped.

Those who weren't getting shot were falling to their deaths into the canyon. We were barely even hitting them and they dropped like flies.

Somewhere between an instant and an eternity later, the canyon fell silent.

Not a single living soul remained in sight on the rim. Everything was still, even Tezca, who had taken to calmly lying down on top of the bullet hole-ridden picnic table.

"Is it over?" Paige whispered.

"Highly doubt that." Rori checked her ammo, then motioned to me, Carter, and Santos. "Hunter, you stay with her. You three with me."

Santos and I fell into position on either side of her and later, I would recall how natural and seamless the formation had been.

We stayed just on the edge of cover, heading toward the main elevator that carried us in on our first trip here. I guess for me, it still was my first trip, and hopefully my last one.

The elevator cage was at the top, the inside of the glass walls now covered with some kind of stiff, gray sheet. I assumed it was some kind of bulletproof shield for getting people out safely.

The four of us kept moving toward the panel with the button that would bring the elevator down. Carter, in front, kept sweeping his gun back and forth in front of him, and I did the same on Rori's left. On her right, Santos' remained hypervigilant with his machetes at the ready.

Once about ten feet away from the panel, we heard a metallic clanking and an electric hum.

"It's moving!" Rori hissed. "Someone's coming down!"

Without another word, the four of us pressed into a dipping curve in the canyon wall, covering ourselves but within full view of the elevator door. The three of us with guns pointed at the slowly descending elevator and waited.

"That shield sure is a cock tease," Carter muttered.

"So this is what guys feel like when they're about to see some titty," Rori mused.

No one else commented as the elevator made its descent. When it gently touched down on the floor pad, we collectively sucked in a breath and tightened our hold on our weapons.

The door slid open and...a *dog* came loping out?

No, wait. That was a wolf. And one I'd seen before.

"Lupa?"

The wolf ran straight toward us, tongue lolling out and lips pulled back in a canine smile.

Rori stepped in front of Carter and shoved his gun muzzle down. "Put your weapons down, they're allies."

"How the, what—"

Her cousin was still sputtering his disbelief when Gwen stepped out of the elevator, her smile a bit more reserved. "Hey, Rori. Torr. You guys really should get better at accepting help when it's offered."

Chapter 12

Rori

"I'm so, so grateful you didn't listen to me on the phone," I said, pulling Gwen into a hug for at least the third time.

"I just knew the resort had more tricks up their sleeve that they'd never reveal to guests." She returned my squeeze, then pulled back with a cheeky grin. "Plus, I had to return your bikes."

"Oh, Gwen…" My motorcycle was my baby, my most prized possession in the world. And it was crazy to think that I hadn't given her a thought while I was hellbent on rescuing Santos and Torr. But now, thinking of reuniting with my treasured steed, controlling and riding her in the way I only knew how, brought tears to my eyes.

"My dads' riders' brought them out of storage and rode them over," Gwen said with a reassuring look. "I promise your bikes were well taken care of."

"Oh, I trust you. I'm sure they were." I sniffed and blinked away my emotion quickly. "So, this is your parents' club?" I looked around at the impressive fleet of bikers who'd come to our rescue, who were now helping people up the elevators out of the canyon, searching more of the resort, treating injuries, or just shooting the shit with Carter's men.

"Yeah, Chasing Death MC."

I cocked my head, letting that name bounce around my brain like a pinball. "I think my uncles know them. Sons of Odin MC."

Gwen's eyes widened, and then she bobbed her head up and down in a nod. "Oh, yup. I've heard some stories about the Sons of Odin."

"Don't corrupt my innocent ears." I jokingly slapped my palms to my head. "But seriously, Gwen, I can't thank you enough. We owe you big time."

She shook her head, her artfully crafted eyebrows furrowing. "Just find the people responsible for this. And end them for good."

"That's the plan. Speaking of." I hopped out of Carter's truck bed, where we'd been sitting together. "Nella still hasn't been found. I need to at least see a body before I'm satisfied."

"I'll leave you to it. I'll see if these guys need any help." Gwen headed off to where a group of Chasing Death medics were packing up supplies.

The worst of the injuries had been treated, including Santos' shoulder and Paige's graze. We'd be ready to head to the safe houses in a couple of hours. I couldn't believe all that had happened occurred over several hours. It felt like I had blinked and now dawn was teasing the eastern edge of the horizon.

A handful of gladiators and service staff had died when caught in the crossfire, including two maids. Paige didn't have much of a reaction when I told her, though she may have still been in shock. With a blank expression, she only said she didn't know them. I wondered if she had been discouraged from forming friendships with other maids, just like the fighters were.

Well, she wouldn't have to worry about that anymore.

Torr and some of the others were burying those who had died trying to escape the resort. As for the ones who attacked us? The vultures and other desert animals would take care of them just fine.

I went down the elevator into the canyon to find a disgruntled Santos waiting for me. He was shirtless with a fresh bandage taped over his shoulder, wearing a clean pair of canvas pants and black leather boots. My heart did a little flutter as the elevator door opened. Who knew if he'd ever take it up, but he'd look so damn hot straddling a motorcycle.

"Don't you look happy to see me," I teased, approaching him.

His frown lifted into a smile that took my breath away. "Always, paloma."

The need to kiss him rode me hard, and I was never one to ignore my urges. So I did, rising up on my tiptoes and bringing a hand to his nape, while our lips connected so effortlessly.

He and Torr had been given clean clothes, cleansing wipes, and toothbrushes from the toiletry supply. Just enough to remove the grime of their captivity before getting into a real shower.

As a result, Santos actually tasted and smelled decently. His lips were just as soft and pillowy as I remembered, his tongue slick against mine now that he'd chugged some water and was decently hydrated.

The bossy persona I'd taken on to see this mission through—the reason why Carter had sarcastically called me president—melted away as Santos didn't let me break the kiss, his good arm coming around my back to keep me pressed to his chest.

"Fuck, I'm so glad you're okay," I whispered when he finally let me breathe. "The whole time I was away from you, I was terrified I'd be too late."

"But you weren't." His fingers came to my chin, holding my face while he let his forehead rest on mine. "I believed you'd make every effort to get back here, but holy shit, I had no idea you'd be such a badass."

"What, me?" I laughed bitterly. "People died. I got us trapped in here."

"Everyone knew death would be a risk. The vast majority of us are alive, and thanks to you, free."

I sighed and leaned against his supportive weight, suddenly feeling much more tired. "There's still so much left to do."

"You have more support now. Word of this will spread."

"That's what I'm afraid of." I leaned away, reluctantly stepping out of his embrace. "On that note, this entire canyon needs to be combed from top to bottom for Nella. She needs to be found or else we have to assume she escaped."

Santos' face hardened. "There's still no sign of the Ghost—I mean, Devin—either. I'll bet you anything he's hunting for her."

"Why, something personal there?"

He blew out a long breath. "You could say that."

That sounded like an off-limits conversation to me, so I grabbed his hand and laced my fingers through his. "Want to search for them together?"

There was that smile again. I swore just touching him, talking to him, validating him in any way, made him happy.

And that made me happy.

"It's a date." Santos brought our connected hands up and kissed the back of my palm.

"Hunting for an enemy together, so romantic." I grinned at him. "Let's check with the others and see what areas have already been cleared."

Some of the Chasing Death guys had found hidden corridors to a maze of underground garages. Santos asked one of them if they'd seen Devin, and the man pointed down a corridor they hadn't cleared yet.

We headed in that direction, our path illuminated by security lights in the ceiling and along the walls in a vast tunnel reinforced by concrete pillars.

"Did you know any of this was here?" I asked Santos.

"Not a clue," he said.

"They really cut deep into the rock here." I turned to glance behind me. "This whole place must have taken at least a decade to build. It's amazing no one found out."

"If they did, they were probably paid off," Santos muttered. "Or captured or killed. Any of those seem likely—whoa."

We stopped at the same time. The tunnel had opened up into a flat expanse of steel and concrete. A parking garage.

"Holy shit." Santos walked up to one of the few cars that remained, a sleek red sports car that looked as though it could barely fit two people. "I used to watch street races of these things. Never thought I'd see a real one up close ever again."

"The guests must have panicked and piled into the bigger vehicles when we showed up," I mused. There were only a handful of other cars in the garage, all compact and flashy. The air had a slight burned-rubber smell, and dark tire tracks criss crossed all over the concrete floor. A bunch of guests definitely left in a hurry. Good fucking riddance.

Santos cupped his hands around his mouth. "Devin! You in here?" His voice echoed off the ceiling and floors in the mostly-empty garage.

Something prickled along my senses on the left side, like fingers skimming lightly down my arm. I looked in that direction, seeing only a bright blue car before swinging my gaze in the opposite direction.

The prickling only intensified, and then I heard Astarte's voice. *Look closer.*

A flash of movement caught my eye and drew my attention back. All at once, my instincts roared.

"There!" I sprinted toward the blue car just as Nella took off, running away from it.

She ran hard but not fast. It seemed she'd been running and evading someone for a while because she was clearly gassed, breathing hard in her effort to get away. I pumped my arms and legs, gaining on her quickly. She had a head start, but I'd be caught up to her in seconds.

I was so focused on catching her that I'd forgotten about Santos' friend, Devin.

"Devin, don't!" I heard Santos yell.

Something bright silver flashed in my vision, and then with a cry, Nella went tumbling down. I had so much momentum that I nearly tripped over her, but I was able to jump over her crumpled form instead. When I turned back to her, Nella was clutching her leg where the handle of a knife stuck out of her calf muscle.

Devin emerged from a dark side corridor, as silent and deadly as his gladiator name, the Ghost. His face was stony, determined, with a knife in each hand at his sides.

"Devin." I stepped in front of Nella, blocking his path to her. "Listen to me, I can't let you kill her."

"Move." His voice carried a dark edge of calm. "I have every right to kill her."

"I need her alive for information." I extended a hand in an attempt to calm him. "If she dies, so do the secrets of Mystic Canyon. They'll be able to start up again, somewhere else. We need to shut the whole operation down for good, and we can't do that unless she talks."

Despite her stab wound and the fact that she must have been in extreme pain, Nella let out an indignant snort. Without taking my eyes from Devin, I said, "Santos, secure her, will you?"

"You got it." I heard his footsteps, a scuffle, and then a screech of pain and the sound of him dragging Nella across the floor. Hopefully it was by her injured leg.

"Look, I don't dislike you," Devin said, which seemed to be a high compliment coming from him. "But you don't know everything she's done to us, to me and him especially." He nodded at Santos. "And I'm really fucking sick of taking orders from women. So, no offense, but she's not leaving this garage alive."

"I get it, Devin. I really do." I brought both hands up now, palms out toward him. "She's hurt you, and you want revenge. I completely understand, and I'm willing to let you have it." My heart kicked a furious beat in my chest while I tried to focus on Devin's face instead of his knives. I knew exactly how deadly he was with those. "But I'm asking you to look at the big picture here. If she dies, more women just like her will continue to mistreat innocent men, just like you two. It won't stop with her, Devin. Do you understand?"

He didn't answer, but there was a tiny flicker in his expression. I would have missed it if I blinked. Devin wasn't a dumb guy, he wouldn't have survived being a gladiator this long if he was. He had to see my reasoning, and I could only hope that some thread of rational thinking was breaking through all the hurt and aggression clouding his judgment.

Finally, his dark eyes lifted to meet those of the man standing behind me. "You in favor of this?" he asked Santos.

"I trust Rori." Well, if that didn't make me swell with satisfaction. "I agree that Nella needs to be questioned. But once Rori has the information she needs...maybe we can work out a deal."

Devin's gaze returned to me, snide and resentful. "So I'll have your permission to kill her after you're done? Should I be grateful for this?"

"You can feel however you want," I told him. "But yes, I'm in charge, so you'll need my permission. And I'm willing to make a promise to you now, with conditions."

"Of course," Devin scoffed.

"If you give me your word that you'll give her a swift death—no torture or rape—I'll hand her over to you after I'm done with her."

"Torture or rape?" Devin's lip curled like those words were the most distasteful he'd ever heard. "What kind of person do you think I am?"

"I have no idea. All I know is you're a gladiator. But I'm willing to make a bargain with you, Devin. So there's my offer." I folded my arms, relaxing now that I'd gotten him to think a little more rationally. "You can have your kill, a clean kill, if you can wait for me to question her. What do you say?"

There was a long silence, during which Devin's eyes went Santos again. After an eternity, he said, "Fine. I agree."

I sagged with relief and felt Santos do the same behind me. "Thank you. Now how would you like to leave this place?"

Devin holstered his knives into his belt. "What was your name again?"

"Aurora. But I go by Rori."

"Like the aurora borealis," Santos chimed in, hoisting Nella up by her arms so she could walk—or rather, limp—out of the cavern with us.

"The what-now?" Devin fell in behind Santos and Nella while I led the way out.

"You know, the northern lights. They light up the sky way up north where it's fucking cold all the time."

Devin made a scoffing sound. Then he muttered something that sounded like, "The light and the guard."

"What was that?" I glanced over my shoulder as we came up to the tunnel's exit.

"Nothing," Devin called back. "Just something I heard once."

Chapter 13

Santos

After getting her stab wound treated, Nella was hogtied and thrown in the bed of a pickup truck, which was damn satisfying to see. She wouldn't be tortured or abused, but nobody gave a shit about making her ride comfortable.

Once the canyon was ransacked and everyone's injuries patched up, we loaded up and headed for the safe houses. And for the first time in my life, I rode a motorcycle.

Well, hung on the back of one, rather. I got paired up with Torr while Devin rode with Rori's cousin, Carter. Rori led the pack, her ride occupied only by her. When everyone figured out where they were sitting or riding, Rori raised her arm straight in the air, whistled so loudly that it echoed across the landscape, stomped her foot down against the side of her bike, then tore off with a roar.

Everyone followed in a steady procession. Torr's bike jolted forward, prompting me to tighten my hold around his waist. He gave me a little pat on my hand and I laughed, flipping him off.

Once I got used to the speed at which we were moving, felt the wind racing across my skin, it hit me like a brick wall.

We were out. Fucking out. We were free.

The thought was just as overwhelming as it was liberating. I hadn't seen the outside world in years. Hadn't just...done whatever the hell I wanted in years. I felt like a child surrounded by toys, not knowing which one to pick. The fact that I was completely free now left me paralyzed.

I didn't even know *what* I could do anymore. How much had the world changed since I'd been captured? I'd been a criminal before. It was all I knew. One thing was certain—there was always a living to be made as a mercenary. But I wasn't sure if I wanted to do that anymore, not that it'd been much of a want in the first place but a necessity. I needed to survive, and my first job fell into my lap at 19. Turned out, I was good at it. So I kept doing it.

Round and round my thoughts went, focusing on nothing in particular. At some point, Torr hit the brakes and we slowed, my chest leaning lightly into his back. Up ahead, Rori was sitting on her idling bike, talking to a man in a small shack next to the road. He looked to be in his early forties, had a black leather vest on, and carried an automatic rifle almost as long as my arm span.

They talked for a few minutes and then Rori burst out laughing. She and the man embraced like they were family, and then he settled back into his gatehouse. Rori signaled for us to continue forward, and on we went.

"Who was that?" I asked Torr as we pulled forward.

"Family friend," he answered. "Well, biker family, not blood. Slick rode with Rori's fathers back in the day, so he's basically another uncle to her."

Slick was not the only guard we passed, he was merely the first. Our whole caravan went through three more checkpoints, all manned by armed, black-vested bikers. All of whom seemed to know Rori like she was their sister or daughter.

Our elevation changed constantly too. It was a never ending up and down, the gears on the motorcycles putting in the work to make us climb and descend. We didn't go through any more canyons, thank

God, but stunning mountain passes and valleys that became greener the longer we rode. The air became cooler too, a sign that we were leaving the blistering heat of the desert for somewhere more temperate.

When Rori stopped her bike for the fifth time, it wasn't at another checkpoint but a cleared plot of land set with a few buildings and tons of open space. There were two houses facing opposite each other on a gravel road cul-de-sac. Between them was a detached garage, which didn't seem entirely necessary because each house had its own garage door.

Nonetheless, a black pickup truck was parked in front of the detached garage. A dark-haired woman sat on the edge of the truck bed pulling bungee cords free and folding back a tarp over the bed's contents. She looked up and grinned as everyone pulled into the cul-de-sac.

"Bitch! Took you long enough!" The dark-haired woman cackled as she jumped gracefully to the ground, arms wide open to the sides as she approached Rori.

I tensed, only because I could clearly see the two guns in their holsters under the woman's leather jacket.

"Fuck you, bitch!" Rori laughed in return as she hopped off her bike, spreading her arms in the same gesture.

I only relaxed when the two women embraced hard, nearly knocking each other to the ground. Rori was a few inches taller, so she would have won that fight, but the other woman had a similar air of not-to-be-fucked-with.

"Everyone!" Rori turned to face us all, her arm around the other woman's shoulders. "This is my cousin, Valorie. She brought the lion's share of supplies for you all, and we're going to divvy it up fairly. Everyone will get the very basics that they need, but if there's anything else like meds, phones, what-have-you." She wrapped her arm playfully around Valorie's throat, holding her in a headlock. "Take it up with this bitch."

Valorie laughed, wrestling out of Rori's hold. "We've got a mobile clinic with a nurse and a doctor arriving soon too. So anyone with more serious injuries will be tended to."

"If you're not injured, start lining up with Val for supplies," Rori said. "There are clean beds and showers inside both houses and food in the pantries. But please, do not take more than you need. There is enough for everyone." Her expression went serious, eyes sharpening as they scanned over the roughly two-dozen faces that needed refuge. "If I find anyone stealing or hoarding anything, that is where my generosity will end. Medics?" She lifted a hand, motioning for those riders to come forward as she walked to the driveway of one of the houses. "Let's assess the injured here to hold over until the mobile clinic arrives."

"Goddamn it." Torr sounded angry as he kicked the bike into motion again, driving forward slowly to get out of the way of traffic. He headed for the edge of the driveway where Rori and the medics were setting up.

"Something wrong?" I asked when he parked and shut the bike off.

"She's treating the injured when she's fucking exhausted. Look at her, I bet she's been awake well over twenty-four hours."

Now that I could see her up close, Rori did look burnt out. There were large, dark circles under her eyes, and she moved slower than she had at the resort. Her smile as she snapped on a pair of sterile gloves had no light behind it.

"You go talk her into getting some rest. I'm gonna claim a bed and some food for her." In the work of a moment, Torr was off the bike and heading into the house through the garage, which was now open.

Rori and the medics used folding tables to set out a random mix of medical supplies, which looked like a bunch of first aid kits that had been combined into one pot. I took a seat on the folding chair next to Rori and got straight to business.

"You need to rest," I told her.

As if I hadn't said anything, she made a little spinning motion with a gloved finger. "Turn and sit the other way so I can check out your shoulder."

"Did you hear what I said?"

She said, "Yes. I'm just choosing not to listen."

"When did you last sleep?"

"I don't remember. Doesn't matter, I've been running on caffeine. Turn the other way, Santos."

"Paloma, you're exhausted. What if you accidentally stick a toothbrush in my shoulder?"

The laugh that erupted from her began as an adorable snort, then she slapped a hand over her mouth and laughed louder. She was too tired to hold back any of it and started wiping tears from her eyes. "Oh God, my mom would kill me."

"Why's that?" I wanted her distracted. Maybe if she wasn't so *go-go-go* all the time, she would realize how exhausted she really was.

"Because she's a doctor." If anything, that seemed to make Rori more focused on treating me. "If you're not gonna turn around, I'm just gonna check your shoulder out this way." She clicked on a pen light and stuck it behind her ear before proceeding to unwind the bandage at my shoulder.

"She the reason you're a medic?"

"I'm not, really," she said. "I know first aid and CPR, plus she taught me how to treat injuries in the field. None of my training is formal, except technically, I'm a phlebotomist. I'm certified to draw blood and stuff, but that's about it."

"How'd you get into that?" I watched her face intently as she spoke, taking note of her fight to keep her eyelids open.

She shrugged, inspecting my shoulder wound with the pen light. "Just something I did while trying to figure out what to do with my life."

"And did you? Figure that out."

"Nah. Kind of got interrupted by a talking bird telling me to come on this grand adventure."

I smiled at her. How could I not? She was checking out my wound while trying not to nod off where she stood.

"Well, I gotta say, you're pretty good at the whole 'riding to peoples' rescue' thing."

Rori snorted. "Yeah, 'til I totally forgot to watch our asses and we got trapped for a hot minute."

"Hey, it was your first time. And you still gave all these people their lives back."

"Mmhm." She rubbed her eyes against her upper arm and blinked several times. If her hands weren't busy, I was certain she'd slap herself to stay awake. "Your shoulder looks good. Doesn't look infected, and it's healing up super fast, looks like."

"Thanks, doc."

She huffed at that and started wrapping a fresh bandage around the wound. "Make sure you have a real medic look at it in a couple of days. Speak up if you get a fever or it starts hurting more."

"And *you* make sure to get some rest. Your man will have my ass if you don't, and he was just starting to like me." I angled my head, looking up at her. "Don't make me look bad, paloma."

Rori started to laugh just as Torr returned to the garage. "You." He pointed menacingly at her. "Come here."

"Torr, seriously. I'm okagh—hng!"

While her mouth was open, he jabbed a slice of buttered and jellied toast between her lips. He had folded it in half to ensure the toppings didn't go everywhere in the ensuing fight. "Chew," he ordered. "Then swallow. Don't worry, I've got water too."

Rori rolled her eyes but obeyed, devouring the toast quickly in several bites. She even licked a drop of jelly off of Torr's thumb.

"Good girl," he purred. "Here."

She accepted the bottle of water, acting like it was the last thing she needed, but she barely took a breath as she gulped the whole thing down.

"Was it necessary to be so dramatic?" she asked dryly when finished.

"With you, yes." His hands went to her waist, where his fists curled into her leather jacket and pulled her forward. "Now, I've claimed a bed for you—"

"No, I don't want a bed," she argued. "Give it to someone from the canyon. I'll crash on the floor or somewhere." She angled her head toward me. "Let Santos have it."

"Nah, Torr's right. You take a bed, you deserve it." I insisted. "I'll find Devin, and we'll figure out a place to crash. Don't worry about us."

"Thanks, dude." Torr beamed in my direction before returning to look at Rori. "See? You're outvoted, and you're falling asleep on your feet. Go. Lie. Down."

"Everyone else is tired too! Why are you two ganging up on me?"

"Because there's still shit to do later, and you need to be sharp for it." Torr picked her up by the waist, spun around, and set her back down facing the door leading into the house. "Like questioning that prisoner and figuring out what we're going to do with everyone in the long run."

He started to gently push Rori toward the door, but she stopped short. "Wait, Nella! I forgot! Where is—"

"Carter's got her in the basement," Torr said. "He's got a 24-hour guard rotation on her, don't worry. See what I mean though? You wouldn't have forgotten about her if you were at peak energy."

Rori sighed, her body swaying as she finally allowed herself to be pushed by Torr. "Fine, fine. I'll take a little catnap."

"Nope, you're getting eight hours minimum. Hopefully closer to ten."

"I swear to God, if you don't stop acting like *another* father to me..." Their voices faded as they went into the house, and I abandoned my chair to go in search of Devin.

I found him in a little copse of trees behind the houses. He was throwing knives into one of the skinniest tree trunks with Tezca hanging out near him. It was interesting, how the jaguar seemed to go wherever he was needed most. Since finding Rori, I didn't feel like I needed as much of his guidance. I had found what I was looking for.

Devin, on the other hand, seemed far from content. He was on-edge, using all of his strength to sink his daggers deep into the tree trunks. If his targets had been men, he'd be decapitating them.

"Hey," I said casually, keeping clear of his throwing zone. "You find a place to sleep?"

"I'm not staying here." To any normal person he would have sounded calm, but I heard the seething anger in his voice.

"Where you going, then?"

"I don't know, but not here." He glanced at me, wiping one of his blades with his sleeve. "I don't trust them."

Tezca yawned then, as if he'd heard this conversation before and was tired of it.

"I trust them," I said. "Torr was in the dungeon with me. Rori kept her word on coming back for us. That doesn't mean anything to you?"

"No." He let fly three blades at once, and they sunk into the wood in a perfect vertical line. "You've always been too quick to trust, Santos. To me, the only thing I'm sure of is that people act in their own best interests. They didn't free us from the canyon out of the goodness of their hearts."

Like Tezca, I wanted to yawn, and not just because I was exhausted. This was the same old argument and the biggest sore spot between Devin and me. Despite proving myself the deadliest fighter in the pit, not to mention fucking whoever I had to to survive, he thought I was too soft-hearted. Like I only trusted Rori just because she was pretty, or good in bed, or whatever. No, I was a realist. I could tell the difference between sincerity and manipulation. Tezca himself had told me Rori was the real deal.

Devin was just so damn prickly and such a cynic that all he saw in anyone were liars and manipulators. He probably wouldn't recognize a sincere act of kindness if it stabbed him with his own knife.

"What about Nella, then?" I asked him. "You're just gonna leave without taking your chance to kill her?"

He had brought his hand behind his head, ready to throw again, but ended up dropping that arm to his side. "That's the main reason why I haven't taken off yet."

"Main reason, huh?"

He turned to face me, a smile pulling at his lips. "Like I'd leave you behind, dick."

"Give them a chance," I said. "I mean, we don't have to fucking fight anymore. Can we just relax and celebrate that?"

Devin scoffed, his smile growing. "I don't know what the fuck I'm going to do tomorrow."

"Anything you want. That's the beauty of it." My hands rested at my hips, hovering over the handles of my machetes. There was no doubt in my mind I'd be keeping them. The world wasn't any kinder just because I was free. I was certain Devin felt a similar attachment to his knives. These weapons had been our only instruments of power, had kept us alive to see us through this escape.

"I think I'm gonna sleep in. Let the sun wake me up." I crossed my arms over my chest. "You know how damn long it's been since I've gotten out of bed whenever the hell I wanted?"

"I don't know if I ever have." Devin dragged a fingertip along the edge of a knife.

"Stay a while then. And try it."

Devin's expression hardened, his dark eyes like obsidian as he looked up at me. "She gets one chance to fuck us over, got it? One. Maybe you'll be able to forgive her or whatever, but that's not me, Santos. I am *done* with women trying to control me."

"I hear you," I said with an affirming nod. "I think that's fair."

"Do you?" he challenged. "Because you look perfectly happy being a third-wheel boy toy."

I glared at him. He could talk shit about me all he wanted, but I wasn't about to let him slander Rori. "That's not what it is."

"No? I'm not blind, Santos. You hook up with her like three

times, get locked up with her man for a few days, and now you think you're part of a happy throuple? Come on, you're not *that* naive."

I started to regret coming out here, shaking my head as I looked at our surroundings. "You know what you sound like, Dev?"

"Like I'm right?"

"Like you're jealous."

He barely reacted, but I knew his tells, as subtle as they were. A twitch of his eyebrow. A slight hardening of his mouth. A squeeze of his knife's handle.

"Whatever." Devin faced the tree trunk again, preparing for another practice throw.

"Yeah, whatever," I agreed. "I was gonna suggest we room together, but it doesn't sound like you're keen."

"What, you mean Rori and Torr haven't made space in their bed for you? Color me shocked."

I shook my head again, turning back toward the houses. "Get some rest, man. We all need it."

"Like I can get a wink of sleep in this place," he muttered before letting his blades fly.

Chapter 14

Rori

I slept way too long. I knew it immediately from how refreshed I felt when my eyes fluttered open, from how good it felt to stretch and groan.

"Goddamn it, Torr." I rubbed my eyes and brought my feet to the floor, stretching once more now that I was upright.

I was annoyed that he let me sleep for so long but grateful too, I had to admit. He'd insisted I get the biggest bedroom in the house too, which was a total waste, especially when everyone else had to share rooms. I had been too tired to fight him about it yesterday, but soon I would have the energy.

Through the window, the sun peeked over a distant mountain range. I couldn't tell if it was rising or about to set. The room felt a little chilly, so I guessed it was early morning.

That meant I slept—damn—around twelve hours? Yep, way too long.

Rummaging through a duffel bag set near the bed, I found a pair of sweatpants and a hoodie that were too big but would be comfy. With one deep inhale of the hoodie, I knew—these were Torr's clothes.

The smile could not stay off my face as I pulled the clothes on. *Look at my guy, being all thoughtful and shit.*

I heard a soft murmuring of voices as I came down the stairs and found Carter, LJ, Valorie, Paige, and the Hunter all hanging out in the kitchen.

"Mornin', sunshine!" LJ called as he saw me come down. "Want coffee?"

"Oh God, please," I groaned.

"Nice cowlick, Alfalfa." Valorie grinned at me over the rim of an ancient, chipped mug that said, *Save the Tatas* next to a faded pink ribbon. "You slept like the dead, by the looks of it."

I felt the back of my head and, sure enough, my hair was sticking straight up right at the crown. "Wasn't by choice, but yeah, I guess so."

"You deserved it," Paige told me from where she sat next to the Hunter.

"You sound like Santos," I grumbled but smiled at her as I took a seat between Carter and the Hunter.

"Who?" asked the ex-gladiator, his brows drawn together in confusion.

"Oh, um, the Butcher." I raked a hand back through my hair, probably making it stick up some more. "I probably should've asked him if it was okay to give out his real name."

"I saw him going around saying hello and introducing himself by name last night," Carter piped up. "Seems there isn't a need for gladiator names anymore, right?"

"I dunno, I do kind of like being the Hunter." The man in question extended a hand to me. "My given name is Levi, by the way."

I shook the hand he gave. "Great to meet you. And thank you for taking such good care of my girl, Paige, by the way."

The two of them blushed as they exchanged glances. Yeah, such a cute couple.

"I was honored to do it," Levi said softly, his eyes rapt on her. "I only regret that she got hurt at all."

"Stop." Paige gave him a playful smack on his bicep. "You couldn't have done anything to stop it."

"I could have taken that bullet myself."

"Ugh." Paige rolled her eyes and looked exasperated but couldn't hide the blush that deepened. Or the smile twitching at her mouth.

"They were just telling me the story." Valorie finished off her coffee with a smack of her lips. "Damn, I wish I could have been there and shot some slave-driving assholes."

Carter snorted. "Your ass would have been shot within the first minute of arriving."

"Why, 'cause I'm a girl?"

"No, you're just fucking loud. They'd hear you a mile away."

"Aw, fuck off, Carter."

Their bickering served as amusing white noise as I nursed my coffee. When there was a lull in the shit-talking, I asked, "Are Torr and Santos asleep somewhere?"

"Yeah." Val nodded. "They helped me dispense supplies and get people settled after you went down."

"'Course they did," I grumbled through another slurp of coffee. Those two made *me* quit working, then ran around like busy bees themselves. Hypocrites. Sweet, lovable hypocrites.

I turned to Paige after my first cup was drained. "How are you feeling?"

"Oh, better!" she beamed. "My leg is still a little sore, but I can walk without much trouble. Would you like me to tidy your room?"

"No! I mean, sorry, I don't mean to yell, but no, Paige. Focus on recovering." I smiled at her, absolutely loving the way she kept sneaking glances at the fighter next to her. "You can do whatever you want now, including *not* tidying up after anybody."

She returned my smile nervously. "That's the thing. After being, um, in service for so long, I'm not sure what to do. The other maids have said similar things. Maybe it's silly, but I'm a little anxious, to be honest. I have no idea what's next, and I have no idea where my moms and sister are."

"It's not silly at all," the Hunter reassured her. "The fighters feel the same way. Many of us don't know what to do with all this free will."

"You guys don't have to worry," I said. "We have resources that can put you in touch with your families. If you don't have people, you're welcome in Sevier, where Valorie's from." I nodded across the table to my cousin. "Or Four Corners, where I grew up. Both territories are very friendly to refugees from all kinds of situations. They have streamlined paths for housing, education, career opportunities, the whole thing. You'll be making your own choices for everything, but there's a structure to it all, so you won't be overwhelmed. You guys will be fine, trust me."

"Oh, that's such a relief." Paige released a long sigh, like she was no longer carrying a heavy burden. "A new territory sounds amazing. If my family's found, I hope they're already there or will be willing to move."

"Once we find your people, we can ride out to retrieve them, then escort them back to ensure safe passage," Valorie piped up. "It's one of the many services the Valkyrie Network provides."

"Thank you," Paige breathed with a hand to her chest. "I can't believe this nightmare is over."

"The world is your oyster now." The Hunter's eyes brightened as he stared at her. He was so smitten, it was adorable. "If you could do anything in the world and there were no limits, what would that be?"

"Oh, um..." Paige looked down at the table, focusing on folding a napkin. "It's nothing big, kind of dumb, actually."

"No activity is dumb if you're passionate about it." He nudged her gently. "Come on, what is it?"

"Well, um." Paige shot a nervous glance at me, and I gave her an encouraging nod. "I really like...doing makeup. I'd love to be a makeup artist."

"And you are incredible at it," I said. "I loved every look you did on me back at the canyon."

Paige took a whole second to beam with pride before staring

down at the table again. "Oh, thank you. It just feels silly because it's not a 'useful' skill, you know?"

"Bullshit," the Hunter said. "I don't know anything about it, but it's like art, right? It's creativity. And the world needs more of that."

Yup, they are one-hundred percent getting married, I thought as their eyes met. And that led to a lightbulb going off in my head.

"Would you ever do wedding makeup?" I asked.

"Oh yes, I love bridal make up! I've never done a look on a real bride before, just practiced, but I'd enjoy that very much."

"My twin brother is getting married in six months. And I'm pretty sure his bride doesn't have a makeup artist for the wedding yet. Would you be interested?"

Paige's mouth dropped open with nothing coming out for a long while. "You mean that?"

"Of course I do. I'll have to check with Lily, but I don't see her saying no. It'd be one less task for her to do."

"Oh my God, I would be honored! Please yes, check with her first, and if she's already found someone, that's fine. But if not, I would be thrilled to."

"I'll give her a call later and let you know." I squeezed her shoulder as I got up for a second cup of coffee.

Carter was right on my heels, leaning in close to speak quietly. "Thought you should know that Nella has been refusing food and water since we arrived. Anything you want done about it?"

"No." I refilled my cup and stirred in some sugar. "Let that bitch starve if she wants to."

"Roger the fuck that," he answered, amusement lighting up his eyes.

"How's everyone else?" I turned my back to the table, keeping my voice low. "Is there any friction or is everyone getting along?"

"Getting along pretty good for the most part. Couple little scuffles here and there, but nothing we can't handle. My people are keeping an eye out, so is Chasing Death."

"Scuffles between who?"

Carter paused to take a long sip of coffee. "The one who calls himself the Saint seems to think he's in charge."

"Keep an eye on him. It's not that I get *bad* feelings about him, but I don't get good ones either."

"You got it, Pres."

I punched his bicep, not enough to hurt but just enough to threaten spilling his coffee. "Stop calling me that. People will start to believe it."

"And?"

I gave him an exasperated look. "It's misleading. I'm not the pres of anything."

"You could be." When I went to punch him again, Carter caught my fist in his palm. "I know I give you shit, Ror, but truth be told, you're handling this whole thing extremely well. You're a natural leader, and people want to follow you. On top of that, you care. You follow through on your promises and show that you can be trusted. I've seen a lot of presidents who have one or the other but rarely both. The last one I saw who had a backbone and a heart like yours was Reaper."

My throat tightened at the mention of my father's name, choking off any response I had. God damn, I missed him. All of them.

"My old man would have followed your dad to the deepest pit in hell without even a moment's hesitation. I guess he did, back in their day. And you know what?" Carter dropped my fist to point his index finger at my chest. "I know for a fact that Torr and Santos would do the same for you, and not just 'cause you're their woman."

I brushed that off with a wave of my hand. "Santos doesn't know how to ride."

"So? He can learn, he's devoted to you, and he's a deadly fucking fighter. Shit, if that Ghost guy comes with him, you'll have a better weapons combo than the Steel Demons ever did."

I opened my mouth to say that was impossible, then quickly shut it. All of my dads had been good fighters, but none had the other-worldly accuracy, speed, and skill as Gunner and Shadow. I heard countless stories of them hitting impossible targets with deadly aim. Thinking about it now, it would be fun to see Santos and Devin compete against those two.

"What about you?" I scoffed, changing the subject. "You're talking me up like I'm pres material, but would *you* ride into hell with me?"

Carter gave me a crooked smile as he put his coffee down in the sink. "I'll ride with you at every opportunity, but the Valkyrie Network is where I've pledged my loyalty. This fight you have?" He circled his index finger in the air. "I respect it, but it's not *my* fight."

"I get it. I was just messing with you."

"Think about what I'm saying. This is only the beginning for you. You're going to need to get organized and have a group you can trust."

I shook my head. "I barely know what I'm doing here, Carter."

"Well, you're faking it pretty well. Just think about it." He coughed and leaned one hip against the counter, then in a louder voice said, "So how long you want to have these folks here gettin' some R&R?"

"Another couple of days, I think." I mirrored his pose, also talking louder now that our private conversation was over. "Let people relax for a bit, and let it all sink in. If they want to leave sooner, they can. Of course, anyone who's injured should stay as long as they need to recover." I lowered my voice again. "I'll talk to Nella tomorrow. Give her another full day to throw tantrums about our hospitality."

"Sounds good to me. What're you doing today?"

I polished off my second cup of coffee, placed it in the sink, then headed out of the kitchen in search of a shower.

"Hopefully that question becomes a matter of *who* I'm doing."

Chapter 15

Rori

After a shower and a more substantial breakfast than coffee, I headed over to the second safehouse to check on things there. This was where most of the solo fighters seemed to gather, whereas the female service staff and couples kept to the other house.

The first thing I noticed when I stepped outside was men working out everywhere. It was still early morning, but the cul-de-sac was abuzz with roughly a dozen men doing push-ups, burpees, sparring each other with bare fists or wooden sticks, and squatting full-grown men on their shoulders. The air was thick with sweat and testosterone.

Old habits die hard, I guess. At least they weren't killing each other.

In fact, they were very polite. Almost everyone nodded or waved hello as I walked past.

Further up the road, it looked like LJ, Gwen, and some of the Chasing Death members were giving riding lessons. A handful of fighters were taking turns on loaner bikes, riding down straight stretches of the gravel road before turning and heading back after a few hundred yards. Paige, the Hunter, and Santos were among them, and so my feet carried me that way.

Santos was just finishing his turn, controlling the motorcycle with a confident ease as he came to a smooth stop. His beaming smile at me was like a hit of sunshine directly into my veins.

Leaving the bike running, he lowered the kickstand and got off as Paige and the Hunter went up to ride next.

"Hey." Santos jogged over to me, that brilliant smile never fading. "Don't you look bright-eyed and bushy-tailed."

"And you look like a natural on that bike," I said. "Was that your first time riding?"

"Yeah. I've always been into cars, though. It's not too different when you get the hang of it."

Oh, I know someone you'd get along very well with. I immediately thought of my dad, Jandro. If he ever got a chance to meet Santos, and not be an embarrassing, overprotective dad, I could see the two of them being like peas in a pod.

"How's your shoulder feeling?" I decided to ask, instead of creeping him out with suggesting meeting my dad.

"So much better." He rotated his arm in a big circle. "I couldn't even do this yesterday. It's still a little sore, but it seems like it'll feel good as new in a couple days."

I stared at him. "That is wild. Like, ridiculously fast healing."

He shrugged like it wasn't a big deal. "I've always been a pretty fast healer. More so when I met this big guy."

Tezca bumped his head against Santos' thigh right then, the jaguar's crackling purr rumbling in a steady rhythm as he rubbed the full side of his body against Santos' legs and then mine.

"Hey, handsome." I ran my hand down Tezca's back, then up again to scratch his ears. "Have you been taking care of our man? Healing him up, too?"

Tezca let out a chuff and licked my palm with his scratchy tongue.

"I like the sound of that," Santos murmured.

"What, the noises your cat makes?" I scratched under the jaguar's chin.

"No." The warmth of Santos' breath heated my neck. "Being your man."

I paused, then turned into him slowly. The heat on my neck had now spread to every part of my body. "You're sure that's what you want?"

"If you'll have me." Santos' voice went low, meant only for the two of us. "I have this thing for badass blondes who save my life."

"And if Torr is mine too?" I met his eyes, keeping my tone serious. "I want you too, Santos, but I need you to understand I'm not built for one partner. I probably never will be."

"I'm good with it, really. I like Torr a lot, actually."

That got a grin out of me. "Really? Because I want to throttle him half the time."

"You love him, though." Santos said it as a statement, not a question. "And you've known each other a long time. You get each other in ways no one else does. It's obvious you two just work well together."

"Obvious to everyone but ourselves until recently." I ran a sheepish hand through my hair. "But none of that bothers you? Please tell me honestly if it does."

He gave me a look that felt like a warm, loving embrace. "I mean, I'm a little jealous that he already knows you so well and has years of memories with you. But I figure we'll reach our stride eventually. Make our own memories."

"Trust me, most of my memories with Torr are stupid." I snorted. "Lots of playing pranks on my brother and being drunk idiots at parties. In a lot of ways, he and I are starting anew too."

Santos looked smug then, crossing his arms with his chin lifted. "Then he and I are on more even footing than I thought."

"It's not like it's a competition, but anyway." I waved my hand toward the house. "You want to go inside?"

"Somewhere more private, you mean?" His grin was slow, sultry. "I thought you'd never ask, paloma."

We joined hands, leaving Tezca to watch the motorcycle lessons, and headed for the fighters' house, which I had started calling the frat house in my head. With nearly everyone working out or learning to ride, I figured the house would be mostly empty.

In fact, that was exactly what I was hoping for.

Sure enough, it was blissfully quiet as we went through the front door. We tiptoed through to the kitchen, holding hands like a couple of teenagers sneaking around our parents.

"Did you have breakfast?" I said, noting the dishes piled in the sink.

"Not yet." He turned and lifted me so swiftly, I didn't notice I was in the air until he sat me on the counter. His eyes burned as he moved in close, his big body filling the space between my legs. "But I'm about to."

His kiss came down, deep and thorough. This was nothing like those fast kisses of relief back in the canyon. No, he intended to stay here for a while and devour me in the process.

I returned each hot stroke of his tongue, glide of his lips, every sigh and soft moan and short breath of air. Every touch was re-learning this devastatingly sweet man I was just getting to know.

"What do you like?" I whispered against his jaw, my hands exploring the planes of muscles on his back. "Teach me how to please you, Santos."

"Mm, you're pleasing me right now, paloma," he groaned, hips pressing forward.

"No, tell me what drives you crazy." I edged my teeth along his earlobe. "Tell me your deepest desire so I can be the one who gives it to you."

He actually froze, a stiffness entering his body, and I started to worry that I offended him.

"Was that too far? I'm sorry, I don't mean to be pushy. I just want this," I squeezed my thighs around his hips, "to be an enjoyable experience for you." *Especially after all that you were forced to do,* was the part that I left unsaid.

Santos shook his head, but the apprehension in his face remained. "You're not pushy," he said with a kiss. "And every moment with you is enjoyable, it's just..." he rubbed his jaw, looking away from me. "If you really want to know what does it for me, it's not exactly...conventional."

"My whole life is anything but conventional." I brought my hands to his nape, running my nails over the buzzed hair on the back of his head. "Try me. I would never judge you."

Santos pulled in a deep breath, fingers teasing along the shirt at my waist while he hesitated a bit longer.

"So, I haven't had the chance to fully explore this, but um." He licked his lips and swallowed. "When it comes to bedroom stuff, I think I lean toward...the submissive end of the spectrum."

"Really?" The word left my mouth in a long, slow stretch of syllables, accentuated by the smile growing on my face. I had no idea what he'd say or how I'd react, but this sensation filling my chest was nothing short of pure elation.

"When it comes to you, I just...I want to please you and take nothing for myself. I want to do everything you tell me because it's what *you* want. When I was a gladiator, my only power was killing others." A long sigh left his chest before he continued.

"I was handed out to the guests for rough sex, but I never got off on that. I've never been turned on by inflicting domination and pain, but it was what I *had* to do. And now..." Santos leaned in until his forehead touched mine. "I don't want power. I don't want control. I want to put it all in your hands and be everything *you* need me to be."

I was struck dumb. Speechless. Nearly moved to tears, I realized as my vision got blurry and I had to blink back to clarity.

As the silence stretched on, Santos started pulling away, and I could sense his emotional retreat as well.

"Sorry, that was a hell of an unload. I know it's a lot, and if you're not into that—"

My fingers curled into his shirt, holding him in place. "Stop talking and kiss me."

His hesitation was for only a beat, and then his sensuous mouth was on mine again. The passion from earlier was dialed up to eleven now, a frenzied desire overriding us both.

"I want you to go down on me until I come, and then you're going to fuck me on this counter." My voice shook with need, but I hoped I sounded dominant enough for him.

"Fuck yes, paloma," Santos moaned, his mouth moved toward my neck.

"Wait, I'm not done." I held his chin, bringing him back to eye-level with me. "You will fuck me good and hard until I come again, but you are not allowed to finish inside me. Understood?"

His throat bobbed with a swallow, eyes dilating as his lips parted. "Yes, paloma."

"Because..." I grinned. "I'm going to suck you off and take your cum deep down my throat."

If he really wanted me to be in control, he was going to have to deal with the fact that I too loved to please my partners.

"Goddamn," he hissed, grip tightening on my waist. "You are my biggest fantasy come true."

I brought his mouth to mine for another kiss, but someone loudly cleared their throat with the obvious intention of interrupting us.

My eyes opened to find the Ghost—no wait—Devin glaring at me over Santos' shoulder. Of course it would be him. If it were anyone else, I'd tell them to move along so I could get laid. But Devin and Santos were friends.

I had no issues with the sharp-eyed, sharp-cheekboned fighter, but he did seem to take issue with me. Especially with my ankles locked at the small of Santos' back and Santos' hands nestled snugly in the curves of my waist.

"Oh hey, Dev." Santos turned to address him casually, not at all embarrassed by our compromising position. "You need something?"

"I would love to make some toast, but it seems I'm all out of counter space," the other man deadpanned.

Santos only chuckled and patted my hip. "I guess we could move."

"Sure." I unwound my legs from him and hopped down from the counter. "Did you sleep well, Devin?"

"Would've slept tons better if the enabler of our enslavement wasn't still breathing fifty feet away." He shot me a huge fake smile. "Unless I now have your *permission* to rectify that?" Everything about his tone was mocking and disrespectful, setting me on edge.

The excitement of being on the cusp of having sex with Santos vanished like a puff of smoke.

Santos took a protective step between us, squaring off in his friend's direction. "Dev, come on—"

"No, it's okay." I put a hand on his arm. "He has a right to how he feels."

"So glad I have your permission for that too," Devin drawled, moving around us to reach the toaster on the kitchen counter.

"I'm interrogating her tomorrow," I said as Devin emptied the tray of crumbs from the toaster. "Figure I'd give her another day to sweat and let her mind go in circles a bit."

"Great. Just fantastic." Devin rummaged through a drawer and I tried to hold back my flinch when he held up a serrated bread knife. "Just let me know when your business is all done. Since you're the one in charge and all, plus you've got *so* much history with Nella. I'm sure you'll have plenty to hash out."

He started cutting slices into a sourdough loaf as Santos bristled next to me. I gave a quick squeeze of his arm and stepped forward, determined not to let him get caught in the middle of whatever issue his friend had with me.

"Hey, Devin, listen. I'm not sure if I did something to offend you. If I did, I'd love for you to tell me so I can acknowledge my mistake and own up to it."

He ignored me and went on slicing, shoulders stiff as he made quick work of the whole loaf.

"Okay, then. Well, if it's not anything specific, I don't see why we can't get along. We want the same thing in the end, we don't have to be enemies—"

"You know what your problem is?" Devin whipped around, loose strands of his long, dark hair following the movement gracefully. He pointed at me and thankfully didn't have the knife in his hand. "You want *everyone* to like you. No, even that's not enough. You need everyone to fall in love with you."

"Man, what?" Santos stepped in front of me again, getting into Devin's personal space. "Where the hell is this coming from?"

"You are the last person who should be saying anything," Devin snapped. "She's got you exactly where she wants you—eating out of her hand. Same with Torr. Same with everyone here who looks at her like the sun shines out of her ass."

"Dev, I don't wanna hurt you, but if you don't shut your fucking mouth—"

"Okay, stop! Come on." I pulled on the back of Santos' shirt, but he stood his ground like an oak tree, so I moved to get in front of him again. Which put me *very* close to Devin.

Funny. I had forgotten how breathtakingly beautiful he was until that moment. The lines and angles of his face were just as sharp as those knives he liked so much. Not even the faint freckles on his nose or the dark beard on his jaw did anything to soften his face.

On top of that, he was angry. At me. Devin's brows slashed down and his lips had all but disappeared with how tightly they pressed together. But there was more than anger that I sensed in his expression. I saw a whole lot of fear, with a generous helping of pain.

I leaned on Santos until he backed up enough to give Devin and I some breathing room. He was sweet to jump to my defense, and it was pretty hot seeing his switch flip from eager-to-please submissive to ready to throw down on his friend for my honor. But Devin was right about one thing. Santos was not the right person to come between us.

"I don't know where you got that impression," I said to Devin. "But I don't need everyone to love me. Or even like me. As long as we can be respectful of each other, okay? That's all I'm asking for."

"Right," he snorted. "So where's my respect? Why do I have to defer to you before I can get my kill in?"

"We talked about this, Devin," I said gently. "I need information only Nella has. Otherwise the machine keeps going, and there'll be another Mystic Canyon within a decade. Nobody wants that."

"Who the fuck put you in charge, anyway?" His glare was downright murderous. "Why do you decide where we stay? Or when someone gets questioned?"

"Look, someone had to step up, alright?" I could feel my emotions running high, coming close to the surface no matter how much I tried to shove them down. "After Santos got thrown in the isolation cell, and then Torr got captured, I had to do something. I felt responsible, okay?"

"Responsible," Devin sneered. "As if we're all children needing a mother hen to keep us in order."

"You want to go back to being a gladiator?" I snapped, flinging my hand toward the front door. "Go. Follow the road out of here. Since you're so self-sufficient, I'm sure you can find your way back to the canyon."

"Way to miss my whole fucking point." Devin's temper was unraveling too, his voice raising as he stepped into *my* personal space this time. "If you think I'm going to roll over and say, 'yes ma'am' just because another woman decided she was in charge, you are sadly mistaken. No one controls me anymore!"

"Hey." Torr picked the perfect moment to come down the stairs, eyes zeroing in on me as he hurried over. "What's with all the yelling? I could hear you from the bathroom."

"Nothing," I said quickly. "We're just getting to know each other. Aren't we, Devin?"

The fighter's eyebrows lifted slightly, like he was surprised I wouldn't rat him out to my boy toy. *Yeah, amazing when people don't fit the preconceived notions in your head, right?*

I was determined not to prove Devin right about me. Sure, I could be petty and bossy, but I wasn't some evil seductress looking for a harem of men to enslave. It seemed like he had a hard time believing that, though. And it wasn't like I could blame him. He didn't appear to have a good track record with women.

We didn't have to be friends, or even acquaintances. But if we could get to a level of mutual respect and trust, I'd consider that a win. He hated me because I was a woman who acted like I ran the show, fine. No better way to lead than by example. All I could do was treat Devin with some basic decency and hope to get the same in return one day.

Torr knew right away there was more to what I said, and he walked over with a puffed-up chest that was soon halted by my outstretched palm.

"It's okay, Torr. Really." I forced a smile at him. "Nothing I can't handle." Devin's issue would remain solely with me. There was no reason for my guys to get involved.

"You sure?" His eyes slid over to Santos, who shrugged.

Devin chose then to leave the kitchen, grumbling as he took with him half of the sliced sourdough loaf with nothing on it. I hoped he'd enjoy choking it down by his lonesome.

"What was that all about?" Torr's question cut through the tension in the kitchen as he headed for the remaining bread loaf. Tension that was now dissipating since the source of it had left.

"Nothing." I eyed the width of Torr's back pulling at his white T-shirt, noted the water droplets in his dark hair as if he'd just gotten out of the shower. No doubt he'd gotten up before the crack of dawn and already got a workout in.

"That Devin guy being a problem?"

"No, Torr. I got it handled."

"I can talk to him," Santos offered.

"No." I spun around to face him. "Really, it's fine. If you guys talk to him, it's just going to reinforce his idea that I send men out to do my bidding. Honestly, I'm not some wilted flower. I can handle him."

"If you insist." Santos let out a soft sigh before gliding his fingers over my neck. I leaned into the touch, grinning and eager to continue what we'd started, before I realized he'd stopped and was staring at Torr behind me. "What you making there, cinnamon toast?"

"You know it, man. You want some?"

"Hell yeah, let me get more butter out. Rori?"

"I'm good, actually. I ate." I gave Santos a little swat as he moved past me to the fridge. "Eat your fill, though. Torr is the toast-master."

I went to work tidying the kitchen while the two of them put a dent in the bread, butter, sugar, and cinnamon supply. My aunt Kyrie had people clean the safehouses regularly, but these fighters had the table manners of wild animals. I felt bad leaving the mess out for others to deal with.

Washing dishes was actually a chore I didn't mind. It was almost meditative. My mind went pleasantly blank as I scrubbed plates and mugs with warm, soapy water. I had spaced out so much in fact, that I didn't notice someone walking up behind me until I felt the weight of their hand.

Torr ran a touch down my back, not stopping until he found my ass and squeezing. I turned in surprise, my senses lighting up with pleasure.

"Looking for something back there?" I asked as he continued to grope and squeeze me.

Torr leaned in close, his nose nudging against my cheek. "Let's go for a ride."

"Mm-hm." I turned my head until my nose brushed his. "And then what?"

He spun me around to face him, then palmed my ass with both hands. "And then you're gonna ride me."

Chapter 16

Rori

With a final, hard squeeze and no other words, Torr released me and headed to where our bikes were parked. I had to just watch him walk away for a moment, those long, powerful legs eating up the distance. His wide shoulders cut through the air with every confident stride, knowing I would follow.

I stopped ogling long enough to find Santos looking at me with a knowing smirk. My mouth opened, the words falling out in a rapid rush. "I'm sorry. Let me go tell him you and I were just about to—"

"No." He shook his head, cutting his hand through the air. "You two should catch up. Go ride."

I hesitated, watching him. He didn't seem jealous or upset but some guys hid it well. "Are you sure?"

Damn it, I felt awful, and this was so hard. Fuck Devin for interrupting our moment. Torr had no idea what we'd been about to do before he came downstairs. If he knew, I was certain he'd find another time to ride.

I figured having to split time with my guys would happen at some point, but not so soon. It made me wish I could take a time-out to call my mother for advice right then.

Hi mom, it's Rori. Listen, what am I supposed to do when I'm about to bang one guy, we get interrupted by a rude asshole, and then another guy cuts in and wants to bang?

Thinking about it that way, the obvious answer was a threesome.

"Yeah, it's fine, really." Santos appeared calm as he walked over and looped his arms around my waist in a light hold.

My hands went to his nape, still searching his eyes as I leaned into his chest. "You could join us," I hedged.

Santos shook his head again, but he was grinning. "Another time." He leaned down and brushed a soft kiss over my mouth. It was so light that I immediately wanted to deepen it for more. "He was your man first. I understand you need some reconnection time."

Technically, Torr wasn't mine first. In terms of being physical, I had Santos first. Then Torr got jealous, and the dams holding back feelings on both our ends had burst. But Torr and I did have a long history, and we were probably both seeking comfort in what was familiar.

"When I get back," I slid out of Santos' hold reluctantly, "we're finishing what we started."

The heated look he gave me sent my heart racing. "I wouldn't miss it for the world, paloma." He made a shooing motion. "Go on now. You kids have fun."

I turned, heading out to where Torr sat on my idling bike. He scooted back, indicating I should drive while we doubled-up.

"No Santos?" he asked, like he'd been expecting the other man to join us.

"No, he said we needed time together."

Torr nodded sagely as I got into my seat, his hands coming to the tops of my thighs as I sat down. "I like him."

Relief and love filled up my chest. "Good." I planted a quick kiss on him over my shoulder. "Me too."

That didn't stop my mind from racing as I brought my feet up and drove off the property. I had been worried about the two of them, and honestly still was. More Santos than Torr, because he'd never been around a family like mine. He was taking it all in stride now, but would this really work for him long-term? Even if I balanced both relationships perfectly and spent an equal amount of time with him as Torr, would it eventually bother him that I loved another guy?

No one I'd ever been with had ever wanted to share me for a long period of time. They either wanted to keep group fun in the bedroom only, or they wanted to date other women as well, which didn't work for me.

I trusted Torr and wanted to trust Santos. But I didn't want to fall head over heels for my sexy gladiator only for the other shoe to drop.

I really needed to ask my mom for advice at some point.

I drove aimlessly, barely keeping track of where I was going. At some point, I got out of my head enough to park on a hill that gently sloped down into a small valley. The valley below was covered in greenery and pops of color—purple, orange, yellow, and pink wild-flowers just starting to bloom. In another couple of weeks, this place would be awash with colors and fragrant blooms. Probably all kinds of butterflies and other wildlife too.

Before I could voice any of this to Torr, he reached forward to shut off my bike. The next place his hands went was my waist, then they slid up to my breasts as his mouth dragged along my nape.

"I need you," he said in a rough whisper, hips already rolling against my ass. "Now. God, I just fucking need you so bad, Rori."

"I need you, Torr."

All thought went out the window as I kissed him over my shoulder, arching and pressing back against the thick erection in his jeans. Sensation and the physical need for him was all that was left.

Torr released one breast to slide his palm down. He cupped the juncture between my thighs, which were still straddling the bike. I ground into his hand, the ache for him becoming more urgent with each rub of my clit against his palm. When his hand pulled away, I wanted to whine in protest, but he was just pulling at my waistband.

"Get these fucking pants off," he growled, releasing me to pull apart his belt buckle.

"I'm gonna have to get off the bike," I told him.

"Fuck no, I want you right here."

It took some creative maneuvering, but I managed to strip from the waist down while remaining on the bike the whole time.

"Next time, just tell me to wear a dress," I said, draping my pants over the handlebars.

"Hmm." Torr pumped his cock with slow, lazy strokes. "I didn't take you for a dress kind of girl."

"I can be for the right occasion." I backed up against him, lifting my ass to rub against his heavy length. "Like being an undercover rich girl and getting fucked on a bike."

"God..." Torr's head fell back on a moan. "You are just the perfect woman for me. I can't believe it took so long for us to happen."

"I love you too, Torr."

A bashful smile crossed the face of my sexy, dirty-talking man. He hugged around my waist and kissed my nape, sensual and sweet. In the next moment, his hands were running over me again, caressing my hips and waist before they disappeared under my shirt. His kisses grew hungrier, sucking and nibbling along my shoulders and upper back.

Though it would have been nice, I didn't expect him to say it back. I knew how he felt, knew why it was difficult for him to say those words. I wasn't upset and would be content to continue telling Torr I loved him. My love for him was selfless, not a tit-for-tat thing. It was here to stay, unlike his birth parents who'd abandoned him and made him feel undeserving of love. And in my words and actions, I would continue to reassure him of that.

But damn, I'd be lying if I said I couldn't wait for that day to come. When he finally felt safe enough to remove that final barrier around his heart and tell me that he loved me.

I closed my eyes, letting go of my thoughts to sink into the sensations of his talented hands and mouth. Reaching behind me, I wrapped a hand around his length and stroked him from base to tip. Torr's soft, shuddering moan turned into a hissed curse as I angled him to my pussy, stroking him against my slick flesh.

"You're getting me all wet," he said tightly. "Are you that soaked for me?"

"Yes," I moaned. My thighs were already shaking from the anticipation of taking him inside me.

Torr didn't waste a moment. He thrust forward while pulling my hips back at the same time. My cry of, "Fuck!" echoed into the valley below as my hands slapped down on the bike's dash.

"Oh yeah, stay stretched out like that." Torr grabbed my hips and started up a rhythm that was already hitting me in places that made me see stars. "Mm, love seeing my girl take my cock on a bike seat."

A motorcycle provided lots of great handholds for leverage as it turned out. My hands gripped the top edge of the dash between the handlebars, feet on the footpegs. Basically, it was the perfect position to absorb Torr's brutal thrusts. All I could do was hold on, and hold on I did.

"Torr," I moaned over the smacks of his hips against my ass with every drive forward. "Let me turn it on."

"Are you kidding? Goddamn, you turn me on so fucking much. I love watching you take my cock."

"I mean the bike!" I laughed. "I have an idea."

He slowed and then paused, smacking a big palm on my ass as he took a series of panting breaths. "Just don't send us rolling down this hill."

I turned the key, bringing the bike to life with a roar that lowered to a gentle rumble. Settling back down, I shot Torr a grin over my shoulder.

"Oh, you dirty girl." He smacked the other side of my ass, returning my grin. "That feels nice on your clit, does it?"

"You know my bike is my favorite toy." I pressed my belly and pelvis down into the seat, seeking the most friction possible from the vibrations of the machine. "Don't you dare fucking stop now, Torr."

"Trust me, I never want to stop." His cock drove through me slower but no less intense with deep, long strokes.

The vibrations seemed to turn up my sensitivity everywhere, amplifying every sensation on my skin and also internally. I felt every inch of him glide through me just as much as I felt his hands on my hips, pressing me down into the bike so I could feel that constant rumbling even more.

My head was empty except for how wildly, insanely good this felt. And when Torr's hand cracked down over my ass, that dialed everything up to a new high.

His hand clamped on my nape, the other digging into my hip, holding me in place as he fucked me with more force, more speed. With my head turned to the side, I watched the hypnotic thrusts of his hips, saw the flex and release of his muscles and my ass bouncing with every impact.

Torr was no submissive, and it was wild to think that I craved his rough hold and punishing thrusts just as much as I wanted Santos' sweetness and eagerness to please.

"Come for me." Torr growled out the command. "I can feel you getting there. Let me feel you squeeze my cock."

"Spank me harder," I demanded in reply.

Torr's rough, sexy moan was eclipsed by the crack of his palm on my flesh. Heat bloomed over my skin like a fever, and he brought his palm down again before I could recover.

Again and again, the sharp heat of pain lit up my senses. Combined with the rumbling vibrations on my nipples and clit, and his cock fucking me at such a brutal, delicious pace, I didn't stand a chance.

The orgasm ripped through me like lightning in a storm, once, twice, and once more. Torr's release followed, kicking inside me and spilling heat that sent more little lightning bursts through me.

The vibrations became too much at that point, and I slapped my palm blindly up in the general direction of the ignition. Torr figured out what I was doing and used his longer reach to turn the bike off for me.

"Thanks," I panted, dropping my cheek back to the seat, then started giggling.

"What?" Torr lowered over my back and brushed a kiss along my nape.

"Nothing. Thanks is just a weird thing to say after sex, isn't it?"

He chuckled and patted my arm like we were no more than acquaintances. "Thanks for the ride, partner."

We burst out laughing together, which quickly turned into moans and body wiggles since he was still inside me and we were both incredibly sensitive.

Torr placed another kiss on my shoulder before he gingerly pulled out of me. I hopped off the bike to get re-dressed and had to lean against the trusty machine on my wobbly, post-orgasm legs.

"I think we both needed that," I said, once zipped and buttoned up again. Nothing like rough sex on a bike to feel refreshed and invigorated.

Torr nodded, his eyes bright and playful. "Aren't you glad I made you rest?"

I rolled my eyes but marched over to him, wrapping my arms around his neck before pressing up on tiptoe to kiss him. "I'm glad you're here with me, period." His arms went around my waist as we kissed a second time. "I love you, Torr," I whispered when our lips parted.

The playfulness left his eyes, showing the vulnerability he hid underneath. His forehead rested on mine, hands tightening on my waist like he never wanted to let me go.

Never *would* let me go.

Again, I had no expectations and felt no rejection at his silence. I stroked his cheek and kissed him with a smile to let him know that I knew, that I understood. That I loved him regardless and would never let him go either.

"I guess we should get back," he said, voice full of reluctance.

"Yeah," I agreed with the same tone. "You want to drive?"

His eyes lit up again, that smirk returned. "I did you that good, huh?"

"Shut up." I went behind him and swatted his ass. "Your ego doesn't need to get any bigger."

In truth, there was no else I trusted more to ride in front of me.

Chapter 17

Rori

I tried not to look too gleeful as I headed down into the safe house's basement the next day. It wouldn't be a good look if I appeared to get pleasure from interrogating someone. But I actually intended to enjoy this. Very much.

Nella had been cuffed around her wrists and ankles. From both points of restraints, a length of chain kept her tethered to a support beam running from the floor to the ceiling. She had been given just enough room to have free range of movement, but no more. She had also been offered a shower and two meals since coming here, both of which she refused.

As far as prison cells went, hers was luxurious. The basement was insulated, and she'd been provided with blankets and sweats for the colder nights. There was even a slim, rectangular window giving her some sunlight and a sense of night and day. Way more than what she gave Santos and Torr in that dark pit.

Nella had more than reasonable accommodations for a prisoner. And I was fully prepared to continue being reasonable, as long as she was.

For some reason, I wasn't holding my breath on that.

I took my sweet ass time coming down the basement stairs, letting each of my steps register on the warped, wooden planks. Behind me came Carter and three veteran riders of the Valkyrie Network. Those three were men that Carter and I both trusted, guys who had ridden with my uncles' and fathers' clubs.

When I hit the concrete basement floor, I didn't acknowledge Nella at first. I nodded to the two men on guard duty—younger ones around LJ's age—and gave them a sweet smile. "Thanks, guys. We'll take it from here."

My posse stepped aside to let them up the stairs, and then it was just us and our prisoner.

"Hi, Nella." I poured every ounce of control into my voice and smile as I grabbed a metal folding chair from the wall, opened it, and took a seat. "How are you doing?"

Her eyes followed me as I moved, the rage pouring off her in waves. No control over her emotions here. "You're wasting your breath," she spat. "I'm not telling you a goddamned thing."

I manipulated my face into a mask of concern. "Hmm, that doesn't sound like you're very happy here. Is it the food? You've refused to eat it, so no, that can't be it. Does the sunlight bother you? Would you prefer a cell in total darkness like the one back at the resort? We'd be happy to arrange it if so. Just say the word."

I crossed my legs and clasped my hands on top of my knee, like a therapist having a heart-to-heart with a patient.

Nella shook her head, chains clanking with the movement as she let out a dry laugh. "You don't get it, child. You're too young to know how things used to be."

"Tell me, then." I gestured a hand imploringly at her.

"The Collapse," she hissed. "Before, during, and after. Do you know how it was for us women? I mean, going back centuries. Do you have any clue what *they* did to us?" Her eyes flicked up to the men standing behind me on the word *they*.

"I have some idea." I picked at my nails, looking bored. "It's still happening, you know. The subjugation of women. Fucking terrible, isn't it?"

"If you know that, then why am I a prisoner and *they* are armed and free?" Nella bared her teeth, pulling on her chains as the veins in her forehead popped. "I don't have just 'some idea', I *know*. I know firsthand how they like to hurt us. Use us. They think they're entitled to our bodies, our labor. We're not people to them, we're cattle."

"So that's what the resort was all about." I cocked my head. "Getting back at men for what they've done to women for thousands of years."

"Yes!" Nella actually sounded triumphant. "The balance has been tipped too far in their favor. Now we're correcting it. Exerting control over them before they can control us."

"Who is 'we'?"

Nella snorted. "Every woman who can see the truth for what it is."

I'd take that answer for now and circle back to it later. "Is it true you kidnapped innocent men off the street? How do you determine which ones to get your revenge on?"

She snorted again, casting a look of disdain up at Carter and the others. "There's no such thing as an innocent man. They're rotten from the day they're born."

I held back the anger that swept over me, just barely. "Seems you like men enough to fuck them. And to have an armed militia ready when you call. Those backup commandos looked expensive. That resort made you very wealthy, didn't it?"

Nella shrugged. "Men can be useful when they're under control."

"You mean enslaved."

"Again, is it any worse than what they did to us?"

Her fanatical beliefs were just pissing me off and not the information I actually needed. I had to focus. "Who owns the resort?"

"A powerful group of women who will bring us into a new era." Her eyes widened like she'd just gotten an idea. "They could use someone like you. A leader who takes charge. You'd be spending your time among your own gender, people with creativity and brains. Not these knuckle-draggers who only follow you because they want what's between your legs."

This wasn't part of the plan, but I shifted in my seat to look up at Carter. "Carter, do you want to fuck me?"

He made a face. "Uh, no? You're my cousin."

My head swiveled to look in the other direction. "How about you, Dan? You want some of this?"

"Respectfully, hell no." Dan frowned. "You're my daughter's age." He was attractive and fit for being in his early forties, but the feeling was mutual. Not my type.

The other guys muttered similar sentiments. I already knew one had a long term boyfriend and the other was newly married with a baby on the way.

"So it seems," I swiveled in my chair back to face Nella, "that the men in this room would *not* fuck me at the first opportunity. So they must follow me for some other reason."

The prisoner only shook her head pityingly at me. "Here's a newsflash for you, child. Men lie."

"I know. Guess what? So do women." I uncrossed my legs and planted my feet wide, leaning forward with my arms on my knees. "So if you and I are so much better than them, help a girl out and tell me what I need to know. Tell me specifically, who are the owners of the resort?"

"You and I are not the same," Nella said. "You're blinded by the world *they* created. We are building a new world. Women like you stand in the way of progress. So I won't tell you a thing. You're just going to kill me anyway."

Showtime, I thought, leaning back in my chair.

"You're wrong there, Nella. I'm going to keep you very much alive. Because while I love having a good bitchfest about how useless men are, I draw the line at kidnapping them off the streets." I leaned forward again, steepling my fingers. "I take issue with forced prostitution. I'm not okay with forcing people to fight to the death for entertainment. The fact of the matter is, not a single one of those men lifted a finger to assault you."

"Of course not! I made damn sure never to give them the opportunity," Nella hissed.

I stared her dead in the face, all pretense of charm and joking gone. "That makes you a murderer, Nella. And a rapist."

She gave me another dismissive roll of her eyes. Fucking psychopath. Which was what I figured.

"So it seems we've come full circle once again," I said with a wistful little sigh.

Nella narrowed her eyes. "What do you mean?"

"You exploit and harm innocent men." I leaned back, holding my hands out to the sides. "These guys get to do the same to you."

Her eyes widened for a second before she put on her air of superiority again. "You wouldn't."

"Who owns the resort?"

"Fuck you."

"That's no way to talk to your pimp." I opened my palms and wiggled my fingers. "What do we got, boys?"

I heard rummaging through pockets and opening wallets as I watched Nella's face morph from bravado to fear. The guys slapped some currency into my hands, and I only glanced down to count what they had paid.

"Hm, it's a little light." I stuffed the territory credits in my jacket pockets and crossed my legs again. "You all can fuck her mouth, but that's it."

"Goddamn it," Carter grumbled as he pulled out another wad of bills and held it out to me.

"'Atta boy." I grinned, accepting the money from him. "You can have her ass too."

In front of me, Nella had gone completely still. And pale.

"Last time I'm asking," I warned her. "Who owns the resort?"

She swallowed and glared at me, trying to put on a brave front, but she had started to shake.

"Suit yourself." I scooted my chair back to give the guys room to surround her.

Dan flexed his fingers, opening and closing his hand into a fist. "Mind if I knock some teeth out? I don't want my dick to get bitten off."

"Mm..." I pretended to think about it. "Not preemptively, no. But if she does bite, feel free."

Nella's teeth chattered from how hard she shook, while the guys closed in and began undoing their belts and jeans. She looked at me through the gaps between their bodies, eyes round and pleading, while I kept my expression passive like I was about to watch a boring TV show.

Dan's cock was already stiff and engorged, his fist wrapped around the base. He clasped the back of Nella's head with his free hand, guiding her mouth to him when she screamed out, "Sisters of Bathory!"

I rocked forward in my chair and the men froze. "Who?"

"Sisters of Bathory..." Nella was sobbing now, curling into herself. "Please don't hurt me..."

I signaled for the guys to step away, wondering why that name rang a bell in my head. "Where are they located?"

"All over...several locations..."

"Do they have a central base? A headquarters?"

"Yes...a compound in the Basin Territory."

"You're going to write down the exact location for me and every single detail you know. How many people in total, including armed guards. Is it another resort?"

"No, it's just..." Nella sniffed. "It's where we live. Where we're safe from..." Her eyes slid over a trembling shoulder to where the guys stood a few feet away.

I snapped my fingers in front of her face. "Focus. And write.

Otherwise, I still have their money. And they'll want what they paid for."

Her expression crumbled into despair, abject fear, and betrayal.

That last one was a doozy. It fucked with my head the whole time her shaky hands chicken-scratched the information I asked for on a legal pad.

She felt betrayed by me. Like there was some code I wasn't supposed to break because we were both women.

When she finished, I scanned the paper and felt satisfied with what I'd gotten.

Nella's head was bent, her defeated gaze on the floor. A few dark spots of wetness had landed on the concrete. Tears.

"Don't let them touch me," she cried softly. "I swear that's everything I know."

Sympathy threatened to rise up in my throat, but I choked it off. This woman had blood on her hands. She'd used and sold dozens of men, including one I was falling in love with. Everyone had trauma, it didn't make them a good or bad person. I'd just figured out how to use hers for our gain.

It worked, and the job was done. But I wasn't sure how to feel about it.

Saying nothing, I got to my feet, taking the legal pad with me. I went up the stairs, the guys following after me, and Nella was left alone.

Once Carter closed the door behind him, I let out a long breath that had constricted my chest like a fist. "Thank you, guys. I'm sorry I asked you to act like that, but...thank you."

They all nodded and grunted through tight-lipped frowns. I picked these men in particular because I trusted them well enough to know that they'd get no pleasure in acting like they were about to gang-rape a woman. They'd follow through on what I'd asked them to do but would never go a step too far.

It never would have happened, but Nella believed it would. That was the whole point, and yet, it wasn't sitting well with me.

"Anything else you need?" Carter asked.

I shook my head. "No, that's it for today. Thanks again, guys."

"Can we get our money back?" Dan muttered.

"Oh, right. Here."

They all grabbed their cash and took off in a hurry, probably in search of somewhere private to rub out those erections caused by the pills I asked them to take.

Alone, I looked down at the information Nella had written, but all the words blurred together in my brain. With a careful pull, I tore the sheet off the legal pad and carefully folded it before putting it in a jacket pocket.

I got what I needed. And I never had to inflict pain on Nella or do any other sick type of torture. I just fucked with her head. Made her believe her worst fear was about to happen and probably triggered some flashbacks.

Hell, that was probably *every* woman's worst fear. Maybe that was why my conscience was all weird about it now.

I wanted to ride. I wanted to drink until I passed out. I wanted to have some very enthusiastic, consensual sex. I wanted to be alone and stare at the ceiling.

What was done was done. But how was I supposed to keep going and be okay with it?

While running on the hamster wheel of my mind, I wandered into the living room where Devin and Santos sat on the couch next to each other.

Their weapons were laid out on the coffee table—Devin's many small throwing knives and Santos' much larger machetes. The guys were clearly in the middle of a sharpening session, with whetstones, oil, and a small pile of cloths near the blades. Both of them paused and looked up at the sight of me.

"Hey," Santos said gently, wiping his hands on a cloth over his leg. "You okay?"

I found it utterly impossible to answer him in that moment, so I looked at Devin.

"I got what I needed. She's all yours," I said before turning and heading up to the bedroom I'd claimed.

Chapter 18

Hudson

I woke up to something hard and cold poking me in the chest. Groaning, I went to rub my eyes but found my limbs still tied down.

Oh, right. I'd managed to free one arm and punched the woman who'd gotten on top of me, which earned my restraints being reinforced by chains now. On top of some other really unpleasant shit.

But it was worth it. I felt a surge of joy lighting up my cold, dead nerves every time I saw that bitch's black eye.

The man I used to be wouldn't have been able to fathom striking a woman. He never would have believed he'd be captured and used as a breeding stud either. My reality was incomprehensible now. Maybe I'd died and this was Hell.

It turned out to be a gun barrel poking me in the chest. The long snout of a rifle, so the woman holding it could still keep a fair distance away from me.

"Wake up," she said, nudging me again. "And wash up. You're going out today."

Out? As in, leaving this room I'd been confined to for months, if not years? I didn't dare ask for clarification, but the spark of hope in my chest was a painful thing. Hope did nothing but ensure more misery later on.

My wrists and ankles were unbound while four rifles hovered in the air a few feet away, all pointing at me. I drew my arms and legs in, muscles screaming at the stiffness and cramping.

"Shower," said the woman, swinging her gun toward the adjoining bathroom. "The water shuts off in ten minutes."

I moved in that direction, timid and slow, until I was in the bathroom and the door shut behind me. If I could still feel anything, I would have wept. A shower, alone, for ten whole minutes!

Not wanting to waste time, I stripped off my clothes and went under the spray. Oh God, it was *hot* water too.

There were no temperature controls, no shower head, towel rods, or anything that could have been used as a weapon. Someone was controlling the water and temperature from another location, but I didn't care. This was a tiny slice of heaven in the hell I'd found myself in.

One small soap bar rested on a shelf, and I ran it over my skin, taking notice of my body for the first time in months.

I stayed clothed when they used me. They uncovered the only part that mattered and then put it away when they were done, so I hadn't taken a good, long look at myself in a while.

I was thinner, paler, unsurprisingly. The musculature I'd once been proud of was gone now, atrophied from lack of use. My tattoos however, were vibrant and stark. Maybe I'd become so pale and sickly that the ink stood out more because of the contrast. I'd forgotten they were there, and looking at them now on my arms, legs, and chest was like finding a photo album of my life from years ago.

The nostalgic memories came flooding, and with them came a physical ache behind my sternum. I wasn't even a person anymore. I couldn't tell some woman to get the fuck off me, let alone choose to put some ink in my skin.

This body used to be mine, and I'd decorated it and worked it out with pride. I used to walk around with my shirt off so I'd get looks and questions about my tattoos. I used to have sex because I was attracted to someone and wanted to feel good. I used to eat whatever the fuck I wanted and sometimes drank too much. Because I was hungry and I wanted to party. Whatever I did was because I just fucking *wanted* to.

Now...I no longer belonged to myself.

I was nothing.

I was a means to an end with lungs, a heartbeat, and a wish that they would shoot me with one of those rifles.

All too soon, my shower ended.

I dried off with a folded-up towel that was left on top of the toilet lid. Underneath the towel was a change of clothes. Just a pair of loose pants and matching long-sleeved shirt that reminded me of a prison outfit.

A metallic tapping came from the other side of the door. "One minute to get dressed," called the armed woman who had ordered me around earlier.

This whole going-out, shower-and-fresh-clothes thing was curious, now that I was thinking about it. It almost seemed like I was being prepared for something. Were they finally going to kill me?

As bright as that thought was, it didn't seem likely that I'd be under so many armed guards if that were the case. Why not just shoot me in my bed?

"Are you dressed?" called the woman through the door. It was almost funny. For as much they liked keeping me prisoner for what I had stored in my balls, they sure didn't want to see me naked.

"Yes," I answered, my voice raspy from lack of use.

"You will be shot if you are lying."

Damn, missed opportunity there.

The door opened, and I was escorted out by my armed detail of serious, stone-faced women. The one in charge led the way out the bedroom door and up a short flight of stairs to a hallway that opened up into a kitchen and dining room. So it was the basement of a small house I'd been kept in, essentially a cottage.

I was led out the front door, and I blinked in the harsh sunlight. Holy shit, when was the last time I'd been truly outside? Looking around, I tried not to let my steps falter as I took in my surroundings.

There were rows of small cottages, all lined neatly along this path my escorts were taking me. Some houses were fairly plain, others were painted bright colors or decorated with gardens. As we continued walking, we passed a larger, fenced-in garden on the right side. Some women harvested fruit and vegetables while others appeared to be propagating or tilling soil.

Everyone stopped and looked when we passed.

I caught the eyes of one woman standing in front of her house with a chubby toddler on her hip. The pink bow in the child's hair indicated she was a girl. And that woman had come to use me many, many times.

My next breath got stuck in my chest and I nearly coughed, my eyes unable to tear away from the woman's child, *my* child, unless there was another poor bastard here in the same position as me.

A rifle barrel jabbed me in the back, and I stumbled forward. "Keep walking," came the command from behind me.

I continued my walk with my head down, my stomach churning with nausea. I had known what they were using me for, knew what the results would be. But I had never seen those results with my own eyes before. Never seen eyes that looked exactly like mine staring back at me.

A cold sweat started breaking over my skin as it all started hitting me at once. There had been so many of them. Nearly every single day. For what felt like an eternity. That child looked about a year old, so how many...

I clutched at my near-empty stomach, my steps faltering. Two rifle barrels pressed into my back now, digging under my shoulder blades to keep me upright.

"You are being brought before the Dark Mother," one of the women hissed at me. "Show some respect."

The what-now?

I concentrated on moving my feet as we wound through the houses, while more women came to watch from their front doors. Some were heavily pregnant or had young children. Others were alone or had older children, I estimated about ten or twelve years old.

All of the kids were girls.

Some math wasn't adding up. Where were the boys?

An answer came to me that was too horrific to fully comprehend. I shoved it away, dismissing it despite the ample evidence of what had been done to me and all the other men I shared space with in this hellhole.

I was brought before a set of stairs leading up to a platform with a slanted roof, held up by four support beams. Four women stood at the edge of the platform, shoulder-to-shoulder. They were all older, in their fifties or sixties, and dressed far better than everyone else.

My escorts with guns and everyone who'd watched us had been in simple, clearly re-used clothes. Not everything fit right or went together, like they'd just grabbed things from a secondhand store.

These women had on long coats that were tailored and looked brand-new, a clear sign of their elevated status, as if being ten feet higher than everyone wasn't enough. The youngest of the group also liked her jewelry, with a gold medallion hanging from her neck and no less than three rings on each hand.

I was shoved to my knees on the ground at the base of the stairs and kept my gaze on the first concrete step in front of me.

"Look at us, male," one of them snapped.

I looked up, blinking at a sky that was overcast but still too bright.

The oldest of the women smiled down at me, sinister and pure evil. "You've done us a great service. So much so that the Dark Mother requested you herself. She is impressed by you." The woman brought her hands behind her back. "And we are not easily impressed by *men*."

She spat out that last word while a tittering laugh rose up from all around. Whatever this was, it seemed that quite the audience had gathered.

"We've canceled the blood sacrifice for this full moon to celebrate instead," said another woman on the stage. "Ten daughters from one source is such a blessing. Praise the Dark Mother!"

My nausea returned while everyone else cheered. Ten...ten fucking kids that I never wanted or consented to. Children I had no rights to. And that was just girls.

While my gut churned like an angry sea, my eyes darted around for something to focus on so I could just fucking breathe. To my right, I saw another woman lifting a baby high in the air as she cheered. Oh God, I was going to be sick...

"The Dark Mother wishes to remind you all," said the bejeweled woman, "that our work is far from done. In order to turn the tide against the men who have taken everything from us, we need more daughters. More sisters in arms. Thanks to our benevolent goddess, our power grows. But we cannot stop here. Not until," she looked down and extended a hand in my direction, "every man is on his knees before us."

More cheering. More bile in my throat.

The two center women on the platform stepped away from each other, and I was forced to my feet. "Come and meet our goddess," said the older one coolly. "Men don't usually get the privilege until right before they are sacrificed."

I resisted going up the steps, but the guns against my back and ass ensured I went up there regardless. Once on the same level as the four elder women, I saw the dark red and brown stains in the gray concrete, all creating pathways toward strategically-placed drains.

Screams filled my head. Memories of waking up to blood dripping on my forehead crashed to the forefront of my mind. Oh God, they did it *here*. Right above where they kept us all prisoner. Every new and full moon, they sacrificed men to their so-called goddess. Spilling as much blood and causing as much pain as possible in retribution for millennia of the subjugation of women.

Only when the guns braced against my back did I realize that I had backed away. I wanted off this platform, off this ride, out of this body that was just a tool for them.

The bejeweled woman extended a palm to me, her smile deceptively warm. "Don't be afraid, male. You will not be sacrificed this moon cycle or the next. The goddess still has much use for you."

"Please, I don't..."

I didn't even know what I was begging for. They would never stop. Never put me out of my misery. Never let me go.

Was this goddess even real? Or was everyone just brainwashed by these cult leaders?

"Don't waste this privilege," the bejeweled woman warned. "The goddess may even let you live long after your service is fulfilled. You could watch your daughters grow up." Her voice grew low. "As long as you understand your place, *male*."

Yeah, right. Watch my daughters grow up to hate and hunt down men? I didn't want to be around for any of that.

A breeze picked up, and the cool air felt like fingers moving along my neck. A comforting touch and a reminder that I wasn't alone.

Hold on, my son. I remembered the voice from days ago, when the wind howled angrily outside my prison. *I have not forsaken you. I am everything their goddess wishes she could be.*

Maybe I was losing it and this sense of calm was just my brain disassociating to protect myself. But I wasn't ready to die yet.

"I understand," I said, lowering my gaze humbly. "I am, uh, honored by the privilege."

The woman looked pleased and turned toward the far side of the stage. "Follow me."

When I went after her, my armed escorts and the others stayed back. There was a shade tent at the far end of the covered platform, even though it wasn't sunny.

But the shade tent was draped in swaths of cloth. Ribbons made of dozens of different fabrics wrapped around the legs. Sitting at the bases of all four legs were flowers, stuffed animals and children's toys, beads and jewelry, handwritten letters and photographs. The items near the bottoms of the piles were dark brown with remnants of dried blood.

Offerings, I realized, swallowing to tamp down my nausea again.

Once we reached it, the woman stood to the side of the tent just outside the canopy. She gestured for me to go inside. "No one but those of us in the Sisterhood has gazed upon a living, breathing deity." Awe filled her voice. "You truly have no idea how lucky you are."

Inside the tent was a wicker bassinet, gently rocking from side to side. A bolt of fear jolted through me. Whatever was in that thing, I did *not* want to see. Only the desire to maintain the illusion kept me inching forward. The woman beamed at me as I walked past her, mistaking my nauseating fear for reverence.

A metallic smell hit me as soon as I ducked under the shade cloth, and I almost turned the fuck around when I realized the entire floor surrounding the bassinet was coated in blood. Fuck, fuck, fuck, I did *not* want to do this.

And with that thought came the helpful reminder that nobody here cared what I wanted.

I approached the bassinet at the pace of a geriatric snail. The closer I got, the more my terror grew, but as I got peeks of the cushion and fabric lining the basket, I became a tiny bit curious. Was their goddess a baby? Some re-imagination of Jesus Christ to fit their anti-men ideology?

After what felt like years, I reached the bassinet. I stood over it and looked down at what was inside.

I lasted maybe five seconds before turning and throwing up on the floor. There was a flurry of movement and voices, then multiple hands grabbing me, guns poking me to move again, but I couldn't get my feet to cooperate. Couldn't get my eyes to unsee the thing writhing in that bassinet.

It looked like...a hunk of raw meat. Maybe a human liver. But it *moved*. It was alive and sentient, and it *knew* I was there. It knew what purpose I served for its devotees. I felt that it recognized me as easily as seeing someone wave at me in a crowd. I saw what it wanted for the world, and the sheer scale of devastation made me feel as insignificant as an ant.

"The Dark Mother was the size of my pinky finger decades ago." It was the bejeweled woman speaking, her smile and eyes bright as she walked alongside me. Except I wasn't so much walking as I was being dragged. "After decades of devotion and sacrifices, her power has grown and she has rewarded us. But there is still so much to be done."

"What...how..." My stomach heaved again, and I coughed up bile and saliva.

"Faith, stupid man. Faith, prayer, and sacrifice." The woman went up to the door of a cottage and proceeded to unlock and open it. "We need only a few months before she can take a vessel, and then our goddess will walk among us." She stood to the side, beaming like she'd won the lottery as my escorts dragged me inside. "And that is something you will *not* want to miss."

Chapter 19

Santos

I watched Rori leave the living room, listened to the bedroom door close, and then looked at Devin. "Shit. What do you think happened down there?"

"Don't know." He did a final wipe-down of his knives before sheathing them. "Long as she didn't take my kill, I don't care."

Liar, I thought. Maybe he didn't like Rori as much as I did, but I could tell he was warming up to her. Slowly. Okay, maybe at a glacial pace, but he was coming around to her and maybe even women in general. I actually heard him say good morning to Paige when they walked past each other.

"I said it to both of them. Her *and* the Hunter," he'd protested when I made fun of him.

Devin was all serious now, his blades tucked away into their various hidden holsters as he stood from the couch.

"You doing it now?" I asked him.

"Why wait?" He breezed over to the basement door, silent and fluid.

"You want to be alone?"

He paused with his hand on the doorknob. "I do, actually." He shot me a glance over his shoulder. "This is for me. Unless you're also itching for a revenge kill."

I shook my head. Killing had been nothing more than survival for me. It did nothing for me emotionally. I never got a sense of closure or vindication from taking a life.

"No, I'm good. Take it, man. You deserve it."

Devin gave a small nod before swinging the door open and heading down the basement stairs. My gaze went up another set of stairs, where Rori had just gone, looking conflicted and gray.

My feet were moving without another thought, taking the steps two at a time until I reached the landing. Only one bedroom door was closed, everyone else was out stretching their legs or learning to ride motorcycles for the day.

I went up to the door and rapped my knuckles softly. "Rori? It's Santos."

"Come in," came the reply.

I opened the door only far enough to stick my head in. She was sitting sideways in an armchair next to the window, the pane opened and her white dove sitting outside on the sill.

"Hey. Just wanted to see how you were doing."

Rori angled her head in my direction, a smile pulling at her lips. "I'm okay, I think. Just working through some shit in my head. You want to sit with me?"

Did I ever.

I closed the door behind me and crossed the room to her. Rori stood from the armchair, allowing me to sit, then resumed her sideways position with her legs across my lap. Her dove flew away as I circled my arms around her waist, tugging her closer.

"Did I interrupt something?" I asked with a brush of my lips across her forehead.

"No." She chuckled, scratching lightly along the back of my neck. "It seems you and I are the ones who keep getting interrupted."

I smiled against her cheek. "Should I barricade the door?"

"No, stay right where you are." The gentle command created a warming sensation in my chest, and I tightened my hold on her. "If anyone knocks on that door, I'll yell at them to fuck off."

The warmth in my chest grew and spread, reaching my belly and my throat. It felt amazing to know she wanted me as much as I wanted her.

"So what is this shit you're working through in your head?" I ran one hand up her back, lightly scratching, circling, massaging, as I studied her face.

Rori inhaled deeply and sighed it all out, looking exhausted. "Ethical issues concerning the interrogation of prisoners, I guess."

"Sounds like a very difficult university class," I said, just to make her laugh. "What's bothering you, though?"

She blew out another breath, and I stayed quiet, ready and eager to listen. "My fathers were tortured. You know, back in the day. They didn't give us details, but they were honest about it happening." Rori's eyes went from focusing on me to staring at a blank spot on the wall. "All of them said the worst part about it wasn't the pain. Not starvation or the solitude. What almost broke them was realizing their worst fears were on the brink of coming true. The idea that everything they fought for would go up in flames. That they'd never see each other or my mother again." Rori's focus returned to me again. "I used that with Nella today. I deduced what her worst fear would be and used that fear to break her."

"Okay," I said. "And that was?"

"Being raped by a group of men."

"Ah." I frowned at her. "Did you—"

"No! It never went that far, and I never would have let it. I just planned it really carefully to make her *believe* it would happen. I chose guys that I trusted and had them pop pills to get hard. Because, you know, they're not the type that would naturally be turned on by that situation."

My eyebrows shot up. Damn, that was crafty. "Oh, wow."

"I had them give me money, told them what they could do to her. It was all an act. They never actually touched her, but fuck, Santos, it got *really* close. And she was terrified. I've never seen a woman so scared. Not even when Paige was under that table in the shootout."

"I see." My palm smoothed up her back. "And you feel bad about doing that to a fellow woman?"

Rori's head tilted back with a groan, leaning into my hand cupping the nape of her neck. "Honestly, not really. But I feel bad that I don't feel bad, you know?"

"Sure, I get it. I've had kills that have made me feel no remorse or anything. And that's a weird feeling in itself."

Rori's features relaxed with relief, her head lifting to face me again. "Exactly. You *do* get it. But it's got me wondering if I'm a sociopath or something."

"The fact that you're feeling conflicted and weird about this is proof that you're not." I rubbed my fingers into the taut muscles of her neck. "You saw Nella for the person she is—someone who has ordered the death and abuse of dozens of people. You were too smart to fall for her sob story of being trampled on by men her whole life."

"Yeah, but the thing is, she's not wrong about that. She and this Sisterhood she's part of, their way of dealing with that is so unhinged." Rori shook her head as if clearing the thoughts from her mind. "It doesn't matter how they justify it. Their fucked up business of gladiator fights and sex slaves needs to end. Nothing justifies treating people like that."

"Seems you already knew that all along." I smiled and rubbed her back again. "See? What do you need me for?"

"Oh, stop." She wrapped both arms around my shoulders and kissed me deeply, a long, passionate press of her lips and tongue that left me breathless. "Thank you for listening," she whispered, then kissed me again. "And for coming to check on me."

"Rori..." I was all heat and coiled up need underneath her. "Can we—"

"Finish what we started in the kitchen? Yes, please." She slid over my lap until she straddled me, grinding down over my zipper. "You remember everything I told you?"

I closed my fist in her hair at the back of her head. Just because I leaned submissive didn't mean I was a passive little bitch. I took control in my own way.

"Eat your pussy until you come screaming my name. Fuck you hard until you come around my cock. Then let your sweet mouth take me until I come down your throat." I brought my mouth to her ear, rolling my hips up so she could feel how hard she was making me. "Did I get all that right, paloma?"

"Y-yes," she said on a shuddering breath, pupils blowing wide. "Good boy."

I surged up from the chair, holding her legs straddled around me, then turned to face the comfortable seat we were just in. Locking our mouths in another kiss, I eased her back down into the chair until my knees hit the floor. Rori's legs hugged around my ribs, holding me exactly where I wanted to be.

She melted into the chair from our kissing and petting, her body languid and fluid, giving me a soft place to land. I was getting used to the idea that Rori was a safe place for me, warm and comforting just as much as she was tough and protective. I only hoped I could provide the same kind of safety for her. It felt like a gift that she opened up to me about what happened in the basement.

"Santos..." She sighed out my name with a frustrated groan, arching her back to press the long length of her body against me.

"I'm getting there, paloma." I nipped at her neck, kneading her thighs and calves on my journey down her legs.

Her shoes were those cumbersome biker boots with shoelaces a mile long, so I had to pull away to undo them. Turned out, plucking at those laces heightened the anticipation, much like unlacing a fancy corset would be. I'd rather be here every time, sitting on the floor, undressing the woman who owned me in the only way that mattered.

"I should tie you up with those laces." Rori laughed as I pulled the last knot free with a flourish and slid the boot off her foot.

"Would you? Please?" I started on her other boot while her bare foot ran up my thigh, her cute little toes dragging over my waistband

411

and zipper. Nothing would make me happier than being tied up for her to use me in any way she liked.

"I'll think about it," she purred coyly, running her foot up my stomach to my chest. "They're certainly long enough."

"Yeah, really. What's up with you bikers and your hundred-yard shoelaces?"

A laugh bubbled out of her before she lifted her chin, arching one eyebrow down at me. "I thought you were undressing me, not making cheeky remarks."

I didn't bother to suppress the groan rising out of my throat. She was so fucking hot when she was bossy and deserved to know it. "Yes, paloma." I kissed the ankle of her foot that had been exploring me which was now resting against my shoulder.

The moment her second boot came off, I reached for the waistband of her jeans. Rori lifted her hips and they slid down easily, along with her panties. Her legs came together to remove everything, and I split them wide again as soon as she was naked from the waist down. Stripteases were fun and all, but my woman gave me a specific command, and I was eager to follow through.

I grabbed Rori's waist and pulled her forward, sliding her down the chair and bringing her knees over my shoulders. As tempting as it was to dive straight down to her core, I wanted to savor her. Ease my way into bliss so that it would taste that much sweeter.

She shivered when I kissed the inside of her thigh, legs coming in closer until I pulled them apart again.

"Sensitive here?" I made sure to run my stubble against her skin as I turned my head to give the same treatment to her other leg.

"You already know I am." She reached down, scratching her nails deliciously over my buzzed hair. "You're so good at pleasing. You don't need me to tell you that."

"You haven't given me a test drive yet." My kisses went lower, and I kept eye contact with her. If I looked down to the spot between her legs, I wouldn't be able to stop myself.

"Because you're going slow and making me wait." Her voice was playfully chiding as she curled her toes against my back.

"You didn't tell me not to tease you." An inch lower on each thigh. Her skin was so warm and smooth here, I couldn't resist flicking my tongue out for a lick.

Rori squirmed in my hold, her hand on the verge of pressing my head down right to where she wanted me. "I'm gonna have to watch what I tell you. I didn't know you'd be such a brat."

"On that note, you should probably know I'm not into spanking as a punishment."

"Mm-kay, noted," she purred. "What would you prefer?"

"Smother me by sitting on my face."

I slid my mouth over her pussy before she could answer, and whatever sexy retort she was going to say became a gasp and a throaty moan that filled the room. And the taste that filled my mouth was nothing short of ambrosia.

I licked a long stripe up the seam of her cunt, stopping just short of her clit. She'd get attention there soon enough, but I wanted to feast on her first. I thought kissing her mouth was good, but I never wanted to stop exploring her with my lips and tongue down here. She was sensitive and thrashing, bucking her hips into my face and clamping her thighs to my ears.

My hands came up and I spread her thighs out to the sides, holding her open so I could taste and see more of her. She loved it when I sealed my mouth over her and stroked my tongue through her entrance, then sucked on her lips as I pulled away for a breath.

Rori was panting now, whimpering and begging, her control temporarily gone while she was on the edge of release.

"Can I please make you come now, paloma?" I whispered over her clit, the little pearl begging to be touched.

That snapped her back into bossy mode. Her head jerked up, cheeks flushed and eyes determined with need. "Yes. Be a good boy and make me come *now*, Santos. Do your job and please me."

"Yes, paloma." I flattened my tongue over the top of her cunt, pressing down while I stroked two fingers inside her. She was so wet, I couldn't wait to suck her taste off my fingers.

I spread and curled the digits inside her, giving some friction to her inner walls while my hand rocked in and out. Down below, I was vaguely aware of my hips moving in the same motion. Fuck, I wanted inside her so bad, but this was what she wanted. Her pleasure overrode mine, always.

"I'm so close...right there...don't stop...oh fuck, Santos!"

Her delirious chanting was music to my ears, the sound I marched to steadily with my tongue and fingers. When the orgasm finally hit her and her body convulsed under my ministrations, I still didn't stop.

Only when she pushed my head away did I release her clit and withdraw from inside her. Still, I lapped at her sensitive skin, kissed all around her gorgeous cunt that was now swollen and flushed with her pleasure. I was content to stay here, licking and kissing between her legs until she no longer needed me.

After a few minutes of that, Rori leaned forward and shoved roughly at my shoulder. Her feet planted firmly on the floor while I remained kneeling in front of her. A small spark of worry struck my chest. Did I do something wrong?

"Take your clothes off, Santos. Now." Rori was already whipping off her leather jacket and shirt. "I need to see you and touch you while I fuck you."

Chapter 20

Rori

Santos hurried to obey me, which sent such a rush through me, it almost resembled an orgasm. He tore his clothes off and flung them to the floor without care. All good with me. I didn't want a slave. I wanted a man who was passionate and wanted to please. From the sight of his cock bobbing stiffly as he stripped off his pants, he was enjoying this just as much as I was.

His fast stripping left him standing, so I decided to fix that quickly. "Kneel."

Santos dropped to his knees in front of me like he was before. Fuck me, was there anything hotter than this huge warrior of a man kneeling at my feet? Right after he ate me like I was the finest meal he'd ever had, no less.

He was beautiful to behold, all scarred, sun-kissed skin and swaths of muscle. A dangerous killer, but no threat to me. Like a wild animal I'd bonded with but could never be truly tamed.

Santos' breaths were relaxed, though his body was taut and alert. His eyes, framed by those incredible dark lashes, followed me as I walked a slow, observant circle around him, though he remained facing forward as I came around to his back.

"Do you like what you see, paloma?" he asked, patient and still while my eyes feasted.

"Very much."

There wasn't as much scarring on the wide expanse of his shoulders and back. If someone managed to attack him from behind, he likely wouldn't be kneeling so nicely in my bedroom right now. He had a perky, squeezable ass too, perfect for grabbing onto while he thrust into me.

"You can touch me anywhere you want." His head turned to the side, revealing the slope of his nose, chin, and luscious mouth. "Please touch me, paloma." His voice took on a pleading tone that was somehow still rich, deep, and masculine. His submission to me did nothing to take away his raw masculinity. If anything, his trusting me enough to relinquish sexual control made him even more of a man to me.

I started a touch in the center of his back, letting my fingertips drag up the length of his spine. Santos' head tilted back towards me with a reverent sigh, like this one touch was all he needed to be satisfied.

"You really want me to use you?" My palm reached the nape of his neck and slid around to his throat, tracing over his Adam's apple and the dip between his collarbones.

"Yes," he breathed, his throat moving against my fingertips.

"Any limits?"

He hesitated. "No violence on either end. No humiliation or degradation either."

"Got it." I leaned down, letting my breasts press to his upper back. My hands slid down over the flat planes of his chest, massaging over the strong drumbeat of his heart. "How about I tie your hands together and ride you? Since you're being so good, I'll let you touch me after I drain your cock of cum. How does that sound?"

Santos closed his eyes on a sharp inhale, dark lashes sweeping over his cheekbones. "I would love that. Please, paloma."

I kissed his neck before standing, taking my time to nibble and pull at his warm, sensitive skin. "You are so damn sweet. I love you so giving and pliant like this."

"Oh, you do?" Santos' voice was teasing, breaking character for a split second.

I had picked up one of my boots and begun to pull the laces free when I realized what I'd said.

Oh shit.

I said I loved him.

I didn't mean it like that, but that didn't make the words any less true. I was in the process of falling for him, that was for damn sure. I probably started falling the first time I watched him fight.

And I was loving this sexual dynamic between us too. I'd never been in the role of a truly dominant partner before. With Santos, it just seemed to work. What I had with Torr was more traditional in a sense, and I loved that too. I guess that put me firmly in switch territory. I loved being manhandled and thrown around by Torr just as much as I loved bossing Santos.

It was such a rush, the control Santos handed over to me. But I had to be careful too. The last thing I wanted to do was abuse this control, and make him feel like this wasn't a safe space for him. He trusted me, and I was determined to make sure that trust was well-earned.

So rather than answer Santos' question of if I loved him, I gave him my best stern expression while yanking my shoestring through the eyelets of my boots.

"Put your hands together above your head."

He slapped his wrists together, tongue darting out to lick his lips as he watched me with greedy eyes. I stood in front of him, my breasts at his eye level while I bound up his wrists in the black cord.

His warm breath teased my skin as he stretched forward, testing his limits while I took his hands away.

"May I please give you a kiss while you do that?" he asked, low and husky, his mouth within inches of my nipple.

"No." I tugged at the knots around his wrists, then slid a finger between the bindings. When I was satisfied the tie would hold him without cutting off circulation, I bent down and took his chin in my hand. "But I appreciate you asking politely."

I dropped a chaste kiss on his lips, which he answered with a needy, frustrated groan.

"How's this?" I tugged at his wrist bindings again. "Too tight?"

"No, it's good." His eyes roamed over me as I stepped back, teeth sinking into his lower lip. "And you are perfect."

"Keep talking like that and you'll get to come in no time." I stroked his cheek, admiring the new flexion of muscles in his arms and chest with his hands trussed up like that. He rested his hands on top of his head, cheek leaning into my hand as he looked up at me, so adoring and eager.

I dropped my hand and brought it to my hip. "Stand up."

Santos rose to his feet with feline grace, all masculine muscle and power as he towered over me.

"Lie back on the bed," I told him.

He walked backward, looking behind him only once so he didn't trip, and I watched with rapt fascination. Using his elbows and strong legs to shimmy up toward the pillows, he somehow made it look hot and not at all awkward.

"Is this where you'd like me, paloma?" His head and bound hands rested on a pillow, long body overtaking my bed with his feet splayed out, relaxed.

His cock, though, was anything but.

It stood straight up like a column, the thickness and slight upward curve promising an incredible ride. The blunt head of him was glossy with precum, just begging for me to spread it around with my hand. Or my mouth.

Damn, did I really have to wait to taste him? I was in charge, right? Who was to stop me from going down on such a beautiful specimen right now?

Patience, I reminded myself. *Stick to what you told him. Don't change the rules.*

"*You* are perfect." I lowered onto the edge of the bed, and Santos beamed at me repeating his words. "Just look at you stretched out on my bed for me. And this gorgeous cock."

I leaned over and circled my hand around his head. With a firm stroke, I spread the wetness from his tip down and around his shaft. "Is all this for me?" I asked in a whisper.

"Yes," Santos hissed, hips rolling up to pump through my fist. "All for you. I've never gotten so hard for anyone like I do for you."

Jesus. How could he expect me to be a stern domme when everything he said made me melt?

Keeping my hand on his length, I leaned up to kiss him and fuck...it had only been minutes but it felt like I'd gone without kissing him for years. The tension between us was as taut as a piano wire, every little exchange of power between us pulling it tighter. My pussy pulsed with a needy ache, and I didn't have to touch myself to know that I was soaked and already on the verge of another orgasm.

Santos clearly felt the same on his end. The passion he poured into kissing me was heightened by his soft moans and the hypnotic rolls of his hips, thrusting his cock through my stroking hand.

Abruptly, his mouth broke away. "You better stop if you want me to last."

I gripped his jaw with my free hand while my strokes of his cock squeezed tighter and slowed down, but I definitely didn't stop. "I stop when *I* want to stop. Your job is to keep all that cum inside your balls until I let you shoot down my throat. Understand?"

He groaned so low that it was almost a growl. "Yes, paloma." The sound was so sexy, so strained from the effort of holding back.

Another bead of precum released from his tip and I spread it down, taking a few slow, measured pumps of him before pausing my grip at his base. Why not give him a little relief? I didn't want to make this an entirely torturous experience for him.

I waited until the tension of holding back left his face before swinging a leg over to straddle him, holding his cock in the perfect spot to sit on. Santos hissed in a breath as he watched me, the muscles in his arms bunching as he pulled on the wrist ties. Squeezing him with my thighs as I would a motorcycle, I lowered down slowly but didn't let him penetrate me yet.

My hips thrust forward and I rubbed my cunt against the underside of his length, letting him feel my wetness and heat without getting inside. His stiff cock felt incredible on my clit, so I let myself grind and rub on him for me and only me.

Poor Santos went crazy. He had no choice but to accept my treatment and not come, and his breaths came in short, ragged pants. His wrists strained at his bonds, his head throwing back on frustrated moans only to lift again so he could watch me.

"God...fuck...*please*, paloma. You're so...ahh..."

"Good at dominating you?" I offered, running a hand up his taut stomach until I reached a nipple to pinch.

"Mmm, I was gonna say you're so mean, but that works too."

I laughed, lifting up until his blunt head kissed my core. "Too mean?" I watched him carefully, wiping the humor from my face.

"No," he insisted, giving me a tight but dreamy smile. "You're perfect."

"Good." I positioned him at my entrance and lowered slowly, finally letting him fill me up.

We both moaned as I sank down all the way. I was so slick and beyond ready to receive him. Once fully sheathed, Santos' erection jumped inside me, the stiff length flexing against my inner walls and hitting a deliciously sensitive spot.

"Fuck..." I pitched forward, my hands on his chest as my hips lifted. The drag of him through me was exquisite, a bliss that bordered on painful. I wanted to savor the sensation but also couldn't get enough, so each slow lift was followed by a quick thrust down to start it all over again.

"I want to touch you so bad," Santos groaned, his eyes following the lifting and lowering of my body.

"You are," I said, giving a playful tweak of his nipple.

"I want to be touching you more," he clarified. "With my mouth and my hands. I want to smack your ass and suck on those cute little nipples."

"Do you want to be untied?" I straightened my arms and took him in a more vigorous rhythm, making my ass bounce on his thighs and my tits bounce in his face.

"Mmm..." His teeth sank into his lip, and it was so cute seeing him trying to form a coherent thought while having his cock thoroughly worked. "Kind of," he decided.

That wasn't a no, and I couldn't find any true discomfort in his expression, so I let my bossy domme side answer. "Too fucking bad."

The ragged moan leaving his mouth was music to my ears. My thighs were starting to ache, so I slowed my ride, leaning down to press flush against him. It would be nice to feel his arms around me, those battle-callused hands gripping my ass, but I loved him at my mercy like this too.

Yeah, I just loved him, period.

Our mouths found each other, the kiss just as passionate and needy as that time we were forcibly separated by the guards back at the canyon. This time, there was no fear of losing each other riding on our backs. This energy with the strength of a monument and fire of a phoenix reborn was purely us. *Our* connection.

The kiss ended with the slowest of separations. My lips skimmed up the bridge of his nose to his forehead as I lifted over him, taking mercy and giving him a taste of what he wanted. What we *both* wanted, more like.

Santos dragged a slow lick over the swell of my breast before his lips closed over my nipple. He gave it the same sensual attention as kissing my mouth, alternating gentle pulls and nips with his teeth. I continued a slow roll of my hips back and forth over his cock, the added friction of our upper bodies together plus his laving on my nipples was bringing on my orgasm faster.

"Santos..." My forehead came down to his, my hip rolls becoming an aggressive, greedy slamming down and lifting in short, shallow thrusts. The pressure building in my clit made my breath tight and every instinct desperate for release.

"Fuck yes, paloma. You ride me so well," he praised. "Come for me. Let me feel that gorgeous cunt grip my cock for everything it needs."

Bless this beautiful, submissive man and his dirty mouth. The orgasm washed over me in waves, taking me under in full-body pulses that gently ebbed away. It was delicious, so fucking good. But my own pleasure wasn't even at the forefront of my mind.

I slid free of Santos when the pulses faded and rolled off his body as best as my shaky legs could manage. "Come here. Sit at the edge of the bed."

He rolled up and swung his feet down to the floor in an instant, bound hands resting atop his head again. I knelt between his legs, coming face-to-face with his heavy, straining cock.

This was where the submissive and dominant sides of me truly overlapped. I loved this, being on my knees before a powerful man to please him with my mouth. I also loved that I was giving my sweet Santos his well-earned release after he'd been such a good boy for me.

My lips slid over his head, tongue pressing along his length as I drew him in. He was coated in my wetness, my own tangy, musky taste filling me with a different kind of pleasure. No other woman would soak his cock ever again.

I formed a seal with my lips as I drew back, eyes lifted to watch the tortured pleasure play out on his face. His mouth was parted on panting breaths, chest rising and falling with exertion.

"Please don't stop. Please...fuck, I'm so close."

To reward his sweet begging, I brought a hand up to massage his heavy balls. They were drawn up tight against his body, his cock like iron wrapped in velvety skin.

I got to enjoy only three, four, five more sucks of him before he couldn't hold back anymore. He swelled and spilled his release down my throat, just as I'd told him to. Again and again, he gave me mouthfuls of hot, salty cum, his orgasm long and drawn-out as I held him on my tongue, my hand continuing to massage his balls until the last of it was wrung out of him.

Santos collapsed back on the bed when finished, the harsh breaths from his chest the only sounds he made. I climbed up next to him, grinning like a cat that swallowed a whole jar of cream as I plucked the knots holding his wrists together.

The moment he was free, his arms came around me, holding me to his chest and cupping my face as he kissed me with such a deep, overwhelming passion that I felt tears prick at my eyes.

"Was that okay?" My hand flew to his wrist, feeling the indent in his skin made by the shoestring. "Does it hurt? I should really learn how to tie sex-safe knots."

"Okay?" Santos sounded incredulous, pulling away to look at me like I was crazy. "I have never in my life enjoyed sex so much."

I blinked at him. "Really?"

"Fuck yeah, really." Hauling me up in his arms, he moved us around until we were lying on the pillows, facing each other on our sides. "Your domme side is just what my sub side has been craving for years." He kissed me again, warm and tender with his thumb brushing back and forth over my cheekbone. "Thank you for trying this with me. I know it's not typical bedroom roles." He pressed a kiss to my forehead before pulling back to look me in the eyes. "What did you think?"

"I really enjoyed it too," I whispered. "It's such a fine balance. I tried to give you what you needed without being cruel. Mostly I'm just floored by your trust. Being your domme is so...humbling. I was nervous about taking it too far, that's why I asked so many questions. I just want to do right by you, always."

"You're a natural." Santos traced my cheekbone and jaw. "And it's good to ask questions and be careful, that's a domme worthy of trust. So many people get off on the power trip. They say they're dominant as an excuse to be an abusive piece of shit."

"I never want that." My hand slid up his chest, resting over his heart.

"I know." He kissed the bridge of my nose before pulling back again, grinning. "You can push me even further next time."

"Hmm, I'll have to think about how." I drummed my fingers on his skin. "No violence or humiliation, right?"

"Yeah, pretty much. I like sensory deprivation. Being tied or blindfolded are my favorites. I loved when you made me kneel and every time you barked orders at me. Fuck, that's so hot."

I leaned into the crook of his neck, laughing lightly. "I almost took pity on you and untied you early."

"Nah, being tied up is great. You know why?"

"Hmm?" I placed a kiss on his neck.

Santos' hands moved over me with slow, intentional movement. Running up the back of my thigh to cup my ass, palming my waist before moving around in front to run up my belly and roll over my breasts. His hand went around my nape and drew me in for another one of those breath-stealing, electrifying kisses. When he eventually broke away, his lips hovered over mine as he answered.

"Because it makes touching you now so much better."

Chapter 21

Torrance

Rori and Santos came down from the bedroom in the middle of the afternoon, both of them looking blissed out and well-fucked. People's heads turned and conversations stopped as they walked past, hands intertwined, but neither of them looked like they were on a walk of shame. It was more a walk of *fuck yeah suckers, we got laid good.*

I was in the kitchen, shooting the shit with Carter and LJ. Paige and the Hunter were hanging out too, and it was hard to not laugh at Paige's eyes bugging out as Rori untangled herself from Santos and came over to me.

"Hi." Rori's arms went around my neck, her smile hidden but smug as she leaned up for a kiss.

"Hey, creep." I let my hands rest on the small of her back, lowering to give her the kiss she wanted. "Have fun?" I whispered against her lips.

"So. Much. Fun." She punctuated each word with a peck on my lips, her smile turning into a full-on grin against my mouth.

"Well, invite me up next time," I said with a swat to her hip.

"I can't wait." Her nails ran over the back of my head as she kissed me again. "I love you, Torr."

I held her fast to me, trying to force those same stubborn words out of my chest. What came out instead was, "Anything for you."

Rori brushed her knuckles over my cheek, her smile warm and loving and not the least bit resentful. "Right back at you."

Our tender moment was interrupted by Santos rummaging through the fridge. "Is there any food left?"

"What, like you didn't get enough to eat?" the Hunter cracked, earning a smack on the arm from Paige.

"Strenuous exercise means calories have to be replenished," Santos replied smugly, closing the fridge door. "I'm gonna check in the other house." He came over, kissed Rori on the back of her head, and gave a quick nod to me before leaving.

"Seems like he gets it," I observed, watching him go out the door.

"He does," Rori said dreamily. "He really does."

"You sound head over heels already," I teased with a pinch to her waist.

She just leaned her head on my shoulder. "Pretty sure I am."

I kissed her forehead before resting my cheek there, loving the feel of her against me, her arms around my neck, and the dreamy relaxation in her voice and face. Sure, it was another man who made her feel that way, but my woman was here with me now. She was happy, and she loved me. Plus, Santos was a good dude. I trusted him with her, so how could I be anything but pleased at this situation?

"I'm happy for you, creep. You two are good together."

"Thanks, but so are you and I," she said into my neck.

"I'm working on it."

"You being a pain in my ass is just another reason why I love you."

I kissed her hairline again with a chuckle. As much as I would have preferred hearing her say she loved me over and over, we had other matters to attend to.

"I think it's time to tell everyone what's next." I spoke low, in a voice meant only for her ears. "It's been a nice three days of R&R, but people are getting restless. Especially the fighters."

Rori nodded, straightening as she stepped away from me. "I figured today would be the day."

"Want me to get everyone together?"

"Yes, please. Is out front in fifteen minutes enough time?"

"If you tell everyone it is."

Rori scoffed just as Devin entered the house, and then her posture immediately changed. She grew stiff, not just straight. The air around her became icy, although her expression remained neutral.

I wanted to block his view of her, to shield her from him. Yeah, I understood why he had issues with women, especially women in charge, but he didn't have to be an outright asshole to Rori. Santos had been through the same shit and he had figured out she wasn't like those whackos running the resort.

Devin came right up to us, and to his credit, didn't have his usual sneer whenever he saw Rori with me or Santos.

"Hi, Devin." She greeted him as cordially as she would anyone, despite her defenses being up.

He stopped a few feet away, hands relaxed on the holster of multiple knives at his hips. The guy didn't even spare me a glance, his focus remaining steadfast on her.

"I wanted to let you know that the deed is done. Nella is no longer alive." His gaze flicked to me before returning to her. "I did as you asked and made it quick. No drawn-out torture or anything of the sort."

Rori nodded at him. "Thank you for honoring our agreement. I hope this kill gives you the closure you were looking for."

Devin lifted one shoulder in a shrug. "Thanks. It helps a little, but there's no undoing what's been done." He straightened again. "I've wrapped up the body, but I didn't know if you wanted anything done with it."

"It doesn't matter to me. We can bury it out in the wilderness tonight, unless you prefer something else?"

Devin seemed taken aback that she would let him decide, but he quickly recovered. "Ah, no. No preference, that's fine. I can help with the burial if you'd like."

"Sure." Rori's smile at him was genuine, her posture relaxing and the iciness in her demeanor thawing. "I'd appreciate the help." There was an awkward silence for a few seconds, and then I cleared my throat to cut in to the conversation.

"We're gathering everyone out front in fifteen," I told him. "Sadly, our little vacation here has to end soon."

"Ah, alright. I'll be right out there. And I'll grab the guys from the other house too."

"Thanks," I told him. The moment he turned to leave, I gave Rori a shocked look, which she just grinned and shook her head at. Once Devin was gone, I said, "Am I high, or was that the most productive conversation you've ever had with him?"

"It was definitely a step in a positive direction," she mused. "Not one that I expected."

"Did Santos talk to him?"

"I don't think so. Even if he did, I get the sense that he doesn't really listen to Santos." Rori shrugged and stepped away from me, her hand running down my arm and clasping my hand until the last possible moment. "I'm gonna freshen up. See you in fifteen?"

"You got it, creep." I kissed her fingers before releasing them, then went to give everyone the message while she headed up the stairs.

"Thank you all for coming out," Rori said from where she stood in Val's truck bed. It was the only elevated spot we had, where everyone could see her. Behind and above her, Astarte was perched on the apex of the roof on the detached garage.

I stood on the ground next to the rear tire, while Santos took up the same spot across from me with Tezca sitting in front of him. The jaguar observed the onlookers with cool, calculated yellow eyes.

Carter, LJ, and Val were seated on the truck's bumper, arms crossed and looking out at the gathered crowd like a trio of bodyguards. With Santos, Tezca, and me, I guess that made six of us.

"Sadly," Rori continued, eyes scanning the crowd, "we can't stay at these two houses forever."

She paused and smiled at the playful chorus of disappointed groans and shouts of, "Boo, this concert sucks!" The Hunter earned another smack from his lady for that one.

"I know," Rori laughed. "But seriously, we're excited to help you all start your new lives. My people and I can take you to your choice of territories, either Four Corners or Sevier, where the professionals there can set you up with housing, jobs, education, or they'll help to locate your family members."

Rori paused and a long silence followed, with everyone staring up blankly at her. She seemed flustered for a moment before resuming her speech.

"Of course, you don't have to take any of these options if you don't want to. Just let our riders know where you'd like to go from here, and they'll take you the closest they can where it's safe."

Another long silence stretched on, everyone's eyes on Rori expectantly. She frowned and glanced down at me. I shrugged in response.

"Um, does anyone have any questions?" Rori called out.

"Yeah," one ex-gladiator answered immediately. "What about the people who run the resort? You're going after them, right?"

Rori squinted at the guy. "Well, yes."

The fighter crossed his arms and looked around at the others surrounding him. "What if we want to come along?" There was a low murmur of agreement and nodding heads.

"Oh no." Rori lifted her hands as if trying to diffuse the situation. "Please, you don't have to do that. You have your whole lives ahead of you and don't owe us anything. I speak for all of us when I say it was an honor to help you get your lives back."

"You misunderstand me, ma'am," the fighter said. "We don't feel as though we owe you a debt. We want to spill the blood of the deranged cunts who did this to us, and our brothers, until none of them are left." He flinched. "No offense."

Rori was too stunned to be offended, shaking her head and planting her feet wide on the truck bed. "You don't have to shed blood anymore, though. You can return to your families, or start new families. Ending this cult will take months, if not longer, and is incredibly dangerous—"

"*We* are just as dangerous," the fighter snarled, punching one fist against his chest. "They made us this way. Most of us don't have much in the way of family to return to, but we all have one thing in common. Every man here is very good at killing. Why not use our skill against those who forced it upon us?"

"We're also not afraid to die," the Hunter chimed in. "Your riders certainly have families that would miss them, a lot to lose. We will take risks in ways that they won't."

"No," Rori snapped. "You are *people*. You're not just expendable bodies anymore. You all could matter to someone else."

"You said it was our choice," argued the first fighter. "This is what I choose to do."

"Fighting at your command, how could we lose?" added the Saint, his smile cunning as he looked up at Rori. "We all saw you liberate us in the pit, your divine bird flying above your head." He gestured to Astarte, sitting on a nearby tree branch. "And the Butcher's jaguar, who led their guns away from us and allowed us to be saved. These gods of vengeance wanted us to find you, Aurora. It had to be for this reason."

The agreement and support was getting louder among the ex-gladiators, the guys nodding, grinning, and moving in place. They were itching for a fight. Rori kept shaking her head, but she was clearly losing this battle.

"Can I just address the elephant in the room, as it were?" The question came from Carter, who stood from the truck's bumper and turned to face Rori. "You know what I'm gonna say, Ror," he warned. "We talked about this."

"Carter, don't," she growled through her teeth.

I exchanged a confused look with Santos across the truck bed. How did the two guys sleeping with Rori not have a clue what this was about?

"Why not?" her cousin challenged, spreading his arms out to the side. "These guys can fight, they're learning to ride, they're loyal to you and will follow you anywhere." He dropped his arms. "Why not form your own MC with these men as your riders," he grinned smugly, "and you as their president?"

The next look Santos and I shared was one of, *Oh sweet holy fuck, how did we not see that coming?*

"Yeah!" The Hunter pumped his fist, and his shout was followed by a wave of support.

"Fuck yeah, let's do that!"

"We follow the light! Aurora for president!"

"I look good in leather, sign me up!"

"No!" Rori waved her arms in an effort to calm the crowd. "It's not happening! I don't know how to be a fucking MC president!"

"Yeah, you do."

Rori's gaze snapped down to me, and the next thing I knew, I was climbing up into the truck bed to stand beside to her. Because that was where I would always stand, especially when she couldn't see the greatness within herself.

"You do know how," I repeated, raising my voice so everyone could hear. The crowd had now gone silen,t but as far as I was concerned, it was just me and her. "You were born to lead an MC, Aurora Wilder. You sat on a motorcycle before you were crawling."

"Torr..." She was shaking her head and her voice had that low pissed-off tone, but I would not be deterred.

"You were raised by four of the greatest men and riders this world has ever seen," I went on. "Since the day you were born, you have been learning how to lead. Not just how to fight and be ruthless but how to be kind and show compassion when it's needed. You know how vital it is to lean on your family and to offer a shoulder when someone else needs that support. Don't you see, Rori?" I held her gaze. "No one is a better fit to lead a club than you."

She didn't respond, only blinked a few times. A breeze rustled some leaves, but it was dead silent beyond that.

"How does this work?" the Hunter piped up. "How do we make her president?"

I looked at Carter, who cleared his throat. "Well, for the inception of a brand new club, presidents are usually nominated. If there is more than one person nominated, members can vote if they want to be civil. The old ways used to have contests of some sort. The would-be presidents would fight hand-to-hand, race each other on a dangerous stretch of road, that kind of thing."

"I nominate Rori!" the Hunter yelled.

I nodded at him. "I'll second that."

"Third," Santos called out.

"Any other nominations?" Carter scanned the dozens of faces, barely hiding a smile. When nobody answered, he asked, "All in favor of Aurora, the light, 'Rori' Wilder as your president?"

Every single hand shot up. Well, every one except Devin, who had remained off to the side, curiously apart from the other fighters. His arms were folded, his expression blankly observant. It was anyone's guess what was going through that guy's head, but he didn't seem thrilled at what was happening.

"Congratulations, Prez." Carter reached over the tailgate to pat Rori's leg, who was still apparently too dumbfounded to speak. "Normally, a president chooses who goes into their cabinet positions. Vice president, treasurer, road captain, all that. But it seems she needs reality to sink in first."

Chuckles rose up from the onlookers, or rather, club members, and there was a new sense of excitement buzzing in the air. I was starting to think I should bring Rori inside, give her some private time to process, maybe a stiff drink, when her hand shot out to clasp my forearm.

"Torr." She blinked rapidly and chewed her lip, like it was just now all sinking in.

"You okay?" I spoke next to her ear.

Rori's hand slid down my arm to clasp my hand. She pulled in a shaky breath and nodded her head.

"I'll, um, decide on the others soon," she said, voice raising to reach everyone. "But this man, Torrance Knight." She looked directly into my eyes as she said, "He's my vice president."

Chapter 22

Rori

I had a couple phone calls to make and decided I might as well get the toughest one out of the way first.

It was unbelievably awkward explaining to my aunt Kyrie that I needed the two safe houses for a little while longer because, well, I was now president of a brand new MC and we didn't have a clubhouse yet.

She, on the other hand, couldn't stop laughing.

"Oh, they really ambushed you with it?" I could just imagine her wiping tears from her eyes. "That's incredible. Wait until I tell your uncles."

"Val probably already has," I muttered. My cousin was yacking on the phone earlier, and I swore I heard T-Bone's booming cackle through the little speaker.

"Have you told your parents?"

I rubbed my eyes. "Not yet. They're my next call."

"Well, best of luck, darling. Don't put those fathers of yours in too early of a grave."

"Wait, before you go."

"Yes?"

I blew out a breath and wished again that I had something to drink. It turned out the fighters had gone through what little alcohol we had on the first day. And now I had the privilege of babysitting them full-time. Fan-fucking-tastic.

"What should I tell Val if she wants to stay with me?"

"If you want her in your club, tell her yes, of course."

"Aunt Kyrie," I groaned. "She's a kid. She's only twenty-one."

"And you're twenty-three. Your point is?"

"She's your only daughter, and we're riding into the heart of a cult. If she was my little sister, I'd be shipping her back home right now."

"Let me tell you a story, my dear niece." I heard a creaking and shuffling noise, like my aunt was crossing her legs and assuming her tall, regal posture. "You know how your uncles and I first met?"

I had heard this story dozens of times. "They were your bodyguards."

"That was the second time. The first time, I had been kidnapped and they rescued me."

Now *that* was news to me. "Holy shit."

"Exactly right. I walked right into a kidnapping plot because my father kept me so sheltered that I didn't know how to look out for danger at nineteen-fucking-years old."

"Whoa." All I had known about Kyrie's father was that he'd been the first governor of Four Corners.

"I decided a long time ago that I wouldn't shield my children from the world to that degree. I would protect them, of course. But Val is grown now, and while of course I worry for her, I'm confident in what her fathers and I taught her. And you know what else?"

"Huh?"

"I know she's safe with you, Rori."

"Fuck." I rubbed my eyes again. "All of you, I swear to God. You all think I'm some badass savior when I'm not."

"Don't believe the lies you tell yourself." I heard the smile in my aunt's voice. "You are capable of far more than what you believe."

"I just don't want to let anybody down." I chewed the nail at the edge of my thumb. "I don't want to fail anyone."

"It's not easy being a leader. And let me tell you, men, and bikers especially, are some hard headed sons of bitches. You're going to get a lot of pushback for every decision you make, especially because you're a woman."

"Great," I deadpanned.

"But remember you're not alone, Rori. That's what a club is, a family and a support system. The right people will stand by your good decisions *and* tell you when you're legitimately fucking up."

At least I could be certain of that. Torr was just as likely to stand by me as he was to put me in my place.

"You can do this, sweetheart," my aunt said softly. "You *are* the right person for this. Trust your instincts. And if you're still not sure, trust your VP."

I sighed out a long, resigned breath. "Okay. Thanks, Aunt Kyrie. I love you."

"Love you too. Oh, and bring back my daughter alive or I'll kill you."

We shared a laugh at that before hanging up, and I realized I felt a little lighter. Like maybe my newfound presidency wasn't a totally unwanted burden. As my finger hovered over my fathers' phone numbers, I started to think maybe *this* call would actually be the hard one.

I hit Shadow's number and brought the phone to my ear, wishing once again for a shot of booze.

He answered on the second right. "Rori!"

"Hey, Dad. How's—"

"Are you okay? Do you need anything? The guys and I can ride out at a moment's notice."

"Oh God, Shadow, leave her alone," said a woman's voice in the background before yelling, "Hey, Roriiii!"

"Hey, Aunt Noelle! What are you doing with my old man?"

"I'm touching up her sleeves." The buzzing of a tattoo machine came through the phone. "So you're good?" Shadow pressed. "You're okay?"

"Yeah, Dad, I'm fine. Hey, Aunt Noelle!" I said to Reaper's sister, who was also Carter's mother. "Your son's an asshole, by the way."

"Aw, what'd he do this time?"

"Made me president of a brand-spankin-new MC."

The line fell dead silent.

"He did *what?*" My father broke the silence first.

"Surprise," I said in a lame singsong voice. "Guess I'm following in your footsteps after all, Dadow."

There was a rustling on the phone, and then I heard Shadow's muffled voice speaking to Noelle. "...later?...moment to talk with my daughter." Another few seconds of rustling and muffled voices followed before Shadow came back on the phone. "What the hell happened, Rori? Your mother's been trying to call you back, by the way."

Yeah, I'd dodged a couple of her calls. Asking for her advice on my guy problems had kind of taken a backseat to my newfound leadership position, and I didn't feel ready to have that conversation with her yet. How funny that I found it easier to talk to my mom about threesomes than a new job.

"I texted her and told her I was fine! Just busy."

"Clearly," Shadow said snidely. "So a mission with just you and Torr turns into you becoming president of a club, huh?"

"He's my VP, if it makes you feel any better."

"Uh huh. Who else do you got?"

"LJ. He's going to be my Sergeant-at-Arms, most likely." I hesitated before saying the next name. "Val, maybe. If she wants to stick around."

"Are you kidding? That girl is *your* shadow."

I smiled at the play on his name. "Also some guys we rescued. I'm still getting to know them, but they want to ride with me." I swallowed hard. "Fight with me."

My father sighed. "Do I even want to know who or what you're fighting?"

It struck me then where I'd heard Sisters of Bathory before, and my heartbeat felt like getting kicked in the chest. *He'd* told me to stay away from them before I left.

A memory surfaced from when I was around five years old. Shadow was holding me, his forearm around my middle. I saw all the lines in his skin, hundreds of scars criss crossing over each other. I knew what they were. Old owies, I had called them. I understood the concept of scars being leftover remnants of being hurt. And he was covered in them from head to toe, even on his face.

Fuck.

Could my father have been an escaped gladiator? A sex slave like Santos?

"Rori? You still there?"

I drew in a pained breath, trying to calm my heart threatening to pound out of my chest. "I'm good, Dad. And no, you don't have to worry."

"Wasn't what I asked," he teased.

"No, you don't want to know. But trust me, I got it." My hand started to ache with how hard I gripped the phone. "They're terrible people, but I'm gonna take care of every last one of them, Dadow. I promise."

"Do you need help?"

"I'll let you know if I do." I tilted the phone away so he wouldn't hear my nose sniffle as I wiped hot, furious tears. "I love you so much, Dad. You know that, right?"

A long silence passed before he spoke. "Rori, are you sure you don't want us to come out?"

"No. No, I'm good."

"Because that sounds like the kind of *I love you* someone says right before a big fucking battle."

I forced out a laugh. "I mean, it kind of is. But I have every intention of coming home. Daren would kill me all over again if I missed his wedding."

"True," he chuckled. "I love you too, Ror. And you know what? I'm always gonna be worried, but I'm fucking proud of you."

This time, I let him hear my sniffle. "Thanks, Dad."

"My oldest daughter, an MC president," he said. "Reaper's gonna be so happy."

"He'll have a heart attack, you mean."

"Eh. Your mom will bring him back."

We laughed together, and then he asked, "So, does your club have a name?"

"Yeah. That's actually why I called you. We need a logo designed for our tattoos and patches."

Shadow barked out a laugh. "Called to solicit my services, did you? I should charge you extra."

"Send the bill to my treasurer." I grinned. "As soon as I decide on one."

"I'll get right on that." I heard rustling like he was shuffling through papers in search of a pen. "Alright, tell me what I'm working with, Miss President."

I grinned wider, the stampeding of my heart turning into excitement. "We're the Vengeful Gods MC."

———

I GOT off the phone with Shadow and left my room to find Val hovering on the stair landing. My cousin was pacing a hole in the floor, looking apprehensive.

"Hey, what's up?" I asked her.

She stopped and turned to face me with the same pouty lips and large blue eyes as her mother, my aunt Kyrie. Rather than her mother's blond hair though, she had thick black hair in a long fishtail braid coming over the front of her shoulder.

"Carter wanted me to tell you that he and the Valkyrie riders are leaving soon. So are Gwen and Chasing Death." Her gaze went to the floor. "Since you have your own club now."

"Right. Guess I oughta say goodbye then."

"They're taking my truck and leaving some loaner bikes for y'all. Until your club gets a hold of their own rides."

I cocked my head at her. "So where does that leave you?"

Val shrugged and played with her braid. "I dunno. Where do you want me?"

I gave a little punch to her shoulder. "You're a grown-ass woman. You decide."

She blinked at me, surprised. "You're letting me choose?"

"I'm your cousin, not your mom."

Val pulled in a breath and lifted her chin. "I want to be your road captain."

I grinned, grabbed the end of her braid, and ignored her yelp as I pulled her into a hug. "I was hoping you'd say that, bitch."

"Ow! Well I take it back if you're gonna pull my hair, asshole."

"That's President Asshole to you." I squeezed her tighter and said into her ear, "Thank you. I need another woman to keep me sane here."

"And I need to be on the road. At your side." She pulled away, her hands on my elbows and her grin ecstatic. "Look at us. A couple of chicks following in our fathers' tire tracks."

"Those poor guys will need therapy." I laughed. "Come on, let's say our goodbyes."

The Valkyrie Network and Chasing Death MC were already packed up and out in the cul-de-sac, trucks and bikes idling as they prepared to head out.

I headed over to Carter first and allowed him to hug me before saying quietly, "I don't know whether to be pissed off or grateful to you."

He chuckled and planted a brotherly kiss on my cheek. "Often-times, we see the potential in someone before they see it themselves."

Both of our faces were serious by the time we pulled away. "I'll look out for LJ," I told him. "I won't let anything happen to him."

"The whole club will," he said. "You all gotta look out for each other."

"Carter," I breathed. "I barely know most of these people."

"You'll get to know them," he said calmly. "And in time, you'll know who to cut, and you'll do it with confidence, no hesitation, and with the support of your inner circle."

"Right," I scoffed. "No pressure."

"You've never been one to be too nice, Rori." Carter smirked. "Just another reason why you'll be a good president."

"You've always been great at compliments," I sneered. "Now get out of here and ride safe, jackass."

"Call me if you need backup," he said before mounting his bike.

When I walked over to where Chasing Death was lining up, Gwen and Lupa hopped out of a black SUV to greet me.

"What, no motorcycle for you?" I spread my arms out.

"Nah, not my thing." Gwen accepted my embrace. "Just runs in the family."

"Thank you again," I whispered against her shoulder. "I just can't thank you enough."

"Sure you can," she laughed. "I kind of started this whole mess for you."

"And it's been a hell of a ride already."

We released each other, and Gwen looked at me for several seconds without saying anything. "May the gods watch over and provide guidance for you, Aurora."

"To you as well, Gwen. May they guard you on your journey and keep you safe."

She smiled. "I have a feeling we'll be seeing each other again."

"I'm sure we will. When this is over, my family will undoubtedly throw a party at our home in Four Corners. You should come."

Gwen grinned and shimmied her shoulders. "I've heard stories of the Steel Demons parties."

"There is nothing like experiencing them for yourself," I promised her. "Take care until then."

I will be seeing you soon, Aurora Wilder. Lupa gave a little yip and a wag of her tail before following Gwen into the car.

I had barely a second to think about that statement before Torr came up to stand beside me. Together, we watched the squad of trucks, SUVs, and motorcycles take off down the road until they were specks on the horizon.

"We should hold our first church meeting soon," Torr said. "Get all the rules laid out, figure out what's our next move."

"Sounds good, VP." I turned toward the houses, giving him a smack on the ass before I started walking. "Get everyone together, and let's go to church."

Chapter 23

Devin

So, was I a gangbanger now? Some kind of motorcycle-riding dude in a leather vest?

Everyone seemed stoked at this spontaneous club formation with Rori at the top, but not me. This shit was so far out of my wheelhouse. I wanted to hop in a car and ride away with the others. Getting dropped off somewhere to start a new life all over sounded perfectly great to me.

But there was no way I was leaving Santos behind, and he was becoming permanently attached to Rori. Who, I'd begun to grudgingly accept, wasn't all that bad.

While I was still annoyed that I needed her permission to have my kill in the first place, she did keep her word. She did seem to care about Santos and Torr equally, even though the fact that she was juggling both of them still weirded me out.

And she did appear to accept the mantle of MC president with a healthy dose of reluctance. She looked tense instead of happy, nor drunk on power, like I would have expected. This position wasn't a goal of hers but an obligation, and she was trying to shoulder the weight of the responsibility as best she could.

I still wasn't her number one fan, but she had more of my respect as time went on.

"Devin, you coming?" Santos clapped my shoulder as he slid past me, heading for the open door.

They were having church, or whatever it was called, in the house with the largest living room. From what I gathered, it was essentially a meeting. Seemed weird to call it church, but again, it wasn't my scene.

"I dunno," I said. "I'm not sure this club thing is really for me."

"Come anyway," called Rori, who stood against the door to hold it open for everyone filing in. "I'm not asking everyone for pledged membership yet, this is still new to a lot of us. But we're going to be talking about hitting the next compound, so you might want to sit in."

Well, I wouldn't say no to killing more of those who enslaved us. Trying not to drag my feet, I followed Santos inside. Rori gave me a small smile and a nod as I passed her. I returned the nod but didn't smile.

She closed the door once everyone was inside, and Torr went to stand in front of it, ever the dutiful guard.

"Welcome to our first church session everyone," Rori greeted, standing at one end of the room. "Just so you all know, this is pretty casual for how it usually goes. Normally, it's an enclosed room. The door is locked so no one can leave early or enter late. Attendance is mandatory for all patched-in members. Nothing that is discussed in church can be shared with prospective members or those outside the club." She paused, scanning everyone's faces with shrewd eyes. "It'll be a while until we have proper protocols in place, and if you decide this isn't for you, that's fine. What I'm trying to get across is that church is sacred. Am I understood?"

"Yes, president," Torr said, which was echoed softly by others in the room.

"Good. Church is where we'll discuss our most pressing business matters. Right now, that is eliminating the Sisterhood of Bathory cult. LJ?"

She nodded at a younger guy who was her cousin, if I remembered correctly. He came forward, spreading out a map on the coffee table in the middle of the room.

"This is the location that the prisoner gave you, president." He touched an index finger to the map. "And here is where we are." He dragged his finger down in a southwest direction. "It'd be about a two-day ride. This area here is a neutral zone. It'd be our safest bet for camping overnight. If the information is correct, the compound is in a valley with a few different lookout spots we can scout from." He marked three different areas on the map.

"What's our worst-case scenario?" Rori asked him.

Her cousin shrugged. "That the resort manager lied and there's nothing there. But Carter and I have ridden the general area before. I know it well enough. Nothing will sneak up on us on our way there."

Rori looked up and scanned the faces in the room. "Anyone have any issues with this plan?"

No one spoke up, so I raised my hand.

"Yes, Devin?"

"What exactly is our goal here? Specifically."

"Find out who the key players are, target them, and take them out. We should be able to gather a good amount of intel from scouting."

"How long do you intend to scout for?"

"As long as we need to. Up to a week if that's what it takes." Rori produced a folded piece of paper from her pocket, opened it, and laid it on top of the map. "This is what I got from Nella as far as guards, rotation schedules, and how many people there are in total. We can use it as a benchmark, but I don't expect all of these numbers to be current."

I leaned over the table, inspecting the numbers scribbled on the yellow legal sheet. "A population of fifty total? That's almost twice as much as the staff and fighters combined at Mystic Canyon."

"And it could end up being more or less." Rori faced me, crossing her arms. Her posture wasn't completely confrontational, but it wasn't exactly friendly either. "We don't have much information to go off of right now, which is why I want us to spy on them for as long as we possibly can. The more knowledge we gather, the better."

I couldn't argue with that logic. It seemed like a sound plan, for what little we knew.

"Do we intend to take any prisoners?" Torr asked from his post by the door.

Rori chewed on that for a moment. "Not at this time. That could change though. For all we know, this could be one of a dozen compounds or more. We should reassess later when we find out more. But my hope is that we hit their operation hard where it hurts. If we ruin them completely, well, that would be fantastic too."

"That's a lot of ifs," I mused. "It's a pity you couldn't get any more useful information out of the prisoner."

Rori's head snapped back in my direction. Her eyes were wide, eyebrows up to her hairline for a split second, before a cold, detached mask fell over her features. "That's a hell of a remark, coming from you."

There were lots more eyes on me now, including Santos' and Torr's. I felt them burning into my skin.

Rori's gaze jerked away to address the room again. "Any other questions?" When none came, she said, "Good. We leave in three days. I suggest you all practice riding and shooting. Torr, LJ, Val, and I will be available for instruction or any questions. Church is adjourned."

Torr moved off the door and opened it for everyone to file out. I had barely turned away to leave when Rori said, "Devin, will you please stay a minute?"

I wanted to keep going, to throw a, "No, thanks, I'm good," over my shoulder, even though it would dig a deeper hole than I was already in. And the truth of it was, I didn't know *why* I wanted to keep pushing Rori's buttons. The moment we fell into a place of mutually-respected acquaintances, I felt an impulse to ruin that. It just didn't feel right.

Fighting with her felt right.

"Want me to stay?" her boy-toy asked. Not Santos, her other one.

"No, it's fine. This won't take long."

The last few stragglers left the room, and when the door closed, Rori wasted no time going off. "What the fuck was that?"

"What was what?"

"*Don't* fuck with me, Devin. For everything you are, I know you're not an idiot. I'm asking you a question. I expect a straight answer."

"You need to make your question more specific."

Rori sighed, brought a hand to her forehead, and muttered something like, "Oh my fucking God." When she looked up again, her tone was seething. "Why. Are you trying to undermine me. In the first fucking meeting of my club?"

"I wasn't," I said with a shrug. "I was just making an observation, that's all."

"Hell of an observation from the guy who wanted to kill Nella before I could get any information at all!" She was shouting now and pacing the room aggressively. "You have no fucking right to have an opinion on the amount or quality of information I got just because you're bitter that I made you wait to get it in the first place."

"Okay," I said passively, strangely captivated by her aggressive body language, the anger roughening her voice.

Rori threw her hands up and tilted her head to the ceiling. "Why are you still here, Devin? No one's holding a gun to your head. You don't like me, don't want to ride in my club, fine! Just fucking leave then."

"I'm not leaving Santos behind." It made perfect sense in my head up until this very moment. Now it sounded a bit silly.

Rori let out a dry scoff. "Santos doesn't need you anymore."

"We've had each other's backs for years, through all kinds of trials. This is just one more." And because I couldn't stop myself, I added, "Besides, I don't trust you with him."

Rori scoffed again, rolling her eyes. "What are you, his mother?

He's a grown-ass man, and believe it or not, I'm not manipulating him into anything. If he doesn't want to be with me, he also doesn't have to stay." She cocked her head, making a blond wave fall across one eye. "I don't know whether to be flattered or insulted that you think I'm some siren with a magical charm that brings all these men under my control." She straightened, regarding me coolly. "Sorry to disappoint, Devin. I'm just a person."

"I don't think there's anything magical about you." Shit, why did I sound so damn defensive?

"I don't care what you think of me, quite frankly. I have more important things to worry about." She walked directly up to me, her gaze and expression unwavering. I had a few inches of height on her, though she was still tall for a woman. Somehow, though, she held the same space and gravity as a seven-foot tall gladiator.

"Hate and antagonize me all you want, I don't care. See what it does to your friendship with Santos. If that breaks down, you'll have only yourself to blame. But what I'm not going to tolerate is you trying to make me look incompetent in front of my club. Am I clear, Devin?"

"Crystal," I said.

She jerked her chin toward the door. "You're dismissed." With that, she turned and walked quickly through the house. I heard a back or side door open, then slam shut. Then it was just the silence of an empty house.

Damn. I had pissed her off so much, she didn't even want to walk through the same door as me.

I went out through the front and decided to do a perimeter walk to clear my head. That...what I'd done in that meeting and just moments ago, was not like me. I had lived this long as a gladiator by *not* stirring shit up, *not* drawing attention to myself. I knew how to keep my trap shut and not poke bears. Okay, I messed with other fighters sometimes, but that was to show that I wasn't timid. We all had to make power plays sometimes. I could hold my own in a fight and was not to be fucked with.

And neither was Rori, evidently.

She was tough for a woman. Crass, hot-tempered, and more foul-mouthed than a lot of men I'd known. For some reason, I found this hard to reconcile with her softer side—the way she smiled at Santos, how protective she was of the maid, Paige, and the rare moments when she actually spoke softly. It was so strange to me, paradoxical even. How could she be both of those people at the same time?

On a logical level, I knew it was possible. Santos was a ruthless fighter, but he also had the warmth and non-violent instincts of a teddy bear. I, too, had just as much capacity to kill as I did to care. People could be opposing things at the same time. I knew this.

So why did Rori's qualities confound me so much?

She claimed to not have any magic, and yet that woman had embedded herself firmly under my skin.

It was so fucking annoying.

Chapter 24

Rori

"They're not ready," Torr muttered under his breath.

"How does that saying go?" I walked up behind Paige, gently lifting and straightening her arms while she aimed her gun at a target, then stepped back beside Torr. "What they lack in experience, they make up for in enthusiasm."

He groaned. "That literally only applies to sex. Not battle."

Paige squeezed off a few rounds. She was still jumpy from the noise of the shots, which affected her aim, but she was getting better.

"Good job, babe." I squeezed her shoulder as she set the gun down to reload, then continued my walk with my VP.

My first love.

My brother's best friend.

My drinking, smoking, riding buddy.

My man, who knew me better than anyone else.

It was crazy to think of all the forms our relationship had taken over the years. I never would have believed second-in-command would be added to the list. And yet, it was a perfect fit.

"We don't want to go in unprepared," Torr was saying. "And we can't exactly have them practice while we're scouting."

"We'll give guns to the most proficient shooters," I decided. "Everyone will play to their strengths. Give Paige a pair of binoculars, and she can be the head scout. She's got eagle eyes and can recall all kinds of details. She'll be the best at noticing patterns of movement. Put her with a skilled shooter so she'll be adequately covered."

"Roger that, president." It was so weird to hear him call me that.

"Even if they don't have guns, everyone should be armed for self-defense. Knives, brass knuckles, whatever they feel most comfortable with."

Torr stopped in his tracks and turned to face me. "You're really sure about riding out in three days?"

I peered up at him. "You don't think we should?"

"I think they need more training, Ror. Riding and shooting are like second nature to you and me because we've done it our whole lives. Only LJ and Val are at a level similar to us. Everyone else?" He swung an arm at the row of people target practicing. "They need months, if not years."

My first reaction was to push back, to get defensive. If I wasn't president and he was shooting down any other idea of mine, I'd let him have it. But things were different now, and he was my VP for a reason. Not only that, he was *mine*. My partner. I had a responsibility to him and the whole club to at least consider his advice. And if there was one thing I knew about Torr, it was that he would never bullshit me.

"I hear you. I really do." Continuing on my walk, I looked over to where LJ was talking to a couple of fighters and pointing out different parts on a motorcycle. "But we don't have that kind of time, Torr. We've got to hit the Sisterhood while it's still scrambling. We can't let them regroup and get stronger. Plus," I spun on the toe of my boot, facing Torr as I walked backwards, "I think you're underestimating these people."

"Am I?" He shoved his hands in his jeans pockets.

"They've been in survival mode for years. They've had to be crafty and think on their feet, make split-second decisions between life and death. They're nothing if not adaptable." I stopped short, and Torr nearly ran into me. "Their instincts are good, Torr. And on top of that, they've got major skin in this game. They don't just want to bring this cult down, they *need* to see it happen. For their own closure and peace of mind."

"Ror, I get all that." Torr rubbed his jaw. "I'm not questioning their passion, or their survival instincts. I'm just worried about their lack of experience."

"Well, they're about to get some."

"This is one hell of a first ride, Ror. I'm not even sure your dads would've been up for this at our ages."

I glared at him. "They weren't much older than us when they saved the whole fucking Southwest."

Torr blew out a breath, scanning the flurry of activity in our surroundings again. "I'd just feel a lot more comfortable going on smaller rides with these guys first."

"No, you wouldn't," I retorted. "You'd find something else to worry about. We have to act, Torr, and not overthink things."

"Says the queen of overthinking," he teased.

"Trust me. I'm still doing plenty of that." I raked my fingers back through my hair until my palm landed on my nape. "But I really think we can pull this off."

He nodded, resigned. "If that's what you feel, I trust you."

We kept walking, observing how everyone was doing with their training, giving occasional pointers and answering the questions of anyone who came up to us. In the quiet moments, my brain was still a flurry of activity.

Carter had wanted to take more time too. Preparation. Planning. He and Torr were of alike mind in that. I fought my cousin tooth and nail on how long we took to attack the resort. He still didn't feel fully prepared when we finally did leave, but if we had been a day late— fuck, even an hour—either Torr or Santos, if not both, would be dead right now.

Preparation was important, sure. I wasn't discounting that. But there was something to be said for diving in headfirst and letting your instincts guide you. Ideally, we would have a balance of both. But time was a luxury we didn't have.

We couldn't prepare for shit we couldn't even see. Scouting would be our preparation. And gods willing, our instincts would lead us on the rest.

I looked up to where Astarte sat on the roof of the detached garage, always watching. "I'm doing it," I said quietly. "Trusting my gut. Following my instincts. Any commentary you'd like to offer up?"

Nothing but silence, as usual.

———

THREE DAYS LATER, the first leg of our ride was delightfully uneventful. The ex-gladiators, now my Vengeful Gods soldiers, took to the motorcycles beautifully, for the most part. Due to the shortage of bikes on hand, they doubled-up without any complaints or squabbles. We took frequent breaks to check in with everyone, and everyone took turns driving.

It was the maiden voyage for us as a single unit, and it went off without a hitch. The thing about first times, though, was that they could hurt like a bitch sometimes.

As the first day came to a close and we set up camp for the night, LJ and Val teased the others relentlessly about their slow, bow-legged walking around, the grimaces on their faces, and the complaints of soreness.

"I can't feel my ass," one fighter muttered as he arranged stones in a circle for our fire.

"I refuse to believe this is the first time *that's* happened!" Val cackled.

LJ shouted, "Ohhhh shit!" Hooting and hollering, my idiot cousins were each other's hype-men. "Hey, Fist!" he shouted at another guy. "Why you walkin' around like fuckin' crab?"

"Just giving room for my dick to swing, Sergeant," the man

replied. And then the ex-gladiators were cheering and hyping each other up.

"They're getting along," Torr observed as he shook out a blanket to lay on the ground.

"They are," I agreed. "Once we get the booze out for these rowdy fools, you'd never know they've not been part of a club before this."

"Who you calling rowdy fools?" LJ demanded.

"You, dumbass!" I laughed.

"Well, that makes you the queen of rowdy fools," Val pointed out.

"Should've made that the club name," Santos said. He was standing nearby, pulling a knee up toward his chest and doing some other leg stretches against a boulder.

I wandered over to him slowly, watching in fascination as everyone continued to rib each other like longtime friends, working all the while.

"How you feeling?"

Santos released his knee to stand normally. "I'm alright. Nothing I can't handle." He tilted his head with a soft smile, angling his body toward me. "Can I give you a kiss?"

I scoffed. "You never need to ask me that."

He lowered his head, his lips making brief, sensual contact with mine. "Just not sure how it all works yet," he admitted. "If Torr outranks me or whatever, or if certain things should not be done in front of everyone."

"Well, I probably wouldn't want to fuck in plain view of everyone." I laughed. "But listen. You and Torr are equals to me. He's my right hand regarding club matters, but when it comes to us, there's no rank. You're both equally mine."

Before he could respond, my arms went around his shoulders and I rose up on tiptoes to kiss him deeply, surging my tongue inside his mouth. And damn, how lucky was I? It was always a pain finding a guy taller than me, and now I had two of them.

At the sound of wolf whistles and obscene suggestions from the rowdy fools that made up our peanut gallery, Santos groaned and palmed one side of my ass in his large hand. I completely forgot about everyone watching us, even as we parted for a breath.

"You're sleeping with me and Torr tonight," I told him.

He grinned, forehead rolling against mine. "As long as you're in the middle."

"Fine. But if you two wake up spooning, maybe that's something you guys should explore."

"Highly unlikely to happen." He laughed and then looked at me quizzically. "You'd be okay with that, though? If two of your guys were into each other too?"

"Hell yes I would. I can only handle so much dick at one time." I crossed my arms, cocking my hip out as I thought about it. "I mean, there'd be rules, of course. Whatever happens, I'd prefer my relationships to be closed. Committed. Not just sleeping around with whoever."

"Gotcha. So Torr and I can't see other women." Santos raised his palms at my glare. "Or men. Not saying I want to, just making sure I'm clear."

"Women, no," I said. "Men?" I tilted my head from side to side. "Depends on if I like them too."

"So you're just greedy," he teased.

"Yeah, and?"

He laughed again, the beautiful sound ringing out across our camp. Devin lifted his head and looked at us. With the distance and setting sun, it was hard to tell if he was glaring or just seeing what the noise was about. In the next moment, he was back to minding his business, sharpening his knives next to the campfire that had just started crackling.

I let Santos return to stretching while I continued to watch Devin for some reason I couldn't figure out. The tall fighter's hair was loose, hanging down one side of his head like a glossy, black waterfall. It looked soft. So did his beard. His fingers were long, his movements methodical as he honed his weapons.

The guy made me curious, but only because he was so damn

confusing. Just when I thought we were starting to get along, he had to go off and be an ass. I didn't buy for a second that he was staying here to watch Santos' back. Santos was fine. He was happy. I didn't wish for the two friends to be separated, but if Devin was so miserable and the MC life didn't fit him, he could just go somewhere relatively close. Santos could visit him at any time.

The club still needed a permanent home, but that would come later. Sevier and Four Corners were both great places to live, and I figured we could settle somewhere in the middle. We'd be near civilization, and I could visit the many branches of my family. MCs truly lived on the road. We'd always be within visiting distance of someone. Devin didn't need to be breathing down Santos' neck all the time. So what the hell?

He got his revenge kill. He got a room to sleep in, a roof, and a fridge full of food. He had choices now, the option to go or stay. Was he just having trouble adjusting to a life that was no longer dictated by someone else?

All of the ex-gladiators needed therapy, I decided. As soon as we finished this mission, I'd see what kind of contacts my mom had in the mental health field. My dads went to individual therapy on and off again. They could probably recommend someone. It would also help, I imagined, if these fighters knew my tough-as-nails, ruthless MC fathers had sat down and talked to people about their trauma. Because God knew it would take some convincing for these guys to accept that you could solve issues with words instead of weapons. And doing that didn't make you weak.

Hell, sometimes I even forgot it was an option.

Chapter 25

Rori

"Ten more minutes," I mumbled, snuggling deeper into Santos' chest. "S'too early."

Torr's body was warm against my back, but his lips were cold as they touched the shell of my ear. "You're the president, not a princess," he said. "You wake up and pack it in with everyone else."

Naturally, I knew that. My dad Jandro was the early bird, but Reaper would be up soon after. Between the two of them, breakfast and coffee would always be hot and ready for my mom when she got up. Damn it. Why couldn't I have been an old lady instead of the fucking president?

And why did Torr, who I guess was my old man, have to be such a hardass? Santos was brushing sleepy kisses over the top of my head, which made it even harder to get up.

Hmm, speaking of harder...

I threw my back into a deep arch, pressing my ass against—yep, there it was—Torr's morning erection. "Let me stay in bed so I can take care of that for you," I said in my best seductive whisper, looking behind me. He was pressed against me, already so close. I ghosted my lips against his neck and gave a nibble to his earlobe.

"Not gonna work on me today, creep. We gotta move out." My VP was all business, and therefore, all-buzzkill.

"Santos," I whined, facing forward again to kiss under his jaw. "Tell him to stop being a dick."

"Mmm. He's right though, paloma."

I let out a fake gasp. "I'm shocked *and* betrayed."

A sympathetic kiss fell on my forehead. "We've got another long day of riding, right?"

"Val says we have a half-day."

"Come on." Santos patted my hip and started to push back the blanket. "We need to set a good example, right?"

I yawned and stretched, accepting my defeat. "I'd much rather have a morning threesome and sleep in, but sure, I guess."

"We'll have time for that later." Torr rose to his knees, rubbing his eyes.

"Promise?" I came up to kneeling as well, reaching for a long-sleeved shirt to ward off the chilly morning air.

Torr grabbed my arms faster than I could react, holding just above my elbows as he came directly behind me. His grip was strong enough to bruise as he pulled my arms back just enough to thrust my chest forward. Toward Santos.

Torr's erection rubbed like a hot, heavy brand against my ass, the sensation too dulled from our layers of sleeping clothes. On top, I wore only a camisole, and my nipples were already pebbled from the cold air. With Santos waking up quickly now, those dark eyes drinking me in, the sensitive tips positively ached for some relief.

"Later, I can hold you like this, pound your sweet ass from behind." Torr thrust his hips, driving his erection over the cleft of my ass. "While Santos takes care of you in front. How does that sound?"

The question was directed at me, but I had no words to answer with, especially as I watched Santos move directly in front of me. His long thighs pressed against mine, that firm chest blasting heat as it came into contact with my nipples. And it was not nearly enough.

"That sounds great to me." My fighter ran his hands lightly, too fucking lightly, over my waist, tracing my contours as he looked over me with awe. Like he was seeing me bare for the first time, and I wasn't even naked.

Between Torr's grip and Santos' legs, I was trapped between them. And there was no fucking place in the world I'd rather be.

"Me too." I finally found my voice, even though it was a whisper. "I'm dying to have you both at the same time."

And just like that, the spell was broken. Torr released my arms and swatted my ass before he crawled off the air mattress. "After the mission. We'll celebrate with threesomes."

"You're such an *asshole*," I groaned, leaning my head on Santos' chest. I looked up at him with a pout, and he gave me a sympathetic ass pat.

"Gotta give you some motivation to work, president." Torr's voice was muffled as he pulled on a shirt.

"Fine. Consider me motivated."

We got dressed and took everything out of the tent to pack it up. The moment I stepped foot outside, it was like putting on another woman's shoes. In the tent, I was just a horny girl who wanted to sleep in and fuck my men. Out here, I was president of the Vengeful Gods MC.

We were nobodies now, but that wouldn't last long. This club would go down in history for wiping an evil cult off the map. And that mantle rested on my shoulders.

These people were my responsibility. To keep in line and to keep safe. I barely knew some of them, but for their trust in me alone, I would treat them like family.

That's what MCs were at the end of the day, a family.

So I greeted everyone I passed with a, "Good morning," and, "How'd you sleep?" and, "Take some hair of the dog for that hangover. We've got a long day ahead of us."

Within two hours, we were on the road again.

The elevation began to change drastically at this stage. What started as a steady incline became a grueling up-and-downhill battle. The terrain grew wilder, with gravel and dirt roads disappearing completely. I had Torr and LJ ride tightly alongside me, to create a wider, easier path for the rest of the club.

"You said you've been here before?" I yelled at LJ as we began yet another grueling uphill climb. Jandro would be having a heart attack if he saw how hard we were pushing the motorcycles. We needed some little dirt bikes for this mission, not these heavy-as-fuck road cruisers.

"Not here specifically but the general area," he corrected, grinding his teeth as he pushed onward. "I knew it was hilly out here, but fucking damn, this has to be the steepest part of the mountain range."

"How close are we?"

"We should be able to see the compound at the crest of this hill if the information is correct."

I nodded and pushed my bike into its highest gear, wincing at the roar of the engine reaching a new, higher pitch. My baby, custom-made by my fathers, was a hybrid design, so she was handling the incline and terrain relatively well, but that didn't mean riding offroad was her specialty.

"Come on, sweetheart, you can do it. You've never failed me." I petted the gas tank as if encouraging a living beast.

The jaguar, on the other hand, was having a great time. Tezca's long body raced up the hill tirelessly, often passing us by and waiting for us to catch up. At least someone was having fun.

At long last, we reached the top of the hill. I squinted through the shrubs and copse of trees and, sure enough, I could make out a small settlement in the distance.

"Cut your engines now," I told Torr and LJ while promptly doing the same. I looked back at the others making their way up, and slashed my thumb across my throat until every single motorcycle was turned off.

On foot, I made my way back down the hill, gesturing at everyone to come close.

"I think we're too far for them to hear us, but I don't want to take any chances," I explained once my club gathered in a tight circle around me. "They could also send out scouts to investigate. We stay put for now, see if they make any moves. Tomorrow, if nothing changes, we hike the ridge line on foot to check them out at all angles. All good?"

"Yes, president," came the chorus of voices.

I nodded. "Rest, relax. It's been a tough ride, you all did good. Let's stay quiet."

While the fighters broke away to unpack food and supplies, Paige stepped forward. "I can begin my scouting now, president."

"You sure?" I eyed her warily.

"Yes," she insisted. "The sooner I can gather information, the better. I figure the trees will cover me."

"Okay," I said. "But if you need a break, let me know, and I'll have someone else take over."

"I will." She gave me a cheeky smile. "I'm stronger than I look, Rori."

I grinned back and playfully knocked my shoulder into hers. "I know you are. I'm just overprotective of my people."

We set Paige up with a telescope on the crest of the hill, while everyone else settled in to hunker down for a while. Because we couldn't have a fire, we drank lukewarm coffee and gnawed on rations of dried fruit and jerky. Astarte stayed near me, creeping closer and bobbing her head while I chewed on some dried mango slices.

"This has chili powder on it," I told the bird. "Don't think it would go down well for you."

"Oh shit, I love chili mango! Can I have some?" Santos scooted from his reclined position to lay his head in my lap.

"You can have anything of mine," I purred, feeding him a piece.

Paige had been watching the compound for roughly an hour at that point and set the telescope down on her pack, rubbing her eyes.

"See anything interesting?" My fingers stroked along Santos' jaw and neck, feeling the movement of muscles as he chewed.

"Not really." Her brow pinched with frustration. "It looks like a homestead community run by women. Everyone's farming, cooking, washing laundry by hand, feeding animals, repairing fences, stuff like that."

"No men?"

Paige shook her head. "Not a single one."

"How about armed guards?"

"I saw a few women with assault rifles, but they weren't at guard posts. They were just walking around doing whatever. One had a baby in one arm and this giant gun in the other."

"A baby?" I repeated. "There's kids there?" Under my fingers, Santos stopped chewing.

"A few, yeah."

I frowned, turning that over in my head for a while. Kids had to come from somewhere, and if they were pimping out men like at Mystic Canyon, that would explain it. But if there were no men at all, where did the children come from? The only explanation I could think of was women being pregnant before joining the cult.

Children also made attacking the compound a much trickier situation. We couldn't go in guns blazing and risk killing them or making a bunch of orphans. Nor did we have the resources to take children with us.

"Take a break," I told Paige. "Rest your eyes. When you get back to it, I want you to keep watching the ones with weapons. Find out how many there are, see if you can spot a pattern."

"You got it." Paige stood and stretched, then smiled as the Hunter approached with a thermos of water and cup of soup for her. "Aw, thank you, love."

"Always," he muttered, eyes rapt on her.

What an adorable couple. I looked down at Santos with a smile that dissipated as soon as I saw his expression. "Hey, you okay?"

"Yeah." He looked anything but, his mouth pressed into a thin line, eyes vacant as he rolled up from my lap. "I need to talk to Devin real quick."

"Okay." I touched his forearm before he could leave. "You know you can talk to me too, right?"

He plopped back down on the ground beside me, his eyes full of that familiar warmth and love as he took my chin and pressed a sensual kiss to my mouth.

"I know, and I will," he whispered. "I just need to hash out something with him first. Ugly gladiator stuff."

"Okay." I ran my thumb over his cheekbone, then leaned in to kiss him again. "Love you."

My eyes shot wide open, realizing too late what I'd said out loud. *Oh fuck.*

Chapter 26

Rori

The words came out automatically, naturally, and easily as breathing. My momentary panic was quelled immediately by Santos' incredible smile, his forehead coming to rest gently on my mine, and the grip of his hand on my nape.

"Love you too, paloma."

With another kiss, he stood and went off in search of his friend while I sat there in wonderment. My ass was firmly planted on the ground, but I felt like I was floating in zero gravity.

It had been so...*easy*. And that felt so refreshing, so freeing.

We loved each other. Period.

Torr and I loved each other too, but that was wildly different. It was still a process with him and I. Not exactly a struggle, but there were obstacles, both in the past and in the present. For some reason, I expected it to be similar with Santos, but it wasn't.

The words left his mouth like a bird taking flight. So natural that it was obviously easy for him.

I would never fault Torr for struggling to say the words. But knowing where Santos stood eased the ache in my heart a little. Hearing him say it gave me the reassurance I didn't know I needed.

Yes, I was a tough bitch, but tough bitches needed to hear '*I love you too*' sometimes.

With a dopey-as-fuck smile, I leaned my head back against the side of my bike and closed my eyes to sink into this beautiful, bubbly feeling.

And then something really fucking weird happened.

My body jolted, like that kicking motion people do when they're about to fall asleep. But when my eyes opened, I wasn't looking at Paige and the Hunter eating lunch a few feet away. I was...up in the air?

I was weightless and soaring over a valley, heading straight for the compound, like I'd just been launched out of a cannon.

What's happening? What the fuck is happening to me?! I tried to scream but didn't seem to have a mouth.

Calm yourself, Aurora, came Asarte's chiding voice. *I'm showing you what you won't be able to see from your scouting.*

Where am I? Am I in...you? I did seem to be flying, and once I calmed my freak-out enough, I could feel the bones and muscles of wings. *My* wings.

Not yours, Astarte snorted. *I'm in control, Aurora. I'm only lending you my eyes.*

You really *don't want me to get excited about this, do you? I'm fucking flying!*

You won't be excited after you see what I'm about to show you. The goddess' voice in my head turned grim, and a brick of dread formed in my gut.

Is it worse than the gladiator fights? I asked.

Yes, came the succinct answer.

I didn't dare ask any more questions, despite my mind racing with them.

Astarte flew us lower over the settlement, and I could see what Paige had been talking about. Women carrying stacks of firewood or huge baskets of laundry. Women inspecting neatly aligned rows of planted vegetables. Animal pens with chickens, pigs, goats, and a couple of cows. I couldn't miss the odd woman here or there with a toddler in her arms or walking with a child's hand in hers. Nor did I miss the ones with assault rifles who meandered too casually around the compound to be doing any actual patrolling.

We passed over the main cluster of trailers and simple, prefab houses, where it seemed the bulk of the population lived. Toward the back of a settlement was a gentle upward slope, too small to be any serious hill, but there was a structure at the top. It resembled a gazebo, with a pointed roof, support beams, and open space instead of walls. The roof and supports were covered in dark paint, like a haunted house looming over the town, which looked cheery in comparison.

Set in the center of the stairs leading up to the spooky gazebo thing was a gutter of some kind. I kept staring at it, the bizarreness of it jarring to me. What was the point of a split-open PVC pipe running down the center of a flight of stairs? The placement didn't make sense for carrying away rain, so I couldn't begin to imagine what it was for.

Astarte perched us on one of the roofs of the nearest houses, a prime vantage point to see inside the gazebo. The floor within it was dark, concrete, and there looked to be a shade tent serving as an altar of some kind. Objects like flowers and small plates of food cluttered the ground in front. And there looked to be a...a baby's bassinet under the canopy?

I'm so confused and already freaked out by this place, I thought.

Just wait, Astarte said in that same grim tone.

A commotion sounded a few minutes later—the slamming of a door, shuffling footsteps, and then panicked shouts and begging.

In a man's voice.

A man had come out of—no, was *forced* out of—one of the houses. His wrists were bound in front of him so tightly that the skin was an angry red and bleeding. Two women dragged him forward by each arm, another with an assault rifle walking directly behind them.

The man was drugged or incapacitated in some way. He couldn't get his feet under him, no matter how much he scraped, dragged, and kicked his heels. The guy was terrified and trying to run. The woman with the large gun drove the butt of her weapon into his kidney, making him freeze up with pain.

Some women gathered along the sides of the walkway to watch, even one with a child on her hip, but most of them carried on doing their business like it was any other day.

They dragged him toward the gazebo and up the stairs with the gutter running down the middle. That was when the guy really started to struggle, and even pulled one arm free of the hold. He spun around but the bitch with the AR was ready, and she crashed the butt of her gun into his face.

He crumpled to the ground with a cry of pain, hands cupped over his nose which was definitely broken. Blood coated his fingers and dripped down his chin.

"You can't escape your crimes anymore, *male*," the woman with the gun said before she spit on him, then slammed her weapon down against the side of his head. And again, against his ribs.

"I didn't commit any crimes!" He curled up to protect himself, the blood mixing with tears on his face.

They had barely gotten started on whatever this was, and I'd already seen enough.

Astarte, we have to do something. How do I get out of your body?

There is nothing you can do for this one, Aurora. Her mental voice was sad, defeated.

Bullshit! We can't just watch this.

You must *watch this, it hasn't even begun. Your human body is too far away to save him, anyway.*

Then you *save him! You're a fucking god!*

I cannot. This one is already lost.

"Your entire fucked-up gender is a crime," the armed woman said to the cowering man on the ground. "Gone unpunished for thousands of years, until now. We're not your victims anymore."

"I never did anything to any of you! Please, this is a mistake!"

"Letting you live one more day would be a mistake," she sneered back. To the two other women, she said, "Get him up."

He was picked up by his arms again, his strength flagging as they continued up until they were under the gazebo's roof. Once there, they forced him to his knees and cut the binding at his hands, only to reshackle his wrists to chains attached to the support beams so that his arms spread out to the sides. His head bent low, defeated.

Meanwhile, I was fighting beak and claw to do something in this dove's body. Divebomb and peck some eyes out. Hell, even shitting on someone's head might be enough of a diversion.

You don't have control over this form, Aurora. Astarte was back to sounding permanently annoyed with me.

Well, this guy is about to get killed, and you're not doing a damn thing! I screamed back. For all my effort, I might as well have been punching a brick wall.

There is nothing we can do for him. Other deities are standing by to guide him to a peaceful end.

He's not dead yet! We can still help him!

Death is the most natural occurrence in the universe, even when it feels cruel. I'm sorry, Aurora, but this is how it needs to be.

Fuck that! This poor man hasn't even done anything wrong, has he?

He was only unlucky.

God, no...

While I continued to deny everything, the scene playing out before me was worse than I could have imagined. The bitch with a gun couldn't just shoot him to end his misery. No, she adjusted the strap so her hands were free while the gun rested against her back and took out a hunting knife from a sheath on her belt.

A small crowd gathered at the base of the incline now, staring up at the bound, bleeding man like he was about to break into a song and dance.

"The Dark Mother is a voracious goddess," said the knife wielder to those below. "No longer is She satisfied with only full moon sacrifices. Now She thirsts for the blood of men at every new and full moon."

The man's head jerked up at that, and he once again struggled to get to his feet, but the two other women held him down by the shoulders.

Astarte, please, I begged, though I wasn't sure what for.

I'm sorry, Aurora. But you have to know what you're up against.

"Too much of our own blood has been spilled by *men*." The woman raised her hunting knife high, catching the glare of the sun on the blade. "Blood from our wombs when they invade us. Bruises on our faces and bodies when they hit us."

"I never touched anyone, I swear!" the man cried out, pulling against his chains.

"And the pain they caused here," the woman tapped the flat side of the knife against her chest, "when they broke our hearts."

Low murmurs arose from the women gathered below, several nodding their heads.

No way, I scoffed inside my head. *They can't be buying this as a justification to kill him. There's no fucking way.*

Young, vulnerable minds are the easiest ones to manipulate, Astarte said sadly.

The gathered women did look young, no older than me. Some of them could have been teenagers.

"When we give the goddess the blood She demands, She wraps us in Her protective embrace," the woman went on. "When we do Her work, ridding the world of these vile creatures who prey upon Her daughters," she pointed at the captive with her knife, "she gives us peace. She gives us safety and a home to raise *our* daughters. She makes sure that no man enters our home unless he is to serve Her, either by his seed or by his blood. Because the truth you were never told is this: men are only useful for those two things."

What. The. Fuck.

"Everything else is a lie." The woman was becoming fanatical—waving her arms and yelling like an impassioned preacher on a pulpit. "Men are monsters, incapable of love and gentleness, though some are good at fooling us for a very long time. But all of you know, you *know* this in your hearts!" She swung her index finger over the growing crowd. "Because in one way or another, everyone here has been hurt by a man."

"He almost killed me," blurted out one woman before bursting into tears. Immediately, a cluster of arms came around her, the others giving her gentle pats and soothing rubs of support.

The woman in the gazebo nodded sagely. "Me too, sweet sister." With that, she refocused her attention on her victim. "She has chosen this one for blood." The knife teased along the man's cheek until he jerked away from it. "From his spilled blood, Her power will grow. And as Her power increases, she will extend Her will and protection to the brave, lonely women who have not yet found their way to the Sisterhood." The knife thrust outward toward the distant horizon, and I suddenly got a horrific idea of what that pipe in the middle of the stairs was for.

"Our sisters scattered across the world will hear the Dark Mother's voice, feel the pull of her embrace, and find their new home." The woman lowered her arms with a serene expression. "Where no man will ever harm them again."

"Yes!" shouted the woman who had been crying a moment earlier.

"Where we'll have *our* turn!" The knife-wielder grew impassioned again, her voice raising as she thumped a fist against her chest. "Where we'll show every one of these animals exactly what it's like to be abused, enslaved, raped, and bred against their will!"

The man shook his head, blood and tears continuing to drip down his face, but he was too defeated to protest with words anymore.

"Yes!" came the chorus of shouts from below.

I can't fucking believe what I'm hearing, I thought, dumbfounded.

Believe it, Astarte said sharply. *They certainly do.*

"Sister." The armed woman stepped out from under the gazebo, descending a couple of steps before stopping and turning the knife so that the handle faced away from her. "Would you like the Dark Mother to guide your hand?"

She was speaking to the one who had been crying, who now looked up at her with such awe and reverence, it was as if an angel were speaking. "Me? I...I don't know if I'm worthy."

"You will never know unless you are tested. Tap into the Dark Mother's power within you." The woman's jaw clenched, and she bit out the next sentence through her teeth. "And kill this man, who would just as quickly kill you."

The woman below started ascending the steps but hesitated when the victim started to sob.

"No..." he whimpered quietly. "Please, I would never..."

"He lies, as all men do." The armed woman thrust the knife handle out farther to the one ascending the stairs. "Make the Dark Mother proud, Sister. Show us all that you are no longer under *their* control."

And that was when the younger woman's hesitancy ended for good and she became a murderer.

She reached the top of the stairs and accepted the knife. The woman with the AR stepped aside, and all I could see of the victim was his outstretched arms while his murderer blocked my view.

I saw her arm thrust forward, the jerk of his arms against the chains. I heard the sound of a knife through flesh, and wet, gurgled attempts at breath.

Blood pooled on the ground, and I figured out then why the concrete floor was so dark. The blood followed the slight downward slope of the floor to find the gutter acting as a small, morbid canal.

He had stopped moving but the woman kept stabbing him, blood coating her arms and the front of her clothes. She had to be in a delusion of some kind, seeing the man who had attacked her in the innocent man she had just now brutally murdered.

Do you understand now what you are dealing with? Astarte's voice cut into the horrified silence in my head.

Yeah, and I've seen enough, I snapped back.

Fuck, that scene would stay with me forever. I had to find out that man's name and where he was from. He had to have loved ones who missed him. How I would obtain this information was yet to be seen, but it was the least I could do when his death had been so needless and cruel.

The goddess stuff is all bullshit, right? I found myself asking. *It's just a manipulation tactic, like every cult leader. There's no way it actually exists.*

Astarte was silent for a long while.

Eventually, all she said was, *Time for you to return to your body.*

Chapter 27

Santos

I found Devin leaning against the loaner motorcycle we'd ridden on together, popping grapes into his mouth, and I wasted no time saying what was on my mind.

"Paige saw kids at the compound."

He stopped chewing. "So?"

I shook my head, my mouth tight in clear sign that I wasn't fucking around. "Come on, man."

Devin finished chewing what was in his mouth and swallowed. "How old?"

"Not sure, but she said women were carrying around babies. So, young."

He pulled in a breath. "Young enough to be...?"

"We've been away for four years, Dev. So yeah, I think it's safe to assume so."

"Fuck." His head tilted back, eyes closed to the sky for a few long seconds. "Have you said anything to Rori?"

"Not yet. I came straight to you as soon as it hit me."

Devin's eyebrows lifted with surprise as he scoffed. "Why? Thought you didn't need me anymore."

"It's not about me. If Hudson's down there, he's gonna need both of us." I sighed out a heavy breath, unable to fathom what our friend had been through over the years. Or if there was even any of *him* left. "I think we should tell Rori together. It's gonna affect her plan for sure."

"You think so?" Devin sounded skeptical, and that lit me up with anger.

"If we say he needs to be saved, she'll do it," I barked. "The only reason she's here is because she wants to do right by all of us." I spread my arms to indicate all of the ex-gladiators who were here. Rori was leading us to our revenge. Why he couldn't get his head out of his ass and see that was beyond me.

To my surprise, he nodded and tossed his plucked grape stems, leaning up from the bike. "Alright. Let's tell her."

Who are you and what have you done with Devin? I wanted to ask, but would rather not give him a reason to stop being agreeable.

Together, we took the short hike up to the crest of the hill and found a terrifying scene.

Rori was lying on her back, her head in Paige's lap, who was bent over her and crying. The Hunter stood behind Paige, his hands on his shoulders as he looked down at our new president with a worried frown.

Torr was kneeling at Rori's side, stroking her arm and face while he stared at her like a man about to lose the love of his life.

"Wake up, creep. Come on," he begged in a rough voice. "Not now. Not like this..."

"What happened?" I demanded, rushing to her other side.

Rori was motionless and unresponsive except for some twitching in her hands and face, mainly in her half-closed eyelids. Only the whites of her eyes were visible through the slits.

"I don't know," Paige sobbed. "She was fine. And then I looked over and she was like this."

"It looks like a seizure. Has this ever happened before?" Devin came over and touched his fingers to the inside of his wrist. Then he leaned down, touching his ear to her chest.

"No," Torr croaked with a shake of his head. "Not for as long as I've known her."

"How long has she been like this?" I looked at Paige.

"Two minutes, maybe three?" she sniffed.

Devin lifted his head, frowning. "I'm no medic, but she has a strong pulse and her heartbeat sounds normal, if a bit fast. I dunno, I think we just need to wait it out."

"We need a *real* fucking medic. What if she's braindead or something?" Torr lifted his head, his eyes landing on me. "Find someone with medical experience. Now."

"Dude, none of the fighters are—"

"*Find someone!*" he bellowed.

"Wait, I think she's coming back!" the Hunter exclaimed, leaning over Paige.

Rori's eyelid fluttering had indeed turned into full-on blinks, her brow furrowing before her eyes opened fully to focus on all of us. "Uh. Hi, guys."

"Oh, thank fuck!" Torr threw himself on top of her in practically a full body slam, embracing her hard. "Thank all the fucking gods you're okay."

"Ow! I *was* okay, but you're crushing me!" Rori shoved at his shoulders. "What're you all looking at me for? What's with all the drama?"

"You were having a seizure." Paige sniffed and wiped her cheeks. "You were unresponsive and twitching for a few minutes."

"Yeah, you scared the shit out of us, asshole." Torr just squeezed around her tighter. "Never do that again."

Rori's eyes widened with some realization, her arms coming around Torr's back to rub up and down. "Oh! I'm sorry for scaring you guys. I was just uh, taking a nap and dreaming really vividly. Seriously, I'm okay. I didn't mean to make you all worry."

Devin and I exchanged a look. Yeah, neither of us were buying it.

"Must've been a hell of a dream," the Hunter remarked as he helped Paige to her feet, then held her against his chest.

"Yeah." Torr released Rori so she could sit up, and her eyes passed over him, Devin, and me with a haunted expression. "I need to talk to the three of you."

Rori comforted Paige with a quick hug, then our president and VP walked us further away from everyone for some privacy.

"I was outside of my fucking body," Rori said in harsh whisper the moment we were alone. "And I was in Astarte, flying and seeing through the bird's eyes. She took me over the compound. I saw...fuck, I saw everything." Rori brought a hand to her forehead, suddenly looking exhausted before looking up again sharply. "You guys believe me, right?"

"Yes." The answer came from Devin, which surprised everyone. He returned our bewildered looks with a shrug. "What? The gods talk to us and inhabit animals, right? Could be weirder."

"If you say so," Torr muttered. "But yes, I believe you too. So what'd you see?"

Rori paled and let out a breath that seemed to take all of her strength with it. "They're killing men as like...ritual sacrifices. I saw the whole thing." She looked to the sky, eyes filling with tears. "And I couldn't stop it."

"Hey, it's not your fault." I followed the impulse to bring her head against my shoulder, kissing her hair. "There was nothing you could do, paloma. I'm sorry you had to see that."

Her arms came around me, fingers curling to grip my shirt. "So you've seen it too." A statement, not a question.

"Not exactly, but we've heard it." I looked over to Devin, who nodded.

"Heard the devotion to their goddess. The screams and the begging. We've even felt the blood drip from the ceiling."

Rori's head lifted from my shoulder to stare at him. "The ceiling? So you were held underground?"

"Basements and cellars usually, yeah."

"Were you two *here?* At this compound?"

I blew out a breath. "I think so. We had hoods on or we were in a box truck when being transported, so it's hard to say for sure." I ran my palm up and down her back, meeting Devin's eye.

"But you two were never sacrificed."

Swallowing the uncomfortable knot in my throat, I said, "We were, uh, tested for other uses. Us, along with a guy named Hudson. My best guess is, Dev and I didn't produce the results they wanted, so they shipped us off to become gladiators."

Rori's eyes ping-ponged between the two of us. "And by results, you mean...?"

"Viable pregnancies. Kids," Devin spat out. "They were testing us out as breeding studs to increase their numbers. So obviously, they wanted to become pregnant with girls."

"Oh my God..." Rori brought a hand to her mouth and turned away like she was going to be sick.

"What the fuck," Torr breathed. "What if they had boys?"

"We never exactly got a chance to ask and find out," Devin answered bitterly. "But since they routinely execute men in public, you can probably make some educated guesses."

"Jesus..."

"If this is the place we came from, we think Hudson might still be here," I said. "And if he is, we want to get him out. He's our friend, and he just..." The fucking lump in my throat would not go away, no matter how much I swallowed. "He just deserves better, you know?"

"Yeah. Yeah, of course." Rori nodded, regaining her composure despite the fact that she still looked a little green. "We can't go in guns blazing, that's for sure. Not with kids and people we need to rescue." She looked at me. "Any idea how many prisoners they could have?"

"Not sure. It was only us three they kept long-term. Then they usually had one or two for the monthly sacrifices at any given time."

"Bear in mind, this was five, six years ago," Devin added. "With how much money they've made from the resort and whatever other projects? For all we know, they could have a whole prison complex at their disposal now."

"Jesus fucking Christ." Rori stabbed her fingers through her hair, pulling on the roots. "How many people has this cult killed? And they've been getting away with it for decades. Fucking hell."

"Hey, listen to me. We focus on one thing at a time." Torr squeezed her shoulder, massaging upwards toward her neck. "Right now, it's pretty clear we have to do a stealth mission. We'll find Hudson and get him out. Maybe that's all we do before we regroup and hit them again later. Hudson might be able to help us."

I chewed the inside of my cheek but kept quiet. It had been years since we'd seen Hudson, and his mental state had already been deteriorating back then. If he was still alive, he was probably so traumatized that he wouldn't be much help at all. If I was being completely honest, I wasn't sure he was savable.

"I'm gonna need some paper. I can draw an aerial view of the compound that Paige couldn't see from that angle." Rori sucked her teeth. "I don't know how to explain to the others how I know this, though."

"They know that gods walk with us," Devin said lightly. "You don't have to give details, just say that your dove showed you."

She gave a passing glance to all of us, but her gaze lingered on Devin. "I need you guys to back me up if the others push against this. I know the fighters want to, well, fight, but it seems like we'll have to tread delicately instead. Can you all do that?"

Devin didn't hesitate to say it with the rest of us. "Yes."

Rori looked relieved, then confused, if also a little on guard. I understood it. Devin being agreeable instead of argumentative always threw me for a loop. But I knew he would keep his word.

"Alright then." Rori put her hands on her hips and jerked her chin down in a decisive nod. "Let's come up with a plan."

Chapter 28

Rori

T he fighters took well to the new plan, for the most part, with only some minor grumbling about not being able to kill anyone on sight. The Saint even sung praises and kissed my ass about my adaptability and compassion for victims and blah blah blah.

That guy still gave me pause. Not alarm bells, but not a strong sense of trust either. He might have just been eccentric, or he had goals of his own in mind. He seemed agreeable to the stealth mission though, and that was all I could ask for. His actions would soon tell me more.

After Torr, Santos, Devin and I decided on a plan, we went over it with the rest of the club for several hours, until night fell. We went over it from several angles, answered questions, and I had everyone repeat it back to me to make sure they understood.

Once everyone broke apart to get some sleep, I thought Carter might actually be proud of me. We had the main plan, the backup plan if shit went sideways, and then the backup plan for the backup plan. Everyone was in agreement and knew their positions. We knew the layout of the compound. There was no reason for this to not work.

Later, when thinking back to this moment, I would laugh at the thought of having any shred of confidence that this would go off without a hitch.

We were supposed to head out two hours before dawn, and I actually managed about three hours of sleep. Torr was already up and moving around when I woke, lighting his way with a small solar-powered lantern as he made coffee on the propane camping stove.

"Did you sleep at all?" I asked him, accepting a mug.

"Nah."

I nudged him. "Something on your mind?"

"Everything. Like what could go wrong."

"You're starting to sound like me."

"I'm kind of surprised you're not more worried." His eyes held mine over the rim of his coffee cup.

"Too tired to be worried," I admitted, stifling a yawn. "Plus, we've talked this to death. I can see the map of the compound every time I close my eyes. Besides, I wouldn't be a good president if I looked worried, right?"

"Well, you're not the president right now. You're Rori. My creep." Torr pulled me forward with a warm palm on my nape, not stopping the momentum until his mouth crashed to mind. Just before I could sink into the kiss, he broke away. "Tell me what you're really feeling."

"I just...really want it to work." My fingers drummed on the tin mug. "This is kind of the first test, you know? We'll see how everyone works together. I'm glad, relieved actually, that it's just a rescue mission, not an all-out assault."

He nodded. "Me too. And I think we're gonna learn a lot about the club after today."

"Agreed." I heaved out a sigh. "You ready to do this?"

"Ready on your orders, Pres."

———

A SMALL TEAM of us headed out on foot to the compound, which was roughly a mile away from the hill the club had parked on. The rest would hang back and wait for a flashlight signal to pick us up on the bikes. I left Val in charge of those hanging back. LJ, Torr, Santos, and Devin came with me. The ones I trusted most, although Devin was still questionable. The Ghost was fast and silent though, which was exactly what I needed.

Santos' jaguar, Tezcatlipoca, also came with us. And I wasn't about to tell the big cat no.

Our plan was to slip in undetected, grab Hudson, and get the hell out. Easy like Sunday morning, right?

Running down the hillside was easy enough. The valley below was a flat, open plain with no cover, so we sprinted across the land-scape. All we could do was pray no one was awake and looking out their window to see six dark figures running toward the compound.

Tezca loped alongside me just as I thought that, his gait easy and relaxed. *You are unseen, daughter. The night cloaks you.*

I was breathing too hard to say thanks, but the shadowy jaguar was gone in the next moment anyway. He picked up speed, running ahead and disappearing into the darkness. The sense of feeling calm and reassured stayed with me though, and strengthened my legs and lungs on my run.

Finally, we made it to the outer bank of houses and stayed out of view of the windows to catch our breaths.

"This is the path up to the gazebo," I said, gesturing around the corner. "The prisoner came out of the fifth house on the left. I say we check for Hudson there first. Santos and Devin will go in for him. The rest of us will look out and provide cover."

"And if people wake up as we check the house?" Santos asked.

He knew the answer. We'd gone over this several times already. He was just confirming that my orders were the same.

"Silence them any way you can," I answered. "Adults by any means necessary, but do *not* kill children."

He nodded, understanding that we could not afford to be discovered. And my sweet, submissive man was prepared to step into the shoes of the Butcher to get the job done.

"Everyone else clear?" At their nods, I un-holstered my handgun. "Positions on three. One, two...three."

I rounded the corner, keeping my back to the wall and staying in the darkest areas of shadow possible. While ducking under windows and keeping light on my feet, I covered ground quickly, moving up the pathway until I was just past the house that the poor, sacrificed man had been removed from.

The road up ahead was clear, as were the side streets, and the main corridor behind me. I signaled to Santos and Devin, then watched them dart across to the house in question. LJ and Torr fanned out at the other end, where we'd come in from. Tezca was nowhere to be seen, but I figured I didn't need to worry about the jaguar.

Devin made quick work of the flimsy front door lock and then they were inside. I went back to checking the area in front, letting my gaze follow the steps up to the gazebo, and nearly gagged.

The sacrificed man was still up there, a grotesque monument to their insanity and cruelty. His arms were still shackled to the posts, the rest of his body hanging limp and slumped down, no longer animated by life.

"I'm sorry," I said in a faint whisper. "I'm so sorry I couldn't help you."

If we had more time, maybe more people and firepower, I'd take his body so he could be returned to his family whenever I found them and given a proper burial. I intended to find his people regardless, but it was wholly unfair that they would never get to say goodbye to him.

I didn't know the first thing about this man, but there was a certainty inside me that he hadn't deserved this. He hadn't been a predator to women or children, and it was sickening that this cult had used him as a symbol for all the evil deeds of men.

I wanted to go up those stairs. The impulse was so strong that I had to dig the treads of my boots into the ground. I wanted to...what?

I didn't know, see him up closer. But why? The curiosity had come over me so strongly and out of nowhere. Never in my life had I wanted to see a corpse up close. Why now?

"Rori!"

A hand came to my shoulder and I nearly jumped out of my skin, spinning around with my gun pointed. Santos raised his hands. "Just us."

Devin was right behind him, sheathing one of his throwing knives and giving me a look that seemed disapproving. I hated it, but he was right. I wasn't paying attention. They shouldn't have been able to sneak up on me.

"Sorry, guys." I lowered my gun. "No Hudson?"

Santos shook his head. "There were a couple jail cells in the basement, but they were empty."

"No children in there, but we silenced the guards." Devin crossed his arms over his chest. "Permanently."

"Okay then." This was the outcome most of us expected but were still dreading. "Keep looking. We got your backs."

"'Til dawn approaches or we find him." Devin leveled his gaze at me.

I nodded. "Whichever comes first."

Neither of them looked thrilled, but I knew they wouldn't stop searching for their friend. And no one was better equipped to do a snatch n' grab job than the Butcher and the Ghost.

Not only did they have the right combination of skills, Hudson would recognize them and be more likely to comply with leaving than if it were me or anyone else.

"If he's here, we'll find him." Santos seemed to be pep-talking himself just as much as Devin.

The other man nodded. "Let's go. Time's a wastin'."

They both turned and then just stood there.

"What the hell's wrong with you guys?" I whisper-yelled. "Get moving!"

Santos turned his body so I could see past him and pointed. "Look, paloma."

Tezcatlipoca was sitting on a house's front stoop, a large cat-shaped shadow with his haunches down and his tail flicking calmly over the ground.

"Well, that makes things a lot easier," Devin mused.

Santos slapped his buddy on the back. "Let's go."

Together, they were off without another word. Using hand signals, I checked in quickly with Torr who was still guarding the opposite end of the pathway, then went back to checking my own surroundings. It wasn't long before the impulse to walk up to the gazebo overtook me again.

I wanted to see...see what? Fucking hell, I felt like a child with no impulse control. This wasn't right, wasn't *me*. I had some anxious tendencies, but I knew how to focus, knew what was important. My job was keeping Santos and Devin safe, so why did I feel pulled away from that task?

They're not important. They're just men.

The thought came out of nowhere, and it took me a while to realize it didn't originate from my own mind. Someone was speaking directly into my head, just as Astarte and Tezca did.

I raised my gun, sweeping it from right to left, but saw no movement. "Who's there?" I demanded under my breath.

No answer came, and my gaze resettled on the man's body hung between the two posts. It was completely unnerving how still he was. Not that I wanted him to pull a zombie act, but I was so accustomed to seeing fellow humans moving, even when they were still. You didn't realize how much life moved you, even just the smallest rises and falls from breathing, a tiny twitch of the face or limbs, until that life was gone.

You don't have to die.

I spun in a circle this time, eyes following the barrel of my gun, and again, saw no one. Not even Tezca guarding the house.

Despite my effort to be silent, my breaths grew louder as they left my chest, adrenaline flooding my system.

"Show yourself," I whispered. "If you're gonna talk to me, show your fucking face."

I would. Unfortunately, I don't yet have a face.

I spun again, my heart beating so wildly I was certain others could hear it. "What are you?"

Why don't I show you, Aurora Wilder.

In the blink of an eye, it was no longer night, and I wasn't in the compound anymore. I was...home?

The sun was bright but not blinding. Instead of the pre-dawn chill, the air felt pleasant and warm. I looked down and saw that I was lounging in a chair, an empty beer glass in my hand.

"Another, paloma?"

I looked up to see Santos, his smile full of love and warmth as he took the empty from me.

"Yes, please," I heard my voice say to him. "But kiss me before you go."

He leaned down and brushed his lips against mine. Something felt so off and strange, like I was watching this happen through someone else's eyes. "I want you to rule me later," he whispered. "After our daughters are in bed, I want you to use me hard."

A thrilling rush filled me, both at his words and the anticipation of what we'd do later. But also...daughters? We had a family? What the hell was this?

Santos left and Torr moved a chair next to my legs. He sat down and promptly took my feet into his lap, where he started to massage my soles with his thumbs.

"I love you, Rori," Torr said, his voice low and reverent. "I was a fool to not say those words sooner. I'll spend the rest of my days telling you this, because you deserve nothing less. You're the mother of my daughters and the love of my life."

Elation, bright and warm as sunlight, filled my chest. It was everything I wanted to hear from Torr.

And yet...that off feeling persisted. Torr didn't talk like that. Some alarm was going off within me, but it felt so far away.

Do not be alarmed. I am showing you what your life could be. Love and family. The most precious cornerstones of human existence, are they not?

"I still don't know who or what you are." My own voice felt far away, not part of this delusion or whatever playing out in my mind.

I can give you what you yearn for more than anything, Aurora Wilder. You feel the pull of me because I am so much greater than the crumbs of approval you seek from men.

"No..." My mind swam with the realization of what was speaking to me, the answer coming in jumbled pieces that were too unreal to believe.

You are a rare breed of leader, strong enough to hold sway over others but soft enough to embody that which makes you a woman.

"I'm not doing shit for you. Let me go. Get me out of this." Torr was gone from my vision, or whatever it was, and the sunlight only grew more blinding.

You are on the wrong side of things, Aurora Wilder. Men are trying to rebuild what they had. They want the same systems in place that drove the Collapse in the first place, because all they care about is keeping their yoke of control over us.

"I'm not part of your 'us'!" I cried. "I don't murder. I don't enslave. Fuck this insane cult!"

Do you know how gods are born, Aurora? Whatever was speaking didn't wait for an answer. *A collective of ideas. A human concept given life, given power. Your anger helped to create me, Aurora Wilder. As did your mother's and your grandmother's. I am the pain of all women who have been hurt by men. You willed me into existence, and I will not allow women to be victims any longer.*

"No!" I screamed. "I love Torr and Santos. I love my fathers, my brothers, my uncles, my cousins. I won't let you touch them."

Oh, but you will. You will lead armies, marching thousands to their deaths. Deities exist outside the boundaries of time, and I have seen it happen.

"Fuck you," I roared. "I will kill every one of your believers until *you* no longer exist before you touch anyone in my family."

Foolish girl. I already have, the voice taunted. *Your father Shadow wears the revenge taken by dozens of my daughters on his skin.*

"I will kill you myself!" I screamed with all the breath in my body. "I don't care if you're a fucking god!"

Your rage is a powerful tool, Aurora. It's misdirected at the moment, but that can be corrected.

"Oh no, it's directed in the right fucking place."

Are you sure? The man you're supposedly rescuing looks like he's about to kill you.

All at once, the blinding sunlight was gone, and it was dark again. I looked behind me just in time to see a thin man with bright blue eyes pointing a gun at me. I didn't need a closer look to know that he was dead behind those eyes.

Santos went to tackle him, but he was too late.

Hudson pulled the trigger.

Chapter 29

Hudson

I woke up to a palm clamped over my mouth. It never even occurred to me to struggle. If someone was about to kill me, well, that would be a relief. If they weren't, nothing was about to happen that hadn't already been done to me.

"Hudson, it's Santos," came a harsh whisper in the dark. "We're getting you out."

No fucking way.

I turned my head toward the voice, my body flooding with the strangest sensation as I tried to make out his features. Later, I would realize that it was pure elation and hope rushing through my system.

"Santos?" I whispered against the palm over my mouth.

"Yeah, buddy. We'll catch up later. But first, we're breaking you out. Hang on, this is gonna be bright."

Santos' hand pulled away and a flashlight clicked on. He swung it away from me to examine my restraints.

"One of them has a key," I whispered through a dry throat.

"No time to find it." Santos pointed at something—a gun?—at one of the bedposts, and I saw a flash of gunfire as he shot the wooden post one, two, three times. The gun made a soft *phew* with each shot. That was one hell of a silencer.

Santos put the gun down and yanked on the post above where it had been splintered. He successfully broke it off after a few tries, then lifted the handcuff up and off of what remained of the stump.

"We'll get those off you properly when we get back," he said, heading for my other hand.

"This is really happening?" I brought my now freed hand to my chest, bending the elbow and rolling my wrist around. The empty handcuff that had been on the bedpost dragged and felt cold against my skin. It felt real.

"It's happening, man. Devin's here too."

I let him do the same treatment to the other bedpost, shooting it, breaking it off, then sliding the cuff up and over before asking, "How? Where did they take you?"

"I'll explain later, man, but right now we've got to move."

He released my ankle restraints in the same way, and within ten minutes, I was free.

"Can you stand? Walk?" Santos grabbed my hand to sit me up in the bed.

"Yeah." I just sat there for a bewildered few seconds, in complete shock that I was being freed by a friend who I thought had long forgotten about me.

"How about run? You got shoes?" Santos took a peek out of the small, high window. "We're going to be running for a bit."

"Just some sandals." I slid down to the edge of the bed, let my feet touch the floor, and stood up. The cuffs still attached to my arms and legs jangled, but holy shit, I was fucking free.

"That'll have to do. Oh hey, here." He shrugged out of a jacket that sounded like leather from how the material squeaked and held it out to me. "It's chilly out there."

"I'm good, don't worry." I couldn't remember the last time I'd even perceived temperature on my skin. Coldness, heat. I was numb to it all.

"Just take it," Santos insisted. "You're skin and bone, man."

I accepted the jacket and put it on. The garment felt strange and heavy, although I caught a whiff of a pleasant smell. Something soapy and floral in the lining.

"Let's go. Follow me." Santos moved toward the door, holding his pistol with its silencer at shoulder height.

I stuck my feet in the sandals next to the bed and trailed behind him. We went up the short flight of stairs to the main floor of the house, where more windows let in the gray, pre-dawn light.

Now I could really see Santos and the muscle mass he'd packed on in the last four years. When he glanced at me over his shoulder, his face looked older than I remembered and his eyes were sharper, the honed gaze of a predator.

Someone else was on guard next to the window, a tall Asian man with dark hair tied up on his head. He was wiping the blade of a small knife on his sleeve when he looked up at me, a familiar smile pulling at his lips.

"Hey, Hudson."

"Devin?"

Santos immediately shushed me, moving silently to the door. "You take care of 'em?"

Devin nodded, sheathing the knife in his chest holster. "Put 'em in the bathtub before they could bleed out too much."

"You killed them?" I remembered to whisper this time. "The ones who lived here?"

Devin nodded. "Hope you weren't too attached," he said dryly.

If I didn't have to be silent, I would have been screaming for joy. Finally, someone was killing these monsters! I would have preferred it to have been me, but they were dead either way.

"I'm so fucking glad to see you guys." It was hitting me with full force now. I was being rescued. By friends! I wasn't a breeding stud anymore. And those who had made me into one were paying with their lives.

"Us too, man." Santos clapped me on the shoulder before addressing Devin. "Is the coast clear?"

"I think so, I'm just trying to get Rori's attention so she can give me the signal." Devin pressed against the wall, then made two sharp taps on the windowpane. "Damn it, bitch. Turn around."

"Don't call her that," Santos chided.

I felt like I must have misunderstood something. There was no way these two would conspire with a woman to get me out. They knew better than anyone not to trust them.

"What's she doing?" Santos demanded.

"She's walking all slowly up toward the gazebo thing, not even checking her surroundings." Devin continued staring out the window with a frown. "We gotta move out. Something must be up, 'cause she's not sticking to the plan."

"Anyone else out there?"

"Just her and our people, as far as I can see."

"Okay, we head out and split up," Santos decided. "You and Hudson head for the rendezvous point. I'll get Rori."

"Look at you being all bossy." Devin smirked. "Sounds good."

Santos cracked the door and poked his head out, looking all around before he signaled for us to come out. As Devin and I filed out beside him, Santos looked west, down the lane toward the sacrificial altar, where a woman with short blonde hair stood in the middle of the packed dirt path.

"Come on." I felt Devin tug my sleeve to start running in the opposite direction, but I resisted.

A wave of euphoria came over me, along with an urge I couldn't fight.

An urge for revenge.

"Hudson, come *on!*"

I ignored Devin and kept looking the same way Santos was. He had started approaching the woman, saying her name over and over. She wasn't listening to him, of course. They never listened.

I wanted to escape this hellhole more than anything, but not until I had a chance to put one of *them* in excruciating pain. Or, preferably, kill one of them. It was the least I could do for all they did to me.

I pulled my arm out of Devin's grip and went up to Santos. He was still holding his pistol with a silencer but had another gun tucked into the waistband at the small of his back.

It was pure instinct that guided me, not thought, as I went for the gun. Old habits kicked in as my hand settled on the grip, my thumb flicking off the safety before pointing it at the woman roughly fifty yards ahead of us. Santos didn't even notice until it was too late.

I lined up the sights on the back of her blonde head and squeezed the trigger just as I heard a shout and something crashed into me with the force of a freight train.

I hit the dirt, but so did the woman.

"What the FUCK, Hudson?" Santos screamed in my face. "What the fuck is wrong with you?"

His face was clearer than ever before. Hair shaved closed to his scalp, stubble surrounding his mouth and jaw, brows slashed down over his eyes in a bewildered expression.

I realized the mistake I'd made then. In giving into the impulse to shoot one of my torturers, it woke everyone up. Santos' face was lit up because lights were turning on.

"Fuck. They know we're here." Devin had run over and was kneeling next to the fallen woman, hastily tying a length of fabric around her lower leg, and I couldn't understand why. She was the fucking enemy. Were we taking her prisoner?

"Just let me finish her off." I went to sit up and search for the gun I'd dropped, but Santos didn't budge. When I shoved at him, he shoved me back into the dirt. Then I felt the sharp edge of a blade under my chin. Santos had whipped out a mean-looking machete and looked more than ready to behead me with it.

"She's with us, asshole!" he hissed in my face. "You're not going near her. You're not even to look at her, understand?"

"No." I was confused beyond measure. "No, I don't understand. Why not just leave her then?"

"I'm more tempted to leave you right now," he growled, sheathing the machete with reluctance. "But then this mission would be for nothing, so let's fucking go."

Devin had hauled the woman into his arms and started to run. "You're gonna have to cover us," he told Santos.

"I can still cover." It was the woman who spoke as she slapped a magazine into a handgun while cradled against Devin's chest. She aimed behind him and started firing at the armed women coming out of their houses. At the sight of that, my confusion only increased tenfold.

Santos grabbed the front of my thin shirt and jerked me upward. "Your one job is to run," he said. "No more shooting. You steal my gun again, you won't have a hand to shoot it with, alright?"

"Okay." I'd fucked things up, that much was clear. And even if there was a woman around, wherever they took me had to be better than here.

We were up and sprinting through the lane between houses in an instant. "Go, just keep running!" Santos shouted. He went slower to cover my back, turning around to return fire with both handguns.

I passed Devin and the woman on my way toward the hills, and she gave me a look of pure venom as I ran by. I'd have to make sure to avoid her at all costs, least of all because I fucking shot her.

"Watch out!" someone shouted.

A couple of sentries jumped out in front of me, their automatic rifles trained directly on me. Panic flooded my nervous system and I skidded to a halt, ready to run in the other direction, but Santos and the woman were shooting at the ones coming from that direction.

We were fucking trapped.

The rapid *rat-a-tat-tat* hit my ears, and I brought my hands up, a reflex that wouldn't do anything to save me.

"Hudson, run!" It was the woman screaming at me. "Keep going!"

I looked down, expecting to see my abdomen riddled with holes. But I was somehow perfectly intact. And once I looked up, I saw the sentries motionless on the ground. One had a knife handle in the center of her forehead, the other bleeding out from a knife wound in her throat.

"Nicely done, Dev," I overheard the woman say as the two of them ran past me yet again.

"Can't say I've ever hit my target while running *and* hauling a sack of potatoes before, but there's a first time for everything."

"Excuse you, I am not a mere sack of potatoes."

"Right, you're a sack of potatoes that's bleeding all over me."

What in the everloving fuck had Devin and Santos gotten into since they were taken from here?

"Oh, thank fuck, there's Torr," the woman said, hissing through her pain.

Another man ran up to her and Devin, who transferred the woman to him. "What the hell happened?" asked the new guy.

"Oh nothing," the woman deadpanned. "The guy we're rescuing just decided to shoot me."

"What?!" He looked ready to set the woman down and take me on himself.

"I'll handle Hudson, you take her," Devin said. "You signal the others yet?"

"Yeah, they're coming. She's not fucking riding like this, though."

The woman waved him off. "I'll be fine for a few miles."

"Like hell you will be," the other guy argued. "Let me drive your ride."

"Fine," she grimaced, wincing as she became even paler.

I had no regrets about shooting her, but everyone else was looking at me like I'd committed some kind of capital offense.

"What are we doing with him?" The guy jerked his chin at me, staring daggers in my direction.

"I'm keeping an eye on him," Devin said, also glaring at me. "You cool if Santos rides your bike solo? That way Hudson stays with me, and you and Rori can double up on hers."

"Sure, that's fuckin' peachy."

It was like listening to a foreign language, and as growling engines became increasingly louder, I knew I was about to enter a world of serious culture shock.

Chapter 30

Rori

It turned out to be a good thing that I didn't drive myself. My lower leg was numb by the time we made it to the clearing where we'd camped the night before. If Torr hadn't insisted I keep my leg elevated and in his lap, I wondered if I might have passed out from blood loss.

Our campfire was still there, the circle of stones and ashes within a testament to how recently we'd been here. Was it only two days ago?

Torr circled around the campfire to face the others, cut the engine on my bike, and waited for everyone else to do the same. "We're not staying," he announced. "No more than an hour. Have a bite, take a piss, stretch your legs. But we're going straight to the safe houses after this."

Santos came over to help Torr get me off the bike, despite my effort to wave him off. "I'm okay. I'm okay, really—aw, fuck!"

The second my heel touched the ground, fiery hot pain lanced up my leg and the guys gave me patronizing I-told-you-so looks.

"Get Val over here," Torr ordered, bracing my dead weight against his body. "She'll know what to do."

While Santos left to do just that, Torr had me lean against the bike while he got out a blanket to spread on the ground. He also pulled out a fifth of vodka, and I would've swayed if I wasn't already hanging over the seat. That shit was gonna hurt.

"Come here." Torr manipulated me like a doll, letting me hang all over him while he eased me down to the blanket with the least amount of impact.

"Look at that, you get to save me for once." I grimaced.

"Seems like Devin already did that." Torr unbuckled his belt and pulled it through the loops. I was about to make a dirty joke when he folded the strip of leather in half and stretched it out in front of my mouth. "You're gonna want to bite down on this."

"Fuck me," I groaned before accepting the belt between my teeth.

"Good girl." Torr smirked, and I rolled my eyes.

Santos returned then with Val on his heels. She carried a small, metal white box with a red cross on it. I recognized it as the kit from the field medic class we'd taken together, taught by none other than my mother.

"Alright, let's see what we got." My cousin knelt next to me on the blanket as she proceeded to glove up. She nodded at the vodka by Torr. "Already got the disinfectant out. Good job, Torr."

She swiftly cut away my pant leg while I looked at Santos who was scowling and keeping his distance.

"Hnnn," I said through the belt in my mouth and gestured for him to come closer.

He shook his head. "It's my fault. I let this happen to you."

Oh, fuck that. I spit out the belt and ignored Torr's annoyed glance. "Stop it. You didn't know what he was going to do. Nobody could have predicted this."

"I should have been watching him."

"You were trying to get my attention. If anything, Devin should have had a hold on him, but neither of you could have thought to restrain him."

"Sorry to interrupt, but you need this now." Torr shoved his belt against my mouth, and I took it again, like an obedient horse accepting a bridle.

Val wasted no time after that. She unscrewed the vodka and proceeded to dump the alcohol over the bloody mess on my leg.

The nearest hills and canyons were miles away, and my scream still made an echo. Tears sprang to my eyes and my legs flailed out to escape the sharpest pain I'd ever felt in my life. Torr restrained my legs, and my distress prompted Santos to move in closer.

My sweet Butcher sat behind me, drawing my back to his chest as his arms came around me. He was restraining my arms so I'd stop flailing, but he also provided comfort.

"Even if you don't blame me, I'm sorry anyway," he murmured with a kiss below my ear.

Val finished her torture and began wiping my skin with a sterile cloth while I breathed in harsh, ragged pants.

"Good news," she announced chirpily. "You have an entry and exit wound. Looks like the bullet went through the meat of your calf muscle and didn't hit any bone. It's pretty clean as far as I can tell. I can close you up for now, but you'll need an actual doctor when we get back to the safe houses."

I spat out the belt, the leather now drenched in saliva and covered in deep teeth marks. "Fan-fucking-tastic, cuz."

Torr fed me water and small handfuls of trail mix while Val packed and covered my wound. My whole right side was throbbing now, the adrenaline wearing off and the pain of reality settling in.

I'd never been shot before. And I still had trouble wrapping my head around the fact that it wasn't from an enemy, nor was it an acci-dent. Hudson saw me, pointed the gun, and fired. He knew exactly what he was doing.

Val gave me some extra-strength pain tablets, which I swallowed down with more water. After she left, I spoke in a low voice to my two men.

"So, is Devin watching him?" I asked Santos.

"Yeah." He rubbed a palm over his short, buzzed hair. "I can't really stand to be around him right now."

"Don't blame you," Torr muttered. "We have to figure out what we're gonna do with him."

What to do with Hudson? Yes, that was ultimately my decision. One I should have been turning over in my mind right then, but pain and blood loss made my brain go fuzzy. I just wanted to sleep until my leg didn't hurt anymore.

"Paloma." Santos paused, hesitating.

He didn't speak again until I prompted him. "Yes?"

When he finally met my eyes, his expression was full of worry. "Before he...did that, I was calling out to you. I called your name several times, and it was like you just...checked out. You didn't respond at all until the moment before Hudson shot you."

Torr shifted so that he was seated right in front of me. "I thought I heard him calling out to you. What happened, Ror?"

Fuck. How to explain the visions I had of them and that I had been talking to...some entity? An entity that wanted to recruit me, by the sounds of it?

I blew out a breath and tried to shift to a more comfortable position, thinking of how to explain myself without making them panic.

"The cult worships a goddess, right?" was the best my exhausted, blood-deprived brain could spit out.

"Yeah, they call it the Dark Mother," Santos confirmed.

"Well, I think their belief has become so potent that it's...real. As real as Astarte or Tezca. And it talked to me."

The two of them immediately stiffened. Torr cursed and brought his face close to mine. "What did it say?"

I shook my head. "A bunch of bullshit. It doesn't matter. What does matter is that these guys were right, and we have to listen to them." I nodded at Tezca, who was ambling over toward us. His coat had a glossy sheen in the bright sunlight, the spot pattern appearing and disappearing with his graceful movements. Astarte was hitching a ride, perched on the big cat's shoulder blades.

"Right about what?" Santos scratched under his jaguar's chin, and Tezca emitted a low rumbling purr.

"This whole fight started with humans, but it has the potential to get out of hand quickly," I remarked. "Especially now that they have a god on their side."

———

AN ETERNITY LATER, we finally made it to the safe houses. It was nightfall by the following day, and everyone was practically falling off their bikes by the time we arrived. I'd have to hold church and talk to everyone at some point, but that could wait until I'd slept for a solid day or two.

Santos and Torr had both fallen into bed with me, and I was too exhausted to even celebrate that fact. When I woke up, the first thing I noticed was that my leg no longer hurt, except for some twinging soreness.

The second thing I noticed was that I wasn't boxed in by two bodies, but three.

My foot hit something warm and furry at the foot of the bed as I turned over, and then I yelped as something hot and scratchy slid over my ankle.

"Jesus fucking Christ, Tezca," I gasped, bringing my hand to my chest as I sat up. "Warn a girl before you start licking her feet."

The jaguar just stared at me through half-lidded yellow eyes, then stretched out long across the bottom of the bed, paws and tail dangling off the edges.

All the commotion had roused my guys and they both stirred, turning in towards me as if their first instinct, even half asleep, was to protect me.

Since I was sitting up, the two of them nuzzled up to my waist. Torr threw an arm over my knees and Santos rested his head on my thigh.

"How you feelin'?" Santos asked sleepily, his eyes still closed as he stroked down the side of my leg.

"Better." I reached down and dragged my hands over both of their heads, enjoying the two different textures—Santos' buzzed scalp and Torr's longer strands. "Good as new, almost."

"Thank fuck." Torr planted a kiss on my hip and hugged around my legs tighter.

"And I've decided I want Hudson gone," I announced.

That got both of them stiffening and then sitting up.

"Can I shoot him first?" Torr rubbed sleep out of his eyes and then stretched. "An eye for an eye and all that shit."

"You want him gone...where?" Santos asked at the same time.

"I don't know yet. But I don't want him near me, and especially not near other women like Val and Paige. Actually, I'm not too worried about Val, but I don't want him in the same territory as Paige."

"He's...not well." Santos rubbed his face and looked tired enough to fall back asleep. "Not just in the head, that much is obvious. But physically, he's not doing great either. I haven't talked to him, but Dev says he looks malnourished."

"So when the doctor comes out to look at my leg, he'll be examined too." I sat up straighter. "Did anyone else get injured?"

"No." Torr shook his head. "Those sentries had big guns but obviously weren't trained on how to use them. You were the only one who got shot."

"Lucky me," I said drolly, and leaned back against the headboard. "Obviously, we need to ensure it's a male doctor we get out here."

"I can make that call." Torr started getting out of bed.

"No, I can do it. I should talk to my mom anyway."

"Fine, but you stay resting, creep." He picked up the jeans he'd discarded on the floor. "I'm getting us breakfast."

"You go with him." I kissed Santos' neck. "Check on everyone for me."

He grinned and kissed my cheek before sliding out. "You just want the bed to yourself."

"Obviously. Now that I have you two, starfishing will be a rare luxury."

My fighter chuckled as he too picked up his pants from the floor and began sliding them on.

"Oh hey, Santos?" I said after a moment of thinking.

"Yes, paloma?" He leaned over the bed, reaching for another kiss, which I gave him.

"If you see Devin, tell him I want to talk to him."

Chapter 31

Devin

My chest felt weird as I rapped my knuckles on Rori's door, then stood back and waited. What was this sensation, all tight like my rib cage was constricted while also feeling light and fluttery at the same time?

Could this be...nervousness?

"Come in," she called from the other side.

I let myself in to find Rori dressed, thankfully, although it was less than her usual getup of dark jeans and black leather jacket. She had on a tank top and shorts and was doing pistol squats next to the bed, her bandaged leg extended in front of her as she raised and lowered herself with the other leg.

"You wanted to see me?" I cleared my throat, unsure why my voice was more hoarse than normal.

"Yeah." She pressed up to full height, then sat on the foot of the bed, looking over at me with a sheepish smile. "I've been told to rest, but I'm just going stir crazy in here."

"Have you tried a disguise to escape unnoticed?" I asked. "Maybe growing a beard and putting on a trench coat?"

She laughed and rubbed at the nonexistent facial hair on her cheek. "Working on it. Come in. Shut the door."

A prickle rose along the back of my neck as I did what she asked. It wasn't alarm or even discomfort alerting my senses. This just...felt all wrong, being in a closed bedroom with my friend's girl. Who he shared with another guy, but that was neither here nor there. They had their triad thing going on, and I was not part of it. Nor did I have any desire to be part of it.

Still, I tamped down the urge to escape the room and stood with my back against the door.

Rori remained sitting on the foot of the bed, looking thoughtful for a while before she spoke.

"I know you and I haven't exactly been friendly since we met. That being said, I just want to say thank you for what you did out there."

Outwardly, I gave a sharp nod. Inside, I was too confused to know what to feel. Brushing it off was always a safe bet, right? "Santos had his hands full, and he would've killed me for leaving you to bleed out in the dirt."

Yep, blame my buddy who was in love with her. It was always the most convenient excuse.

A smile pulled slowly at her lips as if she knew it was exactly that, an excuse. "Well, look at you being so considerate of others."

I ducked my chin to hide my laugh, but it was too late. Aw, fuck, I was in trouble if she could see right through me.

"Really, though. You acted quickly and most likely saved my life, so I'm grateful. This would have gone all cockeyed without you, Devin."

Damn it, now the discomfort was setting in. Her praise made my body and brain send off all kinds of opposing signals. She was being genuine, I knew that at the surface. But every other time I'd been in this position, alone with a woman complimenting my achievements, it had been a manipulation tactic. A means of softening me up before using me.

"Anyone else in my position would have done the same," I answered stiffly. "Is there anything else?"

Rori straightened, her relaxed expression hardening. "How's Hudson doing?"

The question took me aback, and I did not hide it. "I'm surprised you would ask."

"So am I," she said dryly.

"He's...well, not great," I admitted.

"He's dangerous."

Now that got me defensive, and I squared my shoulders in her direction. "He's been through an insane amount of trauma. What me and Santos went through doesn't hold a candle to him. I'm actually shocked he's held on this long. But what he needs most is help, Rori."

Her expression softened by only a fraction. "I can understand that. But we can't have someone around who will shoot at people indiscriminately."

"He won't do that again," I protested. "He will need *lots* of time to adjust to a normal life again, but Hudson is not a violent person at his core. He's like Santos, kind of. He just...lashed out because he's basically a cornered animal."

Rori narrowed her eyes. "I thought we were about to start getting along better, but here you are, defending the man who could have killed me if Santos hadn't jumped him."

"Obviously, that was wrong, full stop." I extended my palm out to her, imploring her to understand. "But all he's known, all day, every day for *years*, is being tied to a bed and raped by women, Rori. He's never even had the tiny freedoms that we had as gladiators. He never got to choose weapons to defend himself. He was never given the choice to fight for his life or die. It's just been endless women in his face, on top of him, touching him, and there's nothing he could do about it. And I'm sorry, but can you put yourself in his shoes just for a minute? What would you do, if that had been your life for six years and you saw a man as you were making your escape? If you had access to a gun, would you take the chance of *not* shooting?"

Rori said nothing and her expression didn't change, but I knew my words had hit home. The silence stretched out between us until she asked quietly, "What do you suggest be done with him?"

I sighed and rubbed my forehead, the responsibility of Hudson hitting me then like a ton of bricks. Who knew if he ever would be able to return to a normal life? Could ever safely interact with women again? Hell, even be in the same room as one?

"I'll work with him," I said. "He'll stay in the other house with the fighters, as long as you and the other women don't mind staying here. I think it'll help if I'm around him and he's around other guys, you know. It'll make him feel safer."

"And then?" Rori prompted.

"I guess we'll have to see."

She sighed, the breath of air deflating her. "I'll see if a trauma therapist can come up here. Frankly, I think you, Santos, and all the other fighters could use some therapy."

"I guess that's fair. As long as it's a male therapist."

"Of course."

She gave me a strange look then, one that got me all kinds of defensive. "What?"

"Are you in love with him?"

"Who?" I demanded.

"Hudson, who else?"

"I—no." Her stare didn't waver, and it felt like being under a microscope. "I...wouldn't call it that," I amended with an awkward chuckle. "I've always carried a torch for him, somewhat. But you know, the situation we were in didn't exactly lend to anything romantic developing."

"So, working with him, as you say." Rori steepled her fingers. "Is it personal to you?"

"I want to see him get better," I admitted. "I want to see him thriving and healthy again. But as far as hoping for something to happen between us?" I waved that away. "It's been years. He's fragile, and I'd never take advantage of him while he's like this. Besides, I'm fucked up in my own way. I'm not what he needs." I shrugged. "I don't even know if he's into guys, to be honest."

A slow smile pulled at Rori's lips again, the one that said she knew more than she was letting on. "We're all fucked up in our own ways, Devin. That doesn't mean we'd be terrible friends or romantic partners. I mean—" she raised a hand, catching herself. "I don't mean you and me but in general."

"I know what you mean." I laughed softly. "And I appreciate the sentiment."

She smiled wider. "The fact that you're willing to look after Hudson this much is a testament to how un-fucked up you really are. As is you saving my life out there."

I looked at the floor, for some reason unable to look her in the eye. "Thank you for saying that."

———

An hour later, I knocked on Hudson's door. He didn't answer, so I opened it just enough to stick my head in. "Hey, just me."

"Hey." He was lying on his bed, staring at the ceiling with his feet out wide. It was eerily just like the position he'd been kept in, only now his hands were on his chest.

"Is it cool if I hang for a bit?"

"Do whatever you want," he said in a flat voice.

I tried to not take that tone personally as I slipped inside and closed the door behind me. "You not hungry?" I gestured toward the untouched plate of food on the bedside table.

"Don't trust it," he answered.

"There's nothing in it, man. Santos made it."

"Someone else could have put something in it."

I marched over and picked up the plate of cold chicken tacos. Standing in front of Hudson, I took a big bite out of one, making a show of chewing and swallowing. The meat was grilled to perfection, though it could have been spicier.

"See?" I put down the plate and spread my hands out. "All good."

Hudson didn't look convinced. Shit, he didn't look *alive,* staring blankly at the paint up there. "Is Santos still pissed at me?"

I stroked my beard. "Well, yeah. He gets why you did it, but he's protective."

Hudson scoffed like that was the most ridiculous thing he'd ever heard. "Protective."

I sucked in a breath, at first unsure of how much to tiptoe around this with him, but fuck it. He was an adult when he got captured, we all were. His brain was developed enough to know that not all women were the enemy.

And so's yours, big guy, I thought to myself.

"Her name is Aurora. Rori. And yeah, Santos is in love with her. She's his woman." I crossed my arms, watching for a reaction from him. "She's the one who led and organized this effort to get you out. So yeah, he's pissed that you shot her unprovoked. And he's not the only one."

"You including yourself in that?" Now Hudson turned his head to look at me, those once electric blue eyes now dead and dull.

"Hudson, man," I sighed. "You're back in the real world now. You're gonna have to interact with women. I mean, we'll provide a buffer for a while and give you some time to acclimate, but that's just how it is."

He shot up and came to stand in front of me almost faster than I could track. The guy had always been quick and decisive in his movements. I almost wanted to say it was a shame that he hadn't ended up in the gladiator ring with us. He would have been honed into an incredible fighter.

And maybe he wouldn't be looking so dead and haunted.

"I don't want *that* woman, or any other, coming near me," he hissed. "Distance is fine. I can control myself. But no woman will *ever* touch me or get within range of touching me again. Do you get what I'm saying, Devin?"

"Sure, man. That's fair—"

"If they do, I swear to God, I won't miss this time." He scowled, the burning hatred in his eyes the only thing lighting him up. "If a woman so much as breathes on me, I *will* kill her."

Epilogue

Rori

I woke up with three animal faces staring at me in the darkness. Astarte, Tezca, and Lupa, Gwen's wolf, were all sitting on my bed, their faces inches away from mine. And yet the bed felt weightless, like there were no animals on top of me at all.

"Okay." I sat up and leaned against the headboard. "I know for a fact that this is a dream. So what's up, guys?"

Astarte spoke first. *Remember what I told you, Aurora. We cannot tell you the events of the future or anything that would alter the decisions you make out of free will. That being said, we are here to guide you. The decisions you make going forward are tantamount to the objective you seek. Listen closely and remember. You will not know what any of this means now, but you will when the time comes.*

I blinked at the white dove, looking like a sliver of bird-shaped moonlight in this dreamscape. She usually sounded annoyed with me, but I barely recognized her tone now. I'd never heard her sound so dire and serious.

"Okay, I'm listening."

Tezcatlipoca's velvety, thunderous voice filled my head next. *You must hold onto yourself, Aurora. Even when your mind shatters and you lose sense of who you are.*

I sat up higher. "Wait, what?"

You must not lose your voice, Lupa said next. *Even when you're choking on toxic sludge and only poison comes out.*

"What the *hell* do you guys mean?"

You must not lose sight of those you love, Astarte said. *Even when your eyes show you horrors that break your heart.*

"What could possibly...okay, I know you said I wouldn't understand, but seriously, what the *fuck*?"

The wolf and the jaguar faded away like they were apparitions made of mist and only Astarte remained.

This will be the hardest battle you, or any living human, will have to face. And you cannot afford to lose it.

I tried to pull in a deep breath, but my lungs felt seized up and unable to take more than small sips of air. "You can't tell me anything else?"

For the first time, I wasn't asking to get on the bird's nerves but because I was scared shitless of what was coming

I can tell you one more thing.

"Yes?"

When it's pulling you under, and you feel yourself losing the fight and letting go, scream.

———

Thank you so much for reading Harmless! The story concludes in the third and final Vengeful Gods MC book, Deathless.

Deathless is available for pre-order now!

———

Want to read about Rori's mother and her fathers? Steel Demons MC is a complete series available now!

Click here to start reading Lawless.

Want bikers and shifters?

Check out my new M/F paranormal romance series, Howling Death MC, on my pen name Sophie Ash!
All books can be read as standalones.

Book 1: **Traitor Wolf**
Book 2: **Enemy Wolf**

———

To keep up with all my releases, join my Facebook group, The Ash Coven:
https://www.facebook.com/groups/ashcoven

Also by Crystal Ash

Harem of Freaks: The Complete Series

Say Your Prayers

Steel Demons MC

Lawless

Powerless

Fearless

Painless

Helpless

Heartless

Senseless

Ruthless

Merciless

Endless

Shifted Mates Trilogy

Unholy Trinity: The Complete Series

For a complete list of books by Crystal Ash, visit her Amazon page.

About the Author

Crystal Ash is a USA Today Bestselling Author from California. She loves writing steamy, heart-wrenching romance with tortured heroes, especially if they're in a reverse harem. Crystal's other loves include animals, mythology, and well-crafted alcohol, most of which can also be found in her stories.

When she's not writing, she's probably drinking craft beer with her husband or trying to coax her feral cat into accepting affection.

crystalashbooks.com

facebook.com/Crystal.Ash.Romance
instagram.com/crystalashbooks
amazon.com/author/crystalash
bookbub.com/profile/crystal-ash

Deathless

Crystal Ash

Content warnings

This book contains the following:

Mentions of infanticide
Suicidal ideation
Human sacrifice
Bodily possession/loss of autonomy
Bondage/rope play
Group sex (including DP)

Chapter 1

Rori

"Come here, sweetheart." My mother lowered into a squat, holding her arms straight out in front of her. Her face was lit up with love and adoration. "Come to grandma."

I looked down and noticed the child in my lap for the first time. A girl, going by the sparkly butterfly clip holding back waves of dark brown hair. She, my daughter, held onto the forefingers of each of my hands for balance. Tiny, chubby hands released me slowly as she started taking wobbly steps toward my mother.

Her grandmother.

"Yes!" my mom praised with a huge smile. "You're doing so good! Come here and give me a hug."

The little girl ventured forward, growing more confident with each unsupported step. She giggled, reaching for her grandma, her other favorite person besides me. My daughter was so happy and loved with the two of us to take care of her.

"Yes! That's my girl!" My mom swept her up on her last step, holding her granddaughter tightly, protectively, as she smothered her in kisses.

I watched, feeling as if it were recording being played. Or like I was a sheet of glass.

"What is this?" I asked, unnerved by the odd detachment from the two people before me, the two people I was supposed to love most. "I'm dreaming, aren't I?"

"It's real if you allow it to be." My mom stood up with a groan, lifting my daughter to settle her on her hip. "Isn't it, my love?" She tapped the child on the nose.

Or at least, it looked like she did. I had yet to see the little girl's face.

"What do you mean?" I looked around, finding small homes, cottages and trailers entering my vision. And women bustling about, some with small children as well. "This is wrong," I heard myself say.

"How so?" My mom grinned at the little girl on her hip, bouncing her up and down as she made funny faces.

"Where are her fathers?" I demanded. "Where are *my* fathers? Your husbands."

"Oh, we don't need them." My mom pretended to bite the little girl's nose. "We're a much better, happier family like this."

"No, we're not. This is wrong." Panic settled in; and I wanted to move, to run. But I felt stuck, as if swimming through thick mud. "What about my brothers?" I demanded. "Where's Daren and Nolan?"

"Where they belong."

"They're your fucking *sons*. What do you mean by that?"

The woman, entity, or whatever was wearing my mother's face, finally made eye contact with me. "I have no sons. Only daughters."

"Give her to me." I approached her with my arms out, even though it felt like I wasn't crossing any distance at all. "Give me my daughter."

The thing holding the little girl seemed to float backwards in space, her arms tightening around the child. "You're not ready, Aurora." It gave me a twisted smile, distorting my mother's face. "But don't worry. You will be soon."

"Ready for what?" I demanded. "Give me back my daughter!"

"All daughters are mine, Aurora. The sooner you accept that, the sooner we can begin."

The little girl then turned to look at me, but in place of her face was just...a moving hunk of flesh.

It was smooth and grayish-brown, expanding and contracting on itself rhythmically as if controlled by a breath or heartbeat.

The faceless child reached its hand toward me and I careened backward, trying to get away. It was wrong. It was evil. It had taken everyone I loved and now it was trying to consume me...

It caught me, gripping my shoulder with a rough hand and shaking me.

"Rori, snap the fuck out of it!"

There was a falling sensation that made me kick, and then I was somewhere else.

In bed, sandwiched between two hard, masculine bodies.

Torr's face appeared in my vision, his hair mussed from sleep and a frown pinching his mouth. "Fucking hell. Again?"

I rubbed my face, my eyes, just to feel something real, solid and tangible. On my other side, Santos seemed to read my mind and placed a warm, lingering kiss on my shoulder. His calloused hand massaged my hip and thigh. The weight and heat of his touch shepherded me back to reality, this place of safety with my men.

"Yeah, again," I sighed in answer to Torr's hovering frown. "I'm sorry."

"You have nothing to apologize for." Santos kissed my temple, his fingers running across my belly. "We're just worried about you."

"I'm fine—"

"Don't say that," Torr bit out. "Not to us. Not when you've been thrashing and screaming in your sleep for two weeks straight."

"It's just bad dreams." I couldn't convince myself of that any more than I could the guys. My hand shook as I rubbed my forehead.

Torr flopped down next to me with a huge sigh. "That therapist guy is coming today, right?"

"He's expected to, yeah." I pushed a lock of hair off of his forehead, then looked the other way at Santos. "You're both talking to him."

"Yeah, about that." Santos turned onto his side, bicep flexing as he propped up onto his elbow. "We think you should talk to him too, paloma."

My gaze bounced back and forth between them. "You two have discussed this?"

"It's like he said." Torr brought one hand behind his head. "We're worried about you. I've never seen you have dreams like this."

"Goddamnit." I covered my face with my hands and groaned.

"Don't tell me you're mad about this," Torr chided. "You can't be a hypocrite and tell us to talk to someone but make yourself exempt."

"I'm not mad. I'm annoyed because I want to be mad. But *noooo*." I sat up and stretched. "You two have to be all sensible and caring and talk to each other because you're concerned about me. I never get an opportunity to be mad at you guys, and that's really fucking unfair."

Santos laughed, deep and rumbling like the purr of his jaguar, as he sat up next to me. "Sorry we're so perfect for you." He dropped another kiss to my shoulder, the slow brush of lips and smolder in his dark eyes making me want to shove his head between my legs.

"You're not sorry." I tried to use my best accusatory tone, but shit, it was hard to *pretend* to be mad too.

"No, ma'am." Santos kissed the crook of my neck and I felt his smile against the curve in my skin.

Still reclined, Torr's hand drifted over my hip and lower back. "You want breakfast?" His touch skimmed up my spine. "Or should we have a lie-in?"

Normally, not even breakfast could get me to skip extended time in bed with my men. It was the best feeling, waking up to the two of them. My head on Torr's chest, with Santos snuggled up to my back.

They were everything I wanted and never thought I'd have, devoted to me and secure enough in themselves to share me. It didn't hurt that they were two of the most gorgeous male specimens I'd ever set eyes on.

But if I was being honest, the dreams were unnerving me, and I probably did need to talk to someone. They were unsettling me to the point of not wanting to spend extra time in bed for fear of falling asleep and experiencing them again.

"Yeah, breakfast sounds good." I leaned over and kissed Torr, then came back up and did the same to Santos on my other side.

As the three of us got out of bed and dressed, someone else started to rouse. Tezcatlipoca yawned, showing off all his teeth before stretching long, the dark spots in his coat shimmering with his graceful movement.

"Good morning, beautiful boy." I scratched the jaguar's neck and kissed the top of his head, earning a chuff and a firm headbutt against my thigh.

Tezca led the way downstairs, where we found Devin already laying strips of bacon in a pan. The lean-muscled fighter was shirtless and his long hair was loose, spilling down his back nearly to his waist in glossy, untangled strands.

Really, it was unfair how some men had such beautiful features. Santos' eyelashes would make mascara companies cry with envy. Devin's hair had the body and shine so many women dreamed of.

"Morning," Santos greeted his ex-gladiator friend with a fist bump to the shoulder. Tezca walked right up to Devin and head-butted him square in the ass.

"Jesus! Trying to kill me here, cat?" Devin swatted at Tezca behind him, but I didn't miss that quick scratch behind the ear.

"That for Hudson?" Santos nodded at the bacon starting to sizzle.

"Yeah." Devin grabbed the handle of another pan and tossed some diced potatoes all casually like he was a professional chef. Though he was likely the best knife thrower in the world, so maybe there was some shared skill there. "Dude needs to put on some calories."

"Invite him to come eat with us." Torr got the coffee started. Our tools were pretty rudimentary at the safe house, so he was putting some muscle into a manual grinder as a pot of water boiled.

"I did." There was a note of annoyance in Devin's tone. "I do, for every meal. Every day."

Silence fell over the kitchen as no one wanted to say what was on their mind. We'd rescued Hudson from the same cult of women who had enslaved Devin and Santos and forced them to become gladiators. Hudson had been so delighted at being rescued that he'd taken Santos' gun and shot me in the leg.

After staying for two weeks at the safe houses of my newly formed motorcycle club, the Vengeful Gods MC, Hudson didn't seem to be improving when it came to being around women. And with me as president, that was an issue.

"Should we revisit the idea that maybe this isn't the best place for him?" I ventured. I truly wanted to be sympathetic to Hudson. I couldn't imagine the amount of trauma he'd been through, being used as a captive breeding stud for this cult for years. But my priority was to my club and the safety of the women within it.

Hudson had shot me in the leg only because Santos had tackled him as the gun went off. While I could understand violence being his first reaction toward me, I did not want my or any other woman's life in danger because of this man's trauma.

Devin flinched at my question as if I had thrown something at him. "And where *would* be the best place for him?"

"I don't know. But it might be worth bringing up to Dr. Corwin when he arrives."

Devin's eyes remained steadfast on the stove in front of him. "He's not dangerous."

Santos snorted at that. "Come on, dude."

"We've kept all the weapons out of his reach," Devin argued. "He doesn't leave his room because he doesn't *want* to hurt anybody. Is that such a bad thing?"

"It's concerning if just seeing a woman will trigger him into a violent outburst." Torr set up the pour-over cone onto the coffee carafe and dumped the freshly-ground beans.

"He used to *want* to hurt people. Now he doesn't. That's an improvement," Devin argued.

"A very impressive amount of progress in two weeks," I deadpanned.

Devin whipped around to glare at me, every long, slender muscle on his body bunched with tension. As much as I loathed to admit it, he was still beautiful even when pissed off.

"You don't get to decide how long it takes for someone to heal," he spat. "Not everything can happen the moment you snap your fingers and command it, *President*."

"You're right. You can explain that to my aunt and uncles if their daughter ends up dead," I replied. "Or to the Hunter if something happens to Paige. He's been through this shit with you guys. I'm sure he will be most understanding. Oh no, wait." I held up an index finger, pretending to think about it. "As president, *I'm* responsible for everyone in my club. So that means any bad shit that happens falls on me."

"So what would you do?" Devin asked coldly. "Stick him in a padded room? Put him on a cocktail of meds? Throw him out into the world to be retraumatized over and over?"

"Like I said, I'm willing to let the doctor give his professional opinion."

"Right. The therapist that a woman recommended."

Oh hell no. This man was not going to insinuate any misogynistic shit about my mother. "Fuck off with that. There's no ulterior motives here," I said. "We all want Hudson to heal. I don't want to punish him or make him struggle any more than he already has. But I'm not going to put my people at risk for his benefit."

Devin faced the stove again, effectively done with the conversation. He turned off the burners with more force than necessary, plated up the food, and stormed out of the kitchen.

"Another highly productive conversation," I sighed at his departure.

Chapter 2

Devin

"**B**reakfast," I called, rapping my knuckles on Hudson's door. When no answer came, I knocked again. "Hud, you up?"

After more silence, I turned the knob and stuck my head inside. "Hudson, you okay?"

Like every morning, his bed was neatly made. Actually, the entire room was neat as a pin, which was a nice change of pace from the rest of the house occupied by ex-gladiators.

Books were stacked neatly on a bedside table. Laundry was either hanging or folded in the open closet. The attached bathroom door was closed, which alleviated my worry at the silence in the room.

"Hey, you taking a shit?" I went inside to put the food down on the table with a single chair next to the window. "I'll get you some coffee if you want."

"Not a good time, Dev!" came the tense reply through the bathroom door.

I paused. "You okay in there?"

"Fine!"

I couldn't place what it was, either just instinct or something in his voice, but I had a feeling he wasn't working his way through his

531

usual morning ritual. Keeping light on my feet, I moved closer to the door. "Hudson?"

"Go away, Devin!"

"If you're really taking a shit, I will. Believe me, I have no desire to interrupt."

He could have just said, *Yes, fuck off.* But he didn't. Instead, a moan floated through the wood. The sound could have been pain or... the complete opposite of pain.

My pulse quickened and I held my breath, not wanting to miss another sound that came through that door. I wanted to make sure he was okay, and if he was, maybe, for stupid, selfish reasons, I wanted to hear that sound again.

"Hudson," I said again, my throat feeling tighter. "What are you doing?"

"Nothing!"

"Are you hurting yourself?"

The silence from the other side of the door spurred me into action. "I'm coming in."

"No, don't—"

I swung the door open wide to find Hudson leaning against the sink's counter, scrambling to tuck his erection back into his sweatpants. He was shirtless and breathing hard, skin flushed under all his tattoos.

"What the fuck, man?" he demanded, blue eyes seething with embarrassment.

I laughed, rubbing my face both with relief and as an excuse to not stare too blatantly. "You could have just said you wanted some privacy to jerk off."

"I wasn't!" The flush raced up his neck to his face.

I stopped laughing, taking in his body language like I was sizing up a target. "Dude, it's okay. Nobody cares."

"No, I was trying to make it go away! I don't want to be waking up with this shit, feeling like..." He trailed off, shaking his head. "I don't *want* that. I mean, I don't want to want it."

It dawned on me what he was saying, and I had to fold my arms to resist giving the poor guy a hug. "Hudson." I gentled my voice as if talking to a child. "It's okay to feel, uh, aroused," I said in an effort to not be crass. "That's totally normal. And if you touch yourself because it feels good, that's fine too. It's your body, you get to have control of it now. No one is going to take that away from you again."

"You don't get it," he hissed. "It reacts like clockwork every day. Like when I used to take cigarette breaks at work, the cravings always hit me at the same time."

"Shit." That was an aspect I hadn't considered, the involuntary conditioning and habits instilled into him after all these years. "I'm sorry."

"I'm losing my shit, Dev. Going through withdrawals for something I don't even want."

"We have a therapist coming out soon. A man," I added. "He'll be able to help you with this, I bet."

Hudson tilted his head back and laughed mirthlessly. "A fucking head shrink. Whose idea was that?"

"Rori's."

His gaze returned to mine, expression going cold at the mention of her name. "And you trust...*her*?"

"With this, yeah." It was a truth I could say confidently. In spite of the friction between Rori and me, I believed she was doing her best for all in this situation. If it were me who'd been shot by the guy we were trying to rescue, I might not be so forgiving. But she was actually compromising a lot, letting Hudson stay here and bringing out a professional to help him. Even I could admit that.

Hudson shook his head. "I don't know how, man. I know I sound like broken record, but how can you believe a fucking word she says?"

"Because that's not the kind of person she is." Obviously I wasn't Rori's biggest fan, but I was astounded at how much defending of her I had to do with him. "She's not the same people who put us, put *you*, through all that shit. She led the charge to get you out. She changed up her original plans to make *your* rescue the number one priority.

And..." I hesitated but decided to go through with that thought. "Santos loves her. Like, deeply loves her."

Hudson gave that a dismissive scoff. "He loves any woman who looks his way."

"Have you lived with him for the past four years? I didn't think so." I crossed my arms. "Maybe in the early days he was a sucker for some female attention, but this life has sucked the soul out of him too. The only difference between him and us is that he still had enough soul left to find happiness when he got out."

I used to be just as dismissive as Hudson when Santos and I were gladiators. His eternal optimism had been so annoyingly naive. Every day, we saw people slaughtered, and Santos refused to believe that would ever be him. He'd escape one day, find a way to make a living, find a woman who loved him, raise a family, grow old together, blah blah blah. I'd made myself blue in the face telling him to snap out of it and face reality—we were gonna die on the sands just like the rest of the faceless, nameless gladiators.

But that didn't happen. And I got up this morning to see him coming down the stairs with an easy smile on his face, hands around the waist of the woman he'd woken up next to. He'd really fucking done it.

Back at Mystic Canyon, I'd joked about being envious of Santos' head-in-the-clouds pipe dreams. Now, I was dumbfounded that he'd actually made it happen.

"Well, good for him." Hudson's tone dripped with sarcasm. "At least one of us still remembers what happiness feels like."

"I dunno, man." I ran a hand back through my hair and noticed Hudson following the movement. "There may be hope for us yet. We're out of that hellscape. The world is our lobster or however the fuck that saying goes."

"Oyster."

"Yeah, that's the one."

Hudson laughed, and this time, there was a touch more humor to the sound. The slightest pull of a smile at his lips. "I feel like getting past this shit would be so much easier if I wasn't attracted to women, you know?"

My throat tightened again while I attempted to keep my focus on Hudson's face, not the tattooed, lean body that had started to fill out ever since he'd started getting balanced meals every day. But shit, he had a heartbreaker's face too. Baby blue eyes. Brown hair with a tint of red.

Don't say it, I told myself. *Don't even think about asking the question.*

But what if you could help him...in another way? asked another voice.

In the end, the weaker side of me won.

"Well, have you ever considered...guys?"

Hudson didn't bat an eye, didn't even seem to notice my internal debate. "Sure, why not? I mean, if I could get this issue," he gestured at his crotch, "resolved without ever having to touch a woman again? Sign me the fuck up." He touched his mouth, eyes focusing somewhere else as gave it some more thought. "If I could ever, you know, learn to enjoy the act again, that would just be a bonus." His gaze fell on me again, eyes narrowing skeptically. "Why, you know anyone?"

Oh, fuck me. Why did I crack open Pandora's box if I thought even for a moment it would lead to this?

Because you want it, that weak, treacherous side of me said. *Because your dirty little secret is twofold: your savior complex and your jealousy over Santos having someone when you don't.*

All terrible, selfish reasons that I was fully aware of. But if I really, genuinely, could help Hudson in this way, wouldn't the good outweigh the bad?

"I know, uh." I cleared my throat and tried again. "I mean, well, there's me."

The guy's chin lowered, his eyebrows going up. "You?"

"Yeah. I mean, I'm the only bi dude I know of around here. But if it's awkward or I'm not your type or whatever, it's cool." And that was how I learned Pandora's box was actually a hole, and I just kept digging myself deeper.

"No, Dev. It's not that. I'm just surprised." Hudson rubbed his lower lip with his thumb, his gaze intense. "Although, I guess I shouldn't be."

"Why do you say that?"

"No reason. It's just…" He stroked his chin. He'd been letting his facial hair grow and it was coming in dense and full. "Whenever I thought back to that time, when it was the three of us, I always thought of you more than Santos."

I swallowed. "You did?"

"Yeah. I just clicked with you more, I guess."

"Look, man." I brought my palms up, eager to backtrack. "Something like this can get messy, so—"

"How do you mean?" he challenged. "Other people in this house are fucking, aren't they?"

"Sure, but—"

"You don't have to treat me like I'm made of tissue paper, Dev." His expression hardened. "In fact, I'd really prefer it if you didn't."

"Okay." I lowered my hands. "How do you want me to treat you then?"

One shoulder went up in a lazy shrug. "I dunno. Like anyone else you'd hook up with."

"Alright. Well it turns out everyone is different. You have to tell me what you expect, what your limits are."

He started to roll his eyes. "Come on—"

"No, this is how it's gonna be." I straightened my spine, firming up my stance. "You have to use your words and tell me what you want and don't want, or this doesn't happen."

"Way to make it fucking awkward," he groaned.

"This is how people make it enjoyable for each other. You discuss this shit."

"Doesn't make it any less weird."

I shoved my hair back and sighed. "Okay, I want you to ask yourself a question. Repeat this in your head: 'Do I trust Devin?' If the answer is no, that's fine, but if that's the case, I'm definitely *not* fucking you."

"I do trust you." Hudson's throat bobbed, and he said more quietly, "You're the one I trust here the most."

"Okay. Then be a little awkward and communicate with me. It's hard to be vulnerable dude, I know. But I'll never ridicule you for what you've been through. And anything you share with me stays between us."

For some reason, an image of Rori popped into my head, shrewd green eyes missing nothing. I shoved her away just as quickly as she came.

Hudson remained silent for a long time until he said, "I don't want you on top of me."

"Okay, that's good. What else?"

"I don't...I..." The poor guy clammed up, harsh breaths rushing in and out of his nose.

"Hey, it's okay." I took a chance moving in closer, standing next to him at the counter. "We can start there, or even ten steps before that. You're in control here."

"That's all I really want," he admitted. "To be in control of what happens to me. And not just there for someone else to..."

"Good. I'm glad you told me that." I knew, even when I thought this would be a far-off fantasy, that I would have to tread carefully with Hudson. To not only show him what pleasure was again, but to make him feel confident and safe. My goddamn savior complex was riding high, and I was too much of a sucker to do the hard thing and think about long-term consequences.

"Can I take your hand?" I asked.

Hudson looked surprised, like he thought I'd want to touch something a lot more X-rated, but then nodded.

I went for his closest palm, then took several steps back to gently pull him out of the bathroom. Hudson followed, cautious but curious. His eyes flicked to his bed when he realized I was heading that way.

Just like throughout our entire conversation in the bathroom, I made every effort to focus on his face and not what was happening in his pants.

Taking a seat on the edge of the bed, I released his hand so I could scoot all the way up the mattress until I was reclined in the middle. Once there, I freed my trapped hair and relaxed with my palms behind my head.

"What are you doing?" Hudson asked in a rough voice.

"Nothing." I tilted my head to meet his eye. "But you can do whatever you like."

"What?"

"Get on top. Use your hands, mouth, whatever you want. Or just sit back and look at me." Only then did I allow myself to drink him in. The handsome face, the tattoos subtly moving with every breath, the slender hips that the oversized sweatpants could barely hang onto.

"Take control, Hudson," I told him. "Do what will make *you* feel good."

Chapter 3

Rori

"You got a cigarette?" I asked Torr.

He patted the inner pockets of his leather jacket. "No, I'm all out."

"Goddamnit," I groaned into my coffee cup.

"Sorry, Reaper." He laughed. "When did you become such a smoker, anyway?"

"Being a leader is stressful, okay? Now I get why Reaper was such a dick when he didn't have his cloves and whiskey." I tapped my fingernails against the ceramic mug, watching the driveway from the front porch. "They should have been back by now."

Torr propped his boots on the porch railing. "Did you try calling LJ?"

"Yeah, straight to voicemail."

"There's a lot of dead zones out there. I'm sure they're fine."

"And if they're not?"

"We can't make decisions based on what we don't know. Only what we do know."

"Thanks, Carter," I grumbled.

Torr just chuckled, all Mr. Calm and Collected while I watched the road like a hawk. Last week, I'd sent LJ, the Saint, and another ex-gladiator, the Bull, to watch the Sisterhood's village. After making sure they didn't follow us, I wanted to know how they'd react to us taking Hudson, their prized breeding stud. Would they increase patrols? Sacrifice or kidnap more men? Those women were nothing if not tightly controlled and organized. I needed to know the ins and out of everything they did.

Scratching my head, I thought back to the dreams I'd been having ever since we'd gotten Hudson out of there. They always started the same way, some idyllic scene playing out like I was watching a film about my future. There was love, laughter, family. Sometimes even children that didn't exist yet. Then it would slowly morph into something horrifying. My men with chains around their necks and limbs, if they were present at all. Me, sometimes with other women, standing on the bodies of men I knew.

And there was always that gross fleshy thing that looked like a cross between someone's liver and a giant slug. That seemed to be the source of everything. It felt immensely powerful and dangerous. Like if I wasn't careful, it was going to slide its way into my ear canal and control me like an alien parasite.

The gods, Astarte, Lupa, and Tezcatlipoca, had given me a warning. And I couldn't shake that it had something to do with these dreams.

A distant roaring pulled my attention back to the road, and I stood at attention, squinting at the horizon. "Do I see riders?"

"Yep. Our boys are back."

I was already off the porch and heading down the gravel driveway before Torr brought his feet down to follow. We passed by Santos, the Hunter, and some of the other guys working out on our way out to the road.

"That them?" Santos sheathed his machetes and wiped the sweat from his face with his shirt hanging around his neck.

"Yeah. Coming?"

He shook his head, grinning as he pointed to Torr. "This fucker owes me deadlifts. I'm waiting here until he gets back."

"I got you, Santos, but it has to wait until I'm done with VP business." Torr gestured to me like it was obvious.

"Sounds like stalling to me," the Hunter chimed in, gulping water down as he leaned against one of the supports of a pull-up bar. "Who knows if he's got it in him to do five-hundred?"

"I'll do the five-hundred and then your ass on top of it," Torr hollered back.

"You guys are all very cute together," I chuckled once we were a good distance away.

"They're good dudes." He rubbed the back of my neck, rough fingers gently pinching and massaging the way I liked it. "I wasn't sure at first, but you've got a good club here, President."

"I hope the same can be said for these two." I shielded my eyes from the sun, squinting to make out the approaching riders. My cousin LJ was the only one I trusted implicitly among them, and I was eager to get a full private report from him later on.

"Who's giving you doubts?" Torr asked.

"The Saint," I admitted. "I can't decide if he's just an eccentric guy or if he's trying too hard to throw suspicion off him."

"I've felt the same," Torr admitted. "Can't get a good read on him. Santos and Devin aren't sure either, and they would probably know him best."

"It's frustrating when you're not sure if you can trust someone. I hope LJ's able to tell us something from this mission."

"It was a good idea to put him in charge of this. That's what a wise president does."

"Don't kiss my ass, Torr."

"Fine." He leaned in close, lips trailing the shell of my ear. "Can I eat it instead?"

I couldn't hold back the grin, even as the riders were coming close enough to make out their faces. "If you're a good boy."

Torr groaned as he leaned away. "Damn, I can see why Santos loves being owned by you."

"Stop." I laughed. "I can't have both of you collared and leashed."

"Why not? You have two hands."

"Too much power going unchecked is a dangerous thing." I bumped into him with my hip. "I need someone to keep me in line, and that can only be you."

"Fair enough." Torr planted his feet wide like the guard he was, eyes on the approaching riders. "But I wouldn't mind a 'good boy' now and again."

"You gotta earn it."

He groaned again. "Trying to give me a hard-on in front of these guys?"

"Stop trying to make me laugh."

We continued bickering playfully until the three motorcycles pulled up in front of us. LJ, leading the trio, yanked down the bandanna tied over his mouth and nose. "Hey, Pres! VP."

"Welcome home," I greeted. All I wanted to do was give my cousin a big hug, but that would have to wait until we were in private. Right now, I was his president and he was my sergeant-at-arms. "What are our friends up to?"

LJ glanced over his shoulder as the two ex-gladiators pulled up to flank him.

"You are a sight for the sorest of eyes, President," said the Saint, leaning over his handlebars with a grin.

"If it's bad news, get it out," I snapped. "You won't soften me with flattery."

"We came up to the settlement as they were in the process of splitting up," LJ said.

"Splitting up?" Torr echoed. "The fuck does that mean?"

"They packed up and they're moving," elaborated the Bull on LJ's other side. "They split up into three groups, all heading in different directions."

Torr and I looked at each other, then back at the riders. "Why would they do that?"

"We were just as baffled as you are." LJ, rarely without a smile, sat higher in his seat, his face stoic. "It makes no sense from a strategic standpoint to divide up their forces."

"What directions did they go in?" I asked.

"Two of 'em headed north, then they split. One heading northeast, the other northwest."

"And the third?" I prompted at LJ's silence.

He chewed his lip, hesitating a moment longer. "South."

"Toward us."

"Yes, but." My cousin dragged a hand through his russet brown hair. "It was the smallest party. Just four older women and a baby. They all fit into one van with a few belongings."

"A baby?"

"Yes, we thought it was unusual," the Saint chimed in. "All the other children seemed to be going with another group, the one heading northwest."

"You're sure it was a baby?" My instincts were stuck on this one detail for some reason, something niggling at me to probe further. "You saw an actual child with them?"

"Well, it was one of those old car seat carrier things. With an arm handle, you know?" The Bull tried to gesture helpfully. "It had a blanket over it, and one of the women kept peeking in there, tucking it in, you know."

"But you never actually saw its face?"

"I didn't." The Bull looked at the other two riders, who also shook their heads.

"Is there a reason why you wouldn't believe it to be a baby?" The Saint narrowed his eyes, compressing the tattoos on the outside corners.

"I dunno," I sighed. "It's just a weird detail. Anything else? Did you see any men with any of the groups?"

LJ shook his head. "None that we saw." My cousin's eyes bore intensely into mine. He walked to talk away from these fighters.

"Alright. Well, good work. We'll hold church tonight, so go ahead and rest until then."

"Ah, the church of Aurora." The Saint made the sign of the cross on himself. "I can't wait to worship."

The Bull snorted as the two fighters rode off together, then there were cheers and greetings as they came upon the second of our two safe houses, the one most of the fighters had taken up residence in. Torr affectionately called it the frat house.

Once there were three of us, LJ dismounted his motorcycle and chose to walk it alongside me and Torr. "Please tell me you have a cigarette," my cousin grumbled.

"No, Torr's out." I patted his back in an apology.

"Son of a bitch." LJ sighed.

"We'll have Val get a whole pallet of 'em on her next supply run."

The three of us walked up to the first house, which was where I, my men, and my cousins stayed. Paige and the Hunter had their own room too, since they were a couple and the frat house consisted of a bunch of single guys.

Rather than go inside, I led our trio around to the back of the house, where a wooded area gave us more privacy. Later in the day, more people would come here to practice shooting, but for now, it was blissfully quiet.

"So how'd it really go?" I lowered onto a tree stump while the two guys remained standing.

LJ shrugged. "Alright, I guess. I had to herd 'em like a couple of cats when the cult groups started splitting up, but that was the biggest friction point."

"How do you mean?" I asked.

"They wanted us to split up as well. So each of us could follow one of the cult groups to watch them more closely, then rendezvous after a few more days. I said no way in hell. The president's orders were clear; we stay together and watch each other's backs."

I beamed at him. "Knew I could count on you." I had said no such thing but told LJ he could order those two around if he suspected something fishy and to say the orders came from me.

"Who's idea was it to split up?" Torr asked him, arms crossed.

"The Saint said it first, but the two of them were pretty gung-ho about it. I had to argue with them about it for a good minute."

"What was your gut feeling?" I asked. "Do you think they were trying to pull something, or were they genuine about this plan?"

LJ let out a long breath, crossed his arms, looked up at the sky and then down at the ground before meeting my eye again. "I honestly couldn't tell you," he admitted. "If it was someone I trusted, like Val or my brother, who'd brought that idea forward, I'd be all for it. But these gladiators, cuz. I just don't know 'em well enough."

"Would you trust Santos out there?" I pressed. "Or the Hunter?"

"Yeah, but," LJ scratched the five o'clock shadow on his cheek, "neither of them would've gone against an order coming from you. These guys were adamant until they realized I wasn't gonna budge."

"We can't let that fly." Torr slid a glance over to me. "They're testing boundaries. Seeing how much they can get away with when you're not around to crack the whip."

"Or they're trying to take initiative and impress me," I countered. "We could learn a lot by watching all three parts of the Sisterhood."

"I wouldn't advise that," Torr said. "That's probably what the cult is hoping we do, and we don't need to be more divided."

"That's what I'm thinking too," LJ said.

"So, this stays between the three of us." I stood from the tree stump. "I want you both to keep close eyes on those two fighters. Especially the Saint." When the two of them nodded, I added, "Let everyone know there's going to be church tonight. We're going to handle the Sisterhood as a club, nothing changes that."

"You got it, Prez." Torr headed for the back door to the house and reached to hold it open just as Devin came out.

"Hey, Dev," I greeted.

"Hi."

Torr and I watched him go by before exchanging curious looks. Devin was fully dressed with his hair up in his normal topknot, but we both noticed something different about him.

The tall fighter's cheeks were flushed. His lips were redder and more swollen than I'd noticed before. His hair, normally without a strand out of place, was a bit mussed like he'd just tied it up carelessly. His eyes even looked brighter, warmer than his usual cold detachment. And was that a *smile?*

I stared. Straight-up gawked as Devin laid out his throwing knives on the stump I'd just been sitting on. His lips were definitely pulling at the corners, a secret hidden smile as he checked his blades' sharpness before getting started on target practice.

"Did you get a blowjob or something since we last saw you," Torr looked at his wrist as if checking a watch, "like an hour ago?"

The hidden cheer in Devin's expression faded away. His dark eyebrows slashed down, mouth pressing into a frown. "How's that any of your business, Torr?"

"It's not, I'm just being nosy. I mean, the only thing that sets my mood on a total one-eighty is a good ol'—"

"Come on." I cut him off with a punch to the shoulder, surprising myself. "Not everyone's sex life is a casual conversation. Leave him alone."

I ignored both men's surprised expressions as I headed into the house.

Chapter 4

Hudson

This was the best day I'd had in a long, long time. I couldn't stop grinning at the ceiling, couldn't stop thinking back to what had happened on this bed a few hours earlier. And thinking ahead to when it would happen again.

Sure, things were better in the last two weeks since I'd been freed, but they hadn't been *good*. Not until Devin came in this morning and offered something I didn't know I'd needed. I'd gone from feeling like my body was still under *their* control, an automated machine dialed in to perform on the schedule *they* subjected me to. Then Devin put the control firmly back in my hands, and I felt like something I hadn't been in years.

A person who could make choices.

Someone with the freedom and permission to explore a partner's body. Devin had encouraged me to touch him anywhere, do anything to him. I was so confounded by the freedom and the trust that I had barely known where to start.

All the while, he never made a move to touch me. His hands, with those long slender fingers, stayed under the back of his head the whole time. Except when his fists curled to grip the sheets at his sides, that was.

I wasn't ready for him to touch me, not yet. But I was starting to think it might feel nice when he did. Kissing him sure felt really, really nice.

"What is happening to me?" I laughed to myself, covering my eyes as if to hide myself from the empty room. I was a teenager with a crush again, but this bright, bubbly sensation in my chest felt so weird despite how good it was. Like I'd been injected with a drug and it was some foreign substance making me feel this way.

Three hard raps came to my door, knocking me out of my daydreaming.

"Devin?" I called hopefully.

"No, this is Dr. Corwin. I just wanted to come up and introduce myself."

My good mood deflated into sour disappointment along with a healthy dose of anxiety. I didn't trust this man, least of all because he was a stranger. Most of all because he came at the behest of that woman, Rori.

"Hudson?" the man called through the wood. "Would you mind opening up for just a moment? I'd like to put a face to your name."

I rolled out of bed, then dragged my feet across the room, hoping he'd get impatient enough to leave once I reached the door. No such luck.

Turning the knob, I pulled the barrier open an inch, just enough to look through. A middle-aged man with medium brown skin, a shaved head, glasses, and a salt and pepper five-o-clock shadow smiled at me.

"Hi there, Hudson." Dr. Corwin gave me a friendly wave. "It's nice to meet you. Would it be okay if I shook your hand?" He held his palm out toward me, but didn't attempt to wedge the door open wider.

He asked the question. Left it up to me to open the door wider if I wanted to. Already, Devin had taught me something important so quickly. If someone gave me a choice, the opportunity to refuse or accept, they just may be worth trusting.

I let the door swing wider and reached forward to clasp the doctor's hand, which he took in a solid grip before releasing me quickly. "It's a pleasure. You can call me Malik if you'd like."

"Um, okay." I stood there awkwardly, not knowing what else to say. Having conversations with other people would be another thing I'd have to re-learn. Talking to Devin felt so natural. I forgot other people would be different.

The doctor, Malik, didn't seem to mind though. "Do you go by Hudson or anything else? I met some of the ex-gladiators, a lot of them seem to prefer their fighting names, which is interesting."

He sounded genuinely interested, without a drop of condescension, and I found myself feeling a little more at ease. "Uh, Hudson is fine. I wasn't a gladiator."

"I know that," Malik said gently. "I just wanted to make sure you didn't prefer anything else." He stepped away from the door, giving me plenty of space. "Well, I'm going to make more introductions and get settled in. Perhaps I'll see you later, at dinner maybe?"

"Oh, I dunno. I don't really eat with everyone else. Usually, I just stay up here."

"I see. I understand Rori is holding a meeting in the other house this evening, so most of the fighters will be there." Malik kept his tone even and light, but I could feel him watching my reactions to every single word. "Maybe if it's quieter here, with less people around, you'd give coming downstairs a shot? If you're feeling up for it."

"I don't know, maybe."

"Sure, give it some thought." He shot me another friendly smile as he turned to leave. "See you later, Hudson. It was nice to meet you."

———

A FEW HOURS LATER, as the sun was going down, I found myself pacing back and forth in front of my bedroom door. For the first time since arriving here, I felt restless. Antsy. Like this bedroom I'd hidden away in was suddenly way too small. Instead of feeling safe here, away from everyone else, I felt...trapped.

"He might be fucking with your head," I muttered to myself, thinking of Malik. I played our earlier interaction over and over in my head, trying to figure out what ulterior motive he might have, and kept coming up with nothing.

He'd been polite. Didn't invade my space. Waited for me to shake his hand. And then left. Our whole conversation probably happened in less than a minute.

Devin made it clear that he'd wished I'd leave my room more often, but that he wouldn't force the issue. I'd never been tempted to leave the safety of these four walls until now, after Malik mentioned there would be fewer people downstairs.

Too many people was overwhelming. I'd get panic attacks. But if there were only a few, in a bigger space than this room, maybe I could handle it.

I stopped the repetition of my pacing to look out the window. Fighters were walking to the other house, talking amongst each other in pairs or small groups. On the porch of the other house, watching everyone enter through the front door, was her.

The woman in charge. Rori, she was called.

Next to her stood the tall, dark-haired man who was always at her side. He was speaking to her, mouth moving with a cocky smirk pulling at his lips, but his eyes were focused on the men walking in. Every fighter got a thorough inspection, whether they realized it or not.

Santos was on the woman's other side, and his focus was entirely on her. The Butcher was clearly smitten, one hand resting on the machete's handle sheathed at his hip, the other hidden somewhere behind her back, probably touching her.

"What's so special about her?" I asked the windowpane. "How is she so different that she doesn't remind you of everything they did to us?"

As if she heard me, the woman's gaze flicked up. Her amused smile fell away, leaving behind a hard mask of disapproval as our eyes met.

I backed away from the window, walking clear across to the other side of the room, as far away from her as possible. My chest burned, pulse and breath tight with adrenaline. I had to force myself to calm down, remind myself that she was roughly a hundred feet away. She couldn't get up here. She didn't even *want* to come up here; she was about to hold a meeting, for fuck's sake.

"She doesn't want me. She doesn't want me," I repeated under my breath to reassure myself. "She wants nothing to do with me."

That phrase, more than anything else, broke me through the panic. Santos could keep staring at her like the sun shone out of her ass. Devin could tell me again and again that she wasn't a bad person. None of it sank in. Nothing could convince me that she was worth trusting.

But as long as she had Santos and that other man, plus all the other fighters wrapped around her finger, she had no need for me. She had all the attention and power she wanted. Why would she bother with me? I was nothing to her.

I would rather be nothing than anything to a woman. Especially this one. Women who had power over men were the worst of all. Better to be forgotten in this case. And for the next hour or so, her attention would be well-occupied by her devoted followers.

Once my heart rate slowed to a normal pace, I returned to facing the door and pulled it open. I moved slowly through the hall of bedrooms, then took note of all the windows and doors on the lower floor once I reached the stairs' top landing.

There was noise coming from below, and I leaned over the railing to take a cautious glance. Malik was the only one in the kitchen, his sleeves pushed up to his elbows as he dried dishes with a towel. He sang something under his breath, whistling on occasion. The guy just seemed...content. Happy, even. I wondered if that would change once the fighters and I began unloading our traumatic stories onto him, or if the good doctor stayed cheerful because listening to horror stories just rolled off his back like water off a duck.

I didn't know which would be worse.

Something must have alerted him to my presence, because he stopped whistling and turned around to look up at me. "Hudson! Good to see you again." Malik smiled like we were longtime friends who hadn't seen each other in weeks, rather than strangers who'd met only a few hours ago. "Are you hungry?"

He made no mention of me coming out of my room, which was a relief. I didn't want to be praised for every little thing like a child.

"Um, I could eat, I guess."

"Good! The rice just finished cooking." He pointed to a pot on the stove with a lid that was too big. "There's vegetables and chicken in the fridge that need to be cooked before they go bad. I figured we could do a simple stir-fry. How does that sound?"

I shrugged. "Works for me."

"Great! Have a seat. Would you like anything to drink?"

"I'll just get water from the tap, thanks." Despite Devin's constant reassurances that nothing was tampered with, I couldn't bring myself to accept drinks from just anybody yet. It was just a few days ago that I'd started to feel okay about the food that was made.

Malik was all over the kitchen in a way that was very energetic but also controlled. He wasn't chaotic in the slightest but actually calming. Whether he was chopping, tossing things in the pan, or stirring up a sauce for the stir-fry, he kept that warm friendliness he exuded when he first came to my door.

It made me feel like I was at my dad's house years ago. He'd make pancakes for breakfast while I sat at the table, my feet swinging because I was too short to reach the floor. And he'd talk to me about anything and everything while he cooked, just as Malik was now.

"My son is a chef, and he taught me this little trick." Malik tapped a white powder from a box into his sauce mixing bowl. "A little bit of cornstarch to thicken your sauce and make it richer. Might sound silly if you know what you're doing in the kitchen, but it was like magic to me! I never learned this."

"I think my grandma told me something about that. Or it might've had to do with baking. I don't remember."

Malik smiled broadly at my reply. "Cooking and baking really are art forms in the right hands, aren't they?"

I dropped into a seat at the table. "Never thought about it that way, but I guess it's true."

"Well, I'm no artist, but I can promise a meal that's edible. Maybe even flavorful." The doctor returned his attention to the stove. "So, what do you like to do, Hudson? What's your art form?"

My fingertips tapped together as I thought about how to answer. An honest response would be, *Sit in my room, hide from the world and half the population in it. Hate everything and almost everyone.* But that was melodramatic, and probably not what the good doctor was looking to hear.

While ruminating on polite responses, it dawned on me how far removed I felt from all that churning, bitter hatred already. It wasn't even like my imprisonment was long ago, I'd only been freed for two weeks. But today, it felt like I'd shed a layer of that anger, discarded it like a shirt that no longer fit. Something transformative had happened today, and it started when Devin helped me take control of my body back.

Fuck, my mind was wandering back to him again, the sight of him stretched out and panting on my bed. And Malik was still waiting for me to answer his question.

"Um, I don't know," I finally said. "I haven't really pursued any hobbies or anything since they got me out." I stared at his back facing me. "You *do* know where I've been the last six years, right?"

"I do," he said lightly. "And I understand it's been an adjustment since you've been rescued. Hopefully I'll be able to help with that process."

"So how's that gonna work?" I placed my elbows on the table and crossed my forearms. "You gonna have me talk about how it felt to raped on a daily schedule, and tell me how it's important to trust women again?"

"No, Hudson. I'm not going to do that." Malik brought down a couple of bowls from a cabinet and began scooping rice into them. "You relive your trauma often enough as it is, don't you think? When you're about to fall asleep at night. When you're alone and your thoughts wander. When you're minding your own business, and then you're suddenly back there with seemingly no trigger. Am I right?"

For a long while, the only sound was the gentle clink and scraping of the pan as Malik poured the stir fry over the rice.

"How'd you know that?" I whispered.

"That's post-traumatic stress disorder, my friend." He turned to face me, holding a bowl in each hand. "Your trauma becomes a monkey riding on your back. A body of water that always feels like it's about to drown you." Malik set one bowl in front of me and the other across the table. As he turned again to find silverware, he said, "What I'd like to work on with you is making that monkey smaller so it's not so heavy on you all the time. After a while, maybe we can turn that drowning sensation into a puddle you step in. Inconvenient, but not constantly triggering your fight or flight response." He sat down across from me and placed a fork next to my bowl. "How do you feel about that, Hudson?"

"That...sounds amazing," I admitted, and then swallowed. "But honestly, a little far-fetched. I don't know how this...being on edge all time, I don't see it diminishing."

Malik smiled kindly at me as he started to dig into his food. "I'm going to ask you to trust the process. It will take time and parts of it may be uncomfortable, but if you work with me, I promise you will have the tools to put yourself in a better head space than you are now."

"Okay. I'll give it a shot." I picked up my fork, twirling it through my fingers before stabbing some well-sauced veggies. "I just want a normal life again."

"First thing I want you to think about." Malik set his fork aside and looked at me squarely. "You already are a complete, whole human being. You always have been. You are *more* than what was done to you."

I froze mid-chew. When I resumed, my jaw worked in slow, methodical movements. "Thank you," I said when I swallowed.

"No need," Malik said. "I'm only saying what's true."

I liked this man already. The perpetual constriction in my chest released a little as we continued our meal together.

All because he'd told me something I never knew I'd needed to hear.

Chapter 5

Rori

Everyone watched as LJ marked three places on a map we'd haphazardly pinned to the wall. "These are the directions we saw the Sisterhood go after they split up." He capped his marker and stepped aside so everyone could see. "The group heading south, obviously, is coming toward us and would be the easiest to engage, if we decide to do that."

"Uh, *yeah*, we wanna do that," Val declared from her armchair. "Shit, let's take out each group one by one. Might as well start with the closest."

"Easy, road captain." To LJ, I said, "Could you tell if these groups were split up in any particular way?"

"Yes. The southern group looked to be four older women with a single baby in a carrier."

"Pffft, piece of cake. Let me handle the grannies by myself," Val said. "I'll be back before lunch tomorrow."

I bit back my laugh. Only a few minutes left of playing president before I could let my hair down. "And the other two, LJ?"

"The northwestern group consisted mostly of children, plus a few armed adults."

"How many?" Torr asked.

"We counted twelve children and three adults." LJ pointed at the other X on the map. "Heading northeast appeared to be the bulk of the adult women, most of them unarmed. We counted twenty unarmed, three armed."

I looked to the Saint and the Bull, the two of them sprawled on one of the couches and having stayed mostly silent during the meeting. "Do you two agree with these numbers?"

"Yes, President." The Saint bobbed his head emphatically while his cohort only gave a slight nod.

"So altogether, this cult is thirty adults strong." I crossed my arms and chewed idly on a fingernail. "Seems like a small operation for all the resources they had to build the resort."

"There may be other settlements," Santos pointed out. "That may be the reason for the 3-way split. They could be reinforcing at other locations."

"I'll bet you the four on their own are the leaders, the ones in power," Torr said. "The armed ones are the muscle, the rest is the flock. The devoted followers breeding the new generation."

"Sure fucking hope they don't have any more Hudsons," Devin muttered. He stood next to Santos, who nodded his agreement. Devin had also been oddly well-behaved for this meeting, which threw me off more than I expected. I'd come prepared for barbs at every turn, having every decision questioned. But he'd seemed content to stand and listen.

"If they do, we'll find them. Well, actually, *you* guys will find them," I said.

"Not too keen on getting shot by the person you're trying to save?" the Hunter cracked, which earned some snickering from the peanut gallery. Apparently, the guys found it hilarious that my first time meeting Hudson resulted in a bullet taking a chunk out of my calf muscle.

Men. Gladiators. Bunch of Neanderthals.

Good thing I knew exactly how to deal with them. I picked up a throw pillow and flung at the Hunter's head. "Exactly! You see what I do for you fuckers?"

Fighters erupted in cackles and crude jokes, shoving playfully at the Hunter as he brought his arms up to block the pillow assault.

"So yeah. It can be one of you assholes getting shot next time instead of your president."

"I will take a bullet for you any time." The Saint placed a hand over his heart. "Send me out, Aurora."

"Alright, let's focus and I can let you animals loose for the night," I said, pointedly ignoring him. "I do think we should scout the closest group. It'll be me with a small team." I scanned the room, weighing my options. "Me, Val, LJ, the Butcher, and the Saint. We ride out tomorrow." I looked at Torr. "You're in charge while I'm gone."

"Yes, President."

He said it with a reverent dip of his head, which sent heat pooling through me. I couldn't help but mouth, *good boy* at him. The look he sent back to me was just as heated, just as promising.

Forcing my attention back to my main responsibility, my club, I said, "Is there anything else that needs to be discussed?" When no one spoke, I said, "Oh, most of you have met Malik already. Don't fucking haze him, he's a family friend. And seriously, talk to him if you're struggling in any way or just need to get something off your chest. Anything you tell him is confidential, even from me. He's here to support you all, and he's great at his job."

"What does confidential mean?" one of the fighters piped up.

"It means he'll talk to you confidently," the Hunter said.

I couldn't hold back the squawk laughter before tearing into him. "I'm going to have your woman put a muzzle on you, *Levi!*"

"She already does that." He elbowed Paige, who was sitting right next to him, while wiggling his eyebrows.

As said woman groaned and rolled her eyes, I answered the other fighter's question without bullshit. "It means Malik will keep anything you've told him to himself. And you can trust him to do that."

The man who asked, and a few other fighters, nodded.

"Anything else?" The room remained respectfully silent. I let a few more seconds pass before clapping my hands once. "Great. Church is now dismissed."

Devin gave a quick, "See ya," to Santos, nodded goodnight to Torr and I, then made a big show of trying to look like he wasn't in any hurry to leave. He slid through the crowd of bodies heading out like a fish through water, agile and sleek. One thing the Ghost was good at? Moving without being detected. I blinked and he was gone.

"How would you say Hudson's recovery is going?" I asked Santos as the last of my club filtered out of the house and to their various rooms.

"No idea." He shrugged. "Haven't exactly been asking for status updates."

"You haven't talked to him yourself?" Torr asked him over my head.

Santos shook his head, his face grim. "Nah. Shooting my woman doesn't exactly put him on speaking terms with me."

"You're so sweet to hold a grudge in my honor." I went up on my tiptoes to kiss his cheek.

Even though it was a joke, the praise made him blush, and a smile teased at his lips. Santos just melted like chocolate in the sun whenever I praised or complimented him, and I loved to make him do it.

"What are we still doing downstairs?" The heat of Torr's breath tickled my ear while he gave a not-so-subtle squeeze to my ass.

I turned to face him, linking my hand in Santos' on my other side. "Lead the way, cowboy."

He didn't hesitate. With a grab of my free hand, he bolted toward the stairs, dragging me and Santos along. The long-legged bastard took the steps three at a time, which was quite a feat for me.

"Hold on, Torr." I laughed, resisting his pull. "You're not gonna get laid if I'm injured doing the splits out here."

"Why not?" he shot back, but paused and waited for us to catch up anyway. "Splitting you in half is exactly what I intend to do."

"Romantic," I drawled sarcastically, even though a shiver of anticipation ran up my spine. Sometimes his ego needed to be checked, but he was so damn good at being rough.

"You got him for being romantic." Torr nodded at Santos as he opened our bedroom door.

I twirled in Santos' arms as we stepped into the bedroom, wrapping my arms around his shoulders and kissing him deeply as we made our way to the bed.

"Anything you're craving tonight?" I asked my achingly sweet, brutal fighter. He would stay on his knees and worship me all night if I wanted him to, but I always checked in with him. Always made sure his needs were met as well.

"Hmm." Santos cocked his head, eyes lighting up as he looked at me. Damn, every woman deserved a partner who looked at her like that. Like she was a meal about to be devoured and a goddess to be worshiped all rolled into one.

"No ropes tonight," he said after some consideration. "I want to soothe you while Torr punishes you."

I grinned, delighted at that prospect. "Want me to boss you?"

"Yes, please," he groaned.

"Then get on that bed and make a nice seat for me."

Santos knew exactly what I meant and hurried out of his clothes. Once he was naked and finding the perfect spot on the wide mattress, I turned to Torr.

"Undress me," he said quietly.

The command was unquestionable despite the low volume of his voice. I stepped closer to him and pushed his jacket off of his broad shoulders, the creak of worn leather the loudest sound in the room. He lifted his arms and I gripped his T-shirt at his waist, my breath hitching at the slow reveal of muscle as the fabric rose higher, like a stage curtain drawing up at the start of a production.

This would be one hell of a show, alright.

I took a moment to drink Torr in, letting my eyes feast on all the swells and dips of his torso. The shadows in the low light made every muscle more pronounced.

"Do you want to sit down?" I asked demurely. "So I can get those boots off for you."

Torr ambled over to an armchair, dropping into the seat like it was his birthright, a king on his throne. His forearms came to the armrests, long legs splayed out carelessly. He asked for nothing, but I dropped to my knees at his boots. If he told me to crawl over to him, I would have.

My submissive instincts weren't as strong as Santos', but in this context, I loved to serve Torr.

I'd gotten both boots off when he reached down to stroke my cheek. "Good girl," he purred. I barely had time to melt under his praise when he added, "Now take care of this belt for me."

Scooting closer, I found myself between his heavily muscled thighs as I pulled apart his belt buckle. The clink of metal was followed by the soft hiss of leather as I pulled it through the belt loops. After dropping it to the floor, my hands rested on his thighs, fighting the urge to cup the thick bulge already pressing at his fly. But Torr was in a mood to give commands, so I waited.

"Santos," he said over my head. "Scoot a little further down, will you? Thanks, that's good."

Before I could react, Torr gripped the short hair at the nape of my neck in his fist, hauling me upward as he stood from the chair. I hissed at the sting, but relished in the sharp sensation all the same.

"Go on over and sit on your other man's face for a bit. With your eyes closed." Torr released me and with the same hand, flicked open the button on his jeans.

"I'm still dressed," I pointed out.

"Then fix that," Torr growled, yanking down his zipper.

"You don't want me to touch you?" I pouted a little, watching his hand dip into his jeans.

"You will," he promised. "But not yet."

Fine. If he wanted to tease, two could play at that game. I would take all my clothes off as slowly as humanly possible. We didn't have music on, so I closed my eyes and swayed to the beat of a song in my head as I peeled off each piece.

I never considered myself an exhibitionist, but the temperature of that room and the buzzing anticipation in my body skyrocketed as I stripped for my two men. I kept my eyes closed, not wanting to ruin the illusion and become self-conscious. Even as I hummed softly to myself, I heard their ragged breaths and the rhythmic whisper of skin-on-skin as they stroked themselves.

"Fuck, you're so beautiful." Santos' voice floated over from my right the moment I stepped out of my panties. "Please sit on my face, paloma. I need to taste you."

Just for the hell of it, I kept my eyes closed and navigated my way to him by sound and touch. He gently directed me to the right place, and when he kissed the lips between my legs, my body rocked with sweet relief and aching need.

I couldn't feel anything in front of me, no headboard or wall, so I planted my hands on the bed above Santos' head, but that was short-lived.

"Stay upright," Torr barked from somewhere else in the room.

My groan was both out of frustration and pleasure with Santos lapping at me, but I straightened as instructed, using my legs to hold myself up. Ever the sweetheart, Santos helped, supporting my ass with his hands while his tongue dragged long, slow licks over my pussy.

Moments later, I felt pressure on one side of the bed like Torr was climbing on. Then I felt a strip of fabric press against my eyes and wrap around my head.

"Since you're so committed to the part," Torr mused as he tied the fabric at the back of my head. The blindfold smelled like him, so it had to be one of his T-shirts.

"Well I *am* a good girl," I said in the direction of his voice.

Santos moaned like he was agreeing with me, the sound creating vibrations against my sensitive flesh. I reached behind me, pressing my palms down on his chest so I could grind against his mouth. He was doing that thing where he avoided my clit, and I was *not* having that.

Still, he sucked on my lips again, teased my entrance with his tongue, but he avoided any direct contact with my clit.

"You know how to make me come, so do it." I injected hardness into my voice, taking on the dominating persona that he loved. "You live to please me, so fucking please me."

A sharp pain suddenly lit up my nipple, the pinching of the sensitive peak making my breath stutter and a whimper squeak out of my throat. The moment it was released, Santos' tongue lashed over my clit.

"Oh, you fuckers planned this," I groaned, hips bucking against his face.

"The specifics only a minute ago," Torr admitted with a chuckle. "With lots of hand signals and mouthing to each other while you stripped so pretty for us."

My retort was cut off by rough treatment to my other nipple, this time by Torr's mouth. There was no softness as his teeth scraped and pulled. The sensation pulsed its way down to my clit, which was desperate for more attention from Santos' tongue. My sweet fighter didn't give it to me until after a short scream left my mouth, and Torr pulled away.

"Too much?" He took my chin in a hard grip, and even though I couldn't see, I could sense him watching me carefully.

"No," I panted.

Fuck, I was so close to coming already. The whiplash of having control and then losing it had me teetering on the edge. This place between them, the balance between my dominant partner and my submissive one, was exactly where I belonged. Exactly where I thrived. I needed to be Santos' domme just as much as I craved being submissive to Torr. And the fact that the three of us found a way to satisfy each other, all at the same time, felt nothing short of incredible.

"Is that all you got?" I taunted Torr. "Blindfold and some nipple play? I thought you were going to punish me."

Just because I let him dominate me in the bedroom didn't mean I wasn't also a brat.

There was a flurry of movement I couldn't track, like Torr was arranging himself on the bed somehow. The next thing I knew, a hand cupped my nape and brought my head down, forcing me to pitch forward. My hands landed on muscular thighs and the blunt head of a cock brushed over my mouth.

"Good girls don't talk back," Torr said. "Open your mouth."

I did as told, and hot, velvety skin pushed past my lips. Torr moaned as I formed a seal around him, making him wet with my tongue. I brought a hand up to grip his base, but to my dismay, he grabbed both of my wrists and pinned them against the small of my back.

"No hands. No eyes," Torr commanded. When I moaned in complaint, he brought a hand down in a hard slap on one side of my ass. "You can do it. Suck me, good girl."

Fortunately, I still had Santos' mouth between my legs. That tongue laved over my pussy, sucking and licking me like it was his full-time job. After Torr's no-hand command and the sting of his palm on my ass lingered, Santos rubbed over that same cheek, his hand soothing the heated, tender skin. Then he brought his fingers to join his mouth, stroking them in and out of me as he finally concentrated attention on my clit.

He was soothing my pains, pleasing me in equal measure to Torr's punishment. God, what more could a girl want? I had sweetness and pain wrapped up in one incredible package deal.

Torr continued roughly playing with my nipples and spanking the hell out of my ass while I took more of his cock down my throat. Every muffled scream, whimper, moan, and slap earned me more of Santos' treatment. Loving passes over my bruising skin, another finger to fill me, and the most perfect suction and pressure on my clit.

My hips ground down hard over his face, my orgasm moments away. At the same time, I felt Torr swell and stiffen between my lips.

"That's a good girl, take me deeper," he urged. "Let me shoot down your pretty throat."

He had loosened his grip on my hands and I took the opportunity to massage his balls. He was too far gone to punish me anymore, his release on the precipice. His curses and groans filled my ears, and Santos' moans vibrated all the way up my body.

It was both of my men combined that did me in, sending me over the cliff in a rush of sensation. Hot spray filled my mouth, and I swallowed Torr's release on the second wave of pleasure.

I removed the blindfold as I lifted away from Santos' face and just had to pause, soaking in the sight of my men. They were both panting, muscled bodies glossy with sweat. Torr's back was against the headboard, with Santos further down the bed and flat on his back.

To my surprise, there were stripes of cum on Santos' stomach and chest. His cock lay against his lower abdomen, softening as the tip dribbled. "Someone wanna get me a towel?" he asked sheepishly.

"Did you...is that from without any touching?" I asked.

"Just barely, at the end," he admitted. "If you and Torr would have taken a little longer, I might have been able to go completely hands-free."

"Now that's talent." Torr tossed him a towel from the bathroom. "I haven't been able to go hands-free since I was like thirteen."

Santos smiled up at me as he wiped himself down. "What can I say? It's pleasing our girl that does it for me."

"Our *very* good girl." Torr dropped onto the bed behind me, bringing an arm around my waist and a kiss to my neck. "You're so fucking incredible, you know that?"

He kissed my shoulder, my upper back, and caressed me with such adoration and care. I knew this was him saying he loved me without using those words.

"I love you both," I said on a contented sigh, kissing Torr over my shoulder first and then leaning down to kiss Santos.

"Love you, paloma," my sweet fighter whispered reverently with a returned kiss and stroke of my cheek.

The three of us shifted into our sleeping positions, scooting and wriggling up the mattress as a single unit. Once I settled into the middle spot, flanked by my lovers and protectors, I closed my eyes and willed my brain to settle down as much as my body had.

No dreams, I pleaded. *No nightmares, just for tonight. Just let me rest before I have to leave.*

I should have known it was pointless to ask.

Chapter 6

Rori

The dream started off normal enough, like all the others. This time, I was in the wooded area behind the safe house. A white dove sat on the mangled stump of a tree, one that had been used for target practice so much that it was little more than an abused fence post.

I came toward the dove, Astarte, my movement not fully perceptible. I may as well have been floating.

"What's happening to me?" I heard myself ask.

The bird said nothing, only stared at me as she moved her head around.

"I can feel something happening to me, but I don't know what it is. I need your help."

Astarte fluffed up her feathers before smoothing them down again. *Do you know the difference between a true god and a false god?*

Her voice in my head warbled, like there was some kind of distortion with the sound.

"I don't know." Some instinct prickled over me, and I got hit with the urge to run. Not just to move at the pace faster than walking but to run for my fucking life.

But where I was practically floating earlier, my feet felt cemented into the ground now.

"Astarte, help me!" Panic edged into my voice. "I don't know what to do."

Yes, you do.

The dove's form broke apart like she'd been made out of sand or pale dust, a delicate sculpture disintegrated by the wind. Now as tiny particles floating in the air, what had once been in the form of a dove came toward me.

I turned to run, putting all my energy into my legs to get the hell away. Whatever the hell that was, I didn't want it touching me.

No matter how hard I pumped my arms and legs, it didn't look or feel like I was crossing any distance at all. I was stuck, running in place from a swarming...something.

You only need to know one thing about false and true gods, Aurora.

My head pounded with the reverberation of the voice, like a bass speaker turned up way too loud inside my skull.

"Who are you?" I shouted at the top of my lungs, though I heard no sound except a constant, heavy buzz inside my head, pressing against my skin, all around me.

When I tried to scream again, it felt like sand was being poured down my throat, shoved up my nose, and rubbed into my squeezed shut eyelids.

This swarm thing was trying to get inside me.

All gods are false except for me.

———

"Rori. Rori! Fuck, come back to us."

I was falling, kicking, grabbing for purchase on anything I could. Something hard and flat smacked against my skull, and I wanted to sob with relief. Finally, something solid! Pain pounded at my temple the moment I finally woke up.

"Shit, she hit her head. I'm gonna get the doctor."

My eyes snapped open to the beautiful sight of the hardwood floor in my bedroom. Relief was short-lived though as I coughed like I never had before in my life.

"Easy, paloma. Take a deep breath."

Santos' voice was the most comforting sound I could have asked for. His broad hand making passes up and down my back were so gentle and grounding. Through gritty eyes, I made out the glass of water he set down next to me.

I was dying for a sip, but I couldn't breathe past the sensations of sand in my throat and nose. Coughing into my hand, I only caught saliva. I swiped a finger into my mouth and only felt the usual suspects—my teeth, tongue, the insides of my cheek.

And yet it felt like I had mouthfuls, fucking lungfuls, of sand that I needed to get out. It was dry, gritty, and everywhere. Fuck, it hurt so much.

Finally, after my throat was completely raw and I had exhausted myself, I could take a shaky controlled breath and a sip of water.

Santos remained at my side the whole time, watching me with a worried expression.

"I'm sorry," I choked out in a weak whisper. "That was a bad one."

He scooted closer to me on the floor, enveloping me protectively with his arms and legs and providing the solid wall of his chest to lean against.

"I don't think we should go on this ride." Santos brought his chin to my shoulder. "Not while this is happening to you."

I pulled in another shaky breath, relying on his strong, solid body to stay mostly upright. "These dreams aren't getting any better. We need to act."

Footsteps thundered up the stairs at that moment, and then Torr appeared in the door. "Malik is on his way," he announced.

"I don't need—"

"Shut it." Torr held up an index finger, his face so grave that I knew he was dead serious. "You were screaming in terror, moving your arms and legs like you were running in your sleep. We couldn't even keep you on the bed. You fell off and hit your fucking head, so you are seeing the fucking doctor."

"I was just telling her that I think we should postpone the ride," Santos said.

"Excellent idea. I agree."

"No! We're doing the ride." I pushed away from Santos and climbed shakily to my feet. "We need to find what these crazy cultists are planning."

"Have you seen yourself?" Torr asked, gesturing at me. "You look haunted. You're in no shape to ride, much less lead."

"Torr, we need to do this. I—"

"Like hell we do. We can scout them again later, but I'm calling it off."

"Will you fucking listen?!"

My frustrated demand came out sounding more like a raspy whine, but Torr's change in expression told me he heard me. As long as I was president, he would hear me out. He went to the bedroom door and closed it.

"Okay, I'm listening."

I took a few more panting, ragged breaths, trying to form my racing thoughts into coherent sentences.

"This has something to do with gods," I finally whispered.

Torr's eyes flicked to Santos and then back to me. "How so?"

"I don't know exactly but..." I went to sit on the edge of the bed, struggling to put it all together in a way that made sense. "That night we rescued Hudson, I heard a voice. It was in my head like when Astarte and Tezca talk to us." I swallowed. "And I had...visions, kind of."

The guys said nothing, just waited for me to keep talking.

"The Sisterhood has their own god. Goddess, I guess." Fuck, if that wasn't terrifying to say out loud. "They...willed her into existence." I felt sick using that deity's words out loud.

"How?" Torr demanded. "We don't just *make* gods, right? Astarte found you."

"It—she— told me she was the pain of all women who have been hurt by men. Like *all* women who have ever lived. We know how far off the deep end the Sisterhood is, they live and breathe hating men. And they've been doing it for decades."

"And making sacrifices," Santos pointed out. "Both the ritualistic ones like in the village and forcing the gladiators to kill each other."

"So it's made from years and years of extreme, single-minded devotion on steroids," Torr mused. "How the fuck is this possible?"

"How are talking doves and jaguars possible?" I snorted.

His head snapped up. "Did you see the animal it was in? What if we just killed the animal body?"

"I don't think it has a body yet," I said. "And even if it did, that feels too easy. What's to stop it from just going into another animal?"

Santos crossed his arms, his face pinched with worry. "How are we supposed to fight a god, then?"

"I don't know, but I'm glad we have two."

Torr pinned me with a hard stare. "So what else did this goddess say to you?"

I blew out an exhausted breath. "She says I'm on the wrong side and I should be a leader for the Sisterhood."

"Fuck." Torr turned away, rubbing his jaw.

"I think the dreams are a tactic to wear me down? Punish me for telling it to fuck off? I'm not sure exactly."

Santos chuckled softly. "You told a god to fuck off, huh?"

"Oh, I told that rotten bitch a lot of things. Like I would kill her and every one of her followers so she'd never fucking exist again." My gaze returned to Torr, who'd begun pacing back and forth. "That's why today's ride is still happening."

"No." He stopped abruptly with an emphatic shake of his head. "No, it's not."

"I'm not arguing about this, Torr." I stood from the bed, already feeling stronger than when I first woke up. "I'm going to shower and get ready for this ride."

Torr made like he was following me into the bathroom to keep arguing, but I closed the door in his face. Moments later, I heard his and Santos' quiet voices floating from the bedroom.

I smiled to myself as I turned the shower on. Santos might have been submissive to me but he was no pushover. He would make sure Torr came around.

By the time I finished showering and re-entered the bedroom, both men were standing with glum faces and Tezca the jaguar between them.

"The cat says the ride still happens," Torr grumbled. "Can't exactly argue with a god now, can we?"

"And this is why Tezca is my favorite boy." I grinned, holding my palm out to the jaguar.

The ancient voice stroked like a physical presence over my brain. *The Ghost is joining us as well.*

My smile and hand dropped, the latter hitting my leg just below the towel I had wrapped around my torso. "Devin? Why does he need to come?"

Tezca ambled over to me then, his forehead bumping into the hand I'd held out moments ago. He opened his jaws just as I went to scratch his chin, taking my hand between those massive teeth.

The pressure was gentle, but it did make my heart rate speed up. Santos told me how many gladiators Tezca had killed. Easily.

I got the message from that soft, warning bite, along with a feeling that seemed projected onto me. I felt like I'd been gently scolded, a child chastised by a parent. *Don't question me, mortal,* was the general gist.

He dropped my hand with a huff and turned toward the door. So polite of him to avert his eyes so I could get dressed.

"Neither of you want me to go, huh?" I dropped the towel and started rummaging around for clean clothes.

"After what you just told us? Hell no." Santos still looked

worried, so much so that he wasn't even watching me prance naked around the bedroom. "At least I'll have eyes on you while we're out. Too bad this poor bastard won't."

He nodded at Torr, who was staring distractedly at Tezca.

"Devin, huh?" Torr mused under his breath, a muscle feathering in his jaw.

The jaguar nudged Torr's hand, as if warning he would get some teeth too if he didn't watch it.

I eyed the sun outside the window as I stuck my feet into my boots and hurriedly laced them up. "Let's go. We should've left by now."

Tezca went down the stairs first, followed by me and my two men. Malik waited for me in the kitchen, eyes shifting from the jaguar to me with a small smile and shake of his head. "You Wilders and their animals," he chuckled.

"What?" I took a bite out of a piece of toast on the counter and washed it down with some black coffee. Malik was a longtime family friend and colleague of my mother's. Naturally, he was a regular at our house parties. "Our biggest animal was a Doberman, this guy belongs to him." I patted Tezca's flank and nodded at Santos.

"I seem to recall a rooster that was definitely larger than expected." Malik shuddered as if the memory traumatized him.

My laugh nearly had me choking on my food. "Foghorn was just intimidated by you. He thought you were going to steal all his ladies."

Malik chuckled, setting down his own coffee cup. "You doing alright, Rori? Torr was pretty concerned."

I nodded, trying to look as earnest as possible while my mens' eyes bore into me like lasers. "I'm good, I swear. Just had a bad dream and a dry throat. Had a little coughing fit when I woke up is all."

Malik was too damn smart and observant. I knew he could tell I was still rattled, but I wasn't about to explain the gods business to him. He might physically prevent me from leaving.

"You're sure? I understand you're going out for a few days?"

"Yeah. I promise you, I'll be fine, doc. I wouldn't put my people at risk."

He spent another good, long minute observing me before nodding. "Alright. Be safe out there, young lady."

"I'll be back before you know it." I gave him a quick hug before scarfing down more toast. "I know these guys can be a handful."

"Oh, they're no trouble. This group is surprisingly open to talking about their experiences. I'm seeing lots of support and camaraderie between the fighters. I'm thinking of hosting a group session soon."

"Really? That's great." A physical weight seemed to lift from my chest. I was really hoping the fighters wouldn't be extremely closed off or worse, hostile to Malik.

As if bubbling up out of nowhere, I got an urge to ask about Hudson's progress but ultimately chose not to voice it. With a final squeeze of Malik's arm, I headed for the door. "See you when I get back."

Torr, Santos, and Tezca followed me out to where my handpicked team was waiting.

"Took you long enough," Val griped. "I could've slept in another half hour if I knew you were gonna drag ass."

"The president arrives when she is ready," quipped the Saint, sitting astride one of the borrowed motorcycles.

"No shit," Val grumbled.

LJ sat quietly on his ride, arms crossed in front of him while he stared daggers at the Saint.

I turned to Torr first, lifting on tiptoes and throwing my arms around his neck in an embrace. "Keep an eye on the Bull," I whispered in his ear. "We need to know if they're shady together or if one of them is instigating something."

"Okay." That was the only thing he said before crashing his mouth to mine, stealing all my air and apparently the bones in my legs as I wobbled. His forehead pressed to mine when he broke away. "For fuck's sake, be careful out there. Call me if you can."

He knew the likelihood of having a signal was slim, and he was worried enough to want a call anyway.

"I'll try." I cupped his face, running my thumbs over those sharp cheekbones. "I love you, Torr."

His lips tensed. Relaxed. Tensed again. He was trying to say it back.

Eventually, he gave up.

"You better fucking come back to me," he growled. "If I hear nothing for one week, I'm riding after you."

"You won't have to," I assured him, pushing his hair off of his forehead.

"I can't fucking lose you. To them, their god, or whatever—"

"You won't." I gave him another kiss, rising on my tiptoes to make it forceful, harder. Pulling away slowly, I was already smiling when we separated. "It's gonna take a lot more than some angry cunt of a god to keep me away from you."

We unwrapped from each other, and Torr turned to Santos. "Keep our girl safe, man."

"You know I will." Santos held out his hand with a smirk. "I'm still the Butcher."

Rather than take his hand, Torr grabbed him in a rough, back-slapping embrace. Santos returned the affection just as Devin came out of the frat house.

The fighter was annoyingly breathtaking as usual, his hair up with a few small braids running through it. Some of his knife collection was holstered over his shirt, but I knew there were plenty more that weren't visible. And why was that knowledge so hot?

"Hey, we match!" Val grinned, pointing at Devin and then her own hair, which was done up in more of a Viking braid style.

He gave a small nod and uneasy smile to her before looking at me. "I assume Tezca told you I was coming?"

"Sure did. Almost got my hand bitten off for asking why."

He gave a nervous laugh but seemed more relaxed. "Yeah, I almost lost my ankle."

"Hudson gonna be okay with you gone?" I blurted the question out before thinking.

Devin shrugged. "He's gonna have to be, I guess. Malik's working with him. He'll survive." Then almost defensively he added, "I'm not sure why you're asking. Hudson doesn't need me for anything."

You two are totally fucking. I kept that thought to myself as I nodded. "Alright. Well, you can grab another loaner bike if you feel comfortable riding on your own."

As everyone got situated and mounted up, I spotted Astarte on the apex of the garage roof. The dove and I only stared at each other. I didn't even have to ask a question. She knew I was wandering into something blind and wouldn't give me a clue as to what it was.

Remember what I said, were the only words of wisdom I got.

I could only imagine what she'd be referring to. The goddess had said plenty of things to me over our time together. What stuck out to me in that moment was what she had told me in a dream the night before all the nightmares started.

This will be the hardest battle you, or any living human, will have to face. And you cannot afford to lose it.

With that happy reminder, I began a slow acceleration down the driveway. Once I confirmed my team was behind me and the open road in front, I hit the throttle and tore out with a roar.

It was all I knew how to do.

Chapter 7

Torrance

Rori's dust had barely settled by the time I started checking my phone for updates. Logically, I knew it was pointless to worry. She wouldn't be Rori if she couldn't handle herself. With Santos, Val, and LJ with her, there was nothing that could stop them.

All of this, I knew to be true. But what I couldn't shake was the sight of her in bed this morning. Watching her struggle to breathe, thrashing around like she was trying to escape a captor. The only time I'd been more scared was when I saw that she'd gotten shot.

My woman was strong. But was she strong enough to fight a god? One who was wearing her down and depriving her of sleep? Who knew what those cult elders could do once Rori came upon them?

Not to mention that weirdo, the Saint, made me uneasy as all hell. She was trying to keep an eye on him, see if he was up to anything nefarious, but I still didn't like him in her proximity without me around.

"Astarte and Tezca better be putting in some overtime," I grumbled, walking back up the gravel driveway toward the houses.

I'd drive myself crazy with worry if I didn't keep myself in check. And the best way for me to do that was to hit the weights.

The workout areas in the courtyard were pretty much cleared out, most of the guys bullshitting elsewhere or having lunch. They'd be getting antsy soon. We needed a real ride, some kind of battle plan after Rori got back. These fighters, whether they were born that way or molded into it, wanted blood. Our one rescue mission was nowhere near enough to sate that desire.

A thought hit me as I changed into workout shorts, leaving my shirt off to keep cool, then headed back out to the courtyard. I wondered if the Sisterhood was arming themselves, getting ready for battle, or if they expected their goddess to handle everything. We already knew some of them were armed, but the vast majority were not.

Another thing to talk to Rori about when she's back, I thought as I chalked up my hands. Either situation needed to be dealt with carefully. The cult members needed to be dealt with, but we'd never stoop to the level of massacring a bunch of unarmed people.

I began with squats, the most difficult and taxing of all lifts. Always best to get them out of the way. I started with sets of lower weights to warm up, gradually adding more to the makeshift barbell. Eventually, I found the perfect mental zone of focus. Or rather, it found me.

That was how lifting always was with me. Once I hit a certain threshold of weight, the mental fortitude snapped into place like a suit of armor. If it wasn't there, I'd be likely to hurt myself.

Time ceased to exist as I pushed my body to the limit. Maybe I had spectators, maybe I was hogging the squat rack while someone else waited. I didn't know or care. My whole world was reduced to adding more weight, seeing how much more I could take.

Lifting used to be a fight to the death with myself. I constantly strived to be stronger, better. Because when I could always lift more, it meant I wasn't enough yet.

Never strong enough. Never good enough. That's why they left you to die. That's why Rori's family had to take you in like a stray dog.

The exertion was a punishment as well as a reward. I got stronger over time despite feeling like I was going to die after every workout. It became an addiction, a punishment I craved and sought out. Like my parents' abandonment of me wasn't punishment enough.

But now I had Rori who believed I was good enough. She loved me. *Actually* loved me.

Was I really though? When she'd told me countless times since we got together that she loved me? When she came back for me and Santos, made me her VP, listened to my advice, had been there for me through thick and thin over the years? Was I really good enough if I couldn't bring myself to repeat the same three simple words to her?

Why did it have to be anything but easy for me? Three single-syllable words held the weight of my whole heart, which felt heavier and more dangerous than the plates on this fucking barbell. The risk of saying those words out loud felt like dropping all that weight right onto my toes.

I knew it was dramatic. It was my subconscious drawing on fears from my childhood. Shit, maybe I needed to talk to Malik more than Rori. She'd never been afraid of putting her heart out there. And I knew, even though I continued failing at expressing what I really meant, she'd never give up on me.

All my shortcomings as a partner made me damn glad she had Santos to make up for it. He was like her, fearless about loving wholeheartedly with no hang ups about saying it. Even after seeing the worst of humanity, of women especially, none of that stopped him from falling headfirst for her and letting her know it. I could learn a thing or two from him.

By the time my legs were screaming, I felt mentally lighter. I was a constant work in progress and the one Rori had left in charge. Sometimes it wasn't good to stay stuck in my mental hamster wheel all the time. What a concept.

Motion caught my eye as I set the barbell on the catches, and I looked over while I caught my breath. *Well, speaking of hamsters in enclosures.*

Hudson had not only left his room but the house. He was outside, in the open.

Trying not to stare, I wiped the sweat off my forehead with my arm. He was using another barbell rack to stretch his shoulders, from the looks of it. He had a T-shirt and athletic shorts on, and the vast majority of his skin was covered in tattoos. Good ones too. The kind that rivaled the quality of mine, done by Rori's dad.

My curiosity piqued even more when he reclined on the bench under the rack, scooting and adjusting it for his reach. After a few warm-up reps with just the barbell, Hudson rolled up and added two plates to each side.

My eyebrows shot up. Two plates. Two hundred and twenty-five pounds. It wasn't an enormous amount of weight, but definitely a lot to start out with. Especially for a guy who didn't look like he weighed two-twenty-five and had spent years confined to a single room.

"Hey." I headed over before I could think twice. "Hudson, right?"

He could have been squinting in the sunlight or glaring at me, it was hard to tell. "Yeah?"

"You want a spot?" I gestured to the bar.

He shrugged like it didn't make a difference to him. "If you want to."

I went behind the rack as he reclined on the bench, his head near my knees. Once he found his grip, I braced myself, ready to stop the barbell from crushing his Adam's apple once he realized it was too much damn weight.

To my surprise, the lower and lift of each rep was incredibly smooth and controlled. As was his breathing and his form. The guy knew what he was doing, maybe even better than me.

He did a set of ten like it was warm-up before setting the bar back on its catches.

"Well, shit." I laughed as he rolled up. "You had me worried when you loaded those two plates, but guess I underestimated you."

Hudson shrugged and brought his arms behind him to stretch again. "I used to compete a little bit, just amateur stuff. It was a hobby."

"I mean, it's a hobby for me too but I've never warmed up with that much." I came around to the front of him, sticking my hand out. "I don't think we've formally met. I'm Torrance. Everyone calls me Torr."

Hudson hesitated, staring up at me for a moment before clasping my hand. "You're the second in command. To her."

"That's right."

Hudson rested his hands on his thighs, elbows flared out in a pose that looked a little defensive. "Gotta admit, I'm surprised you offered to spot me instead of bashing my head in with one of those plates. Or is that still on the table?"

I crossed my arms, taking my time to answer. "I'm not interested in bludgeoning you to death, no."

"And the woman?"

"Her name is Rori. And no, she's not interested in killing you either. Which is pretty damn reasonable, considering you tried to kill *her*. But we're all very sympathetic to your situation, in case the free food, housing, clothes, and other amenities," I gestured to all the workout equipment, "doesn't show that already."

Hudson lowered his head, shoulders rounding down slightly while his eyes remained connected to mine. "I am appreciative. Of all of it. You've noticed I haven't tried to kill anyone else since I got here."

"That's a low bar of gratitude, but we'll take it."

He huffed out a breath, which almost sounded like an attempt at laughter. "It's a nice day out," he remarked after a few seconds of silence.

"Yeah." He wasn't lying. It was just warm enough with a bit of a breeze and a clear sky. It would've been a perfect day for riding if I didn't have to keep an eye on things.

"I almost didn't leave my room when I found out Devin was leaving." Hudson rested his forearms on his legs. "But then I found out the--uh, Rori was going. And the other woman, I don't know her name. Dark hair, blue eyes."

"Valorie," I informed him. "She's Rori's cousin, goes by Val."

"Right, yeah. So I've been able to see this yard from the window. And I figured, if there's less people around, I could see if I still got my technique, you know?"

I didn't fully understand why he was telling me all this. Maybe because I was the only person around to talk to? Whatever the reason, it seemed important to listen.

"It's good to get out of your comfort zone," I said. "Break down those barriers you set up in your mind."

Hudson nodded. "Malik and I talked about that. What's familiar isn't always what's right, even if it feels better to stay within those barriers. Doing what's uncomfortable, taking that risk, that's how I stop being the person I was before coming here." He leaned back, straightening. "So, that's why I decided to leave my room and try some lifts, run the risk of talking to someone, like you."

I studied him, my feelings somewhere between surprised and amused. Damn it, I might actually end up liking this guy. "And how does it feel?"

"Feels..." Hudson paused to consider that, head tilting slightly. "Feels good," he said with a definitive nod. "Yeah. I'm glad I came out here."

I wondered if he'd feel the same way if Rori and Val were around. Or if the mere sight of them would send his hackles up, shutting himself back in his room like a cornered animal. Either way, I didn't need to push it now. We'd find out when they returned. For now, at least, the guy and I were getting along.

"Well, you clearly don't need my assistance with your lifts," I said. "I'll leave you to your workout. Nice talking to you—"

"What's she like?"

The abrupt question threw me off-kilter for a second. "Who? Rori?"

Hudson nodded. "I know what Devin thinks of her. He tries to be very straightforward and objective, but everyone has bias. Especially when it comes to other people. How do you feel about her?"

Well if that didn't make me curious as hell about what Devin said about her, but I smothered that thought with an awkward laugh. "Shit, I don't even know where to begin. I've known her for thirteen years."

"So you know her well."

"Better than most. Doesn't stop me from being biased, though. Your best bet is to get to know her yourself."

"I can't do that yet." Hudson shook his head, blowing out a long breath. "I'm not ready to speak to a woman face-to-face. So I'm trying to learn from those around her. And anyway, your biases are different from Devin's."

All valid points. "Well." I rubbed my jaw. "She's the most loyal friend anyone will ever have. That shit runs deep with her. No one is a casual acquaintance with Rori. You're either a stranger to her or you're practically family. And she's someone who will ride into battle for the people she cares about, no questions asked."

Hudson made a snorting sound and shook his head.

"What?" I demanded.

"So why'd she run in to save me, then?" He met my eyes again, challenging me. "She didn't know me, so what you're saying makes no sense."

"She did it for Santos," I snapped. "Because she loves him and *you* were important to him. 'Til you tried to kill her, at least." Hudson opened his mouth to argue, but I cut him off. "And even if you hadn't been tight with Santos, if we'd have found out about you another way, she'd still want to rescue you because what they did is fucked up. Sexual slavery is wrong, and you didn't deserve that, no matter who you are. It's not that fucking complicated. If something fucked up is going on, any decent person will want to stop it. That's the normal, expected thing to do."

Hudson and I stared at each other for a few tense seconds before he broke eye contact with a sigh. "I definitely don't know what's normal or expected anymore. It's like I need to recalibrate my sense of reality."

My temper ebbed away, and I found myself leaning against the barbell rack. "I can't imagine what that's like. Sorry I got defensive."

"You're really protective of her." Hudson's eyes flicked up to mine again. "They don't call you the Guard for no reason."

"Look, Rori isn't perfect," I said. "In fact, she's a massive pain in the ass sometimes. Stubborn as a bulldog with the bite to back it up. But I'll put my life on the line for her because I know for a fact she'd do it for me."

Hudson chuckled dryly. "You're lucky. I can't say I ever had someone that would do that for me."

"Rori will," I told him before I could think better of it. "You just have to give her the chance."

Before he could respond, a motorcycle rumbled to life. I looked toward the garage, noticing an ex-gladiator straddling one of the loaner bikes, which wasn't unusual. With all the free time the guys had, many of them practiced riding.

The rider turned out to be the Bull, and he gave me a little wave as he noticed me watching.

"Be right back," I said to Hudson as I started toward the man on the motorcycle, some instinct poking at me to stay alert.

"Hey, VP," the Bull greeted me as I came closer. He seemed eager to leave, with one foot already off the ground and his hands twitching on the handlebars.

"Hey, Bull." I meandered casually to the front of his bike, blocking his way. "You headed somewhere?"

"Nah, you know. Just want to hit a couple of practice runs." His eyes darting to the road behind me told a different story.

"Hey, why don't Hudson and I join you?" I glanced back at the man still sitting on the weight bench. "It's about time he learns to ride, and I could keep an eye on both of you."

The Bull ground his teeth. "No offense, VP, but I'd rather do this one alone. Want to clear my head a bit. Next time, though?"

I smiled at him, trying to keep a calm facade while reading into his body language. "Seems like you're in a hurry. You got somewhere you need to be?"

"No," he huffed. "What's with the interrogation? I thought we weren't prisoners anymore."

"You're not, but you also don't know the area. It's not safe to ride off alone."

"Not trying to be disrespectful, but I really need to blow off some steam."

"Why, what's got you riled up?" I pressed. Damn, sure wish I had Santos to check my six.

"None of your business, to be fuckin' honest."

"Hey, no need to have a tone with me. If you need to blow off steam, take a walk. Lift some weights. Shoot some targets around back. But you can't just ride off on a bike that isn't yours."

The Bull snorted out a big breath like his animal namesake. He seemed to relax for a moment, complying with my request. Then he jerked the handlebars and started the bike, kicking off as fast as he could in an attempt to go around me.

Too bad he didn't know motorcycles like I did.

I reached over his dash and hit his killswitch, stopping his ride dead in its tracks. Then I lunged, grabbing the lapels of his jacket to swing him off the bike. He hit the ground, but the ex-gladiator wasn't going without a fight. A meaty fist swung and crashed into my temple, knocking me off him while the world spun.

He scrambled for the bike again, but I grabbed his foot, bringing him back down to the ground with me. He rolled before I could successfully pin him and kicked me in the stomach with his free foot. I doubled over and got clocked in the head once again.

Fucking hell, I really needed backup. Rori had to take all the good people with her. The only one I could really trust here was the Hunter, and he was probably horizontal with Paige right now.

The Bull had knocked the wind out of me and my vision was dotted with stars and black dots, but I held onto anything I could. His jacket, his pant leg. I could not fucking let him get on that bike.

"Gotta warn them," he muttered to himself as he tried to shake me off.

"Warn who, asshole?" I crawled up the backs of his legs, trying to get on top of him so I could get an arm around his neck or something, but he flipped over, pinning me beneath him.

His tailbone pressed directly into my stomach, painful and making it difficult to breathe. I bear-hugged around his torso and tried to get my legs around his, but none of the angles were right. I should have done more of those jiu-jitsu classes with Daren, but that was his thing, not mine.

"Let go of me!" The Bull tried to unlock my hands from their grip, but I held on. "They're keeping her safe! I can't let them, ugh, get to her!"

I couldn't fully process what he was saying, not when my sole focus was preventing him from getting away. But it hit me then as one hell of a delayed realization that we might've been suspicious of the wrong person.

The Saint was weird. Eccentric for sure. But this man, grappling on the ground with me right now, was without a doubt disloyal to us. Maybe the Saint was too, but I couldn't worry about that now.

Despite his size, the Bull managed to wriggle around enough to drive an elbow into my gut. He must have hit a nerve because the pain made me black out for a second and also loosen my grip around him.

He rolled away, and I found myself staring at the sky and part of the garage roof. I tried to find the strength to move, to grab a foot and trip him again, to yell for help, anything. But I should have known better than to fight one-on-one with a former gladiator.

All my limbs moved too slowly and my lungs couldn't inhale a full breath. Fuck! I couldn't let him get away, couldn't let Rori down. Rolling to my forearms and knees felt like it took a full minute, and the Bull was already grasping the side of the motorcycle, pulling himself up.

Hudson moved faster than either of us could perceive. In the time it took to blink, he stood between the Bull and me, hands on the other man's shoulders as he forcibly threw him off the bike.

The Bull was lying prone next to me, palms splayed out and eyes blinking like he couldn't figure how he'd ended up on the ground. Hudson was on his back in the next instant, bringing his arm to lock around his opponent's throat.

The Bull's face started going red and then purple. He gasped for air as he clawed at Hudson's forearm but was quickly losing the fight.

"Don't kill him," I rasped, finally finding air in my lungs. "We need to question him."

"I'm not. He'll just pass out soon." Hudson was calm as he answered, his chokehold rock steady on the other man.

Within another minute, the Bull's eyes rolled up and his body went limp. Hudson released him, and the color immediately began returning to the passed-out man's face.

"Holy fuck." I rubbed the tender spot on my stomach where I'd been elbowed. "Thanks for the assist."

Hudson nodded, his face remote. "We should get him restrained before he wakes up."

"Yeah. Help me take him to the basement?"

As we dragged the traitor across the ground, I could only hope Rori was having an easier time than me.

Chapter 8

Rori

It was three days of riding before we found them.

Aside from the general direction of south, we didn't know exactly where the four elder women were headed. For all we knew, they could have doubled back and returned the direction they came from. But that would have come from the assumption that they knew they had been watched, which LJ would not have allowed. The only other reason for changing course would be paranoia, and while this cult had that in spades, they also had a staggering amount of arrogance.

Whatever this split-three-ways plan was, I was counting on them being confident in it.

LJ and Val had triangulated their most likely positions based on the main road taken by the RV, and the estimation of where they'd end up based on distance covered and potential routes taken. So many of the roads out here hadn't been maintained for decades, since before I was born, probably. We eliminated most potential routes due to the sheer impassibility of them, all overgrown, cracked, and potholed to hell. It'd be suicide to travel those roads in something as bulky as a van, not to mention one carrying supposedly precious cargo.

"You think they'd avoid these towns?" Val pointed out a few settlements on the map. "Because, you know, *men*."

"I didn't see them pack much food," LJ said. "They'll need to stop for supplies, men or no. Safe to assume they'll avoid men if they can, though."

"Here." I dropped my fingertip to a dot marked Portisville. "This place has one of those self-serve stations. You grab what you need and then leave cash or goods in exchange. No need to interact with anyone."

LJ lined up his ruler on the map, muttering under his breath as he did the measurements in his head. "The distance fits within our time frame. If they kept a steady pace, they'll have been there today or yesterday."

"Let's go." I headed for my bike, trusting everyone would follow. "They're not likely to stay in one place for long."

I pulled out my phone the moment I lowered into my rumbling seat. Again, no service, just like every other time I checked. Sometimes I'd barely get a bar of reception that would only disappear in the next second. Regardless, I wrote a quick message to Torr, fully aware of the low chances he'd ever see it. *Connection's bad, but we're fine. Love you.*

Shoving the phone away, I went for the handlebars and hit the throttle, accelerating on the road with a roar. A glance in my mirror showed Santos just to the right and behind me. He looked relaxed on the bike, a complete natural. It wasn't lost on me that he was in Torr's usual spot, my right hand.

I returned my attention to the road with a smile, pleased that my men's formation on the road was just as seamless as it was off. Santos and Torr knew how to cover each other as if on instinct. When one had to stay behind, the other naturally stepped into his place at my side.

Devin hung a few paces behind Santos, and he also seemed at

ease with the formation of our small group. More so than I expected, considering it was Tezca who said he had to be part of this mission.

My gaze shifted to the side, looking for the big cat running alongside us at a speed no regular jaguar could maintain. Tezca didn't like running on the road, so my peripheral vision caught the cat-shaped shadow keeping up with us through the brush, shrubs, and rocky terrain along the roadside.

Somewhere in the sky, Astarte watched over us too. The companion gods stayed with us, keeping us in sight while they remained out of reach. Their steadfastness was the only real confirmation that we were going more or less the right way. It wasn't like they were alerting us to the contrary, which by this point, I figured was as much as we would get.

Portisville stood on its own in a neutral zone, not currently part of any particular territory. At first, it was surprising that a nearby territory hadn't absorbed it, considering the one-stop-sign town had the most well-stocked service station for miles and was just off of a major roadway as well. You'd think some governor would be frothing at the mouth to levy taxes on all those goods. But once we crossed into the town's limits, it became clear why that wasn't the case.

The service station was at the center of town, easy to see from the road leading in. And it was surrounded by armed guards.

"Shit, is there a bank vault in there?" Val mused, parking next to me in the lot.

"No," I answered. "Just the only fresh food, water, clothes, and gasoline for miles."

"If you don't count the safe houses," she chuckled. "What do you want to do, Pres?"

I glanced at her. "We could use a restock for the road. You and I will go in, grab some stuff, and check out the inside." Looking at the guys, I said, "You all stay here. See if you spot our targets or the van."

"And if we do?" the Saint asked, a smile coming to his lips.

"Do not engage. Wait for Val and me to get back."

With that, Val and I headed toward the entrance. If it weren't for all the guns posted at the entrances, it would have been a routine supply run. But the mere presence of those guards had me twitchy, on edge, even if they were there just to make sure no one made off with stolen goods.

"You seein' what I'm seein'?" Val muttered under her breath.

"What?" My handgun felt heavy at my hip and I tried to keep my arm relaxed, resisting the urge to reach for it.

"They're all chicks."

Every one of the guards was armored from head to foot, covered in steel toe boots, bullet and knife proof padding, multiple guns, knives, ammo, and with either helmets or beanies on their heads. From far away, it was near-impossible to tell gender. But getting up closer confirmed that every single guard was a woman.

And they each had a patch on the arm of their dark fatigues. Some symbol that looked vaguely familiar, though I couldn't quite make it out.

"Don't stare," Val hissed at me. "Be cool."

I tore my eyes away, focusing straight ahead. I could feel the guards' eyes on me as we passed through the front door, but they moved out of the way to let us through.

"Fuck, that was tense," my cousin sighed. "Alright, what do we need?"

I looked around, actually impressed by the neat aisles, produce displays, clothing racks, and bank of glass-doored refrigerators. This must have been one of those warehouse-sized supply centers from before the Collapse. There were so few now since such a large space with perishable food required a fuckload of electricity, and most grids weren't stable these days.

"Water," I told Val. "And food. Let's see if they got any whole chickens. Also wouldn't mind an extra blanket or two."

We wandered through the aisles, checking out the supplies while looking around for four older women with a baby carrier. Nada. More armed guards patrolled the inside, as if the ones at the entrances weren't enough.

After gathering our supplies, we made it to the collection box near the entrance. Under the watchful eye of a woman with bandoliers of ammo making an X across her chest, I deposited an estimated amount of currency into the box. Many neutral zone towns still bartered for goods, so prices weren't exact.

"May the Dark Mother protect you," muttered the closest guard as we headed for the door.

Val just about froze in her spot, but I grabbed her arm and pulled her along. "Be cool." I repeated the advice she gave me when we walked in.

"Well, that explains a lot," she huffed once we were out of earshot. "Good thing the guys didn't come in."

"Yeah, that wouldn't have gone well."

Santos, the Saint, LJ, and Devin were huddled in a semi circle when we returned to the bikes, their heads bent low.

"Y'all comparing dick size? What are you looking at?" I said when we walked up.

"This." Devin was the one who thrust the piece of paper at me. "There's a few of them stuck to trees and poles around here."

I glanced at what looked to be an event flyer for some stargazing thing. "'This week, Virgo will be the brightest all year.' That's cool, I guess. I think my little brother is a Virgo."

"You think?" LJ snorted.

"Do I look like I know horoscopes?" I shoved a jug of water at his chest. "Stash this in yours, you got the biggest compartments."

Val laughed. "Typical Scorpio."

"Shut up." To the guys, I asked, "Did you all see anything out here?"

"Just the flyer, President," voiced the Saint.

"I didn't ask you all to look for a flyer, so I guess that's a no."

"You really don't know what Virgo is?" Devin pinned me with a stare that made me want to squirm with discomfort.

"No. Should I?"

"It's the constellation of a woman. A maiden, or virgin."

Silence fell over the group as that information sank in. "You think our targets will be at this thing?" I pointed at the flyer.

"Shit, the whole town might be," Val said. "The flyers are everywhere, and the guards back there said something about the Dark Mother's blessing. The cult probably owns the damn place."

"Where's this stargazing thing happening?" I scanned the paper. "LJ, how far is this from here?"

"About an hour's ride, maybe," he said.

"Let's go there now." I threw a leg over my bike, wasting no time. "We'll scout the location before it gets dark and see if there's a covered place we can watch."

Everyone followed without another word, LJ pulling up next to me since he knew the way. My stomach flipped with anxiety as we hit the road, the complete unknown threatening to make my thoughts spiral. I missed Torr badly right then. His strong, solid presence was always able to ground and calm me.

But I needed to beat my self-doubt now more than ever before. I didn't know what I was riding into, what I was leading my people, my family, into. Regardless, I needed to be their president and stand tall on my own.

Chapter 9

Rori

The directions on the flyer brought us to a series of hills that looked like a miniature version of a much greater mountain range. The stargazing event would take place on the highest one, and we could already see groups of people settling in with blankets and food.

We parked our bikes at the base of one of the smaller hills, making sure to hide them in the brush, then hiked up the hillside farthest away from where the action was happening. We noted other people parking vehicles at the base of the tallest hill before making their way up, but there was no van that we could see.

What if this is all a waste of time? I wondered. *The Virgo thing could be a total coincidence and the Sisterhood has nothing to do with this. They could be getting farther away, or closer to the safehouses to do fuck knows what.*

I pushed on harder, putting more speed and power into my legs as I hiked up the hill. The ache in my muscles and lungs helped to keep the thoughts at bay, kept me here and focused. No wonder Torr used exercise as a coping mechanism.

We were here, so we might as well see it through.

A flapping of wings brought my attention upward, but in the fading daylight, the white dove was a dim blur.

Remember what I told you, Astarte had said.

She said to trust my instincts, to look deep into the divine part of myself, below the surface of anxiety and what-ifs.

I took a deep breath, still pushing onward as I tried to quiet my mind.

We were in the right place. Deep in my gut, I fucking knew we were in the right place.

Everyone spread out once we crested the hill, keeping low behind the cover of boulders, shrubs, and trees. We had an unobstructed view of the neighboring peak where everyone was gathering. Voices drifted over, all feminine. People chatted and laughed, sounding relaxed with an air of excitement. Someone started a campfire, which slowly grew as people fed it dry wood. After a few minutes, it was a roaring bonfire, lighting up everyone's faces with an orange glow.

"Look." Val nudged me. "The two on the left. They were at the service station."

I nodded at her observation. "Did you happen to see what their patches were? The black ones on their arms."

"Oh yeah. Looked like the female reproductive system. The uterus, tubes, ovaries, all that. Just stylized to look cool on a patch."

"Jesus," I muttered. "Real subtle, aren't they?"

Our whole group seemed to collectively hold a breath when four figures appeared on the opposite side of the bonfire. We could only see their silhouettes through the flames, but there was no mistaking them. They stood together, solemn and poised while everyone else looked like they were there to party. And the dead giveaway was one of them holding a large, bulky object with a handle, which could only be a child carrier.

My gaze was fixed on them, unable to look away. I couldn't erase the feeling that they could see me, even through the cover of darkness and our hiding places, and were staring right at me.

Do you know I'm watching you? I wondered. *Did you want me to follow you and see this?*

A hand on my shoulder jolted me out of my trance-like state. "It's just me," Santos said when I startled. He frowned with concern at whatever he saw on my face. "You okay, paloma?"

"Yeah." I blinked and rubbed my eyes, already feeling the strain from staring at the bright fire. "Yeah, I'm good."

His mouth tightened, but he didn't comment further. "What's the plan? Just watch? Or do we engage?"

"Do not engage." I carried my voice to make sure everyone heard. "We're just watching. If we can isolate the four we know are from the cult, we'll go after them. But everyone else might be innocent. We don't want anyone caught in the crossfire."

With that order, everyone settled in for the show.

Stars emerged as the sky darkened. People started pointing up, assumedly at the constellation they all came to see.

I never had much interest in the stars and planets. That was my little sister's thing. On family camping trips, Lucia would have her telescope and book of star charts ready the moment the sun set. She would then map out the planets and constellations, pointing them out to everyone until she nodded off from tiredness.

She would have loved something like this. A bonfire on the top of a hill, gathering with people who shared the same interests as her. Lucia was popular and always making new friends.

A bolt of rage struck through me, surprising me at how quickly it came on. It pissed me off that the Sisterhood would use things like this most likely to recruit and brainwash members. Impressionable kids like my teenage sister.

They probably ran fundraisers that looked like they were supporting women's shelters. Probably gave talks about empowering women and giving them back control of their lives. All things that looked wonderful on the surface but were rotten and evil underneath. My anger rose like a pot of water boiling over, that they could target my sister, or some other girl who was vulnerable and actually needed help. They made it so easy to fall into their trap. By the time they revealed what they were actually doing to men, it was probably too late to get out.

So if their goddess gave them some supernatural ability to see me, I hoped they could read my mind as well.

I'm going to kill you all, and I won't stop until every vulnerable girl, woman, boy, and man is safe from you.

All at once, the chatter on the high hill stopped. Only the crackle and pops of the fire reached our ears. The four figures raised their arms and an eerie chanting began.

"What the fuck?" someone near me whispered.

I was too transfixed by the sight to say anything. The middle one held the child carrier between her hands, high above her head.

The chanting was nonsensical. It wasn't English and didn't sound like Spanish or anything else based in Latin. It was just rhythmic vocalizations repeating over and over.

It was hypnotic.

I could feel myself getting drawn in, my body starting to sway from side to side just like the rest of the bonfire attendees. Their voices started to join those of their leaders, amping up the vibrations and volume through the air.

Something dark passed in front of me, the fire no longer visible. Two hands fell to my shoulders and shook me violently.

"What the—what?" I demanded, feeling disoriented like I'd just woken up from a deep sleep.

"Snap the fuck out of it, Rori." Devin's face hovered in front of me, his dark eyes narrowed in a glare. It was his hands on my shoulders, now digging in with an unforgiving grip. "You start doing that again, I'm gonna slap you. And then Santos is gonna kill me."

"Doing what?" I smacked his hands away, feeling almost...ashamed? Like I'd been caught doing something bad.

"You had joined in, chanting and swaying. I watched you for a full minute." Devin sat back, giving me space. "Whatever they're doing is getting to you."

"Fuck, I'm sorry." I rubbed my eyes, scrubbed my face. It really felt like I had just woken up from a deep sleep. "You don't have to slap me, just pinch me or something." I looked around at my group, finding everyone's face in the orange glow of the fire. "Was anyone else affected?"

They all shook their heads slowly at me, even Val.

It had to have been because the Dark Mother had touched me already, had access to my mind, just like with the nightmares.

Devin moved warily to the side, letting me have a view of the hill again. I watched just in time to see the woman holding the carrier swing her arm and throw it into the fire.

We all let out collective gasps and curses of shock. The chanting and swaying continued as if nothing had changed. But now, black smoke rose from the fire, a dense floating mass that looked like it held more weight, more substance than ordinary smoke.

It hovered above the fire, shifting and writhing in midair. The smoke, or whatever it was, kept its form. It never floated away, never dissipated into the atmosphere. It stayed in place, hovering a few feet above the licking flames like a malevolent spirit.

Suddenly all of the chanting stopped, creating an eerie silence that felt more like a vacuum of sound. I couldn't hear the fire crackling anymore. Couldn't hear my own breathing or my riders if they were saying anything.

Then the floating black mass started to move.

It floated toward me, its dark, ethereal form almost shimmering. It looked like a swarm of bees heading my way.

Every instinct told me to run, but I felt frozen in place. I might as well have been sitting in the middle of a road, watching the headlights of an eighteen-wheeler head straight toward me.

Something touched me, and that was when my self-preservation kicked in. I sprang to my feet and turned, running across the crest of the hill and heading down the other side.

Some president you are, turning tail and leaving your people vulnerable to that thing.

I jerked my head around at the thought and saw the black floating mass heading straight for me. It crossed from the bonfire hill to this one in no time at all. Through it, I could see my riders chasing after it at a much slower pace. Their mouths moved, shouting something. My name, probably.

Facing forward again, I kept racing down the hill. The dark mass from the fire wanted me, not them. Somehow, I'd known that from the moment I saw it rise up from the fire.

And it was gaining on me. I didn't have to look behind me to know that. It started to not only surround me, but absorb *into* me. The sensation was like sandpaper on my skin, tiny pinpricks being pushed into my pores and hair follicles. Every time I dragged a breath in, it felt like I was inhaling sand.

Fuck, this is my dream, I realized in a panic.

I ran harder, even though I could barely see through my eyes feeling sandblasted with pain. I was choking now, my throat working to remove the foreign bodies forcing themselves into me and cutting off my air.

I must have fallen because I was rolling on the ground now, trying to cover my face, my mouth, my eyes. It hurt so fucking bad, and I felt like I was going to pass out from lack of air.

The last thing I saw was Astarte, the dove the only clear object in my blurry vision.

Remember what we told you, she said.

———

As soon as I woke up, I started coughing, my throat seizing up from the dryness. I rubbed violently at my eyes, desperate to get the sand out.

"Hey, hey. Take it easy."

Someone pushed a thermos into my hands and I drank the water from it greedily, gulping it all down in a few swallows. Someone else's palm made circles on my back, soothing me as I returned to rubbing at my eyes.

It took a few seconds to realize my eyes felt normal. Nothing but the usual grittiness from sleep. I blinked and looked around, meeting the worried faces of my crew illuminated by the morning sun.

"Uh. Hi, guys." I scanned all the faces again, noting someone was missing. "Where's Santos?"

"Right here, paloma," said a husky voice near my ear. He was the one rubbing my back, sitting behind me with his legs on either side of me.

"You scared the shit out of us, Pres," LJ grumbled.

"What happened?" I leaned back, letting my head rest on Santos' shoulder. My throat was dry. My legs and feet ached a little, probably from running and climbing the hill. But otherwise I felt...fine. Normal.

"You took off running out of nowhere." Val's blue gaze bounced all over me like she was examining for injuries. "And then you just collapsed. Crumpled to the ground like someone cut your strings."

"It was the smoke! Or the cloud, swarm thing. It was coming straight at me."

"The what?" the Saint tilted his head. It was probably the first time I ever saw him look confused.

"They threw the carrier in the fire and this black smoke rose out of it. Only it wasn't like smoke, it was...it seemed like it was alive."

"We saw them throw the carrier in," Devin said. He was next to me and must have been the one who had given me water. "And there was smoke for a bit, but that was all. Then you took off running like someone was after you with a chainsaw."

The realization hit me with a cold sense of dread in the pit of my stomach. "None of you saw it." I looked at Val, who was frowning with just as much confusion as everyone else.

"Fuck." I rubbed my temples. "Did I dream it?"

No. There was no doubt in my body or mind that it had been real. I had *felt* the grains of sand digging into my skin like thousands of tiny needles. I felt the exertion in my body as I tried to get away, the burning in my lungs as I had struggled to breathe. It was entirely too vivid to be a dream. And minutes ago, before I had woken up, there had been nothing. No dreams at all for the first time in over two weeks.

"Are you okay, Rori?" The question came from Devin, but everyone stared intently at me.

I must have gone quiet for a few minutes while trying to decipher dreams from reality.

"I...think so," I said cautiously. Then more firmly, "Yes. Yes, I'm fine."

It was one thing to let my guard down in front of just Santos, or even my family members. But right now, these were my riders, my Vengeful Gods, and I was their president. I couldn't look like a wilting flower in front of them.

"Sorry to worry you guys." I forced a smile. "But I feel good now." Physically, anyway. At least I was partially honest. "So where are we? Base of the hill?"

"Yeah," Val confirmed. "We didn't want to risk moving you after you passed out. So we just camped out where you dropped. Your vitals were strong, so we figured we'd give you a few hours to wake up."

"I wanted to get you a doctor immediately," Santos muttered.

"In an area that's clearly unfriendly to men," Devin tacked on. "Great idea, that was."

"Well, it all worked out. I'm awake and feeling fine." I planted a kiss on Santos' still-frowning lips before climbing to my feet. "What happened on the other hill? Did someone keep watching?"

The Saint nodded. "Not much happened after they threw the carrier in. They kept chanting for a while until the fire died down, then everyone left."

"I saw the direction the van went," LJ added. "We can keep pursuing them if you want."

I thought for a moment, then shook my head, my head swimming for a moment and my vision becoming disoriented. Rubbing my temples to get clarity, I heard LJ speak again.

"You don't think they—" LJ stopped, his voice catching in his throat.

"Spit it out, cuz." Val squeezed his shoulder, encouraging him to go on.

"Burned a baby," LJ continued, his face paling. "Would they just murder a child like that?"

"If it was a boy, they wouldn't blink." Devin walked over and clapped a hand down on his other shoulder. Even in my state of trying to decipher reality from dreams, I was still pleasantly surprised that Devin seemed to be getting along with the whole group.

"It could have been a new type of male sacrifice for them," the Ghost went on. "But we had no idea what they would do and were too far away to act." His hand dropped from my cousin's shoulder, looking at him sympathetically. "There was nothing we could have done."

"We're not even sure if a child died," I said. "Let's check the fire. If we find remains, we'll give it a proper burial."

"If not a baby, then what was in that carrier?" asked the Saint.

No one answered, but I remembered part of a dream right then. When I thought I had a daughter but it turned out to be a faceless, fleshy mass that moved and writhed.

EMBERS WERE STILL GLOWING in the bonfire's gray ashes when we crested the neighboring hill. We all found long branches and got to work, sifting and poking through the fire's remains.

Pieces of the carrier emerged quickly. Mostly plastic parts that had melted and then cooled. A few metal bits like washers, bolts, and screws. Even a piece of charred fabric from the seat itself emerged. But nothing that resembled human remains.

No bone fragments or even teeth. It was a big fucking fire, but there would have been something more than dust left behind.

We kept searching until we scraped the unburned ground directly beneath the fire pit.

"There was no child in that carrier." I dropped my stick and wiped my ash-covered hands on my jeans.

"So what then?" Santos asked. "Was it even a sacrifice?"

How was I to answer that? Was there even a name, a term for that fleshy blob thing? Was that the god that had spoken to me, inserted itself into my mind and now possibly my body?

I folded my arms over my stomach as if to protect myself. "It might not have been a sacrifice," I said, more to myself than anyone else. "But an awakening."

Chapter 10

Santos

The ride home was long, tense. We left the remains of the bonfire feeling like we had accomplished nothing on this trip. Like we may have been too late.

The closer we got to the safe houses, I became increasingly more worried about Rori. She seemed quiet, withdrawn. On our last day on the road, she also appeared sick. Her complexion was pale, and she began slumping over her bike instead of sitting tall like she usually did.

"Ride with me," I told her on our last rest stop, less than two hours away from home. "You look like you're about to fall over." I pushed a canister of water into her hands.

"So sweet of you to compliment me," she cracked. Despite her fire being diminished, she still had some energy. "I'm fine, just tired," she added.

"You look half dead," I retorted. "I'm genuinely concerned about you being able to drive."

"Don't be." She waved her hand dismissively. "I can ride in my sleep. Besides, I'm not going to abandon my bike out here."

"Val can get it with her truck later. I'm worried about you, paloma. You really don't look well."

I cupped her cheek, which felt too cold against my palm. Touching my lips to her forehead, her skin was cold there too. And clammy.

Rori sighed, leaning her face into my palm as she gazed up at me. "I don't feel so good, but I *have* to lead us home. I'll rest when we get there."

"I'm telling you that you don't have to. You can rest now."

My stubborn woman shook her head, lifting her cheek from my hand. "On the road, I have to be the president. It's only two hours. I can make it."

It was my turn to sigh. There was no fighting her when she was this determined. "Fine, but I'm going to be on your ass the whole way home. If your tires wobble once, I'm running you off the road and tying you to my bike if I have to."

Rori laughed, the sound genuinely amused despite being soft and weaker than usual. "Don't threaten me with a good time."

"I'm serious, paloma."

"I know." She lifted to her tiptoes and kissed under my jaw. "I love you."

"Love you." I let my hand trail down her arm, to her back, then her waist as she walked away.

She walked with purpose, a general leading her troops as she remounted her bike. It couldn't have been easy for her, putting on the image of a strong leader while she felt like shit.

Making her life easier was my job, as far I was concerned. Torr would see to the club while she recovered at home, and I would remain at her side for her every need. We just had to make it there first.

It felt like an eternity on the road before our tires crunched on the gravel driveway leading up to the safe houses. And Rori, with her superhuman grit and resolve, did not wobble once.

Torr waited for us in front of the garage. His face looked grim, even before he saw the condition Rori was in. When she pulled to a stop in front of him, he looked just as worried as I felt.

"Welcome home. How did it go? Oh shit!"

Torr ran up to Rori before anyone could answer, because she was pitching over the side of her motorcycle. All of us that had been riding ran up to her in a concerned rush. Most of them hadn't noticed how bad of shape she was in until now.

"Rori? Rori!" Torr cradled her upper body in his arms while LJ and I carefully removed her legs from their straddle position on the bike.

Once Rori got her feet under her, she started to stand. "Sorry, I'm okay. Feet fell asleep, and I'm a little lightheaded. Just been on the road too long."

"Why are you so pale?" Torr cupped her cheeks, much like I had. "Are you sick? What's wrong?"

Just like with me, Rori waved away his concern. "No, no. Just tired. I'm fine, really."

"You're wobbling like a newborn fawn," Devin pointed out.

"You need to lie down," Val agreed. "With your feet elevated. And you're probably dehydrated."

"You all don't need to fuss over me," Rori snapped. "But I will rest so you all can stop worrying. We'll brief everyone on the mission tomorrow."

Torr leaned down to pick Rori up, much to her grumbling dismay. With her secure against his chest, he turned toward the house. I followed him while everyone else dispersed to go their own ways.

While Torr took Rori up the stairs, I started rummaging through the kitchen for something to feed her. She'd barely eaten the last couple of days, only taking small sips of water on our rest stops. When she'd walked off to take a piss, I'd also noticed her dry-heaving.

I found a sleeve of saltine crackers and an empty water pitcher with a built-in filter. I filled the pitcher, grabbed a glass and the crackers, and headed upstairs with them.

Torr had gotten Rori out of her riding clothes and was tucking her into bed when I entered the room. "This should help settle your stomach," I said, setting everything up on the nightstand.

Torr frowned. "What's going on with your stomach?"

"Nothing." Rori glared at me.

"I saw you dry-heaving," I admitted to her. "I know you wouldn't want anyone to know while we were out there, so I didn't say anything until now."

"What, now you're motion-sick?" Torr asked.

"Maybe, I don't know." Rori begrudgingly accepted a cracker from me and nibbled on it.

"What happened out there?" Torr demanded when she didn't say anything else.

"I thought we were leaving it for tomorrow," Rori grumbled.

"Not with me, you're not."

"Tell him what you told us," I said, holding out another cracker. "What you saw that none of us did."

Torr got laser-focused on her as soon as I said that. "Better start talking, Ror."

"Or what? You'll spank me?"

"I am not fucking kidding around. Start. Talking."

While I could understand her wanting to use humor to deflect, I stood with Torr on this. As her VP, and the one who knew her better than anyone else, he needed to know.

Reluctantly, Rori relayed the night of the bonfire to him. She held nothing back, not even the vision of the hovering, black swarm that had chased her. After she had first told us what she saw, she immediately clammed up. Like she was afraid we'd think any differently of her if she saw things we didn't. I couldn't speak for the others, but I believed every word.

The Sisterhood's goddess had spoken to her, infiltrated her dreams. She was the one being targeted by the enemy's deity. And now my biggest fear was that the enemy had succeeded.

"So you started feeling sick after this cloud thing had caught up to you?" Torr asked.

"No, I felt fine when I woke up. It's come and gone in waves, actually. Like right now, I feel good." Rori sat up in bed, leaning against the headboard as if to prove her point.

She did look better, with more color to her face and her eyes more alert than she had been.

"Why didn't you go after the four women?" Torr asked her. "That was the whole goal, right? You want to eradicate this cult, so why didn't you go after the ones who we're all but certain are the leaders?"

Honestly, I had the same question. LJ had seen the van leave and suggested giving chase. Rori had just woken up then and still seemed a little out of it, but she'd shaken her head and adamantly refused to go after the cultists.

Rori frowned now as she stared at Torr. Then she blinked, looking confused and saying nothing.

"Paloma?" I prompted, worry stabbing through my chest.

"I, um." She ran a shaky hand through her hair, the color once again draining from her face. "I don't remember making that decision."

———

Rori's fatigue took over soon after that, so Torr and I left the room to let her sleep. But that didn't mean either of us felt better about the situation.

"Something's happened to her," he said, pacing the living room downstairs. He was a pacer when he was worried. I was trying to calm my nerves by cleaning my machetes.

"The Rori I know would not have let those cultists get away. It's the whole reason she's out here! She's fucking bloodthirsty for them."

"I agree," I said with a pass of a whetstone over my blade. "But I'm not sure what we should do now."

Torr stopped pacing and stared at the ceiling as he sighed heavily. "I'm not sure either."

A few seconds of silence passed while I finished my first blade and picked up my second. "How was everything here while we were gone?"

His shoulders tensed and he rubbed his jaw. "Something happened here too. But...I don't know if I should tell her about it. Especially if she's got gaps in her memory." He started pacing again. "If it seems like she's there when she's actually not, who am I really talking to?"

"Fuck." I dropped my machete and my tools on the coffee table. "You make it sound like she's..."

"Possessed," he finished for me. "Like Tezca and Astarte have animal vessels. What if..."

"No." I shook my head. "Dude, she can't be. She would never let that happen."

"I'll bet that's the real reason why she was having all those dreams," Torr went on. "To make her sleep-deprived and weaker. To break her down so she would be easier to control."

Fuck me, that was horrifying. It all stemmed back to the night that we rescued Hudson. Their deity must have touched Rori the moment she spaced out.

And had its claws in her ever since.

"Has Tezca said anything to you?" Torr asked. "About how to stop it? How to help her?"

"Not a word," I said with an apologetic shake of my head.

Torr dropped into an armchair like he couldn't handle pacing anymore.

"Want to tell me what happened?" I asked after a few moments of depressing silence.

Torr rubbed a hand over his hair, his gaze staring at nothing. "We had a situation with the Bull. I've got him locked in the basement." His eyes flicked over to me. "How was the Saint on the trip?"

I shrugged. "Fine. His normal, weird-ass self. What'd the Bull do?"

"Tried to leave without anybody noticing. Got all cagey when I started asking questions." Torr rubbed his chin. "I think he was going to the Sisterhood to give them information about us."

"Why?" I asked, my gut roiling with disgust. "Why would he keep any kind of loyalty to them?"

"Dunno. Maybe they have some leverage over him."

"Rori would want his head on a spike," I growled. "And rightly so."

"The real Rori would, yeah." He nodded grimly before pointing to the ceiling. "But I'm not entirely sure Rori is up there."

"You're the VP, you can act in her stead," I reminded him. "And maybe if this Dark Mother has one less minion doing her bidding, it will weaken her hold on Rori."

Torr drummed his fingers on the armrest. "I'm hesitant to do this without Rori's input. Or if she really is not in control, someone's opinion that I trust."

"You trust mine?"

Torr drummed his fingertips some more. "You want to come talk to him and see what you think? He denied everything to me, but maybe he'll talk to a fellow ex-gladiator."

"We were never close in the pit, but sure."

I sheathed my weapons on my belt, which drew a raised eyebrow from Torr.

"You will not be using those. Not until I or Rori give the order."

"Consider it an extra security measure." I rested my hands on the handles, my grip loose and relaxed as I stood. "Shall we go?"

"You're a deadly enough motherfucker without those but fair enough."

Torr stood and headed for the basement door while I trailed behind him. It was the same room where Nella was kept and then ultimately killed by Devin.

The door swung open and Torr had barely taken a single step down the stairs when he froze. He brought his hand up with his index and middle finger extended. I'd also heard what he had and touched my fingers to his to show that I understood.

There were two people in the basement. Voices from down below had hushed as soon as the door opened.

Torr started down and I followed, drawing one of my blades. He was a strong fucker but didn't have a weapon. There was also no other way in or out of the basement, and they already knew we were coming. If we had more room on the stairs, I would have slid in front of Torr so my machetes would be the first things in the room. But our way down was narrow, barely containing the width of our bodies in single file.

We hit the basement floor, and I moved in front of my friend to protect him if necessary. The sight before us wasn't entirely surprising, but it didn't mean there was no threat.

"Saint," I said, eyeing the man sitting on a stack of crates next to the Bull, who was cuffed and tied to the support beam in the middle of the room.

"Butcher," the Saint returned in a bland tone. "And the Guard," he said with a nod at Torr.

"What are you doing here?" Torr stepped around me to address the Saint head on, apparently unbothered by the dagger the other man casually twirled between his knees.

"I came looking for my old friend." The Saint straightened, regarding the Bull with a look I couldn't read. "When he wasn't in the main house, I had a feeling he'd be down here. And I was right."

The Bull ignored us, instead staring at the fighter next to him. "So, you gonna cut me loose so we can kill these assholes and go or what?"

"You two aren't going anywhere," I hissed, drawing my second blade and stepping in front of Torr again. He needed to grab a shovel or whatever else was down here, because no fucking way he'd be running upstairs for a gun at this rate.

"Shut the fuck up, Butcher. You're so deep in her cunt, you don't see what's really happening." He glared at Torr. "Same for you. And fuck you for putting me down here."

"What the fuck are you talking about?" Torr asked with a surprising amount of calm.

"The Bull and I made a pact in the chaos at the coliseum before we left with you," the Saint said, his eyes on the dagger twirling in front of him. "We go way back, he and I. Before the gladiator pits and the prison they dragged us from. We came up on the street together, didn't we, Bull?"

"That's right," the other man said with a metallic clink of his cuffs.

"Once we were captured, we got used by the Sisterhood a few times, didn't we? Tested out to see how well we'd breed them."

"Yeah." The Bull gritted his teeth. "They gave me a daughter."

"And a beautiful girl she was." A faint smile touched the Saint's lips. "When was the last time you saw her?"

The Bull's head dropped, shaking sadly. "Probably about 3 years. I wasn't there for the birth or anything. They just let me see her for a second; I couldn't even hold her." He gave a dry laugh. "She looked like a little old man."

"But they promised you something, didn't they?" The Saint stopped twirling the dagger, his whole body going still as a predator.

"That I could see her again, be present in her life." The Bull's eyes lit up with joy for the first time that I'd ever seen. "I could teach her things, you know? Be an actual fucking father."

"In exchange for what?" the Saint pressed.

"Always remaining loyal to the Sisterhood," the Bull said without missing a beat. "That I would deliver them any traitors of the Dark Mother, male or female." His gaze snapped to the Saint, who had risen to his feet, the dagger gleaming next to his thigh. "And you agreed to do the same. We made a pact! I showed you a picture of my girl, and you said she was worth destroying everything for."

"And she still is." The Saint moved so fast, I'd barely registered what happened until I felt warm droplets of blood speckle my face.

I blinked and saw the Saint holding the Bull's head up by the hair, the red line on the Bull's throat weeping blood.

"Your daughter can still be saved but not by a father like you," the Saint said calmly. "I had a child by them too, a son. You know what they did right after he was born?" He leaned in close, directly next to the dying man's ear. "They smothered him to death. Right in front of me!"

Though he had been calm, the Saint was shouting at the top of his lungs before he was done. Torr and I could only watch as he clamped a hand over the wound he'd made in the Bull's throat.

"Oh no, you don't get to die yet. Not until I've told you everything." The Saint was shaking with rage, adrenaline, grief, and who knew what else. "I didn't tell Aurora about our little pact because I wanted to kill you myself. I didn't expect to have an audience, but here we are."

He didn't even glance at Torr and me as he said that. "After everything we'd been through together, swearing we'd always have each other's backs, you threw it away on *one* false promise from the people who enslaved us. Did you really fucking believe they would let you see your daughter? Did you?"

There was only a gurgle from the Bull as the life drained from him, choking on his own blood.

The Saint pulled his hand away, wiping it on his pant leg as his friend's life continued to fade.

"You wanted to please their Dark Mother so badly, I hope you rot in hell with her." Those were the Saint's last words to the Bull before the ex-fighter's head dropped forward and all motion left him.

With a resigned breath, the Saint looked at us, and Torr and I glanced at each other like we couldn't believe what just happened.

"Well," the VP said. "That was unexpected."

"This kill was not authorized by the president, I know." The Saint straightened, lifting his chin. "She may punish me as she sees fit, but I hope she understands this is proof of my loyalty. And that it was necessary to our cause."

"I'm sorry about your son." It was the first thing I could think of to say. "I can't imagine anything worse."

The Saint's eyes flicked to me, and he nodded slowly. "After it happened, I was on my way to tell him." He jerked his head toward the corpse. "I was so broken, shocked to my core, and I didn't really have anyone else, you know? Then, before I can get a word out..." The Saint swallowed, his face tightening into anger. "He tells me, all fucking excited, that he has a daughter, and they will allow him the privilege to be a father to her." He scoffed, shaking his head at the body of his dead friend. "He was always a self-absorbed bastard, but he was so goddamn happy that he didn't even notice I was a fucking shell of a human being."

Torr cleared his throat. "I won't say you're not justified in this kill. But when you're in a club, that's not something you can do independently anymore. You should have come to Rori or me first."

"I know this." The Saint turned his back on the dead man and his face was calm, if even serene. The very picture of that saying, *out of sight, out of mind.* "It will not happen again. I will accept whatever punishment Aurora sees fit for me. She is the one who saved me, saved all of us. Even if she casts me out of the club for this, she has my unwavering loyalty." Resolved, he jerked his chin down, planted his feet wide, and brought his hands together behind his back. "Take me to her. I will tell her everything I told you."

"This has to be resolved later," Torr said with a shake of his head. "She's resting from the ride."

The Saint's brow furrowed. "The ride wasn't that strenuous, especially for her. Is she not well?"

"She's just resting," I said to back up Torr's point. "She'll deal with you when she's ready."

The Saint's face broke out into a grin. "She's pregnant, then! Well done, such a blessing."

"She's not—" Torr's mouth snapped shut before he went on. I guess we didn't really know, did we? "Anyway, clean this up. Get someone to help you if you want."

"At once, Vice President." Back to his eccentric self, the Saint gave a slight bow and started rummaging around for a tarp as Torr and I went up the stairs. We could hear him whistling cheerfully before closing the door.

"What do you think?" Torr asked the moment we were out of there.

"Honestly? Good riddance. He just did what Rori would have done sooner." I let out a soft laugh. "I almost wish she had seen that."

"Same." Torr smirked. "Do you believe everything he said?"

"I do, actually." I checked myself over for blood before sitting down on the couch. "I think his weirdness is a mask, a coping mechanism maybe. When he was talking about his kid, he dropped all of that. I think that was the real him."

"I agree." Torr sat next to me, sinking down heavily. "Poor guy. Malik would have a field day with him."

He leaned his head all the way back, suddenly looking weary with his eyes on the ceiling. I followed his gaze, knowing exactly what he was looking at, thinking about. Our whole world was up there.

"She's gonna be okay. Right, Torr?"

It took him a long time to answer. "Fuck, I hope so."

Chapter 11

Rori

My sleep was fitful and restless. I went from feeling like death to perfectly fine and back again. I had cold sweats and a roiling stomach, and then I became exhausted and dehydrated.

But my physical symptoms weren't the worst of it. I heard the same voice that had haunted my dreams for the past two weeks. Only now, it was while I was awake.

Just accept me, Aurora. You'll feel so much better if you quit fighting.

"Can't stop fighting," I mumbled. "Have to hold on to...myself." My stomach protested violently, and I leaned over the side of the bed to retch into the trash can someone left me.

I had thrown up those saltine crackers hours ago. At least, I think I did. My sense of time was all distorted, and there were gaps in my memory. I recognized the bedroom at the safehouse but barely remembered riding home.

"What the fuck is happening to me?" I groaned into the sweat-soaked pillowcase.

I think you know, Aurora.

"Stop." I clasped my hands to the sides of my head, balling them into fists as I tugged at my roots. "Get the fuck out of my head. I don't want you here."

Oh, you will. Once you see what we're capable of together. Enough with this ragtag group of men you've collected. Don't you want to be worshiped? By thousands, no, millions of women? Women we have saved.

"No!"

I rolled in an attempt to escape the voice that followed me everywhere and landed on a hard surface, probably the floor. Crawling my way to the chair where my clothes were, I fumbled around for my holster.

Now, now, the voice chided. *We're not doing that.*

I blinked, and then suddenly I was back on the bed. Some time had passed, and it was now dark outside. Another black-out.

"Fuck!" I cried, sitting straight up.

Santos and Torr weren't in bed with me, but a massive, dark shape with golden eyes was.

"Tezca." I reached to the jaguar for comfort, instantly soothed by that velvety pelt and the rumbling purr that started up.

"I'm scared, Tezca," I confessed. "I don't know what's happening to me."

Yes, you do, the jaguar god said mournfully. *And I'm sorry, daughter. I wish I could prevent this.*

My hands froze on his back before they started to shake. "What do you mean?"

I know you can make it out through the other side. He headbutted my hand, then licked his sandpaper tongue across my palm. *Be brave. Don't lose sight of who you are. Remember those you love.*

"I can't—I don't—" A migraine hit me like a punch to the jaw. Pain radiated up my jaw, exploding behind my eyes. My stomach roiled again, spasming around nothing.

The next thing I saw clearly was Tezca, not on the bed with me but on the ground. His back was arched, fangs bared with a low, constant growl emanating from him. When I reached for him, he hissed and swiped a huge paw at me, claws extended.

"I should make a rug out of your pelt, useless male."

My palms clapped over my mouth in horror. I said that. Not *me*, the voice leaving my mouth was not my own. It was the one I always heard in my head. The one that first spoke to me in the Sisterhood's village.

Are you understanding now, Aurora?

"No. No, no, no, no."

I ran to the bathroom on wobbly legs, slamming the door against the wall as I crashed through it. Holding onto the pedestal sink for support, I glared into the mirror.

"Get out." My horror had given way to rage. My own, familiar anger felt good, felt like me.. I drew on it as a source of strength, a connection to myself. I hated this cult, and I would not allow its fucked-up deity to take up residence inside my skin.

"Get the fuck out," I repeated. "I'm not your fucking vessel."

"Mm, but you are," my reflection said cheekily back to me. "You're the perfect vessel, Aurora Wilder. I've waited decades for you."

"I didn't consent to this," I growled. "I don't want you. How are you better than a man, huh? Invading my body like a fucking parasite?"

"I'm a deity, child. I exist outside of the boundaries of time and space. Your limited senses can't perceive existence like I do. But if you allow me, you can. Don't you want to be divine, Aurora?"

"No!" I screamed.

The mirror cracked, and I slumped to the floor. I didn't know if it was the Dark Mother or me that did that, but I felt truly in control for the first time since I woke up after the bonfire.

Only I knew something was different.

I had control for now, but that rotten deity was still inside me. She had retreated for the moment, but she would come back and fight me. For control of my own body.

I rubbed at my arms, curling into a ball on the bathroom floor. I'd never felt so utterly violated in my life. My own skin was not a safe place to be.

I couldn't let her win, couldn't let her have full possession of me. But she had been right. My human body had limits, and it already felt like I was there. I was exhausted, weak, and felt so small. A kitten scratching at a full-grown lion.

There was only one solution my exhausted, pain-addled brain could think of, and it brought tears to my eyes. No, there had to be another way.

"There isn't," I whispered aloud to myself, looking out the bathroom door to the gun holster in the chair I'd almost reached.

The Dark Mother wouldn't let me do it. She'd stop me again. No one in my club would, especially not my men. Devin might've been happy to once upon a time, but things had changed between us. We were practically friendly at this point.

Even if I explained what was happening, if I said this was necessary to prevent the Dark Mother from gaining a vessel, they either wouldn't believe me or wouldn't be able to bring themselves to do it.

There was only one person who could do it. And he would be the only one willing to.

I climbed shakily to my feet, again grasping the sink for support. I avoided looking in the mirror as I splashed water on my face and rinsed out my mouth. Then I pulled on some clean clothes, as well as my holster with the gun still in place.

Tezca had disappeared, and I felt truly alone as I left the bedroom. The house was quiet as I reached the ground floor, but there was activity out front.

It sounded like a barbecue, with the sounds of conversations and the sizzle of something cooking on the outdoor grill. Through the window, I saw Santos throwing a football to someone. He was smiling, laughing, then running to catch the ball as it was thrown back to him.

Torr was at the grill, idly snapping a pair of tongs as he talked to LJ.

I ached to go out there, to greet their smiling faces with a grin of my own. To accept embraces and kisses, to be pulled into conversations and maybe even a touch football game. I watched it play out like a movie. Like I was outside of my own body, a ghost of my former self.

I couldn't bring myself to go out there. I wouldn't be able to hide the heartbreak of what I was about to do, the sorrow of never seeing them again. I couldn't subject them to that. I should just let them be happy.

I turned away from the scene in the driveway and headed for the back door. Going through, I closed it as quietly as I could behind me.

It was an unseasonably warm night, probably why everyone was outside.

I looked at the back porch of the house next door. He was standing there, looking up at the stars with his tattooed forearms on the railing, a beer bottle dangling from one hand. The fact that he was the only one out back solidified the belief that this needed to be done. And I needed him to do it.

"Hudson," I said, stepping off my porch.

His head snapped over to face me and he straightened, guarded and stiff at the mere sight of me.

"I'm not going to hurt you. I promise." I lifted my palms as I approached. "Can we talk?"

He didn't answer. His jaw was clenched tight, as was his grip on that beer bottle. Sharp blue eyes fell to the weapon holstered at my hip. Of course, my open palms meant nothing.

Moving slowly, I kept one hand raised as the other went for my gun. I placed it, barrel facing the woods, on the railing in front of him, and then walked away from the weapon. "That's my only firearm. You can hold onto it if you want."

His gaze flicked to the gun, though he didn't touch it. After a few seconds, he unclenched his jaw enough to mutter, "What do you want from me?"

I took a deep breath, trying to ease the tension in my chest. "I need a favor from you."

Hudson flinched like I'd physically touched him. "I don't do things for women anymore."

"It's not like that," I protested. "I don't have much time to explain but I..."

Oh God. Would I even be able to say it?

"I need you to take my gun." My voice shook as I nodded at the weapon between us. "And..." I closed my eyes and forced the words out. "Shoot me. Shoot to kill."

Hudson's eyebrows slashed down with confusion. "Why the fuck would I do that? What are you setting me up for?"

"I'm sorry. Really, I'm so sorry to pin this on you. To put you in this situation." I blinked back tears and sniffed. "But you have to. Please, Hudson."

He just stood there, staring at me like I was speaking nonsense.

"Please just get it over with," I whimpered, letting the tears fall. "Before I have too much time to think about it and back out."

He didn't move a muscle. "Why do you want to die?"

"I don't *want* to, I *have* to," I sobbed. "Or it's gonna use me to destroy everything."

"What is?"

"Their goddess. The Dark Mother." I was full-on crying now, so afraid that I didn't care what I revealed. "Their deity is...inside me. She's trying to possess me, and I can't let her, Hudson."

Chapter 12

Hudson

Holy shit, was she really asking me to do this? To finish what I intended to do the first time I saw her?

I looked at the weapon she put in front of me, then slowly picked it up. The gun fit comfortably in my hand, the weight of it dense and satisfying. With the grip nestled into my palm, I let the barrel rest on the fingers of my opposite hand.

Guns used to excite me. I'd nerd out about the mechanics and specs of various models. It wasn't even so much about the power or damage potential for me, but how the weapon was built. What kind of recoil did it have? What made one weapon feel like an extension of my arm while another felt clunky and awkward?

This one, Rori's, was nice. I knew immediately I'd be comfortable shooting it. My aim would be accurate. But as I held that weapon in my hands, there was none of that excitement from years ago. It was just a tool, a means of causing irrevocable harm. Harm I had no desire to do, but that was exactly what she was asking of me.

I didn't know how much time had passed before I looked up at Rori again. She stood there, waiting, shaking like a leaf and with tears streaming down her face.

"Please." She hugged around herself and took a shaky breath. "I can't let her control me. She'll use me to hurt Santos and Torr, all of you. Please, Hudson. I can't ask anyone else."

"What's to stop her from taking over someone else?" I struggled for a moment to recall the names of the other women. "Your cousin, Valorie. Or the Hunter's woman. If you're gone, wouldn't she just take over one of them?"

"I don't know, maybe. But doing this might buy us some time. Kill me, and then warn the others. Tell them what you did and why."

"Are you fucking mental?" I hissed. "They'll kill *me* as soon as they know what I've done! Did you think this through at all?"

A sob choked out of her as she wiped tears from her face. "I don't know what else to do!"

Her display of emotions was so jarring and strange to me. Everyone talked about how tough this woman was, that she was a natural born leader and nothing could faze her. I found that hard to reconcile with the terrified woman standing in front of me, pleading with me to murder her.

I felt...bad.

No, bad was too bland of a word. I felt terrible for her, and that in itself was one hell of a shock to my system. I was feeling sympathetic. Toward a *woman*.

I hated that she felt this was the only way forward, a premature end to her life that was so full of promise. I hated that she was scared. Scared of death, scared of hurting the ones she loved, scared of losing the life she would never have.

And I hated that she'd come to me for this. Because I was the woman-hater who had tried to kill her before. I hated that she saw me that way. I was...ashamed of it. I didn't know when the change in me had occurred, but I didn't want to kill her. I didn't want to use this gun, and I didn't want to see her cry.

So I pressed the magazine release on the gun and caught the slide as it fell out. Then I set the two pieces on the porch railing and stepped away from them.

"I'm not going to shoot you."

Rori let out a noise of despair, rubbing her eyes angrily. "You *have* to! Think of what she'll make me do to you. You don't deserve that, Hudson!"

Images of my past captivity flashed through my brain for a moment before I shoved them away. Malik taught me some refocusing techniques today, and I was already finding them useful.

"I don't want to hurt you," Rori continued. "I don't want her to use *me* to hurt you."

"That's not going to happen," I found myself saying as I stepped off the porch toward her. For some reason, I wanted to ease her and reassure her, make her less afraid. It was almost like a compulsion to be strong for her while she was falling apart.

"It could," Rori argued. "If she gets control of me, that could be the least of what happens. They want war, Hudson. They want to kill or enslave all men."

"And you want to prevent that?"

It might have been a weird question to ask, but some nagging feeling needed to hear it from her mouth. I might have grown more tolerant of being in her presence, but I still found it hard to believe she was truly different from the women who had abused me.

"Of course I do," she said, exasperated and without hesitation. "I *love* the men in my life. I love Santos, Torr, my fathers, my brothers, all the men in my family, even my grumpy-ass Grandpa Finn. I like the Hunter because he's funny and he treats Paige so well. I like and respect all the ex-gladiators who want to ride and fight with me. Shit, I even like Devin! I just want all of you to have happy, fulfilling lives like everyone else."

She started crying again, and I let free the weird impulse that had been gnawing at me since I first saw her tonight.

I came down from the porch, walked right up to her, and put my arm around her.

Rori resisted when I tried to pull her toward my chest. She looked up at me, her face tear-stained and confused. "What are you doing?"

I wasn't sure how to answer, so I said, "I don't like seeing you cry."

She continued to stare up at me, then let out a little scoff and muttered something like, "Whatever, fuck it," and let her forehead fall to my sternum.

Her hair smelled nice, so I lifted my face away in order to not be weird and inhale more deeply. My arm rested across her upper back and shoulders, and she leaned into me until her chest was against mine. My other arm itched to wrap around her waist but I kept it at my side.

At some point, Rori's arms went around my waist, palms resting on my back. She gave a gentle squeeze and sighed.

"We'll figure this out," I said. "But killing you is definitely not the answer."

She gave a little snort of laughter. "What changed your mind on that?"

"Well, I got pulled out of a brainwashing cult and into the real world. That tends to fix your perspective a little."

"You're already a completely new person," she said. "I mean, this is the last thing in the world I expected." Her fingers lifted from my back and tapped down again.

"Me too," I admitted.

My thumb rubbed over her shoulder. The embrace felt nice, different from the affection I'd started exploring with Devin. She was taller than I expected, her hair almost tickling my chin. The slight weight of her leaning against my chest felt good, grounding, like a heavy blanket.

We stayed like that for a while, not speaking. A shaky breath escaped her after some time, and she seemed to lean on me a little more.

"I'm glad you told me no," she whispered.

Before I could think about it, my hand passed over her upper back, rubbing up and down until I stopped abruptly with a realization.

"Have faith," I told her. "We'll find another way." Apparently, I was including myself in that *we*.

"Faith? Are you religious?" She glanced up from my shoulder.

"We all are somewhat, aren't we?" I leaned back from our embrace to meet her gaze. "We have them." I nodded at the jaguar, barely visible at the dark treeline. "Our vengeful gods."

Rori looked toward the big cat, her arms still around my waist in a loose hold. "Does he talk to you?" she asked, her tone curious.

"Just once," I said. "While I was in there. He told me to hold on, to not give up. That my suffering was ending soon."

Rori looked at me, her expression brighter than it had been all night. "He came through for you."

"I guess. He made sure you did, anyway." I rubbed the back of my neck with my free hand, the one that wasn't still around her upper back. "It's given me a lot to think about. How fortunate I really am. So many never got rescued."

"Did you see them?" Rori's voice went low. "The sacrifices?"

"Some of them. They'd drag me out to watch sometimes. I heard pretty much all of them." The look in her eyes wasn't pity but commiseration. "Did you see one?"

She nodded. "Got a bird's eye view." Only then did she step back, bringing her hands to her hips as she looked thoughtfully at the woods. "I want justice for them too. And the gladiators that died. Everyone who's been hurt by the cult since the beginning."

"There's too many to count," I told her with a shake of my head. "Not just men, either. Women who have tried to run away. The blood bags, the—"

"What?" She cut me off. "What are blood bags?"

"Men that they keep alive just to cut them so they bleed. It's how they indoctrinate the young girls. Once they start their period, they cut the blood bag and make him bleed every day they themselves are bleeding."

Rori's mouth fell open, her face going pale. "You mean, like..."

She trailed off, swallowed, and tried again. "It's a bunch of shallow cuts all over their body?"

"Yeah, usually avoiding areas with big blood vessels to prevent permanent damage. Nothing on the neck, wrists, the chest near the heart, but everywhere else is fair game. They want him to stay alive. That's his whole purpose, to bleed."

I hadn't told anyone about the blood bags yet, and it felt good to get it off my chest. When I occasionally saw those men covered in thousands of tiny slashes, both old and fresh, I sometimes wondered if my position was better or worse than theirs.

"God fucking damnit." Rori raked her hands through her hair before balling them into fists.

"Sorry," I said. "I probably shouldn't be so graphic."

"No, it's fine. I'm glad you told me." She gave me a weak smile, but her eyes still looked haunted. "I'm...pretty sure I know someone who was a blood bag."

"You do? Here?"

"No, someone from back home. A family member. He's, well, older than us."

"How much older?"

She shrugged and wobbled her head. "Fifties."

My eyebrows shot up. "Damn. He must have been one of the first, then. How'd he escape?"

"I don't know. He never talks about it. Not to me." She crossed her arms, frowning. "I suspected he'd been a victim of theirs after I started to learn more, but I had no idea it was...like that."

"It's a fucking nightmare," I agreed.

She glanced at me. "You've been having nightmares?"

"Oh yeah. They're routine at this point." I shrugged. "Talking to Malik is helping. So is waking up next to Devin."

A slow, knowing smile spread across her face. "So that's happening, huh? You and Devin."

I hesitated before answering. He and I never talked about keeping our 'thing' a secret or being open with it. I suspected he had a crush on Rori, so maybe he didn't want her to know? He wasn't the type to sneak around, though, unless he was being the Ghost and putting knives in people's throats.

"I had my suspicions," Rori said in my silence. "He did mention feeling something for you, from before."

I gaped at her. "He did?"

Rori's eyes went wide, and she placed her fingers over her mouth. "Oh. Maybe I wasn't supposed to say anything."

"Whatever." I waved it off. "It's out there now."

She cleared her throat. "Well, I'm glad you two are making each other happy." She sounded a bit stiff but otherwise genuine.

"Thanks." I glanced down at my hands, unsure where else to look. "Maybe one day, I'll be able to be with a woman again, but not for a while."

"Oh yeah?" Her eyebrows went up in surprise. "So this thing with Devin is temporary?"

"No. I mean, I don't know. I don't want it to be, but I don't know what *he* wants. I'm a mess mentally, and with everything going on… we haven't really talked about it."

Rori nodded, a smile touching her lips. "Well, I hope you two are together for as long as it makes you both happy."

Footsteps crunching over the ground made both of our heads snap to the side.

"Paloma, there you are." Santos approached with a big smile of relief on his face. "Torr and I have been looking for you." Once he realized who she was standing with, his smile disappeared and he hurried to her side. "What's going on?"

"Nothing."

"Nothing."

Rori and I blurted out the word at the same time, only making ourselves look more suspicious.

"We were just talking." She turned into him, accepting being tucked under his arm and leaning against his chest, closer than she had been with me.

"Talking?" he repeated like he'd never heard bigger bullshit in his life. "*You* two?"

"Yes," Rori insisted with a glance back at me. "We're actually getting along alright. Aren't we, Hudson?"

"Yeah," I agreed, nodding my head under Santos' hard glare. "I don't mean any harm to her, or anyone."

"Then why is there a fucking gun right there?" Santos jerked his chin at the forgotten weapon lying next to its removed ammo on the railing.

"I brought it," Rori said before I could answer.

Santos looked at her, his confusion mounting. "Why?"

Rori opened her mouth to answer just as someone pushed the sliding door open behind me and Devin's husky voice floated to me.

"The hell are you doing out here?" One arm came around my waist, the other over my shoulder to stroke my chest. His teeth had just barely nipped my shoulder when he noticed Santos and Rori. "Hey guys. What's going on?" He went stiff when he too noticed the gun and clip of ammo. "What *the hell* is going on?"

"It doesn't fucking matter." The voice came from Rori, but it wasn't her speaking.

She pushed Santos away with so much force that he lost his balance, windmilling his arms and eventually landing on his ass.

He returned to his feet just as Rori turned her gaze on me. Devin's grip tightened around me as he muttered, "Fuck," in my ear.

Fuck was right. Rori's eyes had gone completely black, no irises or sclera visible at all.

"Oh, now she's fighting me hard." The strange voice from Rori laughed. "Making quite a racket up here." She tapped an index finger against her temple. "So protective over these *men*, that's her biggest flaw. But don't worry. I'll make her *perfect*."

"Shit," Santos gasped. "It's taking over her."

"Hey!" Torr was jogging toward us now, and I didn't know if that was a good or bad thing for the deity gaining control of Rori. "You found her." He slowed, confusion hitting him as he took in me, Devin, Santos, and then Rori's demonic black eyes.

"You were right," Santos told him quickly. "She's being possessed."

Out of nowhere, Rori crumpled to a heap like a marionette whose strings had been cut. Santos and Torr ran toward her, and Devin released me to do the same. Her eyes, their normal dark green color, snapped open with a gasp of breath.

"You have to get away from me," she said in a panicked rush. "All of you, everyone. Get them out of here. She's taking control of me, and I can't stop her!"

"We're not leaving you," Torr insisted. "We can keep you restrained. We can—"

"That won't work!" Rori screamed in his face. "You can't win against a god! Get everyone to safety before she makes me kill you all."

"There has to be something—" Santos started.

"Yes! Killing me," Rori cried. "I came here to ask Hudson to do that, but he wouldn't, and now it's too fucking late." She stared straight at Torr, darkness creeping into her eyes before she blinked the inky blackness away. "If you love me at all, you will either shoot me right now or get the hell away. Those are the only ways we keep going."

"Hudson." Devin took hold of my arm, his feet moving like he was trying to lead me away.

But I was transfixed, held in place by some kind of grim fascination. I'd seen lots of terrified expressions, my own included. The brain moved the muscles of the face to express fear and terror all in similar ways, whether that was fear of death, torture, or the unknown. And yet, Rori's fear was unlike anything I'd ever seen before.

She was rapidly losing control of herself to something already inside her. I saw her hands working like she wanted to grab her men for comfort, yet she refused to draw them any closer for their own protection. Even now, consumed by her fear, she was only thinking of them.

"Don't be fucking idiot heroes and try to save me," she said. "I'm done for. Go save everyone else."

"Fuck everyone else," Torr spat. He reached for her, she backed away, and he only advanced closer. "You're all that matters in this."

"You're not fucking listening!" Rori screamed. She dropped to the ground again like a ragdoll and sprang back up before the guys could get much closer.

This time, Torr and Santos backed away, their eyes meeting Rori's soulless black ones.

"Are you really surprised, Aurora?" The entity used Rori's mouth to speak as she went to the porch railing and picked up the gun. "Men never listen." She slapped the loaded magazine into the grip. "Not when we say 'no, stop, it hurts'." With ease and proficiency that could only come from Rori's muscle memory, she pulled back the slide. "When we're smarter than them, they ignore us or steal our ideas."

Her eyes were black as tar now, without a flicker of the real Rori left.

She was really gone.

And the thing animating her body held a loaded gun.

"Hudson," Devin hissed, tugging at my shirt.

Everyone tensed as Rori lifted the gun in the air, a sinister smile on her face as she pointed the barrel at the sky. "Maybe you'll listen this time. *Run.*"

The gun fired and, like the start of a race for our lives, we scattered.

Chapter 13

Devin

The moment she raised that gun, my only instinct was to cover Hudson. I shoved at him, forcing him to start running while I stayed on his heels. Another shot fired and that kicked up our speed, our heads ducking low. The bullet never touched us, but it was close enough that I could smell it in the air.

"We've got to get everyone out!" Torr yelled, drawing his own gun which he aimed behind him as he ran.

"No, don't!" Santos grabbed at his arm, trying to wrestle the gun away.

Torr kept the weapon out of his reach, pushing on Santos' chest with his free hand. "Stop. It's not her anymore," he told the Butcher.

Santos started faltering. He couldn't stop staring at Rori, who was advancing on us at a leisurely pace like she had all the time in the world.

"She's still in there," he protested weakly. "We can't abandon her like this."

"Santos, listen to me." Torr clapped a hand on the other man's nape, dragging him along to keep him moving. "We *will* get her back.

But that thing is going to kill us all if we don't get out of here right the fuck now."

Another shot rang out, making Torr and Santos jump as a small dust-cloud erupted at their feet.

"Keep running," the odd voice called from Rori's mouth. "Run as far and fast as you can. You can't escape me."

Torr looked at me. "Evacuate the frat house, no time to pack anything. Double or triple up on bikes, I don't care. Just get everyone to leave. We're taking the main road out."

"Okay."

That was all I said before shoving Hudson again, forcing him to take a hard left toward the front door of fighters' house.

"You get everyone in the common areas. Open up the garage and get the bikes started," I said. "I'll go room to room."

We entered the house together and immediately parted, him yelling at the men lounging around the kitchen and living room while I hoofed it up the stairs.

I didn't bother knocking, just blasted doors open with my foot or shoulder, screaming at the top of my lungs that we needed to move. Thankfully no one was delaying too much, and the commotion I heard from downstairs indicated that Hudson's evacuation was working as well.

I opened the final bedroom at the end of the hall, expecting it to be empty, but stopped dead at the sight before me.

Rori held a fighter with an arm around his neck, her gun barrel pressed directly into his crotch. He struggled like hell, grabbing at her forearm to pull it away from his throat, while his lower body jerked and spasmed as he tried to get away from that gun. Apparently, possession came with superhuman strength.

The thing wearing Rori's body grinned at me, wild and maniacal. "I was hoping for an audience," it said in that strange voice.

Her finger curled around the trigger, and it went off before I could so much as say, "Stop."

The fighter's scream hit my ears painfully. Rori released him, leaving him slumped over to bleed out as she went out the open window. I heard scratching on the exterior walls, the groaning of the gutters and siding as she climbed.

She's getting on the fucking roof? I could barely process anything, not the possession that just happened or the poor, bleeding man on the floor.

I dropped to my knees, crouching over him as I withdrew a knife and cradled the back of his head with my free.

"I'm sorry," I told his wide-eyed, shocked face. "I'm so sorry. Go peacefully, friend." Fuck, what had he been called again? The Iron. I hadn't known him well, but he was a solid man, as far as I knew.

I brought my knife around the back of his head, and with a few quick motions, severed his spinal cord just below his skull. He went limp and quiet, and I closed his eyelids as I released him.

Severing his brainstem was the most painless, swift death I could give him. I hated that that was the last kindness he ever got, and right after something so horrible. He trusted Rori, believed in her and chose to follow her. Now that he was no longer confined to his body, I hoped he understood.

"I'm sorry," I said for a final time before getting up from the floor and heading back downstairs.

Hudson had successfully cleared out the lower part of the house, and I heard the distinct sounds of multiple engines running in front of the detached garage.

I burst out of the front door, sprinting toward the fleet of vehicles. "She's on the roof!" I yelled. "Fucking go now!"

Three shots rained down, making everyone duck and scramble. Several people were in the bed of Val's truck, which tore off down the road with a roar of the engine. I saw a riderless motorcycle and went for it, throwing my leg over and gripping the handlebars like my life depended on it.

"Hudson!" I called. "Where's Hudson?"

A weight settled behind me as a pair of arms squeezed around my waist. "Go, go, go!" he yelled in my ear.

I started down the gravel road with a jerk forward and could only hope everyone else was making it out too.

Some nagging impulse told me to look back, and in my mirror I spotted Rori on the roof of the fighter's house, her gun trained not on anyone escaping on the ground, but on the horizon.

I wrenched the bike over, turning it to the side. Ignoring Hudson's screaming at me, I followed Rori's line of sight to the white dove, flying away like a ghostly apparition.

I tapped into all my instincts, my practice, my muscle memory, because something told me I had never needed it more than this moment right now.

I let a knife fly at a distance I'd never thrown before. I put all my strength into that throw, hoping my force would resist gravity just long enough to...

The blade stabbed Rori through the hand, forcing her to drop the gun just as the shot fired. Hudson was now silent as Rori locked eyes, pure black soulless eyes, with us. She pulled the knife from where it stuck her, squarely in the back of her palm, and the wound instantly seemed to close back up.

Like waking from a dream, I jerked us into motion again, turned onto the road and sped to catch up with the evacuating fleet of vehicles. It wasn't long before I came up on a bunch of red brake lights stopped on the road.

"What's the hold up?" Hudson demanded, his grip tightening on my waist.

"They're talking to the guard at the checkpoint." I had to stand on the footpegs and crane my neck over Val's giant-ass truck to see. "They're basically dragging him into the truck."

"They need to hurry up."

It would almost be funny if the situation wasn't so dire. We were escaping for our lives from a sadistic deity set to enslave or kill half of the human population, and we were caught in a traffic jam.

The vehicles finally started moving just as a thought hit me.

Where could we even go? It was the only coherent question in my mind as we drove through the night.

———

NEAR DAWN, our fleet of vehicles drove up to what looked like a warehouse and a few trailers in the middle of nowhere. I was bleary-eyed and exhausted beyond belief but managed to follow the flow of traffic into the warehouse and park the motorcycle in the available spot.

Engines shut off and the large space was filled with the echoing shuffle of people getting off bikes and the low murmurings of conversation. The guy who had been at the checkpoint, he went by Slick or something, broke away from the crowd to address everyone.

"The trailers don't have much, but there's bunk beds, sleeping bags, maybe some air mattresses you gotta blow up. But before you go." He raised a hand and scanned the crowd like he was looking for someone. "Someone needs to tell me what the hell is going on and where the hell Rori is."

"We can do that." Torr walked up to him with Santos at his side. The two of them looked beyond exhausted. They looked haunted.

I nudged Hudson's shoulder. "You find a place to sleep. I'm gonna back them up, and I'll find you later."

He shook his head stubbornly. "I'm coming too."

Slick led us all to a sectioned off area of the warehouse. There were folding tables and chairs set up to make it look like a small break room or office.

The older biker wheeled around on Torr. "Start talking any time," he said, crossing his arms. "Starting with, where is my niece?"

Torr let out a big breath that seemed to deflate all his strength. "Rori's been taken."

"By who?" Slick demanded.

"A cult that really likes to murder people, especially men."

"And you chose to bring all these former gladiators *here* instead of fighting to get her back?"

Torr was silent for a while, as were the rest of us. We were waiting for his cue, knowing that he didn't want to just tell anyone what we were really up against.

"You were with the Demons, right?" Torr asked quietly.

"Still am." Slick lifted his chin proudly. He was in his late forties maybe, but only the graying at his temples and in his beard showed it. "What's that got to do with my niece?"

"You were there?" Torr pressed. "During the war that saved Four Corners, you *saw* what the enemy did?"

"Yeah. Some kind of entity that had a bunch of people under mind control. Craziest fuckin' thing I ever seen. Thousands of people moving in perfect sync, like some kind of hivemind."

"That's what has Rori," Torr explained. "She's under the control of this...deity that the cult created. It has her, and it's going to use her to lead them."

Slick went silent for a long time, his face draining of color. "You're telling me it's back?" he whispered.

"We think it's something new," Santos spoke up. "This thing has never possessed a human before. It wanted Rori. Like it was...waiting for her."

Slick's eyes snapped to him, then scanned over all of us. "You all saw this?"

The four of us nodded. "Rori had been fighting it for a couple of days," I said. "But it had been breaking her down over weeks, giving her bad dreams so she couldn't sleep."

"Fuck." Slick tilted his head back, eyes closing wearily. "We have to tell the Steel Demons."

"I'm sorry, I disagree." Torr lifted his chin, meeting the older biker in the eye.

Slick glared back, the two of them looking like they were getting ready to square off. "She's their *daughter*."

"I know. Exactly why we shouldn't call them," Torr said.

"They're going to rush in to save her, all four of her fathers. Probably her mom and brothers, too. And wouldn't this cult just *love* that? At least four, maybe six, men to kill, abuse and torture. All while Rori has a front row seat to it all."

"They won't be rash," Slick argued. "We're all far more seasoned in war than you. We've seen our loved ones taken, tortured, controlled, and been forced to keep a cool, strategic head about it. You're the one not thinking this all the way through, Torrance. You just don't have the experience under your belt yet."

"But we do." I stepped up next to Torr and Santos did the same, the two of us loyal soldiers. "We've seen it all in the gladiator pit," I went on. "And we support Torr. For their own safety, Rori's family should not get involved. Not yet, at least."

"This is our fight anyway," Santos added. "The Steel Demons have done their part. Let the Vengeful Gods finish what they started." Slick eyed each of us, even Hudson, who had come up to stand by me. I'd have to tell him later how much his quiet support meant to me. He didn't have to be part of this at all but was choosing to be.

"Alright," Slick finally relented. "Come up with your plan then, and quick. I don't want to tell my brothers you left their daughter behind to die."

With that, Slick walked off. He still wore a Steel Demons cut, the old leather soft and worn, his patches faded and fraying. I tried not to think of that grinning horned skull on his back as mocking us.

Chapter 14

Torrance

The warehouse and accompanying trailers turned out to be a temporary shelter for Valkyrie Network riders and refugees. I half-expected to see Rori's cousin, Carter, but he wasn't present among the small crew who was running things. I would have loved to get his advice, because I felt utterly lost.

I was president now, until we got Rori back. It was never supposed to be this way. I was supposed to support her, be her right hand. The fearless Aurora Wilder was never supposed to be taken out of the equation. And now that she was...

I stood from the bench, heading over to the barbell on the ground to do another set of deadlifts. My few hours of sleep had been broken and fitful since we'd arrived. My stomach was a block of cement, so I'd barely eaten any of what was rationed out.

I was not mentally, nor physically, well enough to lift such heavy weight, but it was the only thing I *could* do. My solace and my punishment.

The last thing Rori had said to me was that I wasn't listening. And that was so painfully goddamned true. Two people lost their lives because we didn't evacuate fast enough. Devin told me about the guy he had to mercy kill. Another fighter got attacked in the mad scramble for motorcycles. He'd been shot in the leg from the roof, then pulled off a bike and dragged away behind the garage. I could still hear that laughter coming from Rori's mouth, that unsettling inhuman sound that was not her at all.

Was she present during everything that happened? Could she see and feel what her own body was doing while she wasn't in control? I hoped for her sake that she wasn't there for any of it, that she wouldn't have to deal with the horrifying recollections that 'she' had murdered two people she had promised safety and refuge to. Controlled or not, she would never forgive herself.

I did deadlifts until my lower half was jelly, then I let my ass plant on the concrete floor of the warehouse. Sitting there in that moment of total physical exhaustion, the one thought I had been avoiding slipped to the forefront.

Would I have to kill the woman I loved?

My stomach turned on itself in protest, and my palms slapped the hard floor as I doubled over to fight the dry heaves. My skin broke out in a cold sweat, and that stubborn beating muscle in my chest squeezed with a painful ache. Every cell in my body rejected that thought, hated it.

I couldn't do it. It didn't matter if I had a guarantee from the gods themselves that it would eradicate the cult for good. I didn't care. I was not sacrificing her for some greater good bullshit.

Not only that, I'd prevent anyone else from doing it too. I'd kill Santos, Slick, anyone who tried to say it was the only option. I'd let the cult enslave every man in the world before I lost Rori for good.

I was getting her back alive and whole. The only question was how.

How the hell would I expel a god from its vessel without harming the vessel?

Once my legs got stable enough to support me, I worked my chest and arms. The repetitive movements became a blur, nothing but white noise to my thoughts going around and around again.

If Rori were here, we'd bounce ideas off each other. We'd just say what was on our minds, no matter how ridiculous it sounded.

We'd be serious, devolve into stupid jokes, then get serious again. We'd offer counterpoints to the other's ideas, things we never would have thought of on our own. She and I had completely different thought processes from each other, but together we could form a complete picture.

At some point, I stopped moving and just let my arms dangle. Staring up at the ceiling, I found it ironic and cruel that figuring out how to get Rori back alive and well was the moment I needed her feedback the most.

I needed her toughness, her compassion and level headedness. I even needed her anxiety, those racing 'what-ifs' and worries that she never shared with the rest of the club.

She was alone, lost, and it killed me that I couldn't be there for her, couldn't talk her through her fears and reassure her that it would all be okay.

It might never be okay again.

A side door opened, the hinges loud and squealing. Footsteps approached me that I recognized as belonging to Santos.

"Hey," I said without looking at him.

"You couldn't sleep or eat either, huh?" I felt his weight lean against one side of the rack.

"No. It all feels like a waste," I admitted. "Like every minute I'm not thinking of how to get her back is just time being pissed down the drain."

"She'd call you all kinds of names for saying that." He chuckled. "Talk about how rest and fueling yourself is important and you're an idiot for not doing that."

"Of course that applies to everyone but her," I replied. "You know how she keeps going until she's about to drop dead."

"Yeah," he said quietly. "I know."

After a few minutes of silence, I asked, "So what have you been up to instead of eating and sleeping?"

"Begging Tezca for answers," he admitted. "You'd think having a companion god would mean something now more than ever, right?"

"So I take it you didn't get much out of him?"

"Nothing." Bitterness hardened Santos' voice. "He kept saying I'm asking the wrong questions, asking for the wrong thing. Tried going to Astarte and got the same shit. Now I know why Rori was so annoyed with that bird."

I sat up from the bench, narrowly missing getting hit in the forehead by the barbell. What Santos had said alerted me to something, ringing some kind of bell. I just didn't know what exactly.

"What did you say?" I demanded. "Tell me exactly what you asked Tezca."

Santos frowned, confused. "Everything I could think of, really. Why this was allowed to happen. Why Rori, of all people. What did we need to do to get her back. How are we supposed to fight a god without hurting her. I mean, I kept going until I was literally out of questions to ask."

"And he said you were asking the wrong questions?"

"Yeah. I can't even imagine what that would be, though."

"So he *did* want you to ask something specific." I rubbed my temples. I was too sleep-deprived and hungry to be thinking about this, but I was onto *something*. I just didn't know what it was. "Did he say anything else to you?"

Santos scratched his head. "No, but Astarte said something like, 'To ask, you must also give'. What the hell, right?"

"To ask, you must also give," I repeated, thinking on it hard. "We need to ask some specific question, and in doing so, give them something in return."

"Like what?" Santos asked. "A sacrifice? An eye for an eye kind of thing?"

"No, that's not it. They've never asked us to do anything like that before. That's what sets them apart from the cult goddess. We've never needed to prove our devotion to them."

"Because they're much older," Santos said. "Tezca was worshiped by the Aztecs. Rori told me Astarte is even older than that."

"Yes, but they also weren't born out of ideas like revenge or hatred." I felt like we were straying from the original point, so I tried to refocus, despite a headache building in my temples. "I feel like the answer is right in front of our faces. What are we missing?"

Santos unsheathed his machetes and rolled out his wrists, making the twin blades dance in the air. I got the sense that he leaned on those blades like I did on weights. They kept him honed, focused.

"What's something that you give when you ask for something?" he said, more to himself than to me.

"I keep thinking of that expression, better to ask for forgiveness than permission." I shook my head. "I'm not sure if that's the right train of thought, though."

"Asking for forgiveness is also giving...what?" Santos began juggling his machetes, and I was forced to look away. "Giving someone another chance to trust you?"

"That's not yours to give, though," I pointed out. "The other person has to decide whether or not to trust you again. That's their gift when you ask forgiveness."

"Okay, what about permission, then?" He stopped juggling, and I breathed a sigh of relief. "Same thing, right? You ask permission and someone else has to give it."

"Yeah..." Something about that nagged at me. The answer was right in front of us and we were dancing blindly around it. "Permission is another word for consent," I mused.

"Uh-huh." Santos went back to twirling his blades, the sharp metal becoming a silver blur.

"What if you're not asking for permission to *do* something, but asking for something to be done *to you*?"

Santos' blades stopped abruptly, then he turned to me. "So by asking for this thing to be done, you're giving consent."

"Yes!" I jumped up from the bench. "That's it! The asking and giving at that same time."

"I still don't get it," he admitted. "What are we asking for? And giving consent to?"

I looked him squarely in the eye. "We're becoming vessels for the gods."

Chapter 15

Rori

It was such a weird sensation, being unable to use my own body. I felt like I was floating through space, weightless and adrift. I would have preferred to have felt bound by rope or even chains. At least then I would have felt something.

But I didn't even feel my toes inside my shoes or my hands shoved into the pockets of my jacket. When the Dark Mother used my lungs to breathe, I couldn't smell the trees, couldn't get a sense of the air my body pulled in to stay alive.

I could still see and hear, but I got the feeling that was only because she allowed it.

Despite all the nothing I was able to do, I kept fighting. I willed my body to punch and kick. And because I had no use of my physical throat, I screamed endlessly inside my own head.

Get out! Getoutgetoutgetout! Get the fuck out of my body!

She ignored me, but I knew she heard. She was like a parasite that had infiltrated my brain. A squatter coming in to make themselves at home where they were not welcome.

It was the morning after she had taken full control, and we stood on the front porch of one house, watching RVs and Jeeps pull into the cul-de-sac where my motorcycle club once stood.

All the motorcycles were gone now, even mine. Someone must have taken it in the chaos of the evacuation, which was good. I didn't want anyone in this cult touching my ride, not even if it was my own hand controlled by someone else.

The door to the biggest RV opened and a woman probably in her sixties came out, her gray hair spilling loose over her shoulders. She wore dark red robes that looked almost priest-like, with details in gold thread on her cuffs and lapels.

"Mother..." she whispered in awe, taking hesitant steps toward me. "It worked. Goddess in all of us, it worked!"

"I told you it would," her goddess answered using my mouth. "Come here, daughter of mine." She extended a hand, *my* hand, and the woman eagerly came forward. The Dark Mother held the woman's shoulder and bent forward to kiss the top of her head from our elevated position on the porch.

I felt none of it. Not the solidness of a shoulder under my palm or the woman's hair against my lips.

"You've done well for me, daughter," the Dark Mother praised. "So well that I have a gift for you."

"A gift?" the woman parroted. "Dearest Mother, seeing you in the flesh is the greatest gift of my life. I could not possibly ask any more of you."

"Even so," her goddess answered with a chuckle. "I've secured a man for a sacrifice tonight."

The woman's eyes lit up while dread filled my soul. "A sacrifice, how wonderful! We'll make it the biggest celebration yet. For our new home and your new form."

"See that you do," my voice said, as if such a thing was to be expected and a human fucking sacrifice wasn't absolutely barbaric. "This is far from over. They will attempt to take back these homes and this body."

I was screaming all kinds of obscenities and wordless rage, but my parasite ignored me like I wasn't even there.

The woman nodded sagely. "Should we wait before bringing the children, then?"

"Yes. Keep the children where they are for now. The men will try to reclaim their home and bring bloodshed, as they always do. And we must keep our future secure."

Folding her hands in front of her, the woman made a noise of agreement. "Where is the sacrifice, mother? I'll start preparations for tonight's rituals immediately."

"Come with me, daughter. I'll take you to him."

I felt something then. Not a physical sensation but a feeling being pushed at me so strongly, it felt like a smothering blanket. The Dark Mother was feeling smug, superior, and she wanted me to know it.

What is this? I wondered as she led the woman into the house. *How can you have a sacrifice? He already died.*

This one didn't, she answered me for the first time, heading for the basement.

She must have allowed my sense of smell to reach me, because the air was thick with the tang of blood. The woman following had no reaction, like she'd been here hundreds of times. How many sacrifices had this woman overseen to have no reaction to human suffering and to manifest a goddess that controlled a human body?

Heavy lengths of chain wrapped around a man's torso, tying him to the support beam in the center of the basement. There was a dark stain on the concrete under him, like a massive puddle of blood that had been cleaned up. What the fuck had happened here? The man's head jerked up as soon as we came down the stairs, and the hopeful look on his face broke my heart.

"Rori! President! Thank God you're here."

The thing in my body reached up to grab a chain and pulled it, turning on the bare bulb and casting the whole basement in an eerie yellow light.

Immediately the man shrank away. "President, what happened? What's wrong with your eyes?"

Ignoring him, the woman hummed approvingly at my side. "He'll do nicely."

The ex-gladiator looked at her. "Do nicely for what? Who are you?"

"I shot him through the shoulder and bandaged the wound, so his damage is minimal. He should last a while through the ritual."

The fighter's brow furrowed in confusion. "You're the one that shot me? And dragged me off the bike? What the hell is going on?"

I screamed the whole time and was ignored like I was in a sound-proof cage. My anger became panicky and I was begging, even bargaining for the man's life. I screamed at him to run, to fight, save himself. But no one heard a word.

Why don't I remember him? I wondered. *I remember the other guy she shot, but I don't remember this one.*

Because I wanted to surprise you, the Dark Mother deigned to answer me. *You thought all but one of your men escaped, so I just allowed you to keep thinking that. But don't worry, you'll watch the entire ritual too.*

Please let him go. If I had control of my face muscles, I would have been sobbing. *I'll...I'll get the others not to attack you, just don't kill him.*

I won't. My followers will, in devotion to me. And they will make sure it lasts the whole night.

Please, I begged. *Just stop all of this. I saved these men. Please, I'll do anything you want.*

You're already doing just that, the deity said gleefully.

I'd never felt such hopelessness before. Not even when Santos and Torr were captured. At least I was in control of my actions then. But now? This cult would find my men, kill and abuse them, while I could do nothing to stop it. Even worse, their fucked-up goddess would make me watch.

We left the basement as the man cried out and called for help.

The house was filled with women now, moving in and out of bedrooms, poking through the kitchen, and rearranging things like a bee colony taking over a new hive.

You can't do this, I protested weakly. *None of this is yours. You and your fucking cult have no right to be here!*

The houses will be well-maintained and taken care of, the Dark Mother replied with false reassurance. *They would have looked like landfills in another month if you'd continue to let men live here. Consider our occupation a favor.*

These are safe houses for people who need refuge! I screamed. *My family built these so people could escape from things like you.*

And now they'll provide refuge for the victims of those you housed here. Poetic justice, isn't it?

You're insane. How can you be so powerful and have your logic so twisted? My men were your *victims!*

Your human perspective is so limited. Of course you don't understand.

She had walked my body outside again to help with some of the unloading. A woman with a modest baby bump, probably early in her second trimester, was carrying in a basket of laundry when we approached her.

"Dear daughter, let me take that from you," my mouth cooed, taking the basket from the stunned young woman.

"Oh no! Dark Mother, please! It's no trouble. You shouldn't bother yourself with things like this."

"And you shouldn't be carrying things when you have back pain," the deity chided gently, taking the basket. "Get off your feet, dear one. Take some time to connect with your daughter."

The woman's face lit up with joy as her hands fell to the gentle rounding of her stomach. "It's a girl? Oh, thank you, Dark Mother! I've been praying."

"I can't reveal what is not meant to be known." My lips curved with a smile that felt like someone sticking their fingers in my mouth and pulling my lips apart. "But all things are either a blessing or a lesson. I know you will be ready for what comes."

My feet turned away, walking back up the porch with the laundry basket, when I came to a realization.

You don't actually know, do you? I said. *Being a god doesn't make you a fucking ultrasound machine. You don't know if she's having a girl or boy, and you can't control if that happens because even you can't fuck with how biology works.*

It's just as I told her. The Dark Mother set the laundry basket down in an armchair. *She will be blessed or she will be tested.*

You're really gonna make her kill her infant if it's a boy? And you don't see how fucked up that is?

I allow some males to live. The smugness in her voice returned. *Like your father. Like Torrance. Really, you should be thanking me. Neither of them would have been in your life if I hadn't allowed them to live.*

The confirmation that Shadow had been a victim of her cult was heartbreaking enough. But Torr's name was the last thing I'd expected to hear.

What's Torr got to do with you? I demanded.

His mother was a failure. Her tone became disappointed. *She was recruited too late and could not see the truth. She snuck away multiple times to see a man who was not one of our breeders. At our colony, she pretended to use the breeder but never did. When her pregnancy began showing, she led everyone to believe she had conceived in our way, the only approved way.*

I thought back to what Torr had said about his early life. He barely remembered anything before he was twelve years old. If he did, he never mentioned it.

She went to be with her man to birth the child, the Dark Mother went on. *Girl or boy, she would not have raised her child with us.*

Good for her, I declared. Whoever Torr's birth mother was, I was insanely proud of her in that moment. She probably couldn't leave the cult voluntarily, but she did what she could to keep her baby safe.

I was a mere spark of consciousness back then, but I could see all. I knew what she did. The Dark Mother sounded spiteful. I let her think she could keep up her double life for ten years. As my power grew, I inspired my true daughters to interrogate her. They worked her over for hours, but the bitch didn't crack. She was released just to use the bathroom, but she made a run for it. She hit one of my daughters with a crowbar and stole a car, then drove straight to her man and son.

And they evaded you. I couldn't help the glee in my mental voice, the pride and pain I felt for Torr's mother. How I wished I'd known her. *For at least two more years, right?*

Oh, I let them believe they did. Every so often I would ransack Rochelle's mind and give her terrible nightmares. It was how I learned to perfect you as my vessel.

You've got a knack for that shit, I'll give you that.

Eventually, she caught on that I was real, I was in her mind, and I would never let her escape me. So she talked her husband into leaving their son behind, because she was afraid of what I would do to him through her.

Smart woman, I thought.

I was not capable of taking a vessel at the time, and even if I had, I never would have chosen her.

I wanted to roll my eyes at how much this deity was sneering like a high school mean girl.

But I was capable of fucking up her mind, so that's what I did.

I hesitated before asking. *Is she still alive?*

Wandering the streets of Blakemore with extremely advanced dementia at only 52 years old, but yes.

If only I could close my eyes to squeeze out some tears. If only I could hit something, feel the ache in my chest that I knew was there, scream until I felt a satisfying, painful rawness in my throat.

You're so fucking cruel, I said with despair. *How can you really believe you're making a better world?*

Because I'm rooting out true evil and everything that enables it.

She just wanted to keep her son safe!

And let him grow up in a world where he can take what he wants without consequence, simply because he's a man. She would enable him, no matter what he did, because he's her little prince who can do no wrong. Sound familiar?

The need to cry and scream was building up inside me with no outlet. Yelling inside my own head was nothing like being able to use my body to express my rage. There was no catharsis, no way to process all this emotion. I was stuck in an endless loop, tied up and shut away while someone else took the wheel.

Men can live alongside women one day. The deity said it like she was conceding a point to me in a debate. *But that day is centuries from now, when all of their current programming is long removed. Their violence and oppression will be long forgotten, and they will revere women as the divine beings we are. Only then can we permit men to exist with us.*

I didn't know why I even bothered to argue. This being didn't care, didn't see reason or ethics at all. She talked about the divinity of women while puppetting my body, while telling me about how she tortured a woman to the point of dementia. She called infanticide a test and a lesson.

Nothing to say? the Dark Mother taunted me. *Good. I was waiting for you to be quiet. The less you think, the faster this goes.*

Faster what goes?

The binding of myself to this vessel. The longer I'm in this body, the more your physiology adapts to my being here. Your skin, bones, and blood will become my permanent home.

And what happens to me?

Oh, you're coming along for the ride, Aurora, she informed me gleefully. *I could shut you down and end this swiftly for you. But I enjoy your amusing little head noises too much. For as long as you're with me, you will bear witness to my new world. You will be deathless.*

Chapter 16

Santos

Torr only told his plan to three of us—me, Devin, and Hudson. What he proposed was shocking, and yet somehow made total sense. It felt right. As he spoke it aloud, it cemented into my mind as the only answer. This was what we had to do, what was meant to happen.

"Only the four of us can go." Torr's voice was steady, a general confident in his battle plan. "No one else gets involved. We don't even tell anyone else about it. This has to be us, because we were chosen for this."

Hudson, the only one of us who seemed unsure, scratched the side of his head. "I understand you three, but why me? I'm not part of your little group. I barely even talked to her last night before it all went down."

"And it was a pretty significant conversation, wasn't it?" Torr said.

"I don't know. I mean, I guess."

"You're also good with a gun," I reminded Hudson. "So you and Devin will be our backup with the more traditional weapons."

Torr looked across the table expectantly at me. "Are we ready?"

"In a sec." I looked at Hudson. "Can I get a word with you?"

He looked surprised but nodded.

"Make it fast." Torr rose from the table, his footsteps echoing over the warehouse floor. "The sooner we get that thing out of Rori, the better off we'll all be."

Devin followed after Torr, but not before giving Hudson a reassuring squeeze of his hand. Without another word, my former friend and I went to stand by a stack of wooden pallets for relative privacy.

"So, what's up?" Hudson tried to sound casual but there was no hiding the eagerness in his voice.

I pulled in a long breath, gathering my thoughts before speaking. "If you can promise me now, and mean it, that you will never seek to harm Rori, or any other woman, again, I can maybe forgive you for trying to kill her."

He opened his mouth to reply, but I held up an index finger. "I'm not done." Abruptly, his mouth closed and he nodded, waiting for me to continue.

"It doesn't matter if it's with a gun, your hands, or your fucking words. You are somehow important to all this, so I gotta deal with you being around. It's really fucking inconvenient to hate you if I gotta see your face all the time, so that's why I'm extending this olive branch. But only *if* you can guarantee that women, especially mine, are safe around you. I don't care what kind of relationship you have with Rori, if any. But if you even break her shoelace, I will banish you myself. That'll be the end of her hospitality. Got it?"

Hudson just stared at me for a while, then blinked a few times. "Yeah. I got it, but—"

"Good. I'm glad we could have a productive conversation after what happened."

"Santos, my dude." He huffed out a laugh. "You realize she's not exactly the damsel in distress type, right? She can boot me out herself if she wants."

"She can." I rested my hands on the hilts of my machetes. "But she shouldn't have to. She shouldn't have to raise a finger to exile the man who shot her on sight."

"I am sorry about that." All humor dropped from his expression. He looked and sounded sincere, the regret weighing heavily on his shoulders. "I really am. It was wrong."

"Why?" I wanted to hear the reason from his mouth.

"Because she was innocent. She was helping you guys rescue me." He shrugged. "She had done nothing to warrant me almost killing her. I realize that now, and I regret being so reactionary."

I took several seconds to inspect him, sizing him up from head to toe like I would an opponent in the fighting pit. "You're really different in such a short time," I observed. "That's a good thing. You look better, more alive. Well, even."

Hudson shrugged. "Devin's been the biggest help, honestly."

"Devin?" I noticed the flush that creeped up his neck. "How's that going?"

"Um, good." He blushed darker, avoiding eye contact with me.

"Just good?"

"Fuck, Santos." Hudson dropped his forehead into his hand and groaned. "I think I'm falling for him. Hard."

"Nothing wrong with that," I said. "I fell hard and fast for Rori. If you two are happy, then—"

"I think *he's* in love with Rori."

My mouth fell open and nothing came out for a long beat of silence. "Oh."

"And it's like, I can't even hate her for it." Hudson ran a frustrated hand over his head.

"Wait, what makes you think he feels that way?" Now I was confused. "They're either at each other's throats or ignoring each other."

"I dunno, it's just a feeling I get. He's...really, really good to me. But I'm a fucked-up mess, you know?"

"Who isn't a fucked-up mess?" I countered. "Even if the three of us hadn't been through the shit we had, we'd be a mess in some other way."

Hudson shook his head. "Just sucks when you're so fucked up that you're not enough for someone."

"Has Devin told you that?" I argued. "Or done anything that would make you believe such a thing?"

"Well, no, but—"

"Then it's not fucking true. It's your own brain telling you lies." I put a hand on his shoulder and squeezed. "You deserve to be happy, dude. Is that so hard to believe?"

He let out a long sigh. "Sometimes, yeah."

"I get that." I said with a release of his shoulder. "But try to let yourself be happy with Devin, as long as he's good to you. The longer you're there, the more you'll believe it."

"But what if I'm right?" He looked at me with a hard expression. "What if he wants to be with me *and* Rori?"

I thought on that for a moment. Devin in our dynamic wouldn't be so bad. In the rare moments that he and Rori got along, they had some chemistry. But I couldn't see him doing that if it was detrimental to Hudson. Devin had essentially appointed himself Hudson's caretaker, and it was a role I knew he took seriously. He wouldn't let anything interfere with Hudson's emotional progress, especially not if romantic feelings were involved. It could get messy though, I had to admit.

"That's a bridge we'll cross if we come to it," I said. "Rori will be the one who ultimately decides. And believe it or not, she wants you to be happy too."

"I do believe it, actually," Hudson said softly. "When we talked before you showed up last night, she was...nice. I might even like her."

"Well, holy shit." I crossed my arms, unable to suppress my grin. "If that isn't progress, I don't know what is."

"Yeah, well." He was blushing again, a small smile playing on his lips. It almost seemed as though he more than liked her. Hudson had a crush. On a woman. *My* woman.

No wonder he had all kinds of conflicting feelings.

I initiated this talk with him feeling skeptical, but now my fears were completely assuaged. He was far more likely to kiss Rori than kill her. And I wasn't worried about him with other women either.

"You'll be alright." I gave him a slap on the shoulder. "Thanks for talking with me."

"Yeah." He smiled as we headed to where Torr and Devin were waiting. "Not to get all mushy or anything, but I'm glad we're friends again."

I grinned at him. "Me too."

Torr and Devin were just outside the open warehouse door, next to the motorcycles we rode in on. Tezca sat off to the side while Astarte was perched on Torr's handlebars.

"We doing this?" I asked Torr, then glanced at the animals.

"Now or never." He looked at the dove, who cooed and stretched out her wings.

Likewise, I stared at the jaguar, unsure of what I was waiting for. "Uh, do we do this at the same time? Is there some kind of procedure?"

Just ask what you need to ask. Astarte sounded like she was sick of our shit. *We can't do anything until you ask.*

"Okay, well, you've given us no direction or help, so thanks for that," Torr grumbled.

You sound like Aurora, Astarte griped back. *As I've told her before, we cannot interfere with your decision-making. You must make these decisions on your own, with no influence from us.*

"Alright, I'm going." I kneeled in front of Tezca, meeting those golden eyes that seemed to carry all the wisdom in the universe. He returned my stare calmly, waiting as I braced myself with a deep breath.

"I'm asking you to possess me," I said to the jaguar god. "I give my consent for you to use me as a vessel."

For what purpose? Tezca's voice breezed over my skin and spoke directly inside my head.

"For the purpose of killing a destructive god," I answered. "And to return Aurora to us safely."

A new sensation came over me then, one that was strange and a little uncomfortable, but not painful. Something pricked my skin, like it was trying to get inside of me through my pores. Something entered my mouth, funneling its way down my throat. The same thing entered my sinuses, then my brain. I felt a gentle pressure on my eyeballs, and then blinked at a gritty feeling like sand or dust.

My occupation of you is temporary, Tezca said, now entirely inside my head. *I will only control your functions and perform my abilities when necessary. Even with me along for the ride, your free will remains intact.*

I blinked several times until the grittiness cleared from my eyes. My palms were planted on the ground, as were my knees. Like an animal, I was on all fours on the ground.

I sat back on my ass, meeting Devin and Hudson's bewildered expressions.

"Well, that was the freakiest shit I've ever seen in my life," Devin remarked.

"What happened?" I demanded.

"Tezca disintegrated into, like, this smoky form, and you basically absorbed him." Hudson nodded at Torr. "Same for him."

Torr and I looked at each other, then looked around. The dove and the jaguar were nowhere to be seen.

"How do you feel?" Torr asked.

"Alright. You?"

"Yeah. Pretty much the same." He placed his hand on his chest, then cocked his head like he was listening to something. "Astarte's like, 'What did you expect? This is real life, not a movie.'"

"Hah." I did feel normal, if even good. I felt sharp, alert, strong. Like right before a good fight in the pit.

There was something else there, a subtle presence other than myself if I paid close enough attention.

"I can feel Tezca in here." My hand came to my chest, much like Torr's gesture. "He's quiet, though. Almost lurking."

Torr snorted. "Astarte is *not* lurking. She is making her presence very well known. No wonder Rori can't stand her." He brought a hand to his temple and squeezed his eyes shut. "Okay, okay, okay. Sorry, geez." He didn't elaborate on what the dove goddess had said, probably for good reason.

"So that's it, then. We good to go?"

Devin and Hudson nodded. "Ready when you two are."

Torr and I gave one last look at each other. "Let's get our girl back."

And eliminate this unhinged god killing our sons and daughters. A low feline growl rippled over my mind. It took a moment to realize it was an audible, physically made sound too, not just in my head.

"Whoa, Tezca." Devin held a palm up. "Easy."

I rubbed my throat, wondering how he was able to make that noise through me. "This vengeful god's ready to kick some ass."

With that, and a final nod from Torr, the four of us mounted up and hit the road.

Stay strong, paloma. I focused the thought toward the horizon as we sped toward our destination. *We're coming for you.*

Chapter 17

Torrance

It was fucking weird, having a god just hanging out with me under my skin. The best I could describe was that sense of someone sitting near you, maybe behind you or just over your shoulder. You couldn't see them but you could *feel* them there. That was what it felt like, only inside of me.

Although she was a smartass when she spoke, Astarte was a quiet passenger for most of the ride. I got the sense that she was thinking hard about what was to come.

"Do you know what's going to happen?" The rushing wind over me and the motorcycle stole the volume of my voice, but I didn't need to be loud for her to hear me. "Like, can you see the future?"

The future doesn't exist for me. Neither does the past. Time is...well, it's not something that applies to me.

"But do you know?" I pressed. "What will happen when we get there?" It was the best way I could ask if we had a snowball's chance of getting Rori back without losing my shit.

I can see several outcomes. The end result will depend on the choices you make.

"Helpful as always."

You are welcome to fight this other deity yourself.

"No need to get sassy."

Astarte actually didn't reply with a cutting remark to that, keeping silent instead. Could gods be nervous? Because that was the sense I got.

"So you've seen all of human history, pretty much?" I wasn't sure why I felt so chatty, but what other time would I be able to ask questions like this?

Not all, but a sizable portion of it. I've seen genocides, wars, and the rise and fall of many civilizations.

"What's your favorite thing about humanity?"

An odd sensation tickled my nervous system, and I got the sense that Astarte was laughing.

What are we, on a first date?

"I'm just curious." Could gods even have favorites?

Your tenacity is astounding, she said after a while. *It's almost paradoxical, your ability to carry on and adapt. You keep surviving but pass on your trauma and coping mechanisms to your children, whether or not you realize it. It's fascinating how the youngest generations carry the wounds of several generations past.*

"By fascinating, do you mean sad?"

Sometimes it's sad. But also fascinating.

"Do you know about my birth parents?"

For years, I'd convinced myself I didn't care about them. They left me, so why should I care? I'd just lift to get strong as hell, sleep around, and keep my heart out of anyone's reach. No one could hurt me because I was emotionally untouchable.

But ever since Mystic Canyon, when Rori and I broke down our long-standing walls, I started to figure out that I *did* care. I wanted to know why. Why did they leave? Why didn't they want to keep me? All my life it had been eating at me and I shoved it down, pretending like it didn't affect me. But everything I did, pushing my body to the extreme and never letting anyone get too close, was a direct result of that hurt.

I see them, yes. Astarte's tone was low, almost mournful.

"See them?" I repeated. "They're still alive?"

You can't afford to be distracted, Torrance, she chided me. Then more gently, *Your past isn't going anywhere. You can meet it when you're ready. But if you want Rori in your future, you need to focus.*

A future with Rori was all I wanted. I still needed to man up and tell her I loved her.

Don't fight me during the moments I must control you, Astarte added. *Trust that I will not harm you as my vessel.*

"And Rori?" I asked.

The deity was silent for a while. *I will do my best.*

———

Dawn approached when we entered the valley where the safe houses were hidden. I didn't know exactly where to go, but Astarte guided me. Not like she was giving me directions but gently steering my body and therefore bike in the right direction.

I brought the bike to a stop at the first checkpoint on the road leading up to the houses. The little guard station was now empty, but it seemed as good a place as any for a final pep talk.

Angling the bike to address the others, I waited until Santos, Devin, and Hudson drove close enough to hear me.

"I don't know what we're getting into, so use basic common sense," I said. "If they're armed, shoot them. If they surrender, keep them detained. If they run away, follow them. Injure them if you must, but try not to kill anyone who's not trying to kill you." I paused to level a stare at Hudson, who stared back impassively.

"And if it's Rori that's intent on killing us?" Devin asked.

Santos' eyes went completely black, much like Rori's had when she got possessed. From Santos' mouth, Tezca thundered, "We will deal with Aurora and the parasitic creation inside her."

Santos' eyes returned to normal and he shook his head as if clearing it. "Fuck, that's weird."

"But can you make sure she survives?" Devin demanded, his jaw clenched.

It wasn't the first time I'd seen him so concerned about Rori. He was the one who bandaged her leg and carried her out of harm's way when Hudson shot her. The guy didn't make his concern for her obvious, except in the ways that counted most.

Astarte used my mouth to answer him while my mind processed those thoughts. "That depends on how far gone Aurora is already. We can extract the parasite from her body without causing injury. But until that happens, there's no telling how much of her is left." Devin's face hardened even more, a muscle feathering in his jaw. "What are we waiting for, then?"

I turned my bike to face forward, accelerating on the narrow dirt road to what had once been our home.

"What are the chances?" I asked Astarte. "That we'll get Rori back?"

I don't know, the deity answered. *She was possessed violently and without consent after being broken down for weeks already. I'm sorry, Torrance. The chances aren't good. Even possessing you as we are now, done in a way that is minimally invasive, is damaging long-term. The prophets of your ancient times were not stable because they had been possessed by their deities for too long.*

"Huh. Well, that explains a lot." My fist clenched on the throttle. "Rori's a fighter. I know she's still in there. She hasn't been possessed for long. She'll be okay."

I didn't know what the fuck I was talking about. But believing the alternative was not an option.

As we pulled up, the safehouses looked the same as when we left them. A couple of idyllic, two-story cabins with a detached garage between them, an open gravel driveway in the front, with trees surrounding the sides and back.

Only this time, a couple of RVs sat parked in front of the garage. Instead of motorcycles filling the driveway, there were Jeeps, pick-up trucks, and vans.

We parked the bikes and headed for the house on the left, all four of us on a single-minded mission. Santos was at my side, his steps falling into sync with mine. I couldn't quite tell if Astarte was in the driver's seat as our boots ascended the porch or if it was a mix of us. Either way, I felt like a well-oiled machine sent out to do my one purpose.

I shoved open the front door, making it bounce off the wall with a loud bang. The few women inside, maybe three of them, scattered, diving behind furniture with shrieks. Santos and I moved through the house which had once been so familiar but had already changed so much. Hudson and Devin fanned out behind us while we headed for the back door, as if pulled to the area behind the house on instinct.

We only took a few steps through when the women opened fire. They hadn't dove out of fear, but to grab hidden weapons that were stashed.

Devin and Hudson disposed of them quickly, without mess or fuss. A single shot of returned fire and the quiet, wet sound of a blade slicing open a throat.

We went through the back door, where we found the rest gathered in the wooded area before a grisly scene.

"Shit," Devin muttered from behind me.

Twelve women sat in a circle around a central figure, who wore a flowy white dress. The garment clung to a feminine body, thin fabric hugging hips, a waist, and breasts that I knew. That I had held, worshiped, and adored.

Santos sucked in a breath of shock beside me before a low, rumbling growl began emanating from his throat. Tezca was pissed, as was Astarte.

The remaining details of the scene filtered through in slow motion, like my brain needed extra time to process everything I was seeing. The lower half of the white dress and the figure's hands and forearms were stained dark red with blood. Behind the central figure was a man's body, strung up between two trees. And the ground was soaked with so much blood, I could see the reflection of the tree branches in a small pool of it.

But nothing shook me more than that easy, careless smile on the central figure's face. Because it was Rori's smile, Rori's face. It was Rori, walking barefoot through the bloodsoaked ground toward me and holding her bloodstained hands out in a welcoming gesture.

"I'm so glad you boys could make it," Rori said in a voice that wasn't hers. "You just missed the first ritual, but don't worry. We'll take volunteers for tonight."

"You will sacrifice no more of our children," Astarte said through me. "We're here to put you down. Cull you like the bad seed you are."

The grin on Rori's face faltered for a moment, her all-black eyes flickering like a lightbulb going out. And just as quickly as it happened, the maniacal expression returned.

"This is no place for old gods," the Dark Mother said flippantly. "Go back to your crumbling tombs and dust-covered idols behind museum glass. You are no longer relevant."

"You are no god," Tezca snarled, turning Santos' eyes fully black. "You are fanatical obsession with a voice and a body that you stole. You are murdering our sons and daughters because you have no true devotion, no real power."

"I've gathered more devotion in decades than you have in millennia. My people called me forth because they *needed* me. Where were you during the humans' Collapse? Didn't your sons and daughters need you then?"

"You're as short-sighted as a child," Astarte sneered. "You know nothing."

"And you," the Dark Mother raised a bloodstained finger to point at Santos and I, "are too late, old gods. I'm what today's people need. I'm creating a new world."

"This world is already here," Astarte replied. "And it doesn't need you."

Right then, my control was yanked away. Astarte had been true to her word that she'd only control me when necessary, and that time was now.

I lost all feeling in my limbs, all sense of space and balance, though I could still see and hear. Energy hummed through me, creating a pulsing pressure that wasn't entirely unpleasant.

Tezca had gone behind Rori, Santos' form visible over her shoulder. I lost track of Devin and Hudson and could only hope they were handling the other women as planned.

Rori took off running at an impossible speed. Astarte surged after her, the trees whipping past us in a blur, as if we were in a moving car. Tezca was on her as well, nearly on her heels. In a puff of dark smoke, Rori vanished.

"Are you tracking her?" Astarte immediately asked Tezca.

"Yes." The jaguar god stilled, only turning Santos' head as if to listen. After a few moments, he drew one of Santos' machetes and hovered his free hand over the blade, muttering something under his breath.

He held the weapon out toward Astarte, and I watched my own hand hover over the razor-sharp blade. My mouth moved and made sounds that I couldn't begin to decipher. The pulsing energy that I'd felt before seemed to find an outlet through my palm and went into the machete.

Internally, I started to panic. *Don't kill her. You said you wouldn't hurt Rori!*

This will not harm her physical body, the goddess answered me. *This will sever the connection between them. Rori's parasite will be forced to leave and no longer maintain a physical form.*

Relief filled me, but only briefly. *Rori will need to regain control for this to work,* Astarte went on. *It only needs to be for a moment so we can seize the deity and cut it from her, but Rori has to be aware of herself and fight like hell.*

She will, I insisted. *She'll do it. I know she can.*

Astarte was quiet for a while. *I only hope there is enough of her left to fight. I will give you control of your voice. Tezca will do the same with Santos. If she hears you two, it might rally her strength just enough.*

And if...there isn't enough of her left? To fight? I was terrified of the answer but still had to know.

We can still extract the parasite, but the vessel will have to be destroyed, Astarte answered gravely. *Aurora will die.*

"I found her," Tezca announced before I could reply.

He made some kind of gesture in the air, fingers curling into a fist, and then made a pulling motion with his whole arm. Rori's form appeared before us again, and the two gods taking us for a ride didn't hesitate.

With inhuman strength and speed, they each took an arm and pinned her to the ground.

The Dark Mother kicked and thrashed so hard, she was creating a human-sized crater in the ground. Pushing and fighting to get free against two other gods gave her the strength of an excavator in a human woman's body. Tezca and Astarte used that same super-human strength to keep her down.

Now, Astarte instructed me. *Use your voice to reach her.*

"Rori!" I called out. "Rori, it's me. It's Torr. I know you're in there, creep."

My woman's body surged hard against her restraints. She kicked a leg out and hit me in the thigh. The force of it would have broken my femur if I didn't have god-armor on. Astarte dropped my leg on top of Rori's pinning her down flatter.

Keep trying, Astarte encouraged. *Keep talking to her.*

"Come back to us, paloma," Santos urged, his voice aching and desperate. "We need you." Bravely, he lowered down to Rori's struggling form, brushing his forehead against hers. "I need you."

The Dark Mother spit in his face. "Fuck you, *male.* Get away from me!"

"Rori!" I yelled to draw her attention away from him. "I know you're not weak. Take back control of your body right the fuck now."

Something flickered in those empty black eyes, and another surge of pulsing energy filled my limbs.

It's working. Her awareness is rousing, Astarte said. *I can sense her, but we need more. She needs to fight harder.*

"Rori, we need you to fight harder." I hovered over that pissed off, snarling face with the soulless black eyes. "You need to kick this rotten cunt to the curb right now."

"Toss her out on her ugly ass," Santos chimed in. "You're strong enough. She wouldn't have chosen you for a vessel if you weren't a fucking badass. Show this bitch how strong you really are."

Rori's head threw back and let out an animalistic cry of fury.

Fuck. For the first time, Astarte sounded truly worried. *I can feel her fighting, but she's not getting the upper hand. What little control she has is slipping. I'm sorry, Torrance, but she's almost gone.*

A new kind of desperation overtook me now. A sense of such utter helplessness, knowing that what little I had left to give wasn't enough. And still, I'd offer it up anyway, because it was all I had left.

Give me one of my hands, I said to Astarte.

That isn't a good idea. Strong as you are, it's not enough to—

Just give me one of my fucking hands! Let me touch her before I lose her, for fuck's sake.

There was a moment of hesitation before I felt control return to the palm and fingers of my right hand. I used that hand to cup Rori's cheek. Her face turned toward me with surprising ease, those soulless eyes somehow amused in their lack of expression. Leaning down, I touched my forehead and nose to hers as Santos had earlier.

"Listen, Rori." My throat was impossibly tight with a choking knot. I was all but saying goodbye to her and had to get the words out.

"Listen, you need to come back." My thumb stroked over her cheekbone, still so warm like she was very much alive. "You need to come back not because you're strong and we need to save the world or some shit, but because I—" I swallowed, but the knot wouldn't loosen. So I forced the words out. "Because I'm too weak to go on without you." Something about saying it out loud made the floodgates open, and the rest came pouring out.

"I need you to come back because I can't fucking handle you leaving me, okay? Not you. You swore you wouldn't. You asked me to trust you, and I did. You said you loved me, that you'd never leave. So don't become a fucking liar, Rori. Don't you dare fucking leave me like they did."

Nothing else registered as I closed my eyes, unable to look into that face that was no longer hers. "I love you too much to let you go."

Chapter 18

Rori

A young man sat next to me. He was handsome with russet brown hair, green eyes, and a cheeky, dimpled smile. Some of his features, like the shape of his nose and chin, reminded me of my father Reaper.

"Hey, kiddo," he said quietly.

"Uncle Daren?" I tried to look around but couldn't get a sense of where I was. I wasn't even sure I had a head to turn. "Am I dreaming?"

"In a sense."

"Am I...dead?"

"No. It would feel like a mercy if you were, but it's not your time to die yet. Hades told me himself."

He was speaking words that I recognized but had trouble making sense of. I tried to lift my hands to see them, to stand up, to look around and observe my surroundings again. But the more I tried, the more it seemed like I didn't have a body.

"Where am I?" Panic frayed my voice, even though I couldn't physically feel any anxiety. "If I'm not dead, how can I see you so clearly?"

"It's alright, Rori. Just listen carefully." My uncle's face was solemn as he spoke to me. I'd never met him before, he'd died before I was born. But ever since Reaper told me about his younger brother, I'd felt an inexplicable bond to this man. Another father figure whose spirit guided me through dreams.

"You're not in control of your body right now," Uncle Daren told me calmly. "Someone else has taken over, so you've retreated to a safe place." He gave me a lopsided smile. "Turns out, that's with me."

His words began to make sense, and I nodded as the memories returned. "I always did feel safe with you. When I had nightmares as a little kid, you told me to come find you so the monsters wouldn't get me."

"That's right." My uncle smiled. "I figured, if I couldn't be around to protect my nieces and nephews in the physical world, I'd protect you in your dreams."

"Well, a real-life monster did get me." I tried to run my hands through my hair but felt nothing. It was trippy not having a body. "So, is this it for me? You and me, hanging out in Dreamworld?"

"No, Rori." Uncle Daren's smile disappeared, his stoic expression reminding me of my father again. "Your story is not over. But you have to fight your way back, harder than anyone ever has. It will hurt. You will be confused and disoriented, but if there's one person on earth badass and stubborn enough to fight off a god's possession, it's you."

If I had corporeal hands, I would reach for his. I would hug him in an attempt to seek comfort and strength. But all I had was this ghostly, detached feeling.

"Come with me?" I asked, despite knowing the answer.

Uncle Daren shook his head, the hint of a smile returning. "I have no body to return to, sweet niece. My place is here."

"I don't know if I can do it alone."

"You're not alone, Rori." A gentle sensation of pressure wrapped around me, and it felt like this was my uncle's way of hugging me. "You've got those men who love you on the other side. Your whole family. Fuck, every person alive right now wants you to win, whether they're aware of it or not." His non-corporeal squeeze became a little tighter. "And you've got at least one not-alive person rooting for you too."

Never before had I wished I could cry so badly. I wanted to make myself small and let him rock me until I was soothed.

"You'll still come see me, right?" I said. "When I'm dreaming, after this is all over."

"Hell yeah. We'll do the impossible stuff we can only do in dreams, like ride motorcycles over the ocean and shit."

I laughed despite my fear. His sense of adventure and fearlessness was infectious. What I would have given to ride with him while he was alive.

"You ready, Rori?"

With my nod, the pressure of his embrace released me, and I felt myself floating away. "See you soon, Uncle Daren."

His smiling face became smaller, like I was actually traveling a physical distance. "Knock 'em dead, daughter of Demons."

I STARTED to rouse as if waking up from a deep sleep. Some noise was breaking through the thick fog that had settled over me like a suffocating blanket. The sound was muffled at first, fuzzy and muted. Slowly it grew sharper. Clearer.

"Rori!"

I tried to blink, tried to wipe away whatever was blurring my eyesight, but neither my hands or eyelids moved. Where was I? *Who* was I?

It felt like I was at the bottom of a muddy, murky lake, looking for the surface. There were ripples and distortions, and everything was so dark, so unclear. I thought I could make out a man's face but wasn't sure.

Why couldn't I feel my body? Was I dead? Somewhere between life and death?

"Hello?" I tried to call out, but I didn't seem to have a voice.

Shut up! A harsh voice reprimanded me that seemed to come from everywhere. *Just be quiet, Aurora.*

Aurora. Was that my name? It was pretty.

"...back to us, paloma..."

Paloma. Was that also me? A nickname? It meant something in another language. How did I know that?

Memories and thoughts tickled at me with the more questions I asked, the more I became aware of myself. The answers were there, just out of reach. But as I woke, I stretched and grasped for them. Who called me paloma?

Santos! I realized with a start. My sweet fighter, the Butcher. A brutal killer by necessity and my loving, eager-to-please partner by choice. He was here. He was trying to reach me.

"Rori!" Someone else called my name, and an overwhelm of emotion flooded me at the sight of Torr. My first love, the one I never believed would be mine. He'd come for me too.

I tried calling out to both of them, but the fog blanketing me darkened and became heavier. It dragged me down like an anchor, and the faces of my men became murky again.

Wait, who were they?

Torr! Santos! Voicelessly, I screamed out their names, trying to reach them while also keeping them in my mind, my memory. But they were slipping away so easily, like water through my hands.

I was grasping at hundreds of tiny, fragile threads, trying to keep everything together without losing again. My own name. My men. Who I was. My family. What happened to me. What I was fighting for.

Hold onto yourself, Aurora. Another voice that seemed to come from everywhere, but different than the first one. This one was masculine, warm. Somehow incredibly powerful and gentle. *Hold onto yourself. Do not lose sight of who you are.*

Who are you? I tried to scream into the silent, empty void pressing in all around me.

Louder. Use your voice. A third person was talking to me, feminine and familiar. This person had made me feel...annoyed. Frustrated. And yet I had immense respect for them. *No matter what she tells you, do not stop fighting. You're a daughter of Demons, so give her hell.*

"I don't know what's happening!" The sound of my own voice was shocking to me. I could hear myself!

At the same time, I felt myself pulled down further, the oppressive weight on me even more restrictive. My memories, my loves, and my awareness were further away than ever.

Look at his face, this man you love, the third voice commanded me. *Don't lose sight of him. Don't you dare forget him, Aurora.*

He was barely visible through the fog and the vast distance between us, but I saw the tension in his brow, the slope of his nose. His lips trembled as they moved and I strained to hear him. A tear tracked down his face. Why was he crying? Who was he, again?

"...don't become a fucking liar, Rori. Don't you dare fucking leave me like they did."

A tear dripped from his nose onto my lips, and holy shit, I could *feel* it.

"I love you too much to let you go."

"Torr!" I cried out with all the strength I could gather. "I'm never fucking leaving you, meathead. You're mine. I love you. I will never be someone who abandons you."

It felt like trying to push a house off my chest, but I fought against that oppressive force holding me down with renewed vigor.

Torr's face became clearer, his heartbroken beautiful face. One day I would roast him for crying over me, but I needed to reach him first. He thought he was losing me, and I couldn't put him through that. I needed to kiss those tears away, hold him and tell him I was here, I was coming. And I would never leave him.

The more I fought against the current trying to drag me down, the more I remembered. The more of myself I regained.

I'm Aurora Wilder, president of the Vengeful Gods MC. I'm the eldest daughter of the Steel Demons MC. My twin brother is Daren. My two lovers are Torr and Santos. A deity has possessed me against my will, and for that, I'm one pissed off bitch.

For every new piece of myself I remembered, the invasive force inside me tried even harder to drag me back under.

Your vessel is mine. You are my prisoner, Aurora!

"Fuck you!" I screamed back. My throat, my actual physical throat ached from the scream, and it felt good. "Get the fuck out of my body!"

You can't get rid of me! You are mine.

"Go cease to exist, you rotten cunt! Fuck the hell off!"

I was *just* there. I could feel cool dirt beneath me, felt the weight of limbs pinning me down. I moved my own eyes, my own head, and I could see my men's tense faces.

"Torr! Santos!" I screamed so loud, my lungs ached. "I'm here! I see you!"

But something was wrong. Santos' eyes went completely black and Torr's completely white.

Over my body, which seemed to be lying face up on the ground, Torr held his hands out, palm up, as if offering something to Santos on the other side of me. In response, Santos raised his machete over his head.

"No, what are you doing?" I demanded, now overrun by fear. "It's me! Santos, I love you."

He brought the blade down in a smooth arc with no hesitation. I felt the blade tear through me and screamed at the blinding pain.

I felt like I'd climbed up the rocky face of a cliff bare-handed and maimed to reach them. I'd used all my strength, fought to hold onto every little scrap of myself, only for them to toss me back down, hurtling toward my death.

That machete severed the last tie I had. The final thing connecting me to the men I loved.

In a freefall, I hurtled through darkness until there was nothing left.

Chapter 19

Hudson

The sight of Rori was terrifying. She was every bit an evil apparition from a horror movie. The white slip dress covered in blood. Those empty black eyes. I felt the evil from her like the weight of a boot on my chest. She was pure hatred, not the scared woman who ran to me because she wanted to sacrifice herself.

Torr and Santos closed in on her while the circle of women jumped up and tried to scatter.

I fell back on my weapons training and my orders from Torr. A cluster of women darted to the left, and I raised my gun to fire warning shots a few feet ahead of them. They stopped short, lifting their arms to cover their faces as they shrieked.

"Come quietly and you won't be harmed!" Devin called out.

The women slowly lowered themselves to all fours, hands splayed on the ground in a clear picture of surrender. I relaxed, allowing my aim to lower, and that was when they struck.

One was faster than the others, pulling a gun out of seemingly nowhere and firing off a shot before Devin or I realized what happened. By the second shot, our brains had caught up and we went diving for cover, flattening ourselves against a tree trunk.

"Well, so much for that," Devin hissed. He had two knives in each hand, slotted into the space between his fingers like claws. "You alright?"

"Yeah, you?"

"Fan-fucking-tastic. I love it when guns are just hidden in the leaf litter on the ground."

My breath came hard out of my chest and I tried to quiet it, listening for footsteps, voices, any clues about where our enemy was located.

"Shoot to kill," Devin reminded me. "And don't let any get away. Pretty sure they're all armed at this point."

"I know."

A month ago, that would have thrilled me. How many times over the years had I fantasized about killing these people?

Now, there was no pleasure, no surging satisfaction at the prospect of taking lives from those who had taken so much from me. I only wanted to see this through, to do what was necessary to get through another day. And maybe see a future where this cult didn't exist.

"Hey." Devin was distracted, peeking around the tree, and didn't answer me. As he pulled back to cover himself, I made sure he paid attention.

The kiss was short, but I made it count. I took my fill of his lips, swiping my tongue against his, and pulled away before he could react.

He stared at me, surprised and a little breathless, before he smirked. "What was that for?"

I shrugged, re-checking the ammo in my weapon under his heavy stare. "Just good luck, I guess."

He slid a hand around my neck, squeezing my nape as he leaned his forehead on mine. "We'll celebrate properly when this is over." It was a promise of delicious things, of touch that felt good. Orgasms for pleasure, not as a means to procreate.

Devin was exactly what I needed, when I needed it. He was both a friend and a welcome reset of my sexual hardwiring. I never thought I'd be into men. And maybe I wasn't, generally. Maybe it was just him.

I thought back to the conversation I had with Santos before riding out here. The swirling mess of my thoughts over the last few days had culminated into that conclusion the moment I voiced it. The guy I was sleeping with also had a thing for Rori.

And...maybe I did too.

That conversation would have to come much later though, if Rori or any of us even survived to that point.

Devin and I took turns covering each other, shooting at our attackers. He was decent with a gun, though I was better. He wanted to save his knives for guaranteed kills, so they stayed in his spare hand while he shot with the other.

I was damn lucky to be with an ambidextrous man.

After exchanging fire for several minutes, a flurry of movement caught my eye on the far side of the house.

"They're up to something over there," I said to Devin once we back-flatted against the tree again.

"Gonna have to be a lot more specific." He peeked around and let a knife fly, dropping one of our attackers in an instant.

"Don't know, I just saw movement around a corner."

"Well, shit. We're pinned down here for a minute." He returned to our cover and glanced at me. "How do you think Torr and Santos are doing?"

"Hopefully better than us." The worst thing about a shootout like this, where we were outnumbered five to one, was that it was time-consuming. I had no doubt we'd win. We were the better shots for sure, but there were simply more bullets flying toward us than away. We had to be careful as we decreased that number and gained the upper hand.

So far we'd dropped three of the women shooting at us. Only seven more to go. I could tell they weren't particularly experienced or skilled, but they had more than a rudimentary introduction to guns.

"Did you hear that?" I could barely hear it over the ringing in my ears, but there was some new sound in the air.

"Yeah." Devin cast a worried glance toward where I saw movement earlier. "Sounded like a car starting."

Not even a minute later, a Jeep shot out from where it had been hidden on the far side of the house. There were two women inside, the driver white-knuckling the steering wheel as she drove onto the main road, heading away from the safe houses.

"Fuck!" I trained my gun on the tires, firing at those increasingly smaller targets as they got further away.

Bark and splinters exploded near my ear and I ducked on instinct, covering my eyes. Our shooters had taken advantage of the distraction.

"We have to go after them." Devin grabbed my shirt at the back of my neck to lift my head up. "You alright?"

I blinked several times. "Yeah." Probably got some splinters in my cheek and ear canal but my eyes were fine.

"We gotta run for the bikes," he said. "You with me?"

"Yeah, I'll cover you. On three. Ready?"

We counted together, then I sprang out from behind the tree, running as fast as I could while returning fire. One more woman dropped.

Devin reached the motorcycles, starting mine and then his own while I blocked their line of sight to him.

"I got you, let's go!" he hollered.

Putting all my trust in him, I turned my back to our attackers to mount my motorcycle. All I saw was a flash of metal catching the sunlight before three more dropped dead.

He was already tearing off down the road, and I leaned down over my handlebars, accelerating hard to catch up. We were still being shot at, and I wouldn't put it past them to climb into another vehicle and pursue us.

As chaotic as everything was right then, we had to keep our eye on the prize in front of us.

I caught up to Devin, slightly behind and flanking him. We were driving through the dust cloud kicked up by the Jeep ahead of us, our targets a dark silhouette just on the other side.

"You shoot their tires!" Devin yelled. "I'll cover us from the back."

I nodded and sped up to get ahead of him. Dust and gravel were killing my eyes but I needed them. I didn't dare blink as I came within twenty yards of the Jeep's bumper. Driving the bike with one hand, I raised my firing arm and tried my best to take careful aim. I could not afford to fuck this up. They could not get away.

The car started swerving just as I fired. Yeah it sucked for my aim, but that would be a boon if they rolled that damn Jeep for us. Even better if they went into a ravine or something.

I kept steady, following their movement with my eyes and my gun. When a clear shot lined up for me, I didn't hesitate. I fired.

And heard the click of an empty magazine.

"Fuck!" I roared. I needed two hands to reload and didn't feel confident about going hands-free on the bike. Reloading would take a split second though, and I fucking *needed* these shots.

In the moment I lifted my hand away to reach into my pocket, a cry of pain had me wrenching around to look behind me. Devin was nearly facedown on his dashboard, clutching his shoulder, which was wet and stained with dark blood.

That was all it took for me to lose control of the motorcycle. Not thinking about anything else, I tried to turn my whole body. I forgot I was driving a vehicle at all and tried to *run* to the man who drew me out of the darkness, who showed me what it was like to be human again.

The ground hit me hard with a full-body slap. My back, my chest, my ass. I got hit all over as I went rolling. Eventually I stopped, but the world kept spinning. Still, I forced myself up, knowing we were still being shot at.

"Devin!" I called, scanning the wobbly landscape for any sign of him as I fought to get my feet under me.

A massive dark shape zoomed past me, kicking up a massive cloud of dust. Another car?

"Devin!" I spun around helplessly, a sitting duck for our attackers, but no way in hell could I function in this fucked up place without him.

"I'm okay!"

The relief took nearly all of the strength from my legs, but I stayed upright as I went toward the sound of his voice.

Devin was still straddling his motorcycle, his feet planted on the ground, engine at a low rumble as he breathed hard, gripping his shoulder.

"They got a lucky shot on me," he panted, grimacing with pain. "But I think it went all the way through, so there's that silver lining."

Once I knew he was okay, reality hit me like that fall I'd just taken. "I let them get away."

Together we looked at the horizon, where a now-distant dust cloud surrounded two vehicles shrinking on the horizon as they drove away.

"Fuck." My hands tore through my hair, which I wanted to rip out in frustration. "Goddamnit, I fucked that up so bad."

"We'll figure something out," Devin said wearily. "It'll be okay, Hud."

But I wasn't ready to stop being pissed off yet. I wanted nothing more in the world than to eradicate this cult. I was a sharpshooting champion in my teens. Sure, I was out of practice, but I was still fucking accurate enough to make hits. This should have been the easiest fucking task for me, and I fucked it up.

"You were worried about me." Devin could sense the anger pouring off me, it seemed. "I shouldn't have yelled like a little bitch and distracted you."

"Not your fault. Getting shot fucking hurts."

"You're telling me," he groaned, tentatively lifting his hand from his bad shoulder.

Guilt shot through me. Here I was, throwing a pity party for myself, relatively unscathed, while Devin had actually been injured.

"Come on, let's get that taken care of." I pulled off my jacket and then my shirt so he would have something to stem the bleeding with.

Once we had his shoulder wrapped up, I got on his bike and he settled in behind me, holding my waist with his good arm.

"Do you think they got Rori back?" Devin rested his chin on my shoulder.

"Guess we'll find out in a sec." I accelerated gently, heading back for the safe houses.

"She'll chew us the fuck out for failing if she is back," Devin said. "Thing is, I'm kind of hoping for it."

"Me too," I admitted.

Once I parked in front of the house, Torr and Santos came around the side, both of them looking as somber as pallbearers at a funeral. Torr held a limp, unresponsive Rori cradled to his chest.

"Oh God..." Devin trailed off mournfully.

I helped him off the bike, then we hurried over to the two men who looked like broken shells of themselves.

"Is she...?" I didn't dare finish the question.

"She's breathing and has a pulse," Santos said flatly, his eyes vacant. "But we don't know if she's...there."

Torr carried her wordlessly into the house, assumedly to bathe her and put her in bed. She was covered in dirt and leaf litter on top of the blood that had already coated her arms, legs, and dress.

"What happened?" Devin demanded. "Is Tezca still...in you?"

Santos shook his head. "The gods left us as soon as the deed was done. They drew the Dark Mother out and cut her away from Rori, but..." He pulled in a shaky breath, looking as if he was moments away from tears. "She fought so fucking hard. We don't...we just don't know if there's anything left of her."

"Can you find out?" I asked.

"If she wakes up."

"Fuck." I was saying that a lot today. "I'm so sorry, Santos."

He pulled in another breath, clearing his throat as he composed himself. "How'd you guys do? I saw some bodies. You get 'em all?"

"No," I said on a big sigh. "Two vehicles got away. I ran out of ammo, heard Devin take fire behind me and I just...couldn't keep it together."

Santos' head jerked toward Devin, as if noticing his injury for the first time. "You okay?"

"All things considered, yeah." Devin tried hard not to grimace. "I'll live."

Santos returned his focus to me. "How many people total got away?"

"I think five. There were two in the first car we chased. Then I'm pretty sure there were three in the one after us."

Santos nodded. "I'll let Torr know as soon as...you know, as soon as he's ready to think about something else."

"Yeah, of course."

"I'll see who I can call to get that looked at," Santos said to Devin before heading into the house, no doubt to check on his woman who may or may not be lost for good.

I turned to Devin with a sigh. "Let's find some clean gauze and alcohol until you can get some real medical attention."

"Sounds great."

We searched through the fighters' house, going through the motions while the big picture situation began to sink in.

The Sisters of Bathory might not have their goddess anymore, but they would regroup and, eventually, retaliate.

And we just might have lost our best weapon against them.

Chapter 20

Torrance

Rori wasn't waking up.

I lost track of everything outside of her. It might have been a few days that had passed or a month. I didn't know. When I didn't keel over from exhaustion, I spent every waking moment staring at her face, willing those eyes to open, those lips to part.

I was only distantly aware of the movement around me. The club had moved back into the safehouses. I must have called them back at some point. Or maybe Santos did. It was all a haze outside of Rori.

Astarte returned in her dove form, as did Tezca as a jaguar. They often watched over her with me.

"Please tell me," I implored the gods. "Just tell me if I'm getting her back or not."

That's her decision, Astarte told me helpfully.

"Decision? She's fucking comatose; she can't make decisions!"

She has the power to return. She only needs to find and seize it, Tezca added, only slightly more helpful.

"So she *can* come back." I said. "If she can, then she will."

She is lost. She must find her way back.

I dropped my head into my hands, but that meant I wasn't looking at Rori anymore, so I lifted it up again.

"Come on, creep." I'd forgotten how many times I had repeated those words to her. "I know you heard me back then. I *know* you won't leave me."

Not a single twitch of movement on her face. Time passed. Santos entered and left the room. Motorcycles roared in the distance. None of it mattered.

At some point, I felt the weight of someone's hand on my shoulder, Santos' hand.

"Torr, you with me?" Apparently he'd been saying my name for a while.

"Yeah." I rubbed my weary eyes. "What's up?"

"A couple of guys just rode up. They say they're Rori's dad and uncle?"

I shot up out of the chair, panic lighting a fire under my ass, and stared at him. "What are they doing here?"

Santos shrugged. "I dunno, just coming to say hi, I guess."

"Shit." I rubbed my face hard. "Fuck. What do we tell them?"

"The truth, I assume." His eyes scanned over Rori as if looking for any changes in her condition. "They did this kind of thing back in their day, right? Maybe they can help—"

"First, they'll murder us for letting this happen to her," I groaned. "Although it's not like we don't deserve it."

This was going to be a shitshow. Aside from calling her aunt about the safe houses and supplies, then her dad about the logo for the club, Rori had been insistent that she did not want her family involved. Both for their protection and, I imagined, her own pride. She'd never admit it, but I knew she wanted to prove that she didn't need older adults for this situation.

Her family let her be independent, for the most part, but they had always known about these safe houses. She hadn't checked in for a while, naturally, so they were probably doing the regular concerned parent thing and decided to swing by.

At least there was the small miracle that they hadn't shown up during the brief time this place was under the Sisterhood's control.

"Let's get this over with," I grumbled to Santos, moving past him to the bedroom door. "Should I get shovels?" he asked, following me down the stairs. "They're probably gonna have us dig our own graves, right?"

How he could muster up a sense of humor right now, I had no idea. But I was grateful for it, and a small snicker left my mouth. "Yeah. Better check the garage."

As I had feared, Shadow was the dad who'd decided to show up. Rori always said he was the biggest softie of her fathers, but from my outside perspective, I knew he was also the most protective of her.

Shadow's half-brother, Rori's uncle Grudge, stood next to him. Grudge was an OG member of Sons of Odin and one of Valorie's fathers.

The two older bikers sat astride their massive custom rides, relaxed and talking softly to each other as if they were guests waiting to be greeted. Grudge's hands moved in a fluid sign language while Shadow responded with his voice and an occasional gesture of his own.

Their bikes were shut off, and Shadow's had several compartments loaded onto his. Most of the fighters had made themselves scarce, unsure of what to do with these two strange men in the driveway.

Val headed for the front door just as I was, and she shot me a worried look that spelled out exactly how I felt.

"What do we tell them?" she whispered frantically.

"The truth," I answered, grabbing the front door and holding it open for her.

"Fuck," she muttered before stepping outside and plastering a huge smile on her face. "Heyyy, Dad! Uncle Shadow. What are you old farts doing here?"

Grudge made a disapproving grunting sound, then his face split into a wide smile as his daughter approached. "Is that any way to respect your elders, young lady?" he asked her in sign language.

"Shut up. You know I love you." Val laughed, signing as she spoke.

"Torr," Shadow said to me by way of greeting, holding his hand out. "You look like shit."

"Yeah, I'm—I, uh—"

While I stammered, hunting for the right words to say, he gave me a small punch on the shoulder as he dismounted his bike. "You haven't been lifting. I can tell," he added with a teasing smirk as he walked around me to greet his niece with a hug.

"What brings you guys here?" Val's eyes darted between the two of them, her voice taking on a higher, nervous pitch. "We, uh, weren't expecting you."

Shadow gestured to the compartments on the back of his bike. "I got your club gear. Finished the logo and made it into patches. Brought some leather cuts in a few sizes too, we figured not all of you would have them. And," he turned, making sure to catch my eye as well as Val's, "I brought my tattoo equipment."

"Wow," Val breathed, wringing her hands. "Everything to make us official."

"Rori deserves nothing less," Shadow said with a smile. "Where is she, by the way?"

"Can we see the logo?" Val said in answer. I didn't know if she was trying to stall for some reason or was just that damn nervous. Either way, Shadow was catching on that something was wrong.

"I really think Rori should be the one to unveil it." He turned to me, his scarred face hardening. "Is she okay? I figured she'd be out here talking my ear off by now."

"She's...I..." Even though I wanted to hold nothing back, hide nothing from this man I respected immensely, what could I say? How did you tell someone their daughter was technically alive but not with us?

"Torrance." Shadow growled out my full name in warning. "Where the fuck is my daughter?"

"She's upstairs. In the bedroom," I managed to spit out.

"And?" he pressed. "Is she sick? Injured? Down for a nap? You need to tell me what the fuck is going on."

"There was a battle," I forced out through the knot in my throat.

"Okay." The calmness drained from his voice. "So she got hurt?"

"No, she...she got possessed."

"Possessed?" Shadow's eyes sharpened with understanding. "By a god?"

"Yes. We got it out of her, but...she hasn't woken up in..." I glanced at Val.

"Today marks five days," she supplied.

"Who possessed her? Where the fuck are your gods? And who the fuck were you fighting?" Shadow's rapid-fire questions were the ones of a frantically worried father, and I fought to compose myself to answer everything for him.

"Our gods possessed us, Santos and I, to draw the one out of her and sever it. She was possessed by something called the Dark Mother, which is worshiped by an all-female cult called the Sisters of Bathory."

Grudge made a sound of disbelief and shock, while Shadow's mouth dropped open, his face going pale. "You did *not* just fucking say that," he whispered after a long silence.

I nodded. "We're all just waiting for her to wake up."

Shadow's gaze went somewhere else, focusing on nothing in front of him. He must have gone deep inside his own head, maybe even his past. Scrubbing one hand down his face, he traced the long scar cutting through one eye, the one that turned white, I assumed from said injury.

Rori had never gone into detail about what caused her father's scarred appearance. I got the sense that she didn't know the full story herself. Although with his current reaction to the cult's name, I could start to make some educated guesses.

"Fucking hell!" And just like that, Shadow was back, pacing around like a caged animal. "I told her. I fucking *told* her not to engage with them!"

"Shadow—" I started toward him, holding an arm out for...comfort, maybe? I didn't entirely know but was stopped abruptly by a large hand clamping down on my bicep and pulling me back.

Grudge leveled me with an expression that was somehow both calm and intense. He lifted his hands and signed to me, "Leave him be. He needs to process."

Of course Shadow's brother would have more insight into his emotional state, so I was inclined to listen.

Abruptly, Shadow stopped pacing. His massive chest and shoulders heaved with every ragged, strained breath. "I need to see her," he said and immediately headed for the house.

My own protective instincts surged. I was already distressed enough that I wasn't at her side at this very moment. "I'll come with you."

Shadow grunted disapprovingly but didn't argue. "Just don't get in my way, Torr."

What could I do but obey? Silently, I followed him through the house and up to the bedroom. The moment he entered and saw her, his whole demeanor changed. His shoulders lowered on a long, slow breath, and his hands relaxed from their clenched position. He moved quietly to her bedside, as if taking care not to disturb her in sleep.

"Hey, Rormeister," he whispered, taking her hand as he sat next to her. With a quiet laugh, he added, "My stubborn, impossible daughter. Why didn't you listen to me? You need to do what your old man says sometimes."

He spoke to her softly for a few more minutes, then moved some hair off her forehead and bent to kiss her there. When he stood from her bedside and looked at me, the loving, doting father was gone. He was once again a hardened biker.

"Rori told me she made you VP," he bit out, crossing his arms.

"That's right."

"Since she's currently incapacitated and I'm one of the two most experienced riders here, I'm overriding that decision."

I stared at him. "What?"

"You're no longer in charge in her stead. Grudge and I are." He cocked his head, regarding me like I was mud scraped off his boot. "If you don't like it, you're welcome to challenge me."

Yeah, right. Shadow being thirty years older than me didn't change the fact that he was one of the deadliest assassins that had ever lived. He'd wipe the floor with me.

"You can't just override the position *she* put me in," I argued. "Rori trusted me, and you're going against her wishes."

"You are not worthy of the position she put you in," he answered coldly, then pointed to the bed where she lay motionless. "And *that* is precisely the reason why."

Chapter 21

Hudson

The whole atmosphere changed when Rori's dad and uncle showed up and decided they were in charge. Now, instead of just waiting anxiously for her to wake up, we were taking orders from a couple of strangers.

Torr made introductions, explaining who they were and that we could trust them. But the guy looked like the ghost of a dog who had been beaten all his life. With Rori still unresponsive and now being stripped of his VP title, he was a shell of his former self.

The day-to-day of being under Shadow and Grudge wasn't all that different from before, just more regimented. We worked out, practiced shooting and hand-to-hand combat, and learned more about motorcycle mechanics. The days were busy, but we still had free time to chill, talk to Malik if we needed to, or my preference, practice shooting some more.

When we faced off with the cult again, my shots needed to be guaranteed kills. I would not fuck up again.

I spent every available moment of daylight target practicing. Even when the sun went down, I'd go by the house's exterior lights until someone yelled that my shots were too loud and they were trying to sleep.

I'd gotten up before sunrise one morning and decided to try arranging the targets so the rising sun would be in my eyes. I had to prepare for everything.

I'd gone a few rounds with two different handguns when the low voice came from behind me. "You're a good shot."

Out of habit, I set the gun down and removed the magazine before looking over my shoulder. "Thanks."

Shadow stood watching with his arms crossed, the bright sun lighting up the hundreds of tiny scars criss crossing over his forearms and biceps. The biggest scar, which cut through his face, made him look especially menacing.

"Why are you shooting into the sun?" He didn't sound anything but curious as he came forward, squinting and shielding his eyes with one hand.

"Just trying to prepare for anything."

He made a small grunt of acknowledgment as he scanned the selection of weapons I had laid out to practice with. "It's good to challenge yourself, but staring into the sun will cause permanent damage. Let's clean these while we wait for sunset, alright?"

He had already opened a cleaning kit, sat on a tree stump, and taken one of the rifles across his lap. I had little choice but to follow suit.

Shadow waited until I was settled in on the stump next to him, cleaning a .40 caliber handgun, before speaking again. "Ask me what's been on your mind."

I froze, my hands holding two pieces of my weapon.

"Go on," he urged with a gentleness I didn't expect from such an intimidating man. "It's alright. I can talk about it."

I braced myself with a deep breath, praying to Tezca and Astarte that I wasn't misreading him. "You were a blood bag, weren't you? For the cult."

"Yes, I was." He smoothed an oiled cloth down the rifle barrel with care.

"For how long?" Going off of how extensively scarred he was, I'd have to guess years.

"First twenty years of my life, give or take a few."

I dropped the pieces I was holding, feeling a strange mix of awed and horrified. "Twenty years? From childhood to…"

Shadow nodded, continuing with his calm, almost meditative cleaning of the weapon. "I was born into the cult and had just reached adulthood when I got out. At least, I think so. I never did find out exactly how old I am. They don't keep birth certificates for us, you know?"

The evidence sat right in front of me. He knew what a blood bag was, and that horrifying reality was all over his skin. And yet it didn't make sense with…*him*. This family man and father. This person who was calm and in control, whose presence held power and the confidence to use it.

Despite Shadow's scarred appearance, he was…normal. If even well-adjusted.

"How?" was all I could ask.

"You're going to have to be more specific." He reassembled one weapon with practiced ease, then took another one into his lap.

"How did you…" There wasn't one word or phrase that could sum up the transformation this man must have gone through. Survive? Heal? Escape? Get over it?

"It started with a very persistent woman." A smile pulled at Shadow's lips. He seemed to know what I was getting at. "She said good morning to me every day that she saw me. It…unnerved me. Made me suspicious. Defensive. But also curious."

"Rori's mother?" I asked.

"Yes." That single word from him was filled with pride and warmth. "To this day, I still don't know why she put in the effort to talk to me. But she changed everything for me because she *chose* me."

He paused, straightening as his face went solemn. "It wasn't easy or painless by any means. There were lots of setbacks and I almost lost her, multiple times. I can still feel the blades cutting me in dreams sometimes." He paused again, mismatched eyes focusing on me. "What I'm trying to say is, it's a long, hard road with many pitfalls. The love of a good woman wasn't the only thing that got me through it, but...I wouldn't have been able to do it without her. She was my reason and my strength."

"I'm happy for you," I told him with a nod. "But I don't have anyone like that."

"Sure, you do. You've got Devin, your whole club." He pointed a finger at my chest. "You were also an adult when you got captured, if I'm not mistaken, so you know this cult is batshit. You *know* they're not how the majority of the world is. You didn't have to learn that like me."

"I know. I know, but I—"

"No excuses. You can't take out your trauma on others. You're out now, you have to do the work to heal."

"That's what I'm doing. Why I'm practicing. I need to take them down because I need...closure."

Shadow's gaze fell from me to the weapon in his hands. "Yeah, maybe I do too," he muttered. Putting it aside, he added, "Are you willing to fight alongside my daughter and niece, even trusting them with your life?"

"Yes," I said without hesitation. "I don't know Rori that well, but the people I trust believe in her. She's only shown that she wants to do the right thing."

"Good man." Shadow nodded. "And listen, Hudson." He was quiet for a while before speaking again. "What they did doesn't define you. It's not part of you. It's not what you are. *You* decide who and what you are, and no one can take that away from you. Remember that when you feel lost."

I nodded, unable to respond verbally with the sudden emotion that swept over me. I felt acknowledged and seen. Eventually I grunted out, "Thanks."

He nodded curtly and stood, quickly re-assembling and reloading his weapon. "Sun's down. It's good practice to shoot at dusk. Try the fifty-yard target with this one."

He placed the gun in front of me and just like that, we were back to business.

I shot targets under his instruction until it was too dark to see. Once we started to pack it in and head back inside, a door slammed forcefully. With rapid footfalls, a figure cloaked in shadow ran toward us.

"What's going on?" Shadow called, stepping in front of me as if to protect me.

The figure's face became illuminated under the porch light as he approached us, the Hunter.

He panted when he stopped. "Been looking all over for you...sir." Meaning Shadow, not me.

"I'm here. What happened?"

The Hunter's face broke into a grin as he delivered the news. "Rori's awake."

Chapter 22

Rori

My eyelids were heavy as I blinked, fighting through immense fatigue to make sense of my surroundings. When I started to push myself up, someone grabbed me, bringing me to their chest in a crushing embrace. My senses were still coming online but it could only be Torr.

My arms went around him in return, the feel of him strange and unfamiliar. Had he lost weight? How long had I been out?

Lips brushed my cheek with a whisper of my name, and then I was kissing him desperately. I kissed him like I needed his air to live, the press of lips and stroke of tongues making me more alive than oxygen ever could.

The unfamiliarity didn't bleed in until we broke away. This mouth was different. The rasp of his beard was softer, the bristles longer than Torr's or Santos' stubble.

I pulled away to find Devin staring back at me.

The tenderness in his dark eyes gave way to full-blown panic.

"Shit. I'm sorry. Really, I'm sorry. I don't know what—"

He stood from the bed, backing away on clumsy feet to crash directly into Torr's chest.

The sight of him broke a dam of emotion that I hadn't even been aware of. A sob breaking through my chest was all it took for him to maneuver around Devin and take me into his arms.

Always so strong, the love of my life held me, rocked me as I shuddered out tears and ugly sobs. I cried for his parents, the childhood that I now knew thanks to that parasite that had been in me. I had no right to know, but I did anyway. I cried at the sheer bone-deep relief that he was here. Mine. My north star, steadfast and constant.

"I love you," he whispered repeatedly into my neck, stroking my hair and back with a heavy, comforting hand. "I love you, Aurora Wilder, and I will never let you go."

"Took you long enough," I said on a sniffle and shaky breath.

He laughed softly, pulling back to cradle my face in his hands and rest his forehead on mine. "It's so fucking good to have you back."

"I'm never leaving you." My hands drifted all over him, like I couldn't get enough confirmation that he was here, real and solid. And that *I* was in control of my own body again. *I* could touch him, feel him with my own hands.

"I know." He brought one of my hands to his lips and kissed my knuckles. "I know you won't."

A throat-clearing sound pulled my attention away from him, and I looked up, my mouth open with the intention of telling whoever it was to fuck off. The last person I expected to see looming in my doorway was my own damn father.

"Dad?" I choked. "What are you doing here?"

Shadow wasn't alone. He was flanked by Hudson on one side and Devin on the other. There was more activity behind him, like people were coming up the stairs to see for themselves that I was awake.

"Rori..."

My name, choked out in a rough whisper, was the only warning I got before getting wrapped up in a tight hug that took me right back to childhood. Torr must have darted out of the way in a flash with how fast my father moved.

Shadow felt like an impenetrable shield surrounding me, his

strength protecting me from all of the evils of the world. Worn leather and gunpowder filled my nose, and I burrowed into that safe, familiar place. After the hell I'd just endured, there was nowhere else I wanted to be.

All too quickly, he pulled away and straightened his spine. Subtly, he did the same to me, hands on my shoulders pushing back until I sat up tall enough to meet his eye.

"Welcome back, President," my father said, his gruff voice returning. "It seems you have a lot to catch up on."

———

"So the Dark Mother is gone?"

After being able to shower and eat, I was surrounded by my club just like in those early days that felt so long ago. Only now, Shadow and my uncle Grudge joined, watching us like judgmental chaperons overseeing a bunch of unruly kids.

Yes. The answer came from Tezca, sitting at the edge of the couch next to Santos, who all but held me in his lap. He and Torr were extremely reluctant to lose physical contact with me ever since I woke up. I could feel Devin's eyes on me like a physical touch too. His embrace and kiss remained imprinted in my mind, even lingering on my skin like an echo of what happened. But that was not where my focus needed to be right now.

When we severed the Dark Mother from you, we also severed her personhood. She is no longer a self-aware entity.

"So that's it?" The Hunter straightened in his chair, excitement brimming in his voice. "It's over?"

"Not until the cult is eradicated," I said. "Otherwise, they'll be able to continue sacrificing men, rebuild their resort, and eventually bring their goddess back." I cocked an eyebrow at Tezca. "Am I right?"

You are.

"So there's still work to do." I scanned the faces of my people, my riders. Even now, after everything they'd been through, they looked as solemn and focused as soldiers awaiting orders. "Seems these old men have been keeping you all in shape while I've been down for a nap." I cocked my head toward Shadow and Grudge. "Are the Vengeful Gods ready for some action?"

A chorus of shouts rang out from the others, ranging from, "Fuck yeah!" to, "Goddamn, finally," along with a bunch of crotch-grabbing and obscene gestures. I laughed at the antics, realizing just then how much I'd missed my crew of animals.

"Grudge and I will be joining you," Shadow said when the noise ebbed. "You'll be in charge, of course. But this is personal for us too." He and my uncle shared a glance. "This will be...the closure that we've needed. An act of finally putting this behind us for good."

I nodded, the understanding passing between us silently. This was my mission, what I had been called to do. But my father and uncle also needed to be there. Maybe they had always meant to be. Only the gods knew for sure.

"We ride out in the morning, then," I decided. "No point in dragging this out. We've got guns, so do they. We're human, and so are they. Time to find out whose sense of vengeance is stronger."

"They also have children with them," Santos reminded me. "That's worth exercising a little bit of caution, right?"

"Their armed soldiers won't be the ones guarding the children, too much risk for a mistake. Those children are their future, so they'll be kept safe at all costs. We take out the armed guard first, then we find the kids."

"How do we know where to go?" someone else called out.

My gaze slid toward the window, knowing full well what I'd see. Astarte sat on the ledge, preening her white feathers like she was any other bird.

"We have eyes in the sky," I answered. "A guiding light."

Chapter 23

Rori

"You okay?"

I kept my forehead on the windowpane while glancing back at Torr, who stood in the doorway. "Now why on Satan's scorched earth would you ask me a silly thing like that?"

He chuckled on his way over to me, his expression almost bashful. "Guess there's no easy way to ask how you're holding up after a coma and possession by an evil god."

"Guess not." I returned his smile. The sensation felt weird on my face, but I felt a little bit of joy returning. That easy comfort that we shared. "I'm okay, I guess. Just taking it minute by minute. I still get these moments where it suddenly hits me that I'm *me* again. And how hard I fought just to get back."

Torr gave me an uneasy look. "We don't have to ride out in the morning, you know. It's okay to rest, Rori. You're allowed to recover from this before putting on your president's cut again."

"No." I rolled my forehead from side to side on the windowpane. "I'll recover when this cult is wiped off the earth. I can't even start healing until they're gone." My head lifted from the glass. "I've reinstated you as VP, so your advice from now on better be good."

Torr chuckled again. "Just thought I'd try. And to think I was worried about you because you're not the staring-out-the-window type."

"I just might become one. Feels like I can think better with cool glass on my forehead." After a while, I turned around to face Torr, tucking my feet underneath me in the armchair. "Did you see Devin kiss me?"

He nodded calmly. "Yeah, I did."

"I thought it was you, at first," I admitted. "I thought you felt different."

"Is that what's got you staring out the window all longingly and shit?"

"Fuck you." After a few seconds, I added, "That's part of it."

"I'm fine with it, if that's what you're wondering."

"Fine with what?" I wanted to hear him say the words.

"You and him. Him being one of yours, along with me and Santos."

"He's with Hudson, though," I pointed out.

Torr grinned. "I think Hudson likes you too."

My knee-jerk reaction was to reject that notion, to hotly deny it. *Me? Hudson? Pfft, no fucking way.* But my clearest, most recent memory of him prevented me from saying that out loud. He'd talked me out of ending my life. He had hugged me, comforted me in the last few moments I had control of myself.

"He's alright," was the admittance I allowed.

Torr gave me an, *Uh-huh, sure,* look as he unlaced his boots. Wordlessly, he reclined on the bed, and I immediately went over to join him. Together, we shifted into a position that was as natural and familiar as breathing. My head on his shoulder and leg over his. His arm around my back until his hand nestled into my waist, with his opposite hand resting on my knee.

We let out a sigh once we found a place to settle, relaxing into each other for the first time in what felt like years. But even while nestled against him, my mind couldn't relax.

"Did you ever find out what happened to your birth parents?" I already knew the answer but had to start the conversation somewhere.

"No." Torr's thumb traced the dip in my waist. "Why, what's up?"

His patience was saintly as I worked up the nerve to speak. "She told me."

His thumb abruptly stopped moving. "The Dark Mother?"

"Yes." My fingers curled into his shirt. "I'm so sorry, Torr. I couldn't believe this cult had affected your life too."

"Tell me."

He was quiet as I relayed what the Dark Mother had told me. Like me, Torr's body became gradually less relaxed. His hand drifted from my waist up to my shoulder, which he squeezed almost painfully when I said where his mother was now, the condition she was in.

"They never abandoned you." I smoothed a hand over his chest, trying to read his expression. "They knew the cult would kill you or worse, torture you to set an example. They didn't have many choices, but they gave you the best possible chance of survival."

He might as well have turned to stone for how much he was responding, so I continued running my palm up, down, and across his torso. "And I couldn't be more grateful to them for doing that, for being brave enough to lead the cultists away from you." My hand stopped while I stared up at the side of his face. "Because if they hadn't, I might have never had you in my life."

After what seemed like an eternity, Torr brought his lips to my forehead. "Will you help me find them? After all this is over."

I hugged tightly around his waist and felt the crush of his arm against my shoulder. "You know how I am about family. I'll be happy to."

———

IT WAS biker club tradition to throw a raging party the night before a long ride, or especially, a big battle. Said party would usually consist of, but not be limited to getting tattoos, drinking, and fucking. By sundown, I had started at the top of the list and planned to work my way down as the night carried on.

The kitchen table served as my father's tattoo station. I was sprawled on my back, shirt and bra straps pulled down and off my shoulders to give Shadow access to my chest, where he proceeded to ink the vengeful god, the icon of my club.

"It really needed to be this spot, huh?" Shadow grumbled over the buzzing of his machine as he traced the pen drawing below my collarbones.

"Don't be weird," I snorted. "You've inked tons of womens' titties."

"I'm nowhere near *that* area, daughter mine."

"All the more reason for you to not be weird about it." His brooding silence continued without answer, brow furrowed over his eyes, rapt with concentration on his work. "Are you mad at me, Dadow?" I asked in a softer voice.

He straightened with a heavy sigh, and the buzzing machine quieted as he lifted the needle from my skin. "I'm not mad, I'm—"

"Don't say disappointed. That's even worse."

He let out a dry chuckle while resuming his work, touching the needle down to my sternum. "I distinctly remember telling you to stay away from this cult."

"I didn't know who they were until after the whole thing with the resort," I argued. "Besides, it's not like you gave me any context or reason. 'Watch out for the men-hating psychotic bitches' would have been a great heads up."

Shadow shook his head, eyes following the lines of his ink. "I thought I was being paranoid. I never thought you'd actually run into them. I never—shit."

He straightened again, setting the tattoo gun down as he started at some blank space on the wall.

"They were never supposed to touch you," he said after a long silence. "You were never supposed to know a world with this kind of evil. Fuck, Rori. I never wanted this to be *your* fight."

"But it is," I told him quietly. "This is what I was chosen to do. To finish what you started."

Stubbornly, he shook his head again. "We should have protected you from this. Years ago, Grudge and I should have done this ourselves rather than burying our heads in the sand."

"You didn't bury your heads in the sand, you were healing." I sat up, swinging my legs to dangle over the edge of the table. "You were being our dad, Mom's husband. Running your tattoo shop, taking care of your family. You did everything right, Dadow. By living so well, you told this cult, 'fuck you, right in the eyeball'."

He chuckled softly at that. "I wanted you and your siblings to have what I never had. We all wanted that. You grew so fast and we loved you so much, I never wanted to miss a single moment." His face darkened again. "But if I had taken a damn minute to consider the future—"

"You couldn't have predicted a damn thing. Seriously, Dad." I angled myself to face him head-on. "I really believe this was how it was all meant to play out. You were meant to escape them, to live and survive. To meet the love of your life and become a hero and a father. Then it was my turn to carry out the next phase. So that's what I'm going to do."

Shadow sighed heavily, but his eyes brightened and a smile played at his lips. "How did you become so wise?"

"Being possessed by a deity manifested out of hatred has a way of putting things into perspective."

He chuckled again, picking up his machine. "So you want your tattoo or not, President?"

"Yes, sir." I swung my legs to extend them along the length of the table again and reclined back into position.

"Don't underestimate them," he said as he resumed tracing a line. "Especially not now, so close to the end. They didn't have their goddess back in my day."

He didn't need to worry about that. Having the Dark Mother inside me had taught me more than I ever expected.

Chapter 24

Devin

"**I** kissed her."

Hudson's expression didn't change. I almost thought he hadn't heard me. He sat on the porch railing, holding a beer on his knee as he watched some of the guys play a drunken touch football game in the driveway. Half of the shirtless team were proudly sporting their freshly outlined Vengeful Gods tattoos on their chests, stomachs, or backs.

At some point, I'd get mine as well.

I wasn't sure exactly when my loyalty to Rori became ironclad. Maybe it had always been there, an invisible motive hidden beneath my frustration at being attracted to her. Something that only came to the surface when I realized we could lose her, and then in the soul-shaking relief when she came back.

All of that was stuff I had to work through. But I also owed loyalty and honesty to Hudson.

If I were to gain something with her, I didn't want to lose him. It would kill me to do so. He felt a certain way toward Rori as well, and while it felt like a pipe dream for all five of us, Torr and Santos included, to end up a happy family, I remained clinging to that hope.

"Did you feel something?"

"Hm?" Hudson had finally spoken and pulled me out of my swirling mess of thoughts.

"Did you feel something when you kissed her?" he repeated.

"Yes," I admitted with a resigned nod.

"Similar to what you feel for me?"

"Similar but different." I yearned to touch him, to comfort and reassure him, but his posture was stiff and I knew he wouldn't be responsive. "It doesn't diminish what I feel for you at all. You're two different people, so what I feel is just...different for each of you."

I wanted to apologize for what I'd done, but it would be a lame attempt at absolving myself of responsibility and a lie on top of that. Hudson deserved better.

"I'm sorry for hurting you," I decided on instead. I was still an asshole, but at least that sorrow was genuine. "I never intended to go behind your back. I only wanted you to feel good."

"Jesus, stop."

I froze, taken aback as Hudson took a long pull of beer.

"We just decided to fool around. It's not like we got married. I never expected you to never want or touch someone else."

It took a moment for those words to sink in. "Oh."

"Honestly, I saw you falling for her from a mile away." He passed the beer bottle between his hands. "Probably since that night you all got me out, when you wrapped up her leg and carried her off like she was your bride."

"Well, she couldn't exactly walk."

"Right."

He didn't say anything else for a while, so I dared to keep going. "So you're not upset?"

Hudson pulled in a deep breath, his gaze still trained on the running, tackling, and laughing going on in front of us. "I almost want to be, but I'm not."

"Because...?" My worst fear in that moment was finding out he actually didn't feel as strongly for me as I did for him.

"Because I knew it was bound to happen." He set the now-empty beer bottle aside on the railing next to him. "Because I knew on some level, you started up this thing with me to distract yourself from her."

"That's not true," I protested. "I had always wanted you, since before her, before all of this. I won't deny that I was selfish. *I* wanted to be the reason you healed. I wanted to be the one who made you feel pleasure again, feel strong and confident again. *That* was what I always wanted. I...I didn't expect her."

Hudson let out a soft little laugh. "It's funny how the things we're meant for are the last things we expect."

I stared at his side profile, completely lost as to what to feel. "Are you saying I'm not meant for you?"

"What do you want, Devin?"

"What do *you* want?" I shot back. "You're a whole person, remember? You can make your own choices now."

He shook his head as he swung around, hopping off the railing to stand next to me. "I'm still too fucked in the head to really know what I want."

I moved closer to him. "Then I'll stay with you until you figure that out."

"But what do you *want*, Devin?" he pressed.

"I want you both," I admitted in a whisper. "I don't want to choose."

"What are you two doing moping out here?"

We whirled around to see Rori striding out onto the porch, a thick white bandage taped across her chest from her collarbones to underneath her T-shirt. Her face was flushed, probably still riding off the adrenaline from her tattoo session. She approached us with a short tumbler of liquor in her hand, though her eyes were sharp as they darted between us. She looked battle-ready and not the least bit inebriated.

Even so, I couldn't resist poking the bear. "Doesn't alcohol thin the blood? You'll need a fresh bandage if you keep that up."

"Oh, fuck off. This thing's halfway healed already." Rori couldn't resist biting back, as I knew she would. "Everyone's is healing super fast." She gave a small smile that almost looked sad. "Can't help but feel like it's a final gift from our vengeful gods. Better get your ink done soon if you want the superhuman healing."

"I've hardly got any room left." Hudson chuckled as he rotated his thoroughly inked arms.

"Yeah, right. You've got this big open spot right here." Rori yanked down the front of his shirt, touching her forefinger to his sternum. "Perfect spot. Big ol' empty canvas."

"You sure it's big enough?" He smirked at her and didn't look the slightest bit uncomfortable with her standing so close, nor with her touch on his bare skin.

If anything, he seemed to be flirting right back.

"It'll do the job." Rori returned his smile and stepped back, releasing her hold on his shirt. She clearly didn't want to crowd him, didn't want to cross any boundaries he may or may not have established. "Your skin holds ink beautifully, by the way."

"Thanks." Hudson actually blushed. "Helps when they don't see much sunlight for a few years."

Rori had been in the middle of taking a sip from her drink, then promptly choked and began coughing.

"Easy." Hudson actually patted her back when she doubled over. "No need to swallow it all at once."

Rori wheezed like she couldn't figure out whether to cough or laugh. I too was dumbfounded by Hudson's flirting and innuendo. He seemed different since Rori had woken up. Happier, even.

"Well, aren't you full of surprises tonight?" Rori mused when she recovered. " Dark humor and dick jokes. Anything else I should know?"

"I just told him."

The two of them looked at me when I spoke, though my breaking the silence didn't seem to break the tension between them. If anything, it felt more like the chemistry between them expanded outward to include me.

"Told him what?" Rori asked.

"What happened when you woke up," I said. "Between you and me."

"Ah, when we kissed."

"Yeah."

Her attention returned to Hudson. "And how do you feel about that?"

He pulled in a long breath as though taking the time to ponder a big decision. "Weirdly not jealous about it."

"Well, that's a promising start," Rori observed, her eyes flicking back to me.

"He's all torn up about it, though." Hudson jerked his chin at me. "Look at him."

"Hey, I'm not—"

"He's in love with both of us." Hudson steamrolled right over my protest. "And he's conflicted because he thinks he has to choose." While I wanted to disappear into the floor, Hudson gave Rori a knowing look. "But not choosing is kind of your thing, isn't it?"

"That's...true," she said tentatively. Finally, someone else who looked as shocked as I felt. "With all consenting parties, of course. Sharing partners isn't for everyone."

"He wants us both." Hudson shrugged. "And you're a pro at the whole sharing thing. Sounds like a perfect solution to me."

"You don't need to put words in my mouth," I finally spat out. "I can decide for myself what I want."

Hudson spread his hands. "Is any of what I just said untrue?"

It wasn't, and I was only trying to protect my own ego. To no longer find myself bared to Rori fucking Wilder, the woman I tried so hard and failed to convince myself I wasn't batshit crazy for.

In all the times I'd been held, used, and humiliated by the Sisterhood, I'd never felt as vulnerable as this.

Rori approached me slowly, as cautiously as she would a wild animal. "I wouldn't make you choose, Devin. I'm open to this, as long as the two of you are."

She glanced toward Hudson, who gave an affirming nod.

"What about Torr and Santos?" My voice came out huskier than intended.

"I think they've always known this was a possibility." With a small smile, she then turned to Hudson. "What surprises me the most is you."

He nodded as if expecting that. "Your dad and I had an interesting talk just before you woke up. It put a lot in perspective, you know? Gave me a lot to think about. And even before then, I just..." He paused for a long time. "I just like you," he said with a shrug. "I admire and respect you. I don't know if my feelings go beyond that or if they ever will. But Devin," he inclined his head toward me, "means a lot to me. And it's hurting him to be without you. So why would I deny him that?"

Rori's smile grew wider. "You're a good guy, Hudson." She looked at me, a teasing glint in her eye. "Your boyfriend's a good one."

"He's—" I stopped myself, blowing out a breath. "Okay, yeah. I guess he is my boyfriend."

It felt strange, but also freeing, to not be secretive or even subtle about being with Hudson. We were supported, accepted. Neither of us were tools for some evil purpose anymore, we could just be us.

"That's right. Can't deny me anymore." He threw an arm around my shoulders and planted a big kiss on my cheek.

"When have I ever denied you anything?" I grumbled out the words but the sensation in my chest was light, bubbly and giddy, as I turned my head to find his mouth.

Rori was beaming, her warmth toward us genuine. "I'm happy for you two. As for the other part of this equation," she motioned between me and herself, "we can take it slow if you want. Being with multiple people can be strange."

Before I could respond, Torr came out of the house with a slam of the front door. He was shirtless with a large bandage taped across his chest just like Rori.

"That was fast," she remarked as he came up behind her, arms snaking around her waist as he planted a kiss on her neck.

"Your dad's the best at what he does. Hey, guys." Torr nodded at Hudson and me before bringing his chin to Rori's shoulder. "How are you, by the way?" he murmured, turning his face toward hers.

Rori snorted. "Never been better."

"Seriously, creep."

"I'm...actually okay, yeah," she assured him. "Even better than when you checked on me hours ago. I'm just ready to wipe these crazy bitches off the planet." Her smile at him was earnest, if a little wobbly. "I promise I'll work with Malik on how traumatic this was after we're done. But I have a job to do first."

"We all do," I piped up. "Every person here has a score to settle with this cult. We're not just taking back our own lives," I squeezed around Hudson's forearm, "but the future."

"That's right." Torr held his fist out for a pound, which I gave. "But before we do that..." His arms re-wrapped around Rori, his mouth going to her ear. "Santos and I have a surprise for you upstairs."

"Oh, really?" She grinned, arching subtly to lean against him. "What kind of surprise?"

"One we're pretty sure you'll like."

"Hmm." Rori's gaze slid to me and Hudson, eyes sparking with delight. "How would you feel if these two joined us?"

"Joined? You?" I choked out in disbelief.

"You two can watch and just play with each other," Rori added quickly. "See how it feels to be part of a bigger group. If it's not your thing, you can leave. We won't be offended."

"Baby steps," Torr added with a nod, as if they had already discussed it. "I'm good with it. I'm sure Santos would be too."

My voice was lost with awe, excitement, nervousness, disbelief at what was being offered, a whole mix of emotions. So I was grateful when Hudson answered.

"Yeah, I think we'd be open to that." He kissed my neck, one hand sliding into the top of my shirt. "But you have to use your words, Dev," he chided playfully.

Finally, I found my voice. "Yes, we'll join you."

Chapter 25

Rori

I paced on the landing outside my closed bedroom door. Torr and Santos were on the other side of that slab of wood. Torr said he had to, "Get Santos ready," and proceeded to shut the door in my face. That was almost twenty minutes ago.

"This better be fucking good," I grumbled impatiently. I had been excited, my fantasies playing out all kinds of delicious foreplay scenes in my head. But as time stretched on, I was beginning to feel seriously blue-balled.

Devin and Hudson waited with me, the two of them adorably wrapped up in each other. While my boots wore a hole in the floor, they kissed, embraced, and spoke softly to each other. At times, I could feel Devin's eyes on me, maybe even Hudson's too.

Once we were all in that bedroom, some touching might happen between me and one of them. But I didn't want to get between them out here. It would be their choice if they wanted me involved.

"How much longer?" I yelled through the door.

"Couple more minutes!" Torr called back.

"I bet it's food," Hudson said confidently. "He's laying Santos out on the bed and covering him in whipped cream and cherries that you can eat off him."

"I hate cherries, so he better not," I muttered.

"What? How can you hate cherries?" Devin demanded.

"'Cause they're gross!"

Finally, the door creaked ajar and a grinning Torr poked his head through. "Ready for your surprise?"

"Man, what do you think?" I was brimming with so much anticipation, I couldn't even think of a proper smartass answer to that question. I just wedged my body through the gap, forcing Torr back as I stepped inside.

I was solely focused on the bed, which turned out to be empty and neatly made. But the moment I turned, my jaw fell open. "Oh. My. God..."

Santos was sitting in a chair, wearing nothing but boxer shorts. Or rather, he was *tied* to the chair. This wasn't a quick-and-dirty tie-up job, though. The only way to describe the ropework was *stunning*. A work of art.

An intricate pattern of ties and knots held Santos in place, from his ankles and calves being held to the chair legs, to the harness-like structure stretched over his chest and torso.

"Hey paloma," he said in a soft voice that was vulnerable, almost shy, but full of want.

That sound immediately pulled my focus from the aesthetics of his bonds to him, my Santos. "Hey, handsome. Was this your idea?"

"We both came up with it." He nodded at Torr.

"Look at you." I breathed in awe, drinking him in from head to toe. "You like being trussed up for me like this?"

"More than like." His constricted chest strained against the rope as he took a breath, the binds pressing into his skin. "I *want* this. With you."

"You're sure?" I couldn't stop taking in all the details. The contrast of the straight lines and uniform knots against the organic contours of his body was beautiful to behold. Pale threads against tan skin. His slight movements under so much restraint. Restraint that he wanted.

"God, yes." His voice became a plea, one that sent heat flooding to my core. "Your control is the only kind I've ever craved. Your pleasure is all I care about giving." His big shoulders pulled slightly at the ropes, and fuck me, why was that so hot? "So please, paloma. Use me. I'm yours for the taking."

Speechless was an understatement. I was absolutely floored by the display of devotion and trust. And not just by Santos. Unable to find anything to say, I walked a slow circle around my gift. My prize. I was only distantly aware of other movement, probably Devin and Hudson making their way into the room.

Once behind his chair, I paused to admire how Santos' arms were tied behind his back. Ropes looped around his forearms and were held together by an intricate braid of knots between the two limbs.

"You like your gift?" Torr asked, arms crossed with more than a hint of smugness.

Looking back down at my bound gladiator, I kept noticing more ties and patterns that I didn't see before. The rope went over Santos' thighs and hips and under the seat of the chair to hold him in place. Torr needed to have gotten *very* close, touched him in intimate places. I knew the two of them weren't sexually attracted to each other, but that kind of trust and comfort between each other was moving in its own right.

The thought of Torr leaning over Santos, pulling lengths of rope around his hips, securing it, and snaking the lengths up his waist, was practically foreplay in itself.

On top of all that, they had done this for *me*.

"You're not saying anything." Santos' voice hardened slightly, losing some of that sweet, sexy begging. "Are *you* okay with this, paloma?"

"I'm just...speechless," I admitted. "I've never received such an amazing gift. Especially one wrapped so beautifully." I looked at Torr. "When did you learn how to do this?"

"When you were out for a week," he said. "I couldn't lift to cope, couldn't leave your side for a second. All I had was a length of rope, so I tied knots and made patterns."

"Amazing," I mused, returning my attention to Santos. "Can I touch you?" My hand hovered over his shoulder.

"Please," he purred.

His skin was warm under my palm. I slid a finger under the rope binding his elbows, testing its tightness. The digit slid under easily, though the rope left a clear mark on his skin.

"You're not in pain anywhere?" I asked, circling around to the front of him again. "Or going numb?"

He shook his head, tongue wetting his lips. "The only thing that hurts is that I'm not pleasing you right now."

"Oh, gorgeous man, you *are* pleasing me." I hooked a finger under the knotwork in the center of his chest and pulled slightly, until the tension snapped the rope against his skin with a soft crack. "You are just a feast for the eyes. I hardly know where to start with you."

A soft creak coming from the bed reminded me that we weren't alone. Whatever I'd be doing to Santos, I'd have an audience. Maybe even some extra participants, if I was lucky.

"You guys still good to hang out?" I said with a tilt of my head toward Devin and Hudson.

"Oh yeah."

I wasn't sure which one of them answered, but that was good enough for me. My attention was solely on the beautifully bound man in the center of the room.

"You've got to promise me one thing, Torr," I said while walking another slow circle around Santos, gently pulling and testing at his binds as I did so.

"Yes?" Torr's voice was raspy, practically a groan already.

"Next time you wrap my present for me," I stood behind Santos and ran my palm down his chest to his firm stomach, "I want to watch you do it."

"Sure, I'd be happy to show you." Torr's eyes followed the movements of my hands as I caressed Santos. "Maybe even teach you how."

Santos dipped his head back and moaned. "Uh, yes." His body surged under the ropes.

"You would like that?" I brought my mouth directly against Santos' ear. "Feeling me tie you up before doing whatever I want with you?"

"God, yes," he breathed.

"Oh, but what to do to you now?" I kept contact with him, letting my fingers drift over his warm skin as I circled around to stand in front of him again.

"Anything you want." His shoulder muscles bunched as he watched my every movement like a hawk. "Please. All I want is to please you."

I took him in from head to toe, vaguely aware of the grin spreading on my face. *If only you could see the Butcher now, Nella.* Her fearsome gladiator, her prized possession, was exactly where *he* wanted to be. Mine.

"You see, the problem with that is," I moved one leg between his spread thighs and dropped my weight to sit on one of his knees, "All I want to do is please you too."

Santos pulled in a breath as I slid higher up his thigh, brushing my leg against his crotch.

"Make me please you," he choked out. "I'm your toy to use. Please."

"Quiet." I brought my thumb to his lips, pushing the digit inside. "I don't want any words from you for the next ten minutes. Understand?"

"Mm-hm..." His lips wrapped around my thumb, tongue licking and teasing it as if it were the most erogenous spot on my body. When it came to Santos, any body part could become a sweet spot.

"But I do want you to make noise." My heel lifted off the ground, arching my foot and rubbing my inner thigh against his growing erection. "No words, but I want to hear exactly how much you love what I'm giving you. Understand?"

"Mmm..." Santos' quad muscles flexed, his skin biting into the ropes going across his powerful legs. He wanted to thrust, to roll his hips into my touch. But the restraints kept him in place.

I skimmed a hand down his stomach, tracing the ropework framing his hips before settling my palm on his length. He pulsed against my hand with a gasp, legs straining for more contact with me.

"Fuh—ah, hmmm..." Poor Santos was so vocal and expressive that *not* using his words served as a unique challenge to him. Good thing obeying me was a higher priority.

"We'll find something to gag you with if you can't obey simple commands." I freed his cock from the snug boxer briefs with that warning and enjoyed the sight of his head lolling back on his neck. A long, wordless moan poured out of his throat as I stroked him with a firm grip.

"Good boy." I leaned in to nip his Adam's apple and found a comfortable place to curl up and lean briefly.

The crook of his neck fit my forehead perfectly, so I rested there, kissing the hollow of his throat, enjoying the warmth of his skin and the fresh scent of him.

"I'll never get over how right you are for me," I whispered. "I'm so glad to be back and that you're still here."

He was so solid underneath me, a protective, deadly force despite his submission in bed. The kiss he brushed over my forehead promised his strength and devotion without words.

"I love you too." With a final kiss under his jaw, I slid down his body until I was kneeling between his legs. He had allowed me a moment to melt, but I was back in my domme headspace now, gazing up at him with his cock in front of my face.

He made those moans and ragged breaths again as I pumped him from base to head. I opened my mouth and let the blunt tip brush against my tongue with every stroke. It was driving him wild, and I wanted to see if I could get a word out of him.

"Fuck," he groaned before sinking his teeth into his lip, knowing he'd messed up.

"Aw, bad boy." I released his cock with an exaggerated sigh of disappointment and looked up, finding the eyes of the other men in the room for the first time.

Torr leaned against a dresser, arms and ankles crossed in front of him. Devin and Hudson were on the bed, shirtless and spooning in a tangle of limbs. I had to jerk my attention away from them, from the shapes, lines, muscles, and tattoos that made up their bodies.

"Torr?"

"Yes?" he purred, like he thoroughly enjoyed watching my struggle.

"What can we gag Santos with for breaking the rules?" I asked.

Torr grinned evilly. "How about your panties?"

I smirked back at him as I stood, already flicking apart the button on my pants. "You were hoping for that, weren't you?"

"Not hoping. I would've made it happen. Come here."

He yanked me forward, pulling me into a rough, handsy kiss. With both hands, he palmed my ass hard, bringing them down in a slap on either side. The next thing I knew, my pants and underwear were being shoved down in rough pulls.

As soon as my bare ass was exposed, Torr slapped each side again hard enough to leave handprints. I couldn't even cry out from the sting before his mouth was on mine, hands smoothing over the bruised skin to soothe the ache. His kiss plundered my mouth, possessive and all-consuming.

The difference between my two men could not be more apparent. Torr's dominance left me dizzy, off-kilter and breathless. Santos' submission made me powerful, fired up and confident enough to rule the world. And I could not be me without them both.

With my pants and underwear off, Torr placed my panties in my hand, spun me around, and sent me back to Santos with another, lighter, slap on the ass.

"Punish your man, then torture him some more until you're dripping wet enough for me to wreck you," Torr growled.

Weak-kneed as I was, I managed to stand tall in front of Santos. "Open your mouth."

He obeyed, nearly panting as he stared up at me with huge, dark puppy eyes.

I shoved my balled-up underwear into his mouth and he moaned, accepting the slip of fabric with my taste and scent on them.

"That'll teach you to disobey orders." I returned to kneeling in front of him. "As further punishment, I'm going to deep-throat you and you're not allowed to come. How does that sound?"

His answering moan was pure sexual frustration. I watched him carefully for any signs of genuine discomfort—a shake of his head, a look in his eye, but my man was in heaven being ruled by me.

My lips slid over his blunt head, mouth stretching around his girth as I made my way down. I opened my throat to take all of him, focusing on breathing through my nose as my lips finally met my fist wrapped around his base.

Santos moaned around my panties, and I knew he'd be begging to touch me, thrusting up to fuck my face if he were free to do so. But as long as he was my toy to play with, I'd enjoy putting him in my mouth.

And he was an absolute mouthful. Solid and burning hot, twitching when he hit the back of my throat. He wanted to come so badly, but I knew my good boy wouldn't disappoint me this time.

I was so orally fixated on him, I didn't notice Torr come up behind me until a pinch on my nipple made me squeal.

His hands were underneath my shirt, groping and grabbing with a touch that was both reverent and possessive. My shirt and bra came off, and then I ripped off the large stretch of gauze covering the fresh tattoo on my chest.

Torr's hands ran down my sides while I returned my attention to Santos' cock, showing no mercy as I resumed taking him down my throat and pumping him with my fist. His gorgeous face was in a grimace of pleasure and pain, muscles straining under the ropes. He was solid as iron on my tongue, no doubt incredibly sensitive and teetering on the verge.

"You're being so very good for me," I praised, giving him and my mouth a moment of reprieve.

He groaned around my panties, head falling back as he took ragged breaths through his nose.

Torr's hand went between my legs, a rough groan leaving his chest when he found how wet I was at Santos' submission. I spread wider for him, arching and pressing back, resting my arms and head on Santos' thighs.

"You love sucking his cock this much?" Torr purred approvingly as he dragged slick fingers to my ass, teasing my back entrance. "You like seeing him all wrapped up like a present for you?"

"Yes..." I arched deeper for him, lifting my hips.

"How would you like to ride him?" Torr's fingers pressed inside, working and stretching me while the other hand lazily stroked my pussy. "Ride both of us?"

"Yes, please," I whined.

"Come for us first." He zeroed in on my clit while stretching my ass with another finger. "Look at him while I get you ready for both of us."

I gazed up at Santos, fingers gripping the ropes at his hips to hold on through the onslaught of sensations. He met my eyes, head and shoulders angling down as much as he could, like he wanted to curl around me.

I reached up and took my panties from his mouth, discarding them somewhere on the floor. "I want to hear you when I'm riding you." A moan left my mouth, my grip tightening on his ropes as pleasure built from Torr's ministrations. "I love hearing you talk when you fuck me. It's one of my favorite things."

Santos' smile was radiant. "And I love watching you come. I love it when you hold onto me while Torr is working you. So keep looking at me, paloma. *That* is my favorite thing."

I rested my cheek on his thigh, gazing up toward his face, but my orgasm was ratcheting up so fast I gave into the impulse to shut my eyes.

Torr slapped my clit in response, the sharp, painful pleasure making me cry out. "Keep your eyes open," he growled. "He said he wants you to look at him."

The display of his dominance combined with the tender, loving look from Santos did me in. My pleasure lashed out like a lightning strike, nearly making me crumple to the floor if it wasn't for Santos's legs holding me up. Torr kept his motions up until I was begging him to stop, the aftershocks licking through me to the point of oversensitivity.

"So good," Torr praised, stroking down my back. Then he said the words that sparked a thrill in me like nothing else.

"You're going to take us both so well."

Chapter 26

Rori

Fuck, just hearing Torr's words felt like they could spark another orgasm from me.

My gaze rolled toward the bed, once again remembering our audience. Devin and Hudson were facing each other now, kissing aggressively. Their bodies rolled and hands were hidden between each other. Hudson's back was to us, his inked skin rippling across taut muscles.

Hudson's fist gripped the hair at Devin's nape, which was making the long, dark strands come loose as the men plundered each other's mouths. With a groan, Hudson kissed the other man's jaw, making his way down Devin's neck.

And Devin looked over Hudson's shoulder to stare straight at me.

His dark eyes were hooded with lust, but no less sharp as they focused on me, his hand gripping Hudson's ass to bring the other man's leg over his waist. Devin's torso rolled and I could imagine their cocks sliding against each other, just on the other side of Hudson's hip. I wondered if they were making a sticky mess with precum, how each of them would feel in my hand.

"Like what you're seeing?" The question came from Torr, his

hand running along my shoulders and upper back. "You like watching them fuck each other?" His mouth came to my ear. "Or do you want them to fuck you?"

I shuddered at the question, fresh desire lighting up my spine and all my sensitive points.

"Keep watching them while we fuck you." Torr gripped my nape, massaging and squeezing. "Let their pleasure become yours. And who knows?" He nipped my earlobe. "Maybe one of them will let you finish him off if you're lucky."

A soft moan left my throat. Devin. It was Devin I really wanted to touch that way. That would be up to him and Hudson, but from the way he continued to watch me, I had a feeling he wanted it just as much as I did.

"Paloma." Santos' sweet, pleading voice cut into my thoughts. "Please ride me. I'm dying to feel you."

Hearing him beg was like a shot of power through my veins. Instantly, I recalled my control, my responsibility to dominate him well.

I stood from the floor, breaking eye contact with Devin to turn to my powerful gladiator, trussed up and helpless only to me. "I'll use my good little fuck toy whenever I damn well please."

Santos' eyes lit up, his cock standing even higher at attention with a cute little twitch. "Yes, paloma," he purred.

"Lucky for you," I braced my hands on his shoulders, straddling my legs over the seat of his thighs, "I could go for a nice ride right now."

"Oh God, yes," he hissed. "Ride me like you own me."

I hovered over him, just barely letting his wide head kiss my slick folds. "You don't have the right to make demands," I reminded him sternly. "Ask correctly, or I'll leave you here."

"I'm sorry," he panted, squirming under his bonds. "Will you please ride me, paloma? I'm dying to worship your sweet cunt with my cock. Please, I would feel so honored."

How could a girl say no to that? I kissed him deeply, wrapping my arms around his shoulders as I slowly lowered down. His reverent moan into my mouth was delicious and full of longing.

"That's my good boy," I breathed when we broke apart, raising my hips only to lower down and take him fully. "You're so good to me, Santos."

"You're everything to me," he said roughly, his forehead on mine. "The world, the sun. Absolutely everything."

I knew he meant every word, and for a moment, it was just us. I held his face through another achingly perfect kiss. Giving this man everything he wanted and deserved would never make up for what he had been through. But I would spend the rest of my life trying my best.

The moment I lifted up again, I felt the heat of Torr's chest on my back. "Stay there for me," he whispered darkly.

My thighs were already burning from the effort, and I was practically on my toes.

"Lean on me," Santos urged. "I got you, paloma."

"You do," I agreed, letting my weight rest on him while Torr nudged at my back entrance. "You have me, always."

"Tell me if I need to stop." Torr nipped at my shoulder while he pressed through in short thrusts.

"I'm good, I'm good...wait."

He paused to let me adjust, teasing the sensitive nape of my neck with biting kisses, hands roughly kneading my thighs.

"You're not new to this." I could hear the smirk in his voice.

"Neither are you," I shot back over my shoulder. He and I hadn't done anal together before, but we'd both been fairly experienced before getting together, so I wasn't surprised. I was actually glad he knew enough to be considerate and slow.

"Okay, I'm good," I told him.

"You're fucking incredible is what you are," he groaned, pushing in a little deeper.

Even with Santos supporting me, my legs were tiring to the point of lowering down over his thighs and taking him deeper as well.

"Holy...fuck." By the time both men were seated inside me, I felt so full that I could scarcely breathe.

"I'm gonna start moving," Torr rasped against my nape. "Gonna start fucking this sweet, little ass. Tell me if I need to stop."

"No fucking way," I gasped, clutching Santos' shoulders for dear life. "Don't you fucking dare."

"That's what I like to hear," Torr praised. "Let me hear you beg for it."

Giving in to his demands was automatic, instinctual. "More," I whined. "You can go harder. Give me more."

Torr picked up his pace with a curse, the pressure of him filling me just as punishing as it was satisfying.

"Oh fuck me, I can feel that too," Santos hissed. He could only rock his hips in a slight cant, but coupled with Torr's brutal fucking, it was all I needed.

I was speared between them, helpless to do anything but take what they gave. The three of us were slick with sweat and panting, an expanse of skin, muscle and rope. I never wanted it to end.

The heat, sweat, and pleasure make me sinewy, all loose and languid. At some point, my head lolled and caught sight of our voyeurs.

Hudson and Devin were spooning now, the two of them facing us. Devin locked eyes with me again, the lower half of his face hidden by Hudson's shoulder. He had an arm around the other man's chest, a lean-muscled forearm cutting across an expanse of tattoos.

Hudson was panting. His blue eyes met mine briefly but quickly moved on, like someone taking in a large painting on the wall. He liked the details but also wanted to see the whole picture.

And I did the same to him. Starting at his face, then letting my gaze travel down his body. A tattooed hand clutched at Devin's arm. A pale stomach expanded and flexed with every ragged breath. My eyes followed the trail of hair below his navel further downward...and were rewarded by the sight of Devin's hand stroking up and down a long, thick cock.

Pleasure spiked through me and I cried out, my body surging with a new intensity between my two men. When I looked at the two on the bed, I saw the whole picture, not just the details. And it was nothing short of the hottest thing I'd ever seen.

The two of them lying there, Devin with one arm braced over Hudson's chest and the other hand jerking his cock. Like me, Hudson was helpless to do anything but take, feel. Watch.

Devin's eyes never wavered from mine. It almost felt like he was daring me. Like this was some kind of challenge to quit the staring contest and actually do something.

"I'm going to come," Torr growled, still stretching me to the limit. "Your ass is too fucking good."

He reached around and nimbly stroked another orgasm out of me, using me to clench around his cock so he could spill inside my ass.

Torr had barely staggered away and cleaned up when Santos called out, "Think you can untie me? I'm kinda numb in places."

"Oh shit, I'm so sorry." Mortified, I started to lift up. "We shouldn't have left you tied up this long."

"It's fine. Sit down." Santos' voice was forceful, a commanding quality that I didn't often hear from him. But one that I liked. "I want you to stay right where you are."

"Demanding," I teased, lowering to take him fully inside me again.

Torr came around with a knife and carefully cut away the bindings. I was sorry to see the beautiful rope work go but already couldn't wait to play like that again.

Worry struck me again when Santos hissed and grimaced in pain. His arm came around my waist as he started to slide from the chair.

"Santos! What's wrong?" I tried to pull away but his strength was unmatched.

"Fine," he bit out. "Just circulation coming back, it's gonna hurt for a bit." We ended up on the floor, him flat on his back and me still on top of him.

"You sure you're okay?"

"I'm perfect." He did a small roll of his hips, making me gasp. "When I'm with you like this, it's impossible to be anything short of that."

I couldn't help but admire the indentations in his skin left behind by the rope. They would fade soon but were beautiful reminders of his devotion to me.

Tracing them with my fingers, I said, "You have been very good, and still haven't come yet."

"You told me not to, paloma." He said it like it was so simple, his broad hands spanning my hips and running up to my waist. "Use me to make yourself come, and let me touch you. Please?"

"Touch me all you want," I purred, pressing my palms into his chest. "I'm just as much yours as you are mine."

His grip clamped down on my waist as he bucked into me. My head threw back with the impact. As I crashed back down, my eyes found the two men on the bed again.

Hudson's skin was flushed, his breaths coming in fast, desperate pants as Devin jerked him with a quickening rhythm. I found myself riding Santos at the same pace of Devin's hand, my breaths finding sync with Hudson's. When he let out the first strangled groan of his orgasm, I was right there too.

Santos' fingers dug into my hips as I convulsed along his length, but my good boy remained solid as iron inside me. On my descent from the high, I folded over him and pressed a breathless kiss to his mouth. "Come with me on the next one," I whispered.

"Won't be long," he groaned through clenched teeth.

I sat upright just as Devin wrung the last jolts of pleasure from Hudson, his hand now taking a smooth, leisurely journey from the swollen head to the thick base.

"Devin." His name left my mouth like an incantation.

And like he was being summoned by me, he gave Hudson a final squeeze and a kiss before rising from the bed. His erection was heavy and taut, bobbing stiffly as he stood. My eyes traveled up Devin's body until our gazes met. I felt the need to say something, to ask for permission to touch him or ask if he was still okay with everything.

But before my scrambled, already well-fucked brain could string together a sentence, he stepped forward, bringing that jutting erection right in front of my face.

I leaned forward, lips parted, with my gaze never wavering from his. My tongue could dart out and taste him, but I paused mere inches away. He did not step back, nor did he look conflicted in the slightest. Instead, he brought his fingertips to the side of my face. With that small, tentative gesture, he urged me forward.

And I gave in to the temptation I never thought would happen.

My lips stretched around him, tongue leading the way. With a groan and a slight thrust forward, Devin's hand on my face became a more solid, sure touch. He cupped the side of my cheek, long fingers brushing back my hair like I was the most precious thing.

Santos began a slow, deep roll of his hips beneath me, holding me steady. While I crashed down to meet him, I began a tentative exploration of Devin as I took more of him in my mouth. A hand trailing up the long, lithe muscle of his thigh, fingers spreading wide when I reached the front of his hip and lower stomach. I followed the diagonal lines from his hip bones to the base of his cock, where I wrapped my fist around that stiff length.

The three of us got swept up in a rhythm of grunts, moans, ragged breaths, and slaps of slicking flesh. It was messy and pornographic. My legs ached and I was exhausted, wrung out on all the orgasms I had already, but I would not stop this for anything.

I looked up at one point to see Hudson standing behind Devin, their mouths locked in a brutal kiss as tattooed arms snaked over Devin's body. One hand slid down, caressing over Devin's stomach and hip, heading lower. That hand found its prize a moment later, cupping and massaging Devin's balls.

Desperate moans came from above me and his cock swelled in my mouth. Pleasure coiled in my clit despite my fatigue, and Santos' cock kicked inside me, urging me toward that peak. When a cool chest pressed against my sweat-slicked back, I would've grinned if my mouth wasn't full. Of course Torr had to rejoin us for the finale. It only felt right this way.

"Come for us," he commanded in my ear, fingers running down to my pleasure center. "For all of your men. Give us one more."

My final orgasm unfolded slowly, pleasure bursting at each point of contact. Santos' wet heat spilling inside me, Devin filling my mouth as Hudson handled him, and the weight of Torr's hand at the center of it all, his voice guiding me to bliss.

Chapter 27

Santos

Devin and I moved silently through the dark. It should have been pitch-black, but I was somehow able to find my way without issue, and he followed me with no complaint. Perhaps Tezca was lending me some of his night vision. Either way, I wasn't about to question this gift.

We had gotten out of bed way too early for this, didn't get anywhere near enough sleep after that incredible night with Rori. But I didn't feel sleep-deprived, and I'd venture a guess that Devin didn't either.

I was alert and as sharp as the edge of my machetes. All of my senses honed in on my surroundings. I was a primed and ready weapon, just waiting to be used.

I was the weapon they made me, but if today went well, it would be the last time. If everything went our way, the skills I'd learned in the fighting pit would end those who had made me a gladiator in the first place.

Rori and the others were not far behind, but Devin and I were chosen for this specifically because of our close combat skills.

The enemy would never see us coming.

We had left and hidden our bikes roughly a half mile back, where Astarte had perched on a tall boulder. Devin and I knew it was a signal to stop like we'd known our own names. From there, Tezca guided us silently through dense forests and steep hillsides.

I couldn't see him at the moment, he blended in too well for even my eyesight, but I could feel him nearby. Our compass and companion from the moment he showed us his power on the sands.

Near the edge of the treeline, Tezca stopped abruptly. Those large, yellow eyes were intense with warning as he turned his body to cross our direct path. He didn't need to speak into our minds to say, *This is as far as you go.*

I looked to Devin to discuss what to do next, but he was already moving.

Like a damn squirrel, he was climbing up the trunk of a nearby tree, barely testing the branches as he hauled himself up higher and higher. I almost laughed. Another way he was a ghost? With how fast he shimmied up that tree, he could have been weightless.

He stopped once he found a spot, and I kept an eye on the ground past the treeline while he observed from up top. All I could make out was a clearing in the distance, maybe a fence and buildings of some kind, but it was hard to tell. I could also make out small light sources, like flashlights or lanterns, moving around, though we were well out of their range now.

Devin came back to land about five minutes later and slowly moved his hands in the modified sign language Shadow and Grudge had taught us.

"There's a fence making a big square. Inside is freshly tilled earth, like planted crops. Rotating patrols all around the fence perimeter, I counted six. All armed with long-range rifles."

"What are the lights?" I asked, my hands moving just as slowly.

"Patrols have headlamps on. They look..." Devin paused as if trying to remember the sign, then he gave up and clumsily finger-spelled it. "Stupid."

I suppressed a laugh. "Roger that. What's beyond the fence?"

"Some buildings. Looks like mobile homes. Trailers and RVs. Didn't count many, but hard to see that far."

"So we're handling these perimeter guards, yeah?"

"That's what I'm thinking."

I dropped my hands and used my mouth to speak in a low whisper. "One last time as the Butcher and the Ghost, huh?"

Devin grinned and knocked his fist into mine. "For the right reasons this time."

With a soft hiss of steel, I unsheathed my machetes. A throwing knife appeared in each of Devin's hands without a sound. And with that, we were off.

We paused at the edge of the treeline to study the rotation pattern of the guards, which wasn't anything to write home about. They stood at the corner of the fence for about fifteen minutes, then the leader gave a signal and they all walked to the next corner.

Devin knocked his elbow into my arm. "Wait until they've been in one spot for a few minutes," he whispered. "Give 'em a chance to get comfy."

I nodded but felt worry needling in my gut. Something about this felt too easy. Although that was the point, wasn't it? We were here to make it easy for Rori and the others to crash through like a battering ram.

At the next rotation, Devin and I took off to find suitable positions to lie in wait before we struck. He headed for the outermost line of fencing, so I went for the back, closest to the buildings of the settlement. After we took care of the patrol, we'd go door to door and take care of the rest.

A week ago, I wouldn't have loved the idea of murdering people in their sleep, but nothing was off the table now. Their goddess had nearly taken Rori away from us. The Dark Mother did to her what she claimed she wanted to protect all women from. For bringing *that* into existence, there was no more mercy for these cultists. Only the children would be spared.

Since taking back our safe houses, we were operating under the assumption that every adult was armed anyway.

A few cars were parked between the fence and the trees, so I took cover behind one to stalk my targets. Devin was nowhere to be seen, but that was to be expected.

The guard closest to me was talking to someone further away. Their grips on their rifles were loose, and they leaned against the fence instead of standing at attention. In other words, painfully easy kills.

Their heads turned away from each other once there was a lull in conversation. My feet started moving, knowing Devin would take the opportunity to strike as well.

There was hardly any sound. No scream, not even a gurgled groan. Just the sound of a body slumping to the ground, and even that was softened, probably by Devin laying the body down gently so as to not be heard.

Still, it was enough for the woman in front of me to turn toward the sound. I was on her before she had the chance to call her friend's name, probably before she fully realized her fellow guard was no longer at her post.

One hand covered her mouth while my machete sliced cleanly through her neck like butter. She collapsed like her strings had been cut. I caught her fall, eased her to the ground, and moved on without a second thought.

The remaining patrol knew something was happening now. Their headlamps whipped around like fireflies in the night. But Devin and I were both nimble enough to stay out of range of those lights. We were as quiet as shadows and moved just as quickly. Systematically, we disposed of the patrolling women one by one, before they had a chance to wake anybody. Devin nodded at me once he laid the final body on the ground. It was time for phase two of our assault.

With a returned nod, I pulled the small flashlight from my pocket and pointed it toward the darkness away from the settlement. I clicked the light on and off in a distinct pattern--our signal for success. The sky was lightening to a rich, dusty blue as I repeated the signal two more times. Dawn would be here soon.

A small, flickering light came alive in the darkness, clicking on and off in an answering pattern.

"They know we're good," I told Devin. "They're coming."

A flutter of wings brought our gazes skyward to the white dove flying overhead.

"Hey, paloma," I whispered. Somehow I knew it was Rori up there, watching over us and looking for the best direction to launch an attack.

A shot rang out, shattering the peaceful quiet of the pre-dawn day.

"Shit!" The white bird veered sharply off course, wings beating in panicked desperation. Another shot fired, the sound's echo crackling like lightning, and the bird dropped like a stone from the sky.

"Someone's awake. They know we're here." Devin grabbed my shoulder in a rough squeeze, bringing me back to focus. "Let's take care of that shooter."

"Rori," I choked. "If she was up there—"

"She's fine. She's back in her own body," he insisted. "The bird is just a vessel. Astarte is still here too." He shook my shoulder harder. "Don't choke on me, Santos. This is it. Let's do our job, okay?"

I nodded, rolling my wrists to swing my blades, to feel the weight of those weapons like extensions of my arms again. "Yeah, let's go."

We headed for the heart of the settlement, which was just a corridor between the two rows of structures. As Devin had said, they were mostly mobile homes plus some RVs and pop-up campers. Some spaces were made, marked with stakes and nylon rope like they were planning foundations for more permanent homes. Too bad that would never happen for these people.

Devin and I stayed out of view of windows and doors, creeping in the narrow alleys between structures. The shooter had to have been sitting on a roof or something—

The sound of something large dragging through the main corridor made me freeze, locking up every muscle in my body while I listened hard. Devin and I were back-flatted against the side of a house, the source of the sound just around a corner. He took a peek first and then made a noise that sounded distinctively like a snort.

"What?" I demanded.

He resumed his position next to me, grinning. Then he jerked his head to the side as if to say, *Take a look.*

I peeled off the wall, placing my feet carefully so as to not make a sound. What I saw around that corner was Tezca in plain view of all the homes, sitting calmly in the center of the temporary village.

His jaws were clamped around the throat of a woman, pale, limp, and unmoving. She still had the rifle strapped around her torso.

"That was our kill, damn cat," Devin muttered.

"No," I said, the understanding hitting me. "He's a vengeful god, and that woman in his jaws just killed Astarte's vessel."

Beyond the black jaguar proudly displaying his kill for all to see, there was a flurry of movement behind windows and doors. People were rousing, shouting at each other inside their homes. A window slid open and a rifle barrel poked through the crack.

"Tezca!" I shouted.

But he was already gone, tearing off like a shadow. The barrel lifted to point at me, and I darted around the corner just as a chunk of siding broke off from the house.

The roar of a dozen engines was a constant hum in the air now, a vibration that energized my blood. More shots fired, and I knew some of them had to be our people.

"Which direction are they coming from?" I asked Devin, eying that rifle now lying unused in the middle of everything.

"Sounds like it's directly east." He cocked his head from one side to the other. "Yeah, behind those houses." He indicated the row opposite from ours.

"Perfect."

The four cult leaders had now emerged and were shouting

orders. "We're under attack! Eastern side, eastern side! Take your positions like we taught you!"

"Do it for your daughters!" yelled another woman, raising a rifle in the air before climbing up a ladder to the roof of an RV. Three more followed her, and other groups climbed up more rooftops. Some wore bulletproof vests and had hardened, battle-ready looks in their eyes. Others were wide-eyed with fear, still in their pajamas, holding their rifles like it was an animal about to bite them.

"Some are in the village! They got past the patrol, find them!"

With a quick nod, Devin and I separated, heading for the cover of cars, storage crates, and other items stacked behind the homes. Footsteps quickly crunched after us, loud and telling.

"We know you're hiding!" The woman fired a warning shot that was close enough to make my ears ring. "Come out, and we may still honor you as a sacrifice." She fired another shot that shattered the window of the car next to me.

"Could you be any louder?" chastised another woman. "And don't waste ammo." The next sound she made was a gasp and then a gurgle.

"Gladys!" cried the first woman. "Oh, Dark Mother, help us!"

I took the opportunity to dart out from my cover, machetes raised and thirsty. It took me a fraction of a second to reach her, and she had no idea until I drew a red line across her throat. She'd been too distracted by Devin's knife sticking out of her friend's neck.

"Your Dark Mother is dead," I told the woman as the last of her life drained away.

"Come on." Devin slapped my shoulder before she even stopped choking on her blood. "Let's back up the others."

We ran together back into the fray. A full-scale battle was waging now, gunfire and shouts ringing in my ears. Women were lined up on the roofs of the homes and RVs, shooting into the woods. It became clear quickly that our side didn't need much help—the women were being picked off at a brisk pace.

"Damn, Hudson," Devin muttered. "Leave some for the rest of us."

"That's probably Rori and Shadow too," I mused. All of our best shooters were likely at the front line.

"Smoke them out!" one of the cultist women yelled. "Give them smoke!"

Devin and I braced together, weapons ready. "Oh shit," I said when I realized what was happening.

The cultists had matches and lighters and they were lighting strips of cloth on fire. Strips of cloth that had been stuffed into glass bottles full of clear liquid.

Devin grabbed my shoulder roughly. "Guns. The two we just killed. We gotta grab their guns and stop them from setting the whole forest on fire."

He didn't have to tell me twice. We ran back behind the buildings where the two bodies lay. In the mere seconds it took to grab their weapons, the air was filled with the unmistakable smell of burning.

We ran back to the central corridor, and a wall of fire and smoke was already building between the structures and the woods. Shit, they must have set up a perimeter around the whole place. I looked around, noticing the straw laid out in what looked like a border path that seemed to go around all of the buildings. Piles of chopped branches were laid out in several places along the straw path as if they were being gathered for firewood. But these branches were young and freshly cut, which would create lots of smoke if they caught fire.

"Shit," I said again. These cultists were craftier than anticipated.

The smoke billowed out over the village, making the landscape eerie and unsettling. Also pretty much useless for shooting. My eyes watered painfully and my throat was already feeling the effects.

But over the chaos, I heard motorcycle engines approaching and male voices shouting. Our people had been flushed out of the woods and were heading into the village to finish this up close and personal.

Devin and I stayed low and covered, shooting at dark figures on the rooftops who were now scrambling down to get out of the rising smoke. It was much harder to tell who was friend or foe now, so our shots were cautious, hesitant.

With a deep mechanical roar, two massive, black figures burst out of the smoke from the north end of the village. Shadow and Grudge emerged on their bikes like a pair of henchmen from Hell, coming to take sinners to eternal damnation with them. One look at them and cultists on the ground started running. The two veterans picked them off easily, almost like they were bored.

Once the shock and awe wore off, Devin and I ran out to meet them.

"Anyone hurt?" I asked immediately.

"So far, so good, but we're on borrowed time until smoke inhalation fucks us." Shadow's mismatched eyes roamed everywhere except for us, tracking sound and movement through the smoke. "How are you guys? Okay?"

"Fine," Devin answered curtly. "Where's Rori?"

"Not sure. Everyone scattered when the smoke came. Torr should be with her, though."

Shadow lifted his rifle suddenly, pointing it at one of the rooftops. But the figure hiding in the smoke dropped dead from someone else's shot before he could fire.

Another figure took shape in the smoke, striding toward the edge of the awning and dropping gracefully to the ground.

"You gotta be faster than that, Uncle Shadow!" Valorie's voice was muffled by a bandanna tied around the lower half of her face.

Grudge signed something to his daughter in fast, aggressive gestures. Val rolled her eyes and signed back as she spoke. "Yes, Dad. I'll stay off the roofs."

"Hey!"

Torr rode up to us then, braking his bike with a harsh jerk. "You all seen Rori?"

"I thought she was with you," Shadow growled.

Torr shook his head, worry and regret taking over his features. "We got separated in the smoke. Can't see for shit."

"Split up. Find her," Shadow ordered. "My daughter will *not* end up in their hands again, you fucking hear me?"

Our small group took off in different directions without another word. Devin and I headed toward the southern end of the village, where we'd picked off the night patrol on the fenced-in area. Parts of the fence were already broken down, like motorcycles had crashed through them.

Another shootout was happening, the Hunter squeezing off round after round with grim determination at cultists hiding behind the same cars I had.

A woman's head popped up behind the hood, and she returned two more shots before her gun clicked empty. The Hunter holstered his weapon with a triumphant grin and returned his hands to the handlebars, driving his bike forward through the tilled earth.

"Don't worry, Hunt. We got them," Devin yelled as we made our way to the cars.

But the Hunter either didn't hear or was too hopped up on vengeance and adrenaline to care. He picked up speed, heading straight for the enemies, and disappeared.

It happened so fast, I thought I was hallucinating. One second he was riding, the next, he pitched forward and disappeared like he'd been swallowed by the earth.

Fortunately, Devin caught on faster than me. "There's holes in the ground! Don't drive over that, they'll trap you!"

The time it took for us to realize what was really under the tilled earth was enough for the cultist to reload and fire at us.

A bullet whizzed by my ear, and I hit the ground, scrambling for cover. More bullets sent mini explosions of dirt and fence splinters all around me. This bitch was actually a decent shot.

"Hey, you dumb cunt! I'm over here!" More gunfire, but this time, the bullets pinged off a metallic surface.

"Fuck, Rori!" She was barely visible in the smoke, her black leather jacket and short crop of blonde hair the only features I could make out.

The beautiful, ruthless, and insane love of my life spread her arms wide in a taunt to the other shooter. "I'm the one you want, right? Come stuff your stupid goddess back in me, I dare you!"

The shooter remained silent behind her cover, but she was definitely alive and moving. Rori could see it too, and when she was this pissed, she was *not* patient enough to wait out her prey.

She stuck the gun in her holster and gripped her handlebars, jerking her wrist to accelerate the bike forward.

"No!" I screamed. "Don't drive across, you'll fall!" But the smoky air had already wreaked havoc on my throat, and my voice couldn't cross the distance between us.

Devin tried too. "Go around! Don't drive through, it's a trap!"

Rori was already several yards deep into the tilled earth patch. When she heard Devin, she actually slowed the bike and lifted her head as if looking for him.

I cupped my hands around my mouth to yell at her again, but I couldn't scream louder than the shot that rang out.

The shot that hit her in the shoulder, making her body jerk to the side with the motorcycle following.

And then the ground swallowed her whole.

Chapter 28

Rori

Well, this was just fucking peachy.

My dominant shoulder was a throbbing, burning ball of pain. I was pinned under my bike in a damn hole in the ground, and there was dirt in my eyes, mouth, and ears. Oh yeah, and there was the fact that I'd taken a cheap shot by a cultist and had fallen into a literal trap.

"Fuck," I groaned, trying to breathe through the pain like I was going into labor. I couldn't feel my legs from the knees down, and that was also a bad sign. My back was also massively uncomfortable, like something was underneath me.

"Come on, Wilder." With my right arm useless, I had to throw everything into my left side to get the motorcycle off my legs. For a touring bike, it was pretty lightweight. That still didn't make it easy to move a four hundred pound metallic contraption with one fucking arm.

After several tries, I got just enough leverage to turn the handlebars and front wheel and pull my left leg free. With gritted teeth to brace for the pain, I wiggled my toes inside my boot. When that worked, I tried rolling my ankle. Then I flexed my foot up and down. A little sore, but it didn't feel sprained or broken.

"Alright. Now the other." I didn't know when I'd become a person that gave myself pep talks, but no one else was going to get me out of this. All my men were up on the surface, fighting for their lives. And I needed to get back up there and help as soon as possible.

Now that I had one good leg in addition to my arm, I used both to push the motorcycle off my remaining leg. I tried wiggling my toes in that boot and—

"Oh fucking Christ! Fuck me!"

The pain shooting up my leg was blinding, leaving me breathless and shocked.

"Okay," I panted when the pain reduced to a manageable level. "Not riding any time soon. Or climbing out of this hole myself, I guess."

It drove me mad that I was stuck and had to wait for help. I was the president. It was my job to lead the charge and protect my people. But my crew was capable, skilled, and not to mention vengeful. I knew they'd finish what they came here to do, then come find me when they could.

I didn't dare yell for anyone to get me out. Santos and Devin saw me fall, they knew where I was. And I didn't want to add to the noise and potentially distract someone in a life-or-death situation.

So I listened to the sounds of battle raging above me while moving as gingerly as I could. My whole right side was fucked, from ankle to shoulder. And that was damn annoying when it was my dominant side. Even with being in as much pain as I was, it was hard to shake the habit of depending on that arm, that leg.

It reminded me of one of the many lessons my dad Gunner had taught me. He made me do shooting drills over and over with my non-dominant hand until I was just as accurate with my left as I was with my right. When teaching me hand-to-hand combat, he'd even tied my right hand behind my back and had me throw punches and knife strikes for an entire month like that.

"What if you got captured and they broke your dominant hand?" he'd say whenever I complained. "What if you're tied up and you can get more leverage on your left side to wiggle free? You just going to give up because that side is weaker? No, you're not, Rori. You know why?" Then he'd pulled me into a hug after seeing how tired and frustrated I was. "Because you're *my* daughter. And no daughter of Demons is going to give up on herself."

His words repeated in my head as I leaned my weight into my left side, finding balance and steadiness in my good leg while my hand braced against the dirt wall. For the first time since falling in, I was able to get my bearings and look closer at the hole I'd found myself in.

It was big, obviously. Big enough for me and my bike to fall cleanly through, and deep enough that I wouldn't have been able to climb out even with two good legs. By my estimate, I was about eight feet deep, and the space around me couldn't have been more than six square feet.

They'd been expecting us on our bikes, it seemed. Even so, digging multiple holes of this size had to be a hell of a job. The opening had been covered by thin plywood and loose earth, disguised to look like part of a long row of tilled earth. Even I had to admit it was clever.

Loose dirt and broken pieces of plywood littered the ground where my bike and I had fallen. My bike which now had a bent frame and scratches and probably even more damage that I couldn't see.

"Don't worry, baby." I leaned my good shoulder against the wall while I reached out with my left foot to give the front tire an affectionate stroke. "Jandro will get you right as rain when this is all over."

The bike leaned at an odd angle against dirt mounds of various sizes. I remembered the discomfort on my back, like I hadn't fallen against packed earth but something else instead.

Curious and with nothing better to distract me from the pain, I gingerly moved closer to the dirt mounds. Cradling my right arm against my chest, I used my good arm to toss aside the broken pieces of plywood and start wiping away the loose soil.

When I uncovered the face of a man, I forgot all about pain for a single instant.

I screamed and scrambled away, my right foot shooting a reminder of its condition all the way up to my skull. My breath whistled through my teeth, both because of the pain and the shock of seeing that face I couldn't look away from. He stared blankly up at the sky, eerily unmoving.

I didn't need to feel for a pulse or wipe away more dirt to see the gray of his skin. The poor man was dead. There was no other reason he'd be at the bottom of a hole, dirt carelessly thrown onto him.

It took a few more minutes of pained breathing to come to terms that I was in a hole with a dead man. Once the shock wore off, I could start to think rationally again. He wasn't stinking or decomposing yet. So he must have died recently.

Somehow, I got up the nerve to brush more dirt off of him. I wanted to see this man as he had been, as a human being who once had a life. Most likely, I wouldn't be able to tell much, but I wanted to find out what I could about who he had been.

I uncovered one of his arms and turned his hand over. God, his body wasn't even stiff yet.

The sight of his palm brought fresh tears to my eyes. The skin was broken and raw in so many places. He'd been bleeding from his hands before he died.

That explained how these holes had been dug.

"I'm sorry." I squeezed his hand as if he could feel me doing it. "I'm so sorry we were too late for you. I hope you're at peace now." With some effort, I bent his elbow to place his hand on his chest. "If you have family, we'll find them. We'll return you to them, I promise."

I closed the man's eyelids just as a small shower of dirt and pebbles rained down, like someone was at the edge of the hole. Shielding my eyes, I looked up and squinted. The sun was rising and it was especially bright at the opening of my dark, underground prison.

I couldn't see exactly who was standing at the edge of the hole, but I did catch a leather jacket and a motorcycle helmet with the visor pulled down.

"Hey, is it over?" I called up.

The helmet nodded but otherwise stood there without saying anything. There was too much pain coursing through my body to give it much thought. All I wanted was some relief and to see that my men were unharmed.

"There's gotta be a ladder around somewhere. In one of the houses, maybe. But someone might still have to carry me. I'm kinda fucked up."

The helmeted biker again said nothing and just stood there. My reflection in the visor was tiny, a muted blonde head in a pit of darkness. Only then did I start to sense something else through the pain. My thoughts raced through the faces of my riders, especially the ones I knew the least. Who wore a helmet like that? I couldn't think of a single one.

"Who are you?" I tried to keep the pain out of my voice as I angled my bad arm and leg away from the figure. "Take your helmet off. Show yourself."

The person dropped to their haunches at the edge of the trap, then lowered their feet to dangle over the side. I backed as far away as I could while the person slid carefully down the dirt wall and landed gracefully in the hole with me.

It had to be a woman. She looked shorter than me, despite currently standing on the side panel and rear tire of my bike. She even scraped mud off her shoe against the treads of my tire. If I had use of both arms, she wouldn't have been standing up any longer. Such disrespect.

"Who the fuck are you?" I demanded again.

Two small, feminine hands went to the sides of the helmet and paused there, as if drawing out the suspense to tease me. I gritted my teeth and continued to wait, refusing to play into her game.

The helmet lifted slowly, revealing a chin, lips, nose, and finally an entire face. One that I didn't know but vaguely recognized. It hit me as she shook out shoulder length brown hair.

"You're one of them," I realized. "One of the cult leaders." She had to be the youngest one, somewhere in her mid to late thirties.

"So you do have some sense after casting out our Dark Mother." She tucked the motorcycle helmet under her arm. "And I thought you'd make this too easy on me."

I didn't dare flick my gaze up to the top of the hole, even though that was all I wanted to do. But I was injured with one of the crazy cult leaders right in front of me. I wasn't taking my eyes off this bitch for a second.

"Call for your men if you want, but they won't hear you." She put the helmet down and proceeded to shrug off the leather jacket. Everything about her movement and tone was so casual, it was eerie.

"I'm not calling for anyone," I said. "You can hide down here, but it's just a matter of time. Your cult is gone. We've won."

"Are you so sure about that, *President?*" Her tone turned mocking as she tacked on my title. "The biker queen stuck underground with a gunshot wound and a broken ankle doesn't bode too well for your side."

I swallowed, refusing to give in to her taunting. The Sisterhood outnumbered us, but we were better skilled and experienced fighters. Santos and Devin even took out their patrol so we'd catch them unaware, although it seemed they were ready anyway. Still, I had confidence in my people, especially with my dad and uncle joining us.

"I thought I'd be impressed meeting you face-to-face," she went on after my silence. "The Dark Mother insisted you were the one, the perfect vessel to lead us into our new age but," she shook her head, her expression falling into one of disappointment, "you're just another woman weakened by men."

While she spoke, my good hand moved slowly to the gun holster under my jacket. "I would say sorry to disappoint but I honestly don't give a fuck."

In the blink of an eye, I drew and fired, but even in the small space, she managed to dodge it. She came at me with surprising speed, head and shoulders low as she tackled me around the middle. Blinding pain shot up my shoulder as she slammed me into the wall. I fought against it for clarity, for all the fighting instincts I'd been taught by my fathers until they were second nature.

I pressed the barrel of my gun against her head, but she anticipated the move and pulled it from my weakened grip. Maybe it was the desperation of the moment, maybe she didn't know guns well enough to use it, but she tossed it to the other side of the hole rather than turning it on me.

The woman clearly wasn't an experienced fighter and left so many openings I could have exploited. She exposed her neck when she tossed the gun and had me pinned against the wall in an awkward, easily breakable position, had I been at full strength. Her only advantages were my damn injuries, and she was exploiting those in full force.

She would wait until I was trapped and maimed to fight me head-on. Cowardly bitch.

Numbness was setting in now, my vision darkening as my consciousness wobbled on a tightrope. If I passed out, she would certainly kill me. I had to gain the upper hand somehow, and fast.

I sagged against the wall, moaning and whimpering. Everything hurt like a bitch, so it wasn't entirely an act, but she fell for it anyway. Her hold let up on me just slightly, and she raised her head to look me in the face.

With what little remained of my flagging strength, I headbutted the bitch right in the nose.

The crunching sound of cartilage and her resulting cry of pain were satisfying to be sure. But what I really needed was for her to back away, to be lost in her own haze of pain for a moment.

She doubled over, clutching the front of her face, and like a dumbass, turned her back on me. It gave me just enough time to pull a switchblade from my boot, the last weapon in my arsenal. What I would give to be Devin right then, with hidden knives strapped all over my body.

Ha. I'll have to tell him that, if I see him again.

I held my knife out, staring at the woman's bent over back. Fuck, I could stab her so easily. Get her in the kidneys, her spinal cord, if only I could walk a few feet straight ahead without falling over. Throwing the knife was another option, but that wasn't what it was meant for. Plus, that wasn't my strongest skill set. I could miss, or just nick her, which would be a waste.

Another thing to learn from Devin, if I ever made it out of here.

The woman started turning back to me, and I opted to hide the knife up my sleeve. I needed her up close to use it, needed her thinking I was weaker than I actually was.

A genuine bolt of fear struck when she went for my gun that she'd tossed aside. To my dismay, she released the magazine to check the remaining ammo before slamming it back inside. She even pulled back the slide to make sure a bullet was in the chamber. This bitch knew what she was doing.

"Wait, wait." I held up my good hand, feeling the knife handle slide down toward my armpit. It wasn't too hard to sound desperate. "Let's just talk, woman to woman. I get it, okay? Men are terrible. They're entitled, stupid, and can't even wash their ass correctly."

"Too late for any of that." She trained the gun on me, eyes alight with hatred above her swelling nose bridge. "We have no use for you now. Any of you. You may have decimated our numbers but we *will* rebuild. The Dark Mother will regain consciousness through our devotion, and she will find another vessel, a better one. One that doesn't—FUCK!"

The handful of dirt I flung in her face bought me precious little time. I screamed through clenched teeth as I dragged my whole body forward, caught my knife handle in my palm, and shoved the blade into her stomach, twisting and pressing as far as it would go. She dropped the gun in her shock and I kicked it away. I saw the punch coming but didn't expect it to land so hard. My jaw lit up, as did my vision. Dots and lights sparkled like it was Christmas.

The world faded in and out, darkening and lightening up with detail like a TV screen being switched on and off. The woman was on top of me, drawing her bloody fist back again and again. I tried to hit back but couldn't tell if I landed anything. I just felt so heavy and tired.

Don't you dare. You're almost at the end, don't you dare stop fighting now. The voice came from within my own head, but those weren't my thoughts.

Astarte? I thought you died.

I'm a deity that has been self-aware since the Bronze Age. I can't die, genius. And today, neither will you.

Even then, I wanted to laugh. But my mouth wasn't working right. And it was full of something.

Turn your head. Spit out all that blood before you choke on it. There you go, little human. Now stay alive a little longer.

Easy for you to say, I thought.

Do not give in, Aurora.

You almost sound worried about me. I'm touched.

Think of your men. Your family. They will all need you for years to come.

Much like with the Dark Mother, it felt like fighting against an impossible current. A tidal wave against a grain of sand. I was being pulled under, and this time, I truly didn't have any strength left to fight it.

I'm so tired, though...I've been fighting...so much...

Aurora!

Chapter 29

Rori

The weight on top of me had to be the woman. She'd succumbed to her injuries and somehow, I was still alive.

I shoved at her, forgetting that my right shoulder had been shot until a deep, throbbing pain pulsed all the way up my arm into my skull.

"Hey, hey, easy," a familiar voice said above my head while a soothing hand pressed down on my good shoulder. "You're safe, cuz. Come back slowly. That's just Tezca on you. He's been healing you."

"Val?" I croaked, my brain coming online slowly.

"None other. Here, have some water."

She pushed a straw between my cracked lips, which I sucked on greedily until she took it away.

I wasn't ready to open my eyes yet, but I processed my surroundings slowly, piece by piece. Reaching down, I found Tezca's head on my belly and scratched that velvety fur. His purr started up as he licked my hand, the healing rumble soothing all my aches as my injuries announced themselves. There was another rumbling too, a vibrating sensation underneath and all around me.

"Where are we?" I rubbed my eyelids, which felt like they had been welded shut.

"In my truck bed. Torr's driving. Santos and Devin are up front with him. Right now, I'd say we're, oh, about three hours away from Four Corners."

A wave of relief immediately washed over me knowing that Torr, Santos, and Devin were okay, but the first thing out of my mouth was, "Four Corners? The fuck?"

"Yeah, you've been out for a minute." Val's hand returned to my shoulder. "It's over, Pres," she whispered. "We did it."

I wanted nothing more than to sit all the way up and demand that she tell me everything, but my injuries forced me to move slowly. And when I finally did open my eyes, I was in for another surprise. Val, Tezca, and I were not alone in the truck bed.

My eyes met those of four girls sitting against the right and left sides, all looking to be between the ages of three and eight.

"Uh, hi."

None of them replied as I slowly sat up. The younger two seemed curious. The others, suspicious.

"I went back to the safehouses for my truck after they got you out of the hole," Val explained. "Then Torr and your dad agreed we should find the kids immediately, and Tezca led us straight there. So," she nodded at the four silent girls sitting with us, "here we are."

"Was..." So many questions hit me at once, and it was a struggle choosing which to ask first. "Was there another battle?"

Val lifted one shoulder. "I wouldn't call it much of a battle. We...took care of most of them at the settlement." She spoke carefully, eyes flicking toward the children. "And the remainder were not a problem for us. The kids were kept hidden away, and once we found them, we didn't let them see what had happened."

"She won't tell us anything," declared one of the older girls, mean-mugging me as hard as she could with her arms wrapped protectively around one of the smaller children. "You kidnapped us!"

Val gave her a sympathetic look. "I know it seems that way now. But one day, you'll understand we are not the bad people in this situation."

"You have *men* with you!" the girl argued. "They're going to hurt us just like mama said!"

"No one is going to hurt you." This time Val cast her eyes toward me, a weary expression on her face.

Yeah, that look said it all. It was going to take years of patience, love, and therapy to un-indoctrinate these kids.

I wanted to ask Val more about what happened after I'd fallen in the hole, but gruesome battle details probably weren't kid-appropriate conversation.

So I opted for more basic questions instead. "How many kids?"

"Twelve in total," Val said. "Paige is riding in the other truck with the rest. None of the guys are in close proximity to them, for obvious reasons."

I nodded. "Did we lose anyone?"

Val shook her head, and I sagged with relief. "Some injuries, but you were the worst off." My cousin's expression went grave. "I had to restart your heart in front of your men and your dad. Talk about working under pressure."

I brought my hand to my chest, feeling the bruised flesh around my sternum for the first time. "You always did love to tit-punch me."

"Yeah, well, it was actually necessary this time."

A sudden thought hit me as I remembered blank, empty eyes and a hand that had been scraped raw. I scooted closer to Val, keeping my voice low so the children wouldn't hear. "A man's body was in the hole. The cult forced him to dig it before killing him, and there's probably more. We have to recover him, and the sacrifices—"

"We will." Val took my hand and squeezed. "I promise you we will, cuz. But we have to get you and everyone home first. Get these kids checked out. The dead will be honored, but they can wait a little longer."

I was quiet for a long while, letting it all sink in. "It's really over then, isn't it?"

Val squeezed my hand harder and grinned. "Yeah. It is, President."

———

Torr didn't stop driving until he pulled up to the hospital in Four Corners. The kids were ushered into the pediatric ward, and I was immediately sent to emergency surgery to get the bullet out of my shoulder. I kicked up as much of a fuss as I could, telling the doctors to look over my people first, but they were having none of it, and I was out like a light before I knew it.

When I came to, my head felt like it had been stuffed with cotton, but the pain was blissfully gone. It was also much easier to open my eyes now, but that didn't prepare me for the person I saw sitting next to my hospital bed.

"Welcome back," Hudson said softly. He started to rise. "I'll get Torr and the others—"

"No, wait." My protest was a breathy whisper, so I tried again. "Wait. Not yet. Give me... a few minutes before they all rush in."

Hudson froze on his way to the door, then rushed over as I started to sit up. "Here. The bed moves so you don't have to."

He pushed a button on the side of the bed and the head started to lift me into a sitting position, making me chuckle in embarrassment. "Oh, that's right. They can do that."

"I can raise your feet too. I can also see if it'll make you breakfast, but I don't think we're there yet."

That kept me smiling. "That's okay. I'm good, thanks."

Hudson nodded and resumed standing awkwardly next to me. "I'm glad you're feeling better."

"Me too. Drugs are awesome like that." We laughed a little together before silence returned. "Did I say anything funny while I was under?"

"Uh, well." He rubbed his jaw, trying to hide a smile. "You woke up a couple hours ago saying no one better tell your mom you were here because that'd be embarrassing. Torr broke the news that your mom already knew, and then you started talking about building a house on the moon to hide from your family."

"Wow." I laughed. "That's absurd but also makes total sense." My eyebrows lifted. "Have you met my mother yet?"

"Not yet. Someone said she was helping the pediatricians do check-ups on the kids."

"That sounds like her." I noticed his face going remote. "Hey, you okay?"

"Yeah, just..." He dragged his chair closer and dropped into it with a sigh. "They're going to run DNA tests and I know..."

He didn't have to explain it. Some, if not most of those children, will have been fathered by him.

"Hudson, look at me." It was hard to ignore my heart beating faster when those blue eyes lifted to mine. "My mother understands. Everyone who was there with us is behind you. No one is going to force responsibility or anything onto you regarding those kids."

"I still feel responsible," he admitted. "They're here now. They're people who exist in the world. What kind of person would I be to not at least acknowledge my part in that?"

"Well, you don't have to decide right now. But anyway, I haven't asked yet. How are you? How's everyone?"

Hudson shrugged and gave a small shake of his head. "We're all fine. Just worried about you. Torr and Santos haven't slept since before we hit the settlement. I told them to go find a bed somewhere, but I think they crashed in the hallway."

I laughed at that mental image. "It's sweet of you to stay with me."

He shrugged again like it was no big deal. "Told 'em I would."

"So Devin's good? The Hunter? Paige?"

"Everyone is alive and well. We all got checked out by doctors. Some of the guys are staying at the hotel down the street, checking out the town." His gaze got heavy. "Just waiting for their president's orders."

I scoffed, looked at my right arm in a sling and my right foot elevated and in a cast. "Don't think I'm riding for a while."

"You're still our president, though."

"That 'our' sounds an awful lot like you're including yourself."

"I am." He was dead serious, his face solemn and his gaze steady. "Your dad's with your family, but as soon as he's free, I'm getting my Vengeful Gods tattoo. I'll follow you anywhere, Rori."

My throat tightened with emotion, and I blinked rapidly to keep the tears at bay. Did he have any idea how significant this moment was? He must've. The amount of trust he was placing in me was beyond my wildest dreams. It almost felt too good to be true.

"Why?" I asked. "You know you can be with Devin without following me. I would never ask you to—"

"I had a choice," he cut in. "When we cleared out the settlement and were looking for you... We swept over the field where the holes were hidden. I was the one that found you."

Hudson brought his palms together, eyes focused on his fingertips. "I looked over and saw her hitting you over and over. You were limp, just taking it. You must have been unconscious already. And I realized something." He paused as if he had to push himself to continue speaking. "I could've let her kill you, and no one would've known. Then I'd kill her myself. That would have meant two less women in the world, and the old me would have found that something to celebrate."

His eyes lifted to mine and I was stunned at the emotion in them, a stark contrast to the coldness in his words. "As soon as that thought entered my mind, I realized I couldn't let it happen. After everything you did for me, for the gladiators, I couldn't let you die. I didn't—" He swallowed and struggled again to speak. "I didn't want to live in a world without you in it."

There was a long, tense silence until I broke it. "So you saved my life."

He shook his head, refusing to look at me again. "When Val had to restart your heart, I almost lost my shit. I thought that one second of hesitation made me too late. I still can't believe that thought entered my head."

"Stop that. Come here." I held my good hand out for him to take. When he just stared at it, I added, "As your president, I order you."

That got a small smile out of him, like I'd hoped. His fingers were warm as they clasped around mine in a gentle squeeze.

"First of all, like those kids, you're undoing some indoctrination too. You've felt nothing but hate for women for years, then got thrown into dealing with *me*, of all people. It's okay if some of those old thoughts intrude, because they shaped your reality for so long."

"It's not okay, though," he argued. "Not when it comes to life and death decisions."

"I'm not done." I gave a cheeky squeeze to his hand. "Second of all, you're not perfect and nobody expects you to be. No one is policing your thoughts, and it's your actions that matter anyway. You acted quickly enough to save my life. And third of all." I released his hand and held my arm out in a *ta-da* motion. "I'm alive and on some damn good painkillers. So don't beat yourself up when it all worked out in the end."

Hudson laughed, and it sounded like actual joy bubbled out of his chest for the first time in a while. "You make it hard to argue, President."

He looked happy, genuinely so. It looked good on him, and I couldn't stop smiling. "I'm glad you're here, Hudson."

"Me too, Rori."

The next thing I knew, he was smoothing my hair back and placing a kiss on my forehead. Only then did I think about how shitty I must have looked, considering how many punches to the face I had received.

Hudson lingered with his lips on my forehead for a moment, long enough for me to wonder if he'd consider becoming more than just one of the men who followed me.

Would he ever join the ones who stood beside me?

Before I could venture any kind of questions in that direction, he straightened and backed away. "I'll let the guys know you're awake."

Then he turned and left the room.

Chapter 30

Hudson

Two weeks after arriving in Four Corners, Rori and Devin waited with me in the doctor's office. Rori paced around the room, seemingly unable to sit still despite the walking boot on her foot. When she did sit down on the doctor's little rolling stool, her left knee bounced up and down.

"Will you stop?" Devin grumbled at her. "You're making *me* nervous."

"Sorry." She drummed her fingers on her knee, looking toward the door. Her right arm was no longer in a cast, though she still held it tucked close to her body. "I don't know why I'm so worked up."

"It's okay." I knocked my shoulder into Devin's, who was sitting beside me on the exam table. "Watching her fidget keeps my mind off of whatever the news is gonna be."

"See?" Rori held her hand out toward me. "I'm helping."

A knock came to the door then, and it opened from the outside a few moments later.

"Hi, everyone," came the friendly greeting from the doctor, an attractive woman in her late forties with olive skin and long, brown hair. "How are we doing?"

"Hi, Mom," Rori answered. "They seem good, but I'm on pins and needles over here."

Dr. Wilder chuckled as she planted a kiss on her daughter's forehead, then playfully smacked her shoulder with the paper folder in her hand. "Move it, mija. You're in my seat."

With an exaggerated sigh and groan, Rori stood from the rolling stool and crossed the room to stand by Devin and me.

As her mother took her place on the stool and wheeled closer to us, I could see the resemblance more clearly. She and Rori had the same cheekbones, nose, and lips.

"So," the doctor placed the folder on her lap, "are we ready to know? Do you have any questions for me first?"

I felt Rori and Devin's eyes on me as I shook my head. "Just give it to me straight, Dr. Wilder."

"Of course. And please call me Mari."

There was a warmth about Rori's mother that I felt the moment she came in. She had a calming, comforting presence, to the point where I felt no anxiety when she opened the folder's cover. No wonder Shadow's uneasy soul had been so drawn to her.

"Of the twelve children rescued from the Sisterhood," Mari's eyes scanned the document in her lap, her finger trailing over the DNA results, "four of them are biologically yours, Hudson."

"Four," I breathed, letting the information sink in. "That's...actually less than I expected."

Mari nodded. "The oldest is five. The youngest is six months."

Devin cleared his throat. "The other kids that aren't his. Are any of them, uh..."

"None are yours or Santos'," Mari said with a gentle smile. "They all have different fathers, actually. I imagine most of the mothers came to the cult while pregnant or after their children were already born."

"Where are the kids now?" Rori asked.

"And are they safe?" A protective urge rose up in me that I didn't expect.

"They're in foster homes and are completely safe," Mari assured us. "The foster families are vetted and interviewed extensively. We also have a team of nurses who go out and do check-ups on the children weekly. Along with any medical issues, they're trained to look for and report any signs of abuse or neglect. I promise you, the children are as well taken care of as they can be."

The doctor focused her gaze on me. "As for the ones sired by you, you have choices, Hudson. You can meet them, if you'd like, and decide if you want a relationship with them. The families they're with have been told a very basic overview of your situation, and they're open to visits from you, if you'd like. If you're not ready for that at this time, that's okay too."

The room fell silent, waiting for an answer from me.

"What happens if I...I don't?" I clasped my fingers together, searching for words that were oddly difficult to spit out. "If I don't...claim them as my own?"

"After some time to adjust, they will be eligible for adoption," Mari answered. "The territory is giving you priority and a grace period to decide, since you are the biological father. But if you don't seek parental rights after twelve months, they will seek to place those children in adoptive families."

Devin wrapped a hand around my upper arm and placed his chin on my shoulder. "No one will blame you if you're not ready to be a parent in a year. You never wanted this. You never agreed to have kids. And they'll still be happy and cared for."

Mari nodded sagely. "The territory and adoption agency are sympathetic as to what happened in that cult, but they must act in the best interest of the children. These kids need stability and a very gentle introduction to normal society so they can thrive."

"I want to meet them." The declaration was out of my mouth before I could give it much thought, but it felt right as soon as I said it. "Well, maybe one of them to start."

Mari smiled warmly again. "How about two? The two older ones are with one family and the two younger ones are with another."

I swallowed and nodded, nerves lighting up my stomach. But if anything, that was just further proof I was doing the right thing. "Okay, sure. Two of them. Maybe the older two first? I don't know, I've never spent much time around kids."

Mari closed her folder and beamed at me. "Just be yourself, Hudson. You'll do great."

———

Rori and I pulled up to a small house three days later. She wasn't in riding shape yet, so we borrowed her brother's car to make this visit together. It didn't hit me until right then that this was what couples did. Partners in love met children for the first time, not friends or... whatever we were.

Really, it should have been Devin with me. But the kids were still distrustful of men, if not absolutely terrified of them. Mari and the social worker I talked to recommended that I have a woman with me when I met my children for the first time.

My children. I was still getting used to that idea.

But I wasn't bothered by the idea that Rori and I looked like a couple. There was actually no one better to do this, and I was glad she was here. My feelings were complicated, but for now, I was just grateful for her support.

"Cute little place," Rori remarked when I cut the engine.

The house did look cozy and well-maintained. Flower bushes of some kind lined the walkway. The exterior was painted a soft blue with an off-white trim and had painted shutters framing the windows. It looked every bit like a warm, happy home where kids were loved and content.

A stab of inadequacy hit me. How was I the number one candidate with rights to these children? I had nothing. No home or way to make a living. Even the clothes on my back were borrowed. Just because we shared blood didn't mean I could be a father.

"You good?" Rori asked gently. "We can try another day, if you want."

It was a fair question. Was I actually ready for this?

I was here now. Uncomfortable and completely out of my element, yes. But if I left now, would I really come back? Or would I just avoid this discomfort, this massive potential responsibility being held out to me? I was getting stronger in trusting myself but wasn't all the way there yet.

"Yeah, I'm good," I told Rori as casually as I could manage.

I gestured for her to go ahead of me, an idea we'd discussed with June and Lisa, the foster parents, over the phone. The children would be more at ease seeing another woman first.

Rori gave my arm a squeeze as she walked past me, heading up the charming mosaic-tiled walkway to the front door where she knocked gently.

A Black woman almost as tall as Rori and with long, multicolored braided hair opened the door, smiling warmly as she stepped aside to let us in. "Hello, come in! I'm Lisa. June's watching the girls out back."

"Thank you for letting us come over," Rori answered. "I'm Rori, this is Hudson."

"Well, I can see the resemblance," Lisa said as she shook my hand. "Maia, the older one, looks just like you."

"Thanks." I laughed nervously. "That's promising, I hope."

I was antsy to meet these kids, I realized. I wanted to learn about them, their likes and dislikes, their dreams and fears.

"Please make yourselves comfortable." Lisa gestured toward a cozy living room with deep set couches. "I was just making some tea, would you all like some?"

"That would be lovely, thank you." Rori took a seat and smiled graciously. It was a trip seeing her this way, all warm and polite. I almost couldn't believe this same woman was the foul-mouthed biker president with a thirst for revenge.

But that thirst had been sated now, I reminded myself. The nightmare was really over.

Once settled on the couch with tea, I could see through a bay window to a large backyard. A Caucasian woman with dark hair up in a messy bun sat on the other side of the window. We could hear her talking to the two girls, though they weren't in view.

"Sounds like they're settling in well," Rori remarked.

"Every day is a little bit better," Lisa said with a nod. "The younger one, Elodie, probably won't remember the cult. But Maia is old enough to remember, and she struggles to understand some things. She asks about her mom a lot. We try to tell her that her mom wasn't a bad person, but she had brought Maia into a dangerous situation. So she had to come with us to be safe."

"Do they have the same mother?" I asked.

"No, different mothers," Lisa said. "Those two are like peas in a pod, though. Very emotionally close, like true sisters." Lisa placed her mug down on the coffee table and brought her hands to her lap. "Are you ready to meet them?"

"Yes," I said. "I would like to."

"Are we still okay doing it as we discussed?" Lisa's gaze shifted from me to Rori.

"Yes," I said again. "Whatever it takes to make them feel more comfortable."

"Alright then."

She stood from the couch and headed for the backyard, with Rori and me following. After opening the sliding door, she and Rori stepped outside while I stayed behind.

I could see and hear the kids from where I stood, but they wouldn't see me until I was signaled to come out. The children had been taught by the Sisterhood not to have any interaction with outsiders and that men were especially unsafe. So our plan was to introduce them to Rori first, and then, based on their reactions, see if they were open to meeting me.

"Hey hun, Rori's here," Lisa said to her wife. "Girls, this is our friend, Rori. Can you say hello and introduce yourselves?"

"Hiii!" Elodie, the almost-four year old, waved and smiled brightly at Rori. "We're playing sandbox."

The younger of the two had russet brown hair curling around her face, much like mine had at that age. Her expression was open, happy, and curious about her foster mothers' new friend. Maia, on the other hand, remained silent and withdrawn, watching Rori suspiciously. She *did* look like me, down to the blue eyes and furrowed brows.

Lisa and June didn't push Maia for an introduction, and Rori seemed to take note of her frostiness, crossing her legs to sit on the grass just outside of the girls' sandbox. "I like all your shovels and tools in there." Rori gestured to the brightly colored plastic buckets, rakes, and other sandcastle building supplies. "Can you show me what you're making?"

Elodie babbled happily about her sandcastle process, showing Rori everything she used and what it made. Maia, however, silently continued her own project in the far corner of the sandbox.

"This is so cool." Rori was engaged and attentive to Elodie the whole time. "You've got a whole workshop. My dad has a workshop too, only his stuff is for building motorcycles."

"Dad?" Maia asked in shock, speaking up for the first time. "You have a dad?"

"I do, four of them actually." Rori smiled at her. "And I love them just as much as I love my mom."

Damn, that was slick. Way to shift the conversation in an age-appropriate way.

"My mom said all dads were bad, and that's why we didn't have any," Maia argued.

"Some dads are bad, that's true. But so are some moms. Moms and dads are just people, so there are good and bad ones out there."

"I had an amazing dad." Lisa had sat on the bench next to June and clasped the other woman's hand. "He supported us through everything. I miss him every day."

"I'm sorry you lost him," Rori said gently.

As the conversation progressed, Maia gradually moved closer to Rori. "What's it like having a dad?"

"Well, it's different for everyone. But for me, it was great. Sometimes a little overbearing because I had four of them, but they taught me so much. How to defend myself and ride motorcycles. How to treat other people and care for the ones I love. When I was really little, it was like having four superheroes. Big, strong guys who would protect me from anything."

"They protected you?" Maia's attention was rapt on Rori, like she was learning the secrets of the universe.

Rori nodded. "A good dad will always protect you. Sometimes even when you don't want protection," she added with a laugh.

"I wish I had a good dad," Elodie sighed wistfully as she smacked a plastic shovel on her sand tower.

Rori looked at the two foster mothers first and then at me, mouthing with a smile, "Ready?"

I nodded, my heart pounding in my chest.

"If you two would like to meet him, I know someone who'd be a great dad." Rori grinned at the two girls. "He'd love a chance to be yours."

"A dad? For us?" Maia looked suspicious but also intrigued.

"Not just any old dad, but an excellent one. He's a great protector, he's big and strong, and he won't let anyone hurt you." Rori's smile softened and her cheeks darkened with a flush. "He's also smart and funny, and he's honest. He's a good listener, and he gives great hugs. I know for a fact you girls will be safe with him."

I was so floored by everything she'd said, I almost missed the head nod she did as my cue to come out. Even as I walked over, my thoughts were in a daze. She knew I could hear everything, but she wouldn't lie to those kids, right? Rori Wilder would never speak so highly of anyone unless she believed it was the truth.

"Girls, this is my friend, Hudson." She tugged at my pant leg a bit, and I took the invitation to sit on the ground next to her, eye level with the two children.

With my daughters.

"Are you a dad?" Maia gave me a hard stare, already starting the interrogation.

"Well, I've never been one before," I answered. "But if you give me a chance, I'd like to try."

"What's that?" Elodie pointed at a tattoo on my wrist, a compass rose. Her little finger rested just above the point for North.

"These are tattoos." I extended my arm so she could see more of them. "They're drawings that will never wash off."

"What?!" Maia was so bewildered that she came right next to her sister for a closer look. "How do they never come off?"

"Oh, I can't wait to hear this." Rori stretched her legs long in front of her and planted her palms behind her. She relaxed and listened with a smile as my children and I got to know each other.

Chapter 31

Epilogue

Rori

One year later

"I can't believe he finally did it." Devin lay diagonally on our bed, bare feet crossed at the ankles, hands laced behind his head. "He's been hemming and hawing at it for months. I was about to decapitate him myself out of frustration."

"Oh, come on. You know you can't push him if he's not ready." I inserted the silver hoop earrings into my lobes, then stepped back from the mirror, angling my body from side to side to check my reflection.

"If I didn't push, you wouldn't be dressing up for a date with him right now," Devin retorted. "It would have been five years from now." He turned on his side, propping up onto his elbow. "You look incredible, by the way."

"You think so?" I swayed my hips, making the long skirt swish along with the movement. My leather jacket was slim-fitting and cropped, more for fashion than actual riding. It added a little edge to my feminine dress and earrings.

Lucia picked out the dress and jacket for me. Even my fashion-loving little sister knew I couldn't go full girly-girl for a date. And I was pretty sure Hudson was going to pick me up on a motorcycle.

"I know it for a fact." Devin came up to sitting on the edge of the bed, meeting my gaze in the mirror. "You don't even have to try for him, you know. He's already crazy about you."

I turned away from the mirror to face him, bringing a hand to my hip. "He needs this sense of normalcy though, and honestly, I like it." I brought a hand to the back of my neck as my face heated. "I've never been asked on a date before."

"No?" Devin's eyebrows shot up. "Torr, Santos, and I will have to fix that."

"It's different with you guys," I laughed. "I mean, I'm not saying no to that, but Hudson needs this, you know? He's worked so hard over the last year."

"He has," Devin said quietly with a nod. "I'm really proud of him."

I gave him a stern look. "I hope you tell him that."

"I do." Devin smirked deviously. "Usually while he's sucking my cock, but—"

"Oh, fuck you." I grabbed the nearest thing that wouldn't cause permanent damage, a makeup bag, and threw it at him.

Devin caught it easily and brought his arm up to throw it back. He cackled when I brought my arms up, shielding my face.

"No! You are not allowed to ruin my face, hair, or outfit!"

"Well shit, I think that's the first time I've seen you cower from anything."

"I am *not* cowering!"

A knock came to the door before we could continue fighting. Which was a good thing, because arguments with Devin usually led to intense, passionate sex. Which was always incredible but probably not the most appropriate thing to do right before a date.

Devin turned out to be that perfect medium between Torr and Santos that I didn't know existed. He liked to push my buttons and get me to react, but he didn't want submission. Sex between us was a battle, a rough, tumbling, push and pull until we were both sated and exhausted. That was just the dynamic between us. Instead of butting heads, we bit each other's lips, shoved, grabbed, groped, and tested each other's limits.

Most of our verbal arguments weren't serious now, and we actually did get along the majority of the time. But neither of us wanted to have fight-sex all the time, so it worked out perfectly that we had other partners.

If tonight went well, however, his other partner could become mine too.

"I'll get the door." Devin stood and smacked a kiss on my lips before I could react.

"You jerk, now I have to re-apply it," I groaned, turning back to the mirror.

"Worth it." Devin chuckled as he left the bedroom.

While I carefully tried to fix the lip color Lucia had put on me, I tried to ignore the fluttering in my belly. Why was I nervous? I *knew* Hudson, had gradually gotten to know him better over the last year. When he wasn't working or spending time with his daughters, he was with me and my guys. We both fucked Devin, for Christ's sake.

He had been especially busy as of late, though. I hadn't seen him for a few weeks, so when he asked me—and only me—to dinner the other day, to say I was pleasantly surprised was an understatement.

It felt like this might be a turning point for us, a new chapter in our relationship. And I couldn't lie, I felt nervous, like a longtime crush had finally noticed me.

Hudson and Devin's voices were a soft, comforting murmur as I finally left the bedroom, trying not to let my nerves show as I walked down the hall. I kept my chin lifted, my steps assured and confident, trying to channel the strength of my domme persona.

Hudson looked, well, really fucking hot. He'd gotten a haircut and his face was clean-shaven. The blue shirt he wore under his leather jacket brought out his eyes. His boots were polished and his dark jeans were slim-fitting, hugging his muscular thighs in all the right places.

The smile that lit up his face when he saw me did nothing to assuage my belly flutters. "Hey, Rori."

"Hey," I returned more breathily than I intended. "Long time no see."

"Yeah, hope I can make up for that tonight." His eyes continued to drink me in, and I never wanted him to stop looking at me. "You look amazing."

"So do you." My heart jumped into my throat as I said that, but I never was a girl to hold back what I felt.

"Yeah, both of you are hot as hell." Devin grinned smugly before fixing Hudson with an icy glare. "I want her home by midnight—"

"Oh, fuck off." I shoved at his shoulder.

"But if that means you come home *with* her," he continued, ignoring me. "I certainly won't mind."

Hudson laughed, a blush creeping up his neck. Over the past year, he'd been a branch extending off our group relationship. Sometimes he and Devin would spend time alone, other times he'd hang out with us as a group. But he'd always maintained a little bit of distance. Devin was the only one he had a sexual relationship with. So far.

"We'll see where the night takes us," Hudson said coyly before accepting a kiss from Devin.

"Have fun." Devin kissed me on the neck this time. "I'm meeting up with Santos and Torr at Bryce's. Join us after your dinner." He smirked. "If you don't suddenly get *busy*, that is."

"Alright, we're out of here." I wrapped my hand around Hudson's bicep with a dramatic sigh. "He's been doing this all day."

"You poor thing." He laughed.

We headed out the door with our arms linked together. "How does an MC president feel about riding on the back of my bike?" Hudson asked, his tone playful.

"I have no problem with letting a gentleman lead every once in a while." My arm wrapped a little tighter around his. "Honestly, it's nice to not be in the driver's seat all the time."

"Should I keep dinner a surprise, then? Or would you like to know, and possibly veto, my choice?" We came to his bike and I released his arm to let him climb on.

"I'd like to know." Once he was seated, I swung my leg over and allowed my body to press snugly into his back. "Not to veto your choice, just because I don't like being kept in suspense."

"It's Nina's." Hudson spoke to me over his shoulder, our faces close. "The new place downtown. Lisa and June are friends with the owners, and they said the food is incredible."

"Sounds great." I wrapped an embrace around his stomach and propped my chin on his shoulder, wondering if he'd take the chance to kiss me right then.

He didn't, but that was okay. We had all night.

———

HUDSON and I were seated by a friendly hostess and then ordered drinks and appetizers from a very attentive server. The moment we were finally alone at our table, Hudson blurted out, "So, I want you to be the first to know something."

"Okay. I'm listening." He looked nervous but also on the verge of bursting with happiness.

He broke out into the widest grin I'd ever seen on his face. "It's happening. I'm officially adopting Elodie and Maia."

"Oh my God, Hudson!" I immediately slapped a hand over my mouth, realizing my shriek had attracted some curious stares from other customers. "Hudson, that's fantastic," I said more quietly. "Congratulations!"

"Thank you." He rubbed his palms together, shifting in his seat. "I'm kind of terrified but also really excited to be a dad full-time."

"You are so ready for it," I told him. "You've worked so hard over this past year. Not just on yourself but getting to know them, learning about what they need. You'll do great, Hudson. I'm so happy for you."

Our conversation paused while the server returned with our drinks and appetizers.

"What a thing to celebrate." I held my drink out to him. "Cheers to that."

After we toasted and drank, I asked, "How's it going with the younger two? Is bringing them home with you on the horizon?"

Hudson sighed, a frown making his brows pinch. "It doesn't look like it right now. We've tried some bonding activities, and they're just not very responsive to me. I get it, they're really young, and I'm still basically a stranger to them. They're really attached to their foster parents. Who are great, don't get me wrong. But it's clear they're not choosing me, and that sucks a little."

"I'm sorry." Without thinking, I reached across the table and put my hand over his. "They are still babies. I'm sure they'll understand more when they're older. You'll be able to keep seeing them, right?"

"Yeah. It seems like their foster parents are hoping to adopt them, and they said they want me to continue having a relationship with them. So, I'm sure we can work something out."

"That's good to hear."

He nodded, stroking his thumb over my fingers. "I want to start bringing Maia and Elodie to see them too. They're all sisters, so they should get to know each other."

"I think that's a great idea."

There was another pause in the conversation as our main dishes were brought out.

"How's Torr's mom?" Hudson placed his napkin in his lap. "Any improvement since the last update?"

I gave him an uneasy smile and his frown deepened. "Not much has changed," I admitted. "She has her good days and bad. She is remembering Torr more often though. The doctors say he just needs to keep seeing her, stay consistent so he'll stick in her memory. It's hard on him, but he keeps showing up for her. That's just the man he is."

"Shit, I'm sorry."

"It's not all bad. When she's lucid, she's so spunky and hilarious. We're just taking it one day at a time."

We turned to lighter topics as we ate, talking about work and what else we'd been up to since we last saw each other. Since moving to Four Corners, Hudson had found his calling in tech communications. Thanks to him and a small team, the town had reliable internet for the first time since my parents were in their twenties. It wasn't very fast yet, but it was a booming industry that was constantly advancing.

As for me? I was still running Vengeful Gods MC with primarily the same crew of ex-gladiators. We aided Four Corners and other neighboring territories with the transportation of goods, usually as escorts to deter any theft or violence.

"If your girls are ready for it," I said when I was nearly finished with my food. "Maybe they can come to one of the parties at my parents' house. There's lots of kids around the same age."

"Um." Hudson cleared his throat and wiped his mouth with a napkin. "That's kind of something I wanted to talk to you about too."

I had been relaxed most of the evening, but now that fluttering in my stomach returned. "Okay."

"I..." Hudson pulled in a deep breath and tried again. "I want you in the girls' lives. You, and the guys too."

Neither of us said anything for a moment. "In what way?" I asked.

"I'm not asking you to become their mother," Hudson said quickly. But I...they..." He swallowed and tried again. "The girls love you, Rori. They idolize you. Maia wants to be exactly like you."

"I love them too," I admitted. "They're such sweet, smart people. And they've been through so much at such a young age. I'd go to war for them, and I'm a hundred percent serious."

"They're amazing," Hudson agreed. "I still can't believe they're mine sometimes. And I'm, um, rambling and stalling, but what I'm trying to say is..." He paused and took a deep breath. "I just want *you*, Rori. I want us."

"Us," I repeated, trying to calm the fireworks lighting up my chest. "You mean like *us* us?"

Hudson grinned, sheepish and adorable. "I want to share you with the three other men who love you, who I also love, are my best friends, and the people I want my daughters around. I want you with them, and I also want you alone. Like we are now." He reached across the table for my hand and I placed it in his. "What do you say, Aurora Wilder?"

"I think," I said coyly, "that we can do much better things alone than just sitting and talking."

He didn't miss a beat. "Then I'm getting the damn check."

We paid our bill and headed out of the restaurant in a hurry, going straight to his motorcycle parked out front. Hudson spun to face me the moment we stood next to his bike. His hands went to my waist and mine went around his neck as we came together in a deep, all-consuming kiss.

That kiss was a release of a year's worth of pent-up attraction, of growth and setbacks for both of us. A year of orbiting each other, of processing our individual traumas both privately and with others, before we were finally ready to collide into each other.

And what a collision it was.

Breaking apart for a breath was barely a separation at all, we remained wrapped up in each other, our mouths hovering mere inches away as the heat of our breaths mingled in the space between.

"I want us too, Hudson," I whispered. "I just need to know that you're sure. Us sharing Devin is one thing, but—"

He cut me off with another kiss, a lighter, more playful one that I could feel his smile through. "I want it all. Everything, as long as I have you. You saved me, Rori. And I don't just mean the night you got me out of that house."

"The night you shot me, you mean."

He chuckled, because that's what it was to us now. A memory so distant that it became a joke. It almost felt like that night happened between two other people, not us. "If that's how you want to remember it, fine."

I pressed my smile to his, winding my arms around him tighter. "It's a good thing you saved me too, then."

His hands slid around my ribs, molding to my sides. "I'd say that makes us even."

"Mm, well, I never shot you, so I dunno about *that.*"

Hudson laughed and dropped his forehead to my neck, which allowed me to say into his ear. "You come with some pretty cute kids though, so I'll let that even the score."

He took a shuddering breath, wrapping me into an embrace that crushed me against his chest. "Thank you for...waiting," he whispered. "For letting me get my shit together, learn how to become a father, and put that whole ordeal in the rearview mirror. Thank you for allowing me to become a man worthy of you."

I blinked away the sudden tears that rose, not expecting him to go from joking to all swoony and romantic.

"I would've waited forever," I admitted. "Not for my chance or anything, but for you. More than anything, I wanted you to heal. I would've waited forever to see you whole and happy again. And if you found happiness with someone else..."

"But I didn't," he said when I trailed off. "I found it right here."

"So did I."

I smiled up at him, and we came together in another kiss.

One that would be followed by many more that night, and for the rest of our lives.

———

Thank you so much for reading Deathless! Not ready to stop going on wild motorcycle adventures? Ride with Mari and her four biker husbands in the Steel Demons MC! This series is complete and available in Kindle Unlimited!

Start the Steel Demons MC series:
https://books2read.com/SDMC1

———

If you're craving a standalone story with three chaotic bisexual men, Valorie's parents have a book too!

Read all about Kyrie and the Sons of Odin in Their Property:
https://books2read.com/theirpropertysonsofodin

Also by Crystal Ash

Harem of Freaks: The Complete Series

Say Your Prayers

Steel Demons MC

Lawless

Powerless

Fearless

Painless

Helpless

Heartless

Senseless

Ruthless

Merciless

Endless

Shifted Mates Trilogy

Unholy Trinity: The Complete Series

For a complete list of books by Crystal Ash, visit her Amazon page.

About the Author

Crystal Ash is a USA Today Bestselling Author from California. She loves writing steamy, heart-wrenching romance with tortured heroes, especially if they're in a reverse harem. Crystal's other loves include animals, mythology, and well-crafted alcohol, most of which can also be found in her stories.

When she's not writing, she's probably drinking craft beer with her husband or trying to coax her feral cat into accepting affection.

crystalashbooks.com

facebook.com/Crystal.Ash.Romance

instagram.com/crystalashbooks

amazon.com/author/crystalash

bookbub.com/profile/crystal-ash